I0709383

A LIFE CALLED SCARLET

A Life Called Scarlet

HARRISON HICKMAN

Harrison James Frank Hickman

Copyright © 2023 by Harrison Hickman

All rights reserved. No part of this book may be reproduced in any manner whatsoever without written permission except in the case of brief quotations embodied in critical articles and reviews.

First Printing, 2023

For Lissette

Contents

1990

A Farewell

1 January 1990

She doesn't realise it yet, but this is the decade that will make or break her.

She pulls herself up from the floor, feeling queasy. How much was she drinking last night? It started off with a couple of cans of cheap lager, but it quickly escalated.

The room is full of bodies, snoring gently. The Edwardian-era room still echoes with the farewell music to 1989. And some party it was. Lots of drinking, some snorting, plenty of sex.

She remembers making out with a guy. What was his name? Jace, Jake? Something like that. Posh guy. Right out the front they were, passionately kissing. Fun stuff. Until the moment his girlfriend came along. Megan or something. Screamed her head off.

She makes sure that she doesn't disturb anyone. Nearly tripping over a half-empty bottle of vodka, she leaves the room. What did they call this room during the posh era? Drawing Room, or something like that. She starts tip-toeing down the stairs.

Her stomach's playing the bagpipes.

She inches past more snoring bodies and opens the front door of the house. The typical grey scene of Croydon greets her.

Who was it who hired the mansion? She plays this question around in her head, taking deep breaths and putting one foot in front of the other. Must've been Mickey. His dad's got loads of money. So much that Mickey went to the States for a year. He was supposed to be doing a course in engineering or something, but spent his time chatting up girls. Did he make a pass on her last night? She can't remember.

The street is devoid of life. Dawn is still in the process of lighting up the day.

She is tempted to stop and take in the surroundings, perhaps as inspiration for the art project she's working on. But she doesn't.

Last night's party was a good way to end the Eighties. Duran Duran was on for most of it. They got a bit irritating after a while.

She wonders what the decade ahead will bring in music. The decade is a black hole and she's standing on the edge of it. She's scared to jump in, but she knows she has to. If she ever wants to be a part of it herself, she has to face the darkness in order to see the light.

She's meeting the girls on Saturday. She hoped to see Josephine last night, but she didn't turn up.

She gets to the end of the road, remembering that she's got that family dinner later. She wants to fall down and smash her head off the pavement. That won't solve anything, of course, she knows that. She's just got to roll with things today.

Turning left, she heads to where she knows there's a taxi rank. It's going to cost her, but what choice does she have. There won't be any public transport on today.

She laughs when she remembers a guy last night trying to fry eggs. "I'm fucking starving, you posh nutters!" he yelled at the laughing crowd. "Didn't get dinner this evenin'!"

She's just spied the line of taxis when she sees a fried breakfast in her mind. Covered with thick grease. Oozing beans. Thick, red sauce.

A family – young dad, young mum, young daughter – emerge from a side street. The daughter has a balloon with a Disney picture on it. She's running full pelt. Mum and Dad try to stop her, but she's too fast. The girl runs into her...

Fried breakfast is the tipping point.

The drawbridge to the castle is down.

She vomits over the girl, carrots in the mix.

Screams.

Mum, red overcoat and thick spectacles, and Dad, steel eyes and raincoat, try to calm the girl down. The balloon's on its way to the heavens. Bye-bye, Disney.

"I'm sorry," she splutters.

"Can you not watch where you are going, you stupid bitch?!" screams the mum.

"That's quite enough!" the dad shouts, holding tightly onto his howling daughter. The girl is red-faced, clawing the sick from her face.

"I'm really sorry!" she pleads with them. "Look, accept my apologies!" The she runs; they'll call the police no doubt. She goes for the nearest taxi and calmly yells her address to the driver. She keeps her head down as the car pulls away into the road. The driver turns the vehicle into the opposite lane. She makes sure there's no way she can be seen by the family. She sits up when she knows it's safe.

The city begins to slowly merge with the countryside. It's beautiful, in a way, how green patches splash themselves in the city, growing larger until they expand into fields. How sullen-faced Londoners become slightly more cheerful. How busy streets open up into country roads. How the sky becomes less opaque and more relaxed, as though it's proud to be itself, not fearful of any consequences.

She's lived in Kent all her life. It's part of her identity, that yearning to leave, fly across the Channel, into France. She's been to a fair few countries, yes, but that desperate freedom to be somewhere else, to be so far away – it's something that'll always be with her.

On and on the taxi drives. The meter does its little dance, climbing up and up.

She's thinking about the day planned ahead. Her parents no doubt want to have a family lunch and talk about rubbish: "Alastair, are you looking forward to a career in law?" She's worried about what she needs to say to convince everyone that she's got a practical mindset. Her dad wasn't keen on her doing that course at art college, learning "how to waste money and life on creating images."

But she doesn't want to have a practical mindset. She wants to be free.

She sees a sign for Sevenoaks.

It won't be long now. And it isn't.

The taxi takes her through the streets, past the train station, left turn, right turn. All the while, more details come back.

There were three big bowls of peanuts last night for everyone to help themselves to. "Stuff ya faces," someone said. "And quench ya thirst!"

When she gets to her street, she wants to be sick again.

"Anywhere along here," she says to the driver, who promptly stops, as if glad to be rid of her. She pays him and heads up to her house. She fumbles around for her key, but there's no need. She hears voices from inside and pushes the door open. The house is so dark, her eyes struggling to adjust to the dimness.

"You're finally home!" says Alastair. He's walking up the stairs with a steaming mug of tea in his hand. He's got his cardigan wrapped around him and his beige slippers nestles against his toes. "Good party last night?"

"Amazing," she says. "Should've been there..."

"Well, I needed to keep my head together." He waggles his fingers and continues up the stairs.

She remembers the timid little creature from the Great Storm of 1987 and smiles. She makes to go up to her room, but stops. She's stopped dead in her tracks like a rabbit caught in headlights, because she's been called by her mother.

Grudgingly, she puts one foot in front of the other and starts toward the kitchen, unsure of whether her tongue will play ball.

"How was the party?" says Mum.

"It was good," she says. "Excellent. Lots of people."

"Glad you enjoyed yourself." Mum wipes her hands on a dishcloth and switches on the kettle.

She looks to her right, through the archway, to the dining room. Her father's sitting with a book on law, reading glasses on, mug of coffee to his lips. As soon as he sees her, he places the cup down, puts his bookmark in, snaps the tome shut, and then pulls off his lenses, folding them neatly into his shirt pocket.

"Where were you last night?" he asks.

"Party," she answers.

"Did you enjoy yourself?"

"I did. Nice to get out once in a while."

"In your case, every other day."

Now it starts. Now she's going to be eaten alive. She wants to turn away, run for her room, but his icy stare keeps her here, a stone statue.

"Look, your brother and I are about to have a talk about stuff. Go and do whatever it is you need to do. We will talk later."

She takes the hint and leaves, leaves before she can be insulted anymore. It's going to get to the point where she will have to walk away, but that won't be for a long time.

In her room, she falls down onto her bed, letting out a deep sigh. She wants to scream at the top of her lungs. But she's so low right now. Looking around her tip of a room that reeks of beer, cigarettes and soiled underwear, she decides to get a bit of air. She creeps to the bathroom, swirls mouthwash, ridding her gums of the taste of vomit, and then strides out of the house and into the winter morning.

It's surprising the number of cars on the road. Everyone's out to make a bloody killing. Everyone. Everyone's addicted to adrenaline and stress. It's something she fails to understand. She'll understand it someday, when the decade is nearing its end. She'll understand why people prefer to wear shirts and ties and drive fast cars and collapse in front of the television on a Friday night with wine and Chinese takeaway, complaining to their spouses about how stressful life is. She'll understand why some people prefer this over a life of freedom, where you can get pissed regularly and fuck from dawn until dusk. But it won't be for many years yet, not until she's forced to confront it.

The cold bites into her neck like a vampire.

The world turns.

She fumbles for yet another cigarette. The smoke being dragged into her lungs soothes her flaccid muscles. So good.

"All right, darlin'?"

She turns, wanting to kick the officer in the face. In her haste to get to the outskirts of Sevenoaks, she's failed to notice the police car parked by the kerb.

"Happy New Year, Scarlet." He's smiling his vicious toothy grin at her, as he's often done for years.

She resists the grudge to swear at him, knowing she'd get herself nicked. She walks on. The officer's partner is standing in front of her. He's younger than the other one; by his appearance, he's only recently joined the force. Clean-shaven, spotless uniform, all that.

"Excuse me," she whispers.

He doesn't try to stop her, instead gesturing for her to walk on by like a good officer of the law. "Whore," he says after her.

She could report him, but the officers would no doubt respond by digging things up. The older one has known her since she was a child. She can't risk it. She keeps walking.

She thinks about going into her shack, but decides against it. She's still in holiday mode. Instead, she goes to a field she's loved since childhood. It's right outside Sevenoaks, very spacious. She goes through a hole in the hedgerow and plonks herself down onto the grass.

The sun's warmth tingles her skin.

Art

3 January 1990

It's now or never, she realises, breathing in the stale air. She stretches her arms over her head and sits up. Too tired to argue with her conscience, she slips to the floor, tugging her guitar out from under the bed. As it clangs against the bedpost, it makes that wonderful hollow noise.

Ten minutes later, guitar strapped to her back, she's wandering through the dark streets of Sevenoaks. She needs some breakfast, but she'll have to make do with the energy bars she's got stuffed in her pocket. And she's not going to eat them until she gets to the shack.

"Fuck's sake," she murmurs, as dawn begins to spill out across the sky. By this time, she's out of the streets and into the countryside. The sun is harsh and bright – maybe a little too much.

She lights a cigarette and keeps walking. She's eager to get the paintbrush in her hands and start whipping the blank canvas with strokes of colour. She'll be able to be herself in her shack. She won't have to worry about not doing something right.

It's great she'll finally be able to be alone.

There are things she's longed for, things she'll know she'll never get, but that only makes the longing more painful. More in your face, you could say. But she's got her art, her photography. Surely that will make things dissipate for a while. Even if it doesn't, it's worth a try.

When she arrives at her shack, her back's twinging. She's simply not used to the exercise. She's going to have to change that soon.

Her shack's in the corner of a field, secluded and hidden from the world – the shack, that is. No, the field is very open and welcoming. It's got everything that a young artist could ever want.

Inside, she washes out her coffeemaker. She's never really cleaned it properly before. No doubt it's full of mould. No doubt. But when she sets it going, it works fine. The coffee tastes all right as well. Munching on one of the energy bars, she sets about erecting the easel. It's such a familiar routine, one learnt by repetitive repetition. She hums as she prepares the paints. She's on the brink of whistling as she stirs her brush in the colours. But when she begins to paint, she finds that she can't. There's no connection. No bridge of safety.

Suddenly, she realises how chronically alone she is. She's frozen. The fear has made a timely appearance. So, she packs away her paints and easel, and then proceeds to remove her guitar from the sleeve. It's been a few weeks since she's played it, but now she's finally got some time to play, she can't help wondering if this will be the last time.

"Take it away then," she says to herself. She strums the chords, feeling that intimate connection with music waltz down her spine.

To the casual observer, it would appear that she's merely making nonsensical noise. But to her, it is simple beauty. How can there be words to describe the happiness she feels right now? Each note is a rung on a ladder that climbs farther up into the sky.

"Keep it going," she whispers. "Keep it going."

Her fingers glide effortlessly across the strings. It's so soothing to her nerves. She doesn't want to feel like she belongs. She wants to feel lost, if only for a little while. And in this world of notes and finger movements, she's able to let her guard down. There's nothing here to hurt her. When she meets the girls on Saturday, that will be the time for emotional pain. But right now she's happy in her own little world. Her eyes begin to water, not with sadness, not with frustration, but with peace. The pain in her cunt recedes.

How long passes? An hour? Two hours? Several hours? Does it really matter? Does it?!

She's feeling peace right now! She's happy! Can't the world just give her a fucking break?! Why is it when we see a woman, tormented by nightmares, playing a beautiful piece of music, we can't help but wonder *why* she's playing? Can't we just leave her alone? Can't we? But we just can't.

Outside, the world turns on. Midday comes and that's when Scarlet realises she has to stop playing. Her fingertips are red, unsure of whether to bleed. She's panting. Her coffee is cold now.

She knows that peace is something few find. Maybe she'll find it herself. Maybe she won't.

She goes outside, breathing in the freshly warmed air. She feels – what is it? – inspiration. She needs it.

What's she going to say to the girls this weekend? Gina will take some convincing. She's always sceptical. Josephine will be up for it, no doubt. Emma will be a bit shaky, but she'll do it. Susan won't blush – she'll want to fit in. She's that type.

Scarlet takes a moment to observe her surroundings. She sees the farmer trudging along the field. He'll get snappy with her later, probably. She's only allowed on his land, because the art institute has paid him a lot of money. There he is, stomping away, looking grim and unhappy at life.

She goes back inside, pours herself some (fresh?) coffee, and sets up the easel once more. She paints and this time, this time it works.

You see, we have such an issue with free-thinking spirits. We see them, no, we don't see; we look at them like they're grotesque gargoyles. We wonder why they're doing something practical. Yes, practical. We have one hell of an obsession with that word. Can't someone make things for the sake of making them? Can't someone be left to their own devices? We have no right to judge her. The decade ahead will test every fibre of her being. No, maybe you're right: maybe she does need to be *practical*. But at least let her have this day in peace. By the decade's end, yes of course, she'll be less of a threat to you.

After she finishes painting, she packs her easel and paints away again and locks up. Slinging her guitar into her case and throwing it over her back, she heads home. She's rehearsing what she'll say to the girls on Saturday. She's written four songs over the holidays, so that will be a good start.

Now, she's whistling to herself as she walks back home. She's starving, so much so that she's dizzy as hell. Not long now, she thinks. She's ready for this.

Interlude

You're still feeling a little uncomfortable, right?

We've spoken about this, haven't we? I made it very clear to you: let her have this day in peace! She's been judged enough already!

But you're still feeling uncomfortable with the fact that she's a free spirit, painting pictures and playing music, instead of focusing on normal things. Even through you've probably got a few of the band's albums downloaded. You might even listen to them on your iPod when you're in the gym. Maybe when you're driving to work. Maybe –

I'm still not getting through to you, am I?

Perhaps a minibiography is in order.

Scarlet was born on the 15th of January, 1970, at 4.01 A.M. She was a healthy weight and had no childhood illnesses, apart from a bout of chickenpox when she was six.

She attended a local primary school in Sevenoaks. No issues there at all. Okay, she had a scrap in the playground when she was nine, but nothing serious. She got good results in her schoolwork, demonstrating a fascination with art.

After leaving primary school, she attended a nearby high school, where she met Susan. They became instant friends, going on sleepovers, camping trips, you name it.

Scarlet continued to pursue art, painting and drawing in every spare moment. She attended a fancy art college in London, meeting Emma and Gina there. It was Gina who introduced her to Josephine. They were local to London, if such a thing can be said. They came from *various parts* of London, but what does it matter? The fact is they could all meet up for coffee and drinks, double-date, pretend to do coursework, you name it.

Scarlet graduated from the art college and was given two years of funding by an art institute to paint the countryside and produce a few sculptures. And now she wants to start a band.

But you know she's hiding something. There's something about her that doesn't seem quite right. I know that you want to dig it up. Because that's what you are.

I don't judge people. If you hate her, hate her. It's not my place to dictate that. You have two options. If you want to stop reading, stop. Throw the book in the bin. Never think of Scarlet again. Go on, it's easy...

Or, you can stay with me. You can read Scarlet's story. Find out how she and the band became a major part of the 1990s music scene. You know she's going to fail in the end. There's no surprise finish.

So, come with me. If you get uncomfortable, well that's too bad. Remember, this is Scarlet's story. Don't worry, you'll get your money's worth. I wouldn't want to deprive you of that now, would I?

The choice is yours.

Take five minutes. Then decide.

I'll be waiting.

The Girls

6 January 1990

So, you decided to stay. Jolly good.

Scarlet sits at a table, the biggest in this funky little coffeeshop, sipping her latte. She watches the others, waiting to see who will break the silence first.

And it has to be Gina: "Don't get me wrong, Scarlet, I think it's a wonderful idea, but there is the issue of money."

"Come off it, Gina!" Josephine shouts. "You always think of money! Money, money, money. Always money. Scarlet has got a good idea. We're all musical, aren't we?"

Emma says, "I've been playing the drums since I was ten."

"I'm pretty good on the guitar," says Josephine. "You've all seen me play."

"Not very well," says Gina. A really dumb attempt at cracking a joke. Was it last year – yeah, it was last year when she had that episode and stayed in bed for six days. Depression plays a very cold instrument. Now it's trying her hand at humour. Badly.

Josephine fakes a laugh and continues: "I definitely think it's worth a shot. I mean, if we screw up, we screw up. What's there to lose?"

"Our dignities," mutters Gina, knowing at her nails. She's avoiding eye contact.

"Come off it, Gina!" When Josephine does that exasperated laugh/sigh, she *really* goes for it. "Our dignities are already fucked!" She smiled naughtily and Scarlet can tell that she's thinking about the time when she fucked Mickey a couple of years ago... in the car park of an old people's home at four o'clock in the morning after a heavy night out. She and Scarlet stopped talking for a few weeks, because: 1. Scarlet thought that the elderly should be treated with respect. And 2. Scarlet liked Mickey.

Gina snaps back angrily, and the two bicker angrily for a few minutes, until Emma tells them to shut up.

"We need to get some kind of a plan together if we're gonna do this," says Emma. "Maybe we need to exchange schedules."

"That's not enough," Josephine says with a spark of citrusy energy. "We need to... How do you say it? Go full steam ahead on this."

Emma continues, casting a *Help me, for fuck's sake!* glance at Scarlet. "Let's review our schedules. It's a starting point."

"Okay then," says Scarlet. "Saturday nights? How are we all for that? I'm free at that time."

"Saturday nights work out fine for me," Josephine tells all.

"Me too," adds Gina.

"I can do that," Emma says in a half whisper.

Then there is a really eerie silence that seems to explode like sheer mayhem. It's as if the coffeeshop is no longer a coffeeshop, but a maze of sharp glass daggers. Scarlet can feel them surrounding her. She knows Gina can't cope with tension. It's the tension of Susan's silence, her ability to remain on the edge of an argument.

Oh, Susan, thinks Scarlet. Betrayed at every corner. Stabbed in the heart so many times. A strong girl, though, nonetheless. Strength is such an unusual friend. Sometimes it's there, sometimes not. It's like a passing ship in the night. The ocean is so cold. It's black like the night.

Oh, Susan.

Susan sits off in the corner. She wears a strange smile, that kind of smile you only see once in your whole life. She's only ordered sparkling water. She's clutching her knee and swaying on the sofa. The leather crinkles under her weight.

"Susan?" Emma mutters. "Susan?"

"Yeah, Saturday nights are good," Susan says at last. Her voice is lost. It's not quite shaking, but it could be if this was a shit film.

"That's settled then!" Josephine exclaims, downing the dregs of her coffee. "Are we going to count tonight?"

"May as well," says Gina.

"Maybe it's better to wait till next week," says Emma. "Gives us all a chance to brush up on our musical skills."

"Good," agrees Josephine. "The boyfriend's agreed to fuck me senseless tonight anyways…"

"So, a week today then?" says Scarlet.

When the girls are together for a fairly average amount of time, Josephine always has to spoil it with her sexual adventures. The dirty bitch. "We need to get our research done on the record industry, etcetera. We all need to input."

"Cool," Gina tells them all. "Cool, cool, cool."

With that, the meeting is declared over. The girls finish their drinks and begin the process of dissipating like something that won't dissolve in water.

On her way out, Scarlet makes sure that Susan *happens* to run into her. She knows that Susan always tries to hide away, but not this time. The plan works perfectly. Scarlet catches her just as she emerges from the ladies, head in the clouds.

"Scarlet!" Susan almost squeaks. The girl's been crying, eyes, red.

"I never got the chance to wish you Happy New Year! How was your holiday?" asks Scarlet.

"Oh, fine."

"Get up to much?"

"Oh, usual. Turkey dinner. Family. Champagne. What about you, Scarlet?"

"Much the same."

They begin walking out of the coffeeshop and down the street, cold air whipping at their ankles. The roads are slowly beginning to breathe. The world is turning. Scarlet can see fresh tears falling down Susan's cheeks, but she doesn't dare say anything to her. She knows what happened, knows how Susan was betrayed, knows how truly broken Susan is, knows that Susan put her trust and faith in *him*.

Scarlet wants to say something to Susan, but what can she say? "Sorry your true love dumped you before Christmas. Hope it wasn't too lonely for you." So instead, she keeps her mouth shut. She wants to make sure that Susan's okay, yes, but she doesn't want to push too far. So instead, she lets the matter drop.

"What're your plans for later?" she asks, her resolve gone.

"Not sure. Probably grab an early night. Mum's not too well at the moment."

"Aw, I'm sorry to hear that."

"Don't worry about it, Scarlet. She'll pull through. She always does. It's just −" Susan's eyes are watering again. She's stopped dead in her tracks. "It's just, Dad isn't taking it too well. Comes home drunk nearly every night."

"I'm so −"

"Just don't say you're sorry. Everyone says that." Susan gulps, clutches Scarlet by the elbows, and breathes in and out, in and out. "Look, I, I know what you're trying to do, okay, but this is something I need to cope with myself, okay? Look, I really need to get home. I'll get on with practising my stuff and try to call you in the week."

"Okay," replies Scarlet, knowing full well that she could try to reel Susan in, knowing full well that she could try something. But she's silent and she watches her friend walk away.

She wanders around Sevenoaks for a bit, considering whether to go home. She's about to go to the train station, when she realises that her guitar is in the shack. She didn't bring it to the meeting, didn't want to surprise the girls too early. Didn't want to cause any unnecessary tension.

She heads off to her shack, her mind restless, bitter with frustration. Now she's walking, fresh air filling her blood. She's rerunning the whole scene in her head, wishing she could have dominated things a bit more. But it's too late to go back, words she'll be repeatedly telling herself in the decade to come. However, let's not jump ahead.

Scarlet spends the rest of the day in the shack, painting, trying to be inspired by the view out of the window. She actually gets something done, which is a relief to her, and probably to the funding body as well.

There's a point where she can paint no more. It's not that she's running out of ideas. Oh no, we couldn't have that, could we? Not, it's because of a burning sensation in her stomach. The desire to be truly animalistic with herself. But if she does that, she'll spend the whole day confused and tearful.

So, she decides to go to a place she's known since childhood. It's just a short walk from her shack. A good brisk kilometre. So, being as it's a nice day, she goes to it. Why not?

There's a part of her that's always been a bit childish. A part that's always wanted to hide beneath the blankets. She's not scared of things changing, only when they change too fast. Only when they spiral out of control.

The place is an oak tree at the side of the road. It's a strange little scene: a groove in the side of a grand old oak. It's a handy place to stop, think, and reflect. She's been sitting in that groove since childhood.

It's not the past that scares her, she realises, crouching in the groove, resting the guitar over her knees, it's the answer. Only the future possesses the answer. Will the band succeed? She'll know in the next few weeks. Initial momentum will determine the trajectory it will take.

It's like when you fall in love with someone. You can't imagine a life without them. But you don't have the courage to tell them to their face. So, you send them a letter explaining everything: How your life was so empty, then they wandered in and lit things up. You know full well that you will see them in two- or three-days' time. You spend those days pacing the house, waiting. Deep down, you know it's going to end in disappointment. But the truth is you enjoy the waiting. The sense that things will or won't be. You feel a bizarre sense of hope.

That's how she feels, watching and waiting. She sits for hours, as still as the branches in the oak tree. When she's falling asleep, she walks away. She needs a night off.

First Practice Session

13 January 1990

"Are we ready?" says Josephine.

"I am," says Gina. "Dunno 'bout you guys." She finetunes her guitar for the umpteenth time.

The others gradually murmur their replies and then Scarlet realises that Josephine wants her to lead.

"I wrote a few lyrics to a song," she says, pulling her guitar strap over her head.

"Let's hear it," says Emma.

Gina and Susan shuffle about in their seats.

Scarlet begins strumming, singing her lyrics. It's about a boy called Jacob who she knew when she was a child. She liked him. But it was not meant to be. He moved to West Germany. When she finishes, she looks up at the others.

Gina seems impressed. She exchanges glances with Susan. Emma gives the thumbs up. Josephine, however, does not seem remotely enthused.

"Not quite right," she says. "You have to really make it something special. Like, like, your life really depends on it."

"Very imaginative," says Emma.

They all play various notes for an hour, random little tunes that make little or no sense. Susan suggests a few lyrics. Emma puts forward a few ideas for the first album: design, number of songs, etc. Gina raises the possibility of acquiring more members – swiftly rebuffed by all (including Gina). Josephine thinks she can get some good publicity; she knows a couple of people who can help. Scarlet says she'll think of some more lyrics.

They're in Scarlet's house right now. Everyone's out: Mum and Dad have gone to London to buy Alastair an expensive suit for his work experience in March. Gold watch, leather shoes; they're buying him everything. He's going to be the future, so they say.

After a second hour of casual chat (Josephine got fucked well the other night), they decide to break up for today. Scarlet sees them off at the door. They promise to think things over and have more material for next week. When they've all departed (she's so worried about Susan, the poor girl), she heads back upstairs and continues playing.

Later, when it's so dark it's like depths space, she reflects on the first practice session. Not bad, she thinks.

She hears the click of the door.

"Home!" says Dad. "Scarlet? You in?"

"Yeah! In my room! Coming down..." She heads down the stairs. From the number of bags already piled in the corridor, she guesses there's been a big shop.

At dinner – beef and kidney stew with boiled potatoes and steamed peas – Mum and Dad relate the story of how they purchased a first-class suit.

"Bond Street really is the place," says Mum. "You should see the range of stores there..."

"Fantastic range of antique shops," Dad says, pouring everyone a refill of the French red wine.

Scarlet hates this stuff, but it makes her lightheaded: she's able to dream her way through the conversation. She thinks about music. How she'll feel when she's on stage in front of thousands.

The subject then moves on to the Cold War.

"It certainly has been a tense decade," remarks Dad. "I swear there were times when I thought the bomb would drop."

"Do you remember *Threads*?" says Mum.

Dad is quick to reply: "I do indeed. Scary as anything."

"Do you think that Gorbachev is a good man?" asks Alastair.

"I think he is," answers Dad.

Mum nods in agreement.

"I think the whole Cold War was a mistake," Scarlets interrupts.

The three of them look at her, eyes puzzled. How dare she suddenly interrupt like that?

"Why do you say that?" Dad, naturally, is the first to respond.

"Well, look at what the Americans did to Hiroshima and Nagasaki." Scarlet sips more wine. "You really want that to happen many, many times over?"

"That's a very weak argument. Why don't you read an history book sometime?" Dad's obsession with history books… "Nuclear weapons were use *deter*…" He really emphasises that word. "…not to be used to kill. If you have them, no one is going to dare use them against you. That is the principle of nuclear deterrence."

"But what about misinterpretation? Say, the Soviets thought that NATO was about to fire a nuke at Moscow?"

"Okay. The alternative would be total disarmament. Let's suppose that the West scrapped all of its nuclear weapons. What do you think would happen? Peace on Earth? More likely the Soviets would wipe NATO off the face of the map."

"Though," says Alastair, "there's always a possibility that the Soviet Union may be interested in unilateral disarmament. Maybe not the hardliners…"

"Ever the young lawyer…"

The conversation has finally shifted away from Scarlet.

Second Practice Session

20 January 1990

"Fuck!" screams Gina from the kitchen.

Scarlet knows what this is. So do the girls.

Emma's looking panicked.

Josephine gives a sigh of resignation: it's her flat they're practising in, and there's no doubt that the crashing noise that preceded Gina howling the f-word was indeed a china mug.

"Fuck!" Gina screams a second time. "I fucking hate tiny mugs!" There's more smashing. Smash. Smash. Smash.

"Well, that's the last time I'm getting her to make the tea," says Josephine.

Susan is in solemn silence. It's obvious that she's used to outbursts.

Scarlet heads through to the kitchen. She can tell Susan's right behind her. Even in these familiar dangerous situations, Susan appears to feel safer with Scarlet. Or is it the other way around?

Gina is sitting on the floor, cross-legged. Broken china islands surround her in a lake of tea. Tears blot her cheeks. Her hands are spread out, fingers as wide as they can be.

"It's okay," Scarlet reassures her, putting an arm around her shoulders.

"Jesus, fuck!" shouts Josephine. "Gina! You stupid fucking bitch!"

"Give her a break!" Scarlet responds, as Gina sobs into her armpit.

"Why? She's ruined my fucking kitchen! Look at it!" Josephine is fuming, eyes almost teary. Emma is stood behind her, clearly unsure of which side to take.

"I'm sorry," Gina cries through tears.

"You listen to me, Gina," says Josephine, walking up to her. Gina's eyes glisten with terror.

"You listen to me right now. My flat isn't a place for you to have mood swings. If you carry on like this, we'll kick you out of this fucking band. You get me?!"

"I get you."

"I didn't hear you!"

"She understands!" shouts Scarlet. "Guys, come on. Let's cool things! Look, I'll take her home, alright?"

"What about this mess?" Josephine paces around the kitchen, suddenly kicking a piece of china against the skirting.

"It's just a few broken cups and some tea," says Emma, trying to be helpful. "Nothing serious."

"Yeah, but they cost money!" Josephine bellows. She storms out and returns to the living room.

"I'll get Gina home," says Scarlet. "Emma, see if you can calm Josephine down."

"I'll do my best." Emma's nearly torn in two at the doorway. It's as if there's a division sewn into the band already and she's at the stage where she's confused about which side to take, knowing that this moment is something she'll reflect on in years to come.

Susan's at the kitchen window, looking out. Is she lost?

"See if you guys can work through a few tunes or something," says Scarlet. She starts helping Gina to her feet. The poor girl is shaking and sobbing. Scarlet can smell the odour climbing up through her t-shirt. Damn it, why doesn't Gina take care of herself...?

She steadies Miss Trembles towards the exit, kicking aside a couple of beer cans and a wine cork. (She, very briefly, tries to wonder if it's a French vintage.)

By the time she's helped Gina to the ground floor, she realises that Susan never said goodbye. What's got into that girl lately?! Crazy! But she can't worry about Susan right now. There's too much wrong with Gina.

On the streets, the Saturday afternoon traffic rids Scarlet's musical ears of strums and notes, replacing them with steel and practicality. She can feel the world spinning.

"Fancy a drink?" she says to Gina.

"Yeah, I'd like that."

It's funny how Gina suddenly straightens up and smiles at the mere mention of alcohol.

They walk until they find a pub. It's not for the youth of today. They go inside and see a row of traditional ales. Old men – war veterans by the look of them – are drinking thick, black stuff.

"Two of your best," Scarlet says to the barman, a bearded man in his mid-fifties, cigarette resting between his lips. She hands him the money and pushes Gina GENTLY in the direction of the nearest table.

"I'm having a get-together with a few friends on the Second of February," says Gina as she sits down. Two dripping glasses of ale are planted on the table. The barman shuffles off, towel over his shoulder.

"I'd love to," says Scarlet, "but the Second of February is the annual pilgrimage to the Casseldens in Liverpool. Fuck, it's not long now. Fuck."

"Sorry, I should've remembered. What's the latest with them?"

"I heard a rumour that Paul's bought himself a new car." Scarlet rolls her eyes and takes a long drink of the pale stuff. "Hits the spot. Look, are you okay?"

"I'm fine. It's just..."

"Mood swings again," finishes Scarlet.

"Yep."

"Look, don't worry about Josephine. Give her a few days."

"I know."

"She cares about you." Whether this is true or not, Scarlet doesn't know. But she's gone too far to stop. "We all care about you."

"Thanks."

A group of three young women suddenly burst into the pub. There's excited chatter amongst them. Evidently something big has happened in one of their lives.

"I'm just so excited!" exclaims one of them – evidently the lucky one. She flaps about in her seat like a seal. Brown hair does its own routine.

"So you should be!" shouts one of her friends. "When's the big day?"

"We're thinking of Autumn sometime, but, oh girls, let's get drunk!"

"What'll it be, ladies?" asks the barman, approaching them.

"Champagne all round!" says the third woman in a thick Mancunian accent. "And some nibbles. Crisps or something."

Scarlet leans close to Gina and whispers: "Shall we get out of here?" She downs the last drops of ale.

"Sure." Gina drinks the remnants of her pint.

They stand up and Gina returns the glasses to the bar.

Scarlet is about to lead the way out when she lees a lone woman sitting in a corner booth. She has a quarter-full pint of lager sitting in front of her. She's wearing sports gear, glistening with sweat. She has a broadsheet piled up next to the glass. Long, black hair is tied in a ponytail. Her face is one of concentration. She's licking her lips at Scarlet.

"Scarlet?" Gina's tugging at her elbow. "Let's get going."

She forces herself to follow Gina out of the pub, glancing back at the dark-haired woman. The woman (*My God*, thinks Scarlet) is licking her lips even more. But Gina is eager leave.

They head back the way they came, but Scarlet decides to drag Gina into the city centre. After all, it's a beautiful day...

Walking along Embankment, Scarlet feels the burning desire to gauge Gina's opinion on something.

"That woman, back there in the pub..."

But she notices that Gina's sniffling again.

"Yeah, what about her?" says Gina. "She give you a dodgy look or something?"

"No, not exactly dodgy... Oh, Gina..." Scarlet wraps the girl in a thick hug. She's momentarily pissed at herself for being so self-centred. "Look, you've done nothing wrong, okay? Give Josephine a bit of time."

"I need help. I'm sick."

"You'll get help soon. We'll all help you get through this."

They hug for a few more minutes. With every passing instant, she becomes aware of an insane warmth inside her. It's the warmth of friendship. As they pull apart, she glimpses the watery eyes of Gina.

"Fancy another drink?" says Scarlet.

"Yeah, sounds good."

"There's a great place I know." She picks up her stride. "Come on!"

"Where are we going?" shouts Gina. "Scarlet?!"

"Covent Garden! Come on, Gina –"

"I can't." Gina stands still, leaning on the railing.

"Why not?" Scarlet knows her brashness will not win her any favours, but she can't help it.

"Because I don't feel the need to get blind drunk anymore. I'm not a pisshead."

"I never said you are. I wasn't planning to get drunk. Just have a few beers."

"Look." Gina seems so frail. There's an almost picturesque quality about her, as if she's perfect for preserving in this moment. A punk angel with baggy jeans and trainers and dark-set eyes. No doubt Gina sees the same in Scarlet. "Look, I've got some shopping to do, okay? I'll see you later." She starts walking away from Scarlet. She's a silhouette in moments.

Scarlet stands there for ten more minutes (or so she thinks), and then heads to Waterloo Station. As she walks, she thinks of the girl in the pub.

There was a mysterious awe about her. So mysterious. She could go back there now, see if the girl's still there.

She decides against it.

She gets on the train, having the misfortune to sit next to a politics student with John Lennon glasses and frizzy blonde hair. He's wearing an orange cardigan and a pair of corduroy trousers. It turns out he's heading to Sevenoaks as well. There are a few student flats on the outskirts of Sevenoaks which are good for postgraduates, she finds out from him.

"I'm staying with two guys," he says excitedly: "a lawyer who's taking a break from practice to do a Master's in American Law, and a doctor who's decided to do a PhD in protein synthesis. Good couple of guys..."

He's onto politics in a second:

"The Cold War is pretty much over. There're so many questions. There is freedom." He continues rambling: "George Bush has certainly got his work cut out."

Then he does a little side talk on NATO.

"You see, when the organisation was set up in Nineteen-Forty-Nine, the world had just recovered from such a disastrous war..."

Beethoven:

"Now, Moonlight Sonata is such a beautiful piece... I often have it playing when I have hefty studying."

Punctuality of the trains in 1989. Will we ever go back to the moon? The Kennedy assassination.

Eventually, Scarlet's had enough. After nibbling her tongue, she asks, "Are you gonna be using the train a lot?"

"Oh yeah – every day. If you use it regularly, we should start a discussion group of some sort."

"You don't wanna do that. What you really want is to stick your dick in my cunt, isn't it?"

The student looks shocked. Well, he is. His face goes pale. Scarlet isn't sure what he says next, but it comes out in a half-squeak.

"How much money do you have saved up?"

"Sixty-thousand." Oh, he's stuttering now, the poor boy. "Yes, sixty-thousand pounds."

"Good, so this is what's gonna happen when we get to Sevenoaks, we'll go your flat and fuck like animals; then you are going to leave your studies and travel the world for a year, with your sixty-thousand pounds. Is that fair?"

"Are you being serious?"

"Yes, I am."

"Very well."

"Oh, and one more thing, you must never set foot in Sevenoaks again... ever."

"I can agree to that." *Now* the student appears agitated. He's perspiring. And he's starting to get hard. The mountain is rising up from the sea.

When the train arrives in Sevenoaks, Scarlet leads Mr Geek by the hand. He's like a drunkard back in the good old days. The gentlemanly drunk. They don't act rough and violent. Instead, they lag behind, staring blankly at the sky, as if terrified of where they're being led to.

The apartment is located very near the station, as it happens. Just across the road – and along a bit. Very convenient.

"Why am I fucking leading you?" she snaps, pushing him in front of her. "I've only got a fucking hour."

He fumbles with a set of keys that clang like village bells.

"Just imagine my wet mouth around your dick," she whispers in his ear. She puts her hand between his legs and can feel him stiffening even more. He drops the keys. Swearing, he bends to pick them up.

"You guys are useless," she sniffs, taking the keys off him. She has no trouble finding the right one. Nudging him inside, she gropes her cunt, trying to make herself wet.

They tiptoe up a plastic staircase to his flat. She's not going to give him the keys this time. At his door, she shoves them in one by one until she scores.

"Home sweet home," she declares as they go inside.

The flat is warm and unclean. Soiled garments present tripping hazards to all concerned.

"How can you live in this fucking place?" she blurts out. "Now, where's your fucking room?"

"Just here," he tells. He pushes open a door on the left. His room is remarkably clean. "Just made the bed," he tells her with gleeful satisfaction.

"Then let's unmake it," she says, shuffling her coat off. She lunges forward and makes out with him, grabbing his crotch in her hand. "Let's make the fucking walls scream." She takes off her t-shirt and touches her nipples. "Come on, fuck's sake." She starts undressing him and pushes both of them into bed.

He enters her slowly and she shuts her eyes, listening to his moans. He comes shortly after she digs her nails into his back.

"Fuck me, that was good," she huffs.

"Yeah," the student replies, falling next to her. "Damn, that was fantastic!"

"Of course it was." But her mind is drifting back to the pub, to the woman in her fitness gear. She's imagining, just imagining, what those lips taste like.

She's thinking about going back to that pub in the near future. She's thinking about tracking the girl down.

Suddenly she tells herself that she's not ready for this. She's not ready to take such a leap into the unknown.

The student lies with his face staring at the ceiling. He's still stiff. Scarlet's tempted to suck him off and drink away the rest of him like he's an exotic substance. But she wants to be gone.

She nudges him awake and says almost menacingly: "Remember what I said."

She gets out of bed and pulls her clothes over her sweaty body. One last look at the lump of flesh on the bed and she creeps out the flat.

When she gets home, she finds that everyone's out. According to a note left by her mum, there's a council meeting and they want to put in an appearance.

She falls onto the sofa and drifts off to sleep for a bit. She wants to dream of the girl in the sports gear, but crazy images come into her head of the band crashing and failing before they've even left the ground.

Pursuit

27 January 1990

"Much better this week," says Josephine.

Their practice session has just concluded. Gina's in the kitchen, making tea; she's apologised a thousand times for her actions. Emma's practising her drumming technique; her hands move so rhythmically. Susan is testing a tune on her keyboard.

"Well done, guys," says Scarlet.

"I'm still unsure of a few things," Susan speaks up. "I mean, this song is simple. Girl meets boy. Girl falls in love with boy. Boy dumps girl. Yet, we're filling this song with all sorts of weird and wonderful lines. '*She looks at him like he's a fish in a tank/He looks at her like she means less than nothing.*' Guys, we've got a great song, but really, do we need lines like that? They're a bit off-putting."

"I agree," says Emma, flicking her hair.

"We need to think of a name for the band," says Josephine, spitting out sunflower seeds. "And a name for the debut album. Gina, you're the best at these sorts of things."

"I am?" stutters Gina.

The girl hasn't really talked to Scarlet since last week. She's guessing it's due to the stress of what happened, but she knows it's deeper than that. Did she, Scarlet, appear to be hitting on Gina?

"Let's get that kettle on," says Josephine. She still doesn't want Gina anywhere near that kitchen.

"Guys, I'm gonna have to jet off." Scarlet hoists herself to her feet and slaps her trousers. "Family fucking dinner tonight. Dad's bringing some lawyers around."

"Have fun," says Josephine. She doesn't notice – none of them do – that Scarlet's told a lie. Their friend has deceived them.

Scarlet waves, smiles, and leaves the flat. When she's sure she's out of sight of any prying eyes from Josephine's windows, she breaks into a run.

The pub comes into view as if no time has passed. It's busking in the chilly afternoon.

She goes inside and sees the barman, who appears to remember her ever so slightly.

"I need a favour," she says. "The girl who was in here last week with the sports gear. You remember?"

"Yeah, I remember." He looks extremely gruff.

"Has she been back?"

"Ain't seen her since last week, love."

"What about before that?"

"Never seen her before in my life, until last week. Look, darlin', I've got patrons to serve..."

She sighs

She feels at a loss. She's confused.

There's nothing more to do, but to go home.

The burning desire won't leave her. She realises, quite suddenly, that she's in love. Oh, fuck, it burns like the sun.

Are there tears running down her face?

She has this incredibly dirty fantasy of licking this girl, running her tongue over that hot body with the muscles pulsing beneath the skin. She doesn't want the girl to be squeaky clean: she wants to taste the sweat and filth; drink it in like the juice.

"Fuck," she groans.

There's a gym across the road. It looks cheap and fairly rundown. But the girl would go to a gym like that.

Scarlet, in her infinite wisdom, wanders in. Loud music punches her eardrums. There's a sorry-looking tattooed man sitting behind a grotty desk.

"Yes?" he says in a tough east end accent.

"I was wondering, mate, could you do me a favour?"

"Sure. Girl as gorgeous as you, wouldn't hesitate."

"Oh, fuck off. Look, can you help me or not?"

"I might. Soon as you give me a nice, wet, sloppy kiss."

"Look, I'm trying to find this girl. Dark hair. Goes to the pub after she works out here."

"Oh, that'd be Layla." The man sniggers violently and smacks the table. "Yeah, she often went for a drink after boxing class. She's a little slut. Fucks every guy in sight, so I'm told. She actually left this gym and changed to another one in the West London. Well, given that she's knocked everyone senseless over here, she really needed a switch."

"What gym?" demands Scarlet.

"I keep forgettin' the name of it. It's by this new hospital. Think it's called – oh yeah, that's it... Grinding Pain! Silly name for a gym, but, yeah, that's the place..."

Scarlet's running. The man shouts something after her, but she doesn't give a damn. She gets a taxi and she's pleased, overjoyed, thrilled when she tells the driver where to go and he knows the place. The traffic moves in her favour! It flows like warm, soothing water. She's got an itch between her legs. She's going to make Layla hers, whatever happens. She's going to caress the girl and make them both happy in every single way.

No one will complain.

The taxi arrives rather quickly at the gym. Grinding Pain, how shall we say, looks derelict. White paint falls off the outside in great flakes. Rubbish bags sit outside, stagnant. A cat strolls along aimlessly, as if it's praying that the pavement will open up and swallow it whole.

Scarlet pays the driver and rushes inside. She's worried, quite obviously, that the grubby man was mistaken about the girl (after all, more than one girl *must* go to the pub after exercise class), or that he deliberately misled her. But her fears are quashed when she sees a photo of the girl proudly proclaiming itself on the desk.

"I need a favour," she says breathlessly. "A big one. I need to find Layla..." Her voice drops. Something in the back of her mind warns her about the photograph. It's so beautiful, too beautiful, too perfect, with a frame that's too perfect. Layla's on a mountaintop somewhere, crouched, big gritty smile on her face. Two candles are burning silently at either side of the frame.

The receptionist, a young woman with red-rimmed spectacles and blonde hair tied in a bun, says words that Scarlet dreads, but that she's expecting:

"I'm sorry, but Layla was killed yesterday in a traffic collision. Did you know her?" The words drift in and out of the ether like a dying flame that behaves like a stampede that is fading out like a swarm of bees dissipating into a nothingness. "Did she mean something to you? I'm so sorry..."

Scarlet is running out of the gym. She stumbles on a loose paving slab and nearly falls over. She's crying, heaving, wanting to disappear.

She finds a taxi, tells the driver to get her to the station. She needs someone to hold her so desperately. Oh, she needs it. She wants to fall into Layla's arms.

Oh, Layla, that *had* to be her name. She's a ghost, a spirit of a lost chance at forbidden, dirty love.

Fuck, she thinks. Fuck it all.

Somehow, she makes it to the train station. Somehow, she keeps it together as she boards the train. She sits in sullen silence as she is taken back to Sevenoaks.

When she arrives, she sees the two policemen, who love nothing more than to dig up her past, sitting in their patrol car outside the station exit. She avoids looking at them, pointing her face at the floor. She stealthily heads to the flat of that politics geek. She rings the bell and is admitted by, she presumes, the medical student – judging by the Oxbridge look.

"I'm looking for your politics friend," she says, pleading, on the brink of tears, fighting to keep them buried.

"Oh," says the student, "he left yesterday. I believe he's in France, trying his hand at hostelling." He smiles and slams the door shut, as if sensing her torment and taking advantage of it, like bacteria in a wound.

When she gets home, her mother's on the phone. Thinking the call is about insurance, she heads upstairs. Her mother yells up at her, "Josephine on the phone for you, Scarlet!"

She goes back down and takes the receiver.

"Hi, Scarlet." Josephine's voice is dark and critical.

"Yeah?"

"We've got a spot at a music festival on June Fifteenth. It's in the north of Scotland. I can't think why, but they want us. Listen, I don't know what's got into you; you seemed a little distracted this afternoon. But we need you to focus if this is gonna work. This is our big break, Scarlet. I want your full attention. Do I have it?"

"Yes," says Scarlet. No hesitation.

Interlude Number 2

Well, Scarlet is having problems, that's for sure. She's lost a chance to find happiness.

This can be said for certain, because Layla had fallen for Scarlet, right there in the pub. Such a beautiful chance at happiness... lost. Burned.

Layla had been cycling to the gym when a car cut across her. Her neck was broken. Death was instant.

A doctor at the scene would later say that the girl's death had traumatised him, caused him to leave the medical profession, and write bestselling books on the numerous failures of the medical establishment of Great Britain.

By coincidence, he'd also been flatmates at university with Herbert Buxton, a prominent music journalist in the Sixties. He will play a big role in Scarlet's life, but we're getting ahead of ourselves. It's not until several years later that he comes in.

The point I'm trying to make is that Scarlet has been affected by what's happened. This will affect her music and, more importantly, the band's fate.

The story will fast-forward now to June 13th, when Scarlet and the others are travelling north.

Nothing much has happened. Yes, you may want to know how Scarlet coped, but there's nothing much to it. She cried a lot, and drank herself unconscious a number of times.

Oh, wait, I nearly forgot. We're not quite ready to go to June 13th. First, we need to go to February 2nd, when we meet the Casseldens.

Now, let's return to the story...

The Casseldens

2 February 1990

The alarm is made even more painful by the two pints she had after band practice last night.

Her dad's up already. He probably has been since Five A.M. Five cups of coffee, straight down.

Mother's probably been getting a little bit of beauty sleep. Then again, she's probably got herself a cup of coffee also. She needs to be alert today.

Scarlet looks at her alarm. 07:01. For a moment, she forgets what day it is. But, of course, she remembers pretty quickly. February 2nd. Groundhog Day in America. But here, it's the annual pilgrimage to the Casseldens in Liverpool. Dreary fuckwits.

She pulls herself out of bed and stumbles to the bathroom. She needs to work on her guitar a bit more. Josephine's been so critical of her lately. The two of them, according to Susan, will end up coming to blows someday. But –

"Scarlet!" Dad calls up. "Are you up yet? We leave in an hour. I'm not being late for them!"

Grudgingly, she showers, massaging her breasts, trying to get rid of the sweat and fatigue from last night.

Since Mum and Dad met the Casseldens six years ago at a funeral, they've been in separable. Boring chitchat seems to take precedence over humanity with them. No wonder they've bonded like ships lost in the night. The Casseldens visit London frequently and they often have dinner together in the city; but every February 2nd, Dad insists on visiting them at their home in Liverpool.

By the time she comes down to breakfast, her family has nearly finished theirs. Alastair is spooning the last of his porridge into his mouth. For a wannabe lawyer, well, neatness isn't his greatest strength.

"How did Paul get on with that deal in France?" he asks.

"I'm not quite sure yet," says Dad. "Though when he phoned me last week, he seemed confident in the whole thing."

"I'd be surprised if he didn't have any luck," says Mum. "The damn French are the problem. I bed stupidity has gone straight to their heads."

Dad seems to have the answer, as always: "You under-estimate Paul, my dear. He is a smart and capable insurance broker –" He glances at Scarlet.

Scarlet pours herself some coffee and sits at the table. She grabs a slice of toast from the Toblerone holder and butters it. It tastes rubbery, but it's so good she has another one. She listens to tales about insurance and investment and banking, all capped off by Paul's ingenious new purchase of a 1989 Volvo 240 DL.

"You ought to pay attention this time," her dad says, "instead of having your head in music."

"I'm breathless with anticipation," she mumbles sarcastically.

"That's quite enough," snaps her mum. "James, isn't it time we hit the road?"

"Yes, we'd better start moving." Her dad is rising from his seat. He sips his coffee and disappears upstairs. He's there all too briefly before he returns, car keys, thermos and overcoat in hand. "Let's go!" He adjusts his shirt and sweater as he leads the way.

Scarlet doesn't get the chance to brush her teeth. It's merely a case of grabbing her coat and following her brother to the car.

Mum and Dad argue about the best route to Liverpool. Mum locks up whilst Dad rushes to the driver's seat. As soon as Mum's inside, he starts the engine, forgetting that: 1. He's left the car in gear, and 2. He hasn't put the clutch down. The car jerks forward. He slams the brakes just in time before they roll dangerously into the road.

Scarlet hates cars. They're so claustrophobic. They remind her of the corporate life she doesn't want. She'll fight to the death before she becomes part of the corporate mass. She wants a life of music; she's chosen it and it's chosen her.

They leave Kent, a county where she feels safe, and head towards the north of England. It's the first time she's been up this way since the new decade commenced. Already she's dreading what awaits her.

Last year Paul criticised her for wearying a stud earing and dressing in punk clothing. Apparently it wasn't *normal*. This year she's made sure to wear a larger stud earing and the gayest punk t-shirt she can find. If he doesn't like it, he can go fuck himself... tightly.

She's so determined to be who she is that she's drowned the rest of the world out. Her proud ability to be who she *is* will be severely tested in the years to come. The Casseldens are nuisances, but they won't be the ones who drag her down.

She will experience so much pain and hurt before the decade's end. Some challenges will bring her down, others will propel her forward. Some people will love her, but, deep down, most will have a dislike of her. She's beautiful, lovable, but she's only human.

The closer they get to Liverpool, the more excited her dad becomes. He's muttering about whether Siobhan has persuaded Paul into buying that conservatory. Or whether Paul is serious about that cruise in the Pacific he mentioned to them just before Christmas.

"What are our holiday plans this year?" asks Alastair.

"I've had my eye on Spain," says Dad. "Apparently the north coast is beautiful."

According to Paul, Scarlet thinks. She's hoping to get away with the girls this summer. She needs time away.

"Do you think there will be anywhere to park?" says her mum. "Last year we were mucking about for over an hour trying to find a space!"

"Ah," says her dad, "the Casseldens have had their driveway completely redesigned! They've even got those little LED lights lining it!"

Paul and Siobhan don't know about the band. She wants to keep things that way.

As they journey up the motorway, Dad's mood becomes more erratic. The first meeting with the Casseldens since the dawn of the new decade is bound to bring some new boring shit to discuss.

She realises, all too late, that she's left her Walkman at home.

Her mind drifts. She wants to be back in Edinburgh. She misses that place. The three weeks she spent there with the girls last year were pure bliss. They were happy days. They drank pint after pint in the pubs, drawing perverted attention to themselves. She allowed herself to be picked up several times. An interesting way to see Edinburgh...

She remembers one of the guys she met. A photographer. He was up from London to get some pictures of Scotland's capital for some magazine. A nice guy, a true gent. Someone who would always watch over her. But she told him she was too busy for a relationship when he asked her to dinner. She didn't even catch his name.

They arrive in Liverpool only half an hour behind schedule. A little congestion on the motorway, but not a massive deal.

Winding their way through the roads and streets, they edge ever close to The House Of Sheer Boredom. Just a few minutes until the lectures begin.

Paul's standing on the driveway. He's wearing a peach shirt, a cardigan with little patterns on, and grey trousers... complete with soft leather shoes.

"Welcome!" he booms as they pull into the driveway.

Her father turns off the engine, applies the handbrake, and steps out, shaking Paul firmly by the hand.

"Happy Nineteen-Ninety!" shouts her father.

"Same to you!" replies Paul. "Same to you!"

Scarlet gets out of the car reluctantly, but knowing she has no choice. She can only embrace the inevitable.

"Marianne!" greets Paul, rushing Scarlet's mum into a tight hug. "You look in excellent form, if I may say so." He gives Alastair a firm shake by the hand. "I haven't congratulated you on your graduation from law school last year. Well done!" Lastly, he turns to Scarlet. "I'm looking forward to seeing how your... band... develops." He waves them all in like Peter O'Toole in *Lawrence Of Arabia*.

They go through a drab, dark hallway, full of ornaments, oil paintings, photographs of the Casseldens on various trips to France, mock sea navigation instruments, and a couple of muskets. Paul leads them through to the living room, inviting them to take seats on the leather sofa and companion armchairs. Scarlet takes one of the two chairs: she likes being by herself, sealed off from the others.

As the others take their positions, Paul goes off to search for his wife. Scarlet hears him mumbling about the weather forecast for the next few days.

Her dad's sitting excitedly, constantly fidgeting, impatient for it all to begin.

Paul returns with his wife, who promptly embraces them all. Scarlet hates the smell of lavender that comes off her. Siobhan has had her hair treated with every chemical known to man. Siobhan has dressed well for this occasion: white shirt, dress, bangles, earrings. Siobhan is trying to make an impression, no doubt about it. Siobhan has money on her mind.

Coffee and biscuits are brought in. Everyone's seated. Dad and Paul are primed for launch.

Paul kicks off: "Ladies and gentlemen, welcome to the new decade. There are plenty of exciting opportunities ahead. But there is also uncertainty. Gone are the yuppie times of the Eighties, gone are the safe days of the Seventies. We live in the age of uncertainty. Over the next few years, I predict that this uncertainty will become the dominant player in business. Everything's about getting ahead now. If you're not ahead, you're nowhere. Remember that."

Scarlet zones out now.

She's terrified.

At lunchtime, they're all gathered in the dining room. Roast dinner is on the cards today. They're in their places. Even

Scarlet – for the tiniest of tiny moments – feels she's part of the crowd.

"In Nineteen-Sixty-Two, when Siobhan and I were a young couple, just starting out, we went to America for a period." Paul likes to begin with a story. "There we were, in New York City, glittering lights, you name it. We toured the States, met people, visited businesses, tried to get a sense of the environment. So much happened, including, of course, the assassination of JFK. America in the early Sixties was a fantastic place for investment. But..." he throws up his hands. "...those days are gone. This decade ahead will be scary, but opportunistic. You have to make your mark... hard. All this rubbish about liberalism, cast that aside. It's of no use. Getting on top is all that matters."

"But, surely enjoyment in life comes into it?" says Scarlet.

"Enjoyment?!" Paul exclaims. "Bloody hell!" He bursts out laughing, as does his wife. "Enjoyment? Enjoyment?! There's no fun in getting to the top, trust me!"

"Then, why do it in the first place? If you don't enjoy doing it, there's no point." She knows she's put herself on the line by saying this, knows that she could be humiliated beyond all belief.

"When we were in America, we saw one thing, Scarlet." Paul's response is far calmer than she expected. "People clambering to reach the top like ants going up a pyramid. Imagine you're on that pyramid..."

She'd rather not. She's thinking about the lyrics to a new song.

"...clambering up and up and up. Then you pause – just for a moment – to have a bit of fun. Someone runs past you. Before you know it, another one goes by. And another. And another. And another. You're at the bottom. Up and up and up. There's only one way to survive: money, money, money."

"What about security against financial loss?" says Mum, as if on cue.

Scarlet's hungrier than she realised. She gouges at the roast potatoes with her fork. Siobhan is a very good cook, it has to be said.

Lunch goes on and on and on.

Dad and Paul end up talking about the future of the American economy.

"Oh, but I don't particularly think George H.W. Bush is the right man for the job," says Dad.

"But I disagree on that," replies Paul. "I disagree most heartily."

After debating American politics for the next half hour, Siobhan changes the subject to what is for dessert: "Lemon meringue pie."

Scarlet hates this vile stuff. Why does she get the feeling that Siobhan's made this just for her? It's reprocessed sick. They should feed this to prisoners! But Scarlet has no choice. She must.

Then the conversation switches to Thatcher.

Paul is unmistakably pro-Thatcher. He launches into how her reforms made Britain stronger and more prosperous. He also defends her actions over the Falklands.

Dad's position is mildly different. He is very supportive of the way Thatcher reformed Britain, but he believes that she went too fast. He also believes that she should have placed massive standing armies in the Falklands after the conflict.

For a moment, Scarlet's distaste dissipates. She watches the two men debating times past, as if afraid of the future. But the moment is a moment. It is brief. So brief that you could debate as to whether it existed or not.

Paul has just been given an update of Scarlet's music.

"How many records have you made?" he asks.

"None so far. We're going studio in a couple of months to audition."

"And you've been together since...?"

"January."

"Wow. That's very fast."

"I thought the John Harvey-Jones's of the world lived life at such an extreme pace," she responds. She knows that she's falling. The day will come when she will lose her resolve to use such phrases.

Dessert is cleared away and everyone moves through to the living room. Siobhan brings through some filter coffee in a silvery pot: a great tall thing with handles and a rod poking out the top. She sets it on the table and jams the rod firmly down. There's bubbling inside. She goes back to the kitchen and returns with a tray of coffee cups and a sarcastic smile.

The subject moves to something that is of mild interest to Scarlet: entertainment. But there's an obvious catch: *what Paul Casselden thinks* is the best entertainment:

"I've been reading a lot of Lynda La Plante at the moment. Excellent storylines, must be said. I do love crime fiction. It's so... to the point."

"That I agree," says Dad.

The rest of the afternoon is taken up discussing a bloody great variety of things: up-and-coming crime writers; U.S. deployment of tactical nuclear weapons in Europe; new business opportunities in Scotland; the weather; more about Thatcher; Paul and Siobhan's planned cruise next year to South America; Alastair's future career in law.

"I must say, young man, you've done bloody well," says Siobhan.

This is the point where the second pot of coffee has come in. Siobhan, bless her soul, has provided dark chocolate biscuits wrapped in silver foil as well. This is the point where Paul Casselden really digs his heels in:

"So, how is your career going?" he asks Alastair.

"Very good. My firm has looking at case studies, including Ruth Ellis. To give us some further training..." Alastair has been jittery like this ever since he started back in mid-January. Is he trying to get Paul's approval? "But I've been doing great. I'm really fitting in well."

"Excellent."

"This is a man of the future," says Dad. He sips his coffee noisily and starts unwrapping a biscuit. "Ten years from now, he will be a big name. Mark my words, Paul."

Scarlet thinks where she might be in ten years. She hopes to be in the midst of glittering lights on a stage somewhere. The reality is, she won't be. It will all end in failure – apologies if I've spoiled the story for you, dear reader – and she will be left with nothing.

Let's take a few minutes.

The Casseldens are what you might call a 'career couple'. I won't go into much detail about them: they have two sons who are off somewhere working for insurance firms. They love their French wine, luxurious cruises, business books, that sort of stuff. The family lives a quiet, uninteresting life. Well, it depends how you define 'uninteresting'.

What Scarlet is experiencing right now is difficult to describe. It's one of those extremely bizarre sensations. But it's fair to say she feels a sense of deep sadness and pain, and fear. She swells up in the fear of failure. What if she never succeeds? What if the band becomes nothing except a footnote somewhere?

Whilst everyone talks about their careers (Paul has recently done business with a car dealership), Scarlet lets her mind drift. She's on top of a hill somewhere looking upon her fans below. Does she feel herself slipping? Can she feel anything anymore?

Something Siobhan says to her snaps her back.

"I'm sorry?" stutters Scarlet.

"I was wondering if you'd considered another career path," says Siobhan, refilling her coffee cup. "Music doesn't seem the right thing. No chance of making a penny."

"We're going to give things a good shot; I mean, if it fails, it fails."

"I think what Siobhan is trying to say," interjects Paul, "is that you need a main bread-and-butter career. Keep the music as a pastime."

"I have my art," she finds herself protesting.

"Yes, but that's not –" Paul, normally able to have a lively debate, is obviously struggling to find the words. Eventually though, he finds such a precise set of words which seem to fit perfectly, so perfectly. It's as if this whole world can fit him and his whole ego in. "It won't get you anywhere," he tells her.

"Paul's right on that," says Mum. "You have to think about your future."

"But music is the thing I love," Scarlet shoots back. "It's my true love."

"I'm not saying *abandon it*," Paul's on fire again. "Just keep it on the backburner. The world of business is not as dull as you might think..."

"Yes, it is," she answers him. "Tell me, where is the joy in it?"

"In making money," Paul and Siobhan say in unison.

"That's my question answered," Scarlet mutters. She can *swear* Siobhan is raising her eyebrows bitterly. Bitch. Sour, vile bitch.

"Think about what we've said," Paul tells her. "Bloody hell! It's been a lengthy day!"

"We could chat for hours more, Paul, but..." Dad's glancing at his watch. "We do need to think about getting on our way. The traffic's going to be a nightmare." Dad's not in any hurry though. His face is pained. He wants another hour here, at least. But he knows that London traffic isn't the nicest. He knows that he has a busy day tomorrow.

After some minor spitter-spatters, asking about how various family members (after all, they met the Casseldens at a funeral six years ago. Funny how bereavement can bring people together. Oh, fuck! Auntie Mary is dead! We barely fucking knew her, but oh, what the hell, we have to go to the funeral. Let's be as miserable as humanly possible. On the plus side, there's a buffet...) they head to the door. Hugs are exchanged. A few pecks on the cheek. Scarlet shuts her eyes as the Casseldens embrace (wrong word) her.

Mum, Alastair and she go to the car, whilst Dad has a last brief conversation with Paul. Siobhan skulks in the doorway like a cheetah about to pounce.

After about ten minutes of farewell chat, Dad finally waves goodbye and gets into the driver's seat. Just as he's about to pull (reluctantly) away, Paul comes to the window. Dad quickly winds it down.

"We'll have to grab lunch sometime," says Paul. "I'll try to rendezvous with you in London one of the days."

"Sounds good, Paul. Right, better be on our way. I'll give you a call in the next few days."

"Very good, James. See you!"

The car leaves the Casselden's driveway with a damp thud as slope meets flat. Scarlet refuses to glance behind her. Oh, she won't dare risk seeing Siobhan at all, that final glance which can seal everything like concrete.

They motorway is pitch-black with a hint of sodium orange.

Scarlet thinks of titles for new songs. She's determined to get an album ready for submission by the summer. Obviously, she'll succeed. I mean, you've no doubt listened to all of their songs. You know that their debut album sold like wild rain. Forgive me, I'm having issues with telling their story. It kind of goes with the territory, when you're describing the life of a band that had such extremes. But I try my best.

The journey back is long and uneventful. No congestion or traffic jams, thankfully. Even around the outside of London, the traffic level is agreeable. (This isn't quite the 21st Century.)

When they arrive home, it's nearly Ten P.M. Scarlet goes straight to her room. She's unwilling to be sucked into the 'review' of the pilgrimage that's always discussed in the living room.

Later that night, she finds herself dragged in front of a documentary about the future of the financial markets. Surprisingly, it gives her focus. She's thinking of new lyrics. The lights are turned off and the T.V. gives that fierce glare that makes your eyeballs burn.

Finally, it's time to go to bed. And she's very glad to do so. She says goodnight to everyone, brushes her teeth, and collapses, fully clothed and facedown, into her bed.

She wants to dream of songs and lyrics, but she finds herself trapped in a never-ending lunch with the Casseldens.

A Life Called Scarlet

13 June 1990

"Fuck's sake," Josephine curses as she loses another game of Snap with Gina. "Fuck you!"

"Hey, keep it down!" says Emma. "I'm trying to sleep!"

They're on a coach passing through the Lake District, on their way to Glasgow. Outside, it's dark. Other people on the bus are gently snoring away, all in a state of bliss, as if they don't care about the journey or the destination.

The girls have got a hotel booked in Glasgow for one night. The festival organisers have agreed to pay for the accommodation in Inverness. But the hotel in Glasgow (which they're using as a stopover on the way back) has come out of their own pockets. It was Josephine's idea to have a full day in Glasgow, give them an opportunity to get some practice in and relax for a bit.

Scarlet has been doing well since losing Layla.

One of the things she's been doing over the past few months is trying to pursue Emma. At first it started as a mild wonder at what the girl would look like minus her t-shirt. But now she's trying to find ways of cornering Emma behind the stage after they've been on and trying to say things which will get the girl to fuck her. She's decided on a number of approaches:

1. *The Gradual Incline.* She sits down with Emma and says a number of things which involve lesbianism. *Gradually,* Scarlet increases the lesbian content until Emma wants it.
2. *Straight Up.* Simple, she tells Emma that she wants to fuck her.
3. *Extreme Risk To All.* She leads Emma to a secluded spot, probably a hotel room, takes her t-shirt off and presses her breasts into Emma's face.

But Number 3 would, of course, be wrong. Yes, she knows that.

The card game continues its merry little course until Josephine and Gina (the wound has healed well between them) give in to each other's cleverness. The game ceases with as little grandeur and splendour as it began. The two of them fall asleep so soundly and softly and sweetly that, well, quite frankly, it could pass off as nothing. Yes, that's right, dear reader, a nothingness. You may, dear reader, have had such an encounter during your life, i.e., a kiss with a random stranger during a night out with friends, or a smile from a pretty lady across the street – yes, that's it, a smile. Such wonderful moments exist for such brief moments, and then they are forgotten about, going away forever. That's what it was like for Josephine and Gina. That moment was there; it was beautiful; now it's gone. It's like that for the other girls. Moments. Gone. Pride. Gone.

Scarlet is the last to fall asleep.

14 June 1990

Their arrival in Glasgow is not marked with anything special. Why would it be? They're not famous yet. They're barely known, even to themselves.

It's Six A.M.

"Right, girls, get your shit," snaps Josephine, as they alight from the coach. "Fucking hell," she groans. "What a dump this place is."

"Stop being so bitter," Susan tells her. "We've only got one night here anyways."

"Has anyone been here before?" asks Gina.

The group of them have left Buchanan Bus Station and entered Sauchiehall Street, bemused and befuddled.

Josephine's got directions to the hotel; she stands with the map in her hands, looking to be on the brink of swearing and losing her temper. "I think we need to go to the right," she says. "Yeah, to the right."

They wander along like a group of tourists, adrift in their own dimension. Scarlet is feeling what can only be described as wanderlust. She's never been to Glasgow before, never really cared for the place, but she feels drawn to it now, in love with it. She knows she'll be coming back. Indeed, this city will prove to be a major influence in the band's music, as well as providing them with several major venues in the years ahead.

After a bit of searching, fighting, swearing and arguing, they find the hotel. Actually, it's a cheap, funky, grotty little place. More appropriate. There are two of them to a room (apart from Josephine, who's arranged things to get her own space). Scarlet was asked by Gina if she wanted to share a room with her. This was weeks ago, way before she realised that she was developing an attraction for Emma. Scarlet is therefore overjoyed and a little scared when Gina tells her that she, Gina, has decided to bunk with Susan instead.

Fuck.

When Scarlet goes into the hotel room (it's a bit shit: two single beds and a small coffee table, complete with kettle and sachets, plus a cramped-looking bathroom), she feels pangs build up inside her. Emma's bending over her bed, fishing stuff out of her bag. Scarlet wants to go over and –

She snaps out of it.

No.

Emma turns around and smiles, saying in what seems to be a taunt, "You don't mind sharing with me, do you?"

"Not at all," Scarlet replies. "Emma, there's something... I need to talk to you about something."

"Sure. Is everything okay?"

Before Scarlet can answer, there's a knock at the door. Josephine tells them that they're going for a spot of breakfast.

"Tell me later," whispers Emma.

"Sure."

They find themselves in George Square. My God, they look lost, strangers in the morning. They've just had breakfast at a local café and are sightseeing to pass the rest of the day.

"Not bad," says Susan.

"The city's a nice place," Gina adds.

They're about to get into a conversation about the architecture, until Josephine shouts, "Will you two shut the fuck up? Let's pose for a family photo."

They gather together, Scarlet and Gina kneeling, Emma and Susan standing behind. Josephine finds a passer-by, a man strolling along in his own little world; she drags him over into their world and gives him the camera. Quick as a flash, she takes up a position next to Emma.

Click and flash.

"Nice one, girls," remarks Josephine, taking the camera off the man. He smiles and heads off.

Ten minutes later, as the man walks around a corner, head in the clouds, he will knifed in the back. Ambulances and police cars will descend on the scene. It will cause mass hysteria in Glasgow; a few protests will call for the return of the death penalty. How dare a thug attack an innocent man and steal away his life!

But Scarlet and the girls will be well away by the time the first police sirens wail. In the murder investigation, an inspector, on the basis of witness reports, considers bringing the girls in for an interview, but decides against it.

As they leave the square, Emma says, "We should rendez-vous here in ten years, whatever happens. June Fourteenth, Two-Thousand."

"I'll stick to that," replies Scarlet.

The others agree.

But that reunion will never happen. The very fact that Emma's suggested such a thing clearly shows that fragments are appearing already.

Interestingly, on September 19th, 2014, the day after the Scottish Independence Referendum, Josephine will come to the square.

But she won't be same woman she is now. She will be middle-aged, overweight, and a bitter alcoholic, traumatised from several abusive relationships. She will wander through the crows, reminiscing about the days of the band. She will be a shadow of who she once was, a downtrodden shadow that drinks spirits from the bottle.

But that's years from now.

In this moment, the girls are tight.

They mill around for the rest of the day, visiting museums, eating a hearty lunch just outside Central Station. Josephine's attempting to get them to *unwind a little*. But it's not working. In the end, they wind up back at the hotel. They do a little bit of band practice in Josephine's room, but are told by the landlord that they are "disturbing the peace and quiet". Eventually, after a meal out and a few quiet drinks, they get an early night.

So, Scarlet is in bed. She stares at the ceiling, glad that their first performance is so near, yet also swelling up with a mild dread. She made sure she got changed and cleaned up before Emma returned from a trip downstairs to complain to the management about something or other, just in case there was an accidental viewing of naked or semi-naked flesh. She's hoping Emma's forgotten about the chat earlier.

But, just as she's about to fall asleep, she hears Emma say, "You wanted to talk about something?"

"Oh, it's nothing," replies Scarlet. "I just wanted to fly by some lyrics to this song I've been working on."

"Scarlet..." Emma's voice is sharp through the streetlight that streams into the room. "...I'm not stupid. Something's up. Tell me."

"It really is nothing, Emma."

"No, it isn't. Scarlet, I know you."

Scarlet's mentioned nothing of Layla to any of them. It's almost like they *were* lovers, and it's an affair that must be kept secret, lest it destroy a holy marriage.

Scarlet doesn't answer Emma's provocative statement.

Then Emma says it, as though the words were carved on a tablet by the Mayans, destined to be read at this exact moment in this exact room: "Scarlet, are you attracted to me?"

"Yes," she answers.

There is silence.

A pinprick of sweat falls down Scarlet's side. She's done it. She's destroyed the band. She consigns herself to the lonely slope back to the *real* world.

The lights turn on, so bright.

Emma storms over and Scarlet thinks that she's going to get slapped. But Emma lowers herself down and presses her lips against Scarlet's. They taste of melons and salt.

Scarlet's not sure if this is real. She watches as Emma takes off her nightclothes and climbs under the duvet with her. Emma begins undressing her, soft hands caressing her chest and thighs. It feels like every single sense of relief rolled into one.

"I've wanted you for a long time," says Emma. "We don't have to tell the others. This is *our* relationship. No one else's."

"I want you too." Scarlet can feel Emma breathing on her neck. She reaches overhead, fumbles for the switch, and casts them into darkness.

15 June 1990

"Let's go, girls," says Josephine. "Long ride north."

The lot of them are standing in the hotel lobby, bags ready. Scarlet's only got a small rucksack and a little shoulder bag — as well as, of course, her guitar. The others have got considerably more stuff. Gina probably gets the gold medal: four large bags, all shoulder ones, plus her guitar. Susan has a shoulder bag and a pink wheelie case. Josephine and Emma decided to share the weight, but it clearly hasn't worked well: they're both clearly pushed down by the enormousness of what they're carrying in unstable rucksacks. Josephine is clearly looking pained as she manhandles her luggage through the door.

The rest of the girls follow through. It's a torturous process and they are being given harsh looks from the manager and two of his desk staff as they try to fit through the opening. Yesterday, both doors were open, but today only one is. And it's Five in the morning and they are shattered as hell; Scarlet is, anyway.

The head back up Sauchiehall Street towards the bus station. Josephine is saying something to Susan: something was on the news yesterday about the demolition of the Berlin Wall officially beginning. Oh, dear reader, politics is *so* exciting...

However, when they reach the bus station and get on the coach, Josephine starts on about The Stone Roses. She and Susan sit together near the front of the coach. Gina is on her own, reading a book. It's not a crowded coach, thankfully. Scarlet and Emma are near the back, pinkies interlocked. They listen – well, they don't have much choice, do they? – to Josephine's verdict on The Stone Roses:

"God, I love 'em. The boyfriend loves 'em too. They've got so much rhythm in their music. Just flows like water." She goes on for a few more minutes and then starts doing renditions of the songs.

Scarlet feels Emma nudge her.

"Funny old year, isn't it?" says Emma. "I mean, look at what we've achieved!"

"Yeah, it's incredible. We've nearly got an album ready to go. Emma, we owe you one for this, getting this slot at the festival. It can't have been an easy thing to do."

"I did it for the band."

"No – you did it for us."

"Of course." Such feeble words from Emma. "I had this song stuck in my head. I dunno why. There're no lyrics to it, none at all. But there's the tune. Plus, I thought of the title..."

Scarlet's taken aback. She presumes that the song was something Emma had heard on the radio. But, oh no, it's something *original*.

"I think you'll like it," Emma continues. "But, it's not something that should be produced until a few years down the line, assuming we're successful, of course."

"We will be, don't worry. What's the title?"

"I wrote it about you." She hands Scarlet a small notebook. It's empty, judging by its crispness. On the first page, in Emma's neat little handwriting, right at the top: *A Life Called Scarlet*.

"Beautiful," says Scarlet. "I can't believe you'd..." The words trail off. "When will you find the lyrics?"

"Give me a few years." Emma grips Scarlet's hand. "I want to find out about you first. You're my inspiration."

"Thank you. You're mine too." Scarlet watches Emma as the girl's eyes close. If there is ever an instance of perfection, it's here, it's now. It's in the air between them.

Scarlet falls against the window and stares out, watching as urban turns into countryside, the hills growing like teeth, the sky opening into blueness.

She begins to fall into a trance, a darkness of the soul. She flashes half-in, half-out. What is she seeing?

She is flashing back before she realises it. Maybe it's the beautiful mountainous scenery. Maybe it's a car. It doesn't matter. She's flashing back. She reaches out for Emma, but the girl's not there. She's flashing back.

She's back.

She won't go there again. That was the day that set her on the dangerous path, trying to impress. She did something very bad trying to impress him. Too bad, if such a thing can be said. But she has to look forward, if such a thing can be said.

She has to focus on tonight. Those two cops at home can wait. Tonight is what's important.

They pass through a town called Aviemore. It's a sleepy looking place with its inhabitants shuffling about their daily business like the slaves of ants.

Scarlet would love to get out and stretch her legs. But there's no chance, obviously. The bus is making very good progress and they're expecting to arrive on time in Inverness. The traffic has been favourable. There was some congestion outside Stirling, but nothing too bad.

They leave Aviemore and continue north. The world outside is empty and fresh.

Scarlet can feel Emma shifting her weight, snoring lightly. She clutches her hand. A rough cough sounds behind her and she turns just in time to see an elderly woman snatch her head away, giving a rough squeak of disapproval. She's wearing a pink hat and glasses, as well as a dress decorated with awkward summer flowers.

Arriving in Inverness, Scarlet feels a renewed sense of optimism. Her band will soon get its kick-off, a much needed one. Everything has gone so swiftly to plan.

There's a newspaper folded up in the pouch on the seat in front of her. The main headline piece is about the demolition of the Berlin Wall. Interviews are promised inside. She thinks of the politics student, but immediately shuts such thoughts away.

Opening the paper, she intends to turn to the music section. But she's distracted by an article in the books section. An image shows a thickset man in his early fifties. He wears thick glasses and a chequered shirt. He's been photographed in his living room: a piano and a set of French windows dominate the background. The title says: *Music Journalist Publishes Debut Novel*. A small image of the front cover showing a woman running down a dark street is next to the picture of the author. It's called *Murder, Florence and Wine.*

She reads the article, nearly smirking:

By Jeremy Newcombe

Music journalist Herbert Buxton has taken his first venture into fiction with the publication of his debut novel Murder, Florence and Wine.

Set during the summer of 1976, it tells the story of a young student who travels to Florence on a language exchange. On a night out, she witnesses a murder by a local gangster. What follows is an intense thriller as she tries to escape the city and get back home.

I had the privilege of speaking with Mr Buxton when I went to visit him at his home in North London.

I asked Mr Buxton about his inspiration for the novel.

"Well, I was very interested in writing about 1976," he said. "It was such a hot summer that year and I wanted to write a story set in it. At the same time, well, I kept conjuring this image of a young woman alone in a city after witnessing a horrific murder. Also, I'm a fan of wine and Florence."

Mr Buxton was born in Leicester in 1940. He attended the University of Cambridge, studying English Literature, before drifting into music journalism. After graduation, he moved to the United States and worked for a large number of music magazines.

"It was a good time," Mr Buxton told me, as his wife brought us coffee. "I arrived in the summer of 1962 and left in 1970."

When asked about the reasons for leaving, Mr Buxton recounted that he felt the music industry in the U.S. was losing its kick.

"I spent the summer of '69 in New Orleans living with this amazing reggae singer. It was part of a project the magazine was

doing with him – I was to spend the summer living with him as he produced his new album"

Mr Buxton was then very keen to nudge me back to the book. He stated that his music journalism days were coming to an end. Instead –

Scarlet puts the paper back in the pouch. Boring. She will think back to this article a few years from now, but right in this moment, her thoughts, quite rightly, are focused on tonight.

When the girls arrive in Inverness, they feel lost. It's not surprising. They've never been here before.

Their hotel is located just outside the main railway station. What can be said about their accommodation for tonight, apart from the fact that it is a two-star establishment, fairly ordinary and relatively comfortable. They check in, the same room format as before. Scarlet and Emma are only too happy. They have a quick bout of aggressive lovemaking before heading to Josephine's room for a quick practice session.

After the guitars have been strummed and the words sung, they head to a small restaurant opposite the hotel for an early dinner. They eat in nervous silence, counting down the minutes until the performance.

They are due to be picked up at Ten P.M. from the front of the hotel and taken to the venue in the north of the city.

Josephine is eager to be ready at Half-Five, so she hurriedly gets everyone to eat and then pushes them back to the hotel. Gina complains, but then again Gina complains. Susan obeys, but she's very quiet about the whole thing. Scarlet and Emma work extra hard to be ready in time.

They stand in the hotel room, still as ancient statues. Scarlet has her guitar over her back. Emma, now Emma has her drums at the venue itself: she's ingenious enough to have sent the equipment on ahead.

They exchange one firm kiss and head downstairs. The others are waiting. It's not long before curses are directed at Josephine: they're outside when they could have slowed down a bit, eaten their dinner slower!

Just before six o'clock, a minibus pulls up. The driver looks gruff and dishevelled, bored of life to such an extreme that he may as well commit suicide.

"Let's go, girls," says Josephine, as the driver opens the back door.

They pile in like a bunch of hippies about to sing for peace.

Scarlet feels a sense of optimism like she's never felt before. She has a lot of faith. For a moment, she's tempted to talk to God (even though she doubts He exists).

"Are you ready girls?" Josephine chants.

"Yeah!" they all cry in unison.

The venue is like a carnival city. Tents poke up like castle turrets. The people stream around like rats. And there's something otherworldly about the jollity of the incredulousness of the place: the way the stalls offer candyfloss with a zest for life; the groups of young people on their well-earned nights out, talking without getting plastered; the lines of lights hanging in the air like a map of heaven. Then, of course, there's the bandstand...

It's plainer than she expects: a small platform of wood surrounded by black curtain. But there's an essence of invincibility about it, like it can turn a nobody from the street into a superstar.

The minibus takes them around the back of the platform. A man with wiry grey hair and a threaded cardigan waves his hand, signalling them over. They get off, their instruments deadly swinging weapons.

"My name is John Chandler," says the man with the grey hair, digging his snakeskin boots into the ground and rocking on them. "I'm managing the show tonight. You guys have the opening ten minutes of the show before the main act."

"Cool," says Josephine. "Cool."

"Okay, you guys better get set up."

A heavy looking bouncer with fat, pudgy hands appears from an entrance. "All clear," he informs them in a deep Scottish accent.

Scarlet can tell that this man, with his large form and eyes swallowed by big red cheeks, has known a life of pain and hardship. "Girls are good to get set up," he says.

"On you go then," John Chandler snaps.

"Let's go," says Josephine, hurrying them along. "Come on guys."

They go up a staircase that tunnels through the stand and step out on the stage. The curtain, drawn over their view of the audience seats and the world beyond, like a protective mother, flaps in the wind. The girls take their stations. Emma sits on the stool behind a set of silvery drums and gently taps each piece with a stick. Josephine strums her guitar lightly. Susan is touching the keyboard set up for her, stroking it, bizarre. Gina is pacing around. She flings her guitar strap over her neck.

There's the dull thud of cheering coming from behind the curtains.

"Do we know the firing order, girls?" says Josephine. "Two songs are all we've got time for, okay?"

"Two songs," says Emma.

"Do we know the order?"

Emma tells her the suggestions.

"Yes," the rest say, one after the other.

John Chandler enters the stage; one could say it's the scene of life. "Thirty seconds, girls," he informs.

Scarlet stands centre-stage, carefully positioning her guitar, moving the strap away from the skin of her neck. The microphone is throbbing in front of her. It's a brutal stain in her vision. All her life, she's waited for this. Now it's finally come along and all she can think of is Layla. The curtains slide apart and she is exposed to the world. A voice over the speaker system announces who they are.

Scarlet plucks a note and the first song begins.

"That's was incredible!" Emma booms.

It's much later now, you see, dear reader. After they had done their two songs, the big bouncer with sad red eyes escorted them away. Josephine wanted to stay and enjoy the main act, but the girls persuaded her that it would be better to go back to the hotel and relax, before hitting the town later. The minibus took them back like excited little hatchings and there was a big group hug in the lobby. Josephine, Susan and Gina went out for drinks, whilst Scarlet and Emma proclaimed exhaustion.

Far from it.

Scarlet and Emma are both naked, looking at each other. They haven't made love yet; they're too tired at the moment.

"He looked like a really unhappy guy," Scarlet blurts out randomly.

"Who?"

"The security guy. Looked on the edge of crying."

"He was probably tired or something." Emma strokes her fingers over Scarlet's back.

"He was just so sad. I dunno. Maybe I should go back. Maybe I should buy him a drink or something."

"Why would you do that?"

"I dunno." Her voice is faltering.

"Do you trust me?"

"Yes, of course."

"Roll onto your stomach, Scarlet, and spread your legs."

Scarlet does so, pushing her nose into the pillow. She feels Emma move over her, resting her elbows on the insides of Scarlet's kneecaps. A tongue runs between her bumcheeks, sliding into her anus. She tries to pull back, panicked, but a hand forces her back down.

"Relax," murmurs Emma. "You're so fucking tense. She licks again.

Scarlet shuts her eyes. She's not enjoying it, but then she lets go, falling into darkness, as the tongue slides deeper and deeper. She's spinning into memory like a screw in an old rusty building rigged for demolition. She's falling, tumbling, twirling like a petal caught in a rainstorm.

Scarlet comes out of her reverie. She knows that Emma has finished. The girl is pulling back, kissing Scarlet's thighs as she does so. Scarlet turns over and pulls Emma close.

"That was amazing," she says to Emma. "I'm so fucking wet right now."

"I bet you are," laughs Emma. "So, what did you think of tonight's performance?"

"Yours or the band's?"

"Ha-ha." Emma begins touching Scarlet's cunt. "I thought it was pretty good. The crowd seemed to like it."

"They did. Josephine seems confident that we'll get a deal with a record company soon."

"She's always confident." Emma gets out of bed and heads to the bathroom. "She's a confident woman, I'll give her that."

Scarlet sits up and watches the naked figure of Emma wash her mouth out. It's even more beautiful at this distance, skinny and spotted. Imperfection has its own unique tenderness; it doesn't have to impress a panel of judges. It is its own.

Then she sees Emma's bags. It didn't occur to Scarlet earlier, when they set off for Scotland, they're large, like the ones you see two-car families take on holiday.

"Going somewhere?" she questions.

"Yeah," says Emma, following Scarlet's gaze. "My gran's not well, so I'm going to stay with her for a few weeks. Sorry, I should've mentioned it earlier."

"It's okay. Everything all right with her?" Scarlet knows that Emma's gran, living alone in a cottage in Orkney, is often unwell. Her husband died five years ago from cancer, so the poor old woman is often bitter and miserable.

"Yeah," replied Emma, coming back to bed. "Just needs a bit of company."

"I need company right now," Scarlet tells her. "I've gone dry again."

"I bet."

Secrets and Hopes

1 July 1990

Since her return home, Scarlet has been a bit worried. There's been no word from Emma. Scarlet doesn't know the number of Emma's gran. She hopes the girl is okay.

It's morning. Eight o'clock. Scarlet's in her shack, painting away.

On Friday, she received a letter from a small gallery in London wanting to buy one of her pictures. Unfortunately, quite recently, she sold all of her paintings to various cafés, restaurants, bars, small galleries, smaller galleries, and tourist centres, so she's had no choice other than to start one from scratch. The gallery needs it by Tuesday. Funny how creativity flows when you're under pressure.

It's nothing special, the one she's painting right now. Nothing that should take too much time. There's so much stuff to do with the band.

Their performance in Inverness was highly praised. Reviewers called them *incredible, dangerous, amazing.* The girls have all been pleased beyond belief. They're actually getting somewhere!

Josephine's been busy making enquiries to record companies. Now that they've made their first mark out there, they shouldn't find it too difficult to get a record deal. They have an album ready to go, just as soon as they get serious interest.

Susan and Gina have been helping out where they can, spreading the word that there's a new band on the scene.

All of them understand that Scarlet is busy with real work at the moment, so she's been excused from band duties.

The morning passes quietly as she paints. Her hands and forearms, flecked with colours, move quickly and deftly. She's beautiful. She's always been beautiful.

It's probably nothing, but she thinks she's left the door unlatched. She turns, nearly knocking a plastic paint bottle over. As she huffs at herself for being so gullible (how could she have not looked at the door?), she notices that her painting trousers have come loose and shrivelled halfway down her arse. Her skin is so white. Now, it would be utterly wrong for her to touch herself here and now, but the bottle has been opened, so she's got to drink from it. She can spare five minutes, surely?

Knock. Knock. Knock.

She pulls her trousers up and unlatches and opens the door. It's one of the boys from three doors down. He's only nine, yet acts as a teenager sometimes.

"This came to our house yesterday, Scarlet, by mistake." He's avoiding eye contact as he hands over a small brown envelope. "See ya." The kid runs off, scampering away like a rabbit.

She shuts the door and goes back to her desk. She still feels wet and horny, but the letter takes precedence. She notices Emma's handwriting on the front. She has a feeling about what's inside, a sort of premonition. Nevertheless, she pulls it out and reads:

Dear Scarlet,

By the time you read this, I will be far away. Somewhere in the world. I left this letter with my grandmother to send after I had departed.

Scarlet, you made me happy. What we had together will remain with me for the rest of my life.

The truth is, I've been planning this for some time. I want to get out, go and see the world. You should do the same.

The band meant something to me, but I couldn't stay. I'm no musician, Scarlet, I never was. But when we stood on that stage, I felt like one.

I love you. I always have and I always will.

I know that you're probably angry with me for doing it like this, but telling you to your face would have made things harder for both of us. Much harder.

And you're special, Scarlet, very special. You have a talent that goes far beyond my own. The band has potential and I know that you will succeed. But never forget that there is a bigger world. Never forget that you can choose to walk away whenever you want. You are not a prisoner.

With Love,
Emma

Scarlet folds the letter up. First comes puzzlement, then anger, then frustration, then hate, then self-loathing. Emma is gone. Scarlet is pissed for letting her guard down. The cunt. The little fucking cunt. She scrunches up the letter and throws it into the corner. She's fucking angry.

No one, you see, can really know the precise moment when what happens, happens.

And there is such a thing as precision. It's in the dust motes and the bees and the whistling noise when you put your ear to a seashell. It's in the fragments of life that become fragments in your very fragmented memory. You can't see it; you only feel it for such a brief moment of time that you don't even register it.

That's why you can't know exactly when the door to her shack opens. But it does. The two police officers walk in. They're like distant family right now, rather than enemies.

"Just checking up on you," says the older one. "Heard you went away."

"I'm fine. I'd like you to leave me alone." She's fighting back tears.

The younger one sneers and walks out. The older one warns her that the past is never past and follows soon after. He's always been bitter.

Scarlet snarls, waits an hour, and then masturbates. There's no room for comfort. When she's done, she's angry at her sexuality. It's a sore that needs to be healed.

She finishes her work, heads for home, and waits some more.

She makes a brief excuse about her funding body inviting her to an art show. She'll be back late – and the funding body is paying for the train fare.

She showers, dresses in her leather gear, off to the station. She lets her hair down, shaggy, loose.

She's going to fuck tonight.

She thinks of the student only briefly as her train creaks in the direction of the big city. Is this the same set of seats they were in? Nah. Can't be.

In London, she goes to the nearest cashpoint and gets some money. She goes to a pub, downs eleven pints and

God only knows how many spirits, and then stumbles across London.

Somehow, she ends up at the same bar where she met Layla. She's ordered out before she's even placed her order.

"Too drunk!" the landlord yells.

She finds a club, but they won't let her in either. So, she goes to another one and this time she gets in. She dances, drinks shots.

She sees a guy. Floppy black hair, glazed face, red t-shirt. She goes to him. The music pounds her eardrums. She doesn't care. She grabs his crotch and smiles. Strong hands seize her and drag her from the music. Too drunk. She feels herself slumped on the cold wet ground. Thick voices call her a bitch and tell her never to come back.

She walks, half blind. She laughs. She vomits over front and screams that she's a slut that needs fucking.

Walking, stumbling.

She's somewhere. It's Seven Dials. Streets are empty; vacant, devoid. She goes to the central point and pukes again.

She sees someone running towards her. Real or not real? Imagine? The figure is panicked and he's funning full pelt. He heads into the darkness as though he never was. An echo.

She vomits again, legs giving way. The ground is cool and damp. There's a light drizzle in the air. She heaves and more wet sticky stuff comes up her throat. It's then she realises she's lying faceup. She's choking. It fucking burns!

She wishes she was gone.

She hates her existence.

Wanting to be consumed by the past, she drums and pummels and scrapes. There's a fight going on, but the past relents and lets her in.

The Monkey Cage

2 July 1990

Scarlet knows she is in a hospital before her eyes are opened. She can hear bleeps and fast feet. She feels sick. Her throat tastes of acid.

There's music in the background. She recognises the song. Recognises the singer. The album has only just been released. *I'll Be There*... Mariah Carey. Her debut, self-titled album.

As she opens her eyes, she can see the worried looks on her parents' faces. Alastair is skulking away in the background, his posture that of a lawyer's.

"Where am I?" she croaks.

"In hospital," says her father.

"Why?"

"You didn't come home last night, so we got worried," her mother informs her.

"This art thing..." Her father looks angrier by the second. "...it was an excuse, wasn't it? To go and get drunk. Why?"

Scarlet tells some story of a bad bottle of wine, how she was left by her friends with no money for a taxi. She knows that she's caused an embarrassment. She knows that she's overstepped the mark.

Today is no major drama. The doctor gives the all clear and warns her to watch her drinking levels. Unfortunately, he's not giving her anything for the hangover: she should take it as a lesson.

There will come a time when doctors who condemn female drunks are branded *misogynists* and other sorts of terms, but that day is not today. He files his paperwork and formally discharges her.

The family leaves the hospital, heading straight for the car. Dad's driving: he always claims that he is the better driver in London.

"Are we going to your sister's for Christmas?" he asks, as he navigates a large roundabout.

"Yes, I think that's the plan." Mum coughs into a hankie. "I think she is bringing her entire extended family over."

"I do admire your sister. She very family orientated. She recognises the importance of children going away and building up their own worlds and their own families, but everything always comes back to the main family, the elders, the men."

"Well, she's just become a grandmother, so you can bet you'll hear her talk about that. Doris tends to go on a bit, you know that, don't you?"

"Oh, I know that."

It occurs to Scarlet that they're taking the same route she took in the taxi on New Year's Day.

Mum and Dad go on about Christmas plans. The rivers and fountains of normal, everyday conversation have returned. The drama is over.

You see, dear reader – and I think you've guessed this already – Scarlet hates Auntie Doris. She lives up in Kings Norton, what Scarlet believes is a very ordinary part of the world. She had a fear that were going to stop on their way to visit the Casseldens earlier this year. More will come on this later, but you should be aware that Auntie Doris is very old-school: she believes that men are superior to women. Women should stay at home and bear children for their husbands. Anyways, let's not get ahead of ourselves. Patience, dear reader.

They continue out of London, driving coolly and in a state of selfish bliss.

Oh, I know you can't wait for December. We could skip ahead if you want. I know you secretly desire to see Scarlet's interactions with Auntie Doris, but this story is about more than just that.

Stay with me for a few chapters. And don't skip ahead, as tempting as it may be.

When the family arrives home, Scarlet is first out. She vomits on the driveway. Damn, she's hungover. She really needs some water.

The house seems to offer a cooling refuge. As soon as the door is open, Scarlet dives in, goes to the downstairs bathroom, vomits some more, tries to rehydrate herself. She thinks and cries so hard about Emma.

But Emma is gone! Does she not get it?!

When she feels a little better, she makes it a priority to phone the other girls, letting them know about Emma. They're shocked and horrified, but Josephine is mortified: they need a new player on the drums. It's easily sorted: Gina has some experience of playing the drums. Plus, do they need *three* guitarists? Of course not! No problem, it's sorted.

Meanwhile, their album is nearly ready for submission to record companies.

By the end of the day, after twenty or so frantic phone calls, things are finally cleared:

1. Gina is going to brush up on her drumming techniques and go over each of the songs.
2. Each member will promise to forget Emma. She chose to leave. She has to live with her decision.
3. They're going to have a lengthier practice session this Saturday.

As soon as things are settled, it begins to rain outside. She looks out, seeing the brutal devastation that rain causes to the road. It's flooding!

She's bored. Impatient. In truth, she's tired of the lack of success. She wants the band to be out there, making big sales and performing all over the world. Right now, she feels a sense of obscurity, as though she doesn't matter to anyone or anything.

She is like a monkey in a cage, screaming to be let out, hammering on the bars. She so desperately wants fame and fortune. Isn't that what everyone wants?

It might interest you to know, dear reader, that there's a small pub in west London on the end of a suburban street. A man sits on his own, drinking a pint of ale, bored of his miserable, lonely life. If he and Scarlet met, they would fall for each other. They would be happy, have a nice family. But they don't meet. They never find each other. He attends one of her concerts five years from now, but by then he is married. He jumps along with the music, but he goes home with his wife and thinks of Scarlet as nothing more than a good singer.

Love lost...

She spends a few minutes watching the rain and then goes to bed. Tired. Unbeaten. Unbeaten by the twists and turns of life.

Finalising The Debut Album

7 July 1990

"It's a wrap!" Josephine announces with glee. "Well done all! Especially you, Gina – you did very well."

"Thank you." Gina begins putting her drums away.

Susan goes to make them all tea. She's cursing about something, though it's clear the others can't hear what she's saying.

"What are you girls up to this weekend?" says Gina.

But Josephine cuts across. "Some news on the album front. There's a record company who might be interested in us. We've got a slot in their studio. October Eighth. I think – yeah, that's a Monday."

"When did you find out?" asks Scarlet.

"Oh, last night." Josephine flashes a quick smile, a rapid dismissal. "So, girls, make sure you brush up on all your skills. If we're confident, we'll get the record company's support."

"You should have told me about this!" Scarlet's eyes flash red.

"Why? Knowing you, you'd go out and drink yourself stupid."

Scarlet is speechless. Can you imagine that? Crazy, isn't it?

Tea is brought in. Gina's looking perplexed, as Susan (who obviously hasn't heard the argument) proceeds to put the tray down.

The confrontation is over before it lifts five feet off the ground. Soon enough, it's back to business. They talk mostly about getting ready for the submission. They agree to step up the practice sessions. Each one must be strict, business-like, and well-behaved. They have another, extremely quick run-through of two songs and then decide to call it a day.

Scarlet is determined to have a quiet word with Josephine. Why has she decided to take control of the band? It's like it's her pet project, a school experiment. Answers are what's needed.

Gina and Susan depart like mourners leaving a funeral before they get roped into going to the wake.

"Why didn't you tell me, Josephine?" she asks, following her into the kitchen.

"Bitch didn't even bother washing the fucking mugs," snaps Josephine. She turns on the water and puts some detergent int the water bowl. "Can you believe that?" She plonks all four mugs into the bubbles and begins the arduous process of washing and scrubbing.

"You gonna answer my question?"

"You gonna dry the fucking mugs?"

"Sure, I'll do anything you ask." Scarlet takes the offered tea towel and starts wiping the mugs dry.

"That sarcasm in your voice?"

"Maybe. You didn't answer my question."

"What, am I being fucking interrogated?"

"I just want to know why you enjoy taking the fucking piss?"

"I don't take the piss." Josephine shakes her hands, the specks of water cold sparks. "The truth is, I'm worried about you. Your commitment has been shabby, to say the least, and I worry."

"My commitment is strong. Just remember, this was all my idea."

"I know that. I haven't questioned your creativity." Josephine makes an uneasy pause. "It's just, shall we say, your other interests with Emma."

"Excuse me? What the hell do you mean?"

"I know about you and Emma." Josephine stands firm, still as a statue.

"Excuse me?"

"Oh, come on. I could see it a mile off. I always knew that you were a lesbian, Scarlet. You don't have to deny it in front of me. Come on, you know I'd never tell anyone."

"Dunno what you're talking about."

"I heard the two of you in Inverness. Grunting away in your hotel room like pigs."

"You're fucking sick!"

"Am I?" Josephine fills up a glass of water. She sips it slowly, watching Scarlet's every move.

"I loved her," Scarlet admits. "I loved her. I loved her so fucking much."

"And she's gone, isn't she? Did you drive her away?"

"No, I fucking didn't!"

"But she's off –" Josephine makes a wide berth with her hands. "– somewhere in the world. Hanging around with Chinamen, or pissing in a rainforest. I dunno. She's gone. Gone!"

"So, you gonna tell me why you hate lesbians?"

"I didn't say that!" Josephine's protest is sharp and volatile. Sick, disturbed, afraid.

"Well, you've implied it!"

"Oh, for Christ sakes!" Josephine rests her hands on the sink and hangs her head. She breathes in and exhales deeply. "You really think I'm such a bitch, don't you?" she says at last.

Scarlet looks at her with condemnation, at first. Then, she feels a smile begin to crack. Does Josephine see that too? She must. Of course she does! They both fall into hysterics!

"I can be a bitch at times!" laughs Josephine.

"Oh, ya bet."

"Christ, I'm shitting myself about this record thing."

"We'll be fine."

"I'm not so sure." Josephine straightens her back. "Do you think this was all a mistake?"

"What d'you mean?"

"Well. I mean. This. The band."

"Don't say that!"

"There's a lot of competition out there," Josephine says in a manner indicative of the emotional whirlpool that comes when you stand on a ledge over a waterfall. "Have you listened to New Kids On The Block, their album *Step By Step*? Christ, it's incredible! Fleetwood Mac's *Behind The Mask*? How can we beat those guys?"

"They had to start from somewhere," Scarlet responds.

"True. Maybe I'm just being a total bitch about it."

"Maybe. But you seem to be the only voice of reason."

"Ha!" Josephine shouts. "Very funny."

"No, I mean it. Look at the others. They never would have organised anything like this."

"You did."

"No, I came up with the idea. You're the one who's made the wheels turn."

"I suppose."

"When's your boyfriend back?" asks Scarlet. "I don't want to outstay my welcome."

"He's away at his parents."

"Oh, cool."

"Due back in a couple of days."

"How is he?"

"What more can I say? He's still looking for a job. Honest, he's really trying."

"He's trying, and that's the important thing."

Josephine goes for her coat. The change in pace is so fast that there's almost an aggressiveness to it. Scarlet, for a few tiny moments, is alarmed, afraid that Josephine wants to do something bad. But the oldest member of the band is cool and collected. She'd never do anything silly.

Josephine lets out a yawn and says, "There's a party in Camden Town. Tonight. A friend's. You're more than welcome to come."

"That's probably not a good idea," says Scarlet. "I mean, after what happened."

"I understand. I'm not pissed at you, don't worry."

"My parents'll be worried if I don't come home tonight."

"Like I said, don't worry."

As Scarlet begins to walk out, Josephine places a firm hand on her shoulder. She clutches it, holding it tightly in place. There is a fear going through her heart: don't let go. Just don't. Don't fall. Don't cry.

They leave the apartment, head down the stairs, enter the street in a daze.

Do any of these drivers, speeding past in their cars of professional characteristic, not see that these two girls are part of a band that will one day ascent to the dizzy heights of glorious fame? Honestly!

We're not exactly in Britney Spears territory yet, though! That's not for a good few years! No, dear reader, this is the end of 1990. The shackles of the 1980s are still being shaken off.

Scarlet and Josephine head to the end of the street and realise that they must part ways.

"Well, it's been a good day," remarks Josephine. "Fairly productive."

"Enjoy your party," says Scarlet, looking down. Afraid to meet Josephine's eyes?

"I will." Josephine gives Scarlet a soft pat on the elbow. She turns and sets off at a pace.

Scarlet makes her way to the station. She's quite clearly upset. Who wouldn't have guessed? She feels so fragile. Maybe for the first time in her life, she is aware of the femininity that's constantly here and there, sometimes shouting to the world, often not. In the years ahead, this conflict will present challenges. Some she will overcome. Others will drown her.

A cyclist brushes past her, on their way in such a hurry that it seems like the world revolves around them. She wants to swear, but cuts the urge. What will it achieve?

When she gets to the station, she finds she's missed the train. "Oh, shit," she mutters angrily, seeing that she has too much time until the next one.

What is there to do? There's a bookshop nearby: it would do her good to get a decent book and have a bit of a read. Yes, she'll do that!

She heads back out of London Waterloo East and sets off along Cornwall Road. She sees The Old Vic up ahead. Some sort of theatre troupe is gathered outside. Their colourful, fantastical, beastly costumes contrast with their tired looks. They're run into the ground.

One of them, a bitter-looking man with potted skin and white makeup, dressed as a ladybird, is trying to keep some sort of order amongst the group. Without success, it should be added. He looks like a Roman General – portrayed in an old classic movie – who has just lost the most important battle of his career. Suddenly, he slumps to the floor and gives a silent cry to whatever lives in the clouds.

Scarlet starts approaching the building like it's hypnotised her into being there, as pretty as a picture. She wants to say something, anything, to appease her inner demons.

"Beautiful, isn't it?" a male voice says.

Scarlet jumps and turns to face the speaker. The ladybird man. She noticed him approaching her from the side, but her heart still bypasses a few beats.

There is something important for you to note, dear reader. It's happened right here, right now. Scarlet thought that the ladybird man was a gruff, mid-fifties sort of bloke. The kind any twenty-year-old woman would see in 1990. These men long for the now dead Eighties, when anything could happen; they are still unable to let it go. Still unable to accept the death of a man's world.

So...

That's what Scarlet imagined him as. Instead, he must be mid-twenties. She can see that even through the makeup.

"Very beautiful," she replies.

"Far better than this soppy bunch," he says, gesturing with his elbow at the troupe.

"Ha-ha. What are you guys meant to be doing?"

"Theatre production. *Alice In Wonderland*. I know, it doesn't look like it. We're a bunch of twats. Pardon my French."

"Didn't know The Old Vic did stuff like this. Thought it was only –" She puts on her best posh accent. "– serious drama."

"Well, we've got this special arrangement with a local school. The headmistress, now she's a bloody lady, has paid us a lot of money. The Old Vic, I mean, she's paid The Old Vic. She's paid for her kids to have the experience of a lifetime." The man's shiny face is glistening with sweat. "This bloody government."

Someone calls over to him. It's a young girl, still unsure of life. "Darren, we've got five minutes."

"Alright. Tell the guys inside we'll be right there!"

"Busy day?" says Scarlet.

"You can say that again. Oh, I'm Darren, by the way."

"Scarlet." She shakes his hand. "Good to meet you." A very silly thing to say!

"Wait, don't I know you from somewhere?" says Darren. "You're that singer, aren't you? You were at that music festival, weren't you? Inverness?"

"Yeah. But, I'm part of a band. I don't really like to take the full credit."

"Of course. You're starting to ring a few bells now."

"How'd you find out? How d'you know?"

"It was in one of the papers. Can't remember which one –"

"Darren!" The girl who's unsure of life and (probably) herself looks angry. Somehow, the mushroom costume she's just slipped on has amplified this.

"Gotta go," says Darren.

"Take care," comes Scarlet's weak reply. She watches as the assortment of fantastical imagination files inside the building like marching ants. When she's alone, standing on the street, she smiles. First taste of fame?

There's a brutal vacancy about the street now. Moments ago, every colour in the rainbow stood outside, swirling around on the pavement. Now, there's an absence. In a way, it hurts. It's like the knife's been retracted and the gaping wound spurts blood.

Submission

8 October 1990

"She's done well for herself, I'll tell you that," says Josephine.

"Oh, not again!" groans Gina. "Can't you talk about something else?!"

"How can I? Maria McKee is in the top five hits. That song of hers..." Josephine starts humming *Show Me Heaven*.

The girls are obviously not too happy. This is their big day, after all. In a few hours, they'll know. This record company lets you know pretty damn quickly if your band's submission has been successful, so they've heard.

Then Susan has to say it. Well, someone always does. "You really believe we'll do this?"

"Shut the fuck up!" shouts Josephine. She nearly hits the kerb, but rights the car just in time. The other girls swear. "Not my fucking fault!" she protests.

"Girls, let's focus, come on," says Scarlet. She hates when Josephine drives. Every moment is a tense film in itself.

"Forgive me, Scarlet, but it's hard to focus right now." Josephine slams the horn down as a cyclist pulls in front of her. "Bitch!" Whether the rider has noticed or not, well, dear reader, that's another story for another day. She might have. She might be in total ignorance. If she's wearing a Walkman, well that's obviously the reason. In the years to come, the Walkman will be everywhere. The iPod will come soon after. Everyone will be silenced, drowned out, beaten down.

"We can do this," Scarlet snaps, trying to keep order in the chaos. "Just keep fucking focused."

"Yes, sir!" Josephine says mockingly, doing a silly salute with two fingers.

They drive on, their movements more like fidgets, barely doing anything. Have they already resigned themselves to failure?

Half an hour later, thanks to heavy London traffic, they arrive at the record company's office in Croydon. It's a dismal little building, a couple of small warehouses thrown together. The joining line is like a festering wound, peeling apart, sick.

"Here we go, girls," says Josephine, turning off the engine. "By the way, Scarlet, put Emma out your head." A vicious, poison dart.

Scarlet's ready to strike back, but she hesitates. By the time she's ready to retaliate, the girls are already out of the car and Josephine's telling her to get moving.

"Let's do this!" yells Gina.

Scarlet has barely noticed Susan. She does so now. Oh, the poor girl is hanging at the rear. Face drooped. Eyes moist.

"You okay?" Scarlet asks.

"Yeah. I'm fine." Susan feigns a smile.

"We haven't really had a chance to speak since Inverness," Scarlet casually remarks as they stand before the entrance. She watches Josephine knock angrily on the grey door.

"Not really," says Susan. "Well, you've had a lot to deal with. We all have. With Emma leaving us..."

"Yeah, it's been tough."

The door opens with a wooden creak and a fat man wearing a red and black checked shirt, corduroys and black-rimmed glasses emerges. He confirms who they are and then admits them inside.

"There's been a bit of a cockup with things," he says, his Cheshire accent thick and greasy. "The boss ain't here. He's been called to Los Angeles. One of our other bands has just been offered a slot in a big music festival over there. Not the kind of thing Roger should ignore. So he's taken everyone, except me."

Scarlet feels brutal sense of dread. She's seen the dog-eat-dog nature of the music industry already. The guy in charge has pissed off to the States, rather than listen to their music.

The record studio complex is filthy, untidy and disorganised. The fat man, who quickly introduces himself as George, shows them through the reception room, which is littered with magazines, mouldy coffee cups, and a thick computer sitting on a chipped wooden desk. They enter a corridor, piled high on both sides with LPs and CDs. The entire place has the feeling of the dying 1980s.

"Through here, ladies," says George, taking a thick bunch of keys out of his pocket. He curses as he flips through them, trying to find the right one. When he succeeds, he rams it though a lock in a door marked *Recording Studio* and opens up.

"Scarlet, go back to the car and get the instruments, will you?" says Josephine. Then, to George: "Are the drums here?"

"As requested."

When Scarlet returns, her arms full of the instruments, she feels irritated. Is Josephine staging a fucking coup or something? Christ's sake!

George beckons them inside the studio and shuts the door behind them. "Okay," he says. "Get yourselves set up."

The room is the size of a teenager's bedroom. A recording desk is situated behind a large glass panel, sealed off from the rest of the recording studio like a tropical fish tank. The rest of the studio is empty, apart from the drum set and a few mikes hanging from the ceiling.

"Okay, girls, take your positions," commands Josephine. Yes, she commands. This is a fucking coup!

When they're all set up, Scarlet tries to imagine things from George's perspective. What would he see? A group of young women, scared shitless, scared witless, shaking, about to burst their hearts open.

"Quick question, George, when will Roger hear our little performance." Oh, how the sarcasm in Josephine's voice threatens to derail everything!

George responds, "Good question. I probably should've explained that. He's entrusted a lot to me. I'm gonna hear you do a couple of songs, then I'll decide whether to recommend you to Roger Miser."

"Sounds cool to me," agrees Josephine, casting a gaze at Scarlet. "Girls, let's do that one we all agreed on doing back at the flat."

George goes behind the glass and plonks himself down at the recording desk. He fiddles with a few controls. "Ready when you are," he says at last. "Go for it."

The girls all look at one another.

Josephine leads off, then the others follow. The song begins smoothly, a perfect ricochet of parameters. A complex mathematical question that, quite simply, doesn't need an answer.

But they're barely halfway through, when George bursts up from his chair, rapidly waving his hands. "Stop! Stop! Stop!" he cries out.

Silence befalls this tiny island.

Scarlet knows it's over. The dream. *Her* dream. Destroyed by a fat man named George.

He comes up to them, shaking his head. He doesn't tell them to piss off. He doesn't make fun of them. What he does so is ask the strangest question ever in these circumstances: "Was this the song you performed in Inverness?"

"Yes," says Gina.

"Well, I have to ask this, and please don't take this the wrong way." He pauses and pushes his glasses up the ridge of his nose. "Why the *hell* weren't you the main act?!"

"Excuse me?" stutters Susan.

Tears creep from beneath George's eyelids. "Your song, it awoke so many fond memories. Ladies, you have a record deal. Not one album, but *three*. You heard me right. *Three* albums. I'm going to telephone Roger with the arrangement."

There's a reluctance to accept what's happened.

Scarlet looks through the windscreen. The rain pitter-patters against the glass. The wipers knock it away, but it comes back with a vengeance.

They are stunned.

Whining silence.

"We did it," says Susan. "Scarlet, you've helped thrust us into the limelight."

"Hey, what about me?" snaps Josephine, but no sooner has she said it, when she breaks into a grin. She's kidding. She lets out a loud hoot and the others join in. By the time they're in Central London, the car is shaking.

"Let's get our backsides to the fucking pub!" shouts Gina. "I'm in the mood for some serious drinking!"

"Sounds good to me," agrees Susan.

"Well, I'll drop you guys off, then I'll get back to the flat and deposit the gear." Josephine talks so matter-of-factly. "Meet you in the pub? Our usual haunt?"

"Cool," says Scarlet.

"No, I need you to come back to the flat with me, Scarlet. I need to finalise a couple of things with you. With regards to the lyrics."

"Can't we do that in the pub?"

"No, we fucking can't."

"Why not?"

"Just do as I say."

They drop Susan and Gina off outside the girls' favourite watering hole. The pub's midday atmosphere is gathering pace. Josephine waves them off, and then lunges forward in the roar of first gear.

When they get to Josephine's, it's a case of the following: engine off, up the stairs, through the door.

"Sit down," says Josephine, shifting a pile of empty beer cans off the sofa. "Sit the fuck down."

"This isn't about lyrics, is it?"

"No." Josephine stands before her, legs wide open. "We achieved something today. When you gathered us in that café at the beginning of the year and announced the intention to form this band, I'll admit, I thought you were pissed. But I went along with it, because I've always believed in you. I still do. But you and I, we have this dangerous chemistry between us."

"Where's this leading to?"

"There's tension in you. I know what you want. But I'm going to make things clear as day for you. You and I will never be intimate. Am I clear?"

"Yes."

"Good – that's what I like to hear."

"Well, shall we join the others?" Even as she says this, Scarlet can't be sure, but is she feeling a sense of hurt? As though a door, once full of the promise of intrigue, has finally closed.

Family Trip And Time Off

15 December 1990

Scarlet's still in dreamy land and it takes a stern snapping from her mother to properly wake her up.

"And you can wear something smart," she adds. "You aunt hasn't seen you in months."

"Yeah, well, I'm not exactly overanxious for a lengthy stay." Scarlet leans back against the chair and blinks rapidly, so that she doesn't doze off at the kitchen table again.

"You just watch your tongue, young lady," warns Scarlet's father. "It's been a few years since we last spent Christmas with her. I want you to show respect."

"Of course," replies Scarlet.

"And maybe keep quiet about this music business." Her father finishes his coffee with absolute silence.

Scarlet is furious, that much can be said. Why should Auntie Doris's tyrannical reign impact the band?

She watches as her parents and brother finish their breakfasts in a relative state of harmony. Then it's time to brush their teeth, grab their bags, and head out to the car.

They drive out of Sevenoaks without a word of unnecessary conversation. The traffic is slowing, a constant threat to their progress. Will they ever make it?

They bypass London, heading north. Thankfully, there are no major delays and they reach Kings Norton around lunchtime. The roads gradually scale down in size, eventually dissolving into the cul-de-sac that Auntie Doris lives on. It's three doors down, on the right: a single, detached house, somewhat larger than Scarlet's parents' home, but less glamorous, much less so.

They pull up outside the driveway and make their way up. Alastair knocks and the door is promptly answered by Uncle Michael.

"Good to see you all!" he says in his rather deep voice. "Do come in! Sandwiches and sausage rolls are waiting to be eaten." He briskly shakes hands with them all and gestures them inside.

Earlier in the story, I did warn you about Auntie Doris. But let's focus on the house first.

It bears echoes of the Sixties, Seventies and Eighties: vinyl records; thick clunky ornaments on dark mahogany shelves; laminated kitchen cabinets in a state of ruthless staining; over-sized sofas; lime-coloured toilets; dizzying patterned carpets; a chunky television; a casserole pot with a long sad story of its own; and brittle chinaware.

Scarlet curses to herself. Very bitterly, it must be said.

Auntie Doris is sitting in her brown leather armchair. The only one in the house. She gets up when she sees them. She's in a cosy cardigan with little flowers sewn under the breast. She wears a grey dress, with black tights. Her grey hair is done in a pile on the top of her head, a neat display of order.

"Good afternoon, all," she greets curtly.

"Good to see you," says Scarlet's mum, embracing her sister.

"How are you, Doris?" Scarlet's dad gives the woman a kiss on the cheek.

"Hi, Auntie Doris," says Alastair, letting the woman wrap him in a tight hug.

"Hi." Scarlet pats her on the arm and pulls away, hard; she makes sure that Auntie Doris doesn't dig her pink nails into her clothes.

A Christmas tree, the dim multicoloured lights like that flag which is becoming evermore important in Scarlet's life, sits in the corner of the living room next to an orange brick fireplace.

They sit down on a sofa that is situated at a wonderful ninety-degree angle from the aunt's chair. Uncle Michael goes out, announcing that he will bring soon bring food in.

"How are you?" asks Mum.

"Oh, fine," says Auntie Doris. "How was the journey?"

"It was okay. Traffic wasn't too bad. You know how it is."

"It's good to have you here." Auntie Doris suddenly switches to a venomous tone. "Family of Pakis have moved in down the road. They really get on my nerves and make a lot of noise."

"Well, I'm sure they're not too bad," says Dad, smiling grimly.

"And there are a couple of poofs a few doors down!" Doris continues, as though she hasn't heard him. "Fancy that? A man having sex with another man. They should criminalise homosexuality. It's a fucking plague."

"The Gay Society became quite prominent at my university," says Alastair.

"Well, they should be cast into the wind!" snaps Doris. "Repugnant!" She shuffles in her chair and lets out a squeak.

Scarlet is clenching her fists. She'd hit Doris if no one else was around. Oh, she'd strike her good.

"So, I hear you've made a start in the music world, Scarlet."

"Yes, we've secured our debut album."

"You were in Inverness, right?"

"That's right. Really good night. Show was packed."

"I trust that there is a promising young suitor? A lady of your age shouldn't be wearing these leather goth clothes, particularly when visiting family. She should be dressed like a pretty little picture. When I was your age, little cherub, I used to bask in the masculinity of men. Men are the dominant species and women should spread their legs and spit out babies. All this... *feminism*... it's wrong."

At that moment, Uncle Michael brings in a tray of sandwiches. He sets it down on a coffee table and returns with a bottle of sherry and a few glasses.

When everyone has a full glass and a sandwich in each hand, Uncle Michael narrates a story of a shopping trip:

"...after parking at Tesco, we were approached by three youths who demanded that we move out the way for them. I asked if they wouldn't mind going around us. Then they started giving us this human rights nonsense..."

As is often the case in these situations, Scarlet zones out to a new reality.

In her mind, she's travelling. The whole world is an oyster, *her oyster.* Steeped with pearls and wonder. She's a lone traveller, standing on a mountain, watching the miniscule world below. She's standing so tall that there's an infinite number of possibilities of what could be happening on the ground. Two backpackers, strangers from different walks of life, meet in a hostel. They share food and beer, songs and hope, feelings and emptiness. They share the small bunk, the mattress broken beyond repair, springs loose. But that doesn't matter. Really? Does it? As long as they're happy. Oh, she's drifting now, but... falling. Falling down. Crashing.

"Seasons Greetings," says Uncle Michael, raising his glass of red. "A Merry Christmas!"

The picture, very briefly, dear reader: a deep mahogany table; cutglass wine glasses; thick candles in brass holders; cheap-looking Christmas dinner; a decanter (clear glass) of wine; a decanter (even clearer glass) of yellow whisky on a small snail shell-brown table. There will be more details to follow, dear reader.

"It's good to have a family Christmas," says Auntie Doris. "When is Eric coming?"

"Tomorrow," says Uncle Michael. "I forgot to mention, he called earlier. One of his kids' friends was having a Christmas party."

"Pathetic!" shouts Doris. "A disgrace!"

"What do you mean *pathetic*?" interrupts Scarlet. Too late. She's opened her mouth in a cowardly act of bravery.

"Um, I would like more wine, please, Uncle Michael," Alastair says. He's saved Scarlet. A powerful, timely interjection.

Dinner continues. In near silence, save for the occasional requests for more wine.

Afterwards, it's time to break out the whisky. Uncle Michael takes out three glasses from the incredulous, dastardly range in the small cabinet that hangs over the decanter. Scarlet could just use a glass. And she goes for one, but Uncle Michael blocks her off, violently whispering, "For the men only."

"I'm sorry?" To say that she stutters would be one hell of an understatement. I mean, my dear reader, Scarlet is fucking shocked. She drinks copious amounts of whisky all the time with her friends, and her not-so-good-to-be-friends-but-it's-okay-I'll-have-a-few-drinks-with-you-pals.

"A glass of sherry instead?" Michael offers. But he's already getting the bottle for her and is pouring her a tiny measure.

"It's been a funny old year," says Alastair, sipping his (obviously very cheap) whisky.

"It's not over yet," says Scarlet's father.

The group is moving from the dining table into the living room. Uncle Michael, bless his soul, has lit the electric bar fire and soon the warmth spreads. They all take seats, like diplomats trying to avert war.

"It's a changing world, that much must be said." Uncle Michael takes out a silk handkerchief and coughs quite bloody loudly. "Jesus bloomin' Christ!"

"What do you think about Thatcher going out?" says Alastair, snorting.

"Somewhat bizarre, shall we say." Uncle Michael stretches out his fee, tartan carpet slippers camouflaged against the carpet.

"A shame," says Doris. "I really liked her. Very good at politics."

"Not so much with people," Scarlet desperately wants to say. Instead, she makes her excuses, sidles out of the room. She tiptoes outside and stands in the cold air, looking up at the stars.

24 December 1990

"Christmas time, Christmas time," quips Alastair, as the Thompsons pull into the driveway. They're watching from a first-floor window, like old Soviet leaders at May Day Parade.

This is the start of the big arrival. Still to come are the Mortons and the Hopes. It's a bit strange, how they're all able to fit in this house. The answer is simple: everyone doubles up, shares.

Here's how it goes:

Mr and Mrs Thompson squeeze into a single bedroom, along their three daughters. Mr and Mrs Morton (who are currently trying for a baby) fit into another bedroom; they agree to host one of the Hope's sons, whilst the other Hope son stays with Mr and Mrs Hope in a specially designated spare room. Unfortunately, despite the wonderous beauty of this specially designated spare room, it means that Scarlet, her brother and her parents need to move into a single room. Scarlet, reluctant, instead decides to sleep on the sofa.

"It is indeed," says Scarlet.

"You know," responds Alastair, "if you rip away that punk attitude, you might start to enjoy yourself."

"What do you mean?"

"Well, look at you, in that ridiculous t-shirt."

"Well, I secured a record deal. I'm part of something big."

That night, at seven o'clock sharp, they gather. The table – which has a very convenient extension that stretches it to the whole length of the dining room – is packed with all seventeen of them.

"I propose a toast," says Uncle Michael. He raises his glass. "A Merry Christmas and a Happy New Year!"

Everyone chimes in – even Scarlet (with a surprising degree of enthusiasm).

Today is not very significant. There will be some mild criticisms of her – of course there will be – by various family members.

On the 27th of December, she will head home. This whole break with the family is merely an opportunity for her to reset, think.

The next few months will see the release of her band's debut album and her life will change forever. There is – to say the least – on already sincere level of fame. But it's nothing like what lies ahead.

Now, it's simply a case of: farewell 1990! Bring on 1991!

Thank you, dear reader, for sticking with me. We've got past he first tricky section. Now you have to continue. Find out what happens next. Trust me.

1991

Josephine

6 January 1991

I'm shocked. Right through.

There I am, semi-naked, partially hanging from the door-frame. I guess I look fucking horrible and manky.

"I was going to wake you," he says, zipping up the last of his bags. "Didn't realise you were up."

"What the fuck is going on?" I demand. "Are you fucking taking the piss?"

I know he's not fucking taking the piss. Of course I fucking know. All his bags are there, all jammed full with his nonsense. His books; his statue of some American baseball player smashing a ball; his photos of him and his mates out on the piss somewhere; his dirty, filthy raincoat; his Jean-Claude van Damme VHS collection; his mud-stained work boots. He even has a teddy bear he's kept with him since his eighth birthday (a present from his gran).

"I'm sorry," says Robert. "I'm sorry, it's just... you and this band..."

"What the fuck are you on about?"

"I just..."

"Come on, Robert, fucking spit it out!"

"Okay, you want the truth?" Robert slaps the wall behind him. "Fuck! I'll tell you the fucking truth! This whole band thing! It's too much for me!"

"Come on, is this a joke? Tell me it's a fucking joke!"

I know it's not. Truly and deeply, I know this is bluntly bloody real. I stagger back, slump down on the bed, *our bed*. I'm shaking and crying like Veronica Cartwright in *Alien*, the bit when her character gets killed. I'm trying to be steely and reserved like Kurt Russell in *The Thing*, but that's just not working.

Robert comes in and crouches down before me. For a moment, I think... well, I'm hoping he's changed his mind and realises he's made a stupid blunder. But he hasn't.

"Babe, I can't cope with it. I'm sorry." He's adamant. "You're going into the world of fame. I don't think I can follow and not go crazy. It wouldn't be fair on you. I'd be holding you back."

"If you're gonna go, fucking go," I tell him. "Stop hanging around like a spare nut. Just go."

Whether it's the stress or how bloody early it is, I don't know, but I find myself falling into a coughing fit. I snivel in embarrassment.

"Sorry," I say wearily.

"You see, this is the problem with you," says Robert. "Look at you, you're a fucking mess. You're –" He prods me hard in the shoulder. "Christ, I don't know... You absolutely... You never fucking clean up after yourself. Dirty, mouldy dishes in the sink. You wear the same clothes for days on fucking end. You can't even fucking look at me properly."

"I can change," I plead. "If you think I'm not putting enough effort into keeping the flat clean, I will double my efforts. Please, Robert, please don't go."

He looks pained.

"I'm sorry," he says.

"Christ, can't we even talk about it?" I shout. "Can't we sit down over breakfast or something?"

"You really aren't in tune with the world, are you?" Robert holds his Casio digital watch. "It's nearly One in the afternoon. I'm sorry, you and I... we're done. Good luck with the band."

"Where will you go?" I ask, timid as a rabbit.

"I'm staying with my brother in Chelmsford for a couple of weeks, then, well, we'll see..."

"Please don't!" I cry. "Please!"

Robert stands up and moves back to his bags. "There's a taxi coming," he tells me. "I'm going to need to make a couple of trips to get all my stuff down." He moves swiftly and methodically. He ends up taking four trips and looks flushed in the face as he stands there with his rucksack swinging like a monkey from his right shoulder.

"I'm going to post the key to the landlord," he informs me. "Listen, take care, okay?"

"Just fucking go!" I roar. "Fuck off! Stay out of my life, you worthless bastard!"

He gently shuts the door behind him. He's gone. He's fucking gone. Useless waste of space.

I want to cry, but for some reason I'm laughing. He's not good enough for me. That's what they'll all say now. That's what they're fucking like. Those parents, aunties, uncles, grandmas and grandads. They're all the same. *He wasn't good enough for you. It wasn't meant to be. You need to move on. You will find someone better.* I don't want to hear any of that sentimental crap. I don't want it. I just want to stop my fucking heart from coming apart, from breaking like an anvil hitting brittle china.

I'm on the floor, wailing and panting. I feel sick. I want to be sick, but I've nothing to puke up.

"Fuck this," I mutter. "Fuck all of this."

I'm up, staggering towards the shower. I'm feeling light-headed, stupidly lightheaded. I strip off, breathing in the stench of my own body odour. The claggy jimjams I got back in 1988 will have to go. Christ, I'm going to be a fucking superstar before long. The shower takes a few minutes to kick into life. It's freezing at first, like liquid nitrogen. When it warms up to a level that's tolerable, I step in and allow the sweat and grease to be lashed from me. I don't know how long I'm in there for. I don't care. I just need to wash him off me. I just need him to be gone.

After my shower, I go through to the kitchen and rummage through the freezer. I find nothing except a frozen chicken. Christ, a frozen fucking chicken. Nothing else. The fridge is as bare as Gina's eyes when she's not happy.

I'm going out for food. I don't care if I'm putting on too much weight. I'm a bit chubby, but I'm not fat. And I run several times a week. And I'm about to become a superstar. Yeah, I know that.

"Fuck this shit," I say out loud in a phony American accent.

I put on some decent clothes (Christ, I walked into the kitchen without a stitch on) and walk confidently to the door. I'm about to pull it open, when I take a step back. I go through to the living room, pick up the phone and make a call.

"Yeah?" answers a husky voice.

"Scarlet, how are you?"

"I'm okay. You sound exhausted?"

"Yeah, well, the boyfriend just dumped me."

"Are you okay?" No change in the huskiness.

"I'll be fine, don't worry. Listen, are you done living with your parents? There's a room for let here."

Scarlet

10 January 1991

Scarlet's never really been the biggest fan of Sharmaine Bateson, but, well, sometimes you've got to go through the shit.

Sharmaine stands there in Scarlet's shack, her thick, ginger hair billowing, her pale makeup glinting in the dust motes. She's an allegory of mystery, professionalism, intrigue, pettiness, and just about everything one would use to describe the modern woman. Sharmaine is thirty-eight – Scarlet knows this from the press release her magazine did last November to mark her birthday – but she looks twenty. She looks like a teenager. She looks like a teenager's adult fantasy. Sharmaine is cocky. But she's fairly cool. Scarlet's not sure what to think.

"You understand that it's imperative for me to raise these concerns," Sharmaine says in her sweet, raspy voice. "You've just signed a record deal – *three* record deals with this company. I worry about the time you'll be able to commit to your artwork."

"I understand your concerns," says Scarlet. She can't even look at this professional.

"You're a talented artist. God knows you are. But..."

"You're worried about the band getting in the way."

"Don't forget what you said on the phone last night. You're moving to bloody London soon."

Sharmaine steps up to the window and brushes aside a few cobwebs. She gazes out across the fields like Nigel Green in *Zulu*, and sighs.

"Look, I really appreciate you keeping me informed. I really do," she says. "And I also think you did the right thing calling this meeting... but... I'm sorry, but my magazine can no longer be your funding body."

"I understand," replies Scarlet. She knows she's lost. One form of art must be exchanged for another.

"Look, I'll be brutally honest with you." Sharmaine coughs a giggle. "The reason my magazine decided to fund you was because I genuinely thought you were a talented painter. I'll never forget the day I came into your art college and saw you painting away." She shuts her eyes for a brief moment.

Scarlet can't forget it either. She was sitting amongst the other students, her dusty fingers interlocked with the paintbrush, dabbing colours on the canvas. Sharmaine came into the hall and –

"– I took a liking to your work," says the professional. "I was only there to have lunch with Professor Schell. When Doreen gave me a quick guided tour of the place, I caught a glimpse of you. There you were, with the other students. I felt a connection with your work –"

So, Sharmaine offered to fund her. Her magazine was rich enough. All those tea parties and wine receptions. Sharmaine was more than happy to splash out the cash.

"So, you know how I feel." The professional offers a wry smile. "I am prepared to fund an art studio in London for you, but only if you finish with the band. I'm sorry to be utterly blunt. But you've got to know how I feel about this stuff."

"I understand, Sharmaine." Scarlet knows what she has to say, but she's reluctant to form the words in her mouth. "My priority is the band."

"Thank you." Sharmaine dips her head.

The two women fall silent for a few moments. Then the professional hoists her handbag over her shoulder.

"Listen, Scarlet, I'll let you sleep on it. I'm going to head back to the station and return to London. If you could let me know by lunchtime tomorrow?"

"I can let you know now," Scarlet says snappily. "I want to focus on the music. It's what I want. I owe you a lot, you and your magazine. You've done so much for me. I'll clear out this place by tomorrow, so that it's ready for you guys."

"Thanks." The woman looks sad. This professional makeup magazine owner looks miserable. "Well, Scarlet, I wish you the best of luck with your new career. You will do really well. I hope that you – no, I know that you will find success. When's the album out?"

"First of March."

"Well, I'll be on the lookout for it. I'm sure it's fabulous." Her lips twist into a grimace as she studies her Vintage Wrist Watch. "Damn it, I should be heading to the station. I've got to pick my boy up from nursery. Listen, you take care, okay?"

The woman reaches out her hand. Scarlet takes it firmly. A sense of acknowledgement and respect passes between them. There's an honesty like no other like hangs in the air. They say goodbye to one another. Sharmaine exits the shack. Scarlet stays for an hour, clearing up. When she's done, she takes one last look around, and sets off for her parents' home.

No one's in when she gets back. Probably shopping or something. She goes up to her room, smiling meekly at her bags that look like they've been sorted by Greek baggage handlers. All over the fucking place.

Less than two months now.

After they were offered the deal, they finished off the first album in no time. Songs recorded. Cover artwork put in place. Signed and sealed. There's a tour coming up soon. Summertime.

The press releases will be popping up in the next few weeks. She's in the position where she's on the cusp of fame. She's already dipped a toe in and soon the sharks will swallow her.

This is precious time for her now. Very special. Time for her to make the most of a moderately normal existence.

She fishes up her guitar and heads back out again. With the instrument on her back, her hands in her leather jacket pocket, she's an angel of self-determination. There she goes! You see her? She's walking down the street, confident and relaxed. She's got songs and lyrics stuck in her head. She's thinking about nothing and everything.

She goes to a field she's taken to strumming her guitar in over the past year. Damn, it really is over a year since she met the girls in that café and sipped coffee with them! Ah, they thought she was bonkers when she proposed the idea of the band!

She strums away, her bum wedged in the ground. She's had this new idea for a song and she's determined to compose it, then and there. She's going to put it together like she puts everything together.

She swears when she realises the horrifying fact that she's caught in the spiral again. The one that takes her back. She's going back once again. She tries to stay in 1991, but she's falling back in time.

Not again.

Please, oh please, not again.

She pulls herself back. Her fingers are painful, sore, wanting to bleed. But she'll be gone from this place soon, the place of her haunted childhood. She'll be in London, in a new world. For a second, she thinks it's too good to be true, then remembers that she promised to give Josephine a call. She goes back to the road, but forces herself to glance back, back to a field that acts like the gateway to memories: images, thoughts and feelings that should remain buried.

Scarlet

28 February 1991

A late winter morning dawns across London. Some would compare it to a Dickens novel, but it's too pessimistic and too sweary for such a comparison. The buses trundle along. Commuters emerge bleary-eyed from train and tube stations, wondering and, yes, dreading what the day will bring. There is a sense of optimism that briefly hangs, but, yes, it is brief, and it brings a hangover-style grief. The sun emerges like a welcome slap in the face. Big Ben knocks out its famous tune. The city is full of swirling jackets and briefcases. The city is primed with hungry students, jealous teenage crushes, crushed CDs, a few feet of VHS tape across a few too many pavements. Overcoats, raincoats, turncoats, tartan ties, plain ties, chunky golden rings, light silver rings, wannabes and not-wannabes, massive fans of Cher and the greatest fans of Bryan Adams.

People often say this about London, that it is too big. Well, it's an obvious fact.

But, let's do a bit more description:

A dogwalker stumbles. Two old lovers meet after twenty years (a chance meeting whilst queueing up for taxis). A writer gets an idea for a twelve-book series; it might make it, it might not; we don't know yet. A teenager takes a sneaky dip in the Thames. Only lasts for a few minutes, because it's so bloody cold. A woman with a scarlet scarf smokes a cigarette. It's only her tenth and she's doing it to impress a few mates. A bus driver huffs, like he's huffed for the past how many years. A jogger breathes in, breathes out, wipes sweat away, thinks she's invincible, but she's only battling insecurity.

The rooftops of the city are all sleepily puffing away. There's a touch of ice on a few of them. Puddles of smoke billow out and swirl in the air. One rooftop in Marylebone has a smaller cloud on it.

Scarlet's sitting on the apex, sucking away at the last of her cigarette. She's sneaked up here a few times since she moved in. It's a place for her to escape the world, to prepare for solid injection into the life of fame and fortune. Christ, she'd promised Josephine she'd quit the fags. Ah, the girl won't know. She tosses away the butt and heads back, sliding down the roof, feet first onto the walkway that's *supposed* to act as an access for the boiler. She sidles back to the apartment, ambles through the door, returns to the living room, where Josephine has set up the chairs. She's very official, Josephine – wants to brief the girls on what will happen when the album is released at one second past midnight.

"I hope they're not too late," complains Josephine. "I can't take the tension," she says mockingly.

"I'm sure they won't be too long," replies Scarlet.

"We've got the most important night of our lives coming up." Josephine kicks a plastic cup on the floor. It skitters about like its caught in a never-ending draft from a fan. "I don't want anyone screwing it up."

"It's not until tomorrow night," says Scarlet. "Tomorrow."

"Yeah, I know, but I'm still tense. Fuck, where are Gina and Susan?"

"Give them time."

"You know, it's funny," says Josephine, her usual fierce voice lessening, "but I never thought we'd be here. I never thought we'd be doing this. I can't believe anything of the past year and a bit."

"We did it," Scarlet tells for, putting a hand on her elbow.

"No, *you* did it. You're the one who got us together. You're the one who made it all happen."

The doorbell rings, its scratchy squeak hissing through the flat. Apparently, Josephine's been meaning to repair it for a couple of years – another thing she hasn't got around to.

"That'll be them," says Scarlet.

"I'll get them," Josephine tells her. "Take a seat, relax."

"What about coffee?"

"Oh, we don't have time for that. We'll have some after this... briefing..."

"Sure."

Scarlet thinks about nipping out for another cigarette, but can't bear the thought of her voice becoming tainted with nicotine. She's tired of those colourful anti-smoking adverts that cling to the base of wet brick walls on narrow streets. God only knows what she's doing to her body. She's polluting it. She's probably going to kill it off, if music doesn't do it first.

When Gina and Susan arrive, there's a bit of excited chatter (much to the irritation of Josephine), and then adrenaline-fuelled banter of what fame and fortune *might* be like. Eventually, the girls are settled down. Josephine goes up the front and claps her hands together in a deafening splintering crash.

"How are we all going?" she booms. "Thumbs up? Thumbs down?"

"Never been better," says Gina. "Just don't get me to make the tea."

They laugh. Gina's *tea incident*, as it has become known amongst the girls, is now a giggling matter for them.

Susan tells them a quick story about writing a poem. She thought about converting it to a song, but decided it stood beautifully the way it was. She's thinking about doing a collection, but, oh, she's not too sure right now.

"Fascinating tale," mutters Josephine. "Just keep focused, okay? We've got a busy few months coming up.

"Now, as you all know, at one second past midnight, our debut album is officially released. Tomorrow night, we take to the stage in Hackney as part of a big performance Roger thinks will shoot us to fame that little bit faster. He's a strategist, Roger, I like him. So, guys, I wanted to have a little meeting this morning to discuss the next few days. I suggest we take today to relax a little bit, maybe practice a few notes. Roger has said that a few papers and magazines might be interested, so the phone..." She points knowingly to the piece of red plastic in the corner with its transparent rotary dial. "...is hot and ready."

"I've got to be honest, the nerves are getting to me," Susan confesses.

Scarlet wants to wrap her in a tight hug and joyfully slap her rosy cheeks. Susan's the kind of woman, well, you don't know what's happening with her. They haven't really talked much in the past few months, not since they got the record deal. But Scarlet knows there's some sort of trauma behind her. She knows that Susan's frail eyelids conceal a deep hurt.

Susan's just moved into an apartment in Shepherd's Bush. Scarlet knows that Susan now has the time to think and feel her way out of things. In all honestly, she considers Susan her closest friend, but also with suspicious eyes. Oh, yes, she views Susan with the contempt of a Le Carre spy.

Gina's also just got herself a new flat. It's down in Fulham, near Eel Brook Common. A nice one-bedroom cubbyhole with all the necessities you need for 1991, including a Philips wide-screen television and a Matsui VCR. Scarlet hasn't been there yet, but she needs to drop by.

It's strange, how the girls have all come together in London. So old-fashioned, like you expect in a 1980s teen romance. They've all left their pasts behind to start again.

And why on earth has Josephine called this stupid meeting...? She's run out of things to say! She's a damn control freak, always having this Pol Pot do-as-your-told rule over them. Bloody hell!

"Shall we get the coffee sorted?" suggests Scarlet.

"Sounds like a good idea," says Gina. "I could use a cup."

"Unless anyone has any further suggestions?" says Josephine.

"Can I just check something?" Susan interjects. "This might be a stupid question, but do you want us all to remain here for the day?"

"That's probably a good idea. I'd like us all to be on hand, you know, in case we get a call or something."

"Is that absolutely necessary?" counters Scarlet. "I mean, we need to have some time out. As long as one of us is here, that's all that's necessary. I'd like to get out at some point, stretch my legs."

"Oh, babe, you have to do something to spoil the monotony." Josephine rolls her eyes. "Do you really need to get some exercise? Or are you just taking the piss?"

"I genuinely need to get out. I need some fresh air."

"You went out for some earlier, but you chose to puff away instead. Go on then... But don't be too long."

"See you in a bit, girls."

Scarlet grabs her coat, her most worn and worn-out leather jacket. She zips it up and brushes her blonde hair behind her ears. She needs to get it cut soon. She likes it short. She's thinking of having it shaved close to the scalp, but... no... she can't do that. She pulls on her trainers, checks the tiny pin-pricks of makeup she likes to wear in a mirror hanging from the door.

"You're all ready, doll," she mocks herself.

The street is vacant. Only a bird, its claws clipping at the gaps between the paving slabs, gives the illusion of life. She thinks about turning left or right. Yes, she does need exercise. She needs the blood pumping through her veins. She goes left on this occasion.

After a few streets, people appear, like the forgotten extras. A group of businessmen in identical beige jackets burst out of an office, yelling something about the Gulf War ending.

She feels the need to walk faster, and that's what she does. She digs her fists into her pockets. Something wants to burst inside her.

Marylebone Underground is busy with its mid-morning exchange. A throng of people are coming out, a swarm are going in. A loudmouthed American, blue jeans and red shirt, tells his girlfriend to hurry up. Scarlet pushes between them. She feels hot breath on her neck. Damn, the American jock loves blueberry bubble-gum. She keeps her head down as the two sides clash. The parted sea is crashing together. She finds that she has to stop. Yes, that's what she'll do. She'll wait here, wait for the movement to stop. A woman with black hair tied back smiles at Scarlet as she walks into the tube station. A ginger-haired fat bloke with a chubby, greying beard grimaces and snarls as he attempts to weed his way through the crowd.

Hold on!

Scarlet turns around. The woman with the black hair. No, wait. Yes, it is her! Scarlet pushes with a new determination. She shoves people out of the way, creating more anger and frazzled rage with every jolt.

"Hey!" she calls out. "Hey, you there!"

The woman doesn't turn around. She disappears into the chunky mess of the crowd.

Scarlet rushes. She charges like a bull, nips like a bulldog. Someone screams at her that she needs to have a ticket. She's running so fast that she can feel her jacket beginning to dampen with sweat.

No, she's lost her. In desperation, she scans the crowd. The river of heads and scalps bobs up and down. She throws her hands up! She wants to howl and say the most offensive language she can come up with. But she's frozen on the spot.

A loud hissing noise precedes a train inching away from one of the platforms. Scarlet sees the woman inside, hand upstretched. It's not her. The relief and the disappointment make her want to fall over.

Someone says, "Yeah, I think she went down here!"

Damn.

Another carriage pulls in. Scarlet makes for it and slips inside, just as two workers in orange jackets come onto the platform. They look pissed: fuck, they look like they've taken it personally.

She shuts her eyes as the car moves off. She expects when she opens them that they'll be in front of her, ready to drag her to the nearest police station. But all she sees are shoppers, kids and businessmen. They don't look at her. They look right past her. They haven't seen a thing.

Stupid thing to do. She'll get off at the next stop, walk back to their apartment. She's going to have to accept that the girl is gone. The girl from the bar. The one who looked at her with love. She's gone. Buried somewhere in some cemetery. Maybe she'll try and find the grave someday. But it's probably not a good idea. Some wounds need to be closed. She needs to seal this one. She needs to draw a line under what happened last year. If she doesn't...

Scarlet expects Josephine to angry at her when she returns. Truth be told, she knows she deserves it. But Josephine is happy, ploughed with laughter. Susan and Gina have each got a steaming mug of coffee.

"Enjoy your walk?" says Josephine. "Come on, let's celebrate. Do you girls think it's too early for champagne? I don't!"

Why is it that mornings insist on taking so long to slip by? Why is it that they enjoy lagging out, torturing you and drip-feeding you pointless wisdom?

Scarlet sits with the girls. The chairs soon get put to the side and they fling themselves on sofas like they did when they were eleven or twelve. All that's needed is a bottle of pop to kickstart the celebrations, but bottle after bottle of champagne flows. It turns out that Josephine bought a pack of twelve. Gets them used to the party atmosphere they're about to leap into.

Josephine makes sure they don't get too drunk. They want to be fairly sober in case a call comes through, but the jollity and the freedom and the relief and the anticipation, everything flows like water carving away at a dam.

Josephine, well, she eventually gives in, and they end up drunk as lords by lunchtime. She makes them down as much coffee as humanly possible.

"No exceptions," she says, fiercely.

Let's leave the girls to their fun. They'll get a few phone calls that evening from a few interested magazines and newspapers – by which time, Josephine will have them properly sobered up – but that's only the tip of the iceberg.

We're leaving now. We're backing out of the flat, down the stairs, out into the street. The world seems to have taken a bit of a break, yeah, that's what you're thinking. Tiptoe along the road, hover in the air, head towards the Thames.

They're far behind us now.

We're flying along the river. The city is getting ready for its lunch hour. Pubs and restaurants are gritting their teeth for the busy influx. We pass the Houses of Parliament, whizz over Westminster Bridge.

You can see the city with all its characters and stories: a mix of chaos and order that has its own rules about chaos and order.

We pass King's College and London Bridge.

Turn off from the river, pass through the East End and then into Stratford. You're so far from them, you could have forgotten about them.

But remember, that's how they feel. They feel as lost as you are. You're so far from sanity and what makes sense, it's like you've never known it. That's what's in their minds right now.

Shut your eyes. Breathe. Open them when you're ready to continue.

Josephine

1 March 1991

Truth be told, I've never really been musical. I did the piano a bit when I was younger, but I gave that up. I took it up again in 1986, but I've never really been one for letting my fingers tiptoe over keys. I've only become properly musical since Scarlet started this band.

I'm as mystified as anyone why I let Scarlet move in with me. My guess is she won't be here very long. As soon as the money rolls in, the girl will probably get a mansion of some sort. A stable with ponies, a fast car – several fast cars – first-class travel, and as much plush booze as she could want or need. Actually, nah, I don't think so. She's not the kind of girl to do that.

I'll say this for her: she's a lot more focused now. She's got her eye on the ball. She's dealt with that nonsense over Emma. She's loving her music – *our* music.

Well, we're here now, about to do this big performance. I'm in a small storage room by myself, surrounded by old LP records, most of them with dust on. I'm sitting on a case for appears to be a tuba. My knees are hunched and my bare arms catch goosebumps in the cold draft.

I know the girls are by the curtain waiting to be called onstage. There's no hurry. It won't be for fifteen minutes, at least. I wonder how many are out there. Probably ten, maybe twenty. I don't think that a lot of people will have sacrificed their evenings to watch us. I know that our songs were playing on the radio earlier today. I know that this concert has been advertised for weeks.

Truth be told, I know that this is the end for us. I know, I know, I probably should've told the girls my doubts. Yes, we may have gotten ourselves a record deal, yes, but is there a possibility we'll actually *sell* copies? The girls seem so caught up in it, so involved with the moment. But I know the dark, stingy truth: the chances of us getting a massive bunch of fans are next to bloody nothing.

Scarlet comes in. Her jeans are buckled tight and her faded t-shirt hangs loose like used snakeskin. I worry about her sometimes. She needs to eat more.

"Won't be long now," she says. "Are you ready?"

"You really think people are going to turn up?" I ask her.

"What's that supposed to mean?" she snaps at me. "Christ, Josephine, you shouldn't think like that."

"Have you seen the fans pouring into their seats? Have you seen the drinks? Have you seen the signs that scream how much they love us?"

"Look, I'm not having this." When Scarlet's sure about something, she sounds really out of character. "Seriously. You need to get a grip. Now, I don't know if a million fans are out there or one lonely bloke is munching cucumber. What I do know is that I'm going to walk onto that stage and I'm going to sing. We are going to play our music. And if there's no one there, there's no one there. We play our music to an empty room. What are you afraid of, Josephine?"

"I'm not afraid."

"Then prove it!"

"I don't have to prove anything to you, darling. I don't have to prove a single thing."

"Me and you go back a long time." She's fierce with me now. Properly angry. "Talk to me, Josephine. Talk to me."

"You know I'm not good at talking about things like this. I've never really been good at it."

"Well, you're good at venting your anger at me. You should be able to tell me why you don't want to go on the stage."

Now I want to lash out. Those words cut at me deep. I almost wish I was back on that day Robert left me.

"All right, I'll prove myself to you," I tell her. "I'm more than happy to prove my... my worth. Let's go on the stage. Come on, let's do it. There'll be no one there, I guarantee it."

"And I guarantee there will."

I hate it when she does it, but Scarlet follows a mouse's whisker's width away behind me. She's like my mum sometimes, only my mum speaks to me less. I'm like a prisoner in escort. She frogmarches me up a tight corridor to the wings of the stage. Gina and Susan are laughing about something, and then they see me and their smiles fade a little bit.

"It's okay, ladies, I've not got cold feet," I say to them.

You know what, there's no point holding back anymore. The two of them look so eager and excited and full of the joys of imminent success. They have the wise nature of *Alvin & The Chipmunks*. I've got to tell them. Maybe I'll save them some embarrassment.

"Guys, I don't think this is a good idea," I bleat. "I mean, there's no one out there. There might be a few or something. But we'll go on and look like total idiots. Sorry, ladies, I really don't think this is a good idea."

"She's right," says Susan.

Now, I never expected *that*.

Damn, Susan, why don't you try and make eye contact once in a while?

"Look, maybe we should just call it off," she continues. "Do we really think anyone will turn up?"

"That's absolute nonsense!" shouts Scarlet.

I can tell she's panicking. I know she's about to flip out.

"Look, guys," I say, "I have a suggestion. We can't really back out of this. Our instruments are on stage and are all set up. I say that when we go on, we take a look; if there's not a single sorry soul there, we take our instruments and leave. My whole life, I've always been ready for disappointment. It sounds kinda weird, but you've got to bask in disappointment.

Just focus on getting the instruments. Susan, that okay with you?"

"Yes."

The silky curtains behind Gina rustle. A man in a leather jacket emerges. He's not looking too happy. He's got this massive beefy face and seems to be sucking in every breath.

"Shouldn't be too long, girls," he tells us. "Gerard will start his opening speech soon." As he walks into the depths of the maze of dressing rooms and equipment storage, he says to us, "You're in for an absolute shocker tonight, girls. It's not good."

"Shit," hisses Gina. "We're fucked."

"Let's not jump to conclusions," says Scarlet.

We fall into a numbness. Susan keeps clenching her fists. Even Scarlet's beginning to be more pessimistic. Ah, she's just like me, that girl. Just like me.

Minutes pass, but we don't move. We're too scared to budge a muscle. Frigid little gnomes, we are.

Suddenly, a voice booms out.

"Ladies and gentlemen, welcome to the show!" Gerard says.

"Why is there no clapping?" says Gina. "There's no fucking clapping!"

"Just stay cool," says Scarlet. "We'll get through this."

Gerard keeps talking about how great a night it's going to be. He's probably talking to an empty room, but Gerard – he seems like an honest bloke – wouldn't pull a stunt like that.

"– put your hands together and welcome them onstage!"

"I'm off!" shouts Gina, tears on her cheeks.

I grab her by the scruff of her neck and shove her through the curtains. My voice is thick with embarrassment and fury.

"We're not going anywhere, until we get those instruments!" I say in my best threatening voice as we emerge into the blitz of stage lights.

I'm aware of a noise, but I don't know exactly. Something's wrong with sound, I know it. It sounds like clapping, but I know it can't be that, because no one would turn up. Through the blinding light, I can see movement. Hands. Waving.

"I told you," Scarlet mouths at me.

The stage seems so big, like a continent. It takes me seconds and decades to reach my guitar. I nearly drop it out of fright.

The mike's in front of me like an old, bitter lover. I lean into it, shut my eyes, and tell our new world, "It's time for us to properly kick off."

Scarlet

1 March to 2 March 1991

Of course she can't believe it's over, but the clapping and the cheering is too fierce to be dismissed as fantasy.

Josephine waves at them. She ends up being the last one off, blowing kisses to the crowd.

Scarlet's neck is clammy with sweat and her t-shirt is going to have to go in the wash. Is she going to have to wear a new t-shirt for every single concert she does?

"I told you, girls, I promised you," she says with glee. "You shouldn't have doubts. You shouldn't think like that. You should never think like that!"

"So, I suggest that we get a takeaway and head back to mine," says Josephine. It's like she's ignoring her baby-like cries just before the show. She's like that. They never happened – that's how perverted she can be. "Maybe a couple of bottles of wine."

"Sounds good to me," replies Susan, yawning. "That's knocked the seven bells out of me."

Roger appears. Scarlet never saw him earlier. Thought he was in New York, drinking expensive cocktails in the Copacabana. But he's here now.

Roger Miser is a thin, shrewd bloke, with trimmed greasy hair and a face plastered with aftershave. He's from the West Midlands, but has lived in London since he was sixteen. He built his record company up from scratch, weaving it together like a threaded jute basket. He's got a formidable look, but a strange girly kind of laugh. Every time Scarlet sees him, he wears a matte jacket, with trousers the same colour. Tonight's no exception, and he's worn his double cream coloured set. A Hawaiian shirt, two buttons undone, flashes his chest hair and a gold necklace.

"Well done, girls," he says to them. "Very well done. Now, if yow –" He coughs and corrects his Brummie accent to his posh Estuary one. "Now, if you're going to repeat tonight's performance in the future, I see a promising future for you all."

George emerges from somewhere. He's out of breath, panting like a dropout marathon runner. His navy jumper hangs off his flabby body like paper mâché. Roger gazes at him and tilts his head. Instantly, George straightens up.

"Sorry, Mr Miser, but there's been a bit of an incident," he tells his boss. "A couple of lads have had a bit too much to drink and kicked off. Security are dealing with it."

Roger smiles. "Well, that's to be expected, isn't it? The sign of a good night."

"Though, I advise we leave immediately," says George, panicked. "It could get serious."

Roger is calm. He folds his hands over his stomach and rolls his eyes. "Ladies," he says, "a first-class night."

"We're all absolutely shattered!" exclaims Susan. "I think a couple of bottles of wine and pizza sounds just about right!"

"Oh, no!" protests Roger. "Your night's only just beginning! There's a car outside – or, it should be outside. We'll be heading back to my penthouse for the customary afterparty."

"You're joking," says Gina.

"I never joke," replies Roger.

Scarlet's in a trance. Part of her doesn't know where she is. All of her knows that things are changing so damn quickly there's no time to take anything in. Blindly, she follows the girls. Roger and George take the lead. George seems to be doing all the talking. He's always rabbiting on like a powerless, little parrot. He's not happy with the security arrangements, not one bit.

They end up at the graffitied back entrance where they came in earlier.

"Dear God, this place is filthy," says Roger. "Beer cans, crisp packets, swearing on the walls... Who the hell is running this place? Christ." He pushes hard at the fire door. Cold air washes in.

They emerge into the freezing night and huddle together in a tight group.

Scarlet feels the unpleasant sensation of her damp clothes mixing with the arctic conditions.

"Who's going to be at the afterparty?" Josephine asks Roger. She's like a little child now. Impatient. Demanding.

"Oh, just a few friends," he responds, poking his head around, grimacing. "Where's the bloody car? George, where the hell is the driver?"

"I've no idea. He said he'd be here!"

"Well, he's not."

"Is there a phone box nearby?" George asks no one in particular.

No one in particular feels keen to answer him. No one in particular really cares.

"Uh, what about our instruments, Mr Miser?" asks Gina.

"Don't worry about it," answers Roger. "I've arranged for your instruments to be picked up. I'll have them sent on to you."

"We should discuss arrangements for the tour as well," says George.

"I'll leave you to do that," says Roger, more agitated by the second. "*After* tonight, of course."

"Yes, sir, of course."

"Oh, look, here's the car. At bloody last."

It comes around the bend like a serpent with headlights. It's limo, with all the smooth and slick trimmings. It's blacked-out windows are reflecting eyes. The driver's all traditional, like in *James Bond* or something. Grey hat, tails, even fucking gloves. He steps out, gives a courteous, polite nod to Roger.

"About bloody time," curses the record manager.

The chauffer opens the door for them. The inside is so luxurious that there are simply no words to describe it. Every-thing about the plush leather seats and the small array of strong spirits suggests that it has the richness of a Colombian drug lord's empire and the clumsiness of a recorded episode of *The Bill*. They amble inside. Roger sits at the back next to George, whilst the girls sit at the sofa running along the side.

"Well, I brought a little something..." says Roger, raising something in his hands.

"Nice one," says George. "Bollinger."

A frustrated ensemble of clinking glasses sounds through-out the car as they move off. Soon enough, though, soon enough, the girls have a glass each.

"To success!" shouts Roger.

The fizz tastes sour on Scarlet's tongue. She thinks that it might be off, but she's not the biggest champagne drinker. She's never really felt the need to consume this stuff. It's al-ways been fairly immaterial to her. It's always been something that's on a shelf. The kind of thing that the Casseldens would have in a display cabinet

Oh, why is she thinking about the bloody Casseldens...?

They drive south through the streets. A few bands are playing on the pavements. They weren't as lucky as Scarlet. She even feels like she should be there with them, playing on a cold night, earning a few lucky pennies. The less fortunate make her feel a sense of insecurity.

There's some traffic, but they don't need to be in any hurry. The vehicle bangs and clangs against the rough surface of the road. It's 1991 and they haven't fixed the bloody roads!

After seemingly endless trawling through the tight streets, they arrive at a street in Chelsea. Scarlet can see where the afterparty is, and feels the anxiety well up inside her like boiling tar. She can see colourful dresses and leather jackets, attention-seeking pagers and stylish flat caps. There's a big crowd on the road, being gradually shown through a door, like marbles being shoved into a tight tube. Two plump security men are keeping careful watch over things, but there's no need. After all, these are sophisticated people. The artistic sorts. A few cameras flash. Several people try to get themselves noticed, in every sense of the word.

"Damn press," snaps Roger. "George, can you make sure none of them sneak into my home?"

The car grinds to a stop. Mr Chauffer steps out and opens a door. Instantly, the attention of the crowd is on them. Yet, they don't approach. Yet, they keep a smart distance. A few hands are waved, a few cheers are given, but there's no mad rush. After all, these are sophisticated people.

"Follow me," says Roger. "George, have you got the keys to the back?"

"In my pocket, boss," the man says, like an obedient dog.

"Right, guys, stick close."

Roger leads them through a small gulley to the back of the row of apartment blocks. Bats are flying above, blinking out the starlight. It's an incredible display of fruitfulness and fruitlessness.

There's a garden out the back, but anyone can tell it's unused, even shrouded in streetlight and darkness. There's a small bird perch and a rusting green table (and two thoroughly disintegrating chairs).

They go up a spiral staircase to a backdoor which is coated with splintered paint. It's not that much of a grandiose method of being shown into a party; even the keyhole looks like its stepped out of a Newcastle council estate of the early Eighties.

Roger inserts the key, begins to twist, stops.

"Now, girls," he says, peering down at them, "pay attention."

They're all trapped on the staircase like smirking trout.

"This is your last stepping stone before you enter the world of celebrity. Beyond this, there is no turning back. There's no retreat. There's no running away. This is your last chance to have a life where you can be... everyday. In there, you'll meet press, artists, singers, you name it. You will be forever sealed as a celebrity. Yes, you've been seen by the public. Now, you're going to be seen by elite. If you have any reservations, I suggest you turn around. George will see you home safe and sound. No one will know who you are. I will guarantee it."

It's Susan who speaks. The quiet, little cherub finally finds some ground.

"Mr Miser, I speak for all of us, when we say we're ready," she tells him. "We're ready. This is what we want."

"Then, so be it," answers Roger, turning the key. He grips the handle, shoulders the door, and takes them into the light.

There's a wall-to-wall mess of people. There they are, sitting on sofas, feet on chairs, backsides wedged into sofas, elbows on white ledges. They're in heavy discussion about artistic (in the broad sense of the word) nonsense of every kind.

Roger Miser's penthouse is something from the set of *Thunderbirds*: blue leather sofas, ornaments of sportsmen, leatherbound books on a sparkling glass shelf, an uncountable number of modern art paintings, and various other trinkets buried in forgotten corners.

They've entered the living room. A big table with champagne glasses fizzling away is supervised by a woman with a sad face and a longish ponytail. The elite are buzzing around like flies, chattering, winking, clapping on shoulders.

"Hi, folks!" Roger calls out.

The talking and murmuring stops.

Roger introduces the girls one at a time, like they're being introduced to a jury. Someone asks them about why they chose that particular name for the band. Gina gives a meek answer.

"Well, let's get the champagne properly flowing!" he shouts charismatically. "Girls," he whispers, "go and mingle."

Scarlet takes one foot forward, then another, then another. Her fingers meet a glass of champagne. She doesn't see where the other girls go. Doesn't even know what's happening.

"Bloody hell, that was a good concert," says a man with dashing red hair and a blinding, white shirt with the top two buttons undone. He holds out his hand. "Dennis Loud."

"Scarlet," she answers. She feels she'll have to answer a lot here.

"You and the girls certainly have talent. I was watching from the back. Even from there, I got a raw sense of the energy, the pride, the undoing, the fierce nature of the rebelliousness of it all! Oh, you definitely had –"

She can tell he's had a few glasses. He's an eccentric guy. Can't be more that forty. No, strike that, can't be more than thirty. He looks like the kind of bloke who's failed as an actor and now does small roles on nonsensical pantos.

He launches a tirade of how *he* thinks the music world should link with the literary world. It sounds like that. It strangely sounds something like that.

"– but I don't think that there could be any possible collaboration between them. Pearl Jam, on the other hand, now I can see possibilities when it comes to them. I think there's an opportunity for maybe a poet or an essayist to spend time with them and allow their work to reflect of one another. I know it sounds utterly nonsensical –"

"He's not boring you, is he?" says Roger, stepping in. He pats Dennis Loud hard on the elbow.

"Not at all," says Scarlet. She shouldn't even contemplate speaking the truth here.

"Dennis Loud is a lecturer in creative writing and the author of three bestselling books on the Charles Dickens, Jane Austen and... I forgot the other one." The way Roger says this, damn, it's intimidating. "You know what they say. Those who can't do teach. I bet you're wondering why I've got him here. He's got himself a contract to write a book on Seventies rock music. It should be a new frontier for him. Anyway, it makes him a valued guest at this party."

Scarlet's only just seen the glass of scotch in his hand. She knows the smell of it... rather two well. How long has it been? Scarcely a quarter of an hour, yet Roger sounds drunk.

"Scarlet, there's a few people I'd like you to meet." Roger tugs at her arm. "Come on, let's get you away from him," he whispers in her ear as they move away. "He's a bit of a boring cunt."

She's suffocating on the stench of the whisky crashing its way through her nasal passage.

The girls – *her girls* – are spread out, huddled in the middle of small groups.

He introduces her to so many people in so many seconds. There's this guy who owns this record company (a close friend of Roger's); two young violinists who have just released their fourth album; a member of a rock band, who's got thin, stringy hair; an Australian vocalist for this big choir in New Zealand that loves to perform in South Africa, though things are a bit volatile there at the moment. She quickly loses track of who she meets. It's like she's on a carousel, like the horse things she used to go on when she was a kid, the ones in funfairs. She hears comments like: "Your music has that edge." "You touched my soul." "Your band is the future. Trust me on that." She drinks glass after glass of champagne. She's starting to feel a little lucid, a little faint.

"Scarlet, there's a guy I'd like you to meet," slurs Roger, after an unknown while. "Josephine, you should come and meet him too."

Josephine's there. She winks at Scarlet. Pinpricks of sweat are on the bridge of her nose. She looks like she's fully aware – thankfully.

Roger leads them over to a corner slightly neglected corner of his ginormous living room. The bookshelves here have been screwed in at slightly careless angles. A small table dug right into the nook has been permitted to gather just a tiny bit of dust; on it, two cat model supports which prop up some really old-looking academic tomes have been allowed to lose their shine. There are two leather armchairs facing the table, and they look like they've been torn from a BBC adaptation of a Dickens novel, the way they're so faded and lost. Scarlet's surprised Dennis Loud's not over here. On the right armchair, there's a figure sitting; the top of his hair is just visible.

"Ladies, I'd like you to meet Mauro Lane," says Roger.

The figure stands up and gravitates over to them.

Damn, he's cute, Scarlet realises. He's tall, slim, well-built. His blonde hair's just like hers, but it seems less organised and far more natural. He wears a yellow and green punk t-shirt, faded blue jeans, and a pair of... wait... Adidas Court Trainers. He's put a formal element on though, probably to impress his gran: a thick, black jacket. He's rolled up the sleeves, bare arms exposed. No watch. No bracelet. His eyes are gentle blue and his cheeks and lips are ghostly pale.

"Pleased to meet you," he says to them. He's stifling a Mancunian accent and trying to sound more London. "Scarlet, I've heard about you. Your band is amazing. Listened to your album this morning."

"He got an early copy," Roger fills in. "Mauro Lane is one of the U.K.'s top new singers, in my opinion. His debut album comes out next month."

"So my brother keeps reminding me," says Mauro.

Scarlet risks a glance to her left to see Josephine totally perplexed. She really hopes there isn't going to be a fight for this guy, because it'll get ugly.

"I'm Josephine."

Oh well, Scarlet thinks. Here we go.

"Yeah, I thought you were really good as well," Mauro tells her.

"You were at the concert?"

"Yeah. It was totally great."

Mauro looks a bit unsteady. Josephine really launches herself at him, asking about his career, what got him to be a singer. The guy tries to answer as best as he can.

"Right, guys, I'd better go and mingle, or I'll be a piss-poor host," says Roger, excusing himself.

"When's your album out?" Scarlet butts in.

"A few weeks. I'm doing a few interviews and that with radio stations and magazines. Should be quite good. Though my brother says I'll embarrass myself. I keep having to tell Eugene that it's my life, but he really wants a part of it. He won't damn quit."

"Well, I'm sure your brother's wrong about it."

"Oh, he's wrong about a lot of things. Considering he works on a building site." Mauro looks down at his feet, shuffles his trainers. "Oh yeah." He looks up again, a shot of alertness crossing his eyes. "Listen, I'd better head off, actually. I've got an early flight tomorrow. Going to Paris."

"Nice one!" shouts Josephine, rather too loudly. Heads turn. Eyes flicker.

"It's nothing special. Just an interview with a magazine. Listen, it was great to meet you." He shakes hands with them in a business-like manner. He nods to a few people on his way, pats Roger's arm as gently as a feather.

When he's gone, Josephine nudges Scarlet. "Hot or what?" she teases.

"Oh, stop it." Scarlet says this aggressively, but it doesn't seem to work on Josephine.

Oh, Josephine can get fooled in the most spectacular ways.

Scarlet tries talking to people Roger hasn't introduced her to yet. They're mostly up-and-coming singers, some with an album out, others on the brink of scoring a record deal.

Gradually, the numbers dwindle. Some have homes to get to, others have after-afterparties to get drunk at. One guy even has to practice his chords. Soon enough, it's only the girls, George, Roger, and a skinny model of a woman with too much makeup and way too few clothes.

"Well, ladies..." Roger can barely speak. Whisky glasses dot the room like dugout graves. "Well, ladies, it's been a great night. I want to say this, and that... I think you're going to go far."

The model supports him, fragile fingers as touch as concrete bars.

"There were a lot of jokers here, a lot of fakers. But that's all they are. Fakers. You are the real deal. That's why we've given you three fucking deals. You've got a few concerts between now and the summer, but... not much. Start getting on with your second album."

"We will," answers Susan.

"I mean it. You're special." Tears creep out of Roger's eyelids. "You mean a lot to me. Darling," he says to the model woman, "take me to bed. I need to rest."

"The driver's out the front," George informs them, as the record manager is carried and dragged by the woman. "Don't worry, girls, he does this all the time. I'm used to it."

George leads them back the way we came. Is he afraid that there might be some dangerous paparazzi? It seems such a stupid thought. When they're back on the street, the only presence there is the limo.

"Time for bed," says George, as the chauffer opens up for them. "Where do you all live?"

Gina and Susan give out their addresses. Josephine seems a little hesitant. Like she's afraid someone might be listening. Scarlet does it eventually: "We live together."

"As a flatmate!" proclaims Josephine. "Just in case anyone got the wrong idea."

"Well, I'm sure the driver will be so good as to drop us off where we need to be."

There's no need for that, Scarlet thinks, as they set off. Actually, she wants to scream it out loud. She wants to howl it to the moon. Like in a black and white movie from the late Forties.

It turns out it's in the early hours. Funny how time slips by. It only felt like a few minutes in that apartment.

Gina and Susan are dropped off first, murmuring exhausted goodbyes. They're relieved the day's over. They're relieved they'll get some damn rest.

It's nearly Two A.M. when the car pulls up outside their flat.

"We'll be in touch about concert arrangements," says George, spreading out on the backseat. "I'll make sure you guys are kept informed about everything. Don't mind Roger. He can be a bit crotchety, but he really cares about you, all of you."

"He's got a cute girlfriend," Josephine remarks.

"Ha! It's wife number three," returns George. "Sleep well!"

The chauffer shuts the door. He flashes them a smile that's not quite a smile – it's more of a barebones acknowledgement.

"Come on, let's go up," says Scarlet.

Josephine opens up and leads the way upstairs. "Coffee?" she asks, when they get in.

"No thanks, I just want to sleep."

Scarlet starts walking to her bedroom. It's her little hideaway from Josephine's constant rants and tellings-off. It's like a resort for those who need a bit of peace. There's no swimming pool or blue-lit bar with blues music. A pile of unwashed clothes is the main tourist attraction.

"You spoiled things with that guy tonight!" Josephine calls after her.

"What are you talking about?"

"Mauro. I was trying to score. You ruined things." Josephine looks livid. Has she lost weight?

"I don't understand."

"You ruined things. I was trying to get a date with him. You put him off. Just saying."

"Oh, fuck you, Josephine."

"Yeah, you'd like that."

Josephine takes a step closer. It's like she's still on stage. It's like they've forgotten to do one of their songs, and it just so happens to be the one she *really* wanted to perform. She purses her lips.

"What do you want, Scarlet? Is it me you want?" She shoves Scarlet hard, nearly knocking her over. "Hey? You want me?" She pushes again, aggressively. "Christ, I thought you dykes liked it rough. That's what you're all about, isn't it? You like pulling hair and punching and kicking and screaming."

"Oh, fuck off."

"Listen, I told you last year that you and I would never be intimate. And we never will. So, stop fucking doing what it is you're doing. Now we live together. We work together. We're friends, absolutely. I care about you. More than you'll ever know. I'd fight for you if it became necessary. But you listen here, when I'm on a date, when I'm with a guy, you stay the hell away, you got that?"

"Yeah."

"Sleep well, Scarlet."

Josephine turns around and trudges off to her room.

Scarlet wants to respond, but she can't. If only she could see further, some years from now, but she can't. She shakes her head – oh, dear reader, you should see the way she does that – and goes to her bed, slumping down on the covers.

She thinks about nothing else except the concert. The bliss of the stage. The adrenaline. The girls. Her family of fame, music, and devotion.

Josephine

5 April 1991

I can't stand being stuck bored. You know the feeling. When you're sitting with fucking nothing to do, sitting on your backside, stiff and restless.

I've been in this flat for three soppy days, staring at the window, biting my nails.

I think of the tour we're supposed to be going on. A mini one. A gig in Birmingham and two in Newcastle. It's to break us in gently. It's to give us the feeling of what it's like to be going from place to place. It's to give us that shot of adrenaline.

But I've got this sheer void of fucking boredom to get through first. Though we're raking in the cash, though we're literally swallowing it, it always seems like we don't have any. Don't ask me to describe it.

Scarlet's been away for a few days in Eastbourne. She's due back tomorrow morning. We get an early train on Sunday. We're not going in Slum Class anymore. Tickets marked with that prestigious word *First* arrived yesterday. And we're staying in luxury hotels, with a maid to look after each of us.

We'll be out of this place soon, I fucking hope so. The way the money's pouring in, like an endless stream of lager, we'll be on our way soon before we know it. We'll each have our own nice place. Little cottages or something. Fluffy gardens with even fluffier sheep milling about in the background.

Ah, she's not that bad. Scarlet's a bit annoying sometimes, but, yeah, she's okay. She's someone you have to get to know. I sometimes don't know how she's feeling, why she's feeling that way, or who she's feeling towards.

She fancies me. I'm convinced of it. Let me be clear: I'm not that way inclined. Even if I was, I wouldn't get with her. She's too unstable for my liking. You never know what she's up to. The only thing I'm sure about is that she has a dark secret. I know that from the way she looks at me, the way her eyes dart right through me, as if she's hoping I'll guess. She was like that after our first concert, back at Roger's. You could tell that she was looking for a way out. I can't be with someone like that. Who could?

I go into the kitchen and put the kettle on. Fifth cup of tea this morning. The water sloshes and boils and froths. I lean back against the wall, straining to think of something to break the monotony. Practice my guitar? Already done. Take a walk? Already done. After the tea's made, I return to the living room and pick up the phone.

"Hi, Gina," I say, when the other end gets picked up.

"Hey."

"Listen, you want to get lunch?"

"I'd love to, but I'm knackered today. Too much of a hard workout last night."

"I didn't know you went to the gym."

"I don't. I joined a fitness group."

"Gina." Now, please, I really don't want to say this. "Gina, you know it's not right for us to be doing this."

"I'm fully aware, Josephine. I was at George's little lecture two weeks ago."

"Look, just be careful, okay? Can't I persuade you to come out for lunch?"

"I'd love to... honest."

"Go on. My treat."

"Yeah, go on then. Where do you want to meet?"

"How about the Sir John Balcombe?"

"Thought you wanted to be careful where we hang out. You know, with us being celebrities...?"

She's got me there.

"Tell you what, stop the bullshit, and let me by you a pint," I retort. "I'm in the mood for ale today."

"Bet you are. Meet at One?"

"Cool." I hang up.

Maybe I should invite Susan. Actually, no, it's probably not a good idea. Susan's always had something about her that I don't like. She's vague. Actually, that's not the right description. She's perfectly clear in what she wants. Scarlet is always neither here nor there. You can't possibly know what Scarlet's thinking, but somehow, you just do. Susan, on the other hand, well she's so sad all the time. She's always at the back, hiding like a stray dog. But she's clear when she wants to be. And that scares me. That's why I try to avoid her. I'm not getting sucked into her fucked-up little world.

I have to force myself to get a move on when I spend five minutes selecting the right coat. I pick a drab raincoat. Something I'll be chucking out soon enough. When I set off into the day, there's a tiny bit of drizzle hanging like a threatening fog.

I walk with a determination. Not that there's much to be excited about. It's just lunch, after all. It's just two mates – colleagues – having a beer, some pub grub, and a chat. Fuck, there's nothing else to do today.

A cyclist whooshes past me, giving meek, apologetic excuses. A Tom Baker scarf billows out behind him like a torn banner. I jerk my middle finger up after him. Twat.

There's a taxi rank up ahead.

Why the hell am I walking? Celebrities don't *walk*. They *ride*.

I go to the nearest one and fling myself inside.

"The Sir John Balcombe, please," I say.

"No problem, miss."

You know what? It's nice being driven. Sorry to be such a wimp, but my feet hurt a lot these days.

The traffic's on my side today. The rain evaporates and the sun beckons me to be joyful. And I should be bloody happy! I'm in a band! Our music's being played in bars, student dorms, all sorts of places!

Gina's waiting outside. She wasn't lying about being exhausted. She looks so fragile that a wisp of wind could blow her over.

I pay the driver, giving him a nice little tip to make his day.

"Hello, hello," I say mockingly.

"You got here quick."

"So did you. Actually, how did you? You're at least half an hour away from here by car."

"Well..." Gina's face breaks into a cheeky smirk. "A friend gave me a lift on his motorbike."

"Wow, it's a male!" I shout. "So, is there something that you want to tell me, or am I going to have to drag it out of you bit by bit?"

"Maybe we'll drag a few beers out first."

"Right you, inside."

We go in and find the place empty. Everything's neat, shiny, unused.

"I think they're closed," says Gina.

"How did you guess that?"

A woman with strikingly bright red hair pops up from behind the bar. When I say strikingly bright, I mean it knocks the other colours away like a bulldozer. She looks barely eighteen. She looks like she belongs in a story about mermaids.

"It's okay, we're open," she tells us. "You're literally the first people to arrive."

"Two pints," I say. "Your best ale. And if you've got any fish and chips – we'll take two of those."

"How did you know what I wanted?" laughs Gina.

"Lucky guess."

"Take a seat," says the woman. "Wherever you want? I'll get your orders in."

She's quite bubbly. An enthusiastic Daddy's Little Angel. She runs like a little fairy, hopping about, scribbling things with a chewed-up pencil.

We go to a table by the window. I remember being here years ago. A mate's birthday. Way too much to drink. Two of the girls had to be dragged home, vomit spewing every other second. The good old days of the Eighties...

"I'm nervous about this tour in the summer," says Gina. "Fourteen dates. We're going to be knocked out by the end."

"Ah, it'll be fine, Gina. I think you worry too much about this stuff. It'll be a whirlwind."

"Why are you always so confident about these things?"

"What do you mean?" I'm ashamed to say it, but, well, no point hiding it away. "Do you remember me at the concert?"

"Hell yeah. Panicking like a fretting cat. But, come on, you're cool."

The redhead brings our drinks over with a deep smile. I can smell the ale's slightly off, but I don't let it stop me from taking a long drink. Only then I forget to raise a toast. Our glasses clink like two French kissers.

"I actually wanted to have a bit of a chat with you about Scarlet," I said. "Sorry, I know it's not an ideal thing to discuss over lunch, but I have a few concerns, which I think are urgent."

"You and your urgent concerns."

"I care about the success of the band. Look, I'm worried about Scarlet. She was a bit off the other day."

"Don't worry about it."

"You girls okay?" the barmaid calls over to us. "If you want another drink, just raise your hand."

The girl starts wiping the bar with a playful ferociousness. I have to say, it's pretty funny. She's too small to be in this environment, but she acts like she's a giant. Her hair's wavy and thick, almost natural. She looks like an Irish immigrant from the days when they used to flock to New York and all that.

"Thanks," I acknowledge. I roll my lips. "Sorry, Gina, maybe I'm overreacting, but she seemed quite upset, quite lonely."

"She's always like that. Look, if you're really concerned, maybe you should speak with Susan. She's closer to Scarlet than either of us."

"Yeah, I suppose. I dunno. Maybe it's not worth kicking a fuss over. I'm just worried she does something stupid, like get into drugs."

"Oh, don't be silly!" scolds Gina. She sounds just like my mum.

"You're right. But, let's keep an eye on her. Just in case."

"Gotcha." Gina sips her pint. "Right, let's fucking enjoy lunch."

The time goes by too quickly. Though the food is fairly shit and can't leave our systems fast enough. When we walk outside, Gina gives me a polite thumbs up and ambles off. I stay for a few moments, deciding whether or not to nip back inside for another pint. I take too long. I start walking back to the flat. I need to stretch my legs.

I let out a quiet yawn, then a louder one.

The people who pass me... they recognise me, sort of. It's like I'm halfway between commoner and royalty. Fuck knows. Why's the world full of indecision? Why can people never make their minds up about what they want anymore? And why is the guy who nips across my path, darting like a badger, so damn familiar?

I stop and stare at the man in the black suit and brown leather shoes, half-walking, half-skipping down York Street. He's glancing at his watch, repeatedly. I'm probably deaf, dumb and stupid, I start following him, keeping my gaze at buildings on either side. The man stops to check himself in a shop window, and that's when it hits me: it's Scarlet's father. He's really gone for it with the blue stripy tie and the white collar/blue contrast shirt. He's carrying a small briefcase which swings loosely in his grip. I think about saying hello, but hold back. It'd be great to see how these career professionals live. Scarlet's always going on about how she was supposed to be a perfect little poppet, destined to become a leading practitioner of law or medicine or something. Ah, you know what? I want to see what this guy's life is like.

Then he does the strangest, oddest thing. He turns off the street, entering a small alley. Now, if you were in that kind of a suit, you wouldn't do that for all the tea in England!

Cautiously, I stop by the entrance, and follow his footsteps.

They alley goes on for fifty yards, then cuts to the left. As I go up to the corner, I can hear him talking. I get down on my knees and peep around.

Scarlet's father is talking to a gruff, pudgy man in a fleece. He's also got a briefcase, but this one looks battered, like something Paddington Bear would take on a trip with Scousers to Alton Towers.

"All I'm saying is that we can't keep going on like this," says Scarlet's dad. "I mean, how long do you think it'll take them before they find out? This could have serious ramifications. I'm not losing my business over this."

"And how do you think they'll react if we tell them!" the fat man responds aggressively. "Bloody hell, James, you do talk crap sometimes. No one will find out, if we're careful. If we're discreet about things, if we're careful, who's going to know?"

"It's not that simple! I mean, my daughter's becoming a bloody rockstar. She'll be hanging around with Tears For Fears before long, and drinking champagne with Sting. It won't be long before I have the bloody media on my back every five minutes!" James drops his briefcase and groans with frustration. He sounds pissed. "I mean, that's why I've spent the past year trying to slow her down, trying to talk her out of it, but..."

"Yeah, don't forget, I've been helping. But she's a free spirit, James. You can't stop a free spirit."

"I know, Paul. Christ, my wife thinks I'm having lunch with a potential client today. How long do you think we can keep this up?"

"We just need to be careful." Paul takes a step closer to James. "If we have our stories planned, if we take extreme precautions, we won't get caught. And if we do... so what? Two old friends having lunch or dinner. What's odd about that? They're not going to suspect a bloody thing."

Paul puts his case down and touches Scarlet's dad on the shoulder, moving his fingers up to his ear. The two men stare deeply at each other. James puts his hands around Paul's waist, holding him there. Their heads move closer together and their lips touch like butterflies.

I feel sick. Why do I feel betrayed?

"I love you, James." Paul sounds sincere.

"I love you too. Right, come on, how about we grab a pint?"

"Well, I didn't come all the way down from Liverpool just to hear you moan."

I'm panicking. There's not enough time to get out of here. I can't even swear out loud. I slump down and toss my hair over my eyes. I make myself fall to the side.

"You okay, darling?"

I think it's Paul who's said that. I can see his thick features through the fraying strands of my hair. He leans down.

"Christ, do you think she heard anything?" asks Scarlet's dad. He sounds frantic with worry.

"It's okay, don't worry. She's flat-out drunk."

I feel Paul's fingers reach underneath my jaw. If he pulls my hair away... James will recognise me.

"Yeah, she's comatose," says Paul. "I think we should get an ambulance."

"No way. Let's get the hell out of here."

Paul's clammy skin falls away from mine. I hear footsteps and see their disjointed selves head back down the alley. I wait for as long as I dare before rising up. I walk back hurriedly out, melting into the busy late afternoon crowd like a butterfly in a swarm.

I don't immediately think of what I need to tell Scarlet. It's only when I'm back in the flat, back in the living room, that I think about it. I know she doesn't think much of her dad, but this could have serious consequences if it gets out.

Times are changing. Poofs and faggots are now being called homosexuals. We are moving forward. But someone like Roger could react the wrong way. I make a resolute decision, there and then, that Scarlet must never know. No one else must either. If this gets out, it will destroy us. This has to be a secret, one that is actually kept.

Scarlet

7 April to 10 April 1991

She's too tired to argue, so she agrees with Josephine's request to not have a second cup of coffee. She's too concerned about whether or not they'll make the train, so she allows Josephine to harry her out of the flat like a bulldog chasing a rabbit.

"Christ, we're going to miss our train," hisses Josephine, as they head into their taxi. "How much were you drinking last night?"

"A bottle of wine," responds Scarlet. "Celebrating."

"Well, celebrate after our gig tonight. Euston Station, please," Josephine orders.

They hold themselves in silence for a few minutes as the taxi trundles along. They can barely afford to look at one another.

Now, dear reader, you know it's because of Josephine's discovery. You know it's because she's alarmed and scared. Not for Scarlet, but for the band. This morning, she's found it necessary to nit-pick at Scarlet's tiny habits, including that sneaky bottle of time.

"Look, I'm sorry, it was a long journey," says Scarlet. She's broken the silence like a hammer on a pane of glass. "I just needed a few glasses."

"Well, just be careful, okay?"

"I will."

Scarlet's thinking about the trip to Eastbourne. She kept the details secret from Josephine last night, because there was always the possibility of accidentally leaking the truth. No lie can be perfect. Every lie can fall to perfect pieces. She has no friends in Eastbourne. Indeed, she'd never been to Eastbourne before in her life. But it was the perfect place to meet and arrange the necessary business. She'll go back there once this little tour is done, finish everything. She's already sorted it out.

They get there five minutes before the train is due to leave. Gina and Susan look alarmed and annoyed, standing here with their luggage as companions. Josephine offers a muffled apology about the traffic and leads them inside. There's a bit of a mad dash, a few stumbles, but they get on the train with only thirty seconds to spare. There's not enough time to appreciate the beauty and pampering of first-class assistance. Instead, they push their way through to the posh carriage with the clumsiness of a tumbling brick wall.

"Come on, ladies, be seated," Josephine moans.

The four of them have got a table seat, decorated with royalistic cutlery and glasses (plus a virgin-white cloth). Scarlet's by the window, Josephine on her right.

"Now this is the life!" says Gina. "God, Scarlet, when you gathered us in that café the beginning of last year, I didn't think it would work, but..."

"We'll be sipping the richest filter coffee in a few minutes," says Josephine.

The train lurches away like a worm caught in treacle. They pick up speed as they head up north through the pitiful outskirts of London. Everything about the train – this first-class mobile world – seems constrained and freeing at the same time.

Scarlet watches her girls play a game of poker, using the tops of bottles, two-penny pieces, an empty condom packet and half a pencil in the place of chips. She looks at them in admiration, as they deal, bluff, laugh, and get bored.

The ticket inspector comes by. His bristling moustache and uniformed cap ensure that the girls are who they say they are. He's obliged to make sure that they've earned the right to sit in these plush seats. But he merely takes the bundle of tickets, flips through them, autographs them, returns them, sets off.

A few minutes later, a stewardess comes through and stands before them, hands behind her back. She's probably been doing this job for only a few weeks (she's only nineteen) and she definitely can't believe the group that's in front of her. Not her typical rich businessmen. She hands out paper menus. Scarlet takes a long look through. Eggs Benedict, pastries, toast, bacon sandwich, fruit, and porridge.

"Not much on here," says Josephine. "What's to drink?"

"We have tea, coffee and orange juice," the stewardess tells her. "The list is on the second page."

"Yeah, I can see that. I'm after the drinks menu."

"Oh, I see. We don't serve alcohol with breakfast."

"Well, that's not good enough." Josephine looks at each of the girls. "You think that's good enough, ladies? Look, waitress, we want a bottle of your finest champagne. And four glasses. We're celebrating. We're on tour."

"I'm sorry, but we don't serve alcohol with breakfast," the stewardess repeats. She looks alarmed. She's no doubt seen elderly lawyers and the occasional MP sitting in here, but this is something else.

"You look too young and fruitful to be doing this," Josephine says tauntingly.

Scarlet's horrified. She wants to say something, but her throat is caught. She can tell Gina and Susan are the same.

"It must be an absolute fucking nightmare to be doing this job." Josephine sneers. "I should feel sorry for you, but I don't.

Look at you. You wear that white fucking coat like a badge of pride, but you look like an overgrown kid."

"How about I give you five minutes?" The stewardess is avoiding eye contact, trying to keep a firm face.

Josephine's persistent: "I take it you didn't go to university, then. What, your mum or your dad sick or something, and you're doing this shitty job to help pay the bills? No boyfriend? You know something, you've probably never had a boyfriend. You look so fucking stupid, even a fat barrel of pork wouldn't want to fuck you –"

"Enough!" roars Susan.

Scarlet's never heard her go like that before. She's scary. Her eyes are flurried with fury. Her tongue is curled sharp. She looks like a mean, fighting bully. She looks like she could throw something across a room. She looks like she should tear this train in two.

"I'm just having a laugh!" Josephine protests. "Okay, I'd like a bacon sandwich and a cup of coffee. And a croissant. Butter and blackcurrant jam."

The stewardess is fighting back tears, but she keeps a brave face. The others calmly place their orders and the woman walks away, fists unclenched.

"Why did you do that?" gasps Scarlet.

"Because I can. What's she going to do? Report me to my boss?"

"Josephine, I'm going to say this once," says Susan. "I'm going to pretend that you didn't say that. So will Scarlet and Gina. But you mustn't do anything like this again. You promise me?"

"I promise." Josephine raises her hands and snorts. "I'm sorry. I really am."

"Let's try and rest," says Gina. "Don't know why I ordered some food. Already had my breakfast. Christ, I'm going to be fat."

In truth, dear reader, the girls can't believe what's just occurred. To think that Josephine would do such a stupid thing like that, it's something they can't, won't believe. They're celebrities, after all, and they'll be superstars after the U.S. tour in the summer: that means they have responsibilities to behave themselves and respect one another, and the general public.

Scarlet feels the weight of the world on her shoulders. Not just that, but she feels the compression of other people's worlds.

She looks over to Susan. The girl is focused on her feet. She's so shy and frail, like an old woman reborn. It's not right.

Their gig in Birmingham goes well, with a sell-out crowd and only a couple of bottles thrown. Afterwards, there's plenty of champagne in Gina's hotel room. The richest stuff. Courtesy of Roger.

Scarlet's forgotten about what happened on the train, but it's obvious, dear reader, that Josephine hasn't.

They stay up until the early hours, the alcohol flooding their veins like lava. They order pizza, keeping a poor, weary chef from going home. Josephine probably likes that: inconveniencing the common man.

The next day, it's another early train, and they head further north. Josephine says that Newcastle is a wasteland. And she's very vociferous in making sure the girls know that. She says it's rife with unemployment, useless drunks, human scum. Even fellow first-class travellers cast her a look of hatred.

Scarlet really hates the person Josephine's becoming: an arrogant, self-centred bitch. But she knows she needs – the band needs – her. She's aggressive but witty, outspoken but right.

Their two performances in Newcastle go like two concerts should. There's no rioting – which Josephine feared. The most trouble is the limo being five minutes late. In their pampered little nest, they drink more champagne and order more cocktails. Everything seems to come in extra-large quantities. Everything seems to come with a reputation.

Scarlet feels a pang of sadness as they leave the northern city. Its smog smothers her heart. Its smells carve at her throat. Its streets and its songs, its people and its river, its homeliness and its virtue. Everything about it has touched her in some way.

They're on a direct service to London, seated around another table, with the remnants of breakfast scattered across the cloth. As they twist and turn and elbow their way through the morning air, the bright rays of the sun tingle Scarlet's eyelids.

This is what she's been waiting for, she realises. This sense of freedom and fragility. She's slightly hungover from last night, but that's part of the joy. There she was, on the edge of the stage, singing at the crowd, the bright lights upon her. It's a memory she knows will always stay with her.

She's about to nod off, when she sees Susan smiling at her.

"How did you find it?" asks Scarlet.

"Well, our first tour. It's something that should be celebrated."

It's strange, but it's like Gina and Josephine aren't there. Now, dear reader, this isn't some sort of exaggeration or overused idea – this is real. It's like Gina and Josephine have melted away into the seats. It's like the train isn't there either. It's like they're sitting on opposite sides of a picnic blanket, chewing on sandwich crusts and hoping they don't run out of coffee.

Susan starts off on a tale about a guy who gave her a grin in the lobby of the hotel in Newcastle. He was cute, dark-eyed, smart. He was the essence of what she wants in a man. She went to ask him for a drink.

"Unfortunately, he wasn't interested in me. When we were sat in the hotel bar, he talked about how he was a big fan of us, particularly you, Scarlet. He's got a bit of a crush on you, apparently."

"You should have told me," jokes Scarlet. "I'm always eager to meet a random guy."

"You looking forward to America?"

"You bet. It'll be interesting. I just want to get on those stages, sing to the crowds, get our album selling."

"We'll do it, Scarlet. We'll do it"

Scarlet doesn't know if she replies. She's not even sure if she's heard Susan correctly. The last thing she thinks about is the last song she blurted out, the last round of cheering, the last rush of adrenaline, the last pounding of her eardrums. When sleep takes her fully, she dreams of nothing but noise.

Scarlet

11 April 1991

She knows where she needs to meet them. It's the last meeting, the short, brief goodbye to her past. She takes an early train – the first one after the big commuter rush – but ends up arriving around lunchtime, thanks to a nice, customary signal fault. She slights at Hampden Park Station, lights up a cigarette on the platform, and quickly checks the contents of her small rucksack.

It's strange to be wandering somewhere without her guitar. If there's ever a biography written of her, the front cover will be of her walking down an empty street, her instrument strung over her back like an old companion.

She's going to be late for this meeting. But she knows they'll wait. They're like that. They're so patient. She doesn't really want to do this. Of course, dear reader, she doesn't want to give away a thousand pounds – who would? Especially, as it's her first cut of the booty, her first handful of celebrity cash. But this is a worthwhile payoff. Transfer the cash. Buy their silence.

The fear creeps through her, winding its way around her spine. She doesn't have to walk far to the rendezvous point. She follows a main road, all the time watching out for them. She sees the turning ahead: a small lane which goes between two sets of houses like a wound in this town's flesh. She glances around her, just to be sure, before turns off. There's a small grove at the end, a thick mound of chaotic growth. To her relief – and her dread – she sees the two figures smoking.

"About bloody time!" says the elder of the two, tossing his cigarette away. "What the fuck happened? You got a last-minute interview?"

"Alright, guys," says Scarlet, "I'm not in the mood."

"We're entitled to an explanation," the younger one says. "I know you're a celebrity, but you have to explain yourself to us. Since we're the ones propping up your world."

"You're not propping up anything!" she hisses.

She goes into the grove, keeping as far from the two policemen as she can. They're more intimidating now they're not in uniform. They smile gleefully. They've got this power over her that no one else has: they can destroy everything she has, not just her career, but her life.

She takes both bundles out and chucks them at their feet. "That's five-hundred pounds each," she tells them. "You have my word, it's all there. I don't ever want to see either of you again, do you understand? You stay away from me. You don't mention my name. Do I have your word?"

"You've got it," says the younger one. "From me, anyway. I was only a kid when it all happened. I don't particularly care. I was just after the money. My partner in crime here, well, it affected him deeply. He might want something else."

"Don't worry," says the senior cop. "I don't want anything more. I have no desire to ruin you. I don't want to see you behind bars. But remember this: If you do anything that compromises us, if you leak our identities or anything, or say something stupid, I'll be having a word in the ear of the Chief Inspector. I have the evidence I need, stored in a secure little place. Do you understand?"

"I do," she answers.

"Now, go. Go back to your life of rock concerts and stardom. Me and him, we'll be working hard tomorrow. Scrubs like you have never done a day's work in your life. Go on, fuck off. Get out of my sight."

She doesn't need telling again. She turns her back, every footstep faster and harder than the last. It's over. She knows that now. Her past is finally gone. What happened back in 1980 is confined to that year. She can breathe in and breathe out, and she'll never have to look behind her.

She just makes the next train to London. When she gets to the capital, the late afternoon sun has started its glare. A few heads turn and look, but she's still a quite unknown at this point. She's just in the right place. And you know what? She decides to go for a drink.

There's a good pub near Victoria Station. Time and time again, she's gone past it, wandered alongside its intrigue and curiosity. She's resolute in breaking the china mould this time. She's resolute in breaking everything.

The first thing she sees in The Shakespeare is the cute barmaid. She's got blonde hair that reaches down to her shoulders, lapis lazuli eyes, and slim cheekbones. She's smooth, every part of her is tender and calm. Her lips are narrow and her eyes are focused on everything. She watches the sad, lonely souls, the depressed travellers. She's standing with her hands behind her back, blue jeans at just the right height, and a faded green tank top that threatens to tear. Nevertheless, she stands ready. She looks like she'll throw a punch if things get out of hand. When she sees Scarlet, she seems to smile, though whether she really does is a genuine mystery.

"What can I get you?" she asks.

"Got any good ales? Something smooth," says Scarlet.

"I think I've got just the thing for you." The woman takes a pint glass and begins pulling out a dark bitter.

Scarlet reaches out a note, but the girl shakes her head.

"On the house. You look like you've had a rough day," the barmaid says pitifully. "You okay?"

"Just had to deal with a few things from my past." Scarlet puts herself down on the tender barstool. It feels like it'll break if so much as a grain of sand lands on its stapled leather.

"Tell me about it. Ex-boyfriend called me up this morning."

"Oh, shame. Damn." Scarlet takes a swig. "Why can't we just do without men?"

The barmaid laughs loudly, folding her arms across her chest. She reaches out a hand. "I'm Ellen."

"Scarlet."

"Wait!" Ellen's eyes sparkle with an unfamiliar recognition. "Wait a minute! I know you! You're that singer, aren't you? I read about you the other day. God, I can't believe this."

"Sometimes I can't believe it either."

"What brings you to this dump?"

"Having a day off from everything."

"Oh, know the feeling. Wow, I seriously can't believe you're in here! I've got your band's album. Love it so much. Actually, could I get your autograph?"

Ellen turns around and fumbles. A minute later, she produces a pen and notepad, and thrusts them at Scarlet.

"All I can find is this lousy thing used for taking orders," apologises the barmaid. "Please, would you mind?"

"No, of course not." Scarlet signs away and slides it back.

A man's voice cuts in. Aggressive, full of attitude, plied with alcohol. "Everything okay, Ellen?"

"I'm fine, Matt." Ellen sounds different now. Weaker. Further away from everything. A tiny doll. "I thought you were at work?"

"Finished early."

"Well, why don't we get dinner after I finish, babe?"

Matt's a tall, ugly bloke, with hair sprouting from his chin. His skin is covered in acne and seems to be on the verge of splitting. He looks like he's been left in the cold. There's a rage deep inside him – anyone can see that. His crooked, broken teeth, his pulsing eyes, his meaty hands.

"No, I thought I'd join you for a drink!" he shouts.

"Matt, this really isn't the time," pleads Ellen. God, she's really pleading. "Please leave the bar."

"I'm not going anywhere, not until this dyke leaves."

"What the fuck...?" stammers Scarlet.

"I fucking know who you are, you skanky little slut. I know your kind. Well, you don't fucking try it on with her. Or I'll fucking kill you."

"Right, get out!" yells Ellen. "Get out, or I'm calling the police!"

A fist lunges from somewhere – probably Matt's direction. It takes Scarlet in the neck. She feels herself sailing through the air, falling at a million miles an hour. A jolt, a crushing earthquake of pain shoots through her as her cheek makes contact with something. She feels something break. She breathes in. She can't breathe out.

Josephine

30 April 1991

For the record, I'm angry with Scarlet. I've never been angry with her. If anything, I'm disappointed in myself. I'm annoyed I didn't see this coming.

For five days – ever since she came back from the hospital – she's been lying on the sofa in the living room, only getting up to piss or drink. I've never been one to believe in that old *lost for words* nonsense, but I'm happy to make an exception. I can't do anything in this flat anymore. I can't go and watch the telly. I can't put the kettle on, because the slop-slop of the boiling water disturbs her. I can't even leave this place to go shopping or grab a pint. (Susan's afraid that she'll do something stupid.)

Thankfully, Roger's taking care of everything. He's done amazingly, keeping everything hush-hush. After Scarlet was beaten up, the police immediately informed him. He leapt into action straightaway: controlling the media, ensuring she was taken to an isolated ward, and accessing private treatment. Since the incident, he's been sending George over with shopping and other essentials. Anything we want, we can have.

But the story got out eventually, as it always does. The stupid barmaid – Ellen or something – went to the press. Apparently, Scarlet was chatting her up and her boyfriend, Matt, lashed out. At least Ellen – or whatever her name is – is ashamed of what her boyfriend did.

I glare angrily as I read the news clipping. I've got two: one next to the coffeemaker in the kitchen, one in my purse. I'm going to make Scarlet read it.

"I was a little daunted by what the singer was asking of me. Of course, that's no excuse for what he did. But, still, I thought she was a bit open with her sexuality. It's –"

Sanctimonious rubbish, the lot of it.

It won't be long before the media catches on about Scarlet's... interests. It'll be like Freddie Mercury all over again. Christ, how the fuck has he coped?

I won't allow it. Fuck no. Something must be done. Clenching my fists, curling my lips, I storm through to the living room.

"Right, up!" I yell at the sleeping mess on the sofa.

"What the fuck...?" Scarlet stirs awake. The rags she's got on reek of body odour and shit wine. She sits up, rests her elbows on her knees. The brutal gash is still there on her left cheek. She hit her face on the adjacent barstool as she fell. Thankfully, nothing was broken.

"You and I both know this can't go on!" I shout. "Look at you, you're a filthy disgrace! We're supposed to be going on tour this summer. Christ, have you seen yourself?"

"It's healing."

"I'm not talking about your face, I'm talking about the fact that you look and smell like a fucking drunk!"

"I'm sorry."

"No," I say sternly. "No, sorry's not good enough. What were you doing in that pub?"

"What's it to you?"

"Chatting up the barmaid, that's what you were doing, isn't it? Trying to get her under the covers? Scarlet, this can't happen again. We've been lucky this time, with Roger stepping in. We may not be so lucky in the future."

I'm not looking forward to this next bit. But if I don't say it, the band's death warrant has been signed.

"I had a chat with Roger two days ago on the phone. He's got damage control underway, but he's really not happy with what happened. Scarlet, I don't have anything against you with what you are. But you need to keep a disciplined approach in our line of work. Chatting random girls up, well, look at the consequences it's had. So, I'm going to give you an ultimatum."

"What's that?" She looks up at me with puppy eyes.

"I'm going to go out for a drink, maybe a few. When I come back – perhaps in a couple of hours, I'll either find you showered and cleaned and ready to get to work, or you'll have packed your bags and gone."

"I'll stay. I promise. I'll put in maximum effort."

"No, Scarlet. You take these couple of hours. You think about it. You think about it good and hard." I turn away.

My coat and purse are within easy reach. I assemble myself so neatly that Julie Andrews would give me a spoonful of sugar. Scarlet's the opposite of me right now. She looks as messed up as the plane that crashes in *Die Hard 2*.

I walk for a bit to a taxi rank and head to Covent Garden. I must be imagining it – yeah, I probably am – but, as I walk through the thick crowds, I get the distinct feeling that people are staring at me. Flickers of recognition. Who do they think I am? Brian May?

I hear music playing from somewhere. It's R.E.M. Their new album *Out Of Time*. I don't recognise the actual song, but, hell, yeah, I know it's this album. We've got the tape back at the flat. Damn, I love the lead singer's voice. It's almost like Scarlet's, but hers is way smoother.

I go through the doors of The Crown, sort of semi-conscious that people are still giving me the stare. I order a glass of the house wine and settle into a quiet seat next to the stairwell. It's a decent place this, nice people and that. Always a spare seat. But I feel the eyes on me. I feel hands reaching for me. Every time I turn around, they look away. Then I hear the whispers. "She's from that band." "Yeah, it's that guitarist."

"What's she doing in a place like this?" "She sucking up or something?"

The anger that fills me is unpalatable. It makes the wine taste like piss. I scratch at the small ledge of a table build into the wall and feel my brain crying out that it wants to cry. But I'm not enraged at the people behind me.

I know what I'm about to do is so unbelievably stupid, but, you know what? You really want to know what's going through my head? I don't give a shit.

I drink the wine quickly and nip downstairs to the toilet.

"Where's the nearest taxi rank?" I ask the barman.

"Five minutes that way." The overweight, red-faced landlord jerks his thumb behind him.

"Thanks."

I walk briskly with my head down, feet close together, arms folded. The anger's filling me, overflowing like the volcano scene in *You Only Live Twice*. I reach the taxi rank and go for the nearest vehicle.

"London Victoria Station, please," I say.

This is a big gamble I'm taking, but I need to do this. I want the people who hurt Scarlet to suffer. Why do I hate Scarlet? Why have I been like this to her? It's not her fault!

"Keep the change," I tell the driver, when I jump out at Victoria.

I spend a few minutes staring around, watching the busy lines of human traffic intersect with the mechanical traffic. Christ, I must look stupid. Thankfully, it doesn't look like I'm recognised. Even if I was, how much would I care? Would I even notice?

I know The Shakespeare a little bit. Snuck in there when I was 17 and managed to get a half-pint of shandy. I've been back a few times, but... ah... what does it matter?

When I locate it, I hesitate a little. I can see the blonde woman serving drinks. She wears her cheeky grin like a hyena mauls prey. I'll go inside, order a drink, wait until the bitch finishes her shift. Damn, where's the nearest payphone? I won't be back until late... Scarlet will worry.

Wait, something's happening. The girl has come round the front of the bar, a coat draped over her arm. She waves goodbye to someone and comes out. Walks straight past me. Cheeky slut. Fucking coward. I start walking straight behind her. She doesn't even notice me. Even if she does, yeah, she wouldn't care. Scum like her think they're invincible.

It's when I spot an opportunistic alleyway, nice and narrow and secluded, that I act. I lunge forward covering her mouth and nose and throw her hard to the left. She doesn't have time to react. She's on the floor, lying in a puddle of tramp piss, staring up in shock. She retreats on her elbows, shuffling her limp legs like broken dried spaghetti.

I quickly check behind me to see if anyone's noticed us. No one has. They've all got their heads on the ground.

"Do you know who I am?" I ask, throwing a foot down on her ribs.

She tries to get up, but my foot's like a shedload of bricks.

"I'm Josephine. One of the band members. Not sure if you recognise me. I know what you did to Scarlet. If you so much as say her name again, or that filthy cunt of a boyfriend of yours tries anything, I'll find you and break every single one of your fucking fingers. You got that?"

She nods.

I release my foot and hoist her up by her tank top. "This is for Scarlet," I hiss, slamming a fist squarely into her teeth. I let her go and return to the street, whistling as I walk.

Maybe I shouldn't have done that, but, fuck, it felt good. I swear when I see the skin has broken on my knuckles.

What is it about me and alleyways? Every time I go in one, some sort of drama plays out!

Scarlet

7 June 1991

There's a place between the real world and the dream world, where the two interlace like two different kinds of wool. They link so firmly, so precisely, that there's such beauty to it. Dear reader, have you ever had a dream where you meet the girl you've always longed for and then you wake up, and you find to get back into that dream, and the more you fight, the more you become awake? You know what I mean?

Scarlet's like that right now.

Her alarm's ringing, just like a fire bell from her school-days. It's right in her ear, dragging her away from the monot-onous beauty of kissing someone beautiful on a white, silky beach. She swears as she sits up. She breathes in her own body odour and nearly gags.

Why the hell is she living in this sort of dump? Her room's like some Harvard geek's paradise: magazines, mouldy cups, a VHS copy of *Presumed Innocent*, a well-thumbed copy of Stephen King's *It* with the front cover partially torn, soiled clothes, and way too many discarded paper tissues.

"Scarlet, time to get up!" roars Josephine's voice. "We leave in an hour!"

"Yeah, I know!"

"Come on, we're going to be jetting off in First Class! Get your backside moving!"

Scarlet's never been one for empathy. Oh, dear reader, you know that.

How she's ready in time, how she's washed and dressed and sorted, it's beyond the scope of this book to postulate. But she's in the taxi before Josephine.

"Heathrow, please," Scarlet commands the driver.

"By the way, you've got the passports, haven't you?" asks Josephine.

"Right here." Scarlet fishes them out of her leather jacket. "Did you put the luggage in the boot?"

"Both suitcases and our backpacks, don't worry," comes Josephine's reply.

Relations between them now are much better. They're like two sisters who've fallen apart over a stupid boyfriend. But the two of them seem strong and united now.

Gina and Susan are waiting for them, and there's something in their eyes that says they can see the healing between Scarlet and Josephine. They smile and laugh when the two girls drag the suitcases out like dead bodies. They snigger when they see the driver chasing after them, demanding his money.

"Sorry!" shouts Josephine, handing a couple of notes over. "Sorry, mate!"

They're a team now. They're a band.

"Right, you lot!" Josephine says to the others. "I'm not standing about here all day, gawping. Let's get checked in and let's get to that champagne."

They enter the terminal like a lost tribe that's just been found by David Attenborough. There're a few seconds when they just mill about on the spot, totally confused. But this smart-looking bloke who works for the airline – he's got that uncomfortable greasy hair combed with the precision of the Open University – waves to them.

"Please, this way!" he says. "Mr Miser sends his regards and has already checked you in. All I need is to see your passports and then we'll take your hold luggage and speed you through security and to the lounge. If I may say so, I'm a big of your music. I've listened to your –"

"Can you just see our passports?" snaps Josephine.

Scarlet's aware of the long, snaking line of mums and dads, impatient children, crying (and pissing) babies, pushchairs, and fraying tempers. They're watching closely. Some like what they see, others flash envy and distaste.

"Certainly," says the man. "Follow me, please."

The eyes follow them as they're taken to the First Class desk. It's like a small bubble of joy and free-thinking. The woman sitting behind it takes their passports, types a few things into her computer, and returns them with a gentle pompousness. Another attendant – a grim-faced, balding man – puts straps onto their hold bags and hoists them onto the conveyer belt.

"Have a nice flight," the check-in agent says. "Luke, can you make sure you whizz them through security as fast as you can?"

"Yes, of course. Right, ladies, let's go."

The slick guy leads them away from the check-in zone and towards the security area. They're through in less than five minutes. The guy waves them off, then returns to the world of customer service, always eager and compelled to please. Another attendant meets them. She's slim, polite, always talking by moving her arms. She escorts them through the duty-free nonsense, past the caffeine-fuelled coffeeshops, to the lounge.

"Wow," Susan mutters, as they're shown through the sliding glass doors.

It's a paradise of free quality champagne, cheesy biscuits, freshly cut sandwiches, the latest magazines, fake smile attendants – all with an executive view of the roaring runways. The girls have never seen anything like this. Beyond even Stanley Kubrick's wildest imaginative dreams! Everything about the perfectly aligned tables, the buffet with handmade rolls, the leather seats with that virginal smell, it's all like an unwrapped present.

"Make yourselves at home," says their escort. "Champagne?"

"Yes, please," they somehow all say at once. They're like kids – that's right, dear reader. They're like impatient dogs, scratching to get out.

Gina nudges her head to a circular sofa wedged in the corner. It's got the best view in the house. There's no doubt about it. Josephine leads them over – as she always does – and they can't help but laugh. None of them thought they'd be here a year and a half ago.

The champagne is brought over in a cooler – wrapped in a silk napkin. Only the finest cut glass with only the finest bowls of dried pretzels are put out. This is it. They are royalty. They are to be waited upon like they mean something in this world. Josephine raises her glass. She proposes a toast. "To a new beginning!" And they drink the rich substance that's too rich for their tongues.

"How's your dad doing, Scarlet?" asks Josephine.

Well, dear reader, that's a smack back to reality.

"He's fine," replies Scarlet. "He's busy with his law stuff. To be honest, I haven't heard from him much this year. Mum says he's been doing a lot of trips up north for business. I think he's got clients and that in Newcastle and Liverpool."

"Nice."

"You remember that Paul Casselden guy I've talked about? He has been talking about starting up some kind of a partner-ship with him."

"Well, don't let either of them bring you down."

But Scarlet's already thinking of her loathing for the Casseldens, especially the wife. God, she hates the wife with one hell of a bloody passion. But she's thinking more about what Josephine's just said. Why would she bring this up now? A bit odd.

"I always get that sad feeling when I leave Britain," remarks Susan, gazing out. "I mean, it's great to be doing this, don't get me wrong, but I feel a little sad with leaving everything behind."

"Oh, don't get depressed on me!" booms Josephine. "Dear God!"

"No, I know exactly what she means," Gina butts in. "I feel it as well. Slightly sad and depressed with leaving everything behind."

"There's a word for this," says Josephine. "Sentimental. Scarlet, you paying attention? There's a great idea for a song here."

"Well, I don't know about any of you, but I'm starving," Scarlet declares. "I'm going to see what the hell they've got on offer here. I think I smell some bacon rolls frying." She heads over to the buffet area and sure enough she sees a small heap of rolls, all wound up in silk cloth. She grabs two for herself.

"Can I get you something to drink, ma'am?"

A male attendant's voice startles her. He's pretty in his waistcoat and purple tie, flashing that becalmed smile.

"Uh, black coffee," says Scarlet.

"We have Italian, Kenyan, Colombian –"

"Italian filter coffee will be fine."

"Excellent choice, ma'am. I will bring it to your table."

"Thank you."

She's not used to this immobility, this pampering. She's always needed to be someone who's doing something, helping out where she can. This doesn't suit her. Of course, in the years to come, she'll get used to it. For now, she's grateful she can hold the bacon rolls...

"Scarlet, stop daydreaming!" Josephine calls over. "You coming over or what?"

"Roger's a genius for swinging it," says Gina. "How do you think he managed it?"

"The man has many ways," Josephine snorts.

"I don't think Madison Square Garden's that impressive," says Scarlet. She sits back down and starts munching on the first bacon roll. Oh, it'll take her time to get accustomed...

"You're not on something, are you?" Josephine teases.

Is Scarlet imagining it, or is there the slightest hint of aggression in the girl's voice?

"I'm just giving my opinion," replies Scarlet. She's on the second roll now. Christ, does fame make you famished?

The crisp cup and saucer of Italian filter coffee is placed before her with the gentleness of a first kiss. She hesitates, watching for a retort from Josephine, but the girl's talking to Gina about something.

The seconds, minutes and hours pass. Josephine talks too loudly. Gina talks too quickly. Scarlet has nothing to say at all. Only Susan seems to fit in.

Scarlet's just noticed it. Susan's dressed up: formal trousers, bleach-white shirt, jacket. And her high heels aren't too high. She looks disinterested, as if doing her best to give things time to sink in.

Suddenly, yet another attendant is standing over them. She looks like she's stepped off the set of the original *Star Trek*. She's slim, firm, strapped in a dress and lipstick.

"You are ready to preboard the aircraft," she informs them. "When you are ready."

"Let's do it!" says Gina. She jumps up.

"Calm down, darling," says Josephine. "I'm sorry about that," she says to the attendant, *their* attendant. "A little over-excitement."

"Not to worry. Please, gather your things, and follow me."

They do as she asks. Is it a request, or a command? Is the airline trying to get them on the plane, so they can avoid discomfort to other passengers? Is this royalty stuff some sort of con to keep the curiosity down in the lower classes on the plane?

She leads them through the maze of the terminal, past experienced, worn-down travelling businessmen, past backpackers (some lost, some found) who don't care about their life stories, past families who envy their evident special treatment.

They are met by yet more attendants at the gate. All of them smile, except a woman behind a counter with a thick bundle of paperwork. Someone asks for their passports, just for a quick check.

Scarlet can feel the stares on her. Passengers waiting for their turn to board are seated in row after row like sardines. She looks through the window to their plane. It's a 747, the famous bird in the sky.

"Okay, ladies, follow me," says a mean-looking official bloke. He's like that bouncer in Inverness last year. He just seems so low, so unhappy. He hands out a boarding pass to each of them, calmly, swiftly.

The man takes them through the glass doors of the gate to the bridge that links the airport to the plane. His footsteps are heavy. He could be the backup for a panto of *Jack And The Beanstalk*.

Two air hostesses, wearing extra makeup over the normal nonsense they wear, are there to welcome them onboard. They quickly check their boarding passes, then one of them – a petite blonde – says, "We are honoured to have you onboard. Please..." She points to the left. "You are in Row Two, Seats A, B, C and D."

This is a world they have only ever seen in spy movies. The tiny Kingdom of First Class. The seats – so plush, they look like they've been pinched from the House of Commons – form little alcoves.

The girls are all seated together in a row in the middle. A fizzing glass of champagne is set up in each. Even Josephine's aghast.

"It's okay," the blonde tells them. "I think I know what you're doing through. Just sit down, okay? It'll all come to you."

Scarlet's in a trance, even as the girls chatter away amongst themselves, sipping on yet more champagne, playing with the headsets, surfing through the magazines. The blonde's colleague comes through and takes their orders for lunch. There's delicious salmon, a salad with all the trimmings, fresh steak, wine (both red and white), cubes of cheese cut to exact precision, fresh fruit, more fresh fruit, sorbets, cherry cake, and brutalist spirits to wash it down.

She flashes back to when she was sixteen, when she was working at that godawful farm, treated like a piece of shit. Bullied, called names, humiliated in front of visitors. Especially Graham, the lead farmhand. A fat, balding guy, desperately trying to lose weight, he was someone with no prospects, no future. That why he used to get her clean out pig shit with her bare hands. Oh, if he could see her now.

"Can we have another bottle of champagne?" she asks the blonde stewardess.

"Certainly, ma'am," comes the reply.

There's movement behind them as the other passengers begin to board. Except for a man in a three-piece suit, no one else comes into the First Class cabin. The blonde and her colleague (she *has* to be a brunette) do their little safety routine for them; it seems personalised to them: there's none of that stupid sarcasm involved.

The plane shudders as it moves away from the terminal. Scarlet has two glasses of champagne in quick succession as they navigate to the runway. The engines how, scream, stomp their way into life, and they're off, shooting up from the ground. It's like a rebirth for them.

The blonde hostess comes to see them as soon as the seatbelt sign is off. She's nervous, reluctant to speak, way too jittery. Christ, should she be doing this bloody job?

"So, ladies," she says, "I'm quite a big fan of your stuff. I saw you in Newcastle. Your music is so great. I really love it."

"Well, Scarlet'll take the credit for it, trust me," says Josephine. "But we all contributed to it. It's okay, I'm just kidding with you. So, I guess you're wanting our autographs?"

The hostess holds up a CD and grins so inappropriately. "If you wouldn't mind," she teases, sticking up a pen.

They each sign the front cover. To Scarlet, it's like a French Kiss on the cheek. She designed the artwork herself, each and every minute detail of it. It's a small cut-off piece from her former life. Sharmaine would be proud...

"Thank you!" the hostess squeaks. "Thank you! Thank you! I wasn't able to get tickets or anything for New York, but I want you to know –"

"It's okay," Susan tells her, eyes not moving from her book. "Don't worry about it."

There's a light breakfast served: pastries, a bacon roll, fresh French coffee, cubes of fruit. Scarlet's never really liked being drunk when she has breakfast, but, oh yeah, up in the air it's quite cool.

It's when they have lunch that Scarlet realises how far she's come. She's not that fucking farmhand anymore, pitiful wage, neglected. She's a singer on her way to New York, sipping juicy red wine and eating slivers of steak. Yeah, she's free of all that shit. She's free of all that pain and hatred.

Yeah, she's moved on a bit, don't you think, dear reader?

When they land at JFK Airport, the girls are shocked (but unsurprised) to find that they get whisked through immigration, handed their luggage by a dedicated team, and shown to a grey limo. The driver seems like a cross between old and young: he sports a moustache flecked with cigarette ash, but seems to don modern face moisturiser. Scarlet looks at him for a few seconds. She can't quite take in that he's trying to look cool, arms by his side, a trooper for the celebrity cult.

Away from the airport and into the city they go. Everything's so fast, so busy. The limo driver asks them how their flight went. But he's so professional. He doesn't ask it in a casual, happy-go-lucky way. He asks it with a sense of dignity, a sense of respect. Scarlet feels like Marlon Brando in *The Godfather*. All she needs is a cat and puffed cheeks...

The prowess of New York's skyline burns into her retinas – and she knows the other girls are equally dumbfounded. The Twin Towers of the World Trade Centre reach up like two fingers of victory. The traffic, with its customary yellow cabs and bad-tempered flareups, winds and smothers its way past hotdog vendors with customary promises and tramps with definitive dreams.

"I'll need a bath before tonight," says Josephine. "Christ, you think we'll suffocate from the pollution?"

"I'll be taking you do Madison Square Garden," the driver tells them. "I'll pick you guys up from the hotel, about Five, that okay?"

"Fine by us," Josephine answers for them.

"Oh, before I forget, George – that's him, right? He called me earlier. Says to let you know that you've got creams and lotions, products, you know what I mean... it's all in your rooms."

"How long before we get to the hotel?" asks Susan.

"Wish I could tell you, sweetheart, but the way this traffic can be, you gotta show some patience."

The car judders to a halt. The driver slams the horn again. They move, very briefly, but stop again.

"See what I mean, ladies?" he says, exasperatedly. "There's just no goddamn way to predict the traffic."

"You should see London!" Gina's attempt at a joke doesn't work on the driver.

They shift onwards in silence.

Scarlet thinks about tonight. Their first kick in the Big Apple. It must go to plan. Nothing can go awry. Their notes must be pitch perfect, her voice must be exact, their confidence cannot slip. Whether the girls are thinking that same – spread out along the sofa of the limo – that's a mystery. But all Scarlet knows is music. It's her heart. And it mustn't stop beating.

They arrive at the hotel in Manhattan just before noon. It's a grandiose place, a palace for those life has been gracious to. The driver removes their bags, handing them to a man in a burgundy uniform, who promptly lowers them onto trolley. The girls are shown through gold-painted doors by another uniformed bloke. The lobby, with its dangling, cutglass chandeliers and marble reception desks, is quiet and methodical. Hotel staff pace around like they're guarding the kingdoms of the rich and famous. There's a sombre feeling to it.

A man in a suit and tie – not a uniform, dear reader, but a suit that's cost at least a thousand dollars – approaches them. He's forty at least. He looks like the kind of guy who's never had the time to take nonsense. He's someone who's been married several times, disappeared into alcohol addiction at least once, and probably scrapped at least twice this month. He's a kind of celebrity in the hotel world.

"Ladies," he says, "if you will follow me. Your rooms are ready. May I welcome you to this hotel. I trust that you had a pleasant journey?"

"Very much," says Susan.

"What time is dinner?" asks Josephine.

She's said this a bit too loud. Heads turn. Refined people – lawyers, bankers, journalists – glance over, ever so quickly, then swish away again.

"Dinner is at Seven P.M. But I understand that you will be performing this evening. We shall have room service prepared for you when you return."

He shows them to an elevator. Christ, it's one of those with the metal zigzag doors on. The man in the suit gestures them inside, slams both grills shut and presses a cream-coloured marble button situated in a lotus seedpod of others. They're on the 15th Floor, right at the top. The man is humming to himself. He's quietly proud. Anyone can see that.

"I forgot to mention," he says, "I'm Eric Bellini, manager of the hotel. If there's anything that you need during your stay, please do not hesitate to contact me."

When they arrive at the 15th Floor, there's a man in the blue suit. He nods to them in acknowledgement.

Mr Bellini tells them, "This is Ben Evanson, our head of security. He'll be ensuring your safety whilst you're here."

"Pleased to meet you all," says Mr Evanson. "I've taken the liberty of liaising with your security detail. If you have any questions or concerns, please do not hesitate to contact me."

"Thank you very much," says Gina.

"Thank you, Ben," says Mr Bellini. "Okay, let me show you to your rooms." He opens his left hand towards the pale green corridor with pink-rimmed doorframes.

They don't go very far, just a few steps. Mr Bellini withdraws several keys from his deep pocket and proceeds, in numerical and methodical order, to open up rooms 1515, 1516, 1517, and 1518, kicking a door wedge under each for ease of entry. The girls have been allocated their own designated room: there's no having to argue in the corridor for two hours. Everything has been neatly, punctually organised.

"Will you be interested in lunch?" asks Mr Bellini. "We offer a range of culinary tastes, as well as imported wine. On our menu today is calamari, roast lamb –"

"Absolutely," says Josephine. "We're very interested. Can you book us in for Two P.M.?"

"I will reserve a table for you in The Olympia Restaurant. You will most certainly enjoy it –"

"It's in the hotel, right?" checks Josephine. "Right?"

"Yes, ma'am, it is. If I may ask, is everything all right with the rooms?"

Josephine pokes her head in hers. She hums. She comes back out, looks the manager up and down, and whispers to him, "Yeah, mine looks okay. Scarlet?"

Scarlet finds herself doing the same. She's so amazed with the king-sized bed, the silver silk curtains, the small bottle of chilled champagne, that she nearly forgets to come back out. She retreats, startled, looks pitifully at Me Bellini. "Yeah, it's fine," she says.

"Well, that's great," remarks Josephine. "Right, Mr Bellini, is our luggage coming up? And your most expensive bottle of red… make sure there's two of them with our lunch."

"Of course, ma'am."

"That will be all, Mr Bellini."

"I wish you all a pleasant stay." He smiles at them, bows, and then heads towards the lift.

"Right, girls, let's get a bit of rest, then meet back out here Five-To-Two."

Scarlet slams her door shut, resists and gives up on the urge to explore her suite. It is – admittedly – slightly less than she was expecting. She picks up the bottle from the cooler, flinching at its icy touch. She looks around her, as though she's being haunted by a ghost. The bed, with its sheets smoothed and ironed with the discipline of a 1950s National Service re-cruit, faces a television. A small paper programme guide lies underneath the box unruffled. She checks out the bathroom. It's too plain for this place: three bars of soap piled above a small toilet, shower cubicle, a bathtub with no-nonsense spiderweb taps, and towels strapped to a thin rail. She smirks, returns the bottle to the cooler, and flings open the curtains. The trapped oasis of Central Park gazes back, filled and thrilled with the activity of dogwalkers, yoga enthusiasts, and boring old joggers. She cannot help but laugh at how the cut teeth of the metropolis contrasts with the peace and beauty of this stretch of green.

There's a knock at her door.

"At fucking last," she moans, pleased that she'll be reunited with her luggage.

She's startled at the sight of Susan standing there, thin and vulnerable.

"Scarlet, do you have a minute?" she asks.

"Sure, come in. Everything okay?"

"Not exactly."

They sit at the foot of Scarlet's bed. Susan rests her elbows on her knees. Her lengthy, straight hair flops over.

"What's happened?" asks Scarlet, putting a hand on her shoulder. God, the girl feels so frail and fragile.

"Scarlet, we're close, right?"

"Yeah."

"I mean, we've been through a lot together."

"Yeah, of course. Yeah."

Susan sits up. She takes a deep breath, lets it out slowly. She's not shaking, but she's nearly there. She's blinking a thousand times a second.

Minutes pass and there's nothing from either of them.

"Scarlet, I got a phone call last week from someone I thought I'd put in the past," Susan says in a whisper. "Fuck, I really thought they were gone. I don't know how they got the number."

"Just tell me what happened?"

"Do you remember the summer of Nineteen-Eighty-Five?"

"Vaguely," says Scarlet.

"Do you remember that big holiday I went on with my parents?"

"Yeah."

"Don't you think it was odd that I only told you after we went back to school that Autumn?"

"Well," says Scarlet, unsure where this is leading (Susan's probably fessing up to sleeping with a boy Scarlet was with back then), "I remember thinking it was a bit weird, but didn't dwell on it for very long."

"That's because we didn't go on holiday. A week after the summer term ended, I ran away from home. It was stupid, I know. I was just scared of schoolwork and the pressures of everything. I ran away. I managed to get into London and get a train north. Don't know how I managed it, but I got to Bradford. Oh, Scarlet, you don't realise how refreshing it was. I was free of everything, free from all the worries and stresses." The girl looks upwards. Tears collect on her eyelids like small gems.

"What happened?" says Scarlet. "Did someone hurt you? Were you attacked or something?"

"Not exactly. As you can imagine, with only a couple of pounds in my pocket, I couldn't exactly book a stay in the local Marriot. I wandered the city until about Six in the evening, until I saw a hostel for the homeless. You know what I'm talking about."

"Yeah."

"My options were limited. I couldn't get a train back, I couldn't stay in a hotel. I didn't want to go to the police, because I was afraid of facing the consequences. I knew Mum and Dad were probably worried shitless. But I was scared! So, I felt I had no choice but to go to the hostel. I told them that I'd just been made homeless – it wasn't exactly a lie."

"How long were you there for?" Scarlet's afraid of the answer. It'll sting her with a message of abandonment. She should have been there for Susan six years ago. She should have looked after her.

"Five weeks."

"Shit."

"They didn't ask any details. I had a room to myself. A nice room with two beds. I guess I knew that after a while, someone would be occupying the other one, but I felt carefree, happy even. Three weeks, I stayed like that, in blissful ignorance. I'd spend the days exploring the city, pretending to be going to job interviews and the like. I got ten pounds spending money a day for lunch and stuff. In the evening, I'd watch T.V. in the common room with the others. Then this guy moved in. He was seventeen. His parents had just chucked him out for trying to inject his baby sister with heroin: that's what he told me when I was trying to sleep."

"He was in the same room as you?"

"Yep."

"I thought the men and women would be put in separate rooms."

"Yeah, you'd think so."

There's another silence between them. But it doesn't last as long as the previous one.

Susan continues her story with a glorified reluctance: "He was a horrid guy. Obnoxious, aggressive, threatening. He never did anything to me, but the thought might have crossed his mind. But what really got to me was him repeating his lurid story of what he tried to do to his sister. Every night, he'd add in more details. The guy was insane. He was an evil, malicious bastard. I wanted to do something to hurt him. I wanted him to suffer. One night, he came in with some pot. A tiny bag of the stuff. He wasn't going to light up in the hostel, I know that. It was against hostel rules and I don't think he wanted to get caught out."

"Did you report him?"

Susan hesitates. "Yeah. I did. I lay awake until Two in the morning, got my bags and snuck out the room. I told the woman at reception about the drugs and legged it out of there. Managed to hitchhike my way back to London."

"What did your parents say?"

"They were happy to see me, but really hurt. I told them I was sorry. I really did!" More tears cascade. "Oh, shit, I really fucking went down on my knees and begged them to forgive me! When I think of all the hurt I've done... to so many people, it just gets too much."

"You came back, that's what mattered. What about the police? Were they involved with this?"

"Well, my parents had to let them know, as you can imagine. I don't know why they didn't get the school involved. Maybe they did, I don't know, but they never interviewed you. I don't know why. The police didn't want to take things any further after I came home, so I thought I'd just put it behind me. My parents were that way too. I just wanted to move on. And I've really done well, honest. Until last week."

Scarlet takes her hand, squeezes it hard. The atmosphere in the room grows emptier with every passing second.

"Last week, the phone rang," says Susan, "and it was him. Damn, I don't know how he got the number. Rowan, his name is. Rowan Colt. He didn't make any threats or anything. He just asked if I remembered who he was. He told me that because of what I did, he got thrown out the hostel and spent two years on the streets. He said that he's just moved into a council flat in Leeds."

"What else did he say?"

"Nothing. He just hung up. I've had the locks changed and everything and got someone to keep an eye on the flat, but... I'm scared. I'm terrified, Scarlet."

Scarlet shifts off the bed, kneels on the floor in front of Susan, like she's her daughter. She wipes tears away from the girl's face, looks her sincerely in the eyes.

"I promise you, Susan, that nothing will happen to you. Do you hear me? Do you understand? This pathetic loser, whoever he is, he'll never hurt you. If he tries to get in contact with you again, if he tries anything, let me know, and we'll get Roger on the case."

"Okay," whimpers Susan.

Scarlet hugs her tightly. "You're like a sister to me, you know that? I'll always be here for you, whatever happens."

"Me too."

"Right, sister, we'd better get a bit of rest, because Josephine will be pissed if we're tired at lunch, and you know what she's like."

"Oh yeah. At least I don't have to live with her."

They both fall into laughter. Joy through tears. Humour through pain. They hug again, properly this time, like true sisters.

"What's the name of the hostel?" says Scarlet.

"Oh, I think it was called Adler Point. Why do you ask?"

"Just in case this loser turns up again. I think it would be a good idea to have a fact file or something that we could give to lawyers. I mean, they might have to get testimony or something from the people who ran it."

"It won't do them any good." Susan pulls away and goes over to the window. "It burnt down in Nineteen-Eighty-Seven. Scarlet, I don't want to talk about it anymore. It's too painful."

"Sorry, you're right. I shouldn't have asked. Look, I don't think this guy will cause you any more trouble. He probably just wanted to give you a bit of a scare. Forget about him."

"Thanks, Scarlet." Susan pulls away, yawns deeply. "I should get a bit of rest."

"You go do that."

They walk to the door. Scarlet opens it. She's chauffer now.

"If you need to talk, Susan, anytime, day or night, I'm here for you, okay?"

"Thank you." Susan gives a quick wave and passes over the threshold.

Scarlet releases the door, watching it slide into place. She waits until she hears Susan's close, then counts a minute in her head. When the minute passes, she takes her key and ventures out. She tiptoes along to the lift and rides it back down to the lobby.

Mr Bellini is patrolling like a soldier at the DMZ. As soon as he sees Scarlet, his eyes light up. He approaches her, hands behind his back, head bowed. "How may I help, ma'am?" he asks.

"Is it possible to make a long-distance phone call?"

"I do apologise," he says, clearly alarmed, "but we have had technical issues with our phone system. We have two engineers at work as we speak. I will notify you as soon as the system is restored. Please accept my apologies."

"It's okay, it's not urgent. Thanks, anyway."

"You are most welcome."

Scarlet turns to go, hands in pockets. She turns back even faster. "Um..."

"Yes, ma'am?" says Mr Bellini, raising an eyebrow.

"It's okay," replies Scarlet. "It's nothing. I'm just a bit tired."

Lunch in the *Star Trek*-sounding Olympia Restaurant, amongst the distinguished lawyers, academics, (probably a Pulitzer Prize Winner in the midst too), sportsmen, a really obtuse-looking man with the thinnest glasses you could imagine, two twin sisters in identical dresses, three balding men with balding leather jackets, is a quiet affair for them. Josephine doesn't end up guzzling both bottles of wine. It's clear she's making sure that everyone gets their fair share of the tipple. No one talks much, but everyone's afraid of not talking; after all, the entire restaurant is up in arms with conversations about literature, the latest DNA research, fashion, you take your pick. If there's something that's current in this world of 1991, I guarantee it's being discussed in this room.

"I might go out for a bit of a walk when we get back tonight," says Susan. "I mean, it'd be nice to do a bit of sight-seeing."

"Don't forget that this isn't a holiday," cautions Josephine, sipping on her fourth glass. "We're here for work. No time to stop and stare."

"Gotcha," comes the reply. "But, still..."

"If you must, go out tomorrow for a look around. But be back at the hotel for Three P.M." Josephine's so bloody stern when she says this.

Scarlet looks at the empty place that until twenty minutes ago contained thick, juicy lamb. She can't stand to see the fragility of the priceless china and the silver cutlery. She looks around. Is she trying to avoid the girls? The restaurant's beautiful: wooden fish nailed to the walls; black-and-white photographs of times nearly forgotten; a musket with *1792* scratched on; the brittle windows looking out upon the choked-up streets. She almost sees herself working here: little money, but a beautiful sight.

"How many are expected tonight?" asks Gina. "Josephine, do you know?"

"I'm not fully sure, to be honest. I'll say about three quarters of the auditorium. You never know with these things."

When the chauffer with his cigarette-flecked moustache does pick them up, they enter a city that seems to have changed like a butterfly emerging. The rough coarseness of the day has gone, replaced by the thrill and anticipation of whatever the night brings. It's Friday in New York City, after all. White-collar workers followed by blue-collar slaves trudge along the streets, but there's a happiness in their gait, a sort of openness in receiving whatever will be given, whether that's a relaxing beer in a bar or a kiss from the most beautiful woman that the world can provide. Everything's made out of substance here.

As they're driven through the gridlocked streets, Scarlet can't help but be angry with herself. The stereotypical image of New York City is not one of bad tempers, threats, sweat and bitterness. It's lonely desperation for something bigger, something better, something closer.

When they make it to Madison Square Garden – something Scarlet immediately thinks is rundown and disjointed – they're escorted in by five professional-looking blokes in suits. Corridor, open space, corridor, then more corridors. Why don't they call this place a maze and just be done with it? Scarlet thinks. They're shown to a dressing room with its gold star proudly emblazoned on the door.

"Are our instruments out and ready?" Josephine asks one of the suits.

"Yes, they are," comes a steely reply. "Go through the door over there to access the main stage. Myself and my team will be on hand, should you require anything."

"Thank you," says Josephine. "Girls, shall we make our way through?"

"Uh, miss, why don't you freshen up?"

"None of your business. We'll go through, if that's okay with security."

"Actually, I could use a glass of water," says Gina. She's standing half in, half out of the dressing room. She looks delirious.

Scarlet can see Josephine's mouthing, "For God's sake."

"You know what?" concedes Josephine. "Give us ten minutes, then escort us to the stage. And can you bring a few bottles of water?"

"Yes, ma'am."

The girls go into the dressing room. It's a simple affair: blinding bulbs line the fragile mirrors; red leather chairs face tables potted with makeup jars and brushes; a pile of magazines sits in the corner on a spare seat, unread, unwanted. Scarlet looks into a mirror sees their reflections: they all look so shrill, so done in. Must be the flight.

"Right, girls," says Josephine, "take five minutes. We've got a lot to prepare for."

"Oh, Scarlet," comes Gina's bright, chirpy voice. The girl sits before a mirror, thumps her elbows down on the peach-coloured glossy table surface, fingers a makeup brush, then huffs loudly.

"Yeah, what's up?"

"You know that woman who sponsored your art thingy?" Gina says this like it's some sort of test.

"You mean Sharmaine?"

"Yeah. Sharmaine Bateson. Her magazine's gone out of business."

"What?" says Scarlet, avoiding gasping. Not that she would care. "When did you hear that?"

"On the flight over. I got a bit restless, so got a newspaper from one of the stewardesses. Quite tragic, by the sounds of it."

"Oh, it is. Well, thanks for letting me know."

"Are you ladies going to chit-chat all day?" teases Josephine. "You both feeling confident about tonight?"

"Never more so," quips Gina.

"That's what I like to hear. Scarlet?"

"Always ready to kick some."

"Nice."

Just then, one of the suits comes in with a tray of water bottles. He deposits them like many security guys used to do from the 1980s. He puts them down and he doesn't look at the girls. Of course, that's the way it's supposed to be. You know that all too well, dear reader.

It takes a couple of minutes for the girls to have a quick drink each, loosen themselves up. Then Josephine goes outside, asks, *demands*, that they be taken through to the stage. Another security guy comes in a few seconds later and nods for them to come with him. He shows them through two or three set of doors. The set of keys jangling at his side remind Scarlet of one of those old gaolers from fairy tales. Then, after another set of doors, they're inside the auditorium.

"My word," stutters Susan.

Seats and seats are spread out like the world's silent jury. Scarlet wants to make a cheeky remark, but she can't find the words or the excuses. There the stage is, an open beacon of noise and chaos, surrounded on all sides by the rows and rows of tight precision. Amplifiers hang from the sides of the stage and dark red rope creates a line of separation between the musicians and the great slovenly fans. Their instruments are set up and ready. Have they been shined? It looks like it...

"Jesus Christ," curses Gina. "Jesus bloody singing Christ."

"Right, girls," says Josephine, storming up to the stage. She's doing this like she always does. No regard for anyone else. No regard for everything.

It takes them probably half an hour – well, it's most certain – but they strum a few notes, practise a few songs, even come up with the idea for a new one. How the hours pass, they don't know, but they do with a vicious speed.

A suit enters the auditorium, a grim smile worn underneath his thick beard. "There's about an hour before the audience comes in," he informs them. "If you want to follow me back to the dressing room...?"

"Not required," says Scarlet. "We don't use makeup."

"Oh, I understand. Well, in that case, if you want to make sure you have everything you need –"

"We'll be fine, trust me," Gina tells him.

The security guy looks panicked. Every word in his tiny dictionary wants to come bursting out. "In about twenty minutes, one of my team will come out and put the curtain down. You know how you folks are appearing? The curtain's going to roll up –"

"You need a new job!" laughs Josephine. "Honestly, mate."

The man looks a bit sheepish, seems to bow his head, and then walks off. As soon as he's gone, the girls fall into laughter. They're bent over, hurling spit at the stage floor. That's how hard they're laughing. That's how strong their friendship is. It's like an iron bridge.

"Remind me, what's our firing order, for the songs?" asks Josephine.

Gina quickly fills her in.

The sound of stirring feet, of excited and eager men and women, echoes through the walls and the vastness of the chamber. It's here.

Scarlet gulps. Someone else does the same.

When the curtain rolls down, it's Josephine who checks on all of them, making sure they're okay. Making sure they'll do as they're bloody well told.

The seconds tick down to the start of the concert. They dread it like a swarm of locusts, but they revel in it like a swarm of adrenaline. When those curtains go up, they won't just be celebrities anymore: they'll be celebrities who've made their New York debut.

The shuffling of feet. The excited chatter. The pushing and shoving.

It's five minutes to go.

A security man and a technician come in to chat with them. Well, they come to chat with Josephine. That's what all the professionals do. It's Josephine, it's never the others. It's always bloody Josephine. They mention something about the intricacies of how the night will go. They confirm something about the interval at the halfway point. They want to know if she's okay with that.

Then the girls position themselves. A loud voice booms through the speakers, telling the fans to be ready... to... welcome... onstage...

Josephine does a short, swift bow.

The cheers and the screaming and the whistling.

Scarlet takes the centre of the stage, eyes partially closed as the thumping of the audience envelops her. A year and a half ago, she was staggering through Croydon after a drunken night out. Now she's in New York. She's absorbed in everything. She even allows herself to smile. She glances around at Susan, nods, and the first notes of the keyboard sound out.

There's no popping of champagne or wild celebrations as the limo takes them back to the hotel. The night's been too taxing for that. There they are, sitting on the leather seats, covered in cold sweat. Even Josephine's silent. The chauffer tries to make conversation with them, once or twice, but gives up quickly when he sees the tired, weary faces. He's seeing young, talented singers at the start of their career.

When they stagger through the foyer, with only their beds at the forefront of their minds, there's a feeling of collective happiness. This is what they've worked for. Up they go, in the lift with those marble buttons, up to their floor. Scarlet goes to her room, yawning a goodnight over her shoulder. She heads to the bed, grabs the phone, manages to order pizza, and somehow convinces her body not to fall asleep.

She knows she'll never forget tonight, no matter what she does. She knows that she'll carry it with her always.

The margherita pizza and coke comes with mist floating above it. She takes them as though they've always been hers. She does her best to eat, does her best to keep her eyes open. But she only manages a quarter of the circle and half of the can before she goes to the bathroom, runs a toothbrush over her teeth and clambers beneath the sheets. What hour is it? She doesn't know. What's happened tonight? She doesn't know. She's in total, beautiful, blissful ignorance.

8 June 1991

None of them go to breakfast. There's a quick meeting between the four of them in the corridor and they know that they're too tired and wrecked and they need their rest. So, it's room service, which they're all very happy to partake in. Before they disappear back into their rooms, Scarlet gives Susan a smile.

After a meal of pancakes, eggs and bacon, and fresh coffee, she goes downstairs and spots Mr Bellini on his regular patrol.

He seems to know exactly what she's after. He's probably been waiting to say it all night. He comes over, confident in every step and says, "Good morning! Our phone system has been repaired, I am pleased to inform you."

"Thank you, Mr Bellini," she replies. "Actually, I have a favour to ask of you. I have a close friend back home, who has just had a baby. That's why I was eager to make that call yesterday, to check up on her."

"Oh, I do apologise. Forgive me, I was not aware −"

"It's okay, don't worry. It wasn't your fault. Anyway, my problem is I don't have her number with me − I keep phone numbers in a small notebook, and I stupidly forgot to take it with me. I was figuring, if I could find the details of her local council, I could get her details."

"Oh, I see. I would suggest phoning Roger Miser in that case. Do you have his details?"

"Oh, no! I don't want to trouble him with this. I don't suppose you'd have a copy of the U.K. Yellow Pages, would you?"

Mr Bellini grimaces. He quickly turns away to smile back at a passing woman in a frock, but his attention is focused on Scarlet like a sword driving through a heart.

"Unfortunately, no," Mr Bellini says. "You could try – now, I don't know if they will have it – the New York Public Library on Fifth Avenue."

"That sounds perfect." Scarlet looks at the clock above the reception desks. It's nearly Half-Eight. She will need to get moving if she's going to get this to work.

"I shall summon you a taxi," says Mr Bellini.

"Is it within walking distance?"

"It is, but I do insist on a taxi, courtesy of the hotel, of course."

"No, please, I could use a walk to stretch my legs. Do you have a map?"

Fifteen minutes later, map in hand, she's walking down the street. Everywhere she looks, there are people. Everywhere she glances, she sees guys in shorts and t-shirts, joggers, painters and decorators, college kids laughing about inappropriate material, couples on the verge of breaking up, artists with artistic patterns on their faces, street performers, dancers, musicians. She roughly knows where she's going – she hopes so, anyway.

But she loves this place. She should live here, someday. Actually, soon enough, she'll be able to afford it. A nice penthouse in one of those tall buildings. She'll have parties of her own, with distinguished guests, and a glass or two for Roger.

Most importantly, she'll have the girls move out here as well, so they can be near to one another, just like true sisters.

She lets out a small sigh when she sees the library. It reminds her of the art museums and stuff in London. Great academics and fancy cloaks. Pipes and cigars. Brandy and priceless chocolates. She takes a moment to gaze over the pillars and the great steps, watches the young talented minds going in and out, books in their arms. She's impressed, she's curious, but she gets herself focused. She wants to be done with this as quickly as possible. She heads up the steps, catching a few awkward glances. As soon as she's inside, she knows a solid fact: she doesn't belong here.

A security guard is checking passes and gesturing people through a large set of doors.

Scarlet goes to a small reception desk, where a woman with thick Eighties glasses is ticking her way through a mound of paperwork. On all sides, she's surrounded by piles of books, sheets, empty cups, and a dirty grey telephone.

"Hi," Scarlet says to the woman.

"Oh, hi," the receptionist replies. "What's the problem?"

"Do you have any copies of the U.K. Yellow Pages by any chance?"

"If you go through those doors there, one of the librarians will help you out."

"Oh. It's just, I'm not a member or anything."

"Well, I'll have to get you a temporary pass then and sign you in."

"Okay."

The receptionist looks around her, rummaging through the junk that constitutes her workspace. "Oh, crap. Crap. I can't find – What is it you're looking for again?"

"The U.K. Yellow Pages."

"This might sound a stupid question, but do you want to check a copy out?"

"No, it's just one thing I want to look up."

"Oh, that shouldn't be a problem." The receptionist calls over to the security guard, "Hey, Bill, could you mind my desk for me? I'm just going to see to this lady."

"Come on, Annabel!" the guard protests. "You know you can't just walk away from your desk like that...!"

"Sue me! I'm a God damn law student, remember?"

Annabel leads Scarlet through the doors, through high shelves of countless books, through long benches and the keenest academics and students, through wisdom and stupidity, through the sciences, through the arts, through the greatest writers that ever existed. Annabel walks confidently, in smart trousers and a white shirt, with really odd purple shoes. They wind up in a small storage room that, strangely enough, doesn't actually have anything stored inside it, except for a small table.

"What region of your country are you looking for?" asks Annabel.

"The city of Bradford," says Scarlet.

"Hmm. I'm not sure if we have it... Wait here, I'll need to go and have a look."

"Okay, thanks."

Scarlet sits on the edge of the table and waits. She forces herself to breathe. She's hoping, really hoping, that she's out of luck on this occasion. She really doesn't want to have to do this. Oh, damn, she hopes she's unlucky.

She keeps looking down, keeps watching the time on the thing around her wrist. She needs to do this soon. The girls will be getting up before long... If they find out...

Annabel bursts into the room. She's holding something. "It took me a while to find it and I nearly missed it." She slams it down on the table. "The Yellow Pages for Bradford in Great Britain."

"Thanks, Annabel."

Scarlet opens the Yellow Pages and scans through it. She's more methodical here than she is with her music. She finds what she's looking for in sixty seconds flat.

"Do you have a pen and paper?" she asks Annabel.

The receptionist has the necessary items in her right hand. She hands them over with a smirk. "Thought you'd be needing them."

Scarlet quickly writes the number down.

"Hold on!" shouts Annabel. "Hold on a minute! I know you! Damn, I thought I recognised you from somewhere. You're that singer, aren't you?"

"Yep."

"A friend of mine got tickets to see you guys last night. Wow, can't believe I didn't recognise you!"

"It's okay," says Scarlet, blushing. "Listen, thanks for everything, Annabel. I need to head back to the hotel – I've gotta make this call, before everyone back home's at their dinner."

"Oh, don't bother with that!" says Annabel. "You can make an international call from here – I'll pay for it."

"I can't ask that from you."

"It's okay, seriously. There's a condition, though. You have dinner with me and my friends."

"What?" Scarlet isn't prepared for something like this.

"Have dinner with me and my friends," repeats Annabel in such a ridiculously condescending manner.

"I don't know if I can do that. We're performing again tonight, then heading to Los Angeles tomorrow. We come back here in a couple of weeks, the day before we fly home, but..."

"Well, that's settled," says Annabel. She rummages through her pockets, murmuring expletives, then she breaks into a smile as she hands over a small card. "My home number. When you're back in town, phone me and we'll organise dinner."

"Thanks." Scarlet feels something akin to gratitude. Of course, she'll have to clear this with Josephine. She's been getting stricter and nastier about bandmembers hanging around with normal people.

"Right, this call..." Annabel takes the Yellow Pages off her. "Follow me..."

They begin retrace their steps through never-ending construct of books and words, but then take a turning through a small corridor that, quite surprisingly, doesn't have so much as a dotted *i* on it. At the end of this corridor, Annabel opens up another door and shows them into a room that's as disturbingly glamourless as the last one, only this time there's a small desk with a blacked-out computer. A phone sits beside it... gathering dust? Annabel hits a switch and the place lights up briskly.

"I'm going to sort out a few things," Annabel tells her, a slight croak in her voice. "I'll be back in about twenty minutes. Take as long as you need."

"Actually..." Scarlet looks at the phone. "Hmm. I've never placed an international call before... I don't know exactly what to do."

"Oh, sure. Give me that slip of paper with the number on."

Scarlet hands it over, but the woman seems to pinch it off her. Annabel hums as she starts tapping the keys.

"Okay," she says, holding out the receiver to Scarlet, "it's ringing."

"Thanks." Scarlet sits down on the hardback wooden splinter chair. The sound of the purring ringing out across the miles feels like a kiss from her to the island she comes from. She waits and waits. Still it's ringing. Maybe no one's in. She should just call it a day, call it quits, go back to the hotel –

"Good afternoon, Bradford City Council, Angela Brinley speaking, how may I help you?"

"Good afternoon..." Scarlet's only trying to be polite. "I was wondering whether you could help me with something."

"Yes, certainly."

"I'm a youth worker doing a bit of research. Could I ask you whether there was a homeless hostel in Bradford called the Adler Point Hostel?"

"Yes, there was."

"What were the circumstances that forced it's closure? As I understand it, there was a fire in Nineteen-Eighty-Seven..."

"You're correct about there being a fire, but it happened in Nineteen-Eighty-Four."

"What?"

"Nineteen-Eighty-Four."

"Could I ask you to check?"

"Darling, I've lived in Bradford my whole life. Trust me, it was Nineteen-Eighty-Four, June Twentieth, in case you're wondering."

"Thank you for your help." Scarlet puts the phone down.

Oh, she wants to stagger back, but she's stuck in her seat.

A mistake, surely. That *must* be the reason.

She stays like that until Annabel comes back into the room. The receptionist evidently sees the look of horror on her face, because she begins to look the same.

"What's happened?" asks Annabel.

"Nothing," says Scarlet. "Absolutely nothing."

"Okay."

"Annabel, thank you for your help today. I need to head back to the hotel – the others will be wondering where I am."

That night, the concert goes like a fast, swirling molten fluid. Every song oozes adrenaline and ferocity, every round of applause beats the air with appreciation and respect.

Scarlet doesn't think about what happened at the library. It's immaterial now. Whatever Susan's done in her past, it doesn't matter. Her own childhood and youth is potted with scars anyway. In between songs, she risks glances at Susan.

The girl's perfectly content, her hands darting around the keyboard.

Josephine, on the other hand, seems distracted. Though she plucks her notes and wows the crowd with her gimmicks and flashy smile, she's not quite in the moment.

Gina's the most focused of the lot of them. Every drumbeat, every bash of the cymbal shows an attention as sharp is a pin.

Everything turns into a crystal view. Every ounce of sweat and spit clings to the air.

When Scarlet sings, she's screaming into the blinding lights. She can't see the crowd. She can't see them, only hear them. She can't watch them, only be part of them.

9 June 1991

"Take care of yourselves," says Mr Bellini, "and I look forward to seeing you in two weeks."

"Thanks!" says Josephine, pushing the girls through the door.

"Hey!" Gina protests.

Two of the bellboys shift their luggage to the limo like ants moving stones. The chauffer guy is out, puffing out the last dregs of his cigarette. He's got an arrogant streak about him today, a cocky look in his eyes. He's even *sitting* on the bonnet of the car.

Mr Bellini has followed them out, hands clasped behind his back. He tries smiling, but gives up. Is he expecting a tip of some sort?

"Scarlet, are you awake this morning, or not?" says Josephine. "Scarlet?"

"Yeah, sorry," comes her timid reply.

"Get your backside in the car, babe. We're going to be late for our flight."

Why's Josephine so angry with her today? It's not Scarlet's fault that Gina overslept, but, well, someone's got to get the blame for all this. But, she's got to do as she's told, so she goes inside, nodding a farewell at Mr Bellini.

The drive to the airport doesn't take long at all. The chauffer is even *complaining* about the smoothness of the traffic. When they arrive, there's a hefty queue at the terminal entrance. Security guards and police are checking passports.

"I guess they know we're coming," quips Susan. "Right, Scarlet?"

Scarlet smiles back. She tries to form words, but they refuse to create themselves.

A police officer – evidently assigned to look after them – approaches like a forgotten friend. He tells them that there's been a tipoff about some drug trafficking and they're doing extra checks, but it's okay, he will see them through.

People in the crowd are watching them, some in admiration, most in contempt. Even superstars can be hated.

The girls are checked in and sorted within ten minutes. They are chaperoned through security, blind to what's real, blind to what isn't.

They pass from escort to escort as they're moved down corridors and past duty-free shops. Josephine's definitely leading the pack today. Though she has turned her back on Scarlet, though her eyes are pointed firmly away, she can see the smile on the woman's face when they get to the lounge. Opaque glass doors slide open and leather seats greet them. There's low-level music, statues for stewards, and the dimmest yellow light.

Scarlet's thinking: Is this the rest of her life?

9 June 1991 to 23 June 1991

The days pass as a mix of travel, good food, better wine, even better spirits, and concerts with ever-growing audiences. It doesn't feel like two weeks on the road. It feels like one solid waking dream. It doesn't seem like they're being trailed around as celebrities. It feels like they're prisoners. Every bouncer is a screw. Every cheering fan is a dangerous prison gang member. Every meal in their hotel rooms is their daily lot of chow. Every time Scarlet switches the light off, it's lights-out for her and the other inmates.

She doesn't really get time off. She gets a stroll along Venice Beach and that's it. She likes it there, amongst her kindred spirit. Everyone has their own rules, their own way that they choose to live. Yes, that's it. Choice. Venice Boardwalk, with its dancers, singers and artists, it feels like the place she's always belonged. When she dies, she hopes they'll scatter her ashes here. But that's wishful thinking. She's an English girl. That's what the press refers to her as. English through and through.

When they return to New York, the only thing Scarlet's thinking about is Annabel. What will it be like to join the 'normal' world for a bit? By the time they've got back to the hotel, back into the welcoming arms of Mr Bellini, she's thumbing the card Annabel gave her.

The girls check in – or rather, they are checked in by others. That's what they are now: pampered little creatures. They end up back in their exact same rooms. It's like they never left.

Scarlet has a quick lunch of cold meats, cheeses and bread rolls. Apparently – according to the room service menu – it's one of the hotel's chief delicacies. All the while she's chewing, her eyes are resting on the phone at the bedside table. She can't even wait to finish. She punches in Annabel's number like a rabid dog. The line purrs very briefly, all too briefly.

"Hello?" a chirpy voice answers.

"Hi, is that Annabel? It's Scarlet."

"Oh, hi, Scarlet. I didn't expect to hear from you. Are you back in New York?"

"Yeah, just got back this afternoon. I'm really interested in dinner."

"Yeah, about that. Um, I don't know how to say it. I had a chat with my friends and they're not really comfortable with this."

"Why not? Is it because I'm a celebrity?" Scarlet really thinks Annabel's joking. No, genuinely. But it slowly comes into focus. It's the silent breathing on the other end that's the big clue. It sharpens and clears like marbles smacking off one another, like the sea thundering against the cliffs, like a dream twisting into a waking call.

"It's because of... well, they've – we've read a few things about you and your band in the news. To tell you the truth, we don't really like to keep that kind of company. I'm sorry, I know that sounds nasty, but –"

"I'm sorry you feel that way."

"Listen, I've got to go now..."

"That's fine," says Scarlet, the hatred spitting itself out of her. "Honestly. Listen, thanks for helping me out."

"Thanks, Scarlet. Take care."

Scarlet puts the receiver down and collapses onto the bed. She wants to scratch and tear at the walls. She wants to hit the bottle. She wants to punch someone. She wants anything, anything to take her mind off how she's feeling right now. She can feel the tears of frustration collecting in her eyes. But she wipes them away. She signed up for this life. The moment she decided to form the band, she signed up for it. There's no point feeling sorry for herself. This kind of stuff will happen again. She's been shunned by the real world. She's trapped in this one now. This is her life. She can't just go and visit the real world whenever she gets board.

Scarlet gets up and rummages through her back for a cigarette. Her eyes roll up to see the *No Smoking* sign telling her off. Never mind. She flops back down on the bed. Is there a decent wine on the menu?

Her mind's racing over the tour, over the many faces and smiles she's seen. She still hears the amplifiers banging against her eardrums. She still feels the airborne sweat from the crowds. She still tastes the stale beer stuck to the floor. Oh, if she could live like that... Stuck amongst the fans.

But in a way, she's quite relieved she's in silence now. She's even thrilled at the prospect of room service and champagne... to herself. It's no longer necessary for her to be a social animal. She can be who she wants within the confines of her four walls. When she's not performing, when she's not writing music, when she's not sipping the most expensive champagne, she's not really Scarlet anymore. Scarlet's nothing more than a silhouette that lives on the stage. She's a figurehead, a voice. Nothing more.

With those thoughts in her heart, she tries to let herself relax. She's flying home tomorrow. She might see if there are any journalists or singers or the like that she can go to dinner with. Then again, she probably won't.

Scarlet

17 July 1991

Scarlet's suspicion of Susan has gone down a lot, but it's still there. Lingering. Why did Susan get the date of the fire wrong? Scarlet really should have checked up, but she's frightened of Susan reacting in an extreme way. (Assuming, of course, that Susan is lying.) No, Scarlet needs to tread carefully.

There are more important things, anyway. Like the fact that there's another bloody album to record.

She's in a car, watching the summer day drift by. She watches two children arguing in the street over a Gameboy. One of them's in tears.

She can't believe the tour has happened. Actually, she can't believe that two years ago she was sitting in a pub (on her own) in Holborn, dreaming of success and glory. She can't believe any of it.

The day after they got back, Roger Miser phoned the flat. It was Josephine who answered first, relaying his congratulations to Scarlet, drip-feeding it.

She's alone in the car. Josephine went a day earlier, determined, according to her words, to *"see if the place is properly set up."* Scarlet was only too happy to have the flat to herself. She needed the space.

"Soon be there, ma'am," says the driver.

They're going to be recording the second album in this three-storey house in Wandsworth. Apparently, it was George's idea. The common southwest London touch. Yeah, that's what he said.

Just the other day, the band made headline news on the music scene. International news. It was only for a short amount of time, but Roger and George were impressed. (Something else Josephine drip-fed to her from the phone call.)

Scarlet's thinking about when they'll next be performing, when the car pulls to a stop.

The house proudly boasts its three storeys. It's sandwiched tightly between other similar houses. There's a front garden, with various plants and decorations, mutilated with piles of equipment and instruments. A small water fountain (just built, by its appearance) gurgles next to a rhododendron.

Scarlet approaches the building, cautiously, as if she's worried that she might gate-crash a party. Her fears drop when she sees Josephine's head pop out of a doorway. The others appear quickly.

"Wondered when you might turn up," says Gina. She's got her arms folded.

"Aren't we supposed to be getting people to help us move this crap inside?" snaps Scarlet, dropping her bag.

She doesn't know how long they'll be in this place. She's packed for three nights, but she's got celebrity status now. If necessary, she can nip back home. If it's really necessary, there will no doubt be a good few hotels around here.

"That's the question we've been asking ourselves all morning!" shouts Josephine. She ruffles her hair with her fingers. "Christ. We've moved a few things inside, but... look, we're going to have to do it ourselves."

"I'm up for it," says Susan.

"Good," says Josephine. "Scarlet, up for a bit of manual labour?"

Scarlet wants to smile, but finds that she can only grimace.

Gradually, they move the stuff inside the house and set up the equipment. Josephine wants to record in the living room, a spacious place with dusty paintings, vases, plump sofas, and French doors which open onto a patio. Last to come in are the instruments. Scarlet's very careful to lean her guitar in a corner where she knows it won't be accidentally knocked over.

When everything's done, they go out the back for a quick break. Whilst the others stroll off the patio and explore the overgrown garden, Scarlet treats herself to a cigarette. It will make her voice sound scratchy on the finished product, but comfort comes with a price.

Josephine isn't looking too happy. Yeah, she's scowling, almost. Susan and Gina are examining a shrub that's caused its plastic pot to split. Damn, they could even try their hand at being botanists.

About ten minutes later – after Scarlet's smoked another cigarette – they go back inside and start the arduous process of recording the new album. There are fifteen tracks on this one, and they get through six before they decide to wrap up for the day. After a late lunch (boxes of sandwiches delivered during the late morning from Roger Miser), Josephine produces a bottle of red wine.

The house has been clearly disused for some time. The cutlery and crockery are all coated in a thin layer of dust. The rooms and hallways, largely stripped, seem to beckon for love and attention. Whilst Josephine serves the wine, Scarlet ventures to the upper floors. Even more deserted and torn apart than the lower house.

After toasting the success of the new album, Josephine suggests a plan for tomorrow. It's agreed that they want to get out of this place as fast as they can.

Just as they're about to kick back and relax, a man enters the house, a man out of breath. Scarlet recognises him. He works for the record company. She's seen him hanging around with George.

"Hi," he says, "I've got some news from Mr Miser. There's a magazine that wants to interview you, Scarlet."

"What about the rest of us?" says Josephine.

The man doesn't seem to have heard her. Or maybe, like so many others at the record company, he's trying to ignore her. "They want to interview you the day after tomorrow," he tells her.

"Are they based in London?"

"No, they're up in Berwick-upon-Tweed. Mr Miser has the details. A hotel has been sorted out for you and transport's being arranged."

"Don't bother," interrupts Susan, "I'll drive. Can you tell Roger to change the reservation to two guests?" She turns to Scarlet. "I need to get away for a bit."

"Certainly. I'll make sure he knows." The man smiles and turns to leave.

When he's gone, Susan looks around at the others. There's a hint of madness there. She's totally out of character.

"What?" questions Susan. "I really do need a bit of a break."

"Fine by us," Josephine tells her.

They fall silent. The only noise is the rusted ticking of a clock somewhere. Gina takes a deep breath and lets it out slowly. Susan sits down and lets her eyelids droop. Finally, Josephine offers to refill their glasses with the last of the red wine.

18 July 1991

They get started just after breakfast. They are done by lunchtime. They listen through all the recorded tracks, checking, checking again. When they're all satisfied, Josephine happily declares another bottle of red.

A couple of Mr Miser's employees drop off another container of sandwiches. Gina and Susan find an old wooden table in a shed and set it up in the garden. It's crumbling to bits, but it manages to stand. There are a few foldup chairs as well. Josephine sets them up. Scarlet – making herself useful – piles the sandwiches on a plate. She takes the plate outside and quickly returns to get the wine and glasses.

In the early afternoon sun, they feast. There's casual talk about the design artwork for the new album. Gina tells them several times that she can't wait to go back on tour.

In the late afternoon, Josephine goes and phones Roger Miser. An hour or so later, some of the employees of the record company – dreary looking souls – come by to pick up the recording equipment. Scarlet's a bit reluctant to let her guitar go, but at Josephine's insistence, she complies. After all, it's not her trusty wooden one. No, that's kept in the apartment, away from the prying eyes of fans at concerts.

The girls think about leaving, but then Josephine says something about having a night in. They may as well. Josephine phones Roger to tell him their intentions.

The man from yesterday comes by at around Six with the necessary details for Scarlet and Susan. He doesn't smile at all this time, merely unintentionally bowing his head before he leaves.

Gina suggests ordering some food, but Scarlet's hesitant. Actually, she's downright defiant.

"We can't," she tells them firmly. "We just can't."

"What's the problem?" asks Gina. "I quite enjoyed lunch today. I know you and Susan have an early start tomorrow, but –"

"We do," says Susan. "Scarlet, why don't we head back?"

"Yeah."

Scarlet gets her stuff. Christ, her back hurts from sleeping on that camp bed. She should have stayed in a hotel. She's angry, furious at how they've had to record their second album in this dump. She's barely able to conceal her bitterness as she phones Roger and asks him to send a car.

When she's finally standing outside, she wants to unload her rage. She wants to howl and scream and scrape at the floor. She's feeling a hatred for that Annabel. She wants to throttle the bitch for casting her aside like that. But she understands, even sympathises.

"You okay?" asks Susan.

"Yeah, fine. It's just, when Gina wanted to get a takeaway, I mean..."

"I know what you're getting at."

Scarlet says it eventually. She has to. "Susan, we're up a level now. We can't stoop down to ordering takeaways."

Scarlet

19 July 1991

As they leave London, Susan turns on the radio for a few minutes. Bryan Adams is playing. *I Do It For You.* Scarlet likes the song. It suits her well. But she can tell that Susan is uncomfortable with the noise. When the last note plays, the radio goes off.

"Where are we booked in tonight?" asks Susan, picking up speed.

"Hold on..." Scarlet rummages through a small rucksack at her feet, taking out the reservation and handwritten direction notes. "The Royal Hotel."

"Is that in the town centre?"

"Nope, it's on the outskirts. Practically a short walk from the magazine head office."

"Shouldn't be difficult to get to them then," says Susan, flicking on her indicator and shifting lanes.

"You forget something," replies Scarlet. "They're coming to me. The interview will be in the hotel bar."

"It doesn't bother you, does it? What I said in New York?"

"Of course not. Has this guy attempted to contact you at all?"

"No, I haven't heard from him at all. You were right, Scarlet, I think he was just trying to scare me."

A motorcyclist shoots past them. A car in front blasts its horn. Scarlet imagines the profanity being howled by the driver.

"I'm just worried about this thing impacting on the band," continues Susan.

"It won't," Scarlet reassures her, wondering if this is some sort of a test. Is Susan trying to see whether there's any suspicion?

"I believe you." Susan changes lanes again and lets out a massive sigh.

They make good progress throughout the morning, avoiding the bulk of the traffic. But by the time they get into Northumberland, Susan is looking tired and her eyelids are threatening to droop. Scarlet orders her to turn off at the nearest service station.

They take a short walk around the monotonous facilities, stopping only to get takeaway coffees. They stand outside the car for a bit, Scarlet lighting up a stale cigarette.

"When did you get this by the way?" she asks Susan.

"Last week. You like it?"

It's a 1991 Jaguar XJS, fresh off the assembly line by its shiny black appearance. Susan bends to scratch a bit of dirt of the driver's door.

"It's amazing."

Susan's smile leaves her like the steam flying off their coffees. Her lips curl up against her teeth. "We should leave," she says. "Come on, we don't want to be late for this interview."

They finish their drinks in silence, get rid of the rubbish, and then hit the road again. The traffic has increased a little now. It's like there's this hand curled around the motorway, squeezing it, slowing everything down, jamming everything up.

After passing Newcastle, Susan turns on the radio again. Well, she tries to. They can't hear anything.

"No signal?" says Scarlet.

"No, I think the damn thing is just refusing to work." Susan thumps the buttons with the back of her hand and then whistles a tune. "Oh well, we'll glide on in silence."

The motorway disappeared after Newcastle. It's a tight A-Road they're on now, drifting north. After Alnwick, not only does the air seem to get colder, but it feels thinner. Like the life's been sucked out of it. It's almost as if the air doesn't want to be there, doesn't want to be breathed in by these two women.

They stop at another service station for lunch. Scarlet's a bit uncomfortable with it. It's too *commonplace* after all. It's basic: a fuel area with two pumps and a small rumbling burger van. Susan skips over and places orders for the both of them. She returns a few minutes later with two steaming rags. Scarlet feels disgusted as she chews on the sickly meet; she remembers when she brought something like this to her old shack, remembers the vile taste at the back of her mouth, remembers how grease got onto one of her drawings, remembers how she cursed and screamed and genuinely wish she'd never started the stupid picture in the first place.

They drive on, not stopping until they reach Berwick-upon-Tweed.

The hotel is surprisingly easy to spot. Not once do the navigation instructions need to be consulted. Susan pulls them to a stop in the car park.

The hotel has been renovated. Fairly recently, judging by the smell of fresh paint. It doesn't look like the pictures included in the reservation paperwork. Bits and pieces have been changed, quite extensively in some places. The reception desk is a lot larger, painted bright orange instead of the polished oak. There's a white door marked *STORAGE – Staff Only* where before there had been the entrance to a staircase.

Susan starts handling the booking stuff. She's quite proficient at it. Maybe she should be reassigned to the band's administration "department".

They're shown up a tight staircase to their rooms on the top floor, rooms which surprisingly have a strong degree of class about them. A bottle of champagne sits in a cooler, alongside a tray filled with the latest perfumes. All 1991. There's a television with its own VHS recorder embedded underneath. The manager says something about renting tapes. An ensuite bathroom gleams like a cave of crystals.

"Perfect," remarks Scarlet.

Susan's room is on the opposite side of the corridor. By the smile on the woman's face, it's acceptable to her too.

"The magazine phoned earlier," says the manager, on his heavy retreat. "They'll meet you about Seven in the Slaughter Bar."

"The *Slaughter* Bar?!" exclaims Susan. "What kind of a name is that?"

"The name of our hotel bar, ma'am," replies the manager. He sounds serious about it.

"Isn't Seven a bit inconvenient? I mean, Scarlet and I need to eat."

"We'll prepare dinner for you for Eight, ma'am. The magazine has assured me that they will be finished by that time. It's all in hand, ma'am."

"I hope so."

The manager turns and leaves. When his footsteps have dissipated, Scarlet turns to Susan, unsure of whether to be angry or worried.

"What?" says Susan. "I just want to be fed."

"You know something?" Scarlet lets out a snort. "You're sounding like Josephine."

Over a glass of Bordeaux Red (bottled in 1987), Scarlet lets the questions flow across the space between her and the interviewer, a youngish woman with dyed red hair. There's a guy sitting next to her, a bullish-looking bloke, with a jowly chin and small eyes. He's watching the youngish woman, watching every move she makes. He's the senior editor of the magazine. The false redhead is a trainee. He wants to see how she copes with it. It's a trial. Scarlet was briefed beforehand on this. Was she okay with this?

The questions aren't that complicated. How was the band formed? What was it like touring in America? How did the band find recording the second album?

Susan's at the back of the bar, sipping the remnants of a gin and tonic. She's disinterested in the whole affair, most likely wanting it to be over so they can grab dinner.

The interviewer doesn't show any signs of anxiety or fear. Even though her mentor is leaning over her, even though he's peering at every word she writes, she seems cool.

As the session goes on, Scarlet finds herself focused far less on the questions themselves and more so on the interviewer. Nickie, or something. Scarlet answers each query professionally, oh yes, but she can't help but look into the woman's eyes, noticing the way her irises seem to twitch and her skin wants to glow.

When the last question comes, ("What inspires you?"), it's way too vague for Scarlet to answer. She sits there – like she's wearing the Dunce's Hat. She, eventually, gives a half-hearted answer. Something about what she loves. Something else about her daily routine.

"Well, thank you for this," says Nickie – or whatever her name is. They're off the record now. "Phew, I need a drink."

Nickie's supervisor looks worried. His lips twist into a state of frantic, stuttering desperation.

"Is it not appropriate?" Nickie tells all. "Um, sorry, guess I don't think clearly."

"It's okay," Scarlet says, acting defensively. "I don't mind if she stops for a drink. I mean, this wine'll go off, otherwise."

"No, it's okay." Nickie looks embarrassed. "Honestly." She flips a few more sheets on her notepad and scribbles some notes down. "Bear with me." She smiles and tears the paper off, handing it to Scarlet like confiscated forbidden fruit. "Contact details of the magazine, in case you have any queries or concerns."

"Thanks."

"Well, thank you for your time tonight. It's been a great pleasure to meet you."

Handshakes are exchanged. The mentor manages to look mildly relaxed for the briefest moment. The pair shuffle outside like a dysfunctional family, one that's not even allowed on the soaps.

Afterwards, when Susan and Scarlet are staring across from one another, lasagne in front of each of them, one of them casually mentions how smoothly and how professionally the interview was conducted.

"I think it was worth us coming up here," says Susan, shovelling the last of her accompanying salad down her throat. She sips her portion of Bordeaux Red and gulps.

"Even though you weren't the one in the spotlight?"

"Yep. It was good to come up here and spend time with you. We've never really done much together since the band started."

"Maybe we should make it a regular thing?"

Susan seems to scoff at this suggestion. Her eyes grow wide, then narrow. There's a tiny rim of red around her upper lip. "Yeah, why not?" she says at last. "By the way, what did that girl give you?"

"Oh, just some details of the magazine. In case I'm dissatisfied with it. Christ, why did she even bother...?"

Scarlet takes out the slip of paper from her leather jacket pocket. Damn, it's too hot to wear it. She's had it too long. She should consider replacing it with something that doesn't have tears or rips. She sees that there are actually two slips of paper. Once has the contact details, the other has an address.

"So, how do you think it went, you know, with the second album?" The way Scarlet says this makes it obvious that she's trying to deflect attention, but thankfully Susan doesn't seem to sense it.

Susan rolls her eyes, strokes her bottom lip, and launches into a calm tirade of: several of the titles not being suited to the theme of the album; Gina's drumbeats being a little off at times; the band needing a new member, perhaps several. She doesn't stop there. She goes on. It's a shopping list of criticism. Everyone's at fault.

As dinner nears its end, Scarlet starts fumbling for the slip of paper with the address. Every second that passes makes her more afraid that something will happen to this little bit of paper. Christ, will she admit it to herself? She's desperate for this meal to end.

"How about a drop of the strong stuff before we hit the sack?" says Susan.

"Sure, why not?"

Scarlet's fingernails scrape the dying leather over her person. Her impatience is turning into bitterness. She's already thinking about how much she'd like to slap that bitch Annabel. Imagine her smug, little face breaking into sobs.

She doesn't know what they have. It's amber and it's strong, but she doesn't know what it's called. Not even its strength. But it's powerful and uplifting. And it carries her to a higher place.

"We having dessert?" says Scarlet.

"Nah. I'm okay."

"Listen, I was going to go for a walk before heading to bed."

"You go for it." Susan gazes behind her at the clock above the bar. "God, I'm tired." She stands. Her blue t-shirt hangs loose, threatening to collect lasagne stains. "Shit. Sorry, I need to sleep."

"It's okay."

They walk to the exit of the bar. Susan says they'd better head off at Eight in the morning tomorrow, or thenabouts. Scarlet reluctantly agrees. They embrace, the strong friendship holding together, for now, at least. In the years ahead, it will be tried and tested, ripped and torn. But, for now, it's like a rock.

When she's outside, Scarlet consults the address. She has no way of knowing how to find it. No directions. No cues. There's nothing else for her to do except to just walk. She tries street after street. With each failing, she should be feeling downhearted, but she gets a thrill instead. She crosses a bridge, listens to the water swishing below. There are more streets for her to check, more thrills of failing. She wants to find this place so much, wants to see the redhaired woman, wants to kiss her.

She nearly misses the street, counting it as another one of her thrills, then backtracks, smiles. It's Number 6. Damn, she's on the odd side. She crosses. Her heart catches in her throat. Everything stops for her. The houses are neat, detached, and orderly.

The door opens. The woman with the dyed red hair stands there, unimpressed.

There's a small set of stairs that gradually ascends to the front door. Each step is damp from the moisture in the air. Scarlet walks up, hypnotised, dedicated. As she enters, the girl gently closes the door.

"Hey, glad you came," says Nickie. "Glad you're here."

They come closer and Scarlet allows the woman's lips to stroke hers. She tastes faintly of cigarettes.

"Upstairs?" the woman says.

It's a small house, cramped, but tidy. It's one of those places where geese fly up the staircase and floral paper peels from the walls. Scarlet doesn't see any more of the downstairs, because the girl is taking her up the steps, leading her by the hand. They go across a landing, through to a bedroom that appears filled to the brim with teddy bears. They kiss hard, but the girl pulls away. She bangs the wall with a fist and the room is bathed in trembling light.

"Hey, why don't you leave the light off?" says Scarlet, mildly annoyed.

"Why? Won't be able to see your perky little boobs, will I?" retorts Nickie. "Hmm?"

The girl rushes over to the other side of the room and rummages through a heap of binbags, muttering to herself. "Just be a minute!" she calls over. "Yeah." She returns with two cans of beer. "Drink?"

"Sure." Scarlet manages to catch the can as it's tossed carelessly over. It's cheap lager, the supermarket's own. She's way above this stuff, way above it. Someone like her shouldn't be touching this stuff. But she cracks it open, smelling the sweet, perfume-like fizz.

"I want some of your drink," says the woman. "Give it to me." She sits on the edge of the bed and tips her head back, mouth open like a cavern.

Scarlet approaches, cautiously, and begins to fill the opening.

"What's your name?" she asked the redhaired woman. "I'm assuming it's not just Nickie."

"Does it matter?" As the girl says this, beer sloshes down her chin.

Scarlet takes a swig, forgotten memories of low budget late-night parties resurfacing. She leans forward, kisses the woman, pours more beer down her throat. They fall back on the bed. Scarlet allows herself to swill in the moment. She pulls at the thin t-shirt the woman's wearing, tugs it up. The skin underneath is pale.

"Stop!" the woman shouts. "Please!" There's panic in her voice. An upset wheelbarrow of emotions.

"Are you okay?"

The woman stands up. The t-shirt falls back down like a sail. "Sorry. I'm just not ready for this."

"It's okay."

"It's just, I'm not out yet. Listen, can you please leave?"

Scarlet doesn't need asking twice. Angrily, she storms out, yelling something behind her. She flings the front door open, violently. Down the steps she goes, breathing in the cold air, wanting to suffocate. Wanting this rage, this bitterness to go away.

What if this gets out? What if the woman goes to the press about it? What if she talks?

When she gets back to the hotel, she's relieved to find the bar is still open. Gently, cautiously, she asks for another measure of amber liquid. She doesn't drink it in one. She takes it in slowly. She thinks to herself, ponders the question of whether she imagined the past few hours.

She can't quite remember how she gets to bed, can't quite trace her steps.

But she's suddenly lying down, staring at the patterns on the ceiling, a cigarette smouldering in her lips. Is this a no smoking hotel? Will there be a penalty if she gets caught? It doesn't matter. She can afford it.

She should never have allowed this to happen. During the interview, she could tell her guard was slipping. Did the woman's mentor see anything?

Suddenly she wants to get out of this place. She wants to be back in London, where she belongs, not in this northern hellhole. Back amongst the glittering fame she's used to, back writing songs, strumming her guitar, celebrity parties with only the best champagne. That's her home and her heart.

Stubbing out her cigarette, she shuts her eyes. She feels herself panicking. She fears being trapped up here, unable to get out. It's like that film *Papillon*, when Steve McQueen is locked in that tiny cell and starts pulling his teeth out.

But she reasons with herself that by this time tomorrow, she'll be away from here.

Finally, she feels sleep coming on, and allows herself the privilege of a few hours of rest.

20 July 1991

Scarlet is up early, well before Six. She showers, brushes her teeth, writes a few lyrics to potential songs.

Breakfast is served in the Slaughter Bar. It's a buffet arrangement: pastries and cheap bread, orange and apple juice in ceramic jugs, little packets of cereal and cartons of milk. Normally these things don't impress Scarlet that much, but she's ravenous. It's strange, how hope kicks up your appetite. Scarlet raises her hand and orders a pot of coffee. When it arrives, she's disappointed to find it's too weak. Someone obviously got the coffee-water ratio wrong. But it's not too bad.

Susan comes down to find Scarlet with a pile of toast and pastries in front of her. Scarlet feels like Cleopatra, but with a definite direction.

"Morning," yawns Susan.

"Morning. Heading off at Eight, you said?"

"Yep. If that's good with you."

Susan moves over to the buffet and begins putting a selection together. When she comes back, she complains that there's no fruit, and then dives into her cereal.

Scarlet looks outside. It's a beautiful sunny morning. She may be wrong, but the sky looks blue and clear. It's a perfect day for departure.

"You okay, Scarlet? It's just, you look a little bit on edge. Things all right?"

"Yeah, fine. Just really eager to be back in London."

"Me too."

Susan seems spurred on. She quickly ploughs her way through breakfast.

"Where did you end up last night, Scarlet?" she asks.

"Nowhere. Just went beyond the bridge, walked around a bit, then came back. Bit of an upset stomach. I think it was that dinner that did it."

"Thought you might have been after that girl."

"Not in a million years," sniggers Scarlet. "I'm way too good for her."

They talk a little bit more about the new album. Will it sell as good as the first one? When are they next touring? Are they going to be able to manage Roger's ridiculous tantrums? The man has been getting angrier these past days. And the smell of alcohol on his breath seems to be getting stronger. When they last saw him, why was he checking his pager every few seconds? Is the man okay? They know they can talk about this all day, but they need to get moving.

They head upstairs to their respective rooms. Scarlet whistles as she gathers her remaining things, shoving them hard into her luggage. She doesn't waste time doing a final check or any of that nonsense. After all, if she's left a toothbrush behind, well she can afford a replacement easily, can't she?

She heads straight out to the car, confident strides. An eagerness to be on the road. She smiles as Susan trails out of the hotel.

"Beautiful day, indeed!" Susan shouts. She produces her keys and opens up the Jaguar. The gentle scent of leather billows out. They pile their bags in, just as the warmth of the sun increases exponentially.

Scarlet takes one last look around before hopping into the front passenger seat. Too bad her notepad is in her bag – she could have written some lyrics. But it's okay. She'll survive.

The engine starts with a jolt and Susan reverses out of the parking bay. She checks her mirrors, then moves forward. They head slowly out of the town, joining several roads before linking up with the A1. There's little traffic about. A few cars head north, but nothing is travelling south.

"Didn't like the way the interview was conducted, I must say," remarks Susan. Just as the words come from her lips, it seems to get a little bit darker. Up in the sky, clouds seem to roll, melting into black ink.

"Well, you can't fault the girl. I mean, she wasn't very experienced, but she managed to conduct it okay."

"I meant the guy shadowing her. Bit weird, don't you think?"

"How so?"

"A bit overbearing. Quite controlling. I mean, it's not like she's a trainee teacher."

"Maybe the magazine thought she needed a bit of supervision, a bit of mentoring. I'm sure it's not uncommon."

Susan slows the car as a boom of thunder cuts through the air.

"It's certainly taking a turn for the worst," says Scarlet.

The sky has turned into a dirty black and white mixture. It's like tea mixed with grey paint, plundered with cream.

There's a small flash, followed by a crack. Something tiny strikes the windscreen, then something else.

"Here comes the rain," acknowledges Susan.

It's light, at first. Then it starts pounding harder, and harder. Susan moves the wipers up to maximum. Scarlet counts the minutes on her watch. It's been barely a quarter of an hour since they left Berwick. And rain is growing heavier. Susan squeezes the brakes.

"This is getting ridiculous," she moans. "Fucking hell."

They fumble on. Lighting forks across the sky, a one-note musical adaptation of *Dante's Inferno*. Surface water collects like the pooling emotions in Amy Grant's *Baby, Baby*.

Uncertainty builds up inside Scarlet. Will they ever get out of here? How London calls... How London pulls at the heart... More minutes swing by, and the rain fails to lessen.

Flashing lights up ahead. A policeman, huddled in his waterproof gear, has his right hand pushed forward. Susan breaks to a stop and rolls down the window. The policeman looks sodden and miserable.

"Sorry, love," he says through a beefy moustache and pursed lips, "burst watermain up ahead. Road closed. Follow that route..." He points to a small road turning off at their left. "It's a bit of a diversion, but it'll lead you right back to the A1."

"Thanks," responds Susan, shifting the window back up.

They leave the uniform straightness of the A1 and head down a path filled with leaves, twigs and rubbish, and a cover off an LP. Scarlet strains to see the title and artist, but it quickly becomes lost in the wind and rain. Nothing seems to want to hang around here.

"Soon be on our way," says Susan, turning through a steep corner.

The storm isn't letting up.

A car drives past them, lights on full. Scarlet sees the anxiety on the driver's face, even through the teardrops between them. She counts another ten minutes on her watch. She risks a glance at Susan, seeing only concentration, a dedication to getting them home safely.

The road opens up into a field. The soil is clogged with water. The miniature oceans spread out to treelines.

The car picks up speed.

"I think the rain's starting to let off a bit," Susan whispers.

Scarlet knows something's wrong. Before she can reply, the car begins to skid. There's a screech as the brakes are slammed hard. Both of them cry out, that's all they can do. The car veers off the road, plunging into soil and mud. They trundle along, mud slapping the windscreen. Susan's gripping the wheel with all her might. Eventually they stop. Scarlet swears under her breath. She reaches out, takes Susan's hand, moves it off the steering wheel.

"It's okay," consoles Scarlet. "It's okay."

"Oops."

"Listen, there'll be a phone box around somewhere. I'll go off and search."

"You'll get drenched. Look at the weather!"

"Well, I'm not just going to sit here and do nothing!" Scarlet's angry. She takes her jacket off, scrunching up the leather, bundling it into the back. She burst out, into the rain, her frail t-shirt soaked in seconds.

"What are you doing?" Susan demands.

"Put the fucking car in reverse!" yells Scarlet. "I'll push!" She slaps her hands on the bonnet. "Now, Susan!"

The car begins to roar and the wheels slip. Damn, she's not use to doing so much exercise. Actually, she's a fucking stranger to hard work. She imagines herself being plastered with mud, dreads the humiliation. But nothing like that happens. The car begins to shift, and then slams backward, reversing neatly the way it came. Susan gives the thumbs up as she backs the vehicle onto the road. Scarlet slumps forward, knees sinking to the ground.

"Scarlet?"

She can hear Susan running towards her. She knows that she's crying. Strong arms wrap themselves around her.

"It's okay," Susan's voice whispers. "It's okay."

Scarlet's helped up and they amble over to the car. She doesn't know when they set off. Doesn't care. Doesn't even feel the blanket thrown over her. Doesn't even feel Susan's hand touch hers.

Scarlet

5 August 1991

The voice on the other end of the phone is frantic, chaotic.

"What?" Scarlet exclaims, bleary-eyed, half-naked in the hallway. She checks the clock on a table at the far end. It's rested loosely against the wall, uselessly held in place by the April edition of *Vogue*. The woman wrapped in white on the front cover glares back at her.

"This is pretty damn serious, Scarlet," Roger says. *"Listen, I need to know right now, did you do anything untoward up there? Anything stupid?"*

"Well, aside from crashing off the road –"

"No need to worry about that. That's not a problem. Listen, I'm going to phone Susan. Can the both of you come to the office at Eight? It'd be best if we talked this through."

"Okay, sure."

Josephine emerges as soon as Scarlet places the receiver down. "What is it?" she asks. "Things okay?"

"Not really. You remember last month when I went up north to that interview thing? Turns out that it was a prank."

"What the hell?"

"Roger's called me and Susan in. Listen, can't explain now, okay?"

"Tell me exactly what's going on!" yells Josephine. The tiredness has left her eyes now. She's fully awake.

"It's nothing. It's just, well. I can't explain."

"What time's Roger wanting to meet the two of you?" demands Josephine.

"Eight."

"Well, I'm coming with you."

In the end, it's all of the girls. Sunlight dances around them, flutters around their feet. Behind, the skyline of London blisters in the morning heat. Somewhere, lovers reunite. In other places, hearts get broken. They've turned up early outside the record company headquarters. They can tell Roger's in: smoke is drifting from his window. George's car is on the pavement outside, a rusty white Peugeot 205. A crisp packet crinkles away on the dashboard.

"You'll never guess, I was taking a run down by the Thames the other day, and you'll never guess who I saw," mutters Gina, excitedly. "Only for a split second. John Major. Being ferried along in one of those fancy cars. Didn't look too happy."

"When does the guy ever smile?" says Josephine.

Scarlet lights up. She can see Josephine tense up. Blowing the smoke casually away from everyone, she feels her stomach clench. Only a slice and a half of toast for breakfast. Christ, she really needs to eat more in the mornings. How much weight has she lost? It seems like she's half the person she was since Berwick.

George appears, unlocking the newly fitted double glass doors. He downs the remnants of whatever's in the paper cup and beckons them inside. "Roger's waiting for you. Um, I think he only wanted you, Scarlet, and you, Susan."

"Real life has a strange way of playing out," remarks Josephine. "We're all coming."

"Come with me." George shows the girls through the twists and turns of the corridors.

Everything's been done up. Fresh paint on the walls, new furniture. There's a shelf on one of the walls stacked with CDs of all the singers and albums the record company has released into the wild; before, LPs were piled up in slippery towers. The place has a postmodern feel to it. That's what Scarlet thinks, anyway.

Roger's had his office done up a little bit as well. There's a stand in the corner filled framed pictures and trophy cups. Scarlet looks a bit closer. There's a black and white photo of Roger with Glen Campbell; even with the absence of colour, she recognises the flashing lights of Nashville. There's a large image with a shelf to itself showing Roger with a number of important-looking dignitaries in a hotel bar. They're all covered with a thin film of sweat, cool drinks in their hands. She moves closer, trying to make out the details.

"France, Nineteen-Eighty," Roger tells her.

Soon, they're all seated before him, like schoolgirls.

"Actually, I'm glad you're all here," he starts. "I'm assuming you all know what's happened? It's partly my fault, but there's a risk things like this will happen. Right, have any of you had any suspicious phone calls or letters through the post? You know, stuff like that?"

They shake their heads.

"Okay. That's good. I'm going to make an official complaint to the police. I don't know what they were trying to do. Maybe a couple of teenagers playing a prank or something like that."

"I don't think so," says Scarlet. "The person interviewing me was at least twenty, maybe nineteen, and there was an older guy with her."

Roger frowns. He wipes a hand over his oily face and screws his eyelids shut, opening them with force. "Tell me exactly what happened," he says.

"Susan and I came downstairs to the bar about fifteen minutes before the interview was due to start. They'd already arrived. As I said, there was a young woman and an older man. We introduced ourselves. Susan went over to another table and ordered a drink. Myself and the young woman shared a bottle of wine, though she wasn't appearing to drink much. Throughout the interview, the man seemed to be checking on the woman, keeping an eye on her. I thought he was her mentor or something. When the interview was over, they left."

"That's not as bad as I thought," says George, entering the room. He perches himself on a stool. A bit like a poser in all honesty. Arsehole.

"Listen, girls, I don't think it's worth getting too worked up about this." Roger's not looking at any of them.

Scarlet can see the strain the world seems to be taking on him. See the haunted look on his lips and irises. See the anger and futility of multiple divorces, too many broken promises. See how torn and ripped up he is. The booze. The cigarettes. The late nights. Yet, somehow, he continues.

"This is obviously some sort of prank by a few protesters or something. Perhaps they were just seeing how far they could push things. Nevertheless, I'm not planning on taking any chances. I'll be having phone calls with the legal people later. Scarlet, Susan, the two of you might need to give a statement of some sort. However –"

"Hold on," interrupts Susan, "there's something that doesn't make sense here. Roger, you say this a prank. What I don't understand is an older man being in the interview.

He didn't look like... well, a loser. This guy seemed mature, respectful, organised."

"You're thinking too much about it," Gina tells her. She shifts on her seat, eyes up, scratching at the fading makeup on her cheeks. "Look, what is the real risk to us? I mean, did you give anything away that other magazines and news outlets don't know?" She doesn't wait for an answer. "The band's safe. Come on, guys."

There's some murmuring and whispering. Things get a little awkward after a bit. Eventually, Roger calls the meeting to a close. Scarlet sees that some of the strain has left him, but the bitterness still hangs off his shoulders.

She doesn't know how it happens, but suddenly she's alone on the street. She's unsure of where to go, what to do. Remember that time she had a parttime job? Remember when she painted pictures in that shed? She doesn't have those appointments now. There's a small café up ahead, the kind that truckdrivers use, you know, when they're waiting to pick up loads. There are a couple of tables inside, vacant, covered with unfortunate dustings of sugar. The place looks a tip: peeling paint, sweet wrappers lying around, a sticky floor. A heavyset jowly man stands behind a counter, a copy of The Sun draped over his hands.

"Closed, love," he says to her, not looking up.

"Oh, I'm sorry – your door was open."

"Problem with the water."

"Ah, okay. Do you have anything to eat? Only, I didn't have much of a filling at breakfast."

The man's eyes dart up. "Listen, love, are you deaf or something? Did you not hear me? We're fucking closed, alright?" He yanks up his paper. "Stupid bitch," he mutters.

She walks for a bit more, considering whether to go back to the record company, see whether Roger will call her a taxi, but she finds the effort too much. An hour later, she finds a taxi rank, and is glad to be on her way back home.

She doesn't want anything to do with the world of fame, not today. She's still sickened at herself over that girl. Unbelievably foolish and dangerous. What did she hope to get from it?

She ends up sleeping through lunch, waking up around Four. She calls for Josephine, finds she's not there.

Scarlet strums her guitar, tries to find the words, hunts for the notes, but there's nothing coming. She takes a break, goes back, takes a break again. This continues for an hour. She goes through to their living room, spots a tape on the floor. *Child's Play 2.* One of Josephine's, no doubt. She puts it on, lasts for five minutes, tries to go back to the guitar, but there's no point.

Hours later, she orders a Chinese, but doesn't find the need to have it delivered to her. She takes a short walk, picks it up, watches the flickers of recognition. The girl from that band. The one with the short, blonde hair. When she gets back, she eats it straight from the wrappers and tubs. She turns on the television, just in time to catch Michael Buerk's nightly bulletin. She stops, lets the sweet and sour chicken fall from her mouth.

Two policemen have been killed in a car chase in Kent. An absolute tragic affair. Tributes are pouring in from across the country, sympathies directed at the families. Their fogged pictures fill the screen.

She wants to fall over crying, but she feels nothing except relief. The two coppers who know her secret, both dead. She's safe. Truly safe. Nothing can hurt her now. Nothing.

Josephine

5 November 1991

I have to admit, I'm really getting to that point where I'll get bored of the fame.

Ever since Scarlet brought us into that dingy café and told us her big idea, a part of me – really, I'm serious – thought I'd go along with it for a laugh.

A year and three quarters later – Christ – Scarlet and I are boarding the Concorde to New York. We get a few strange glances, but we're going on the plane of the rich and famous. We get handed glasses of champagne by a smiling hostess humming a Kylie Minogue song. Genuinely thinking she has talent.

I'm angry the way Scarlet is looking at the woman. Angry at the look of lust hanging in front of her face. You know something? I want to give her a smacking. More than that, I want to punch her lights out.

When we're in the air, Scarlet begins falling asleep, drifting onto my shoulder. I hate it when she does that as well. Christ, there's actually a lot I don't like about her. Of course, I care for her, like a sister.

As we journey across the pond, I get an increasing sense of dread. I just want to be in and out of New York as quickly as possible.

Scarlet and I have been invited to a music awards ceremony in Carnegie Hall. We're not being given anything, but Scarlet is making a speech. She's been writing it for the past week. *Making Our Debut*, it's tentatively called. She hasn't run it by me, but it's a reflection of how we as a band have adapted to fame, how we've impacted on the world.

It's a load of shit if you ask me.

Several hours later, we touch down. I imagine the desperate eyes of the poverty-stricken as they watch us descend, praying to God for the experience of being in the clouds with us, able to hop on to any flight, hop off in some strange destination.

It's a short limo ride to our hotel. I don't think I caught the name Roger referred to it as, only that it's snug and smug. Pity it doesn't have a view of Central Park.

When I'm in my room, I try to sleep, but I can't seem to nod off. Someone comes by later with lunch, then they come again later with medium rare steak. They come a third time to tell me it's time to get ready for the awards ceremony.

Roger told us not to worry too much about this.

"It's a quick in-and-out," he told us two days ago. "Honest. Just get in there, enjoy the ceremony, and come home again. Ever been on Concorde before?"

Scarlet and I don't talk as we get chauffeured through the streets. All around us, people are going drinking with friends, others are having meals out, all are trying to make their way through the world. Some glance our way. I can tell they're slightly envious of us. If only they knew how I was feeling.

There's something they don't tell you about being like us. Everyone thinks that the glamour, the champagne, the front row seats, the first-class travel, that it makes you happy and content. But they're so fucking wrong. If only they knew how desperately I wanted to burst out of this car, go up to the nearest person and buy them a drink. Fame's not the glorified cloud everyone thinks. It's a prison.

As we pull up to Carnegie Hall, the cameras explode. Scarlet's sapphire dress dazzles the night as she steps out. Reporters scream questions at her. When I emerge, I'm immediately supported by heavy security. I head around to the other side of the car, standing close to Scarlet. We're on the red carpet, pounded on either side by journalists keen to impress their editors with exclusive quotes and paparazzi firing off their expensive cameras.

Everything about Scarlet's face is stricken with confidence, strength and honour. I've never seen her like this before. Her skin has lost its paleness and now, with the makeup applied, it's a beautiful mild red colour. I've always known she was never a fan of the stuff, but she really suits it now. In that moment, I confess to you that I envy her.

We're shown inside. I've always wanted to come here, to Carnegie Hall, where fame and fortune billow out like a swarm of locusts. Yet, it's strange, it's so... normal. I'm used to it. Used to the plush chairs, being seated next to celebrities. I don't even pay attention to the awards ceremony. Don't even know which one it is. The only thing I vaguely sit up to is Scarlet's speech. I'm astonished by what I'm hearing. She's so poignant in the way she does it, she's connecting with everyone in the audience and all those watching via television.

There's a small afterparty drinks session, but we don't stay for long. We thank the hosts, two supposedly well-known actors with careers spanning decades. A few other singers congratulate Scarlet and one or two shake my hand.

You've guessed right. It's Scarlet they're interested in.

We leave just before midnight, chaperoned through the never-sleeping streets. I don't know how this city keeps itself. Don't know how it goes from strength to strength.

I see the Twin Towers of the World Trade Centre blinking away. Each is like its own complex constellation of stars.

Back at the hotel, I try to keep the question in, but it falls out, spewing itself into the world.

We're just outside our rooms when it happens. Scarlet's just said goodnight, stifling a yawn.

"How do you do it?" I ask.

"What?"

"This? I mean, how you delivered that speech and everything."

"Because I don't try," she tells me. She goes into her room before I have the chance to respond. But I don't need to.

6 November 1991

The bad news is delivered to us over breakfast. One of the hotel porters hands us a fax from Roger Miser.

Hi ladies,
Bad news. Your Concorde flight this morning has been cancelled. George has rebooked you onto a flight at 17:00 New York time. It's not Concorde, unfortunately.
See you in London soon.
R.

"Why's he so fucking cocky?" I exclaim. "Always bloody apologising, but I know he doesn't mean it. Tosser."

"Had hoped to be in London by lunch," Scarlet says bitterly. "Oh, well, never mind."

"You working on any new music, you know, for the third album?" I ask.

"Not much. The other day, I came up with some titles. That's about it."

"Well, I've got some ideas."

Scarlet looks up, but seems more dedicated to the bottom of her coffee cup.

"I was thinking about a theme for the next album," I say. "I'm thinking about a theme on computers, how they're beginning to impact society. Pagers and all that. As musicians –"

"No." Scarlet cuts me off with a razorblade.

"Don't you want to let me finish?"

"The problem is, I always do." Scarlet rises to her feet and tosses a napkin to the table. She struts away, hands in the leather jacket.

I go after her. If people weren't around, I'd start calling out names. I watch her go for the staircase, and I'm quick behind her.

"What the hell was that about?" I shout. "Hey? Don't walk away from me!"

"Get some rest," she calls back.

I grab her by the shoulder, turn her to face me. One of her hands slaps my cheek.

"Fuck off!" she hisses.

I nearly fall backwards down the stairs, but hands steady me. A concerned businessman reeking of coffee looks me in the eye. "Are you okay, ma'am? Shall I call the cops?"

"No, it's fine. Just a misunderstanding."

"Are you sure?"

"Yeah."

I need to get away from here. Still struggling to see why she hit me like that. I head back down to the lobby, blindly approach one of the porters. "What time do the bars open around here?" I ask.

"There's a bar on the next block that opens at Five A.M., but –"

I don't care to catch what else he says. I just want to be out of here.

Out on the street, I don't have the luxury to be enraged or to stomp around in frustration. The pavement's too damn full. Where did he say the bar was? Huh. May as well just fall in with the crowd. Pagers go off. A few people have mobiles to their ears, yelling down the lines: stock market information, legal concerns, etc.

I just want to disappear in the ground, fall into the gaps. I'll admit to you, I want to step off this wheel of fame, take a walk in the ordinary world.

Scarlet

7 November 1991

Scarlet's more than happy to be gone from this hotel. How many times is she going to have to keep coming back to this city?

The limo waits for them out front, yellow cabs staying well clear.

"I'm sorry about earlier," she says to Josephine.

"Don't worry about it."

"I just wish −"

"There's no point wishing. I annoyed you. You slapped me. Forget it, okay?"

Porters move bags to the car, human conveyer belts of obedience.

"I'm really sorry."

"Oh, Christ, Scarlet!" shouts Josephine.

Attention is drawn. The porters stop for a fraction of a second. One of their security detail drops his jaw. Other onlookers don't know what response to give: they walk past casting dirty glances to the side.

Josephine thunders on, seemingly unafraid.

Could this be the band starting to fragment, dear reader?

"You've got to stop fucking apologising! Honest!" She calms down, her throat quivering. "Let's just get out of here, okay? We can talk about this back in London. Guys, hurry up with the bags, will you."

A minute later, they're in the flow of traffic. The limo is spacious and comfortable, but there's such an extreme gulf between the two bandmates. Scarlet's tempted by the array of spirit bottles provided for their convenience. She nearly goes for the vodka, but Josephine's voice cuts in: "I deserved that slap, I really did."

"Look, we really can't afford this anymore," says Scarlet.

"It was a stupid idea, really, my thoughts for the next album."

"I was angry. It's just, I've had a lot on my mind at the moment. When we're back in London, let's have a talk about your ideas. I'm not sure how the girls will feel about it though."

They pass a sign for JFK Airport and follow the rough stream of traffic. Horns blare as someone cuts in front of someone else.

It's become a process Scarlet's used to: being hurried through an airport, keeping an eye out for any desperate photographers. This time, they're lucky. The drop-off is quick and uneventful; two guys in suits take their bags and show them inside. Fifteen minutes later, they're relaxing in the lounge. They barely have time to finish their champagne before an apologetic man escorts them to the plane.

"Please accept the airline's most sincere apologies," he tells them, scurrying along. "Your seats are ready for you, and there's a bottle of the airline's finest champagne waiting."

They pass through the gathering crowd of families and children, most of whom stare fixatedly. They're shown onto the plane at breakneck speed. It's as if the airline's determined to get them out the way as soon as possible.

Dusk is beginning to claw the airport.

"Welcome onboard," the stewardess – a middle-aged woman with firm breasts – says as they enter the aircraft.

It's the same routine. Turn to the left. Right to the end. Two chairs, already trussed up with fizzing glasses, wait for them.

"Christ, I need to put my backside down," mutters Josephine.

Another stewardess comes by to check that they have everything and takes their orders for dinner. A third one checks that their champagne is okay.

The two bandmates barely talk, scarcely dare to whisper.

Then Scarlet becomes aware that they're not alone in this luxury saloon. She tilts her head to the left. Across the aisle sit two men, one of whom is familiar.

"Mauro, how the hell are you?" says Josephine. She gets up and goes over to him.

Mauro Lane – the passionate young singer with the blond hair and the deep blue eyes – gets up also. He's wearing a white shirt with cufflinks and faded blue jeans. He's even fitter than the last time Scarlet saw him. The way he looks at her, he makes her turn into a little girl.

"I'm okay," he responds in his smooth voice, kissing Josephine on the cheek.

"Were you at the awards ceremony thing?" asks Josephine.

"Unfortunately, no. I heard it was great though. Saw a few clips on the news this morning. No, I've been in New York to record my new album. We just wrapped up a few hours ago and raced to the airport. Scarlet, how are you?"

She lets Mauro hug her, dreaming that they are alone somewhere, perhaps in a resort.

"I've been all right, but busy. You know how the world of music is." She'll kick herself for days over this lousy response. "How did the release of your first album go?"

"Okay, I guess. I didn't sell as many copies as I thought I would, but I've got a few concerts this month up in the north of England. Hopefully it'll drum things up." Mauro's face twitches.

"Forgive me," he says, like his mouth is in a rush. "Scarlet, Josephine, this is my brother, Eugene."

The second man grudgingly stands up. He's not like his brother, not in the slightest: black hair cut short and an unshaven face. His cheeks are pockmarked and there's thick muscle around his neck. He's in a plain orange t-shirt and jeans, with scuffed trainers and a silver watch. He looks bored, neglected of soulful connections, a wannabe tough guy. His eyes are harsh brown and bloodshot.

"Hi," he says. His accent is thick Mancunian. It's clear that he hasn't found the need to fight it off. Clear that he doesn't care.

They reach out to his offered handshake. Scarlet wants to squirm at the touch of his rough skin. She can tell – you can tell, dear reader – that he's spent his youth and early adulthood on building sites. This is a man who is as far away from the prestige and prowess of fame and fortune as you can possibly get.

"I thought I'd bring Eugene to New York with me," Mauro tells them. "Give him the big experience."

Eugene smirks, wiping the bottom of his lip with his thumb. A gold chain hangs in the flesh of his neck. "And it was great to come. Can't thank my big brother enough for inviting me along."

"Did you enjoy yourself?" says Josephine.

"A question I can finally answer." Eugene picks up his glass of champagne and takes a long drink. "Yeah, it was pretty cool, I suppose. Busy but cool. So, I suppose I should be expecting to see you guys performing in the near future?"

"You should definitely come along to one of our concerts," Scarlet tells him. "Usually quite energetic. You'd like it."

"Well, a couple of my mates are interested. Beats going to the pub after laying tarmac all day."

"So, you're in construction?"

"Sort of." Eugene's eyes shrivel as he says the words. "Listen, guys, I've got to get some kip. Bloody knackered."

A stewardess approaches with another bottle of champagne. She offers it like it's a runner-up prize. They politely decline. Josephine suggests taking their seats, because others are coming onboard now. It's almost as if they don't want to be noticed.

Hours later, when they're all asleep, everyone around her, Scarlet tries to keep herself awake. She doesn't realise how significant this encounter is, not yet. Doesn't even register Eugene Lane, the man who will ultimately change the direction of the band.

Even when they land at the other end, say their farewells as they're being shepherded to different cars, Scarlet doesn't even register Eugene. He's nothing to her, just the strange brother of a singer she's got a massive crush on. That's all.

When she's back home, she scarcely thinks of Eugene. She unpacks her things, lies down, tries to cut out the noise of the aeroplane.

There's a rustle on her shoulder, jerking her awake.

"You okay?" comes a voice.

Scarlet sits up. It's dark outside. Little traffic. She feels hands on her short hair; needles push their way through.

"Josephine, what's up?" she splutters.

"I'm sorry for my behaviour. Don't know how else to put it."

"Stop apologising." Scarlet rushes in and pulls Josephine's lips to her own.

Suddenly, they're clinging onto one another. Scarlet doesn't want to let go. Afraid that this moment will end.

"I've missed you..." one of them whispers.

"Missed you more..." the other replies.

Scarlet holds Josephine as tight as she can. Without warning the smooth skin disappears and she can't breathe. She thrashes her arms out, nearly blinded by blinding light.

"Josephine," she wants to cry out.

She rolls over, tasting the sweet stink of the sweat soaking her pillow. She spreads her bare arms out, angry at the sun. She realises she's naked and it's nearly midday.

"Josephine!" she calls out. "Josephine, what are you up to?"

She pulls on a t-shirt and jeans, pushes into the corridor.

"Damn it," she mutters, seeing the note from Josephine on the kitchen table. "Why do I keep missing you?"

Josephine

14 November 1991

I've never been the one to be fussed about winning awards, not since the egg-and-spoon races in primary school anyway. Yet, as I'm getting trussed up, I think of nothing else except how good it'll be to wander out of the Royal Albert Hall with one of those globular trophies. Roger's told us we've been nominated for three prizes: Best Lead Singer, Best Single and Best Debut Album. Am I pleased that we've been nominated for the Lead Singer one? Hmm.

Scarlet's doing an interview with the BBC, so she'll be arriving at the Royal Albert before the rest of us.

I check I've got everything, double-check the lipstick, and head downstairs to where the taxi is waiting.

Don't get me wrong, Scarlet and I don't have any issues. In the beginning, there was a rift, but it's gone now. In all the time we've known each other, we've sometimes been as close as sisters and other times bitter friends who can barely stare at one another. It was never her that was the problem, it's the band.

You see, I'm much older than the others. I won't shy away from that fact. I won't hide from it. Every time we've done a concert, I've felt that sense of not belonging. Like I've gate-crashed a party. There was a photo of us in a magazine the other day, me looking like a mother watching over her children. It made me twitch.

Clutching my handbag, shuffling in my yellow dress, I stare out at the passing lights of London. Ninety years ago, my great-grandfather walked these very streets, handing out leaflets for his own political party. Days and nights, for weeks on end. He never won a single seat. A life wasted, as my grandmother used to say.

"Beautiful night, isn't it?" the driver says.

"Sure is."

"Mr Miser told me I'll get a decent tip if I get your there ten minutes early, but I'll admit, it's nice taking your time going through the streets."

"You should see New York."

"Love New York. Took the wife there on our second anniversary. Oh, when was that, must be eight years ago now?"

"It's a great place."

"We're nearly there." The driver's tone has changed. He's not serious, but he's lost that sense of distraction.

The Christmas lights are already going up. We pass a Christmas market, where couples sidle along, eyes and noses focused on the delicious treats and ornaments on offer.

"Do I know you from somewhere?" the driver asks suddenly.

"Sorry?" I say. Does he not listen to music at all?

"Your face is really familiar."

"I'm assuming Roger briefed you and everything."

"Yeah, I know *that*. I know you're in that band and everything. It's just, I've got a feeling I've met you somewhere before."

We go on in silence. I'm perplexed. I mean, I've literally never seen this guy before in my life. I'd remember him otherwise. Not the person who forgets.

"Didn't you used to teach at Rainham John Graham?"

"What?"

"Yeah, I remember you now. My daughter went there. Kids used to take the piss out of you, didn't they?" The driver chuckles.

I cringe back in embarrassment, wishing I could soil this guy's cab and refuse to pay the charge. I never wanted this dug up, but I suppose it was inevitable at some point.

"It was a long time ago," I tell him sternly. "I was in training. Couldn't get on with the school. Behaviour management wasn't my strongpoint, what can I say."

"I remember my daughter coming home one day and telling me how a class kicked off and you got told off for it. Really loudly in the corridor. You fled the school in tears or something."

"Yeah, well I wasn't cut out for it. Can you just knock it off?"

"Sorry love, I didn't mean to. I was just joking."

"That's fine. Just don't mention it again, okay? Right, I think that's the Albert Hall up ahead."

I don't even wait for him to stop as I leap out of the vehicle. I'm so determined to escape my past life as a failed teacher – yes, I'll admit that to you – and enter the world of paparazzi and champagne, that I'll risk an embarrassing trip or a broken bone. As soon as we roll up to the beginning of the red path, I'm out, ready to respond to the flurry of questions that come my way.

"So good to be here!" I say to one. "You know what, it's a strong community. Doesn't matter if we win, doesn't matter if we lose," I tell another. "Actually," I say to a youngish reporter, his eyes full of flurry, "there's a good chance we might win after all."

A security guy gestures me inside. Soon I've forgotten about the driver. I'm in the world I belong now. I'm here. Flesh and blood. The cold air licks my bare shoulders. The warmth of handshakes in the pre-ceremony greeting area holds me upright. Someone gives me a glass of champagne. I see Gina in the corner. She's wearing a black dress and even darker eyeliner. Then I spot Scarlet, centre of attention, surrounded by people eager to exchange words with the hottest new singer on the scene. She's in a red dress, skinny shoulders flinching. Only minimal makeup applied. We stare at each other and I know I'm home. This place. Right here. Right now.

Someone touches my arm and moves in front of me. This bloke with longish red hair, arrogant look in his eyes. I've seen him before, I know I have.

"Josephine!" he says eagerly. "I believe we met at Roger's party earlier this year. Dennis Loud, do you remember?"

"Oh, yes, I remember now. How have you been? What brings you tonight?"

"I've been fine, yes, yes. A friend of a friend got me an invite. Such raw talent here tonight! I mean, such raw talent!"

He's in a solid tuxedo, a loosening bowtie clutched around his neck. His hair is at least sorted, but he hasn't bothered with a ponytail. He's chaotic, but the glass of wine tucked in his fingers shows a sense of belonging, a feeling of purpose, like he knows exactly where he's supposed to be, but doesn't care if he's told he's not welcome.

"You see that lady over there?" he goes on, indicating a woman in a pale white dress. "You see? Well, I went to one of her concerts a couple of weeks ago. Her voice, the way she commands the room, the way she connects, bloody hell, it's superb!"

"How's your book on Seventies rock music going? I remember Scarlet mentioning something to me about that."

"Oh, it's okay. I've pretty much done all the research, but the writing is going slow."

"You looking forward to tonight?"

"You bet I am." He bursts into a big smile, the corners of his mouth cracking into deep bits. "You know something, I was in Paris last month, and I saw this street musician. Beautiful, talented violinist. The way she seemed so calm, so perfect, every note resonating with my heart."

"Wow, whereabouts was it?"

"Um, near the Eiffel Tower. A couple of streets away. Really beautiful little scene. Oh, the roar of Paris! The way it mellows! The bakeries and the cafes and the bars. Such a tender place, so tender. A dear friend of mine, a certain professor of English literature, told me something about Paris: *If you've never been to Paris, you haven't touched the icing of the world.*"

"You get to travel a lot then?" I continue.

"Oh, you bet. I had the privilege of visiting Moscow several years ago as part of a literature exchange. Those days of wandering through its streets, watched at all times, you understand, those days were blissful. Now –"

"Ladies and gentlemen, if you could head through!" a loud voice calls out. It's one of the beefy security guys, standing with his arms crossed, a gentle fierceness in the deep recesses of his cheeks.

"I'll see you later, Mr Loud," I say. I gravitate towards the girls. We come together quite naturally.

We're ushered to our seats, asked if we need anything, asked again if we need anything.

Moments after the last person sits down, the show begins. A presenter's voice appears from speakers, appears in the television sets of millions: "Welcome to the 1991 Silver Fenton Awards. Please welcome your host for this evening, Vance Sherman!" I've never heard of him, but I clap with everyone. A shrewd man with wiry, grey hair walks across the stage as music blares out.

"Thank you, thank you!" says this Vance Sherman, fingering his bowtie and opening his arms. "So good to be here, so good to be here! How are you all? How are you?! Well, it's good to be at the Silver Fenton Awards once again. How can we forget the Fentons of Nineteen-Seventy-Nine, when I first hosted it? Oh, none of you will remember, because you weren't alive at the time!"

As Vance Sherman basks in the laughter, I look around to Scarlet. Her eyes are straight ahead, locked on the stage.

"During my many years of involvement with this beautiful industry, I have seen so much unbelievable talent. Looking through the nominations this evening, I had a sudden epiphany. Getting disappointed is going to be harder and harder."

The audience laughs again. Sherman sniggers at his own joke and continues.

"On a serious note though, the talent and the ingenuity of such a diverse range of music and singers and bands has made me reflect deeply. Unfortunately, whilst I want everyone here to be crowned a winner, the decision is ultimately up to the judging panel. Therefore, without further ado, let me introduce a certain up-and-coming singer who will now perform to welcome in the evening. Ladies and gentlemen, give it up for Mauro Lane...!"

Well, this is a surprise. Mauro Lane, his boyish hairstyle flapping in the applause, walks onto the stage. A drummer, two guitarists and a keyboardist, their equipment all at the ready, prepare to strike the opening notes. Strange how I didn't notice it. Why didn't I see it? How could I not? Mauro doesn't waste any time. He's straight into his song, wowing us into silence. When he's done, he takes a small bow, and walks away.

Sherman's back in a flash. "Fantastic!" he says. "Absolutely fantastic! Well, that's certainly set things up for tonight. To present the award for Best Lead Singer, I want to hand over to a man whose name should be woven into the fabric of music journalism. Nominated for many awards, published in many more magazines, winning the hearts and minds of music fans, and delving into fiction, please welcome Herbert Buxton!"

I don't register the man who comes onto the stage...

Scarlet

...Neither does Scarlet. As she sits there, she listens to Herbert Buxton's little introductory speech, not realising the significance he will play in her life – all of their lives.

"...When I started writing about this industry, I had no idea of what would await me. When I was in America, my connection with music became more than writing, it became a link of the soul. Being a music journalist is not just a daunting task, it is a job that demands an understanding of how a musician thinks, what influences drive them, their daily routines, how they feel, what they believe in. Today, standing amongst you, I believe that this hard work has now been fulfilled."

There's a silver envelope in his hands. He starts to prise it open.

"The nominees for this year's Best Lead Singer are..."

As he reads out the list, Scarlet tries to force herself to keep calm. She glances across at Josephine, whose hands seem to be trembling. All at once, Mr Buxton reveals the winner. It's not her. She bows her eyelids in shame as Mr Buxton hands the award over to a skinny girl in a diamond-themed dress. She delivers a short speech, thanking those that gave her the confidence, the band, her new boyfriend and her close friends. In tears she turns back to Herbert Buxton and wraps him in a hug. She holds the award over her head as she returns to her seat. After a few jokey remarks, Mr Buxton departs and Vance Sherman returns.

"Well, that's certainly one for the books!" he says. "Most certainly. A talented young woman... definitely taking her place in the hall of fame. Now, let's move on to Best Solo Artist... To introduce this most prestigious award, I want to hand over to one of the U.K.'s most respected veteran singers..."

Scarlet falls in and out of focus as the evening passes. It's hard to watch fresh and cemented talent snatch awards like sweeties. It's bloody heart-breaking. Best Single comes – something she's hopeful they'll win. For the second time that night, the band loses. Shortly after the acceptance speech, she feels a nudging as Gina passes over a slip of paper.

We're screwed, it says. *Josephine.*

"Well, we're at the beginning of the end of our magical evening," Vance Sherman tells them. "For the next award, it's been decided that I present it myself. Best Debut Album. Now..." He holds up an envelope. "The nominees for this year's Best Debut Album are..."

It doesn't matter. She knows that now. It doesn't matter. She's with the girls. That's all that's important. Nothing else is.

"It's okay," she whispers to Gina. "It's okay. Don't worry about it."

They've won. Is that right? Have they actually won?

Josephine's leading the way, the clapping ringing in their ears.

It's like the first time they performed. Scarlet recalls the anxiety, the panic. She smiles at the thought of it now.

Vance Sherman's hairstyle is a lot more chaotic up close. You know, it's like when you're a kid, and you see a clown or man dressed in a silly costume, and you approach him afterwards, and you see the weird differences, the imperfections in the costume and makeup you thought was so perfect.

Scarlet's the one to take the award. She thrusts it into the air.

She did have a speech prepared, but it comes out in bits and pieces, nonsensical bits and pieces:

"Ladies and gentlemen, thanks... No other words. No words can describe how I feel now. So many people to thank. The girls, for one, my family, friends, Roger, George, all those who inspire me. Thank you."

The audience and the world look at her, returns to applause.

The band will be all over the front pages tomorrow. A flurry of interviews will come their way, bashing open doors to greater opportunity, far bigger wisdom and beauty.

Yes, dear reader, the band are truly famous now.

There's a short afterparty before they leave. Everyone's got a glass of something. One or two of the celebrities are teetotallers: they stand, mingling, eyes focused and sharp, always threatening to be distracted by the prospect of alcohol. Scarlet can see it, can sense it. They're on the edge. One slight move, one careless thrust of a glass of champagne...

The congratulations pour in. Dennis Loud briskly shakes Scarlet's hand.

"So damn brilliant!" he exclaims. "Stupendous! My congratulations!"

"Thank you!" she can only say. "Did you enjoy the ceremony?"

"Words fail me... they truly fail me!"

"Well," she responds, as Mauro Lane appears, "you should definitely write a book on it." She smiles graciously and walks over to Mauro.

"Scarlet, I'm so pleased for you," Mauro tells her. He touches her elbow lightly.

"I thought you performed well. Had no idea you'd be here tonight."

"Well, I was a lastminute addition."

"Is Eugene here?"

"He is..." Mauro scans around. "Hmm, here was here a minute ago. Excuse me," he says to a security guard, "have you seen Eugene Lane at all?"

"Mr Lane has left," comes the reply.

"Oh, that's strange." Mauro glances quickly at the floor. "Oh, well. Sorry, can I offer you a drink? Please..." He stumbles over to a floating tray and snatches two glasses.

"Thank you."

"Actually, Scarlet, I would like your help with a few ideas. Dinner tomorrow night?"

"I'd like that. But maybe just dinner? I don't want a professional dinner with you or anything... Mauro, can I borrow you over here?" She leads him to a corner of the room. She's actually damn certain how she wants to play things. "Mauro, look, are you asking me out?"

She's grateful that no one's eavesdropping. It won't get into the papers. No embarrassing stories.

"Well, I'm doing a bad job of it, aren't I?" says Mauro.

"Yeah, you are. Listen, dinner, tomorrow night. Just the two of us. Now, we'd better get back to this mingling before people start asking questions."

They head back into the crowd. A few photographers snap a picture of Scarlet, one of Scarlet and Gina. The pressure's off now. She meets singers, writers, journalists (with exclusive passes), Vance Sherman, and others with the luck and privilege to be in this arena.

She's worried that Josephine isn't around, but reasons she probably went home early. The wine and champagne flow freely, and eventually the crowd begins to thin, falling apart like a thread.

She's properly famous now, dear reader. You thought she couldn't do it, didn't you? But she's made it. Against all odds, it must be said.

1992

Scarlet

7 January 1992

It's perfect.

The kind of place she's always dreamed of. Where she knows she should be.

She's standing in the hallway of her new home in Chelsea. Everything in this house is empty at the moment, except for the boxes stacked up along every wall.

It's a fairly thin three-story house near to Burton Court. She's already got a glimpse of some of her neighbours: a few football players, a journalist, a T.V. presenter, and a throng of singers. She's been planning this quietly, keeping it from Josephine; after all, Scarlet's a woman who needs her own space.

The keys in her hand, she walks into the home, stopping first at the lounge. Maybe it's a good idea to convert it into a study? No, wait, maybe not. She should have some sort of a socialising area for when the girls come round. She goes to the next room: the kitchen. She'll be doing that Nineties thing soon enough: cutting up fruit and veg on the chopping board with a glass of wine nearby. Gone are the days of maids; the days of do-it-yourself are here.

She goes up to the second floor, bounding up the stairs like she's coming on stage. A couple of smaller rooms lie here: a bedroom and another living room. She'll sleep and relax privately here. No one will be able to come here. Can she seal off the landing?

The third floor is made up of two more bedrooms, according to the leaflet the estate agent provided her with. One of these she'll convert to a study. She's a professional, isn't she?

"Scarlet, you in?" a voice calls up.

She comes back down.

Gina's in the hallway. She's holding a small giftbag marked *Gucci* and wears a cotton trench coat; the wraps are slightly undone.

"Gina, lovely to see you!" Scarlet gestures her into the soon-to-be living room.

"Yeah. Didn't get much of a chance to catch up at that New Year thing."

Scarlet bows her head. Roger Miser's idea of a New Year celebration in the most boring cocktail bar in London didn't exactly fill up her spirits. Afterwards, though, Josephine phoned a friend of a friend, and soon they were at a place in Camden Town, some rich club, dancing in the early hours.

"Listen, it's about Josephine," says Gina, undoing her coat, then realising that there's nowhere to sit. "I'm really worried about her."

"Why?"

"Well, you know she's been dating Eugene..."

"Yeah, I figured that one out long ago, Gina."

"But I'm worried. Eugene – he's not exactly... well, stable."

"I can't control Josephine's life. Mauro and I had dinner with Josephine and Eugene just before Christmas. Didn't see anything out of the ordinary. Eugene's a bit... *common*. He's a bit of a lad, but... Look, what did you see?"

"Well, I popped over to Eugene's flat two days ago. Josephine suggested I come over to lunch with them. I mean, I just didn't feel comfortable. There's something about him."

"But you don't have any definite proof, do you? Proof he's been mistreating her? Or anything?"

"Nothing firm. But I have a really bad feeling something'll go wrong."

"Gina, we can't base things on raw emotions. Look, I'll have a chat with Mauro. He's coming over later."

"Okay." Gina looks around her. "Wow, you've done really well here."

"This house is all that and a bag of chips," Scarlet replies, smirking. "All that and a bag of bloody chips."

When Mauro arrives, hair swishing over his eyes, a bottle of white in his hands, she's hesitant to talk to him about Eugene. In truth, she knows that Eugene is someone who could be abusive in a relationship, but, well, Josephine's chosen him.

"Nice place!" exclaims Mauro.

Scarlet silences him with a gentle kiss on his mouth, and then leads him through to the kitchen. She's assembled some canapes and a few empty glasses. They're going out to dinner later, but she wants to make a proper evening of things.

"It's cold outside, so the wine should be fairly chilled," he remarks, cracking it open and pouring them each a measure.

"I'd love to live in America," she says. "New England."

"That was a bit random!" he laughs. "Why New England?"

"I dunno. Just always liked the openness. Everything sometimes feels a little cramped here."

He wraps his arms around her waist and pulls her close. "You don't need New England just yet."

"Maybe I do."

"Before moving country, at least take some time to think about it. And there's us to think about as well."

"Of course. You know I'd keep you informed, don't you?"

"I know that. You have something on your mind, I can tell."

Scarlet strokes his boyish hair. "I'm a bit worried about Josephine and Eugene. It's just, Eugene's a bit aggressive, a bit of a lad, if you know what I mean. I'm sorry to bring this up..."

"It's okay, I know exactly what you mean. Eugene's always been a bit on the rough side. It's just the way he is. When we were kids, I was always into arts. Eugene was very competitive, you see, and wanted to be the opposite. He loved working out and showing his muscles off, trying to pick up girls, boxing, stuff like that. Yeah, he can be quite aggressive and forceful, but he's not dangerous or abusive. I'll check in on him, though, keep him in check."

"You use those words, *keep him in check*, and that worries me."

"Sorry, wrong words. Listen, don't worry, okay? He won't lay a finger on Josephine, of that I'm certain."

Mauro holds Scarlet tighter. She doesn't want him to let her go, yet she's desperate for another glass of wine.

"Let's get these canapes finished," she whispers. "Then let's get dinner. Spent enough time unpacking crap today. Need to be out the house for a bit. Oh, you fancy stopping by Blockbuster after?"

"I think Blockbuster's a bit below us!" exclaims Mauro. "Well, if you insist..."

"I do."

"We'll see what delights they have on offer."

Josephine

23 January 1992

Always sad moving out. Yeah, don't be so melancholy over it.

I've got the last of my things inside the bag that's come to New York with me on both occasions. It's strange, but this journey to West Brompton feels longer than a journey over the ocean. And it's a new start, because the flat I've bought there is going to be Eugene's as well.

The girls are concerned, especially Gina, but you get to the point in your life when you have to stop listening to those voices. As much as I would fight a duel for Gina, she really is starting to take the piss.

As I head out, I take a final look at the apartment. It's not as though many memories got made here, what with Scarlet hiding away all the time. I'll be glad to be gone. I clench my fists as I think of the day that useless bastard dumped me and walked out. I scowl.

I head outside into the cold where my taxi awaits me. There's a moment of panic when I think it's the driver who took me to the awards. No, it isn't, thankfully. I told Roger about the incident and he's assured me that the necessary *precautionary measures* are underway. He wasn't annoyed that I hadn't disclosed this to him earlier, which I thought was odd. Eugene doesn't know, neither do the girls.

When I arrive at my new address, I smile at the sight of Eugene ordering people around. He's got them in an efficient operation: moving boxes, cases, bags, loose things and instruments with military precision through the entrance to the apartment block and up the six flights of stairs. When he sees me, he thumps his fists against hips.

"My, my, my," he says, laughing. "Got to keep these guys in check."

"Bloody hell, you have," I tell him. "What are you wanting to do tonight?"

"I've heard there's this new posh takeaway nearby. Not your working-class crap, but proper special food. I'm totally up for giving it a try. And I bought a bottle of red as well."

"That's good. Listen, I was wondering if I could talk to you about something."

Eugene steps backwards, spreading his arms. "Sure! I'm an open book."

"Maybe once the guys have left."

"Not a problem."

When we've finally got privacy, I tell him everything. We're sitting at our new kitchen table in our new apartment, and I'm bleeding the information out, profusely. How I applied for the course. The day I arrived at the school to start my training. The initial nerves and excitement. My smile drops as I talk about how I struggled with behaviour management. How I was disciplined by my supervisors. How the kids made my life hell. The day I left the programme after being screamed at in the corridor. The humiliation. The tears and stress. About the stupid taxi driver digging it all up.

"Sounds terrible," says Eugene, taking my hand. "Look, you okay about it?"

"It was a long time ago..." My tongue catches. Even though it was a lifetime ago, it still feels like five minutes. Sometimes I wonder how I stuck it out.

Eugene sighs. "It's great you've told me about this. You shouldn't be ashamed or anything."

"It's hard not to be."

"Well, look at you now. You're part of a really successful band. You go on tour all around the place. Come on!"

"Eugene, I'm having trouble letting it go."

"I've got the perfect cure for that. What was the name of this school again?"

"Rainham John Graham."

"Bloody hell," he smirks. "Fuck. Sounds like somewhere posh nonces send their kids to. You remember the way?"

"Yeah, think so. Why?"

"I'll get the bike out."

"Are you taking the piss?"

"Do I look like I am?"

Eugene dashes off and returns seconds later with his biker's jacket strapped tightly to him. He's dangling his keys from his forefinger, as if he's trying on some level to taunt me. He leads the way down the stairs and then through a narrow road to the car park. This is proper luxurious parking, which we share with this historian guy who lives below us. His blue polished Jaguar winks at us. Eugene undoes the lock around his motorbike and powers it into life. He hands me a helmet at the same time he dons his.

"Don't be shy," he says.

I climb on and pull the helmet over my face. He doesn't waste any time in setting off, revving the engine as far as he can go. I hang onto him as he winds the bike through the dying afternoon. The traffic hasn't built up yet, but it's threatening to get busy soon.

"First time on a motorbike?" he asks me over the roar of the engine.

"Yep. Not as nervous as I thought I'd be, though!"

"Hold tight!"

It's exhilarating. Adrenaline sets my body on fire. I forget about the school, about my past. Even as I'm giving him directions. Even as I pass streets I haven't passed for years. Even as the familiar smell of the tarmac climbs through my senses. Even when we're pulled up outside the front gates.

"Horrors beyond imagination," I say to him.

The school gates are still the same useless rusty things, the spikes like chewed fingernails. There's activity inside and dozens of figures shifting past windows. It's like watching ants. It must nearly be kicking out time. I can see one of the classrooms where I used to teach. Christ, those godawful scarlet roses are still there, overgrown and sagging. Mr Merton's sickly roses. When I was having a really bad class and getting things thrown at me, I'd look at those roses, letting them take me away to some other place, somewhere beautiful and exotic. Then I'd come jetting back to a telling off from Mr Merton.

"I'd like to leave now," I say. "Let's get that takeaway."

"Not yet."

"Eugene, come on."

"Why are you so uncomfortable, Josephine? Why?"

"Let's leave." I hear the bell go. "Eugene, come on!"

"Let this place go," he says sternly. "Tell it to go fuck itself."

"Go fuck yourself."

"A bit louder."

I clear my throat. "Go fuck yourself."

"Better. Wasn't so hard, was it?"

Kids are emerging from the building. They're flocking in our direction.

"Right, Eugene, let's get home."

"Not yet, need to see it for myself."

The kids reach the fence. I don't recognise the teacher on duty in the playground. Hold on, I do! Mr Vernon. Still as cross as ever. Used to help the kids take the piss out of me.

"Eugene, come on." I'm pleading now. "Eugene!"

"You're so scared of this place, and I can't see why."

Mr Vernon's unlocking the gates. Even from here, I can hear him grumbling under his breath as kids push past him, sprinting onto the pavement. My heart pounds in my throat.

"Who was the guy who told you off just before you got thrown out?" asks Eugene.

"Mr Low."

"Sorry, babe, can't hear you..." The engine falls silent. "What you say?"

"Christ, Eugene!"

"What was the guy's name?"

"Mr *Low*!" I hiss. "Now –" I stop talking. Another teacher has joined Mr Vernon and they both enter a dipped conversation.

It's Mr Merton. He looks a lot healthier and fitter. And he seems to have aged down as well.

"You know them?" says Eugene, nudging my leg with an elbow.

"Yep. They both gave me a hard time, if that's what you're after."

"How about we say hello?"

"You're not serious, are you? Eugene, can't we just get out of here?"

The teachers glance over as us, like cheetahs about to pounce on wounded prey. There's recognition in their eyes, but surely they can't see me with this helmet on.

Suddenly the engine jolts into life. Eugene gives it a few revs, turns us around, and launches us off. Seconds later, the school is a fading memory.

"Why are you so afraid of it?" he shouts. "Why? Fuck them. They're a bunch of imbeciles. Look like a group of cunts anyway. So, why you scared?"

"You know something? I've no idea. But I don't want to go back. Never in a million years."

"Wise choice. Now let's get that takeaway."

He's right. I hold onto him tighter. He's absolutely bloody right. Why am I scared of them? Back then, I was young, silly and vulnerable. Not now.

Scarlet

1 February 1992

The restaurant's called something unpronounceable, and it's situated a quarter of a mile from her new home. She was a bit hesitant at first (mainly because of the threatening weather, and subsequently the fear of food poisoning), but Mauro's got this knack of persuading the unpersuadable. His gentle voice, soft eyes. He could talk love to an iron ingot. That's him. That's why he's struck the music industry like a hammer. That's why she loves him. That's why she shouldn't love him.

They walk through the crisp evening, the chill biting at her raw knuckles. Mauro has his arm draped over her shoulders. She likes the feeling of him next to her skinny body, likes how it makes her feel protected.

It should be a good night. A top-notch meal and a bottle of wine.

But she knows he's anxious. She's worried sick as well. They've been in silence for the past two hours, ever since Josephine left. She came by just after lunch to have a chat about song lyrics. That wasn't the problem, dear reader. The fact that she had a black eye, that was a cause for concern.

"Walked into a lamppost, can you believe it?!" she exclaimed, uselessly fighting back tears.

It didn't take long for them to tease out the truth.

"Something will have to be done," Mauro said, after Josephine had left.

"Feeling famished," he tells her as they turn a corner. The restaurant's up ahead. There's a low hum emitting from it. The noise of warmth, friendship and companionship.

He acts like the true gent he is when they arrive, nudging her through the door and handing their coats to the waiter.

It's not too shabby, she realises. Lines and lines of lanterns crisscross the ceiling above cubicles lined with bamboo fences. It's like something from *The Jungle Book*. So much so she shudders at the memories of watching it in primary school, jostling with the others for a clear view. Her breath pauses when she briefly thinks that it's a kids' restaurant. The horrors of children running around, screaming, throwing things. But when the waiter shows them to a cubicle, promotes the *very expensive* wine list, she knows it's okay.

"Chateau Latour," says Mauro. "The bottle, please."

"Excellent choice, sir."

"We're going to have to do something," says Scarlet.

"Christ, can't you give it a rest?" Mauro seems to want to stand up, but Scarlet can see the fight in him. His eyelids flutter, hands clenching. "Sorry, babe, didn't mean it like that."

"We should really report this to the police. I don't think it's right to let Josephine go back home to him."

"The thing is..." He's clearly exasperated. "I don't know how to say this... Josephine's made her choice. She has to be the one to call the shots on this. Unless we see her like this again, we can't really call the police."

"So, you think we should just let this go?"

"I don't think we have a choice. The onus is on Josephine."

"I can't believe I'm hearing this from you, Mauro. This isn't right."

"He's my brother, Scarlet. He's family." Mauro's face is swallowed by his hands. "If you want to do something, then that's your call, but I can't have any part of it. I won't."

The wine is delivered in professional silence. Uncorked with precision. Allowed to breathe.

"I didn't sleep the other night." Mauro's sitting up now, eyes alert. "I was lying there staring at the ceiling. Because I wished you were with me. I'm falling in love with you, Scarlet. I don't know why, I don't know how. But I am."

"You're a strange man, you know. But you're honest. And it's the honesty that I'm falling for. I think I'm in –"

"What the hell do you think you're playing at?!"

Something lands hard on the table, a fist, knocking one of the glasses over, threatening to tumble the other. She just looks at the tight fingers, for a moment thinking that they might be Mauro's. The anger and hatred spews over them.

"Think this is some kind of fucking joke?!" yells Eugene, withdrawing his hand. He's not drunk. Actually, he's never seemed more sober. "That's *my* girlfriend!"

"Okay, calm down," replies Mauro. He's stammering like a lunatic.

"Then don't abuse her!" shouts Scarlet.

"Shut it, bitch!" Eugene yells at her. "Just shut the fuck up! The both of you stay out of our relationship. I'm fucking warning you, you try anything, I'll fucking pull you to pieces. You fucking understand?"

He turns around and storms out, profanity falling over his shoulder.

Diners – celebrity diners – murmur amongst themselves. The headwaiter is telling everyone to stay calm, but his slurred speech shows how panicked he is himself.

"Maybe you agree with me now?" says Scarlet.

"You do whatever the hell you want." Mauro's response is free from emotion. "All I care about is eating. I've decided what I want. Have you? Christ, I'm fucking starving. Can we get some service over here please!" he shouts.

They have another bottle before they leave – the last vintage the restaurant has in stock. They drink until the late hours before they're turfed out at closing time. As they return to Scarlet's home, Mauro starts talking about himself, about his music, about his inspiration.

As if he's giving an interview.

When they reach her front door, he asks if he can come in.

"Why should I let you in?" is her question. "Given the way you've treated me tonight."

"Oh, Christ. Look, I'm sorry. Sorry about my brother deciding to ruin our evening. I mean, I should have known he was going to act up like that."

"Stop with the sarcasm, Mauro. If you want me, you start acting like a man."

"Getting the pep talk now?"

She ignores him. "I want you to spend the night with me. I want you to make love to me. I want to wake up with you tomorrow morning and hear you tell me you love me. Can you do that?"

"Why do you feel you need to ask me?"

She takes his hand. "It's too cold outside. I need you."

She knows he's right. Josephine's on her own. And what does she owe her anyway? Why should she play the knight in shining armour? She's done that enough in her life.

She's not sure when she says this, but she says it close to his ear. Two words that get taken for granted. *I'm sorry.*

Later in the night, it's followed by something else. Something rambling and vaguely incoherent. It's along the lines of: *"Stay with me."*

Susan

14 March 1992

When you're running, you don't feel the wind whisk past you, I don't anyway. You go into the wind. You plough through it, push it aside, like a bulldozer. That's how you should feel when you run. If you're just feeling it pass you, you're not doing it right.

I'm on Embankment, my feet pounding the floor hard. It's early morning, just before Seven. I don't care what time it is. There's a light drizzle in the air, just enough to make my hair cling to my neck, but not enough to warrant giving up.

Hardly anyone's out. Not on a Saturday morning.

I start hitting my breaking point. But this is where I enjoy it the most. When I'm starting to break, when I'm starting to fail. The thought, the fear of failure pulses through me, like the noise of one of our concerts. Every instrument plays its tune. Her voice sings. The audience screams along with her.

I could have gone to my gym instead. Warm, airconditioned, plenty of water, music. But nothing matches running through the crisp air.

Another runner passes me. He doesn't even recognise me from all the publicity.

Someone else does, though. My name is being called. From a distance. I ignore it. They can catch me on television. But the voice doesn't go away. It gets louder. It's following me...

"Susan!"

I turn around, about to blab out the *"Contact the record company if you want an interview."* line. The voice, the face, though, is much too familiar for that.

"Susan, it's been a long time!"

"You!" I hiss. "Seriously, get the fuck away from me!"

"Come on, let's walk and talk for a bit."

He's wearing a thin t-shirt, a raincoat, stained jeans and greasy trainers, and he's aged a bit, lost a little hair, gained some muscle, but he's still the same guy I met all those years ago.

"No, I won't. You leave me alone, okay? Seriously, go away or I call the cops." I start moving away from him. He doesn't control my life now.

He stops where he is, arms folding across his chest. He smiles, that awful toothy grin I remember. "We'll be seeing a bit more of each other soon, I promise you that!" he shouts after me. "Trust me!"

As I run, the rain comes on, hard this time. No, it's not rain. Tears collect on my cheeks as I begin to sob. Soon I stop running and fall down, arms crossing my thighs. Several runners pass me and it's likely they think I'm just out of breath. I glance back. I don't see him.

"Scarlet," I say out loud.

She comes over to my apartment in Shepherd's Bush at lunchtime. I pour us both a glass of white. She declines at first, but I push it towards her and she eventually agrees. I told her everything on the phone, but I tell her again, in full, rabid detail. He's still the same guy, the same loser I met in Bradford.

"He didn't threaten you, did he?" asks Scarlet.

"Not specifically, but his whole tone, his whole demeanour."

My kitchen is smaller than it should be for a flat like this. I've got this white marble table that stretches two thirds of its length and rough purple ceramic tile that covers the floor. We're standing at the black granite countertop, elbows on its surface. The bottle of wine and half-drained glasses form a No Man's Land between us.

"Though I can't understand why he's doing this." Scarlet looks disappointed. "He phoned you up last summer and now he ambushes you while you're out running. All because you grassed him up years ago."

"So?"

"This idiot could have done a hundred other things to get back at you. Why did he contact you once last year and once this morning? I don't get it."

"I'm not sure what you mean."

Scarlet refills our glasses. She leads me over to the table and takes a seat on one of the wooden stools. "I know about the Adler Point Hostel," she says blankly.

"What about it?" I know where she's going with this.

"It burned down in Eighty-Four."

"So?"

"In New York last year, you told me it burned down in Eighty-Seven."

"Did I?" I try to act unsurprised. "Slip of the tongue."

"A massive slip of the tongue, considering you ran away in Eighty-Five." Scarlet empties her glass. "Tell me what really happened, because I know you're bullshitting me."

"I'm not lying to you, Scarlet!"

"Not so sure. You see, if you'd really run away back then, why didn't the police speak to me? I remember Nineteen-Eighty-Five quite a lot. The police didn't speak to anyone, not my parents, not Alastair, not a soul. Why didn't the police speak to any of the teachers at our school? Now, I haven't spoken to your parents, but I'm sure if I did, then I'd get some interesting answers."

I'm defeated now. How can I fight against her?

"Will I get the truth?" she demands.

"Do I need to tell you?"

"Of course not." She clasps my hands. I stare at the fragile fierceness in her eyes. They seem paler than usual, like melting snow.

I guzzle my wine, but I feel her fingers move the glass to the side.

"Tell me," she whispers. "But only if you want to."

"If you'd gone to speak to my parents, you would have found out that they weren't my parents. I was orphaned when I was three years old."

"Oh my God, I'm so sorry." She's genuinely shocked.

"I'm originally from Bradford. I was put into a dingy children's home where I stayed until I was twelve. It was full of the unwanted. Kids whose parents were junkies. Many around me had been abused. You could see it in them. At night, we were locked in this dormitory. Kids around me would cry themselves to sleep. Sometimes Mr Ralston would come in and scream his head off. *I'm tryin' to sleep, ya little shits. Shut ya gobs or I'll smack ya jaw shut meself.'* The beatings were the worst though. But you don't want to know about that, trust me. You want to know about Rowan Colt."

"Whatever you're comfortable talking to me about." She's even more shocked now. Pampered little girl never thought she'd hear this sort of stuff. I don't think she even believed this sort of stuff exists in the real world. "Though," she tells me, "I want to hear about the abuse."

"Trust me, you don't. But anyway, when I turned eleven... my eleventh birthday, actually... this new kid arrived. What I said about him trying to inject his baby sister with heroin, that was true. He'd been disowned by his parents over it. Turfed onto the streets. Anyway, that's what I overheard Mr Ralston saying. Rowan was the same age as me, but he acted like a grown thug." I pause, trying to stop the tremoring in my throat. Scarlet doesn't put a consoling hand on me. "Rowan liked talking to me, but I was scared of him. Weeks and weeks of hiding around the next corner, petrified of his face. Then, I got the news I'd spent most of my life waiting for. I was being adopted. As you can imagine, Rowan wasn't happy. Jealous. He started making threats. *'I'll cut you up.' 'Dig a knife in your cunt.'"* I'm unsurprised I'm doing the voice pretty accurately. "Then, one day, my new foster parents came in, and I moved to Sevenoaks. That's it."

"Oh, my. I can't imagine how difficult it was." Now Scarlet touches me.

"I'm worried about what he might do."

"What can he do? He's probably in some grotty flat, on drugs, with a criminal record as long as this table. He won't do a thing. He's just a pathetic little bully. Nothing more."

I think about those words as I try to close my eyes that night.

I don't think I'll ever get that place out of my head. The fruit juice stains on the carpet. The splatters of blood in the toilets. The cigarette smoke wafting off Mr Ralston's cardigan. I hear the screams of the children in the bed next to me. The howls deafen me even through the silence surrounding me. I bury my face in my pillow, wishing I could forget it. I roll over, face the ceiling, breathing deep.

I manage, somehow, to let it go. I focus on what I am now, the band that I play in, the touring, the excitement, the afterparties.

A piercing ring billows through the room. My hand flies out, picking up the receiver.

"Hello?" I ask. I know who it is.

"Susan, how are you? You were quite rude to me earlier. I was just trying to talk."

"This is seriously your last chance. I'm not being fucking funny, okay? Get off this phone or I call the police."

He's sniggering, cursing me. *"Really? Oh, Susan, you haven't changed one bit."*

"What do you want?"

"Do you know what it was like for me in that place? That despicable shithole? After you left, I used to get beaten up by Ralston. Used to love it. Some of the other boys would help out."

"Can't say you didn't deserve it. After what you did to your sister..."

"I never got adopted. Never found a home. I watched boys and girls come in and then they'd leave. Never really saw the sun until I was eighteen."

"Leave me alone," I tell him as firmly as I can. "Piss off."

"I want you to stay with me."

"You're sick in the head."

"You don't understand me. You will *stay with me. We're going to have a family together, all together in a nice little flat. Enjoy your time with the band, enjoy it while you can. Because*

you're gonna be mine soon. You think you got away from that place the day you were adopted, but I promise you, oh I promise you, your time with me is just beginning. Take care, you little whore. I'll be seeing you soon."

The line clicks dead.

I don't feel threatened. Even though I'm shaking and nauseous, I refuse to allow myself to be frightened. He'll never control me. I won't allow it.

I don't put the phone down. My fingers punch in numbers. Scarlet's husky voice picks up.

"Hey, it's me," I say.

"You okay?"

"Yeah, I'm fine. Come over."

"Has he contacted you again?"

"Nope."

"Look, I'll come over if you really need me to."

"Yeah, I'd like that. Is Mauro with you?"

"No, he's doing that gig in Dorset."

"Come over."

She lets out a growl and I hear the phone crunch down.

I leap out of bed, shower, think about putting on something nice. Not sure what to fling on. Aha. A black mini body-con dress – something I got before my time with the band. I hurriedly throw it on and check my lipstick in my dresser mirror.

It's brand new, this dressing table. Got it from a private auctioneer in Watford. Late 19th Century, from the deep heart of Oxfordshire. The girls don't know.

I have a horrid feeling she won't come. She's probably asleep.

I swill my gums with mouthwash and tidy up the bath-room. I'm not a bloody student. Though the bathroom is small, it should be treated as though it belongs to a queen.

I tiptoe around my apartment. Nothing to do except wait. I check the bathroom once again, tidy magazines in the kitchen, plump up cushions in the living room, cross through to the bedroom where I turn off the unnecessary lights.

The buzzer goes off. I don't even take basic precautions. Moments later, there's a thud outside and Scarlet's voice calls out, "Hey, let us in, would you."

I pull the door open, seeing the surprise in her face when she sees what I'm dressed in. I don't wait for her to back down. I drag her in, slam the door shut, and kiss her hard.

"This isn't right," she mutters.

I can taste the cigarettes in her mouth. Somehow it makes me want her more.

"I don't care," I say to her. "I don't care."

"Just tonight, okay? Just tonight."

I hold onto her, nose buried into her shoulder. Her mouth touches mine. I allow her emotions to wash over me. I don't care anymore about the consequences.

Gina

18 March 1992

It takes me the best part of fifteen minutes to work up the courage to go inside the church. I sit against a cracked stone wall, staring at the spire poking heavenwards, wondering what the tabloids will make of this.

The street I'm on in in Fulham is decorated with leaflets with a smiling picture of a Labour Party candidate on. They catch the wind, flapping around, stopping me from leaving.

I walk up to the church, pass through an iron gate, and nod to the thirty or so headstones scattered in the graveyard.

The church is sealed by a giant oak door, the kind of thing you see in medieval films. A black ring hands at its right. There's a small carving on it, faded by years of abuse. I stare and focus my eyes, but I can't make out what it is. I grip it hard and slam it several times against the wood.

The man who answers it is around fifty, with a balding head and trimmed beard. He wears these really groovy circular glasses that barely cover his eyeballs. He's dressed traditionally, with the robes and everything. I fear that I've disrupted a service: such is the look of angst on his face.

"Yes?" he says.

"Sorry, have I interrupted something? I can come back later."

"No, it's okay. I'm just tidying up. What can I do for you?"

"I'm interested in religion."

"Excuse me?"

"I have developed an interest in Christianity." I try to emphasize the last word, but it just doesn't connect with my tongue in the way it's supposed to.

"You can't just have an *interest* in Christianity, you must believe in it," he tells me. "Look, I know who you are, okay. And I've got a fair idea of why you've come. Touring around with the band, partying until the early hours, it's taken its toll, hasn't it? And you've come for a sense of salvation. You've come here to cleanse yourself of your sins. Well, this isn't a charity."

"Then maybe I should try another church, or another vicar."

He sighs, folds his arms, and nods his head backwards. "Five minutes. Come on in."

As I enter, I swear it gets colder.

The inside of the church is just as you imagine it in children's books. Rows of wooden pews glisten in the coloured light coming through the stained windows; bibles are stacked neatly at the ends. There's an altar table with a silver goblet and a collection of bronze-coloured plates spread out across a silk cloth. A pulpit peers out, ready for the vicar or priest to give his sermon to the congregation. In fact, the whole church seems to have a sense of readiness about it.

"Why does God interest you?" he asks. He heads over to the pulpit and bounds up the steps; at the top, he shuffles a collection of papers.

"I'm searching for a greater answer to things," I say.

"Surely you can find that in your music. My nephew loves your music. He and his friends want to come to one of your concerts someday. He told me recently that it provides so many answers to all his burning questions."

"Are you saying that we are godlike figures then?"

"Of course not!" He looks upwards. "What I mean is..." He tilts his head back to Earth. "What I mean is, if my nephew can see the answers in your words, surely you can find that sense of greater meaning in them."

"For a man of faith, you seem to be pushing me away."

"I'm not doing anything of the sort," he tells me. He looks like he's about to protest. "You must understand, though, that if you want to commit to faith, truly commit, you must have an understanding of what is involved. What are you hoping to get from this? Are you hoping to become a priest or a vicar? Study is required for that, intense study. Are you ready to make that kind of a commitment?"

I try a feeble response, but I'm forced into silence.

The vicar smiles at me. "Look," he says, "here's some advice. Why don't you come along to Sunday Service this week?"

"I'd love that."

"Excellent. We start at ten o'clock, so perhaps if you get here at Half-Nine, before the congregation arrives? I can show you around."

"Thank you. Sorry, I haven't introduced myself. Gina."

"Lovely to meet you. I'm Father Aidan Haynes."

"Take care," I say.

I head to the door. He doesn't bother opening it for me. He stands in the pulpit, a kind smile hanging from his face. He's bathed in the coloured light streaming through the windows. There's a certain beauty about it, an authoritative glimmer that cuts deep within me. Even after I've walked outside, I still fell his presence. It's only when I'm halfway down the road that I realise it wasn't Father Haynes, it was something much greater, something beyond my comprehension, something godlike.

It's a short walk back to the flat. I hear the phone ringing as I enter. I think that I barely pick it up in time.

"Yes?" I answer, breathless.

"Hi, is that Gina -----?" the raspy voice enquires.

"Yes, this is me."

"Hi, I'm from the ----- Magazine, and wanted to arrange an interview with you."

"You will have to go through my record company. We had a bit of an incident recently with a hoax magazine."

"We spoke to Mr Miser earlier and he has agreed. Has he not mentioned this to you?"

I'm eager for my little bit of fame, but I'm cautious. I think I'm the wariest member of the band. It's a wonder they let me join.

"Well, I'll speak to him and confirm, then I'll be in touch. How can I reach you?" I quickly grab a notepad and pen, conveniently rested against a brass ornament of a golfer, and take down their details.

After hanging up, I check with Roger, and soon enough the interview is scheduled in a week's time at their head office in Hackney Wick.

It's good to have the limelight. Scarlet and Josephine are the ones everyone thinks about when it comes to the band.

Kids worship them, men get drunk thinking about them. I'm the silent, obscure soul playing the drums.

I have a good feeling about this interview, and I know God will be with me during it.

Josephine

26 March 1992

Gina and I will be having words later, that's for sure. Can't believe she did that interview without letting the rest of us know. Roger only phoned me last night about it.

"Great success," he said. *"The magazine emailed me across a transcript and I've sent it to you."*

I'm still getting used to emails, and I don't think I'll ever fully get to grips with them. It took me half an hour last night to figure it out. If it wasn't for the three shots of vodka to go with it, I think I'd still be hitting buttons. I read through the transcript, imagining Gina's sardonic voice, as I encountered the mysterious ways of God and Jesus. I snorted at first, then grew the wings of embarrassment.

I'm on my way to confront her now. With only a small breakfast quickly shoved down, I stomp along the street, sweat building around my waist.

Is she openly mocking this band? Is she trying to mock me?

There's something off with her. The warnings signs have been there, ever since the incident with the teacups. I should have kept a close eye on her. The girl's unstable. Won't be long before she's a liability.

For March, there's a distinct chill in the air. I'm imagining it, most likely. I pick up the pace, storming in the direction of Fulham.

Someone calls my name.

I stay calm, remembering what Roger said about these types of situations. *Tell them firmly but politely, "No comment." Then walk on.* I turn around to face whoever it is, but they're clearly not a journalist, judging by their overly formal clothes, and I'm certain they're not a fan who'll jump on me.

"Josephine?" the woman says again. Her handbag swings from her shoulder like a demolition ball. She's got this blonde hair that hangs way too low. She takes out a small band and ties it in a ponytail, never for one minute taking her eyes off me.

"That's me," I say. "I'm not giving any comments on Gina's interview, or any other band-related business. You'll need to approach the record company about that."

"No, it's me, Bella," she says. "You probably don't remember me, but we were on the same teacher training course."

"Oh, yes."

Oh, fuck.

Shit.

Christ, I give Scarlet a good telling-off, but now my tongue hangs like a leaf. This woman, who I haven't seen for years, stares at me like something's growing out of my forehead.

"So, you're in that band now?" she says. "That's incredible. I love your music."

"Thanks. So, are you still in the teaching game?"

"I am indeed." Bella's makeup glistens with her arrogance. "I teach at this comprehensive in Orpington."

"Is it a good school?"

"Yeah, it's okay. Money's pretty good. Hopefully getting a pay rise soon. And..." She holds up her left hand, like it's her own little salute. I see a small ring of metal on her ring finger. "Engaged!"

"Congratulations!" Christ, I want to get drunk right now.

"Lovely guy."

"What are you doing here?"

"Oh, it's a teaching conference. Waste of time if you ask me!" Suddenly Bella gets serious. "Listen, I know you had a hard time at your placement. I heard things got rough."

"Well, it's in the past now," I tell her. "I don't give a shit about it anymore."

"I'm sorry it didn't work out."

"It's for the best." The anger rushes up like vomit. "You know something? I'm glad I failed that fucking course. Every fucking minute of my time trying to teach those vile little shits, every fucking minute a waste. I fucking hated every fucking second in that fucking school. I tell you something, I'd rather open my fucking wrists than go back there. Utter fucking awful place."

"You did have a lot of support on offer," says Bella. She's on the defensive now. Every member of that fucking profession is a fucking coward.

"Did I fuck. Support like: *You need to up your game. You shouldn't be such a pushover. You've got to be consistent.*"

"I should probably leave now."

"Go on then, fuck off."

Bella huffs and starts walking. The rage hammers at my temples.

"Go and tell those cunts at that conference that it's a shit profession!" I scream after her. "The way you treat other people is fucking diabolical!" I pause, allow my voice to lower itself. "You fucking think about that."

I walk again. My feet don't connect well with the ground. It's like the anger and the bitterness and the hatred is pulling me upwards. Twice I nearly stumble. Twice I want to shed tears.

I don't care that people are staring. I don't give a damn that they're seeing the band's guitarist break down. It's like I'm walking over molten iron. I'm feeling myself come apart. I'm trapped in the self-loathing and misery of my time at that school. No matter how badly I want to escape it, no matter how desperate, I'm still sucked in.

I don't raise my head until I'm outside Gina's flat. I quickly work my way through a cigarette and then bash my knuckle against the doorbell.

"Gina!" I growl. "You and I need to have a chat."

When the door clicks open, I'm up like a mad kangaroo.

"Gina," I hiss, when I reach her entrance. My body's shaking so much I nearly knock a plant pot over. I look at it with pity: beautiful, ornate paintings on the side, and something resembling a cactus growing through its soil. What the hell is it doing in this kind of place? This too-clean landing, with its school canteen flooring. "Gina, open up!" I call, just as the door swings open.

"What is it?" she asks, completely uninterested.

God, she's pissing me off. She's standing there, eyes blurry with sleep. She's standing there, wrapped up in a dressing gown that's got way too much fur on. Her hair's a mess, even with the sparkly hairband she's shoved on her scalp. She's totally ignorant.

"What the hell do you think you're doing?!" I shout at her.

"Sorry?"

"Giving interviews to magazines about religion. Have you any fucking idea the damage it'll do to the band?"

"Good morning to you too, Josephine. Coffee?"

"No, I don't fucking want coffee! I want an explanation!"

"You're not entitled to one," she whispers. "Now, are you going to get all moody or will you give me some peace?"

"You realise that they'll be laughing at us because of this? You realise that, don't you?"

"They won't be laughing at us." Gina smirks. "Just you, Josephine." She puts a finger on the rim of her door and pushes it shut.

"Fuck!" I screech. "Christ! Fuck!" I storm down the stairs, emerging into the morning air curling my lips.

There's nothing to do except return home.

I pick my head up, try to fight away the anger. I start walking, deep breaths circulating through me like cyclones.

An old couple on the other side of the street are consulting a map of some sort. The man has an umbrella hooked around his wrist and burgundy trousers that are just a little bit too long for him. Both he and his (presumably) wife are in thin blue raincoats. They see me and cross the road. Christ, they're gravitating towards me. Christ, I don't think they're fans. Shit, shit, shit.

"Excuse me, ma'am," the man says in an American accent. "Could you help us? We're a little lost and —"

"Seriously, just fuck off," I spit at them.

They're aghast. The umbrella nearly tumbles from his wrist.

"Welcome to fucking England," I say as I start walking again.

I arrive home in an even darker mood. The whole weight of the world is pressing on my neck. I'm so enraged, I feel drunk.

Eugene's in the kitchen when I come in. He's filling the coffee machine with powder, humming *Rhythm Of My Heart*.

"Christ in Heaven, Eugene, you wouldn't believe it!" I exclaim. I fill a glass with water and down it in one. "Headed over to Gina's to have a word with her about this interview she did that's totally fucking embarrassed the band. But, on my way over there, I ran into this stupid bitch I did teacher training with. Christ! I'm so fucking angry right now!"

Eugene doesn't respond. I don't think he's heard me. He hums and hums some more as he finishes setting up the coffeemaker. Only when he sets it going does he turn around, a face lacking any emotion.

"Just one of these fucking days," I mutter.

He comes up to me and hums another tune, but I don't know which one this is. His right hand swings hard, striking me across the cheek.

"Christ, Eugene!" I cry out.

He turns away and goes back to the coffee machine. When it's done, he takes his drink and sidles through to the living room. I can hear him opening a magazine.

Tears are snaking down my cheeks. I feel my body shaking. I feel myself falling down. I take deep breaths. Emotion ebbs from me. Suddenly I'm shrieking. I'm on the floor, wishing I could be swallowed by it. All of this is too much for me. It's weighing me down, compressing, crushing my bones. Too much.

Scarlet

7 April 1992

Does she regret what happened with Susan? A little bit, but what's done is done.

She lies on her bed, Mauro beside her as the last few minutes of this night tick away. The remains on an Indian takeaway glisten on the floor next to a used condom. He's nearly asleep, the post-sex exhausting sapping away his spirit. Scarlet's fully awake. She barely remembers anything of their lovemaking half an hour before.

What happened with Susan was wrong, a betrayal of every boundary of their friendship. But it was fun. But it was exciting. Susan hasn't said anything about it. No awkward glances when they all met with Roger and George yesterday. No tears. No regrets.

At one second past midnight, their new album will be officially released. It's been the talk over the past few days. Whispers, magazine articles, newspaper praise and snippets, mentions from fellow souls in the music business (as well as other mainstream celebrities), and pesky offers of interviews on radio and television. At one point, there was the possibility of the girls being invited on *Wogan*, but that fell through.

Scarlet saw a stack of copies of their first album a few days ago in a department store, scruffily positioned next to a stand decorated with the latest Steven Seagal VHS. She watched befuddled as customer after customer came in and bought them. When the stack was depleted, another load was taken from a closet. When that lot was gone, tempers frayed as one of the shop assistants – a pathetic little girl – told the crowd that they were out of stock.

In truth, she's worried about the fame. She thought at first that it was paranoia, but then she noticed the stares as she walked along the street. The eyes on her every footstep. The tentacles reaching out, threatening to snag her and crush her throat.

The pressure's building. How will the new album be received? Will it be good enough? Will it keep Roger happy? Nope. Will the sales and reviews keep Roger happy?

Mauro snorts something in his sleep. Then his head sinks deeper into the pillow. She throws one of her thin blankets over his naked form and lets herself shiver.

She shouldn't have eaten too much either. The spices are doing their familiar dance routine in her abdomen. Sitting up, she reaches to the side and grabs the quarter-full glass of red. She looks at Mauro, sighing at the realisation that he'll feel queasy in the early hours. He was eating like a pig earlier.

They've given up on Josephine. Even though she presents fresh bruises every time they see her. But what can they do? She refuses to leave him. Is it the stability she craves?

When the album comes out, Scarlet will need to brace herself for the rush of praise, the scathing reviews, the increased security. George warned her about this a few weeks ago. He was almost afraid to say the words, as if sensing the rough guys with the thick necks would come pouring in.

She thinks she's set the clock on the wall to the exact time, though she can't be sure. The second hand clicks around like it's taunting her.

When it's one minute to midnight, she thinks about rustling Mauro awake, but she doesn't want to disturb him. She watches the second hand in its final few strokes as it reaches the Twelve. She breathes in... as it leaves the Twelve... and out when it's finally one second past the hour.

The band's no longer a one hit wonder. No longer basking in the joy of their debut album. This is real.

"Is it time yet?" murmurs Mauro.

"Absolutely," says Scarlet.

9 April 1992

Roger smiles bitterly as he goes through the spreadsheet rolled out over his desk. He wears a thick grimace that seems to match his oily hair. He sips his coffee – freshly ground – and coughs loudly.

"Well?" demands Josephine.

"The album was released at one second past midnight yesterday," says Roger. "By close of business yesterday, five thousand copies had sold."

"Wow." As soon as Josephine's said this, she sits back down, running a hand over the split in her lower lip. She banged against into a cupboard door, apparently.

Scarlet barely takes in the news. Of course, she's wondering why they didn't sell *more*, but... She risks a quick glance over at Josephine. The woman looks dejected, but alert. She's the cross between a hangover and a bag filled with regret. Scarlet turns her attention to Gina and Susan. Both of them are smiling widely.

"Congratulations," says Roger. He looks behind him at George, who promptly produces a bottle of cava. "It's cheap plonk," Roger tells them, a comic mocking nature in his tone, "but it'll do for the moment." He nods at George, who proceeds to crack it open with a loud pop.

"My mother would tell me off for drinking this early, but she's not here," says George. He bends down, produces a series of dusty stem glasses from beneath Roger's desk, and begins to serve the booze.

"Listen, I need to shoot," says Josephine. She marches over to the desk, takes a glass, swigs it in one, and heads to the door. Just before she leaves, she turns around, tears in her eyes. "But we should have sold more."

"What the hell's up with her?" says Roger. "Come on, girls, get them down you."

"This can't go on," Gina whispers to Susan.

Scarlet's up in a flash. "I'm sorting this," she says over her shoulder. She winds her way through the building, holding back the urge to spit, fighting it. She shoots a dirty look at the office staff in the reception room, which has mysteriously grown over the past year. Outside, she looks about her, thinks about a cigarette, decides against it, and spots Josephine hunched on the kerb. The woman's keeled over, shrieking, sobbing.

"Josephine?" Scarlet says this like it's a fairy-tale.

"What the fuck you want?" replies Josephine, through a face of tears and mucus.

"Is it him? Has he done this to you?"

Josephine puts her head deep in her hands. Even from this distance, Scarlet can see the gentle nodding.

"Josephine, you can't live with this guy anymore. You need to get away from him."

"And be a fucking lonely loser? Why the hell do you think I live with an abusive loser like that?!" Josephine sits up, baring her teeth. "That's what you want to know, isn't it? Why I'm content living with a guy to punches me, abuses me, humiliates me. Because I have no one else! With Eugene, at least I'm not alone." She gets up. "I need to go now. Go, have a few drinks, celebrate. You deserve it." She's about to say something else, but it's like the tears have clogged everything up. She wipes her face with her knuckles and walks off down the road.

"Josephine!" Scarlet calls after her. "Come on!"

Words are of no use now. She thinks about going after the woman, but instead heads back inside to have her well-deserved glass of champagne.

When she's back in the officer, she finds Roger with yet another stack of papers. Gina and Susan seem to be giggling, like they've told some sick, naughty joke behind Scarlet's back. Even George – always a platonic sort of guy – has a mischievous look about him.

"What is it?" she asks her merry little crowd. All thought of Josephine has gone.

"New tour coming up!" exclaims Roger. "Later this year. Australia. I'll email you all the details. How are you finding this email nonsense, by the way? It's a bit nonsense. Still can't get my head around it."

"Tell me about it," says Gina.

"Right. You've got your U.K. tour next month. London, Cardiff, Newcastle and Edinburgh. Now, you're doing several venues in London. Can't remember which ones... Oh, not a problem. I'll email you all the details. *If* I can ever get the hang of these email things." Roger rubs his desk with his knuckles and takes another small sip from his glass. His eyes are glazed over with ambition and oil. George stands behind him, arms folded.

"We'd better organise a practice," says Susan.

"And soon," says Gina. "Scarlet, is Josephine okay?"

"Not really," comes her flimsy response.

"Listen, I know about what's happening," says Roger, standing up and casting his paperwork down. "Obviously, this can't go on."

"Yeah, obviously," says Scarlet.

"Try and find her before she drinks herself stupid," warns George. "All four of you are going on telly tonight."

"Some new music show on BBC1 that's just started up," informs Roger. "The guy who hosts it used to work on children's T.V. Forgot his name. Ah, it doesn't matter. Listen, Scarlet, go and find Josephine before she does something."

Why is she being ordered about like Private Joker in *Full Metal Jacket*? She nods at Roger, who tells her he'll send a car round at about Six to pick her up, and then heads back out. She gives orders of her own to one of the receptionists for a taxi. Well, she thinks, as she waits, at least she isn't Private Lawrence...

Josephine

9 April 1992

My lip hurts less now, but the mental image of Eugene swinging at me will be forever lodged in my mind.

Oh, I shouldn't be so fucking melodramatic. It's not as if I'm destitute.

Fuck, I'm scared though. I get the taxi driver to let me out at the end of the street, so I can sidle my way up to the front door. But what do I think's going to happen? I can't hide from this. I can't bullshit my way out.

I mean, maybe Eugene's got a bit of a point. I did yell at him a bit too loud last night. He lashed out. He lost control. These things happen. Get over myself. Stop being such a fucking cry-baby. That's what Eugene said last night, anyway.

I open the front entrance and head on up. I'm going to put this right. And he must be in a good mood, because I can hear jazz music humming from the flat.

"Hey, it's me!" I say, as I push the key into the lock and enter.

I hear Eugene's voice, but there's someone else there as well. Actually, a couple of other people. There's panic in their words. I think there's a swearword issued as well.

I go through to the kitchen to find Eugene with a can of beer in his hand, leaning against the countertop like he's posing for a home lifestyle magazine. Two other men are standing at the dining table; both are dressed in faded biker's overalls. It takes me a couple of seconds to realise why they look horrified. On the table is a sheet of aluminium foil. There's a pile of flour or baking powder at the centre, like some nursery child's model of a volcano. On two of the chairs are stacks of cash, held together by elastic bands. Eugene doesn't look worried. Actually, he's trying to hold back laughter.

"Oops," he says, bursting out sniggering. "Um, you weren't meant to see this, babe. I thought you'd be out all day."

"What the fuck is this?" I mutter. "Is this... Is this... *drugs*?"

"It's okay, we don't take the stuff," says Eugene, swigging his can. "I just make it and sell it."

"Eugene, this is our home!" I hiss. "What the fuck is that stuff?" I can't do anything, except point.

"Heroin."

"Fuck! And who are these two?"

"Phil and Ernie," he replies matter-of-factly.

The two men look as if they're about to collapse under the weight of panic.

"Calm down, babe," Eugene tells me, a sweetness in his voice.

"How the *fuck* can you tell me to calm down!" I howl. "This is our home! I've fucking paid for it! What about you, Eugene, when was the last time you worked? Or even applied for a fucking job?"

"Oh, fucking calm down!" he says, the aggressiveness in his tone rising like the sea. "You don't have to worry about anything, honestly. I mean, they paid in cash."

"I want this shit out of here," I say, hands trembling. "And I want you out of here, all three of you!" I see his eyes swell with distaste for me. "Out of here, all of you, or I swear to fucking God, I'll call the police. See how you like prison."

"No, you won't," he whispers. In a flash, he's dropped his beer can, fastened a hand around my throat, and pinned me against the door. "You breathe a word about this, I'll rip you apart. You're not a fighter. You're a pathetic little push-over. You think you can face up to me? You had a breakdown during teacher training, because of some stupid little children misbehaving. You're a flimsy little cunt who can't even look straight. Now you fucking go through to the living room and sit down on the sofa until we finish." He releases me, saliva hanging from his lower lip. "It's okay, boys, she won't say a fucking word about this, but —"

My left fist catches him below his right eye.

And then I'm hurtling away, falling away, falling down. I fumble my way through the flat like I've downed ten bottles of wine. I run, trip down the stairs, screaming, howling. And then I'm out, the clean and beautiful fresh air enveloping me. I'm stumbling along the road, hoping, just hoping someone sees me. I don't care about the humiliation, or what it'll do to the band. I just want to be safe. I just want to be free.

"Help!" I repeatedly yell. No one's listening. There's certainly no one rushing out, or even curtains being ruffled.

I'm wearing block heel loafers – yeah, the worst choice for this kind of activity. They threaten to trip me up, threaten to toss me to the ground.

I only stop when the exhaustion punches me in the gut. I hang forward, hands digging into my knees. No one's following me. Fuck, I need to run more. Take a leaf out of Susan's book. She runs. She was telling me about it just the other day.

And where am I?

I look back the way I came. Just a casual street with over-hanging trees casting their shadows. A car rumbles somewhere in the distance. My stomach rumbles. Clutching my belly, I realise that it's lunchtime. How long have I been going for?

A man walks past me. Normal, semi-rich kind of bloke with a checked shirt and black jeans. He's whistling with every footstep. The way he walks past me, the way he just casually strolls through his day, the manner in which he opens the black gate and tiptoes up a garden path to his pale stone de-tached house, it really pisses me off. Can't he see how screwed up I am?

"Excuse me!" I call out. "Excuse me!"

"Yes, can I help you?"

The door to the house swings inward and two screaming children rush out. They act like they haven't seen him in a life-time. A boy and a girl, around five years old, smiles and tears. Well, what the hell does Josephine know about children any-way? The man nudges the children back inside the house, yells something to (presumably) his wife, and then turns to me.

"Yes, can I help you?" the man repeats.

"Listen, I need help. Just been attacked by my boyfriend."

"Ah." The man's glasses twitch independently of his face. He looks astounded. Curious. His trimmed beard says as much. How old is he? Thirty? Thirty-five? He *is* a bloody academic. "You want to come in?"

"Yeah, if that's possible."

The man nods for me to go inside. I take a few cautious steps, then stride into the house, nearly stumbling over a toy crane. I don't know why, but I stoop down and pick it up. It's a Hornby, a bit like one I used to have as a kid. I gently put it down at the side of the hallway, and then notice how bare and barren the house seems to be: no pictures hanging on the walls; bare lightbulbs hanging from the ceiling, the shades removed like long-lost comrades; a general sense of absence and loss.

"You want a cup of tea or something?" the man offers.

"Yeah," I say.

"Sorry it's a bit chaotic at the moment. We're in the process of moving house."

"Who is it, hon?" a gentle voice screeches. A woman appears in the hallway, a flowery apron tied around her skinny frame. The two children are hanging from her legs, pinning her to the spot like a prisoner of conscience. Her look darkens. "Hon, get her out of here. I don't want her sort near the kids."

"She just told me she was hit by her boyfriend," the man pleads.

"She's in that band, that vile lot. Get her out, now."

The man looks as though he's being pulled apart. His words catch in his mouth. He's like me after I've had a few. Eventually he looks at me with drooping eyes and says with a modicum of politeness, "You'd better leave."

"Fine then," I respond. I turn on the spot and head for the door. Whispers flutter behind me.

I stand on the pavement for a few seconds, wondering which way to go. Before I know it, I'm off running again. Not out fear this time. I'm just running. Strange how these streets are so empty. Despite it being London. I take a right turn, then a left turn, then another left. I find myself on a constricted street that ends in a grove. I slow down to a walk, breathless. Perspiring. Birds chirp away from inside the scramble of trees and light.

It's out of place. That's what's wrong with it. It's *inappropriate* for the thing to be here.

Around me are semi-detached homes. Not so posh. Actually, they look deprived. A Cozy Coupe Classic car toy sits idle in an enclosed and overgrown garden. Cigarette smoke creeps out of a window and up the wall of the house, as if it's yearning to be free of the lungs of its owner. An overweight woman bursts out a front door, yelling behind her, a voice that's so scratchy it makes me shiver. Kind of like Scarlet when I first heard her sing. The woman downs the dregs of whatever's in her cup, wipes her hands on the stained flower petal dressing down that barely fastens itself around her, and lets out a loud, throaty sob.

I tear my eyes away.

I reach the end of the street, cross over a pavement, and enter the shade of the grove. It's like another world. Like something from a fairy-tale. Around me, there's silence. I fall deeper into the grove like it's consuming me. A thin shade of blue surrounds my feet. Blue flowers. Can never remember what they're called. I just need to wear a dress, a pretty one that's all pristine white.

The spotless environment is punctuated only by a small brown shack. It's an old, dreary thing, but, as I approach, I see glinting fresh nails that have been plunged in. I go up to the door, realising that it looks familiar to me. The way the wood is aligned, the scent of moss. I walk around to the other side, where the windows still have their slight cracks at the edges. It's Scarlet's shack. I only went to it a few times, but it's definitely the same one. How the hell did it get here?

A voice growls behind me. Thick and heavy, pushed to the point of becoming broken.

I turn around to see a dishevelled man in a dampish, dark green overcoat. He wears baggy pantaloons and sandals that show unwashed, neglected, cracked feet. A thick beard brushes the top of an orange t-shirt that looks to be coming apart. He's old, but he seems strong, as though his youthful days were spent in constant exercise. His hair hangs behind him in a loose ponytail.

"Who are you?" he asks. "What are you doing near my shack?"

"I'm sorry. It's just –" Do I really want to tell him about Eugene? The last people weren't interested. "I'm just taking a walk."

"Hardly anyone comes in here," he says. "Who are you?"

"Josephine. Josephine –"

"Don't need to know your second name. What do you do for a living?"

"I'm in a band."

"Are you successful?"

"Yeah, we are. Second album just released."

"Excellent. What is your band's name?"

I tell him, slightly reluctantly. As if it's my greatest secret. I watch the man lift his eyebrows, letting out a tiny sigh.

"Never heard of it," he says, after sighing again. "Actually, I don't listen to music at all. Don't read. Don't watch films. Why don't you come in?"

I hesitate, then find that I really want to see the inside, just to be sure it is Scarlet's shack.

"Where did this come from?" I ask, as he shows me inside, inserting a key into a brand-new brass padlock, which somehow I missed earlier.

"You mean my home? It was donated five months ago from Kent Council. Two friends had been wandering through this wood where I was sleeping. One of them, right little angel she was, their dad worked for Kent Council. She got a campaign going, raising money, that sort of stuff. In the end, the council had a rummage around in a few storage containers and found this. Used to belong to some artist. After she'd packed her residence in, the council seized it, but hadn't gotten around to tearing it to pieces."

The interior no longer has Scarlet's paints, easel, or coffee. It's lost that nicotine atmosphere and its sense of neglect and abandonment. Now there is a bunk with mostly clean sheets and a cardboard box filled with energy bars, crisps and sweets. On the top, with their complementary smiling faces, are a few packets of Double Dip and White Mice. Next to the box are three small bottles of water.

"I don't have a kettle, if that's what you're wondering," he jibes. He pulls up a camping stool from the floor and springs it open. "Sit," he tells me.

"I can't stay long," I reply timidly. "I mean, I'll need to rendezvous with the other bandmembers later. Kind of made an embarrassment of myself earlier."

"Then fix it," he says. "Don't spend your time apologising for everything. Seize the moment. I wish I had." His eyes seem to shrink further back into his head. His beard twitches as he sits down on his bunk.

"It's been a strange day." Indeed it has! I started the morning in the record company's office, now I'm chatting to a homeless guy in a grove in the arse end of London!

"You seem unhappy," the man says. "You are successful, but you're unhappy."

"Well, my boyfriend – I should say, ex-boyfriend, attacked me earlier. Came home to find him doing drugs."

"So leave him. Put him behind you. Forget about him."

"It's not that simple."

"Yes it is." He barks a loud cough. "There's something else eating away at you. I can see it. Something in your past is holding you back."

"I don't know what you mean." I want to get away from here.

Across the ceiling, several postcards have been taped and nailed to the roof. Strange faraway places. Tropical beaches. Cities thronged with crowds.

"You don't have to tell me if you don't want," he says. "I haven't exactly earned the right to be a confidante. Cheated on the wife, got drunk at work. Only a matter of time before I lost everything. It took me six years on the streets to sober up."

"I was a student teacher," I blurt out. "Humiliated, bullied, degraded at every turn. It was a long time ago, but I carry the scars."

"I'm sorry, it must have been hard."

"No one knows what it's like to wake up every day feeling sick with anxiety. What insults will be fired at me today? My mentors used to discipline me regularly, telling me how pathetic and useless I was, sometimes in front of the kids. But that wasn't the worst of it..." I gulp. "I mean, there was the day Mr Low yelled at me in the corridor, really yelled at me, reduced me to tears. Or how Mr Vernon used to help the kids make fun of me. Halfway through my time in that shithole, I was..." I hunch forward, digging fingers into my hair. I feel a hand on my shoulder.

"It's okay," he whispers.

"I was sexually assaulted." I don't want to admit to myself that I've said these words. Tears edge down my cheeks. I force myself to repeat this dreaded sentence. "I was sexually assaulted. A Year Ten pupil cornered me outside the toilet, put his hand between my legs. I yelled at him to get away and threatened to report him. Mr Merton saw the whole thing. You know what he did? Took me to his office, accused me of behaving unprofessionally. It's funny, I remember his exact words: 'You need to up your game.' Those were his words. His exact words."

"I'm sorry," the man says. "There are no words that I say, there is no comfort I can give, except this: you have to let it go."

"I don't know whether I can."

"Focus on the music, let your experiences fill the words and the notes. Now, I don't know who this Mr Merton is; he's clearly an idiot. But you have to let it go. Keep faith."

"Do you think I can?"

"I *know* you can." He takes my hands in his and looks straight into my eyes. I see the pain and regret in his face. "You're a beautiful young woman. Never forget that. You deserve so much more than to be trapped in your past. You need to live, not be sucked in by anger and hatred. Go back to your band, go and live. Now, you don't want to be sucked in by an old codger like me." He leads me up and shows me to the door, opening it to the fresh, untainted air.

"Thank you," I say through a mess of tears.

"Take care," he replies.

I start walking through the trees again. Briefly, I get lost, wondering if I should go back and ask for directions, but then I see the opening to the street. Upon returning to urban civilisation, I start the search for a payphone. End up walking down several more roads before I find one. I insert the change, dial Scarlet's number, readying my apologies.

"Christ, are you okay?" she says breathlessly, when I've told her what's happened. *"Jesus! Listen, I'll call the cops. He's going down for this. I promise you."*

"No," I tell her. "I don't want the police involved. It'll mean testifying. And I'm done with that. Just want to get my stuff out of there."

I can hear her sickly breathing. She's been smoking again.

"Okay," she says finally. *"Where are you?"*

Where the hell am I? I look around, desperately trying to identify a marker, then see a street sign partially covered in moss. It's embedded into a stone wall in such a way that it looks like it's being eaten. The rocks around it are rotting teeth.

I tell her. Discreetly.

As kind and calm as I can.

"Stay where you are. We're coming for you."

"Thanks. Scarlet, I'm sorry about everything. I'm so sorry."

"It's okay," she replies. *"Don't worry about it."*

But I'm worrying all the same. That's all I'll ever do now.

Josephine

16 April 1992

Finally, all sorted. The beauty of being rich, I suppose.

Moved into a nice house in Harrow. Upper and lower floor. Nice little garden, with everything to it: brittle plant pots, trimmed grassy edges. Kitchen. Dining room. The girls moved all my gear. Can't thank them enough. Don't think I'll ever be able to.

Yesterday, I went with the girls to the flat to say goodbye. Eugene was smoking a spliff on the sofa, chest bare.

"Good luck," I said to him. "How long do you think you'll be able to afford the rent on this place?"

As we turned to go, he said loudly and coherently, "You'll never be rid of me. I'll be back someday. Bitch."

Gina, Susan, Scarlet and I laughed. I think one of us jerked a middle finger as we walked out the building.

Just so glad to be rid of him. Just so glad.

I'm now sitting in my back garden, resting my bare feet on the yellowish patio stones. I'm sipping the last of my glass of red wine, a sense of freedom washing through me. I can feel again. All this pain, this anger, it's over. And it's time to let it all go.

Susan

8 May 1992

Here we go again.

It's Five A.M. Way too early for most. Not for me though. Arrogant little shit that I am.

Slipping out of bed, I stumble to the pile of running gear on the bedroom floor. I'm partially blind from the sleepiness. I'm totally blind by the excitement of what the day will bring. Fear. Nervousness. I slip the running gear on and head out into the mildly chilly morning.

It takes a few minutes for the drowsiness to wear off, but once it does it feels like I've been born again. I leave Shepherd's Bush and go in the direction of Hammersmith. I'm actually thinking about moving there. Slightly posher than Shepherd's Bush. Prettier and greener.

"Mornin', love!" a man shouts at me. "Nice legs you got!"

"You too!" I quip.

He's overweight, balding, in dire need of a few good runs himself! I laugh on the look on his face. His two mates with him (also overweight with bald patches) also laugh. I don't think he was expecting that!

By the time I reach Hammersmith, cold sweat clings to my neck and stings my eyes. When I reach the bank of the Thames, I force myself to stop and hunch over the railings. It's going to be a beautiful morning: already, the sun is beginning to fill the city with its purple orange light.

Today the tour begins. Four nights in London, then on to Cardiff. We've got a bunch of press things to do – I'm not sure how else to describe it! That's happening at Eleven. Then we get lunch at this ridiculously posh restaurant with Roger. After that, head to the first venue: Cadogan Hall in Chelsea. Tomorrow, it's that Powerhaus venue up in Islington. I know Radiohead have done that place. Good crowd, apparently. After that, it's a night at some place in Forest Gate, and then it's back to Cadogan Hall for the final night.

There's no one near me, except for a Sikh man and his wife opening up their newsagents. They're arguing about something, presumably the price of stock. I often see them out at this time, bickering away like it's the only thing they ever do. I wave hello to them, see if they respond; they don't.

I run along. I'm thinking of getting a digital watch to time my exercise properly. There's this one that's just come out: water-resistant, rubber strap, world clock. When this tour's done, I'm going to hunt one out. For now, I have to use my best guess.

I think I've been out for three-quarters of an hour. I spend another fifteen minutes going along the side of the Thames, then decide to head for home. By time I'm back, I don't think there's a square inch of me that's dry.

I've just exited the shower when I hear the phone ringing. The towel slips off me and I sit down naked on the sofa, water dripping from my hair down my back.

"Morning, Susan." I can hear Scarlet yawning on the other end.

"Hey."

"Listen, you fancy coming over for breakfast this morning?"

"I'd like that. Sure."

"Do you want Mauro to come round and pick you up?"

"It's okay. I'll ring for a taxi."

Mauro Lane smiles as he opens the door. He shows me inside, right through to the dining room with a friendly wave of his hand. Immediately I think that this must be an apology over Eugene... but it should be Josephine who's here. She's not present at the breakfast table, that's for sure.

"See you two have properly moved in together," I remark, as I take a seat.

A pile of croissants in the centre of the dining table glisten in the morning sunlight. There's a bowl filled with fruits, decorated on its edges with illustrations of ancient Chinese warriors. Scarlet brings over a glass pot of coffee, which she lays carefully on a placemat as though it's a flask of boiling oil. She and Mauro sit at the same time, at the head and foot of the table. They look at each other, produce pale smiles.

"Help yourself," says Mauro. He gets up, fills the mug at my elbow with coffee, and serves himself and his girl.

"How are you doing?" Scarlet asks me. She's hiding something.

"I'm fine. Sorry, can I ask what this is about?" I know what's going on. "Look, are you wheeling me out of the band?"

"No!" she protests. "It's got nothing to do with the band."

"It's to do with you," says Mauro.

"What have I done?" I ask, bemused. Of course, I know what this is about. But I'm hoping mouths have been kept shut.

Mauro takes a sip of coffee, runs a thumb over his babyish face, and stares at me hard. "I know about you and Scarlet," he says quietly. "I know the two of you have had sex."

"Shit," I whisper. "Scarlet, why the hell did you –"

"It's okay!" says Mauro. He takes my hand.

I try to stop the panic, then realise that Scarlet is looking relaxed. So is Mauro.

"Honestly, it's not a big deal!" shouts Scarlet, stifling a laugh. "No need to panic. We're not angry with you. Neither of us."

"You mean, you're cool with it?"

They both shrug their shoulders, as if I'm just a fly they've batted.

"Obviously, it can't happen again," says Mauro. "But I'm sure you understand that. As far as I'm concerned, it was a one-night stand; nothing more, nothing less."

"Same here," Scarlet adds.

"And here," I tell them. "Huh." My smile quickly drops. "I sense there's a catch to this."

"There's no catch!" he protests.

Of course there is.

We work our way through breakfast. It's a bit of an uphill struggle, at first, but I soon find that I'm enjoying the food. When we finish, Mauro proudly announces that he will make another pot of coffee. "Why don't we take it through to the living room?" he says. "Kenyan dark roast shouldn't be drunk at the kitchen table." He doesn't wait for us.

"He's such a snob," Scarlet whispers to me. "Honestly." She clicks her tongue and leads me through to the living room. Mauro's dishing out coffee into three extremely brittle-looking cups, so small that you couldn't fit your finger through the handles.

"Good coffee," he remarks, sipping noisily.

"Mauro, are you okay?" I find myself asking. I sit down on one of the leather sofas. Brand bloody new: sharp, black and shiny.

"I'm fine."

"Look, it's not your fault. What happened with Eugene."

"Oh, it's not that! It's..." His voice trails off. Like it's sand falling from the sky.

"Look, just tell me what's going on!" I cry out. "Christ, why can't the two of you be straight with me!"

"Maybe you and I should take a walk," says Scarlet. "Susan."

"Yeah. Sure, why not?" I lift my cup gently and put it to my lips. The coffee tastes that nice kind of sour.

They've done some major redecorating. Judging by the black-and-white pictures of African tribesmen wandering with a sense of purpose, one of them has befriended a travel photographer – a prominent one at that. There's a minimalist sense to the room as well. The walls are painted a very faint shade of grey that seems too perfect. There's a single shelf with eight VHS tapes on, including a *Die Hard* and *Die Hard 2* double pack.

Mauro slumps forward, nearly spilling his coffee. Carefully, he places it on the solid glass table and sits back, confusion washing over him.

Scarlet nips out and returns a second later with my coat. She pulls on her leather jacket, casts a look of defeat at her man, and leads me outside.

"Sorry about Mauro," she tells me, as we walk.

"Christ, Scarlet, why did you tell him about us?"

"I'll explain."

"I mean, I know it wasn't right and everything, but there was no reason to do that! Does anyone else know?"

"Don't worry. The three of us are the only ones who'll ever know."

"Why is he acting like this?"

"I'll explain."

"Well, we need to hurry. It's nearly Nine. Roger's expecting us at Eleven."

"We'll be fine, trust me." She looks behind her, very briefly, then turns around and her eyes light up. "Here," she says, pointing at the entrance to a small park. She goes first and I follow behind.

In the centre of the park is a fountain: a wide basin, with a short spout protruding upwards. Water dribbles down its side, back into the dark liquid beneath. Over the years people have thrown pennies in there; most of them have aged inside the darkness, their resting places forever.

Beside the fountain is a bench. Paling bright blue paint curls off the wood. Scarlet sits down, telling me firmly to join her.

"So, tell me what's going on." I do my best to keep a strong tone, but my voice is breaking.

"Why did you have sex with me? Considering that we're friends, close friends."

"Why did you agree to it?"

"Good question, I suppose."

"Look, it was a one-night fling. It shouldn't have happened. Why did you have to tell Mauro about it?"

"I'll explain."

"You keep saying that."

Scarlet looks away, rests her hands on her knees, and draws in a deep breath. "Mauro grew up in a fairly repressed household. Sex wasn't talked about. You know what I mean. It stunted his development a bit. I mean, you can see it in his music. He wants to... explore his sexuality a lot more."

"What do you want me to do about it? Go and call up a therapist."

"He had a couple of sessions. It didn't work."

"I'm starting to figure out where this is heading. He wants to have sex with me, doesn't he?"

"Not exactly."

"Go on, just say it. What does he want?"

"He wants to watch the two of us have sex."

"Sorry, is this some sort of a sick joke? Scarlet..."

"It isn't a joke." Her eyelids lower themselves. She isn't kidding. I know that look.

"Scarlet, you are off your fucking head!" I scream in a whisper. "All this... Bringing me over like this, subjecting me to that silent interrogation over breakfast, I thought... And it..."

I force myself to lower my desire to howl a few swear words. "All this stress and anxiety you've caused me this morning, just because you wanted to chat to me about your boyfriend's sexual fantasies. And I'm assuming he's not just going to be sitting there. He's going to be... you know..."

"Yes, he wants to masturbate in front of it."

"Scarlet, you always speak plainly, I'll give that to you."

"So, are you interested?"

"Fuck off! What the hell do you think?"

"We'd better go back and tell him then."

"And I won't mind telling him to get professional help. He fucking needs it." I need another cup of coffee. Something strong.

It's strange. I don't feel angry at Scarlet. Not a single shred of me wants to hurt her, or get aggressive, or take her out for a bitch fight. My feelings for her are like the park we're sitting in: green leaves, a gentle flowing fountain, and picturesque beds of flowers.

"Look, Scarlet, you know I can't do something like that," I say to her. "Come on."

"It's okay. Let's break the bad news then." Her hand flutters, brushing gently against mine.

We slowly make our way back, but pick up the pace when we realise the time.

Mauro's still in the living room, sitting there like an eager schoolchild, ears pinned forward. He droops when he sees the expressions on our faces. Disappointment, anger, rejection – a perfect combination – hang from his cheeks.

"Scarlet told me about your little... thing," I say. "There's a condition."

Both of them stop. I swear a heartbeat skips itself out.

"Actually, there are several conditions," I continue. "First, obviously, no one must know about this. No snippets of conversation, no drunken confessions. As far as I'm concerned, it will never have happened. I want the both of you to promise me that."

"You have my word," stutters Mauro.

"And mine," says Scarlet.

"I know, Mauro, the first thing in your head is: *Booyah! Can't wait!* I think it's easy, in the thrust of excitement, to easily promise things, so I'm going to make something else clear. If by some chance this should get out, I will deny everything and sue the two of you for defamation or slander, or whatever the correct term is. I don't care whether it breaks the band apart. I don't care if it fucks up your career, Mauro, and turns you into your brother. I will stop at nothing until the two of you are destitute."

"Susan," comes Scarlet's forgiving whisper.

"These are my terms. If you don't like them, you can forget it. Secondly, this little fantasy thing will take place the day after we get back from the tour, at my place." Something happens in Mauro's eyes. A flicker of panic. I barely register it, thinking he's probably got cold feet. "I would feel a lot more secure if it takes place at my apartment. Scarlet, you are going to tell Josephine, Roger and Gina straightaway, that you and Mauro will be coming over for dinner at my apartment the day after we return. I want that to be open knowledge. Then, should the paparazzi, snap a few photos of you two entering my home, no one will think anything of it."

"Is there a third condition?" asks Mauro.

"Yes. This will happen once and once only. I don't want any further phone calls or letters of teary pleas. This will be the only time this happens. Do I have your word on that, Mauro?"

"You have it."

"You have mine too," says Scarlet.

"I don't need yours. I trust you."

"Thank you for this." Mauro stands up. It's like he's been glued to the seat. He looks pained, anxious, uneven.

"Well, I'd better be off," I say. "I'll see you at Roger's office."

Scarlet

8 May 1992
Fifteen minutes later.

When Susan's gone, Scarlet allows herself a massive sigh of relief. Christ, she's sinning today, isn't she, dear reader?

"Mauro!" she calls out, realising the time. "Mauro, I need to head off in a couple of minutes. Mauro?" She goes to the living room, pokes her head through the door. His indent is still in the cushion. "Mauro?" she calls again. "Mauro, where the hell are you?"

She bounds up the stairs, checks every room. She's puzzled, her mind's twisted. She runs back down, goes to the kitchen. Their breakfast detritus is still there; it seems to smoulder in the sunlight.

A low voice hangs, barely, in the air. It's coming from the garden. As she runs for the back door, she senses something is wrong. Low voices. Has Susan come back? She pushes the door open, enters the green patch.

Mauro turns his head, startled, with the look of someone choking on anchovies. "Sorry, got to go, Rick," he says into the box next to his ear. "See you later, mate."

"Who was that?" asks Scarlet, demandingly.

"A friend." His face brightens. "That's the beauty of these things," he remarks, dangling the mobile telephone by its leather strap. "Have you ever thought about getting one?"

"Not yet. Don't need one. Emails are bad enough." She folds her arms. "Look, Mauro, I need to be heading off. I don't know when I'll be back, but it'll be the early hours."

"Sure." He comes over and embraces her. "You enjoy tonight," he says. "Enjoy it."

"Are you sure you're comfortable with this... experience?"

"I am," he says, after a slight pause. "Thank you."

"You don't need to thank me," she replies. "Maybe buy Susan a bottle of wine, or something?"

Gina

8 May 1992
10:45

I down the last of the coffee, offering a silent prayer, as I watch George and a few handymen do the finishing touches to the pressroom.

It used to be a series of recording studios, but last year Roger ordered the walls knocked down and the surfaces repainted. Four dusty rooms were fused into a pristine, brightly lit hall. A raised platform spans most of the back of the room; there, a table hosts four chairs, one for each of us. In front of the table, there are a bundle of microphones strapped to the floor, pointed up like they're in worship. Opposite the table are several rows of chairs where the members of the press will sit and devour us. Beside the chairs, nestled into the walls, are large video cameras; their lenses are sightless eyes.

"Why don't you go and join the girls?" says George. Sweat is collecting on his temples.

I'm not so keen to be with them right now. Especially Josephine. That whole thing with me talking to the magazine about the Church, I think she's over it now. And I did help rescue her from Eugene, and comfort her. But there's still some hostility. She needs a bit of space from me.

"Well, there's fifteen minutes... fourteen minutes until we go on," I reply. "Anywhere I can get a cup of coffee?"

"The coffeemaker in the staffroom is out of order, as they say. Roger's one, though, seems to be working. Well, it always is..."

"Thanks, George." I turn away, smirking. I whisper behind me, "God bless you." He doesn't hear... I think.

Unfortunately, I don't get anywhere near Roger's office. Josephine's sharp voice pierces the air behind me: "Hey, come and join us."

"You sure about that?"

"Yeah."

Hesitantly, I follow her lead. The room where the girls are gathered is like a holding cell just prior to execution (I've seen *Fourteen Days in May*), except for the table in the centre filled with pastries... and a coffee dispenser. Scarlet and Susan are hunched on the floor.

"How are you feeling about tonight?" Josephine asks me.

"I'm totally okay about it," I reply. "Actually, I'm more nervous about this press thingy."

"Oh, don't sweat about it," says Scarlet. A croissant dangles from her lips. She swallows it inside and grinds away.

"Just follow my direction," comes a deep male voice. Roger's entered the room. Stress and fatigue line his cheeks. "Not too long now, gals. Be ready."

"Do you think they'll ask us any difficult questions?" says Susan.

I dash over and fill one of the cream-patterned cups with hottish coffee. Scarlet grunts when a speck of liquid slams into her cheek.

"How are you settling into your new place, Josephine?" I ask.

"Oh fine. I mean, I miss having a man about the house. But, you know something, I'm glad that waste of space is out my life. I can't thank you enough for what you did. All of you."

"There's no need," says Susan. "We'd all so the same for each other."

"All of you are special," I say. "I know I'm into God and everything, but you're the most important people in my life. I don't know what I'd do without you."

"I wish Emma was still with us," says Josephine. She bites her lip. I can tell she knows she's gone too far.

"Emma made her choice," replies Scarlet. "She has to live with it. Wherever she is, whatever she's doing, I hope she finds peace."

"Yep." Josephine raises her coffee cup. "To us."

I respond in kind. Susan and Scarlet swiftly fill a cup each and return the salute.

We quietly consume our coffee, as if we're eager to let the bitterness slide down our throats, as if we're forced to drink the black liquid and choke on the pastries, as if this room really is the last room before execution.

George enters the room before we finish. Sweat stains the collar of his shirt. His tongue hangs from his lips like a dog's. Yet he seems livelier that he's ever been. "They're ready for you," he tells us.

We don't need telling twice. Even Josephine doesn't rally us. We don't say a word. We merely walk along the corridors without a shred of emotion. We're not vulnerable. But we're not invincible. We enter the pressroom with smiles and waves. We take our seats, facing the blinding flashes and the ruthless screaming of reporters.

Roger's walking around, chatting with a few of the journalists. Does he know them? Of course he does. Is that his woman in the corner, hiding from view? She still has that haunted beautiful nature about her, but there's a sinister sense of duty about her. I can't explain how I can tell this. I just know. Is God telling me this?

Roger moves himself in front of the platform, like he's shielding us. "Good morning, ladies and gentlemen," he announces, bringing the room to silence. "Thank you, thank you, thank you. It's great to have you all here. For those of you who don't know me, I'm Roger Miser and I operate this record company. In Nineteen-Ninety, I discovered this remarkable group of women. I took a chance and I haven't regretted it once. Two albums. Two brilliant successes. Today marks the beginning of this band's U.K. tour. Now, I *know* you've all listened to them, and now you have a chance to hear from them. Get some bits and pieces for your newspapers and television programmes. Right, over to the band."

Scarlet takes the lead, giving the press a brief history of the band. I notice her risking a few glances over at Susan. I know they're best friends and everything, but is Scarlet looking for inspiration or something? When she's done, the first of the questions arrives, of which we're all expected to provide an answer.

This will be a hell of a long session.

Josephine

8 May 1992
20:00

I've made peace with my past. Since that encounter with the man in that grove, I've felt myself heal. Each hour, I grow stronger. I slowly but surely begin to sever the brittle strings that tie me to that school. I don't feel like I'm hiding from anything.

Maybe I should go back to that shack. I should. Thank the old man for his words. His words of wisdom. I can't do it now, though. I'm onstage.

The crowd at Cadogan Hall has just cheered us on. Hooting, whistling, clapping, feet pounding the floor. A fucking earthquake.

Scarlet raises her arms in the air, howling her energy. Together, united, we start the notes, gradually building up the momentum. The first song emerges from the wave, exploding over the audience.

My fingers know the guitar so well that I can look to the side – just for a moment, mind you. Susan seems distracted. No, I don't think that's quite the correct way to put it. It's like she can't shake off the memory of a dream. Don't ask me how I came to that conclusion.

Then, there's a break in the music. I seize my chance. I pick up the microphone in front of me, speak quietly into it: "Come on, guys, you need to up your game!"

If only the girls got the joke. They look at me with a sense of distant weirdness. Then we resume playing.

I wish this moment would last – not *forever* – but for a lengthy period of time. But I know it will.

I've let the past go. My stupid ex-boyfriend. My old life as a teacher. All gone. The painful memories have washed out of me, swallowed up by the cheering and stamping feet of the crowd.

Scarlet

14 May 1992

The last night of the tour, for Scarlet, is not something that sticks out for her. She's tired, worn out, just wanting this damn tour to be over so she can rest. She's forgotten about Mauro's fantasy, well, his *exploration*; in fact, she's forgotten about Mauro. There's so much she simply doesn't have the time to think about. All she's focused on is this last night.

The tour's been a bit of a drag, if she's to be perfectly honest. In Cardiff, a scuffle broke out in the crowd and the girls had to be temporarily evacuated. In Newcastle, a power cut knocked them into darkness. Although it lasted less than a minute, it was enough to upset their rhythm. Thankfully the press haven't been interested in it much – according to Roger, whom she spoke to on the payphone at Newcastle Central Station just before they left. But she's keeping her guard.

The girls, though, seem to be in good spirits. They're clustered around her, pretty heads resting on the seats, disturbed only by the jolts of the train.

"We should go out for dinner tonight," says Gina. "Has George reserved us anything?"

"No, he hasn't," replies Josephine. "Look, we should do something, before the concert. Something we organise, not George."

"What about the Café Royal?" suggests Susan.

"I've heard about that," says Gina, stifling a yawn. She folds up the magazine she's blindly attempting to read, takes up the brittle cup of cooling coffee, and rolls her eyes. "A friend of a friend went there during their student days. Good beer, apparently."

"Then let's do it!" declares Susan.

"I don't care where it is, as long as I'm with you girls," Scarlet adds on. "That's what's most important."

They're met by two security escorts at Edinburgh Waverley Station, who silently escort them through the bustling crowds to the Balmoral Hotel.

Scarlet's slightly awestruck at her surroundings: the old buildings, the crammed traffic, the cheery souls pottering along the pavement. She's trying to recall if she's been here before. She's not sure. Each city she's visited is but a pin in the map in her mind.

Has she been to this hotel before? She's not sure of that either. She watches Josephine check them in. She's aware of the watchful eyes. Those dangerous eyes that spy on their every move. Is it an autograph they want? A contract? Or maybe their deaths. She's being paranoid. But she knows she's been to this hotel before. The days behind her stretch out, unravelling like string. Day becomes night. Travelling becomes resting. She remembers being on a plane, but she doesn't remember where she was going. It's like she's not in control. She's not certain if she ever was.

Josephine's calling for them to follow her. Scarlet follows, keeping her smile high, keeping her feelings in check. But she can't snap out of this daydream. Even if she could, would she?

She's in her room now, dropping her backs. The bed, the desk, the various decorative figurines, none of them have shapes, none of them have definite edges.

Someone enters. "Hey, Scarlet, let's go."

She's not sure who it is.

Sometime later, she's in this Café Royal, fingers curling around a tall glass of flattening lager. The girls are laughing, living in the moment. Living for what is, not for what was or what should have been.

She's aware that she eats something. Aware of Josephine's condemning, comical smile. Aware of Gina's (sometimes) cruel jokes. Aware of Susan's vacant eyes. She's aware that nothing can hurt her here, not whilst she has these people around her.

She laughs and joins in the conversation. What she says or holds back is a mystery, but there's no need for her to remember. All she needs are the smiles and the beauty.

The venue for that night is smaller than she's used to. So much so that she can see the faces. She'll never know their names. She'll never care about who they are, what they've done, what they hope to do. Maybe some aspiring singers are there. Most of these hopeful musicians will give up before they even start, but maybe one will make it through.

The night drags on into blurriness. Their notes ricochet off the peeling plaster walls, shaking the air like thunder.

Scarlet

16 May 1992

Rain collects on the glass. There's just enough to dissuade Scarlet from going outside and lighting up. She hears the shower puffing: Mauro's definitely pulling out all the stops for tonight.

They're going to eat later, after the act is done. She's already pre-ordered something for later.

She tries to breath, but her throat is so dry it's like trying to swallow razorblades. She fills a glass half full with water, but can only sip a quarter of it. She looks at the clock on the wall. Just before Five – about two minutes. The taxi's due at Quarter-Past.

She's wearing her old leather coat and a black t-shirt she bought in 1988; the punk pattern on the front of it has long since faded through countless washing machine cycles. The jeans are new: its dark blue colour seems to leak from the fabric. She stares at her trainers, worried that their dirtied whiteness may soon turn to blue ink.

She perches herself on the edge of the dining table and waits for Mauro to come down. When he does, with his hair combed back and his eyes sparkly bright, she tells him to calm down.

"Getting butterflies now," he tells her, flexing his fingers.

"I just want to get this over with," she says. She sees the mobile in his back pocket as he turns away. "You don't need that thing. Leave it behind."

"Oh. Oh, yeah, sure." He takes it out, hits a couple of buttons, and puts it by their new electric kettle.

"And you're overdressed," she complains.

Mauro's wearing an all-black suit: new and shiny. Adding to that: black shirt, crinkly black leather belt, polished black leather shoes.

"Oh, did you tell the necessary people about that dinner thing?" he asks.

"I did. All of the gang think the three of us are having dinner at Susan's."

"Good. You know –"

The sharp sound of a horn pierces through the walls. Taxi's here early.

"Ah, shit," mutters Mauro. His fists pummel lightly against his thighs. "Shit, shit, shit."

"Look, don't puss out on me now!" she says aggressively.

"It's okay," he says, as the horn blares again. "Christ, this taxi driver's an impatient git, isn't he!" He takes her hand firmly and they head out.

The driver's checking his watch. Bluntly acknowledging them as they climb inside, he asks for the address. The car lurches forward, pulling into the road, into the rain...

...Which grows heavier with every yard. Scarlet watches paving stones become slippery blocks of ice. People – mostly shoppers – run for cover.

It's like *Cinderella*, how they're carried through the rain, safe as anything. Scarlet can't help but watch Mauro become increasingly anxious as they near Shepherd's Bush. Why's he behaving like this? Is he getting cold feet?

"Here we are," announces the driver. He brings the vehicle to a stop, just before some double yellows. He's evidently had the practice.

"Keep the change." Scarlet passes him over a note.

"Thanks, luv."

"I really wish blokes wouldn't call me that."

The driver barely waits for them to get out before he shoots off like a dog after a ball. What was that film she watched the other day? *National Lampoon's European Vacation*. That scene when the dog jumps off the Eiffel Tower. Just like that.

"Let's do this," she says. She goes over to the buzzer and sticks her thumb down hard. "Hey, Susan, it's us. Come on, it's pissing down outside." She turns her head around, noticing that Mauro is on the edge of the pavement looking up and down the road. "Hey! Come on!" she snaps.

"Sorry!" He jobs over, scraping droplets from his hair.

The door clicks open. Scarlet opens up, forcing him through.

Susan stands at the entrance to her flat, in nothing but a t-shirt and jeans. Her bare feet press into the floor like hammers.

When Scarlet and Mauro are inside, Susan bursts out laughing. "You guys are so damn intense. You need to relax!"

"I'm ready," declares Mauro.

"Good. You know where my bedroom is? Go inside. There's a chair. Get naked and sit down. Scarlet and I will be joining you shortly."

"Cool. Why don't we have a glass of wine or something before we get started?"

"That sounds a great idea actually," says Scarlet.

"Oh, we will be," replies Susan, "but *you*, Mauro, won't. You're just going to have to sit in there and wait."

Scarlet's supportive. She finds herself casting a nasty smile at him. "Well, babe, you said that you wanted this to be as authentic as possible. That's what you told me."

"Ah." He goes to Susan's bedroom and disappears into the shade inside.

"There's a glass of wine waiting for you," says Susan, taking Scarlet's hand.

She feels so weak, yet so at ease, as she's led through to the living room. Two glasses of black red are set upon the coffee table. She takes hers without hesitation, falls back into the sofa. She smells Susan's sweet aroma as she cuddles up next to her. Both of them drink at the same time, making the liquid disappear bit by bit.

"I'm glad I've got you," whispers Susan.

"I'm glad we're together."

"You know that's not possible. You have Mauro. I know you love him."

"But I wish I'd had you."

"You can have me. Tonight."

Scarlet

23 May 1992

She's decided to travel by train today, even though, by rights, she should have gone by limo. Oh, the trials and tribulations and general confusion of being an international singing super-star...!

As she nears Sevenoaks, she makes a mental note to herself to do some writing of lyrics later. Much later.

She's home again. Her origin. She grew up here. Seems like a hundred lifetimes ago.

"It's good to be back," she says when the train pulls into the station. It's almost like *Brief Encounter*, but much longer and without the romance.

The usual flurry of passengers alights with her. Everyone going in their own direction. Everyone needing to be somewhere yesterday. She knows she looks out of place, but those thoughts belong to another time. She's past that now.

She sees Alastair at the end of the platform, bobbing his head around. Her parents are behind him.

"Scarlet!" screams Alastair. Oh boy, the lawyer has seen the singer.

She moves forward, allowing herself to be enveloped by her family. She sees her dad's joined the mobile phone club: she feels the brick inside his jacket pocket.

"How's everyone been?" she asks as they begin to make their way out.

"Fine, fine," replies her mother. "How have you been?"

"Touring. That much to be said. Actually, it's been pretty hectic."

"You can tell us all about that later," says her dad, picking out a set of car keys. The family vehicle is planted just outside the station exit, tyres biting into the sharp kerb. Around them, various travellers are looking for connecting bus routes or trying to hunt out their vehicles in the large car park opposite the station.

"You should have parked in there, darling," her mother says to her husband. "It's a bloody wonder we didn't get fined."

"Well, we had better shoot off quick." Her dad opens the car and beckons them inside. "Quick, inside."

It's been a long time since she's sat in this thing, but it's so familiar: the upholstery, the dust on the floor, the gentle lavender scent. Nothing's changed.

As they move off, she asks, "How are Paul and Siobhan doing?"

"They're well," replies her father. "They just got back from Paris yesterday. Quick little holiday. Actually, the son of one of Paul's friends saw you in Cardiff the other night. Really enjoyed himself."

"Well, why don't you come and see me?"

"I think I'm a little too old for a rock concert!"

"Not if the three of you come! Together..."

"That's definitely something to think about," says Alastair. "Hmm..."

"Well, we'll talk about it," says Scarlet's father. "We'll definitely talk about it."

Her room is like a geode, preserved under the ground for countless time. The posters, the unmade bed, the frayed magazines, the one-eyed teddy bear. It's like didn't leave. She slumps down on the bed, curses at the fact she left her trusty old guitar back in London, and resists the desire to light up a cigarette.

Yet it's not as uncomfortable as she thought it would be. Everyone seems so much freer. The silent formality. The dreary conversations about tax. None of it's happened yet.

"Scarlet, something to eat!" her mother yells up the stairs. The same voice from two years ago.

"Coming!"

She finds she's a lot fitter now. More agile. She seems to glide down the steps, cascading into the dining room where a cafetiere, cups and some pastries await. Alastair and her father are seated, very patient. She remembers another time when she was sat before them. She'll always remember it. Stern faces. The bitter taste of knowing her band wouldn't make it. How wrong she's proved the whole world now.

"We're going out for dinner later," says her father. "I've booked a place at this new Indian restaurant that's opened up. It's part of a chain. There's one in Liverpool. Paul swears the food's brilliant."

"Well, let's do it." Scarlet reaches forward and pushes the plunger down. She's not waiting for anyone. She's learnt never to hide what she really wants. Only London can do that. Only fame can drive that true, vicious desire.

They talk about music. About travel. A little about Alastair's career. Scarlet finds she enjoys the boring stuff a lot more than she believes. She's even got an interest in – yuck – tax law. Why's it so complicated and messy?

They finish the coffee and pastries conversation over Scarlet's upcoming tour.

"We get to Sydney first," she tells them, as though she's advertising it. "Three concerts there. Then we zip over to Melbourne for two performances. Our next stop is Perth, where we're doing four."

"Isn't Perth quite cut off from the rest of Australia?" asks Alastair.

"I think so," says Scarlet's mother. "Yes, it is."

"Wherever it's situated, I've been assured we'll get a good crowd," replies Scarlet.

"Who gave you that assurance?" asks her father.

"Roger Miser himself."

"You want to be careful of him." Her dad's changed back into his old self. Over serious, but not so much that it's comical. "He's got a history."

"He's a bit of a character, but I've never had any issues with him."

"A colleague of mine had dealings with him back in the late Sixties, when he was just starting out. Very ruthless nature about him. There were stories about him, things that would make Wall Street seem like a playgroup."

"What specifically did he do? You can't judge Roger on what he was like nearly thirty years ago."

"All I'm saying is be careful, Scarlet."

"I know. But you can't judge someone on their past sins. I mean, Josephine, for instance. She used to be a communist the early Eighties, but I don't worry about waking up under the hammer and sickle every morning. In fact, she's reluctant to talk about it at all. I know she's ashamed about it."

"Just be careful, okay?" Her father clears his throat. Somewhere in the house a clock strikes the hour. "Right, let's finish this coffee, and how about we all head out for a drink?"

"I could do with one of those," says Alastair.

Scarlet laughs to herself as his face grows red. He realises he just sounded like an alcoholic! She can't hold herself much longer and starts sniggering. "Sorry, sorry," she tells him. "You worry so much! What time are we heading out then?"

"Half-Past," says her mother.

"Good." Scarlet stands up. "Mind if I stretch my legs for a bit?"

She's walking into the dreams and nightmares of her past. Though the streets are calm and average, neat and orderly, and excited children play around in gardens, she still feels the cold. She lights up, striding confidently. There's no one here to hurt her now. All ties to her past... gone.

Unfamiliar faces gaze out from behind windows. Dogwalkers and cyclists go past her, a faint glimmer of recognition in their faces. No one asks her autograph. Not that she minds. Not that she cares. One of the pedestrians, an old man with a paper tucked under his arm, wishes her a good day, and she returns the compliment.

She walks until she reaches the spot where she used to paint pretty pictures. The dents are still in the ground where the supports of the shack gouged the ground. She tosses away the fragments of her cigarette and refrains from lighting up another.

Should she have stuck with the art? She was good at it. Sharmaine often told her that she had a unique talent. Scarlet smirks. It was a long time ago. She's moved on. Painting pretty pictures was a path she never took.

She has to go the place. Even though she doesn't want to.

She walks their steadily, as though she's an aged woman afraid of encountering a love once thought countlessly lost. She finds it eventually. Not that she couldn't. The grassy verge with the ditch, all the same. She sees him falling. Everything's shifting into place.

She'll never forget it. Even though it doesn't hang around her neck like an albatross anymore. Even though the threat is gone. Bought out. There's nothing money can't buy.

She smirks, turns around, heads home. No, that's not correct: heads to her *family's* home.

She manages to get back just as everyone else is slipping their coats on.

"I'm glad I came," she says. "Really, I am."

"We're very proud of you, Scarlet," her father says. "I know at times I tried to put you down, but... I'm proud of you."

"Thank you."

"But if you ever fancy a tax inspector internship, do let me know."

"Funny." Scarlet shakes her head. "Back in a second." She dashes up to her room, several steps at a time.

She doesn't know what she's looking for, but when she finds it under a pile of old schoolbooks, she wants nothing more than to play it. David Bowie. *Let's Dance.* 1983 LP. The cover is faded and ripped from all the years of her rough fingers handling it. It feels like her heart. She takes out the disc, twirls it in her hands.

"Come on, Scarlet!" a voice calls up. "We don't have all day!"

She puts it back, carefully, and then heads down. She'll play it another time. When the mood is right.

24 May 1992

She's decided to take one of the last trains back.

At the platform, she hugs her family, wishes she had another few hours with them, and then sadly heads into the murky crowded field of travellers. She turns around, gives her parents and her brother a final wave, and then joins the array of sad-looking souls, all heading back to the city. Fathers going back to the industrial hive to work for a week. Students returning to the world of study. The weekend of bliss is over for them, when they could be amongst their loved ones, free from the pressures that life loves to bring, and now they're back in the real world.

Not her, of course.

Well, dear reader, she has a lot of prep work for this Australia tour, and that *is* going to be somewhat of a drag. But you and I both know, dear reader, that this will not be what breaks the band.

With every mile that she nears the capital, the notes of the last practice session become clearer. Soon she's forgotten about this little holiday. Now she can finally focus. The lyrics appear across her vision. The emotions that she likes to play with find themselves written across boards. She's got a map of it in her head.

Then she gets hungry for the food of the rich and famous. But more than that, she wants to be with Mauro. She needs him. Now that his *little problem* has finally been resolved, he's much more whole. He's his true, honourable self, free from the shadow of his brother.

She's coming back to London. She's back where she belongs.

Gina

The Australia Tour
27 August 1992

I don't think I've ever been so blessed to see such a place like this. Our hotel is right in the heart of Sydney, nestled in its metal forest. My suite is on the top floor, gazing out longingly. Below, the traffic hums and throbs. Unlike New York, there are no angry shouts. No threats. No bitterness. Everyone's equal here.

Technically, we're working, so we have to behave ourselves, but I won't be hesitating to get a quick beer on the promenade. In fact, I think I'll do that now.

I spoke to God the day before we flew. I'm not sure which day it is. Travel does that to you. Was it yesterday, or the day before? But anyway, I spoke to Him, and He told me to keep strong. Not that I'm worried about this tour. Not that I need His support and His guidance.

I spoke to God on the flight over. He told me that this would be a new beginning for me. Don't think I'll ever know what He meant by it. Presumably a solo career, but I can't see myself having one. Besides, I can't sing like Scarlet.

I want to speak to God again, but I can't do it here.

I put on my new sunglasses, top of the range, cat eye ones, oversized. I head out of the room and to the elevator, which seems to be waiting just for me. When I reach the lobby, I already feel the heat wafting over me. It's supposed to be their winter, right? I should move here.

"Everything okay with the room, ma'am?" the attendant at the desk asks me. His eyebrows seem to narrow.

"Yes, absolutely perfect."

"My mate's coming to see you tonight. Tried to get tickets myself, but was too late."

"Never mind. I've no doubt we'll be back down here soon enough."

I head out into the mid-morning heat. It's a struggle at first, but soon enough I acclimatise. When I get to the waterfront, I'm parched. I scan around, trying to locate a bar, just a bit of shade. The Sydney Opera House – where we'll be performing later – reaches up into the sky, towering over the people beneath.

I'm not sure what to say. Never did I think I'd be performing in that building. It doesn't seem real. It's not that I can't take it in, it's just it doesn't feel the way I'd imagined it to be. It's not anticlimactic. It's just emotionless. I do not feel a single thing about going on stage there tonight.

I need a drink. There's a small bar ahead, tables and chairs spilling out onto the pavement. Full of old men. Old travellers. I take my place amongst them without a single moment's hesitation.

"What can I get you, babe?" comes a chirpy female voice.

I don't look "Just a beer. A decent cold bottle. Just off the plane."

"No worries. Be a second."

"You never could say no, could you?" Josephine glares down at me, but there's a suspicious smile growing on her.

She's like an angel. She sits down, waves a hand, and calls, "One beer please!"

"Did you follow me from the hotel?" I demand.

"Yes."

We don't say another word until our drinks are delivered. Condensation clings to the brown glass like exfoliating skin. We watch the people go by. Excited children tug on balloons; young couples are over dinner plans with their respective in-laws; brave joggers slowly suffocate, drown in their own sweat. In the distance, Sydney Harbour Bridge shimmers.

"I can't wait for tonight," says Josephine, lifting the bottle to her lips. "Lots of tickets sold."

"So I heard. A bit nervous though."

"Nerves are good."

We both grow silent. Only the splashing of water, the thump of footsteps, and the sounds of a far-off instrument pierce the air.

"I've let go of my past," says Josephine. "I finally let it go."

"Never let a loser like him define who you are," I tell her, with as much firmness as I can summon.

"I'm not talking about Eugene. Glad that bastard's gone, though. Did you know I used to be a teacher?"

"What? Can't imagine you as a teacher, Josephine!"

"Well, I was a student teacher. Obviously, I didn't consider it exactly a safe career in the end. I was verbally and physically abused by the staff and students at the school, humiliated, degraded. And..." The words seem to catch behind her teeth. "And once I was sexually assaulted."

"I'm sorry."

"It's okay. It's been hard and I've carried those scars with me, but I've let it go."

"What made you want to teach?" I ask. "Sorry, I know I'm digging a bit."

"It's okay. I'm not sure what made me want to do it. Thought it might have been a good career move at the time. I was wrong, I suppose. But I've let it go. The hurt, the abuse, the trauma. It's all gone."

"I'm glad you've managed to let this go. And I'm pleased you've told me about it. It must have taken a lot to say that."

"Yeah." A kindly smug look appears on Josephine's face. It's something I'll remember for years: the sight of a woman who has finally made peace with her demons.

We finish our beers, not needing to exchange another word. The afternoon heat gradually builds until it's too uncomfortable to sit still. We unpeel ourselves from our seats, standing up with the graciousness of a couple of delinquents. Josephine heads into the airconditioned bar and I watch her pass over a note. She presumably shares some sort of a joke with the skinny barmaid, falling backwards with laughter.

"Come on, let's get back," she says, when she re-emerges. "Christ, it's fucking hot."

"Josephine..." I growl. "Please."

"Ah yeah. Sorry."

The night's performance begins with a bang and a cheer as we enter the stage.

"Damn it, you lot, you need to up your game!" howls Josephine. "That means clap louder! Come on, Down Under, you need to up your bloody game!"

We take our places, instruments at the ready. The drumsticks feel like fragile bamboo in my hands. I shut my eyes, wait for the cue from the Scarlet. I wait and wait and wait. The crowd seems to grow anxious. Scarlet stands casually, a hand resting on the microphone, eyes down. The crowd shuffles.

I mouth silently: "Scarlet?"

Everything drops to zero.

There's a scream from somewhere. Somewhere else, a man shouts, "Come on!"

I hear her voice break. It cuts through ice. I know this song. One from our first album. Not as big a hit as the other tracks, but... the crowd seem to love it. There's gentle swaying. It winds its way from person to person, row to row, group to group. We start hitting our notes, building on the rhythm.

We've broken the firing order for tonight. We weren't doing this song until last!

My hands bash the sticks against the skin of the drums. The noise of the cymbals crashes through my ears, cascading through my brain.

I feel my throat tighten with adrenaline. Unable to drink water, unable to shut my eyes. Yet I could do this forever. I don't need to rest. I don't need to stop. God gives me the strength that I need.

We reach the end of the song and Scarlet opens her arms to the crowd. "It's good to be here, in Sydney, Down Under!" she shouts. "Better than fucking England, that's for fucking sure! Now, let's get this night properly underway! Josephine, lead us off on the next track, if you please..."

Josephine starts playing with zest and vigour. We're back on the firing order now. And this track, I absolutely love. She's taking the lead on this, kicking it off with those intro chords that schoolkids have begun to start whistling.

"Come on!" a voice bellows from somewhere. Same bloke from earlier? I can't tell.

Then Scarlet's vocals add to the scene, like the main actor coming onto the stage, curiosity and ambition wrapped up in one. Scarlet's burning. Eyes filled with the tears of pride and triumph. I see those eyes when she turns to face me – ever so briefly – and, to be honest with you, they scare me. I never want to see those eyes ever again. I simply can't face them.

The performance, the night, it wears on, like a tyre gradually shaving itself to a smooth face. We do most of the songs we've written, including ones saved for the next album (cleared by Roger, of course). My body starts to pull apart, like pork cut and ripped to splinters. I'm afraid of failing, afraid of slipping up, afraid to making the simplest of mistakes. But I'm terrified of those eyes. I don't want them to see them. They belong to someone else. Not her.

Susan

The Australia Tour
30 August 1992

Why did I do it? It wasn't an act of stupidity, if that's what you're wondering. I made the conscious choice to help Scarlet and Mauro. Was I wrong? Maybe… But they're happy now — well, they seemed that way when Mauro saw us off at the airport. Over the years, even before I met Scarlet, I've done things that have taken me outside my tiny comfort zone. But I've always done them with a sense of honour, if such a thing can be said about me.

I've done what I believe is right.

I may be wrong, sometimes.

We step out of the airport in Melbourne, skin blistered by the sun. Torn.

"I need a fucking shower!" hisses Josephine. "Fucking hell! So fucking hot! Fucking tortured!"

We're on the pavement outside the terminal building. People — some of whom know us — stare at us, bewildered. Others — presumably the ones who've never heard a single one of our songs — look through our feeble flesh.

Christ, they were serving champagne on the flight.

Our limo – an ugly pink thing – rolls up before us. The kind of thing some playboy bunny in the Eighties would ride around Los Angeles in. Disgusting. Ugly as fuck.

We're inside. And there's no one to help us with our luggage.

Scarlet and I take the back seats, facing our opponents, Gina and Josephine. I feel Scarlet stroke my hand as everyone puts their feet up.

"I wish you wouldn't do that," I say to her.

"Sorry. Just stretching."

Josephine looks our way, but she peers past us. She's got this appearance of peace about her. I've noticed it over the past few days. I don't like it.

That night, at this venue, the name of which does not bear any weight in my mind, we perform yet again. We sing, we cry, we cheer, we howl the others on. Josephine tells the crowd to up their game. Yet, somehow, we've lost energy. I suppose it's a tiredness that comes with long periods of touring, meeting fans, signing autographs, doing as you're told.

Do we have control of our lives anymore? Or is it Roger Miser that has the reins? Is it Roger Miser that tells how and when we sleep, and who we sleep with? Or is it me imagining things?

That's one reason I never fitted into that ghastly children's home: too much of an active imagination. Every second imagining fantasy worlds, knights in shining armour, adventures, travel, galloping over frozen continents.

Oh, if they could see me now! If *he* could see me now...

I lie awake that night, the noise of the crowd still pummelling my eardrums. My throat feels dry and cracked. I think the air-conditioning is gradually packing in. Every so often, it scrapes and cuts. Should I go downstairs and tell the management about it?

Next thing I know, I'm standing on the balcony – a narrow thing with white railings – and looking at the skyline of Melbourne. It expands into the distance, heat lolling over the lights like a tongue.

It dawns on me then that I'm free. The horrors of that children's home are too unspeakable to write down. Dear reader – you really do not want the full, sordid details. What I can say is that those days changed me, but they haven't made me what I am.

This band, Scarlet, Josephine, Gina, *they* are the ones that have made me into the person that stands hunched on the balcony railings. Even Emma did her bit...

Oh, Emma.

She was the friend, the companion, that was lost too early in this story. I'll always think about her. What went wrong? What didn't we do for her? What could we have done? How could we have gotten through to her? Were we guilty of ignoring her?

I scold myself. We did *everything* for her. She chose to leave. She chose to walk away.

She's somewhere on this planet, somewhere distant. Maybe she's here, somewhere beneath this skyline. In a bar with some newfound traveller friends. Or maybe she's unconscious with booze in a ditch in Madagascar. Maybe she's in the building opposite, staring right back at me. Wherever she is, I hope she's keeping it together. Maybe Gina's said a prayer.

But, to me, Emma is someone I just simply have to let go of.

Gina

The Australia Tour
2 September 1992

Still worn down from our opening concert in Perth the night before, I head out as early as I can – just before Six A.M. – to locate this church I've heard about. I don't know much about it, except for rumours of its location at the north edge of the city.

The runners are out, panting like dogs. They make me want to be more like Susan. I hold up a smile as they pass, any attempt to strike up conversation futile.

Erasure's playing somewhere. *Love To Hate You*. Is it a beautiful song? To me it is.

I have no idea where I'm going, but it feels good to be lost. God is my guide. I don't need a map.

It's funny, watching people pass. Runners and very early commuters. They don't seem to know who I am, even though my face has been plastered on so many magazine covers. It's like our fans exist in a different world to them.

There's a taxi rank ahead. God always tells me to be honest and truthful. That's what I do with the cab drivers when I approach them: I tell them the description of the building I'm after. I'm not coy about it. A few laugh, one tells me they don't know, but the last man in the queue knows exactly what I'm on about.

"...Though it's not there anymore, love!" he booms. The driver tosses his cigarette out the window; it flies past me like a torpedo and smoulders on the hot ground. "Sorry about that."

"Take me there," I say. "Please."

"It's your money, love. Hop in."

As the car drives back towards Perth, leaving me standing in the oppressive heat, I gaze at the ruins of this church. The change dangles in my hand like a forgotten friend.

A group of drunk students burnt it down, apparently. Acquitted of arson. According to the driver, anyway. Only a few bricks and black cinders of wood remain – despite it happening more than a year ago.

Is this a test of my faith? To see such a beautiful building devasted in such a manner.

Around me, there's nothing except rocks, dirt and shrubbery. I'm two miles north of Perth, trapped in the blistering heat. No water. No transport back.

I issue a silent prayer.

I shouldn't have left the hotel.

Soon it will be too hot to breathe. I might even die of thirst before I reach the safety of civilisation. Sighing, I pick myself up and start the arduous journey back...

...Just as a spectre of dust and smoke appears in the distance. At first, I think it's a bike, but a car shimmers into view, all four wheels kicking up a storm from the ground. Something deep inside me tells me that whoever's inside the vehicle is coming for me. It's like a memory coming for you, a memory of something that you had left behind.

The taxi screeches to a halt and Josephine steps out, not looking too pleased. She's pissed. Angrily, she hands the driver some cash.

"You do realise we have a press thing at Ten!" she hisses. Actually, she doesn't sound too mad.

"Pray with me," I say.

"For..." Josephine spits at the ground. "For goodness' sake, Gina, we need to get a move on..."

"Pray with me," I repeat, kneeling down. "Please."

Grudging, she kneels next to me. I can smell the perfume departing her skin.

I say the words to God as clearly and concisely as I can. Of course, I have no issue with it. None at all. The words roll off my tongue. I feel God next to me as I say these precious sentences. When I'm done, I take Josephine's hand, and ask her, "How did you find it?" I lead her up.

"Better than I thought," she replies.

"I think the taxi's waiting for us."

I feel something that rolls through my guts, pulsing through me. It's like I've got the spins, but never tasted alcohol. I'm kneeling again, clutching my stomach. There's a loss, a wound that cuts my spine.

"Gina, you okay?!" stammers Josephine. Her hands lift me up.

"I'm fine. Haven't eaten properly today. Let's get back."

Scarlet

25 September 1992

She knows she deserves this, but there's the nagging guilt in her that she hasn't done enough. The Australia Tour was a success, but it was the record company, the security officers protecting the venues, that did the hard work. All she did was sing. So much so that she lost her voice for a couple of days after they came back. But she got private medical treatment. Discreet. Cash payment as well.

It's Four A.M. She's out in the back garden, a cigarette touching her lips. She's wearing her old leather jacket, but she's only using it for warmth. It fits her, but it doesn't keep away the cold. The tobacco burns and smoulders, threatening to scorch her pleat jeans.

Mauro's soft voice shifts away the cold. She knows he's there before he sits on the wall of slate next to her. Their feet dangle over the chasm where a pond will soon be.

"You're up early," he remarks.

"Well, you know what jet setting is like." She smirks, thinks of lighting up again, drops the idea. He doesn't like her smoking.

"Come back to bed for an hour," he pleads. "We don't need to be out the door until Half-Six."

"You go back to bed if you want. I don't feel like sleeping."

"What's wrong? Tell me. You've been like this since you came back from Australia."

"It's nothing."

"Doesn't sound like it."

She has to say it. "It's Emma."

"Look, we've talked about her. You have to let her go."

"I have. But I still miss her."

"There's nothing I can do about that. Look, I'm going back to bed for a bit. If you want to stay out here, that's fine. Otherwise… Well, I won't tell you what to do. I love you, Scarlet."

"I love you, too." But by the time she's uttered the words, he's gone back inside.

She waits.

Waits some more.

She lights another cigarette, but extinguishes it in seconds.

Yet again, ushered through security at lightning speed. Everything's private for them. Express service. No lining up. Every miserable face somehow cracks a smile. Even when their bags are put through the X-Ray machine, and even when Scarlet's brand-named handbag is searched, they're treated with fluffy feathers.

They're taken through a secret passage to the lounge, where champagne awaits and handmade pastries with beautifully whipped cream are served with the most delicate manner. No conversation – except for, 'If there is anything else you require, sir, ma'am, just ask' – needs to be deployed.

Mauro and Scarlet have a spot to themselves – right in the corner of the lounge. The sample place she sat with the girls when they went to the Big Apple for the first time. More pastries are ushered over, planted on the glass table, followed by fresh coffee.

"Thank you for this, Mauro," she says. "It will be good to be back in L.A."

"No worries." Mauro picks up an issue of *Classic Cars*, flips through it, replaces it on the stand next to his seat. He clearly doesn't have the faintest interest, judging by the way he flashes disgust at it.

"I heard you composing last night," she says. "Are you thinking about a new album?"

"I was just messing. Actually, I'm thinking of leaving music altogether."

"What? Why?"

"There are other things, Scarlet. I've spent too long plucking chords. I've actually been thinking of doing some managing. Setting up a record company."

"Come on, don't tell me you're going to become like Roger...!"

"Wouldn't dream of it." He squeezes her wrist. "I just need something different. Something else."

"I'll be behind you."

"Do you mean that?"

"Yes, I do. I'm happy with you."

"That's good."

They don't get a chance to properly finish their breakfast. A man – private security – approaches, whispers something to Mauro.

"Very good, thank you," Mauro responds, waving the man away with a flick of his wrist. "Right, time to board, Scarlet."

Like a couple, confident in who they are, they walk through the airport, onlookers tagging onto them. A girl – must be six or seven – yells something to her mum: "It's her, Mummy! Mummy, mummy, look!"

"Overexcited," murmurs Mauro. "Isn't it term time, as well?"

"Well, she deserves a little leave, babe."

"You know something, I was thinking this morning. It's incredible, isn't it, modern society? A hundred years, ago, none of this was here. VHS stores, credit cards, cheapish air travel. Fast food, you know what I mean? Look over there, bloody Tie Rack. If a businessman forgets his tie, he can get a replacement for a reasonable cost. It's all so convenient, isn't it?"

"Are you becoming philosophical or something?"

"Maybe."

"Well, ten years ago my dad used to travel through here quite a bit. Of course, it was primitive back then. And more expensive."

Their hands link like chains. They're directed down a concourse, through a few corridors, to the gate. A quick check of the documents, and then they're down the gangway and into the First Class section.

When they land in Los Angeles, they suffer more prying faces, more paparazzi desperate for images for their papers. Two police officers keep crowds at bay as Scarlet and Mauro leave the airport to a waiting limo.

"How'd they know we'd be here?" grumbles Mauro.

"Can I have an autograph?" a childlike voice screams. It's a young woman with pigtails, dressed in a pink t-shirt with faded lettering and shorts that are way too short. Flipflops are fastened to skinny feet and painted toenails. She's too young for this life, too eager.

A sturdy police officer, hand resting on his weapon, tells her firmly: "Stand back, ma'am! Stand back!"

"But I just want an autograph!" The girl's look of disappointment seems to resonate.

"Scarlet, let's go," whispers Mauro.

The heat is beginning to enclose them. The distant scent of jet fumes wafts along the road, over the heads of frantic passengers. The limo driver wheels their luggage into the vehicle, hissing through his teeth.

"Just one autograph!" The girl waves a picture of Scarlet as though it's a banner at a soccer game. "Please!"

"Ma'am, back away," the cop says.

Other voices sound in the air. Not the paparazzi – who have been spirited away – but fans. They've seen the commotion. They've seen the limo. And they've spotted Scarlet. They dash over, pushing past one another. Young, old. Men, women. Smartly dressed. Others wearing shorts and t-shirts. Tattooed bikers. Overweight, insecure people. A proper mix.

"We should go," says Mauro. "Scarlet, come on."

"Can't we...?" She looks at the eager woman waving the picture.

A weary-looking man with splintered glasses puts his arm around the girl. Beads of sweat collect on his temples. The father, desperate to take his daughter away from the scene. But for a parent, he seems so aggressive. His face twists into contours. He's mouthing something. Silently. Then he starts shouting. He's looking right at Scarlet. "Bitch!" he's crying. "Bitch! Bitch! Bitch!" He shoves the girl to the side, knocking her to the ground facedown. He charges forward like a rhino, something in his hand.

"Mauro!" screams Scarlet.

The knife ascends above his head, ready to come crashing down. He throws a kick at the policeman and goes for Scarlet as though it's the climax of his life.

"Fucking bitch!" the man yells.

A single shot rings out and he drops like a stone. The crowd panics, fleeing the scene. The policeman lies on the ground, the smoking gun clasped in both hands.

"Scarlet!" a man's voice howls. Is it Mauro's? She can't tell. "Scarlet!"

All she feels – apart from fear – is frustration and bitterness. Maybe it's the shock. She doesn't know. She'll probably never.

The man – who looks so ill – is sprawled on the ground, slowly dying.

"It's okay," Mauro's soothing voice whispers. "Scarlet, it's okay."

She steps forward, ignoring the police officer's orders to stay away.

A hand on her shoulder. "Scarlet, it's okay. It's okay."

"Mauro," comes her weak voice. She's told everyone her whole life that she's not weak. But she's a princess in a fairytale now. A damsel in distress. She falls into her boyfriend's arms, truly weak, crying.

"Ssh. Ssh."

A firm voice, filled with the flux of authority, advises them to leave.

More police have come. Flashing lights. Attempts to hold back the crowd. Time seems to slip. She holds onto Mauro, weeping.

"I can't breathe..." she says. "I can't..."

She doesn't eat for the rest of the day. Who could?

All the police business is done. Two cops came to the hotel about lunchtime to take their statements. They'll be in contact should any additional information be required.

She sits with Mauro in the bar of the hotel, but she's alone. The atmosphere is dark, as black as a beach at night. Two cocktails smoulder on the table between them, dripping cold.

"It wasn't your fault," he says for the hundredth or so time. "Don't blame yourself."

This time she responds: "How can I not? I should have listened to you, when you said to leave."

"Do you want to go home? We can, if that's what you want. We can get on a flight tonight."

"No, I want to stay."

"Do *you* want to go home?"

"No. I want to be here, with you."

"What the hell's that?"

"What?"

"That?!" She points at his hand which rests casually on his trouser pocket. "I saw you try to stash it in your jacket.

"Oh, it's just a bit of rubbish."

"Mauro..."

She feels the defeat leaving him. He sits back, scrapes up a few nuts in his fingers, and stares at the array of gins, whiskies and vodkas piled up on the wall behind the bar.

"Mauro, be honest with me... Is that what I think it is?"

"I was going to give it to you later. Hadn't banked on that shit happening at the airport... Scarlet, I know what I want. I want to spend my life with you. Fuck, I'm not good at this."

"Take your time. Just say what you need to say."

"Scarlet, I love you. Marry me." With that, in a fraction of a moment of a fraction of a heartbeat, he lifts the box up, like he's in an egg-and-spoon race, and presents the ring to Scarlet.

Scarlet

29 September 1992

Extremely hastily organised. That's the way of this decade.

No more than five minutes after Scarlet and Mauro touched down at Heathrow on Monday, a small engagement party was planned for the following night.

Like they're already a strong married couple, they stand at the doorway (most casually dressed), waiting for the guests to arrive.

Roger and his blonde piece are first. Handshakes and congratulations. You'll make a great married couple. Both of them are underdressed. For Roger, that means a blue silk shirt and faded grey trousers, handmade Italian shoes. For his blonde piece – well, a flowery dress, surrounded by a small jacket.

The girls come next, all in the latest dresses and jewellery. Gina has a small crucifix embedded in her throat.

Last: Scarlet's parents and Alastair. They look uncomfortable in these surroundings. They've wandered into an area they never dreamed they'd be in. They're drunk on insecurity and curiosity.

They gather in the living room, champagne assigned to each of them as though they don't have a choice.

"Thank you all for coming," says Mauro. "I know this has been short notice, but Scarlet and I wanted to ensure that we shared our happiness. All of you are important to us. Roger, you've kept this woman on the right track. Tamed, that's the right word."

"Hey!" says Scarlet.

"Scarlet, you're the most important thing that's ever happened to me. Ever since we met, I've wanted to spend my life with you. You're a kind-hearted, honourable, beautiful human being."

"Thank you."

Scarlet's father steps forward, holding his glass in the air. "Well, I think this calls for a toast. To a successful future, to a wonderful marriage, and to a fine young man, who I know will make a great husband to my daughter."

"To the future bride and the future groom!" proclaims Roger's other half.

"We'd better pause there," says Josephine, smirking. "I think George's just arrived."

"He's not coming," says Roger. "Family commitments." He drops his jaw, mouthing, "Unbelievable."

"Well, who's just arrived then?"

The sound of stumbling fills the hallway. Something falls over. Something else breaks.

The scent of booze flies off Eugene as he staggers inside. He's in a suit-and-tie, funeral attire. Top button undone and the tie hanging like a noose. "Hey everybody!" he shouts

"What do you want, Eugene?" demands Mauro, stepping between them and his brother. "You're not welcome here."

"Why not?! We're family, aren't we?"

"Go home, Eugene. Go and drink yourself stupid, for all I care, but not here."

"What are you going to do if I don't?"

"Scarlet, call the cops."

"Whoah!" Eugene raises his hands. "Honestly! Whoah! I'm leaving, okay?!"

Josephine speaks up. She was never silent. "Go away, Eugene."

"Well, well, well!" Eugene's face darkens. His teeth clench like a vice. "You know, I was out at the pub the other night, guess who I ran into? Harry Hough, you remember him? You taught him back in the Eighties. Well..." He stumbles, catches himself on the sofa. Giggles. "Well, attempted to teach him. He told me a lot of shit about you. Christ, if I'd known I was fucking a pushover... You remember when you broke down crying? You remember getting a ticking off in front of the kids? You remember when that Year Ten tried to stick his fingers in your cunt? They still laugh about it now. When they meet for drinks every Saturday, they piss themselves laughing, especially as you're famous now."

"Well, you give them a message from me, and you tell it to them loud and clear, that I've let it go."

"Josephine, just leave it," Mauro warns her, pulling her away from his brother. "Just leave it. Let me handle this."

Josephine tugs her arm away. "You tell them that I've let it go. You tell them that my time in that shithole of a school doesn't define me. And you know something? I forgive them. You tell them that. You tell them that, you fucking waste of space. Now... go."

"Fuck you!" howls Eugene, spitting at her feet. "Whore." He spits again. "Heard about your little mishap in America, Scarlet."

She doesn't rise to it. She looks through him. She won't allow his words to reach her. But they will, eventually, years from now.

"Guy tried to knife you, didn't he? You can't keep out of trouble, can you? Just try not to drag my brother into any-thing, okay sweetheart? And Josephine, I might just finish the job those kids started."

"That's enough!" bellows Mauro. He grabs Eugene's elbows, turns him around, frogmarches him out. Eugene doesn't fight back. It's like he knows he's weaker than his brother and he's accepted that. "Don't every come back here! Ever!" he screams from the doorway. When he returns, Scarlet glares at him.

"Everyone okay?" asks her father.

"James, we should leave," says her mother.

"I'm not allowing that prat to ruin this party." Her father's declaration is filled with holes.

"Quite right," says Alastair. "Let's raise this toast!"

But there's a heavy reluctance in the room. Scarlet lifts back her glass. Everything feels dirty and contaminated to her.

The tranquillity – if there was ever such a thing here – is gone. The house – her home – feels torn and burnt.

"To the new bride and groom," says Roger, taking a sip. The others follow.

They don't move from the living room. Even when Scarlet mentions the makeshift buffet assembled in the kitchen.

"We need to be making a move," Roger's other half says, glancing at her sparkly watch. "It's – er – getting late."

"Okay." Roger grimaces. "Mauro, do you mind if I use your phone to call our driver? I've got one of these mobile things, but bloody well left it at home."

"Sure. It's through in the hallway."

"Anyone want to share a taxi?" says Susan.

"That sounds great," replies Gina. "Yeah."

"Fit me in as well," says Josephine.

"Come on!" protests Mauro.

Scarlet takes his hand, pulls him close, whispers, "Mauro, just let them go."

"No, Scarlet, no! I'm not letting *him* ruin this!"

"Well, you should keep him on a fucking leash!" shouts Josephine.

"I promise you, he won't ever come back."

"Don't take this the wrong way, but your promises don't mean much."

"Then go," Scarlet tells her. "Susan, Gina, you as well. In fact, you'd all better leave."

"Hang on a minute!" her father shouts out.

"Dad, it's okay. We'll do something another time."

"James, let's go." Her mother puts her arm around his waist. Alastair looks around the room, sadly, as though the walls are neglected silent guests.

They don't take long to leave. Scarlet doesn't count the seconds and minutes, but the canapes still feel cold when she goes into the kitchen.

"I'm sorry," is all Mauro can say.

"It's okay." She walks past him with one of the trays and a bottle of wine, a glass fastened between her ring and middle fingers. "I'm going upstairs."

"Look, let's go out tonight. Go for a meal."

"Not interested. I just..." She starts heading up the stairs, pauses, huffs, looks over her shoulder. "Just give me some time on my own, okay?"

"Scarlet..."

"No! Mauro, I watched someone get shot right in front of me. I watched him bleed to death. I can't... I can't do this right now. Why don't you head out to the pub or something? Since you're leaving music, you sink a few jars, talk about football, you know, the stuff normal people do. You're so desperate to fit in with the crowd, please, go, join them."

"Do you want this?" he calls after her. "Do you want to marry me? Please, let me know."

"You know something? I have absolutely no idea."

"Well, maybe I *will* go for a few drinks then."

"Do whatever the hell you want." She goes up to her room, spreads out like an eagle, starts drinking, wolfing down the canape material. She goes through a couple of girly magazines: who's sleeping with who; who's stolen from who; who owes who what. She's surprised that she's not in it. She expects Josephine to be in it, photographed by a sneaky wannabe paparazzi member as she walks out of a bar.

She tries to sleep, but finds herself lost between the real world and the land of dreams. A prisoner of the void. A panic washes over her when she realises it's been two and a half hours. She's up off the bed and she's down the stairs, shouting out his name. In the living room, where earlier the merry party gathered, she finds herself being digested by emptiness.

"Mauro!" she screams as loudly as she can. "Mauro, please! Where are you?"

She doesn't know how she gets outside, but the flecks of rain smash into her cheeks as she runs.

"Mauro...!" She whimpers like a puppy. The faces of the girls appear in front of her. Inside her. All guilt-ridden. All hopeless. All pitiful. "Oh, Mauro."

She sees the lights of a pub. Not a proper one with old men in anoraks, but one that spills out young men who've dressed in too little for the night. A group of them have wrapped themselves in a hug, jumping and cheering. One guy is hunched over a bin, vomiting a reddish pick-and-mix. She doesn't think about the danger. She goes inside, right into the heart of the lion's den. More young men look at her. The barman, a fattish bloke with a beaming, wise old guy face, checks her out.

"Bit dangerous in here for a lass like you," he says, his northern accent thick and unforgiving.

"Have you seen a man called Mauro?" she asks.

"I don't ask their names."

"Blond man. Wavy hair."

"No, love, I haven't. This doesn't sound like his sort of place."

One of the young men grasps her shoulder. His lager-flavoured breath is swallowed by hers. "Look who it is, boys!" he shouts. "Fuckin' hell."

"Leave her alone, Fred," another young man warns.

"Come on, lads, don't you recognise her?"

The information seems to click simultaneously with all the young men. Their eyes and eyelids seem to shift with recognition. Somehow, the collective level of drunkenness begins to dissipate.

"I really should go," says Scarlet. "Sorry to disturb your evening."

"You're not staying to have a drink with us?" says Fred. He's moved his arm down to her waist. "Have a proper bit of male action, instead of those cunt-lickers you hang around with."

The barman steps out, approaching him like a father who's about to discipline an unruly youngest son. "Fred, that's enough," he says. "I know you've had it hard, mate, but... come on."

"The likes of her come in here whenever they like and they just get to leave. No respect at all."

"That's the way it is, Fred."

Another young man is speaking up: "Fred, mate, let her go."

She feels the grip lessening. Instinctively, she moves away, stepping backwards. Heart skipping two or three beats. She gets her first proper look at him. He seems slightly older than the rest. She doesn't know how she can tell this, but he must be late twenties. He's in a t-shirt and jeans, both stained with flecks of beer. He's just like the others, but he's wearing black leather gloves on his hands. His attempt at a costume? His left hand, curled in a loose fist, jabs at her.

"Got nothing to say?!" he shouts. Two of his mates are there in seconds, comforting palms on his spine.

"Let it go," one of them tells him. "Let it go."

The barman's staying put at the side, but ready to dash in. "Fred, come on. She's not worth it."

"Okay," says Fred, sighing.

"Thank you," says Scarlet. "I will go now. Forgive me."

She starts for the exit. Fred's fist is still pointing at her. As she walks past, she angrily pushes it away. She hears a vicious thud as metal and wood make contact with metal and wood. The hand lies on the floor, resting there. Fred's face is aghast, shocked, horrified. His left arm ends in a smooth stump.

The barman intervenes, placing himself between Fred and Scarlet. "I suggest you leave right now, dear. And don't ever come back. He's here nearly every night, drinking himself unconscious. Well, you would be if you'd lost a hand in service of your country. Go."

She doesn't need the instructions repeated. She walks out, breaking into a run. One last look over her shoulder to see the bar vanish into the night. Ironically, it's called The Final Lighthouse.

Never has she felt so alone. She'll never feel that way again, though. She just needs to find him.

She goes to pub after pub, bar after bar; but they're all starting to close. Everything is sealing itself shut. No, she should phone the authorities. They'll know what to do. She knows – vaguely – where she is. A few street corners later, she's at her front door.

Mauro sits in the front garden, face buried in his hands. He looks up, his eyes bleary, tearful.

"I looked for you," she says.

"I didn't go the pub, if that's what you were wondering. I couldn't. Well, I tried. Got to the front door of one. Couldn't go in. Walked around for a bit. Missed –"

"Oh, shut up." She runs over, jumps on him, kisses his lips. "Oh, Mauro, I'm so sorry. I love you, Mauro. I can't live without you. I love you."

"I love you too. Scarlet, I'm sorry for everything."

"It's me who should –"

"Babe. It's okay. Come on, we're both soaking. Let's get inside."

1 October 1992

It takes a day and a half to get herself together, hours and hours to filter out the emotions, but she calls Roger at noon on the first day of October with a sense of sobriety.

"Firstly, I'd like to apologise for what happened the other day," she tells him, her fingers stroking the imposable ears of the stone cat on the dining table.

"No need to apologise. Are you both okay?"

"We're fine."

"How are you coping regarding what happened in Los Angeles?"

"We're both coping well. Just lucky to be alive, I suppose. Listen, I'm phoning regarding another matter."

"Sure. What is it you need?" Funny how he always knows when she's expecting something.

"Do you know The Final Lighthouse? It's near to where I live."

"Oh yes. I know it quite well. Sorry, I know a lot about it. Haven't taken refreshment there myself. You didn't go in there, did you?"

"I want it shut down."

"Scarlet, are you seriously asking me to do that?"

"Can you do it, or not?"

"Well, I've got connections in Health And Safety – I'm sure they'd find a fault or two with it. Scarlet, just think about this. I'm assuming you have some sort of a run-in with a couple of the punters there, but –"

"Roger, for me, can you just shut the place down?"

"Are you sure you want this? That place is the only home for some of the punters."

"Do it." She slams the phone down.

She doesn't care about the young men in that place. She just doesn't want to see it anymore. Doesn't want to have to risk glancing at its peeling walls by mistake. It's a monstrosity. A vile lump of rubbish.

Mauro appears, stifling a yawn. "That Roger you were speaking you?"

"Yep."

"Things okay?"

"Better than okay. Listen, Mauro, why don't we go out today? Somewhere in London we've never been before?"

"What's brought this on?"

"I dunno. A sense of adventure, perhaps. Come on, let's do it."

Gina

9 October 1992

I'm confident that no one knows I'm going on this trip when no special preboarding announcement is made for me. Covered in denim, with a cheap, shoddy pair of sunglasses over my eyes, I'm one of the crowd.

Two of the gate agents are chattering away, their fluorescent jackets artificial glow-worms. They're a mirror image of God's beauty. Though I shouldn't think like that. Father Haynes would condemn me. As would God himself.

A child runs in front of me, nearly catching my knees. She hops around excitedly. Two middleclass parents restrain her, the mother casting me a look of apology.

"It's okay," I mutter. "We were all that age once."

The public address system cranks into life. *"Good morning, ladies and gentlemen, we are ready to begin boarding for Flight 7712 to Paris. At this time, we would like to invite passengers requiring assistance to board and families with small children under five. All other passengers, please wait in the seating area for your row to be called."*

I watch as the elderly and infirm, the very young, and the bewildered head over to the gate.

After a few minutes, the sickly voice states, *"Rows Sixteen to Thirty."*

That's me. I get up, check that no one has recognised me, and then follow the crowd towards the gate. I take a deep breath as I move forward to the lady checking the passports. If my name gets called out here, I'm in for it... But when I get there, she takes a brief look at my boarding pass and passport, ushers me through with the most casual of coarse hands, and then I'm on my way. I gulp when I see the stewardess at the plane door checking boarding passes. I hold a deep breath, exhale as slow as I can, as I approach. My name isn't mentioned once. I find my seat, stow my cabin bag, sit back and relax with one of the inflight magazines.

"All right, love?" an old woman says to me, smiling. She's right above, her shadow enveloping me.

"Oops, sorry!" I exclaim, when I realise she needs to move past me. I shift out of the aisle seat and stand up, gesturing her past me.

A heavyset man with sunken eyes is right behind the old lady. He smiles and points to the middle seat of my row. "Sorry, love," he says. But he doesn't need to apologise for any inconvenience. His green raincoat is off in a flash, his rucksack is stowed, and he slumps into his seat without another wasted second.

"Off on holidays?" he says to me, as I collapse.

"Yeah. Thought I'd get away for a long weekend."

"Nice one. Same here. What about you, dear?" He's turned to the other woman now.

"Visiting my sister in Rouen," she replies. She seems edgy, unfocused. The seat in front of her trembles as a buoyant child slumps down. She clears her throat, gazes at the man and I, as stern as it is possible to me.

"Life's so fast paced these days, isn't it?" says the man. "I'm Rick, by the way." He crosses his hands, jiggling his fingers.

"Gina."

"Helen."

"Good to meet you." Rick shunts himself upwards, looks around him, and then cracks open a small can of beer. "Don't tell anyone."

"Not even Eleven," complains Helens, tut-tutting.

"We can't all be perfect," says Rick. "Bet neither of you can wait to get away from England, eh?"

"I wouldn't say that," I say – probably quite stupidly.

"Why not?"

"I dunno. Maybe there's a sense of loyalty I have."

"What about you, Helen?" Already, the gentle scent of beer is beginning to drift.

"Let's just say, I'm looking forward to some quality time with my sister."

"Good. You'll have a great time. You know something? I don't think we get enough human-to-human time these days."

I'm expecting the old lady to lash out, to complain to the stewardesses, to tell him to mind his own business; but she raises her eyebrows, nods, and says, "Actually, I was reading an interesting article in a magazine the other day. About this... internet thing. I'm too old to understand it, dear. We are facing the risk of being more and more divided, so this article claimed. More distanced from one another. Separated."

"I still like my broadsheets," I say. They flash looks at me. Are they condemning me for interrupting them? Their conversation carries on as though nothing has happened.

When we land in Paris, the odd couple are still chattering away. I don't lose any seconds assembling myself and following the flow of treacle off the plane.

I'm heading to Marseille – a long-envisaged travel destination from my girlhood love of *The French Connection*. I need to get away from the band for a few days. A small break from the hub of music. I probably should have told Roger what I was doing, for my own safety, but what would have been the point of me sneaking away?

I'm a nobody right now. Travellers and businessmen look straight past me.

"I'm looking for the taxi rank!" I say to someone. Their response is in a language I don't understand, though it might be broken up English.

There's a kiosk ahead, right between two currency exchanges. Two blonde women are serving two men in Columbo coats. Above, the kiosk, I think the words 'tourist information' are located, in a multitude of languages.

"Can I help you?"

A police officer, hand on his weapon, has put himself behind me. His voice is soothing, relaxing, the kind of romantic French accent you imagine from films.

"Can I help you, ma'am?" he questions.

"Well, I'm looking for the taxi rank," I reply. "I've got to get to Gare de Lyon."

"Ah, are you heading to Marseille?"

"You read my mind."

The policeman's moustache twitches. He's younger than me, but he acts like one of my old teachers. His English is pristine.

"Be careful in Marseille," he warns. "You should not venture out at night alone. Especially a woman like you, as you are a celebrity."

"Had hoped to get away from that!" I exclaim. "Never mind." Actually, I'm here for God.

"Taxi rank is that way. Through the double doors."

"Thank you."

I allow myself to pray in the moments before I leave the airport, but I find myself feeling lost for words. Why is it that words just sometimes refuse to utter themselves?

The taxi ride is brief, maybe too brief, but nevertheless it's a mad dash for the train. I've always been a stickler for standing around in train stations and letting my mind play wicked romantic fantasies. Not this time. I pelt, trip my way across the floor of Gare de Lyon station. I thrust my tickets in the face of a guard and he points frantically at one of the strings of metal sausages. I run, my bag threatening to bring me down. Lights blink on the side of the train doors. In one gigantic leap of faith, I throw myself inside, stepping onto the grey carpet, the glass sealing itself shut behind me.

"Phew!" I exclaim. I check my tickets. Wrong bloody carriage.

I'm off to Marseille to devote myself more to God. I'm off there to feel closer to Him. Father Haynes told me about a church at the northeast of the city: a neglected piece or architecture badly in need of funds, but it has a cross and the roof still keeps God's tears from soaking the pews.

I have to walk the length of the train several times before I find my seat. I sling my bags into the overhead storage and sit, faking interest in a business magazine sticking out of the seat pocket... which is all in French...

Only now do I feel like I'm actually in bloody France. Now that I'm sitting in a compressed train, fumbling my way through a French magazine (despite the fact that I can't speak a damn word of the wretched language), staring at the disappearing capital city.

My fellow passengers flex back, eyes in their books or crosswords. A gentle hum resonates through the walls and upholstery. I lean back, closing my eyes, then realise that I haven't eaten since the flight. I'm not in a place where the food is brought right to your mouth!

There's a gruff-looking man, with a white moustache and a grey suit, sitting next to me, trying to light up a cigarette. "Is there an onboard restaurant or something?" I ask.

"American?" he says, coughing.

"No, I'm English."

"You sound American." He jerks his thumb behind him. "That way."

"Thanks," I tell him, getting to my feet.

There's a small sandwich bar in the next carriage. Freezing cold sandwiches and softish pastries glisten. I can smell luke-warm coffee. The woman behind the counter raises her eyebrows, speaks French so fluently that I feel guilt-tripped into pretending I understand. I point at one of the sandwiches.

"That and a cup of coffee," I say. "No milk or sugar."

I have over a few notes, hoping I've got the currency correct. She doesn't take her eyes off me as she counts everything out and gives me what I'm owed. I try to smile as I take the sandwich and plastic cup off her. As I'm making my way back, I become aware of the odour of sugar. I sip my drink, realising the woman's put ten cubes in. Diabolical. I nearly gag. But if it's God's will, then what can I say?

The afternoon begins to kick into gear as the train winds south.

The man in the grey suit starts dozing, muttering to himself in his sleep. He's a resting statue, the remains of an old order of chivalry, an order of male honour that is disappearing, vanishing into the thin breeze, being swallowed by the ocean, falling into sand and dust. This is the Nineties, after all.

My fellow passengers, who were so alert when we set off from Paris, are now sitting back with their eyelids glued shut. The carriage has turned into a dormitory.

I watch the trees and fields pass by, so beautifully calm in the late sunshine. A short while later, leaves and branches do their dance for the wind. I clear my mind, think of the church that awaits me in Marseille. Think about the beachfront and the bars. Think about doing a re-enactment of Gene Hackman in *French Connection II*, the bit where Popeye Doyle chases the bad guy and shoots him in the harbour. Best ending scene ever. No soppy bit before the end credits start rolling.

I catch a glimpse of a farmer herding sheep into a pen. Just like you see in those video tapes they play in French lessons: the ones that show situations where normal people speak the basics of this language in staged conversations. Must be a fair wind picking up, because I swear I saw him clamping his hand on his cap.

Why didn't I bring a book or something?

I cross and uncross my arms, forcing myself to watch the windy weather. Some storm! The sky is darkening, clouds forming into tears. Scarlet would have something to say about it. Josephine... something a lot worse.

The train rocks, creaks.

Pink streaks of lightning crisscross the sky. Rain hammers the glass.

Suddenly I'm anxious for this journey to be over. I hope it's not like this in Marseille. Well, at least my hotel – proper posh as it is – might relieve the distress.

The conductor walks past, stumbling as he passes, grasping the edges of seats to steady himself. I presuming he's the conductor anyway, judging from his eccentric uniform and large leather pouch at his waist. And his cap.

I remember our first night performing. That night we thought things wouldn't go to plan. How wrong we were. But I wish that maybe we hadn't been successful. That we'd never lifted off the ground. Here I am, alone, hiding my fame.

Somehow I nod off, losing myself in a vision of one of the concerts, the excited crowd cheering and stamping the floor. It's beautiful, but it's painful. It burns.

Scarlet's smile catches my eye. She bows her head. Turns away like I mean everything and nothing to her...

I wake up to a harsh hand grasping my shoulder.

"You, up, now!"

"What the fuck?" I say.

It's the conductor. His cap threatens to slash my forehead.

"You need to leave the train, immediately!" he hisses in my ear.

"Okay, calm down." I stand up, expecting the scene of Marseille to greet me, but I'm confronted with a black sky vomiting dark rain. We're at a train station – somewhere – but it's literally in the middle of nowhere. Grey plains stretch to the horizon.

"You go now!" the conductor shouts.

"Where are we?"

"Railway track flooded! Train is going back to Paris. Get your things! Now!"

The train is empty. Passengers, bags, and humanity. All gone.

He roughly escorts me down the gangway to the door, helping me out my throwing my wheelie bag onto the platform.

"Excuse me!" I cry out. "That's expensive! You'll be paying for it if it's damaged! I'm in a band, you know!"

"What is the words I'm looking for..." He barks a loud cough. "Yes, I remember. English girl, fuck off."

"Fuck you too," I snap back at him, as I step off. I'm immediately soaked. "Where's the nearest hotel?" I ask. The doors are already closing. The metal string of sausages begins to move.

I huddle myself in the rain, pretty much in disbelief. Maybe there'll be another train, but I have my doubts. Not in this weather. There's no shelter at the station: just a long stretch of concrete and slabs. And no lights. If I don't move soon, I won't be able to.

At the other end of the platform, a small path leads off. I trudge in that direction, swallowing rainwater.

Believe me, they'll be getting a strong complaint. Believe me.

I go as fast as I dare, hoping to see a town or a village. I start shaking. I'll get bloody pneumonia before long. I'm shivering. But I need to keep moving.

I should never have come. Or I should have flown directly to Marseille. Oh, my stupid attitude! Let's see romantic Paris.

The path ends, leading to a road. I throw up a cheer. At least I can flag a passing driver! Maybe even the local police. All roads lead to success.

But the world is getting even darker. The evening light blinks itself into nothingness, leaving me blind. I'm a goner if I don't find shelter soon.

I'm openly weeping, praying to God. Please help me.

I wish I was with the girls, or at least they were with me now. They'd pull me through this. They'd never let me fall.

Memories fill the puddles and floodwater in front of me. I fight back the urge to drown.

Everything is dark now. I'm totally blind. I screw my eyelids closed, trying to see... something.

Totally silent. Apart from the rain. Rain which seems to grow heavier and thicker.

The thought comes to me that I might not survive this.

I don't see the pinprick of light at first.

It's like a candle in a storm.

I blink rainwater from my vision. There are more lights, cropping up like fireflies. It's a village. I can hear distant shouting. I break into a run. Houses, streets come into view, forming themselves in the darkness. I howl and scream. Then my legs stop working. I feel faint. I keep going forward, but my body somehow defies my brain. Everything goes white. I tumble forward, hands outstretched, thinking of nothing except the coldness of the stage after a concert.

10 October 1992

Voices.

French accents. French language. Thick with both.

I think it's two people. Arguing. Bickering. Quite aggressive.

They go on for what seems like forever, before a firm French accent utters an English sentence: "Can you hear me?"

I'm so weak. So weak I think I've drowned in one of those puddles.

"Can you hear my voice?" the person repeats.

My eyes open, taking in the sight of three men – all in white lab coats – staring down at me. Consciousness and strength fill me. I find myself start to move, but gentle hands restrain me.

"Rest," one of the men orders. I think it's the same guy. His brown moustache threatens to tickle the edge of my nose. "You are in the village of St Pierre. We found you last night collapsed. We found your passport in your coat – that's why we're speaking English. You understand me, right?"

"I understand you," I whisper. "What is this place I'm in?"

"The local emergency room. I think that's what you English call it. Can you tell me please... were you drunk last night? Assaulted?"

"If you must know, my train got stuck. They kicked us off. I literally got left in the middle of nowhere. Listen, when's the next bus or train to Paris? I'm going to fucking throttle this train company."

"Alas, mademoiselle, the roads out of here are blocked. Trees have been blown down by the winds and there is floodwater. Unfortunately, you are stuck here for at least a couple of days."

"I have plans! I'm supposed to be heading to Marseille."

"There is no way out." The Frenchman pats my shoulder. "You must remain in the village. We have booked you into the local hotel, if, that is, you're well enough to leave."

"I am. Actually, there were a quite a few people on the train with me. Maybe a few of them are staying in the village as well?"

One of the other Frenchmen speaks up. In French, of course.

"What's he saying?" I ask.

The man with the moustache flutters his eyebrows. "A few cars passed through late last night. Taxis. They managed to get through before the trees and water cut off the roads. Listen, madam, you need to rest."

"What time is it?"

"It is six o'clock in the morning. Rest for a bit, then, if you feel up to it, you can have some breakfast."

"I'd like that."

"Some rest first."

"Nope. I want to get up."

"Please, madam."

"I insist. And I don't know your names."

My friend with the moustache seems to take a short bow. "I am Dr Michael La Rue. These are my colleagues Dr Gustaf Blanc and Dr Eric Garson. And you are...?"

"Gina." I introduce myself properly.

Dr Blanc – really young (almost my age) – lets out a short laugh. He's well-built, confident, got the blue eyes. "You're from that band, aren't you?" he says. His English is almost native.

"Is that a problem? Now, am I a prisoner here, or what?"

"No." Dr La Rue steps back. "You are absolutely not a prisoner. Dr Blanc, please show Gina to the local hotel."

"My pleasure. My pleasure. Gina, please..."

The village of St Pierre is – and I hate stereotypic – the image what appears in old French films.

A large, sandstone-coloured street runs through the centre of the village, broken only by a decaying water fountain right at its heart that seems to have given up its zest for life a long time ago. Thatched houses – I'm not expert on architecture – are situated at irregular angles to the main street. Small gardens bask in the autumnal sun. A local shop, flattered and flattened with advertisements and bits of tape, stands near the centre of St Pierre, right beside my hotel. Branching off from the main street, right beside the fountain, is a smaller road that leads through a tight network of houses, as well as what appears to be a local French bar, to a series of rectangular buildings in the distance. Everything glimmers in the sun.

As for the inhabitants of this curious little place, they seem to ignore me. They walk on by, some on these mobile phones, talking and talking. Others stared at me with only the antagonistic emotion you would show a stray cat.

I look along the main street, seeing what I think is a mirage in the distance: floodwater. I look behind me: where the village ends and the open countryside begins, a pile of trees is blocking the road. I am truly trapped.

I start walking along the main street in the direction of the flooding. It's called Clemens Row. It doesn't sound French; *proper English*, as Scarlet or Josephine would put it. It takes a few minutes to reach the end, but then I'm moving as slow as a snail. The locals who walk past me see me for what I am: someone who doesn't belong. Whispers in a foreign language surround me.

It's just houses at this end. They blink in the warmish sun, showing themselves off. I turn on the spot, trying to see something unique, something that stands out. Wait a minute, I'm looking for a church.

I head back towards the centre of the village, scanning in all directions, becoming for desperate with each passing moment.

"Excuse me." I've stopped an elderly woman. She looks up with watery eyes. "Excuse me, ma'am, do you know where the local church is?"

She moves past me.

A man approaches – not a man, even. A boy. I repeat my question. His blank look says all.

I'll have to find it myself. I'll have to see if it can be found.

I hang around by the fountain for a few minutes, trying to see if there are any patterns in its surface, but it's completely smooth. No carvings of ancient battles or knights with their lovers.

I gaze up, staring at the distant rectangular buildings. I start walking towards them, my feet squelching out the last of the water. I'm looking forward to sorting out the rest of my soaking stuff later...

It becomes obvious after a while what those buildings are: a high school. It's not that it's out of place with the rest of the village, it's that it's been there too long. Like a rusty nail embedded in a tree. As I approach, I see that metal fences have been erected, yellow warning signs strapped to the bars. The buildings – which from afar looked so virginal and pristine – are lumpy, mouldy and splintered. The playground, bitter and broken. The grand school gates, rusted and punished. Windows are smashed. Grass grows between slabs like cancer.

"Terrible tragedy," comes a voice.

A man is standing beside me. He's focused on the ruins of the school, sighing quietly to himself.

"What the hell happened?" I find myself asking.

The man's wispy grey hair peels away from his wrinkled face. "You're English, aren't you?" he says. "So am I. Guilty as charged. Used to teach here, can you believe that? Moved out here in Seventy-Eight, hoping for a new beginning, and look what happened. I moved away after it happened, but the past drags you down, pulls you in. Crushes you. I had to come back to see the place one last time."

It's now that I recognise him. Saw him in the bar as Dr La Rue escorted me into the hotel. Thought he was lonely.

"What did you teach?" I ask him.

"Maths, actually."

"Nice. I was never that good at maths at school."

"Trust me, they always say that. Listen, I'm going to stretch my legs. Take it you got stuck here by the floods? As soon as things have cleared up, get yourself out of here. I'll be doing that. Nothing but sadness and depression."

"Tell me what happened," I say.

"I don't need to," he replies. He starts moving away from me. "Get out of here, doll, get out of here," he calls back to me. He walks with his hands in his pockets, carefree, totally relaxed.

I shout after him, knowing that I sound desperate, but he doesn't turn to face me. I start chasing after him, but pull to a halt before I've even gone five steps.

11 October 1992

My hotel – called some French name I'll never be able to pronounce – has the cosiness of those English inns and pubs, but there's a fragility to it. Old and modern haven't quite come together.

I finish the remains of my breakfast: flaky croissants and decently fresh coffee. The dining room is small, confined.

Wrapped with wallpaper that's threatening to come down. Pictures hang askew.

It's not even Ten, but I need a drink...

I was going to try and find the church this morning, but I got told that the train line has fully reopened. Dr La Rue expressed concerns yesterday that I still wasn't well enough to travel, but I woke this morning feeling like a swishing blue bird.

Last night, curiosity got the better of me when I was having a drink at the hotel bar. I asked the man serving me if he knew about what had happened at the school. Though his English is great (he spoke flirtatiously fluent to me when showing me to my room), he shrugged me off, mentioned something about "the summer of Nineteen-Eighty", and then went about washing a few glasses.

After finishing my coffee, I head upstairs, brush my teeth, and start the checkout procedure. It's not quite New York... but... it'll do. In no time at all, I'm walking back in the direction of the station.

It's warm. It's the south of France. Soon, I'll be in Marseille, walking along the beachfront. In a bar, sipping something nice. Being surrounded by the like-minded.

I saw it. Last night. Just before I left the bar. Pinned underneath a stand of whisky glasses. A photo. The words *June 5th 1980* scrawled upon its surface in rough pen. A set of young people gathered in a woodland somewhere. At the front, seated cross-legged, Roger Miser. Younger – vaguely attractive – but definitely him.

When I reach the station, I see that I have twenty minutes before the train. I look around me, then retrace my steps to the rough gravel path. I glance around once more, tear the crucifix from around my neck, and chuck it as far as my arms will allow me.

Scarlet

28 November 1992

She struggles with the finely cut salmon, at first. It's too watery, too minimalistic.

They're in some restaurant in the West End, properly living the dream. Some eatery she'll never bother to remember. But she doesn't need the food tonight. She's got the company of her lover. Mauro thumbs the stem of his glass of wine, elbow digging at the silk tablecloth. He stares at her, his smile stronger than it's ever been.

She found her way back to him – at the expense of that wretched pub closing – but she found her way.

"How does April sound?" he asks.

"Yeah, I'd like that." She consumes the last of her meal, drinks the final few drops of her wine. "Actually, how about May?"

"I'm thinking April. I don't know, it just feels right."

"Then let's make it April."

"It's a date."

She raises her hand, summons another bottle. Something from Chile. That region, the one she keeps forgetting, she's got a taste for their grapes. But she can't remember the name.

They stay in the restaurant for another hour, taking their time with dessert. When they leave, surrounded by Christmas decorations being raised like drawbridges, the world around them is cold and silent.

"What did you think of Gina's story?" says Mauro, leading her over a crossing.

"Oh, about that place in France. Yeah, I thought it was a bit weird. A bit sad, too. But, well, Roger Miser being involved with it all...? I think it's a bit too farfetched. A bit stupid. He's a bit of a character, but I don't think he was involved in anything... serious. I dunno. Listen, let's keep this to ourselves..."

"Absolutely. You reckon we should go down there, check it out for ourselves?"

"Mauro! Come on!"

When they reach home, Mauro curses, "Damn, left the living room lights on."

He opens the door. They go in, letting it swing shut behind them.

"Thanks for taking me out tonight," says Scarlet. She holds him close, fastening arms around his shoulders. "Thank you."

"Let's go to sleep."

"Not yet..." She kisses him, starts unbuttoning his shirt. "Mauro, I love you, and I can't wait to be your wife."

"I love you too."

"Let's go to bed," she whispers, fastening his fingers in her overtight grip.

Josephine

29 November 1992

Totally not in the mood for this. Grudgingly, I flop over, take the phone, preparing to yell abuse to whoever's disturbed me at... Two-Thirty in the morning!

"Josephine! It's Mauro! Something's happened!"

"Look, have you two had another argument or something? I'm not a fucking peacemaker!"

"No, Josephine, it's Scarlet!" He's coughing sobs. *"She's been taken to hospital. They caught him. They caught him."* He can barely hold his words together.

"Mauro, slow down, tell me what has happened." I sit up, alert, fully alert.

"Eugene tried to kill Scarlet! Injected her with heroin! Josephine, you need to come now! We're in Guy's Hospital."

"I know where that is. Mauro, stay calm, okay? I'll be right there."

"Please come! I can't be alone right now! Josephine, I need you here, please!"

"Mauro! Deep breaths. It'll be okay, I promise."

I don't even shower properly. Ten minutes after being snatched from sleep, I'm waiting for a taxi. I'm not even thinking of Scarlet, not even contemplating how badly she's been hurt, or if she's still alive. I just want to be there. Looking after Mauro.

It's too much. Eugene. Scarlet. My past and my future converging. No. I'm over the past now.

I've never liked hospitals. But that's another story – I won't bore you with it.

The taxi drops me off somewhere by the Accident & Emergency. I hope that's where I'll find her. Presumably so, anyway... I'm through the door, wheeling past old ladies, past worn-out doctors and nurses.

I don't care that I push people out of a queue to get to the reception desk. I hammer the wood, look the startled librarian-type lady in the eye, demand to know where Scarlet is.

"She's in critical care," the lady states. How can she be so fucking calm in a situation like this? How can be so fucking ignorant? "Are you a relative?"

"More than you might think," I snarl.

"Josephine!" I hear Mauro call.

I turn to my right, seeing him start to slide against the door that marks the entrance to Critical Care. I run to him, like he's my lover. I stop him from falling. I catch him, protect him. I hold him close.

"It's okay," I whisper. "She'll be fine, okay? She'll be fine. She's strong." Yet, as these words slip from my mouth, I feel the tears start to stream. I can't hold my breath any longer and allow the sobs to come.

"I can't live without her," he cries. "I need her."

"You aren't going to lose her. I promise you, you hear me? You *will not* lose her."

The cafeteria isn't open at this time, but I sweettalk them into letting us sit down at one of the tables. There's a vending machine nearby. A few annoying moments when I try to put the coins in, but soon I've got two frothy cups of cheap coffee. I set them down between us, a bridge that links our collective torment.

It takes a while, but eventually I get him to talk about what happened.

"We went out for dinner. Came home." He sniffles. "Came home. Went to bed. Woke up to Scarlet grabbing me, scream- ing. Eugene was standing overhead. He had this needle in his hand. Told me he'd injected Scarlet with an overdose of her- oin. She starts foaming at the mouth, vomiting. He's watching. Smiles. He walks away so fucking coolly. I phone for an ambu- lance, told them what happened. Fuck, I can't believe he'd do something like this."

"You say they got him?"

"Yeah. Police arrested him. He'd gone to this party, to sell the remaining heroin. He's being questioned as we speak. Don't care about him. He's not my brother anymore."

We take each other's hands, becoming silent.

Footsteps approach. A grim-looking doctor. They always look grim.

"Mauro Lane?" he enquires. He passes a clipboard from one hand to the other. "I have some news about Scarlet. She's going to be okay."

"That's great!" shouts Mauro. "Thank you!"

"Unfortunately, there will be complications. She's had a massive heroin overdose. I understand she's a singer...?"

"That's correct," I tell him.

"Well, she's going to have to lay off that for a bit. She will need to spend time convalescing. She'll also need to be monitored for signs of addiction."

"Scarlet isn't a fucking addict!" hisses Mauro. "Don't even think about saying that."

"Mauro, don't..." I whisper, stopping a fist from rising.

"It's just a precaution," says the doctor.

"I want to see her."

"That's not possible. She needs to get plenty of rest. Come back later. Two o'clock. That's when our visiting hours start."

"So what am I supposed to do until then?"

"Go home, Mauro," says the doctor, handing his clipboard back to the first hand. "Get plenty of rest yourself. She's in the best of care. You left your number with my colleague earlier I believe? If there's any change, we'll call you on your mobile telephone."

"Come home with me, Mauro. Stay at mine." I probably sound feeble when I say these words, but he nods his head – so does the doctor.

The second he gets through my door, it's a struggle to keep him awake. I move him to my bedroom, tuck him in. I'm like his lover. I wish I was. Treacherous thoughts in a time like this. Wicked, despicable thoughts. But I can't fight what the heart wants. I stop at the door, look at him, watch his chest rise and fall, watch the tears collect in the pillow.

I wish I had him. Unfortunately for me, I ended up with the wrong brother.

It's wrong – I know – but I have feelings for him. I shouldn't. I wish I didn't. But I do. In another life, I would have ended up with him. But this is my life.

"Josephine...!" he calls out.

"Mauro, get some sleep."

"Thank you, Josephine." He sits up.

"Mauro!" I snap. "Sleep, okay?"

Mauro's mobile rings at about Half-Past Eleven. (I took it down with me.) I answer it, kicking off my shoes and digging my heels into my sofa.

"Mr Lane?" A woman's scratchy voice.

"No, it's Josephine."

"I'm calling from Guy's Hospital, regarding Scarlet –"

"Is she okay?"

"She's fine. Actually, I'm calling to say that she is awake, however the doctors do not want her to see anyone at the moment. She's still very weak. They're keeping her under close observation for the next forty-eight hours. I am aware that Mr –"

"It's okay. I'll tell him. He needs to rest himself. Thank the doctors for me."

"Of course. Have a good day. Try to get some rest yourself, Josephine."

"I will, thanks." I hang up. "I will."

Susan

2 December 1992

We're all there when the police inform Scarlet of the news. Two fresh-faced men, holding their hats in the crook of their arms, inform her that Eugene Lane has been charged with attempted murder, as well as a number of drug charges.

"We'll be in touch with any developments," they say. They file out, nodding thanks to the doctors.

Mauro is next to Scarlet, holding both her hands in his. She looks extremely weak, barely in this world.

Josephine, Gina and I surround the bed. Roger and George stand at the back of the room, either side of a table of medical equipment. Scarlet's parents and Alastair are on the opposite side of the bed to Mauro.

"I don't give a fuck what the doctors say," says Scarlet, coughing. Her face is matted in sweat, her hair plastered to the pillow. "I'll be singing soon enough."

"Of that we're all certain," says Roger.

"We should them some privacy," says Gina.

We all murmur agreement.

"Get well soon, we've got an album to work on." Gina ruffles Scarlet's hair. "Get some rest, okay?"

We say our goodbyes and head out, leaving Mauro and Scarlet's family behind. I tell them that I'm going home. I've not had that much rest over the past few days. I tell them that I need space on my own.

I leave the hospital in a hurry for the taxi rank. There's one just next to the Outpatients area. I know, because I came here before just after I was adopted. And that's another story...

There's a bit of a queue – I know my celebrity status won't let me skip it. I wait in line, but I know it won't be too long. That's when I see Gina and Roger walking together.

Gina

2 December 1992

"I think it's great you've dropped this whole religious thing," says Roger, as we move through the car park like lovers sneaking away from a ball. "Not that I have any issues with religion, please understand that. But I think it has put pressures on the band, and us."

His limo is up ahead, occupying several parking spaces. Thankfully the place is reasonably empty – thankfully. George is standing by the bonnet, in deep conversation with the driver.

"I heard things got a bit rough in France," says Roger. He walks with a confidant gait, something that comes with decades of being a frontline music veteran. "Floods or something, wasn't it?"

"Yep. Train didn't even get to Marseille. Ended up stuck in this small town for a bit."

"No wonder you lost faith!"

I'm angry at him now. Even though this guy launched me to fame, I'm so pissed off at him. His arrogance and ignorance. It's suffocating.

"I got stuck in St Pierre," I say.

He stops. Jaw trembles.

"What?" he stutters, turning to face me.

"What happened in Nineteen-Eighty?"

"I need to be getting back." His fingers flex. "Paperwork. Listen, why don't we chat in the week?"

"No!" I realise I've yelled too loud. But it's too late to stop. I go right up to him. "You launched our careers, Roger, you brought us to stardom. We will always be in your debt. But we need to know if there's stuff you're holding back."

"Correction. *You* and only you want to know."

"Roger…"

"Don't!" he snaps. "It was twelve years ago. Over twelve years. I was a very different man in those days. Look, I'd just been through a divorce, I got involved with the wrong woman. That relationship ended badly, okay? Okay?"

"Come on, Roger, I know it's more than that."

"Out of curiosity, what will you do if I refuse to tell you? What will you do?" He smirks. "Nothing. Exactly. Now, I need to head back to the office. Work to do. Go home, Gina, get some rest. I dunno, have a cup of tea. Maybe a glass of the strong stuff. It's what I do to drown the sorrows."

"I might just do that," I say, fighting back the urge to scream.

"Good. I'll forget about what you just said."

I watch him leave. Watch him joke with George about a riot at a concert he organised in Nineteen-Eighty-Eight.

He's right. I should just drop it. What will digging up the past achieve? What happened… happened. I suppose there are more important things in this world.

I set off for the taxi rank. As I leave the car park, I brush past a man in a business suit. "Excuse me, ma'am," he says.

"It's okay," I reply.

"Hold on, you're Gina, aren't you?"

"Yes, that's me."

"Big fan of your music." He speaks with a deep American accent. He's tall, maybe a little too skinny, but he has an aura of strength. "Came to one of your concerts."

"Thanks," I say.

"Anyway, must go. Have a nice day."

I wave and continue to the taxi rank. When I get home, I pour myself a strong measure, curse myself for invading Roger's privacy, and drown everything in one shot.

Scarlet

11 December 1992

For the third time, she ignores the doctor's warning. She assembles her things with rhythmic fashion, slips on her clothes, whistles a tune. One of hers.

"I'm going home," she says to the doctor, a man whose bright white hair threatens him with mandatory requirement. "And you can tell your colleagues that I'll be singing as much as I want. I'm not a heroin addict."

"It's just a precautionary measure," says the white-haired doctor.

"Look, if I feel the need to shoot up, I'll phone the hospital, okay? Thanks for everything."

"We'll inform your family and loved ones that you have discharged yourself."

"Please don't. I'll do it myself."

She waves goodbye and starts walking through the corridors of sickness and death. All she wants to do is get home. Home... the pull of it is so strong.

No one knows she's discharging herself. They still think she's resting, as per doctor's orders. But she's her own person. She makes her own decisions.

She gets to her front door an hour later than she expects, around Three in the afternoon. She pushes the key into the lock, enters her house, drops her gear in the hallway.

"Scarlet?" Mauro emerges from the living room, his skin flooding with colour. "You're home!" He runs at her, wraps her tightly. "I'm glad you're home. I'm glad you're alive. I thought I'd lost you."

She gently frees herself, goes into the kitchen. She fills a glass with water and drinks the fluid of life.

"How are you feeling?" he asks.

She drinks another glass.

"I was thinking, if you feel up to it, we could go away for a weekend. Maybe the Christmas markets in Germany or something."

She fills up a third glass, starts sipping, doesn't reply to him.

"Or maybe go up to Scotland. West coast. One of the islands perhaps." He laughs. "Shortbread and single malt. Perfect cure."

"Why was the light on?" is her response.

"What do you mean?" He goes up to her. "Scarlet, why don't you rest? You look exhausted."

"Why was the light on?" she repeats.

"I'm sorry, I don't understand."

"When we out for dinner, I turned off the lights and locked the door. Why was the light on when we came back?"

"I don't know. Scarlet, maybe you left it on by mistake? Come on, you need to rest!"

"Then why wasn't the door locked?" she demands. "I couldn't sleep last night. Started running through things in my head. Why wasn't the door locked?"

"It was."

"No, it wasn't."

"Scarlet, I don't know what you're getting at."

"You and I both have a key to this house. I locked up. I went to the road to wait for our taxi to turn up. I had my back turned on you for a few moments. Why did you unlock the door?"

"Scarlet, I swear to you, I didn't unlock anything."

"When we came back, you opened the door. But you didn't put a key in. How did you know it was unlocked? Mauro, tell me the truth. Tell me the whole fucking truth."

Mauro sits down, puts his face in his hands. Weeps like a little girl. "He's my brother, Scarlet. My brother. I said he could take a few things from the house. Food and the like. He was a bit short on money. Christ, Scarlet, he's my brother!"

"You let that bastard come into my home. That filthy, despicable piece of shit. Mauro, why did you fucking do that?"

"I'm sorry. I'm so, so sorry."

"Mauro, get your fucking things, and get the fuck out." She tears off her engagement ring. "Here..." She thrusts it into his shirt pocket. "Sell it or give it to some gullible, cheap slut."

"Please, Scarlet."

"I could have died, Mauro! Don't you remember all the shit Eugene said to us? Threatening us? And you said he could come in and take whatever he liked. Why did you take such a stupid risk?"

"I'm so sorry."

"I don't give a fuck." She fights back tears. She wins the battle easily. "Mauro, go. Now."

"Please."

"The engagement's over. I'm sorry. I can't trust you anymore."

"I love you," he says in his wounded voice.

"Don't start that," she says bitterly.

"I never meant for anything like this to happen."

"I know you didn't." She rests her hands by the sink. "But it did. And there have to be consequences."

"I'm not going without a fight. I love you, Scarlet, I always have. And I'm going to fight for you, whatever it takes."

"If you loved me, you wouldn't have done what you did." She turns away from him. She feels his hand on her shoulder.

Such an alien touch. Totally unwanted. "Mauro, if you love me, you'll leave."

"There is nothing I can do to make up for this?"

"No. I'm so sorry, Mauro. You have my word that no one will ever know about you leaving the door unlocked. If the police ask, I'll say that it was left unlocked accidentally. You do the same. You understand?" She turns back to see his head bowed. He nods.

He opens his mouth, starts saying something, but the words refuse to come. He knows he's lost. She can see it. All intimacy between them is gone.

"I'm going out for a couple of hours," she says. "When I'm back, you're gone okay?"

"Scarlet..."

"Mauro, don't make this any worse that it has to be. This is best, for both of us."

She walks past him. He's behind her now. Though she hears the sobs, though she hears the howl of his anger, he's behind her now. She checks that she has her purse, and then starts walking. She goes on. She lives the day.

She stops in a bookshop, peruses the shelves, hopes she can find something to read. There's a small café in the back. She gets herself a black coffee, sits down, amongst the various academic, book-loving souls around her, finds that she has no desire to weep, but she needs consoling.

"Excuse me," a voice says, "but we were sitting there."

She gazes up. A young couple – damn attractive – are looking down at her.

"I'm sorry," she says. "What?"

"I said, we were sitting there." The man is gesturing behind him. "My girlfriend and I had gone to order, and you took our seats."

Scarlet ignores him, sips her coffee.

"Didn't you hear me?"

"Oh, mate," she hisses, "fuck off, won't you?"

"What did you say?"

"David, just drop it," the woman says. "There are plenty of tables."

"Don't care," he says. "Did you hear what she said to me?" He reaches down, takes Scarlet by the collar, lifts her up, tosses her to the side.

"Hey, I'm going," she says, surprised by the man's strength. "Look, just split with my boyfriend, okay?"

"Is there any surprise in that?" he says.

"David, come on," says the girlfriend.

"Okay, just stating the obvious. Have you seen the state of her?"

Instinctively, she runs. She wants him. She stumbles out of the bookshop, knocking over several piles of books. Startled shouts follow her. On the streets, she heads for home, tears now streaming.

She bursts into her house, screaming how sorry she is, how she wants another chance. Silence. The place seems emptier. Not emotionally. Physically. Various bits and pieces are gone: books, videotapes, ornaments. She runs upstairs to the bedroom, checks all the rooms. His stuff is gone.

Then she remembers why she kicked him out. She breathes a sigh of relief. Five minutes later, she's on the phone to Roger, asking him for the latest in security locks, and then gets a bottle of wine out the fridge.

18 December 1992

A week later, she's alone in the kitchen – *her* kitchen – when she sees the mini-interview in one of the music magazines she's forgotten she subscribed to. She found it earlier, beneath the piles of circular notices, damp at the edges. She feels a little sad when she reads the text, but finds herself smirking.

It's a new chapter for singer Mauro Lane, as he makes preparations to move to America. I caught up with him to discuss his fears, his thoughts on Madchester, and what he hopes to learn in the U.S.A....

She folds it shut, pleased beyond belief that he's moved on. It wouldn't have worked anyway. They were too different.

She'll be out of this house soon as well. She did it yesterday: bought a penthouse in the north of London. Absolutely everything she needs.

She's been composing songs for the next album. Knitting them together like wool. Not that she's taken any inspiration from Mauro. He means nothing to her now. Her ideas come from fear...

There's only one thing weighing her down now. The news of her attempted murder has found its way into the papers. It'll get worse in the next few days. No wonder Mauro's fleeing... but he'll probably have to give evidence at the trial.

She's moving to her new home in January. One last Christmas here. But she'll be having it alone. No attachments. Not this time.

Gina

19 December 1992

Yeah, I'm a bit too old for one of these 'blind date' things, but since I've said goodbye to religion, I'm feeling much freer. A bit looser. Footloose. Fancy-free. Josephine's set this up for me. Maybe she felt a bit bad over what happened, how she treated me over that magazine interview. Maybe she's felt bad over a lot of things.

I check myself in the mirror. I can wear as much makeup as I want to this time. Of course, don't go over the top. I gather my coat and handbag, heading into the night. The taxi's waiting for me. The driver calls my name, blankly, without feeling.

"Yeah, that's me," I say, climbing inside.

I was wrong to pry. I know that. Whatever happened back then, Roger Miser's put in the past. Why can I just respect that?

Because I'm too curious. I want to know everything about that summer. It's like I was there myself, but I've forgotten the trauma and the joy. What was it like? Who slept with who? Who broke who's heart? Was it a music festival? Was it just a normal summer? Was there some kind of a French fete that went wrong? Was there... murder? No. Stop it. I should not be thinking along those lines. It's almost criminal.

But I'll never stop wondering. My curiosity is like a fire that can't be extinguished. It's a thirst that cannot be quenched.

My mind races with thoughts and imagination, all the stories of what could possibly happened, as the taxi delivers me to the lucky guy who gets my company for dinner tonight. He's a journalist, apparently. Maybe I'll connect with him. *Don't mention Roger Miser. Don't mention the summer of 1980!*

"Here you are, love," the driver says.

Should I tell him about this modern feminism that forbids phrases like this?

I get out, handing him his cash. Should I call him a bit of a twat?

I think I've made the right choice with the restaurant. It's beautiful. One of those Greek places that have sprung up over the past few years. I step up to the glass doors, pry them open.

"I've got a booking," I tell a girl waiting just inside. I give her the full details, nothing left out. She smiles, escorting me through the maze of tables. Christ, the place is nearly empty. She shows me to a table at the back of the restaurant, trapped in a dark corner. There, a man with circular spectacles sips a glass of red wine.

He's a lot older than I thought he was. Mid-thirties? Oh yeah. But he seems nice, polite, the way he stands up, greets me with a formal handshake.

"Gina," I say.

"Luke," he answers. "Please, do sit. Sorry, I started earlier." He touches the rim of his glass. "Let me order you something..."

"I'll have what you're having."

"Wise choice." Luke waves at one of the restaurant staff, indicating his glass. Two fingers.

"So, tell me about yourself," I say, lowering myself.

"Of course. Well, I'm not a fully-fledged journalist. Just doing a small local magazine. Sorts the rent."

"So you've just graduated from journalism school, then?" I ease my handbag under the desk.

"Oh, yes." His posh accent is hopeful, filled with the fruits of life. "Literally five weeks ago. One of these small courses that's started up. Tailored to the individual's needs."

"So, you didn't get into proper journalism school then?"

"Well..."

"Come on!" I laugh as I say this. I'm trying to have a joke with the guy, honestly. I'm trying to be funny. Why doesn't he see it that way?

His smile drops. Everything about him seems to turn sour. Everything about him twists and writhes. He gets up, takes a long drink, and then walks away.

"Knew this whole thing was a bad idea," he huffs. "She's paying."

I can't help it. I fall forward laughing. I've not been drinking, but it's like I want to be drunk. I head back out of the restaurant, laugh again, stagger up the road. What a pretentious prick! Can't even take a joke, unbelievable.

When I get home, I phone up Josephine to let her know. I can hear her mouth falling open in shock on the other end.

"Oh, well, he's always been a bit of an arsehole," she says by way of a conclusion. She says a quick goodbye, and then hangs up.

Bit of a pointless night. I feel a sense of sadness, deep longing, a desire for companionship. I'm about to wallow in abusive self-pity, then realise that I haven't eaten tonight. Food first. Then I can abuse myself. It'll take the edge off things.

Susan

20 December 1992

I'm still doing these runs. Christ, only five days to Christmas. Time that should be spent filling myself up with shit and booze, but I'm trying to be healthy. I'm trying to keep things together. Christ knows why I'm pushing myself to the brink of exhaustion. Maybe it's the stress of this new album.

Roger's excited chatter when us girls meet him in his poxy office really gets to me. He seems to be bullying us into doing this new album. It does worry me, because our contract runs for three albums. Will he cast us out after this?

On top of that, I swear I saw *him* again. Last month. When I was walking back from the bookstore, about Three in the afternoon. Hunched over a railing, vomit down his front. Though I can't be sure if it was.

That's why I'm running harder and faster. At Six A.M. each morning. No exceptions.

My past is a magnet. It's constantly threatening to drag me in, to punish and torture me. That's why I have to stay focused. Brutal runs in the cold. Until I'm pushed to the brink of blacking out.

Today, I'm going a bit lighter on myself. I want to be vaguely awake for when I see my foster parents. I want to smile and spread Christmas joy. Remind them that they made the right choice when they took me in.

I finish just as dawn is spreading its wings. I stop for a few moments outside my apartment, stretch off, deep breaths. I slowly head up the stairs, pass my affluent neighbours, slip into my lodgings. I make a small breakfast, but quickly decide it's not enough, and head out to a local café.

I find myself sitting alone, sipping French coffee and chewing on dry pastries. Despite it nearing eight o'clock, the café doesn't gain another soul. Rather, it seems to grow emptier and darker.

I should be going. Not long until my train.

I head back to the flat to get my things, freshen up a little. I resist any temptation to put on any makeup, not that I'm hiding. Though maybe I should be.

The train to Sevenoaks is over twenty minutes late. Once I'm on the move, I curse myself that I've left my mobile phone at home.

I get a few stares, a few prods in my direction. A few children tugging at the arms of their parents. Several pairs of hawkish eyes. But I'm someone who's used to all this attention.

They're waiting for me when I get to the other end. They smile and hug me as if I'm their own daughter. I try to act like I am, even though the distance between us has grown wider over the past three years.

"You look exhausted," she says.

"You bet I am."

"How is Scarlet?" he asks.

"Oh, she's fine. She's her usual busy self. Considering what's happened..."

"Yeah, how is she holding up?"

"She's strong. It's not the heroin thing, it's Mauro leaving that still gets to her."

"That's understandable."

My mum butts in, changing the subject, as if she wants to cut me off from Scarlet's world. "We've got some lunch ready for you at home," she says.

The car's outside, right by the exit, kissing the double yellows. My foster dad enters the front passenger seat, shouting at us to hurry up. Some terrible joke about a dodgy traffic warden giving them a fine.

"So, it's been good then?" he asks, as we pull into the road.

"Yep. Just busy."

"Are you seeing anyone?" she enquires.

"No time," I answer. "Way too busy."

"Well, we're concerned you're not getting out there enough." It's Dad's turn now. "You need to meet people."

"I meet people every day. Every single hour."

"Interviewers. Musicians." He counters it with the effectiveness of Willie Thorne potting in the black. "But not other, real, normal people."

"Sorry, is there a problem here?" I stutter.

"No, of course there isn't."

"But I'm beginning to get the inkling that there might be."

"Look, your father and I are concerned that you're not getting out enough..."

"I understand. I know how you feel, doing what I'm doing. I never asked for it myself. I try to get out. I try to meet people. But I'm so bloody busy."

"Have you thought about taking a step back from it?" she says.

"What do you mean?"

"This music lark," he tells me. "All this travelling and performing and singing. You need a decent, fulfilling life."

"I'm having one."

He's about to respond, but he can't seem to say the words.

We drift on in silence. I watch the crowds pass by. I'm a little child again, trapped in the depths of that awful place. Suffocating. Watching the world go by.

When we pull up the driveway, they gesture me inside, as though I'm an invited guest, rather than their daughter. They insist that I go up to my old room, even though I'm just staying here for the day. It's like I'm on the guided tour of who and what I once was.

I get served a salad buffet lunch in our retro dining room. The dying ornaments and decorations of the Eighties have gone, except for the Christmas tree: a weak-looking thing with sickly branches and fading fairy lights. Apparently, salad buffets all the trend now. Healthy social eating. Roger's been talking about hosting one at some point.

"What are your plans for Christmas?" she asks.

"You know, I'm not altogether sure. See what the girls are up to."

"Is that it then?" he says. There's a hint of aggression there. I don't like it. "What about us? Don't we get to spend time with our daughter?"

"I'm here. I'm here, now. Why, what is this about? Ever since I got off the train, you've been edgy. What are you try to...?"

"Should I tell her?" she says to her husband. "Susan, we're worried about you. We're worried about you spending all your time in the company of these women. And –"

"Sorry, what have you got against them? I've known Scarlet for years. Why have you got so much against her? Against them?"

"Don't forget what we did for you." My foster father looks at me with unyielding anger. "We took you in. We gave you a home."

"I cannot thank you enough for what you have done. You gave me a life. That's why I'm puzzled by this line of questioning."

"We took you in!" he explodes. "We put a roof over your head! Even though I was reluctant." He stops, drops his fork. I see his mouth twitch.

"What?" I stutter. "Sorry, I —"

"We've got presents for you." My mother puts on her chirpy voice.

"I should leave," I whisper.

My foster father stays where he is. Hands rest loosely on the table. His salad is untouched. I stagger back, gulping, trying to fight the whimpers.

"Why don't you stay for a bit?" She's pleading.

"I don't think I can. I should go. I'll see myself out. Have a good Christmas, okay?" I don't respond to the shouts and begging. I'm walking out.

I vaguely remember my way to the station. I try not to let the emotion show, but it has its tricks. I shed tears as I take my seat on the first train back to London. Concerned passengers reach out, but I bury my face in the crook of my arm.

I start asking myself a question. One that's uncomfortable. One that I shouldn't need to ask. Is Rowan Colt right?

Josephine

22 December 1992

"Your third album I'd like to be at least fifteen tracks long," Roger informs us. "Fifteen tracks minimum."

It's taken him an hour to come to this. The previous sixty minutes discussed potential recording locations. Why not go international? Record in South America or somewhere? But Scarlet stood her ground. English music should be recorded in England. Christ, she sounded like a right-wing skinhead from the Eighties... What about an old house or something like that? Susan objected to that. She didn't give a reason.

"We've only written seven so far," says Gina.

There's a faint odour of cigarette smoke in the air. Mixed with aftershave.

The office feels smaller today, but us girls feel bigger and stronger. I am, anyway. So much I've let go of. I even crack a smile.

"Josephine, you have something to add?" asks Roger.

"No, just that I think we can do it."

"Excellent! That's what I like to hear." He turns to his faithful George. "Get the girls to bring us in some coffee, would you? And make sure it's the good quality stuff."

"Will do." Bumbling George leaves the room, whistling something under his breath.

"I suppose you're wondering about the big question." Roger sits back in his chair, snorting. "When I signed you on, I signed you on for three albums. So, I know that you're thinking: Will I give you another album? Well, I absolutely want to. But there are certain contractual obligations I have to meet, you see. Now, that's not a problem. Just satisfy the right people. But I need to be certain of your level of commitment.

"Scarlet, may I talk openly?"

"Go ahead." She looks too weak to argue in any case. The meat's leaving her bones and her eyes are sinking. I should really reach out, touch her arm, let her know she's not alone.

Of course, that's not possible. Not now. The space between us is too great. She needs to fight this through on her own.

"You've had a rough ride recently, to put it mildly." The way Roger talks about delicate issues... it's so cold. Gina's giving him an equally frozen stare. "I need to know that you will be able to commit to a fourth album. Come to that, I need to know whether you're going to be able to make it through this one."

"Of course I will," she says. "Look, I need music. I need this."

"You need it. But is that commitment?"

"I promise you, I promise all of you, that I am committed to this. When I started this band, I swore to myself that I'd always be here for it. Look, if any of you doubt me, now's the time to say."

"We don't have doubts," Gina tells her. "Not at all. We love you."

Christ, she sounds religious again.

"I believe you, Scarlet," says Roger. A flash of guilt crosses through his eyes.

They end up coming to my house for a spot of lunch after Roger boots us out for the holidays, with strict orders to get some rest and take it easy. Busy year ahead. Touring. A new album. Expectant fans. I prepare the girls what I have: literally sandwiches and a few cans of beer. So uncivilised.

We're gathered in my living room. Careless feet splayed out threaten to topple towers of VHS tapes and CDs. I've been lazy in not stacking them on shelves. A pile of LPs is gathering dust in the corner, unused and neglected. I've only put one Christmas tree up this year, and it's way too tall, taunting us with is skeletal structure and fading baubles.

"Been a while since I've drunk from a can." Gina lets out a small belch as she crunches up the metal. Belching again, she tosses it to the small waste basket I've installed by the door. Straight in.

"Nice shot," says Susan.

"What's it like living outside London?" Gina asks me.

The question takes me by surprise. It's the kind of thing an interviewer would ask. One who's exhausted all others.

"I'm very much a part of London," I tell her. "It's just, I need a bit of a break from it right now."

Then Scarlet speaks up. Not that she was ever really quiet. "Go and see him," she says. "Robert."

"My ex? Why the fuck would I want to go anywhere near him?"

"He's a good guy, Josephine." She's looking weaker by the second. "Josephine, talk to him."

"No, Scarlet. He's in my past now. Utter waste of space. Terrified of commitment. Terrified of me. I've no time to waste on losers like that."

"But..." She stands up, fingers digging into the material of my plump sofa. Her eyes go moist, pitiful little things. "But..." The can slips from her hands. She tumbles. Like that game. The one with the wooden blocks in.

Susan somehow catches her, lowers the limp form to the floor. For a second – less than that, even – I want to curse at the damage the slowly spreading pool of lager will do to my carpet.

Nothing's wrong with her, but she looks so weak. I take her hand, feeling the clammy cold skin against my own. She's not ill. I think she's craving the attention. I know that childish, arrogant trick when I see it.

"Scarlet, come on, get up." I'm towering over all three of them. "Scarlet, get up. Come on now."

Scarlet's breath catches in her throat. "It's all gone," she whispers. "Everything."

"Nothing's gone!" shouts Gina. "Look, it's going to be okay. Josephine, get an ambulance, will you?"

"She doesn't need an ambulance." I let out a laugh. "Scarlet, get the fuck up. I know how shit you're feeling right now, believe me, but this really isn't helping."

"Josephine, that's enough," Gina warns me. "Honest to fuck, that's enough."

"She'll be fine."

"Look at her!" Susan cries at me. "Look at her! *Look* at her! Josephine, call a fucking ambulance. Fuck it, I'll do it." She's got her mobile out, thumb dabbing the buttons.

"No you won't." I take it off her and chuck it behind me. It hits the wall. That'll scratch the plaster.

"What the fuck are you doing?" hisses Susan.

"Scarlet, get up. Fucking now. Don't waste another fucking second. Get the fuck up."

Scarlet's a spread eagle. A thin scarecrow for a human being. Something that doesn't belong here. Something that isn't right.

"Get up," I order. "Now."

Slowly, she sits up, the blonde hair flapping around her face. She's pale. She's ice.

"Can you hear me?" I say. "Scarlet?"

"I hear you." She's on her feet. She grabs her coat, fastens it over her shoulders, starts walking out.

"Jesus, Josephine," whispers Gina. "What the hell?"

"Isn't that blasphemy?" I retort.

Scarlet

22 December 1992

She did have a childhood, but she never knew how to act like a child.

Always the little blonde girl in a classroom full of dark-haired kids. Always the one at the back, the one who could never take part.

She was never the one for parties, never the one for birthday cake. Never went to sleepovers.

A lonely childhood, but at least it was peaceful.

As she walks, she thinks about the few moments when she didn't feel so alone. Like when Susan came into her life. But those moments were exactly what they were: fragments, miniscule lapses in a desert.

When she was a teenager, all she had was her trusty guitar and a love of all things art. She didn't exactly put herself out there, go to parties, bring home a respectable, respectful boyfriend. She just couldn't fit in like that.

Finally, when the girls started coming into her life, she became more rounded, a more wholesome individual.

She can't even admit it to herself, no matter how hard she wants to open up about it.

But it's so bloody poignant and sharp when she enters the house. Each Christmas decoration, each empty beer bottle, seems to strike against her chest. It burns so much, she can't help but hold her breath. In a sudden throe of rage, she kicks the door shut behind her and falls to her knees. She can't cry, can't force anything out, can't make herself feel the loss. But she does, the carpet becomes moist with her tears. She weeps for the lover she lost, for the life she'll never have with him, and even for his children whom she'll never bear.

She can't make the dreadful, locked-door admission that she's truly alone in this world.

The only way through this is to focus on her singing. She needs that barrier, the stage between her and the real world. Not that she wants it. She needs it. She can't live without it.

Her phone's ringing. She stumbles over. Shaking fingers lift up the receiver. It's a hard male voice on the other end. She recognises the breathing. It's her liaison officer in the police.

"Hi, Scarlet, how are you holding up?"

"As well as I can."

"I've got some news for you regarding the trial."

"Any news on what Eugene will plead? Sorry, dunno if that's the right phrase."

"He's pleading not guilty. They've set the trial for the Fourth of March next year. It's going to go on for approximately two weeks."

"How can he plead not guilty?"

"It's his right, unfortunately. He's denying everything. Listen, you requested that I notify your immediately family and Roger Miser of any important developments. I'm going to do that right now. There's one other thing I think you should be aware of."

"What's that?"

"Eugene Lane has hired one of the top legal firms in London to represent him. I'm not going to lie to you, Scarlet, but they're going to try to rip you to shreds. They'll fire everything at you."

"Christ, how the hell can he afford these lawyers?"

She hears him gulp, swallow and digest any guilt that there is. *"Um, well, his brother is helping him out with the costs."*

"You mean, my ex-boyfriend is paying his legal fees?"

"I'm sorry to have to tell you, but you're better finding it out from me than the papers."

"Yeah, well, my ex is a fucking cunt, that's what he is. Take it he's not giving evidence?"

"We don't need him to."

"Yeah, well, keep me informed."

She doesn't wait for the response. She hangs up, cuts him off.

Gina

23 December 1992

Roger's grabbing his coat as I enter, locking various cabinets, sniffing a quarter-full bottle of whisky. He's searching around, rapidly, furiously, as if cleaning the place with his eyes. He's startled when he sees me.

"Gina, I was just about to lock up for the night!" he exclaims. "Thought you'd be out partying right now. Christmas drinks and whatever."

"Actually, I've come to you for a bit of help."

"Can't it wait until after the holidays?" He's checking his watch now. A face splattered with male creams and lotions winces.

"Come on, Roger, it's not as if you've got a train to catch. Considering you don't take them."

"Gina, I really don't have time for this. It's Christmas, for God's sake."

"I need help, Roger." I see him pick up a satchel. "Now!"

He stops, pauses his brain, looks me up and down. "What is it?"

"Roger, I need just ten minutes of your time. It's something that I feel might be a threat to the band, well, if it gets out. That's why I need your help."

"Tell me." The hurried and fractured nature of his exterior melts. "What's the matter?" He must have seen me pause. "Sit. Please."

I do as he commands, throwing my hands onto my knees, barely able to speak the words. "Roger, I need help. I need —"

"Just tell me. Is it to do with your religion stuff?"

"Nope. Christ, I can't fucking admit it. Roger, I need... I need... Haven't had it in ages..."

"Had what?"

"Had sex."

"Ah." He grits his teeth, shrivels his lips. "Ah. Well, that is a problem."

"Can you help?"

"Gina, I may be a bit off the rails, but I'm not having sex with you in this office. Look, there are certain male prostitutes in London. I can't point you in the right direction."

"Okay."

"Listen, can I get it to you after the holidays?"

"I want it now. Before we start recording the new album. Also, a prostitute might not be a hundred percent discreet, if you know what I mean. I don't want this getting out there. None of the girls know. It's kind of my embarrassing secret."

"Hold on." Roger taps his chin with both hands. "Hold on a minute. I might know who to call about this. It's a long shot though."

"Tell me."

"He's a distant friend of a friend. Used to be a male escort back in the Eighties. Back in the good old days. If I can get in contact with him... He's completely discreet. Which is obviously what we both want..."

I feel sick. No one knows about this. It's my dirty washing hanging on the wall. My lonely sad reality. Christ, it hurts to be honesty, but I need a good fuck.

Roger's not the consoling father-figure you think he is. I don't know exactly the shit he's done, I don't know who he's been mixed up with in the past. Yet he can help me. That's all I need.

"Listen, I need to get going," he says. "Come on, I'll walk you out."

"Thanks for this."

"One more thing," he whispers, as we leave the premises. He's locking up. Hands-on. Totally. "Listen carefully. If this thing doesn't work out, you need to consider the use of... well, you know what."

"I understand what you mean."

"Male prostitutes. Obviously, this is totally confidential. Absolutely. No one will know. Just as long as you don't tell anyone about that place in France." He cracks a tiny smile.

I'm cornered. He's got me. It never occurred to me – and it should have done – that there was something in it for him. I'm fucking cornered.

"Have a wonderful Christmas," he says. "Try not to worry about this too much. Everything will be sorted soon."

I stand and watch him move away, whistling under his breath. Happy as anything. Any idea I had of holding him to account... that's gone. I've lost this fight now, if there was ever one to begin with. And is this individual that Roger knows... is he real? Or did Mr Miser know all along how desperate I was for some action and he was waiting for me to trip up, and now he's got me locked in a vice.

Late that evening, amidst the hubbub of my chaotic Christmassy living room, I end up looking for an escape, a distraction. Not that I have a nice boyfriend or anything like that. I'm ashamed to go out, to have people watch me, because they'll see through to my secret. I decide to watch *Home Alone*, which I've recently bought on VHS. A Christmas present for those stuck in solitude.

It's when the end credits start rolling that I hear a faint ringing noise. Christ, it's probably Josephine, wondering if I'm up for a girl's Christmas dinner.

"Yes, yes, I'm coming," I grumble.

"Hi, is this Gina?" The voice is easy-going, gentle.

"Yeah."

"I'm Karl. Karl with a K. Roger Miser asked me to get in contact with you."

"Are you the... escort?"

"I prefer not to use that word. Listen, Roger Miser has told me the full details of what you need. Regarding fees for my services, he has already paid them in full."

This is blackmail. He's running things now.

"I suggest we meet, just as an introductory thing. Over coffee or something."

"That sounds a good idea. When were you thinking?"

"Tomorrow, actually, if that's okay. Do you know the café off Trafalgar Square, 50 Tables?"

"Yeah, I know it." Actually, I've just passed it, but...

"Excellent. I shall meet you there tomorrow. Nine A.M. On the dot."

"Cool. Is there anything you need to know?"

"No intimate details are required at this present time. Nothing at all. See you tomorrow."

He's gone.

Another film is pulled from my stockpile.

It's something I've got into: sitting down, watching tape after tape. I've got the luxury to pursue it now. No regular job. No commitments. Nothing that holds me down. I can watch what I want, eat what I want.

No intimate details are required at this present time. What's that supposed to mean? Is it supposed to impress me? What a cheeky bloke!

Yet it makes me chuckle.

A Steven Seagal it is tonight. I push in the tape and sit back, kicking the air with my fluffy socks. This is it. A proper, decent night in.

24 December 1992

50 Tables is a somewhat shabby establishment a hundred yards or so away from Trafalgar Square, buried between two

second-hand bookshops. Not even proper coffee. Cheap in-stant stuff from a tin. Out of date crap as well.

I'm there at 08.52, precisely. They don't even show me in.

"Whatever table you want, love," the fat guy behind the counter slurs.

"Thanks," I tell him, placing my order.

It's delivered within two minutes. A godawful ratio of coffee-to-overheated water ratio. It burns as I drink it. It scalds.

A small Christmas tree glints on the countertop. Green plastic pine bits going everywhere. Two of the lights are dead. Snuffed out several festive seasons ago, probably. A blue light hangs up near the ceiling, its dead fly casualties mounting up on the floor.

Nine o'clock comes and goes and he's still not here. Quarter-Past flies into the scene, and he's as absent as the humanity in my coffee.

No intimate details are required at this present time.

My backup plan races through my head. Get a male prostitute. A strapping man at that. But he'll probably brag to his mates who he's fucked. Well, he doesn't need to know the truth, does he? Where do I find the directory? In an alley-way somewhere? Some fucking dump. But those... lists... will only be for men who like something different. Men who like... younger men. I shudder at the thought.

I'm so twisted and contorted. I'm so messed in the head. My hands start trembling. I should go home. Abuse myself for the next few hours. Who'll care?

"Gina?"

I raise my head from my hands.

The man who stands there is definitely older than me. Trimmed greying sort of beard. Painful eyes. Thinning hair. Leather jacket. Slim walking trousers. A faded green t-shirt.

"That's me," I answer.

"Karl. Sorry for being late. Couldn't get parked. You know how it is in central London. So badly timed."

"No worries."

He ignores me. The way most men seem to ignore women these days. He peruses the menu scratched in the blackboard, mulling the limited choices. "Coffee," he's forced to say eventually. "A couple of sugars, if you don't mind."

I try to envision how I'm meant to be attracted to him. Maybe – most definitely – it will come naturally. I hope it does.

"So," he says, a massive huff clogging his throat, as he takes his seat. His coffee is served a minute later. Only when he's had his first sip, does he continue. "So, Gina, great to meet you at last. I think it's important that we take this chance to get to know one another. You're looking essentially for physical sex, right?"

"Christ! Just say that a bit louder, why don't you?!"

"Relax..." The cinnamon aftershave wafts off him. "The guys here know me... This is where I meet all the women who... have needs."

"How will things play out?" I'm still looking around. Just in case someone's desperate to listen in. I cast a glance at the guy behind the counter. He's bent over, grunting as he rearranges pork pies in the display.

"What you mean?"

"The programme. Do we meet five or six times or something?"

"Not quite. Three times, not including this one. Over three days. The first session will be some general talking. Your background, what experience you've had. The next day, we do some touching, kissing, holding hands. The last session, we consummate the relationship. That's the lowdown, rough guide on how I want to go through with things. I think we should move quickly. Say, beginning of January?"

"That works for me."

"Excellent." He retrieves a small notebook from his trouser pocket. Pinkish red cover. Diary of some sort. A pen – lined with golden colours – appears from his fingers. "Let me see..." He scrawls a few notes. "January Fourth to January Sixth. How does that sound?"

"I can do that."

"Good. Please be assured that this is completely discreet. I know that being in a band, the celebrity lifestyle, it interferes with your basic needs, you're constantly worried about being discovered, about your secrets coming to the surface. With me, you're completely fine. This won't hit the papers or the headlines or anything like that."

"That's good to know."

Karl sips the polystyrene cup. He thrusts his fingers through his hair, yawns, puts his lips to the coffee again, takes it deep.

"Good, well, I'll wish you a pleasant Christmas," he says, shuffling to his feet. His ears seem to twitch like a dog's when some festive music kicks into life from the depths of the kitchen. "Have a good one." He starts whistling, moves his body like a slug to the doorway.

"What about...?" I start asking, then realise that I have all the information I need.

I have a few more slurps of coffee, decide that the taste is too sour, decide that it's not going to solve anything.

Well, how hard can it be for me?

I get up, walk out.

The pubs won't be open for a while yet. No chance of picking anyone up. A one-night stand seems a thousand nights away.

The flocks of Christmas shoppers surround me, all happy and merry. All filled with the joys of companionship. What do I have?

My celebrity status seems to have been suspended. They look past me, casually bumping into me, but I'm just an unknown figure to them. A ghost. Even when the tears of desperation flow down my face, even then, they don't see me. I'm nothing to them. I never really was.

I'm fading. I don't know where it is I'm walking to, but soon the people become invisible to me. Then suddenly there are no people. I'm in suburbia somewhere, strolling along casually. Dogwalkers, Christmas music from early house parties, loose bits of decorations. I walk, but I'm always tripping. Twice I nearly fall flat on my face. Four times I think about passing out.

Finally, a voice. Finally, something. "You okay, love?"

Soft hands flex on my shoulders. I should feel in danger, but it's so nice to be touched. I'm turned around like a rose petal.

It's a man with soft-looking skin and deep-set eyes, a look that contrasts gruesomely with his stained shell suit.

"I'm fine," I say.

"You sure? I followed you for a bit. I was worried. You seem really distressed."

"I'm fine. I really am."

"You're not. Trust me. You're shaking." His touch becomes a grip.

"Honestly, just let me go. Please."

"Come on, please. Let's get a cup of coffee or something."

I swing a fist with the carelessness of a child tossing a paper plane. I don't want to be violent or aggressive. That's not me. The thought process that bounds through my brain is just to get this weirdo away from me. My knuckles make contact below his right eye. He shrieks with shock, swears. I move back, break into a run. Profanity comes behind me. I take a corner, another one, left, right, losing myself amongst affluent homes.

I'm forced to stop eventually, collapsing over a railing at the edge of a park. I don't shed tears this time. I've done my crying now. There's nothing left to grieve over.

Susan

24 December 1992
Late Evening

I leave the restaurant early – some poxy, posh place in Soho. Italian, as a matter of fact. If you're a hundred percent desperate to know. There's a cab waiting for me, engine idling, driver looking like he's tempted to light up. I wave at him. He calls out my name, clearly disinterested. He probably doesn't listen to our music.

We agreed on the arrangements for recording the third album. There's a contact who owns an old disused house in East Anglia. We're heading there at the beginning of April, though we still need to confirm the exact dates. Scarlet wants to get the trial out of the way first.

I saw the sense of disgust and betrayal in her over dinner. The rusted nails driving into her heart. The brokenness. Physically, she's better than she was, but her eyes give away the sadness. How would I feel if my boyfriend or husband was paying the legal fees of the scumbag who tried to murder me? How would *you* feel?

I sit in the taxi, slam the door shut, just as specks of drizzle turn the window into fragmented diamond.

"Address, love?" the driver wheezes.

I blurt it out to him, lean back.

She's my closest friend. In some ways, my only friend.

Passing through the dying moments of Christmas Eve, I see lovers and friends and companions milling about in the moist air, all at peace with themselves, the perils of the year swallowed by the raindrops.

I think I see him again. Rowan Colt. Somehow, I don't feel threatened by him. He's on the corner of a street, drenched from the rainfall. There's a massive bruise under his eye, looks almost fresh. I'm not sure if it's him, but does it matter? What can he possibly do to me now?

He's a reminder of what I have to let go of, and that's what I do, giving it away, blowing it into the air outside. Disappeared into the night. Swallowed by the raindrops.

1993

James

9 January 1993

Working in my business – this legal business – carries risks. Anyone who says otherwise is a bloody liar. Since I first started, I must have been on the brink of financial ruin at least four times. They – my family – don't know about this, and I hope they never do. Just like they don't ever find out about Paul.

I'm driving north, destination: Liverpool. It's early – Seven A.M. – and my surroundings are as dark as the Atlantic on that fateful night in 1912. Sorry, inappropriate reference. Deeply inappropriate. I'm meeting Paul for lunch and subsequently dinner – and staying overnight. A few beers tonight, indeed!

My wife wanted to come, but then I conveniently reminded her that Alastair is popping by over the weekend and he needs some time alone with his mum. I need a bit of male bonding with Paul. That's the excuse I threw at her and it appears to have worked...

Paul and I are having a bit of a – oh what do you call those wretched things?! – a heart-to-heart. When he phoned me on Christmas Eve, he seemed in a lot of distress, babbling about a woman he'd known three decades earlier. He said that he needed to open up about it. Could I come over? Yes, of course. Could I come over for lunch and dinner? Yes, why not? Could I stay the night? Well, I don't think that would be a good idea.

It took a few days to organise everything and I was forced to book myself a cheap hotel on the outskirts of Liverpool. Some two-star place.

Don't ever ask me how Paul and I got together. It's not something that I'll ever disclose to you. We're taking a break at the moment, but we're still close friends. We're still driven by the desire and the thirst of insurance and legal nonsense. We love it. It's our passion. Our mutual love.

I need to urinate badly. As if by magic – convenient magic – there's a sign informing me that a service station is half a mile ahead. Too much bloody coffee. I need to cut down. I've been promising myself that I'd slash the number of cups. Lawyers always drink too much of the black gold.

The pause in my journey lasts for less than fifteen minutes. I'm of course not including the time spend stuck behind two mothers wheeling prams in the queue for the café. Takeaway coffee in hand, I'm on my away again.

I reach Liverpool ahead of schedule and start the hunt for that hotel. It takes me half an hour of driving, getting lost, thumping my disintegrating map, swearing at myself, swearing at the world and God, before I manage to locate my bed for the night.

I want to vomit. But, of course, that would be unprofessional. I know they're only trying to make a living.

It looks like a council house, long forgotten from distinct, gentlemanly minds. Littered with graffiti, rusted beer cans, a burnt oil drum, and cigarettes (lots of them), it looks like the concept of disrepair has swept through it, and left in a hurry.

I line my car up perfectly in the empty courtyard and step out, breathing in the stale smell of decay and head inside. Or rather, attempt to do so. The door is jammed shut. A sign begs me to ring a buzzer. This isn't like the Hilton, that's for sure. Surely there's one around here? I press it hard and immediately there are footsteps clunking away inside. An old man answers – Asian chap – and looks me up and down.

I tell him my name and that I have a booking with him. He shuffles his head, says that it's all confirmed and paid for, tells me to come inside.

It really is like a wretched block of council flats in here. The narrow staircase with peeling edges. The rotting carpet floors. I'm tempted to walk out, work on excuses for how I can stay overnight at Paul's. I'm taken up two flights of stairs to my room. It's cosy enough: a single bed, tea/coffee, wardrobe. *Shared* bathroom. My bedroom is somehow not as dirty as the rest of the hotel, but I know that there's always the chance of a nest of bedbugs or a collection of cockroaches.

"Have a nice stay," the man says, handing me a brass key.

"Let's hope so," I grumble, sitting down on the edge of the bed, closing my eyes, imagine that I'm free, on a beach some- where. When I open my eyes, I'm still here... in this room... in this cell.

I become aware of faint laughing outside the room. It sounds far off, like it's being carried across an ocean by a strong breeze. My ears perk up and alarm clenches my fists. The laugh suddenly grows as loud as a foghorn, then fades. I leap up, go cautiously to the door, peer into the corridor. It's all damaged doors and bad air freshener. Nothing alarming. Nothing out of the ordinary.

I open my bag, withdrawing my toothbrush and toiletries, deciding that I don't have time to freshen up. I need to be heading off. I should have left ten minutes ago. Key in hand, I make my way out, striding towards where I know the pub is.

But there's something unsettling. That laugh, echoing through the hotel... it wasn't frightening. It was beautiful.

He's already a half-pint down by the time I enter The Half Moon. He's looking bleaker than he normally is. Now, Paul and

I are very bleak. We're a couple of old legal chaps. I stride across the sticky floor of the pub, tempted – for the briefest moment – to kiss him. One small kiss. Who could that hurt? But mouths tell tales. Barman tells his wife. The wife spreads rumours. Sooner or later, Siobhan finds out.

"Hi, mate, how are you?" I enquire. I turn to the bar. All but one of the ales are off. I quickly place my order to the un-smiling lout and head to Paul's table. "You okay, mate? You've got a face as bleak as anything."

"Fine," he replies, sipping his drink.

I turn around to pay the barman and plonk myself on one of the stools with a frothing pint. "Can I get you something, mate?"

"No, I'm okay."

There are tears collecting at the edges of his eyes, wanting to break free.

"Mate, you sure you're okay? Christ, has something happened with Siobhan?"

"It's nothing. Just reflecting on something that happened nearly thirty years ago."

"That's a long time, mate."

"For sure it is."

"Are we getting food?" I ask, knowing fully how self-centred I must appear. Two of the bald, muscular regulars glance over at us, newspapers and crosswords crunching under fingernails.

"Already ordered it. Two lots of fish and chips."

"Look. Is this...?" I peer around. "Is this about us?"

"Nope." He smiles, running a thumb along the dents in the wood of the table. "It's about... It's about something that happened a long time ago."

With every second, he seems to become more uncomfortable. Gyrating on the spot. Like a million bees trying to burst free.

"You want to talk about it?" I ask.

"Maybe later. First I need lunch."

"You seem quite distressed by it, if you don't mind my saying so…"

"I'm fine, believe me. How is the family?"

"They're okay. Alastair's doing well. He's become a brilliant lawyer."

"I knew he would. I listened to Scarlet's music the other day as well. Oddly beautiful. When's her band's next album coming out?"

"This year. I don't hear from the band directly. No one does, except that Roger Miser. Never really liked him. Something dirty about him. Something that makes me feel uneasy. Don't know what it is."

"Yeah, I've read a few things about him."

Sounds and scents come from deep within the pub. Kitchen voices yell. A blackboard above the main bar proclaims a deal regarding a scotch egg and a drink. £1.50.

We confine ourselves to silence, sipping at the beer like it's poison. Somewhere, one of the old men in anoraks murmurs something inaudible. Two youths walk past outside, spitting and swearing.

"Another drink?" I say to him.

"Sure, why not?"

"Two more bitters, please," I call across to the barman. Heads turn my way. I've been too loud.

"I don't think I'll ever forget that summer," whispers Paul. He turns away from me, staring at the china drinking mugs hung from the ceiling.

"What do you mean?"

"The summer of Sixty-Two."

"What do you mean?" Stupid thing to say. It's damned well obvious!

"Last week, I found out she died. She died alone, with nothing. No family. No friends. The only reason I found out was because of a few contacts I have over there."

"I'm sorry, Paul. Was she a relative or something?"

"No, James, I don't think you understand. I met her in America."

I'm beginning to understand now. It's all clicking into place. The marriage date comes to mind, oh it jolly well does. They were married in 1960. He's confessing to an affair.

"Paul..." My lawyer's head has come on now. "Paul, you need to tell me everything."

"I'm about to. Don't worry yourself, James. I'm going to tell you, everything. When Siobhan and I went out to the United States, we didn't go together. I had to go out first to get everything set up. Siobhan was finishing her studies in Britain. I went over in June, Nineteen-Sixty-Two. She came over at the beginning of September. But you know that... The thing is, James, I'm an idiot. I'm a fucking idiot. I've always been. I've always been. My first time in the United States – all on my own – and I got overexcited. Stupid idiot. I was set up just outside Los Angeles. Long story short, I met a girl. I fell for her, James, I really fell for her. Couldn't control it. I was terrified."

"Why didn't you move to another city or something?"

"I felt I had to follow my heart."

"Paul..."

"I left her in the end. At the end of that summer, just before Siobhan arrived. Told her that she wasn't welcome in my life anymore. Told her to stay away. I swore at her, called her names, did everything I could to make her hate me. Honestly. And it worked. She was so calm when she said it. Told me she understood my pain, my anxiety. She said she was happy to leave, wished me the best of happiness. I suppose that's the end of my little tale. Not that it'll become a bestseller or anything."

"Why are you telling me this?" I ask him. Rather, I'm pleading.

"Because I can't really confess to anyone else, can I? Certainly not my wife. As for my other mates, can't do that either. But us... we're beyond friends..."

"Paul!" I hiss. "Please, don't say that too loudly!"

"Why? Are you ashamed of me?"

"No, of course not."

A third voice intrudes. As harsh as brittle bone. "Two fish and chips?"

"Yeah, that's us," says Paul.

A woman with a thick ponytail and flesh billowing from underneath her uniform t-shirt slaps the plates down in front of us. "If you need anything else, just let the barman know," she says, wheezing as she moves off again.

"I'm not ashamed of you, Paul. I never have been. But I don't want the whole world to know about us."

"It's okay." He looks at his plate with a lawyer's thoughtful manner. "It's quite all right.

"You know, I've often wondered what would have happened if I'd taken a different path. If I'd gone with this woman in America, left my wife. From what my contacts told me, she travelled widely. She lived life on her own terms, choosing and fighting her own battles. Christ, James, she bloody lived."

"She sounds like a character. But you've had a good life with a respectable woman. Siobhan is a decent, honourable person. What more could you ask for?"

"Eat up. Let's be quick. I need a walk." All his wanderlust over a lost lover is gone now. He seems back to his old self. That sly smile is back on his lips.

The environment of the pub has changed as well. Colours have brightened. The stale odour of the ale has sweetened.

We finish our meals – maybe a little too quickly – and allow ourselves a minute or two to crunch the food down, mashing it up with the beer.

"Phew, that was good!" I remark. "Damn it. Damn, we've still got dinner."

"I don't think I'll be able to do dinner tonight. Need a quiet night in."

"Come on, I've already booked the restaurant for tonight!"

"Well, you'll have to cancel it..." The pitiless Paul Casselden is back. Once again. Return of the bloody king.

"I'm not cancelling anything. Oh, you're right. Guess it'll be a takeaway or something in my room."

"We all make our choices." Paul slurps down the last of his pint. He seems transfixed on something. "Just as I made mine. A long time ago. I suppose I'll be seeing you around then." He puts his glass down and scoops up his coat from the floor. "Listen, I'm sorry about this, okay. You just caught me at a bad time, that's all."

I don't register him going. I sit, perched, before the ruins of our meals. I order another beer before I've finished the previous one.

My mind whirrs and echoes with every kind of dilemma. Siobhan has to know. My wife has to know. The truth must be told! This stoic, professional man I've known for so many years has confessed to an affair, a dirty little secret. No, of course I'm not going to tell a soul about it. Why should I? It would ruin everything... And Paul could always respond with revealing our little secret... No one must know.

By the time I've left the pub, the debates of the world have largely subsided. Instead, a general light-headedness has come over me, pushing me down.

I stroll back to the hotel, mildly unwell from the slimy fish and chips. Maybe I need to cut the junk food. But as I near the hotel, I find that the sickness has vanished. Even the effects of the beer. It's all gone.

There's this ridiculous combination I need to enter to gain access to the building. I punch in the numbers against the other thumbprints on the dial and push my way inside.

That annoying giggling, that laughter, is still hanging around. I head up the staircase, holding my breath against the fumes peeling off the walls. The laughter grows louder with every footstep. My frustration starts ebbing away and my curiosity grows. It's coming from one of the shared bathrooms, right next to my room. There's talking as well, muttering. I see through the smudged glass window that there's a light on inside.

"Everything is okay!" a voice booms from inside. It's a soft tone. Full of every colour of flower. Rose petals.

"I'm sorry?" I inch back from the door, gulp.

A woman flings the door open, her oversized t-shirt rippling through the frame. Her hair is soaking, dripping sweet-scented water. Her legs are completely bare, right up to the rim of what she's flung on.

"Are you sure you're okay?" I stutter.

"I'm fine. Honestly." She sounds vaguely Spanish. Very slightly. "I'm just finishing up in here. Give me... another ten minutes?"

"Take your time. I'm James, by the way."

"Portia," she says, reaching out a fairly dry hand.

"I'm down in Room Three."

"Why would I need to know that?" She's giggling, hysterical.

"Sorry, don't know why I said that." I feel like I'm fifteen again, hopeless around girls. Not that I went chatting any girls up, of course. Not someone like me. Not someone who's always carried the aura of professionalism. "I'll see you in a bit."

"See you."

I'm nearly at my door, when she calls my name. Loud and harsh.

"Yeah?" I turn to face her, expecting some daft joke about the state of the hotel.

"What are you doing tonight?" she asks sweetly.

"Funny you should ask me that. I was supposed to be going out for dinner with an old friend, but he's cancelled. What about you?"

"No plans. Watch some television or something."

"Listen, I don't know you or anything..." I'm being really stupid. I'll be condemned by the man in cloth who married us. "Look, I need to phone the restaurant to cancel, unless you want to join me tonight."

"Yes. I'd like that a lot."

"Excellent! Well, the table's booked for Seven, so I'll meet you in the lobby downstairs around Six?"

"Works for me."

I blink and she's disappeared into the bathroom again.

What the hell am I doing?

Visions of my university lecturers condemning me pop into my eyes. *Throwing away a stable life and career for some random woman you've met in a wretched hotel!*

I pace around the room. I make a cup of tea using the small kit provided. It tastes dry, but I force myself to finish it. There's a cracked clock on the wall: a splinter travels like a child's attempt at drawing a diameter.

I try the act of lying down. I fail pretty quickly.

Paul's tale haunts me. I always thought of him as highly professional, never one to break the boundaries. Yet, he's lived more than me. I will never tell Siobhan, never, but this will affect our friendship. How can I look the man in the eye with a sense of honesty and friendship? How can I?

I've got some legal papers to read through. Damn, I'm grateful I've brought work with me. Anything to distract my brain. Legal fees, court dates, claims, failed claims. The perfect cereal.

I watch the hours slowly tick on. I reassure myself that I'm not sleeping with her. I'm not cheating on my wife. I'm not doing anything inappropriate. Just having dinner with a young lady I've met in a downtrodden hotel.

At Ten-To-Six, I brush my teeth, check my complexion, and head downstairs to the lobby. Amongst the rotting leather chairs that sit there smouldering, I wait. Soon, that laughter is coming after me, and she appears. She's completely different. She wears a dress that really belongs to the summer, but I suppose in Spain it's summer all the time. It's a pale-yellow dress that shows flawless bare shoulders. Makeup is applied equally as flawless. She approaches me, bowing her head, a gentle hand fastening in the crook of my elbow.

"So, shall we go to dinner then?" she whispers.

It's an Italian restaurant situated half a mile away from the hotel. Years ago, I took some American clients there. It hasn't changed much, in fact I recognise one of the young waiters who served us. He looks to be headwaiter now.

My newfound friend and I walk in, walking up to the placard that begs us to *Please Wait To Be Seated*. A smiling girl approaches us. I introduce myself, hoping that no one around here is a client, or a friend of my wife's.

We're shown to a table next to a tropical fish tank. A group of young men behind us are laughing about a stag night gone wrong. Our water glasses are promptly filled up with melted ice.

"Something to drink?" we're asked.

"Yes, that would be great." I'm immediately running my hand through the drinks menu.

"Allow me," says Portia. She asks if they have this particular vintage – I don't catch the name – and the waiter calls over to one of his colleagues. A few moments later, after some rummaging through bottles, it's an affirmative.

"Trust me on this," she whispers to me. "Yes, waiter, we'll have a bottle of that."

"You don't strike me as a wine drinker," I say.

"When I was little, my parents and I lived and worked at a winery. I have many fond memories of picking grapes with my mother."

"How long were you there for?"

"Six months. We moved around a lot, you see. Madrid, Marbella, Burgos, Santander. All the places in between. It was rough, chaotic. Fifteen different schools. A few boyfriends... Though none of them were serious."

"Sounds a hectic life."

"It was. And it wasn't."

"What brought you to the U.K.?" I'm suddenly not sounding like a lawyer.

There's an ashtray on the table and I realised I've accidentally booked the smoking section. I smoked once, when I was fourteen. Most stupid thing I've ever done. I'll never get the dry, nauseous taste out of my mouth. Peer pressure, I suppose, given that it was five of my supposed schoolmates who pushed me into doing it.

"I wanted a more stable life. Somewhere to lay down roots."

"You don't strike me as someone who wants to lay down roots." I'm thinking of Paul's mystery lady. I wish I'd lived a life like her; though, it's a wish that quickly dissipates. I'm glad I have what I have. I wouldn't trade my car, my house, my family, for anything.

"You'd be surprised, James. I've spent a life on the road. A life on my own. I need something more, something greater."

The bottle is placed before us and we're given the option of trying our prize, but Portia tells the waiter to fill our glasses. "Trust me," she whispers.

That's the last that's said this evening, except for us placing our orders. We don't need to utter another word. The world around us seems to slow down. It stops when she touches my knuckles with her thumb. I don't worry about loyalty, about family, about a mutual friend walking in and threatening to talk really loudly about what he's witnessed.

I don't register the time. It slips by like an eel. I only know I've eaten, because my plate's empty. All I focus on is her: tanned skin, brown eyes, perfect-fitting dress.

We're standing up to go, the bill paid, and we're heading out. We're walking along, the biting air scratching at her bare skin, tearing at my naked hands. I see the hotel before she does, stare at it, then at her, and she's watching me, and our hands link. She takes the lead, walking me through, taking me through the dingy, unwelcoming building, up the staircase. Inside the room that's the mirror image of mine, she nips into the bathroom and I see her throw water against her face, and then she comes up to me and touches my lips with hers. I taste the pipe-flavoured water from her cheek and hold her face between my palms.

"It's warm in here, isn't it?" she says. She starts unbuttoning my shirt, stroking a finger along my chest. "You're a lawyer, aren't you?"

"How did you guess?"

"Something about the way you act. Christ, it's warm in here." She coughs loudly into the crook of her arm. "Come on, then..." She kissed me harder, uncontrolled, beyond passionate. She undresses herself, tearing off the exterior. She jumps beneath the covers, stretching her arms. She begs me to jump in with her.

Something about her is different. The extravagance and the footloose enthusiasm of her Spanish aura is gone. There's a common touch about her.

I strip myself naked to my shrewd, skinny body, and climb in under the sheets.

"Turn off the light, will you, love?"

"Where is it?" I curse out loud as I fumble for the cord. I stop.

She's a completely different person. Something's been stripped off her skin, leaving pockmarked, scarred flesh. Her voice is different. I can smell the cigarettes. The anger and self-loathing fill the sheets with blood.

"You're not Spanish, are you?" I stammer.

"Christ, I fucking fooled you though, didn't I? I went to Spain once, as a kid, though that probably doesn't count."

"Why did you lie to me?"

"I thought you were old and cute, but you look like the sort that favours exotic girls." She smacks beads of sweat off her forehead, coughing like an old woman into the sheets. "Christ, it's fucking boiling in here. It's fucking roasting. Look, are we gonna do this or not? I'm fucking tired of lying here."

"I'm —"

"Sorry!" She launches herself over me, landing spreadeagled on the carpet. Like a panicked dog, she flails and throws herself to her feet, dashing to the bathroom. I hear her gurgle and choke and stuff land in the toilet.

"Are you okay?" I ask. She's had one too many glasses.

"I feel so sick..." She vomits again, just as I enter the bathroom. "I'm sorry about this. Fuck...!" She goes again. "Listen, I took some pills earlier."

"I'm phoning an ambulance." I'm trembling, because the colour has gone from the girl's face. I'm in serious trouble. Serious bloody danger.

"Fuck," she moans. She throws her head back, casts panicked eyes at me, eyes full of fear and distress. She's petrified.

I step back, watching her naked body go limp, spreading across the floor like butter.

My lawyer's cap screws itself on. I'm not the criminal defence sort, but I know enough from certain colleagues of mine. I need to leave now. I have visions of myself as a miscarriage of justice, fighting to prove my innocence, rotting away behind bars. I have to run. Methodically, I start putting on my clothes, letting the oxygen flood my brain. Get out. Now. Go.

As quietly as I can, I leave, tiptoeing down the corridor to my room. I go in, screwing my eyes shut, slumping onto the bed, my chest tightening.

The fear of the police bursting in and arresting me keeps me awake, stops me from shutting my eyes that night. Every creak is a pair of handcuffs. Ever click the cell door slamming shut on me forever.

10 January 1993

I'm gone before the break of dawn. Well before the first inky rays of light. Before the early joggers and the drunks and the homeless men shuffling to their next destination. My headlights light up the broken pavements and upturned bins.

I put her out of my mind as I checked out, not even glancing at her door. Out of sight, bloody well out of mind. A mere cursory glance at the worn-down receptionist, a slight offhand remark about a hotel in Paris. I walked out confident, head held high. My story's straight in my head: I never met that girl. Had nothing to do with her. Nothing whatsoever. Except for going out for dinner, and there will be witnesses to that. But I know what to do.

I leave the outskirts of Liverpool, joining the frozen motorway, a drained mechanical artery of progress.

I have everything worked out in my head.

The drive home is shorter than I expect. Everything truly goes my way. Even going around and through London... the brisk sun is out and the queues are manageable.

I imagine my wife waiting with open arms, demanding every detail about Paul and Siobhan: Are they off to the Algarve this year? Is he really launching this new initiative? How well is he integrating these mobile phones into his business?

But I don't go home yet. I turn in at a service station near Sevenoaks and use the payphone to call the restaurant in Liverpool. I think it's the headwaiter who answers, the one I still imagine as a boy.

"Hi, I came to your restaurant last night? James –"

"Yes, was everything okay with the service?"

"Oh, it was perfect. No complaints. You see, I am worried about my colleague who came to dinner with me. She seemed distressed afterwards and I wondered if you knew anything."

"I'm sorry, sir, I don't think I can help. We don't have security footage in the restaurant. Um, I can check with the other waiters or something, but, the thing is, you came alone."

"Sorry, is this some sort of a joke? My colleague ordered a bottle of wine. You had to hunt it out from your cellar."

"No, it was just you. I served you myself. You didn't order any alcohol, just tap water."

"You're joking, aren't you?"

"No, sir, I am not. Do you want me to send you the bill for your table? I can have the restaurant post it to you."

"No, it's okay."

It's okay, because I believe him.

I stumble away from the phone, letting the receiver bash against the bashed-in porcelain. Somersaults in my stomach. I run for the bathroom, tripping over myself, zigzagging to the urinals, where I spill my unwanted fluids. No one's around me, thank the Lord. Thank Him, oh Praise Him.

I try to make my way out of the service station with a sense of decency and dignity, but the flashing lights of the gambling zone and the bulging tabloid headlines nauseate me.

She wasn't real. I know that now, because I remember going to dinner alone. I remember the sour flavour of the restaurant's tap water, unchanged after how many years. I remember looking across at the table, hoping that she'd appear, a woman of adventure and intrigue, the woman I wish I'd been in love with, the woman I wish I'd shared a life with. But she is just a figment of my imagination, someone I'll never know, someone who will never know me, or even show the slightest bit of interest.

Josephine

16 January 1993

I'm outside his apartment, downing the last of the instant coffee, anticipating crunching the polystyrene cup between my fattened grip. Yes, I've put on a bit of weight, but I'm losing it as quickly as I can.

This bastard dumped me two years ago. Fucking coward. Snivelling, little wretch. Arsehole.

I go up to the door and hit the buzzer, folding up the cup and letting it fall to my feet. He knows it's me, given the chirpy nature of his voice. Well, maybe not that enthusiastic.

"Come on, Romeo, open the fuck up, for Christ's fucking sake," I hiss.

"I'll come down to get you. Hold on a mo."

I huff and throw my arms across my chest. Bloody fool. And there he comes, at last. I see him through the gridded windows, bounding down the last set flight of steps. He flings the door open, a perfect-tooth smile being forced onto me.

"Robert," I say. I throw a slap – not very hard, just enough to make him flinch in surprise. "That's for walking out on me."

"Yeah, I suppose I deserved that," he seems to admit, stroking his left cheek with the full spread of his palm. "Come on in."

His apartment's on the fourth floor and I'm surprised by how clean, neat and respectful it is. No loose takeaway wrappings or remnants of one-night stands. Everything is in its place.

"How are you finding Colchester?" I ask, as he shows me through to his minimalistic living room. I sigh at the virgin white leather sofa and the pocketsize television propped on a cube of wood.

"It's okay. I mean, it's not got the buzz of London, but, you know..."

"What are you doing with yourself? I mean, I'm assuming you're not a student or anything."

"No, a building job. Construction."

"Not what you'd hoped for?"

"Well, no, of course not. But it pays the rent."

"Maybe you shouldn't have walked out on me then."

"Yeah, that's what I wanted to talk to you about." He jabs a hand at the sofa. "Sit, please. I want to talk to you."

"Look, is this about your Jean-Claude Van Damme VHS Collection?" I say by way of a joke. "I've still got it and I've watched all the bloody films as well. How can you sit through that nonsense...?"

I flinch.

His hand.

It's on mine.

He gently pulls me to the sofa next to him. Suddenly, I flash back to the day we met. His beautiful smile and slender arms, so boyish, so calm. I was drunk. Drowning my sorrows over something or other. I had too much and could barely stand. From nowhere, he came. He held me, cuddled me, even as I punched him in the stomach.

"I'd like to give us another go," he says.

"What?"

"Two years has given me a long time to think. I miss you, Josephine, I miss you."

"Robert..."

"Josephine, I know you're angry with me, I know you despise me, but I want to say I'm sorry. I want us to try again."

"Sorry..." I want to smash his head off that godawful table before the sofa: one of those solid glass constructs. I can't find the words to condemn, no hope of finding the words to praise. No intention of a few moments of respite, because my anger is exploding. "You're a fucking idiot, you know that, don't you! You fucking walked out on me!"

"I know."

"And you think I'm just going to take you back like nothing's happened?"

"I didn't mean it like that..."

"Well, how did you mean it?"

"I don't know. I just... I miss you."

"Missing me is not enough," I tell him, like I'm a stern aunt giving yet another lecture. "You need to want me, to desire me, to want to support me. I mean, would you want to have children with me? Look at my body that's raked with stretchmarks? Hold my hand when I'm overweight? No, I know that. You'd be too scared to. That's the problem with you. You think of love and you see flowers and dinner dates. But you're petrified of the real thing."

"I'm ready to try again."

"And why should I let you in? So you can walk out again when you get a bit afraid? Nah, mate, that's not happening. Besides, I've moved on from you. It's been two years. Two bloody years."

"I know." He looks down, hands between his knees, a stag trapped in the headlights of a bus. Ready to have his heart and soul crushed. Ready to be fucked in the head.

"God, Robert, you really are a stupid cunt," I hiss. "Honestly. Fuck. Do you know how much you fucking hurt me? Do you know what it was like to cry myself to sleep? To break inside? Fuck!" I hurl myself away from the sofa, slamming my hands against one of the many windows in his precious space. Something breaks. Probably a hinge. Hopefully not the fucking glass. It's double-glazed and I can see spiderwebs strung between the two sheets of glass.

His hands rest against my spine. It's so warm, so familiar.

"Don't you fucking touch me, you prick," I say. I try to be quiet, methodical, calm, collected – all that shit they teach you at school.

"Come back to me, Josephine."

My fight against tears is quickly lost. I turn around, look into his eyes. He strokes my chin the way he used to, and for a moment I'm back in the late Eighties, when we first got together. Two young people who had lost everything.

"Oh, Robert..." I gently nudge him away, but catch his hands in mine at the last moment. "Robert, can't you see I've moved on? Can't you see I'm past all that shit? Oh, Robert, can't you see?"

"So, I take it there's no chance?"

"Nope. How can you expect me to trust you again? How can you just ask me to give you another chance?"

Now it's his turn to cry. He's in denial at first, and then he sinks back, collapsing to the floor.

"Robert, I'm sorry." Of course, there's no way I feel remotely apologetic. The prick deserves to know what it's like to be hurt. "Look, I'll see myself out, okay? Robert, you threw me way. You made your choice. Now you've got to live with the consequences. It's gonna hurt, trust me. Goodbye, Robert."

I don't even register walking past his crouched form. To me, he's nothing. He's an echo, a shadow of what once was. He's not even something I think about. He's something lodged at the back of my mind. Something not worth thinking about.

To me, where I belong is in London, or on the inner outskirts, with my girls. I belong in the posh cocktail bars and restaurants. I belong in the recording studios and the magazine interviews and the stage. Oh yes, the stage. Standing before the crowds of the anonymous. I belong with the millionaires and the billionaires. I belong with the fortunate and the famous. I belong in New York and the other great metropolises of this world. Real life, real people, real relationships, well those are things I just don't do.

I tried being normal once. Believe me, dear reader, I did. Once. And it failed. That's all you need to know, dear reader. Christ, losing someone you love fucking hurts.

As I drive back, my mind's as bad as my driving. I'm all over the wretched place.

I want to scream. I want to slam my fists against the steering wheel. Burst open the airbag, Break my nose. Spill blood. Look so fucking stupid.

I don't want to admit it. Not to you, dear reader. Oh, why the fuck am I calling you that? I'm flashing back. Even as I drive forward, I'm being yanked backwards in time. You may as well come with me.

6 March 1984

She landed in the early hours, bleary-eyed and hungry, stomach rumbling. Having spent hours and hours scrunched between two fat guys, she wasn't happy. Sweat clung at her sides and the fragments of the disintegrating left strap of her rucksack became tangled with her hair.

The characters and the strangers she'd met over the past year whispered their phrases in her head as she began to disembark.

It had been a long year. Twelve months of travelling, seeing corners of the world that she had dreamed about as a child. A year of isolation and a hundred friendships. One marriage proposal from a fisherman in Madagascar. A rooftop party in Thailand that lasted from Six P.M. to Six A.M.. A four-day private excursion into Cajun country, where she'd had a fling with the tour guide. A year of moments and fragments of moments.

She'd arrived at the gate where she'd departed the year before. Everything still the same. Was that lump of chewing gum there before? The same scent of faint orange and mango, and the low hum of static.

As she entered passport control, she felt herself shiver. The last place she'd been in was Brazil, where the heat and humidity had kept her sane. She was in her last clean tank top, the others having been sacrificed in the name of makeshift towels and body odour. She'd dug it out from the creases in her rucksack during her last full day in Rio.

She was directed by blank-faced, unsmiling security through line after line, surrounded by signs of more unsmiling men bidding her welcome to this dingy island.

It took longer than expected to get through having her blank pages stamped, and by the time she got to baggage reclaim, the hunger was gnawing at her stomach.

Men and women with placards and banners were waiting by railings in the Arrivals hall. Children crept among them, waiting for their mothers and fathers to return from the great open world. Many would probably not get to see it for themselves. Many wouldn't dare. But she had. And with that, she allowed herself a quick smile.

Her family was waiting, patient and alert. Mum, Dad, and Lauren. They didn't recognise her, at first, eyes shooting past her at the stream of travellers. Finally, things twigged. It was her sister, Lauren, who saw her first. Twelve years old and more alert than everyone else. Then, Mum and Dad. They came over, embracing her briskly. No words. Just hugs. Just connections.

"You've grown since I last saw you," said Josephine, running a hand over her sister's forehead. Lauren looked different, paler. Thinner.

"I'm in big school now," she replied. She sounded weaker.

"I bet you keep all the boys at bay." Josephine ruffled her sister's hair.

"Let's go home," said her dad. "We should go home."

Her room had been tidied a little, but it was still the same: the familiar chaos of the books positioned non-alphabetically; the pile of LPs threatening to topple off her bedside table; the shredded teddy bear she's had since she was three. The smell of old wood and disintegrating bricks was still present in the ether.

She thought about the cabin in Madagascar, right on the beach, where she stayed four weeks. A month in the scorching sun. The fisherman who kept bringing her gifts every day. Gifts that started as seashells and unknown things from the bottom of the sea, and escalated to flowers and woodcarvings, before climaxing with a ring made of crafted stone. The three occasions they had sex underneath the stars, and the five times they did it in the cabin, beneath the splintering wood and the constant chirping of wildlife. She missed that cabin. The simplicity, the isolation, the beauty of that sand and that sea, and the stars.

Could she ever return to the real world, after everything she had seen and done?

She dropped her rucksack and positioned her much larger suitcase next to her bed. She was about to unpack, sort out the gifts she'd bought, when her mother called her name.

To her surprise, there was no food on the table. Just her parents stood on opposite sides of the kitchen, their eyes stroking the floor.

"Where's Lauren?" Josephine asked them.

"She's gone to one of her friend's houses," said her dad.

Her mum then raised her eyes, whispering as loud as a cricket: "Are you planning to settle down now?"

Susan

18 January 1993

I'm going a lot earlier than I normally do. Maybe it's the fact that I'm suffering a lot of anxiety at the moment. I keep seeing him, even though I know he's not there, even though I know for sure he's gone, locked away in the cabinet of my past.

I run with the enthusiasm of an athlete, even though I've been told a thousand times that I would never make the grade.

I find that I've got company. Other runners with their New Year resolutions as intact as steel. Of course, over the coming months, many will fail.

I'm not doing anything complicated this morning. Fifteen minutes running out. Fifteen minutes running back. Simple stuff. Nothing to hurt the spirit. I come to the street corner that's my turning point and start the return journey. I dart over junctions, past bins, between a kissing and loving couple, and allow my lungs to fill and my body to tense.

Lyrics – ideas for lyrics anyway – pop into my head. I start humming, then singing the words. Somehow, they flow. Why do they make sense and why do they sound so damn right?

I'm coming to one of the last junctions on this route, then it's a straight path to my apartment. I make the mistake of not looking as I pass through. The screeching of brakes and a panicked yelling precede a firm punch to the ground and the taste of blood in my mouth.

"Oh, my dear, are you quite okay?" The voice is desperate and fragile. The smell of cinnamon and the heavy breathing clog my nostrils.

"What the fuck...?" I spit.

He's too young to be cycling around London at this time, but there he is: through my blurry vision, I can make out a fresh face and chunky glasses, as well as floppy brown hair and extremely pale skin. He looks a bit like Mauro, except for the total fragility that covers him.

His hands are helping me up, except my legs are like snapped spaghetti.

"It's my fault," comes his babyish voice. "Head in the clouds. As bloody usual these days, for me."

"I don't think anything's broken," I tell him. I can feel the trickle of blood pooling between my lips.

"Let me phone an ambulance for you."

"No, it's okay. Honestly." I know I need help. The ecstasy will soon wear off and the pain will build up and before long I'll be unable to go any further.

"My dear, you're bleeding."

"Honestly, it's fine. Look, you don't know who I am. There are... complications. Look, is there somewhere we can go, somewhere I can get cleaned up? Look, if Roger –" Yep, I've pushed it too far now. This stranger knows the bloody truth.

"Oh, my." He has a beaten-up clown's face. "Shit. Shit. You're Susan, aren't you?"

"Yes, that's me."

A snap in the air hangs between us like a frozen curtain.

"Aren't you going to introduce yourself?" I say. "And help me up as well?"

"Victor," he tells me, rough (almost so) hands raising me by the elbows. "Victor Gully."

"It's a pleasure to meet you, Mr Gully. Now, do you have somewhere I could get cleaned up?"

"Sure. I mean, are you absolutely okay?"

"I'm fine. Just a couple of scrapes. Look, I'm kind of eager to get cleaned up."

"My apartment is just around the corner. I was a friend's last night, you see, and wanted to hurry back this morning. That's why —"

"No explanations are necessary."

He leads the way, an arm poised to outstretch and help me along. But he's a true gentleman and he doesn't do anything that would be considered inappropriate. He smiles and laughs, mostly at his own witty observations of how beautiful the morning is.

His home is in quite a posh place: just like Bloomsbury, with its cream-coloured, straight-faced buildings arranged in a square and its fake sense of companionship. The only imperfection is a workman's van next to the little park in the centre. He fumbles inside his pockets — all of them — and takes out a set of jangling keys, jamming them into the lock with such fierceness I think the metal will snap in the cold.

I follow him up to the second floor, my feet clipping the stone steps and carving out dust. Another door opens and I watch him move his bike through.

"Come inside," he says. "Welcome to my humble home. Please... Do you want to freshen up or something?"

"Actually, do you mind if I grab a shower or something? No, wait, it's okay. Haven't exactly got a change of clothes with me!"

"Ah, not to worry. My sister was staying with me last week. I've got a few of her things with me. A couple of shirts and some trousers, nothing special. And a couple of pairs of shoes."

"Bloody hell, does she live here or something?"

"She works in the city. Investment. But she lives in Yorkshire. She uses my place to sleep occasionally."

"Nice."

He backs away a few seconds, goes through some drawers in his hallway, pulls out items, puts them away. He gets frantic after a few seconds. "Here," he says at last, tossing over a few things. "Bathroom's behind you."

I don't notice how pristine and fragile everything is: the toilet made out of brittle bone; the five bars of soap still in their wrappers; the granite tiles with the plaster in between scraped thin. I suppose my ignorance is due to the fact that I'm used to this sense of luxury. I turn on the shower, step inside, wash away the specks of blood, dirt and sweat. The clothes fit me – they're a little loose, but not too bad. I dry my hair by hand, rubbing away the water as I step out of the bathroom.

"One hell of a place," I say to him.

Victor Gully is standing in front of a gas fireplace, trying in vain to light it. It's the sort of thing I remember seeing in old Bond films: a circular contraption situated at the centre of the room, with a white overhang coming down from the roof and lumps of fake coal arranged in a fake random pattern. Around us, on all four sides, are rows upon rows of books.

"What do you do for a living?" I tease. "Or are your parents paying for this?"

"You wouldn't believe me if I told you."

I notice that he's mysteriously cleaned himself up. He's in light blue jeans and a cufflinked shirt, unbuttoned twice at the top. Hair the length of half a forearm hangs to just about his shoulders. If there ever was a geekiness, it's gone. It went in the last few moments. Christ. Fucking hell. He looks fit. Yeah, he fucking works out.

"I never thought I'd wind up in a place like this!" I exclaim. "Bloody hell, how the hell do you afford it? You're not one of these playboys, are you?"

"Not quite. Susan, I might be overstepping the mark right here. This feminist movement might want to bury me alive for saying this, but can I make you breakfast?"

"You're being so sexist...! Totally unacceptable! But I shall take you up on your offer, Mr Gully."

"You're speaking like someone I know quite well. I'll tell you about them in a few moments. On a serious note, how are you faring? Any injuries or anything?"

"No, I think I'm fine."

"You sure?"

"Yeah."

"Right. I think we'll have breakfast here, in the living room." He jams a thumb towards a small table set before one of the long leather sofas. "Please, do be seated. I'll get some coffee. Colombian Dark Roast, will that be okay?"

"That will be great. Honestly, you're so picky."

"Be back in a sec or two." He whistles, disappears between two bookshelves, and I hear him swear as he drops a cup and china ball bearings clip the floor. I don't know why, but I think about what happened at Josephine's flat, during one of our early band practice days, back before the world took us in.

I start browsing the books from afar, trying to make out the names of the great tomes, trying to understand what they could possibly be about, who would have sat down to put word after word. The authors' names I don't recognise. Certainly not things I read at school. Absolutely not. Way beyond me. I shuffle around like I own the place, like it's my library, my treasure trove of books. I'm still hovering when he comes in, placing a tray on the small table.

"Sorry, decided to go all the way," he says. "Pastries are fresh from the oven."

"What? How did they cook so quickly?"

"Darling, you've been standing gazing at my books for half an hour."

Another half hour later, we're done. Even the crumbs have disappeared. I'm at the point where I'm debating whether to leave, because I see the flickers in his cheeks, the desire that he needs to get on with something.

"So what is it you do for a living?" I ask him. The dregs of my coffee have by now crystalised. I grimace with disgust.

"You wouldn't believe me if I told you. Hardly anyone does."

"Try me."

"I'm a writer. Published. Three books so far. Working on my fourth."

"What kind of books?"

"Fiction."

"I don't think I've seen them in the bookshop. Though I'm rarely in bookshops... Being the singer kind..."

"You mean you've never written music in your life...?"

"Tell me the names of your books." I fold my arms, realise I'm blocking him, reveal myself. "I might think about reading them."

"You might think about it?" He smirks, draws a breath. Draws another one. "Dear, dear. Dear, dear, dear. How about I give you a signed copy?"

"Are you being serious?"

"When it comes to my writing, I take it extremely seriously..."

"I bet you do." And there's a part of me that's suddenly got this massive damn crush on him. The way he looks at me, those soft eyes and tender lips, flawless skin and spiky knuckles.

"Listen, I haven't got any copies with me at the moment, but... what are you doing on Saturday?"

"What do you mean?"

"Doing a book event in Covent Garden. Why don't you come along? I mean, all the tickets have been sold, but I'm sure my agent can squeeze you in." He leaps up, struts towards a door and vanishes into an adjacent room. Ten seconds later, he comes back, a notepad in hand. "I normally use this for noting down ideas. That thing crime writers do... But, it's got its other uses, shall we say... Give me your number, and definitely your boyfriend's or husband's number – I'll get them a ticket as well."

"Very nice. Very old-school. Look, I don't have a boyfriend, but... well, I wouldn't think of it as a date. I mean, watching a toff like you read a few strings of fancy words, how can that be a date? But I tell you what, if it's a good event, then I'll consider allowing you to buy me a drink. How does that sound?"

He's got a pleased look of disappointment in his eyes. As though he's caught halfway between a dream and a nightmare.

"Well, what's your number then?" he says, thrusting the notepad and pen over to me. *New York* is faintly scrawled on both pieces of apparatus.

I write it down, trying to hide the smile that's growing fiercely on my lips. "There you go," I whisper. "What time should I be there?"

"About Seven."

"Excellent. Are you expecting a big turnout?"

"Fairly big. But not for me. For the guy I'm talking to. It's one of those events where two writers are in conversation with one another. You know the type?"

"Not that I've ever been to one, but yeah, I know the type."

"Well, they're all coming to see him. The bloody golden boy. They're flocking like wasps to see him."

"Who is this he then? This golden boy?"

"Herbert Buxton. Used to be a music journalist. Now he's become a novelist. Just had his second book out. *The Vindication*. Romantic love story between a young lecturer and a karate master in Nineteen-Eighties Birmingham. Godawful crap. But much better than his debut, I'll say that. *Murder, Florence and Wine*. Have you ever read it?"

"Can't say that I have." My arm flexes out on the sofa and I accidentally scrape the leather with my fingernails. The scent of books surrounds me – surrounds us.

"Utter lunacy. Yet, the crowds out there seem to love it. Heaven knows why."

"I take it you had to read both of them for the event?"

"Read them and make notes."

I don't think. I'm never good at thinking. It's never really been my strength. I rush forward, kiss him, hands around the back of his neck.

"Sorry!" I fall back, hands over my face. "Sorry, that was –"

"It's okay." His expression hasn't changed. He seems a totally stoic individual. Devoid of vulnerability.

"I shouldn't have done that. Sorry, I mean, to come into your home and behave like that. So unladylike." I want to say more. But I can't help but be consumed by his eyes. I lean in again and he does the same and we kiss once again.

"Are you going to apologise again?"

"No."

"I suppose I'd better let you get home."

"Chivalry never dies."

"It never does." He rises, towering over me, reaching down his hand and helping me up. "Shall I walk you to your carriage, my dear?"

"You may indeed."

Gina

20 January 1993

Just to let you know, I fixed my little problem. All done and sorted. Just need to get out there and start dating again! That's another tiny thing to get sorted.

But, for now, it's band practice. We're gathered in Josephine's living room and it's pissing buckets down outside. We're all sitting drearily on the sofas, our heads full of creative – business – ideas. Creativity is about profit and loss now. Definitely something that mate of Scarlet's dad's would say.

Scarlet, how I worry about her. She's looking much better now. Much stronger. She's eating more. The confidence is re-emerging in her eyes.

We're going to be taking up our instruments in a few moments, but we're still talking about ideas. Not long now until we start recording the third album in April, and we're still coming up with ideas of how we want it to look. We've rehearsed and prepared the selection of tracks, but why is it that there's always the temptation to add more? This little session should really be about the fourth album, assuming we ever do one.

Scarlet's been writing a few tracks, but Josephine doesn't seem too keen on them. Apparently, they're too similar to one another.

Susan's really on top form today. It's like she's always got the last piece of the puzzle to every line of conversation. Since

I last saw her, there's something different in her manner. She's always been the jolly member of the group, but she's louder in how she looks and sounds. I'm getting to the stage now when I know if someone's been shopping. She's definitely in a new shirt. One of these GAP button-down's, worn loose and hanging off all sides.

Our conversation and our ideas suddenly hit a dead end, but at least we've agreed that we're not going to add anything new to the third album. A few moments of quiet and reflection. Then I decide to speak up.

"Maybe we should have a think about moving away from the whole girl-meets-boy theme," I say. "I mean, it's literally been done to death in nearly every damn song out there. What about something else?"

"What do you mean?" Scarlet's perked up like a dog exposed to the scent of cooked meat.

"We could change the theme of the direction we're going in. A new theme for each album perhaps? Humanity. Endurance. Peace. War and conflict. Figures from literature and film. Don't you see? We can go beyond this heartbroken, unrequited love theme. We can do anything."

"Okay," says Josephine, folding up a tissue on her lap. She wipes it over her lips. "How do you propose we proceed with it?"

"Well, like I said, a new theme for each album."

"And do you think that there's a strong money aspect to that?"

"Does there need to be? I mean, we're at the stage now where we can afford to be experimental."

"But Roger will never agree to that." Josephine folds her arms. Christ, sometimes she looks like Miser. Shut off from the world and bitter as a sour lemon.

"Why are we so afraid over what Roger thinks?" I know I'll go too far with this, but the box has been opened. "If we're so fearful over what that guy thinks, maybe we're in the wrong business...?"

"Or maybe you are," says Josephine. She stands up, walks out. Rustles of cups come from the kitchen a short while later.

She's strict. She's angry. Fuck, she's pissed. But not as much as she typically is. She comes back, a cup in her hands (just for herself, of course), and sits down, crossing her legs like she's about to read the paper. All bloody casual.

"So, we're all clear on the third album then?" says Susan. "Right, so what are the arrangements for recording?"

"They'll be finalised in due course," replies Josephine, slurping the drink. Slushing. Bits of hot liquid shoot off in any fucking direction they want to. "Don't worry, girls, you know how I'm like."

"What are we doing for lunch by the way?" I ask.

"There's a new steak place that's opened up near mine," suggests Susan.

"I don't eat steak," replies Scarlet. "Can't stand it."

"Maybe we could order in," says Josephine.

"Look, guys, I need to be heading off now," I say, wishing – for a moment – that I could disappear from this room. "I can stay a while more, but only if it's to practice."

"We've done everything we wanted to today." When she's said this, Josephine shifts herself up, rubs her cheeks. "Girls, I'm sorry I'm a bit off at the moment, but I'm taking time to process things. It's just, Robert told me he wants me back. I told him I wasn't interested, not after what he did. But I'm thinking of him, thinking about giving him another chance."

"Don't, Josephine," I say. Given my own string of failed relationships, I'm hardly the one to be making these kinds of suggestions. "Trust me, don't. He threw you away. You're better than him."

"Gina's right," Scarlet adds.

"She is." Susan stands up and clutches Josephine's hands in hers. "Meet a proper, decent guy, someone who'll respect you and love you for who you are."

"Thanks, girls." Josephine wipes the corners of her eyes.

Suddenly we're all hugging. Arms fastened around one another. Emotions locked together, like we're one being, one voice. We're a collective of reason and sanity.

I was reading something recently about bacteria. (I did a little science at school – nearly went into it, actually.) They can form things called biofilms, which are basically super growths. You get them in drains and gutters and places like that. Quite interesting and beautiful, the way they spread out. Anyway, my point is this: apparently, the individual bacteria are able to communicate with one another, send signals, talk. In essence, they become a larger organism. That's what we're like, right here, in this moment. Nothing will ever separate us. We're part of something bigger, something greater.

The doorbell rings. It's irritating, jangling chimes cause us to break apart. Josephine heads to the door and returns moments later with Roger and George in tow.

"We're sorry to intrude," says Roger. He looks panicked, stricken with exhaustion. His black bomber jacket seems bigger, its cuffs undone and the collar twisted.

"We thought we'd better tell you in person," says George. He twiddles the knot of his tie and flexes his body inside his brown jacket. "Roger, should you or should I?"

"You'd better be the one to do it. I'm still taking it in."

"Scarlet, this concerns you in particular." George looks past me, right at her.

Scarlet stands strong, as if she knows what's coming. She knows it'll hit her like a train. I can see it. Yet, I can see the defiance banging against the inside of her head. She knows what's coming to the platform. And she knows how to deal with it.

George makes his statement as clearly as he can, and there's definitely an element of Roger's steel in it: "Eugene Lane was murdered in jail last night. This will hit the news in an hour. Scarlet, do you have a statement you wish to make at this time? We'll pass it straight on to the media."

"I have nothing to say at the moment, except for this: I would ask the media to give both myself and the other members of the band privacy in this moment. Do you want me to write something down?"

George is holding out a notepad, a pen fastened under his thumb. Scarlet takes it off him and starts scribbling. "Thanks for that," he tells her, giving the words a quick onceover. "Okay, everything seems okay. Right, cool. I'll ensure that the statement is ready to go."

"Thanks, George," she says. "I mean it."

When they've gone, us girls huddle together on the sofa. I stare at the painting of bluebells which hangs just above the curtains. Some artist from decades past. Some long-forgotten face.

"He's fucking gone!" says Josephine. "That bastard's fucking gone!"

We don't shed tears: especially, not those of sadness; but neither those of relief. To us – and I know that I speak for the entire band – he's something that was. Sooner or later, he'll be forgotten, cast into the recesses of our darkest memories, like a discarded toy, or a used condom, a regret, or maybe even a wrong note in our music.

Susan

23 January 1993

I gulp when I see the long line stretching out like string beans. Excited chatter and this 'literary criticism' hangs around in a crowd. I probably shouldn't have left it too late, but I've found I've become increasingly disorganised over this past week. Even my runs have been gradually growing later – though by just a few minutes.

The bookshop is one of a chain that's spread itself up and down the country over the past decade. It'll be the way of things to come – someone was saying that on the radio the other day. Gone are the days of the local independent shops. The era of the mass chain store has firmly arrived. But the link where the event is being held tonight looks a hospitable little place. Books – fresh from the printing line – adorn shelves behind the floor-to-ceiling windows. I can see an attendant wandering around inside, randomly checking things. A poster hangs behind one of the windows, showing the youthful face of Victor Gully – so damn serious – and an older bloke with a trimmed beard and softish eyes. Underneath their photographs, I'm told what tonight is about: *Herbert Buxton In Conversation with Victor Gully*. Well, I'm none the wiser.

I join the queue – something I'm not used to – and wait for the staff to show us in.

Two old ladies are bickering in front of me.

"Have you read Gully's latest book? Honestly – so pessimistic!" one of the them says.

"How can you say that, dear? It was uplifting and beautiful, heart-warming!"

"Well, I thought his influences – particularly the Egyptian ones – did not work well with the theme of the book!"

I zone out, because I know they're academics. University professors. Is Gully a former student of theirs? Wouldn't surprise me at all.

An attendant comes out – I think it's the guy I saw through the window – raises his voice, directing it like a stream of bullets down the queue, mowing us all down: "Ladies and gentlemen, if I can ask you to have your tickets ready for inspection. We will open the doors in about five minutes." His eyes meet me. He briefly turns his head to a fellow attendant, someone much older, who has the appearance of having been trapped in this low-level job for most of his life.

I start feeling the cold nibbling my hands, right through the leather. I hold my breath, as if that will help dispel the anxiety that's coursing underneath my skin. The attendant, his face tanned from a recent holiday no doubt, is approaching. He's checking something on a clipboard. He comes right before me, scans his paperwork again.

"Susan?" he asks.

"Yeah."

"This way please." He's gesturing at the shop.

"Sorry, I'm not sure what this is about. Is there an issue with my ticket?"

"Not at all. Please…"

I walk behind him. Mutterings of complaint echo behind me. I think so, anyway. Then there's the recognition. Someone screams in a whisper: "It's *her!*" Someone else: "Didn't think this would be her thing." I'm shown through a set of double doors into an interior that's bathed with red light. A raised platform with two chairs and a silvery table stands before rows of seats; a decanter of water and two empty, upturned glasses gleam. The place is almost like Gully's apartment: bookshelves surround me on all sides, hundreds upon hundreds of them. It's like being stuck in a shell, crushed in by words. I look at the table on the platform again, just checking if I've missed something, and it turns out I have: two books are propped up like priceless duty-free chocolate. I squint and try to make out the titles: one of them is *The Vindication*. I take a few steps closer, trying to see the second. It's Victor Gully's book; I can see his name in shiny blue writing. *The Nothing Prince.* What?

"If you will come with me," says the attendant. He's sounding firm now. As if I'm a troublesome member of the crowd. He leads me past the seats to the back of the room. There's another table there, with two seats and discrete piles of books, separated by a gulf where another decanter of water and two companion glasses are to be found. The man heads to a blank, grey door and smacks it with his knuckles. A thudding voice from inside asks us to come in.

I'm inside a small room that looks more like a stationary cupboard than an *authors' area* – I think that's the term they use. It's filled with discarded books and reminder notes pinned to the walls. There's a kitchen area as well, where a pile of paper cups is beginning to gather the initial fragments of dust. A kettle emits wisps of vapour.

Victor Gully and this other man each hold one of these paper cups. Instant coffee, by the smell.

"I'm so glad you came!" He stands up and embraces me – in a non-romantic way, of course. "Susan, this is Herbert Buxton. My co-host for this evening." He cracks his face into a forced smile, but one tinted with the enthusiasm for his profession. "Herbert, I'd like to introduce you to Susan –"

"No need to say anymore!" Herbert Buxton has a loud, booming voice that seems to rattle the walls. "Susan, can I just say that I love your music. Beautiful, ornate lyrics. A friend of mine went to one of your concerts once. He told me that you were the most beautiful act he'd ever seen. Anyway, I digress! I'm Herbert."

"Susan." I offer my hand, which he takes firmly.

Herbert Buxton is a tall, mid-fifties man, with a bush-ier beard than the poster. He's heavyset, with a slight bulge in his front and pudgy hands. He wears a white shirt, with thick, golden cufflinks, and a black jacket and a set of blacker trousers. His shoes have been shined to a dark diamond and the scent of diluted cinnamon releases itself from his skin.

"Are the copies of the books stacked outside?" Victor asks the attendant.

"They are," comes the curt, respectful response. The attendant knows his place. They all do.

"Excellent," Herbert answers. "Christ, I've had enough of this coffee. Scraped from the bottom of the tin."

The attendant is standing, all movement stopped except for the infrequent checking of his watch.

"How long?" Victor asks him.

"Two minutes."

"Wait outside and knock when it's time."

The attendant knows his place in this order. He steps outside and closes the door behind him. We're briefly exposed to the murmuring of the crowd, who are now taking their allotted seats.

"So, how come you know Victor then?" asks Herbert.

Of course, neither of us are going to tell him the truth. Victor quickly moves in, his manner firm and brisk: "A mutual friend introduced us."

I continue: "I've had a bit of an interest in this sort of thing for a while. Writing. Been doing a bit of poetry. Victor suggested that I come along tonight."

"Did he now..." The way Herbert smirks, it's clear that he doesn't believe our story. "If you two are seeing each other..." He leaves his sentence open, like a door kicked in at the base.

No one says anything for a few moments.

"Listen you know that dinner you organised?" Herbert's speaking straight to Victor as though I'm not there. "The one that takes place after the event? You know, that one? Well, you know how you booked it for three people?"

Victor's red in the face. "Yes?" he whispers.

"Well, my wife paged me earlier. She says she wants me home by Nine tonight. You know what I'm like. Never one to disappoint. My wife has turned our home into the Soviet Union. Loyalty to the last. All that sort of stuff."

"You should have written drama for the BBC, Herbert," says Victor, trying to supress his laughter. Failing so bloody miserably at it as well.

"I should have been a lot of other things," the bearded man counters. "I was touring across America when I was your age, Victor. So many interesting people. Especially that reggae guy – and that is a story in itself!"

There's a gentle tapping on the door. It's time.

"Oh, shit, where the hell do I sit?" I blurt out.

"Don't worry, he's sorted out a seat for you," says Herbert. "True romance if ever I saw it!"

"Oh, stop it!" says Victor, laughing some more.

I don't know why, but I reach out, touch his hand with mine. It's automatic. Totally out of my control. Only for the briefest moment, but I feel like a gulf of longing has opened within my heart.

Herbert storms forward and opens the door. I closely follow Victor. As we go up the aisle, he indicates an empty seat right at the front. Perfect view.

Everyone knows who I am. More whispers. More dull talking. "That's her." "Christ, I recognise her! She's from that band, isn't she?"

My seat is right next to the two old dears (actually, I should say *academics*), but it will allow me to shelter from prying eyes for duration of the talk.

There's another attendant, but this one is much more on the senior side. He wears the crest of the bookstore chain, very proudly, on the pocket of his blazer. He's totally bald, with thin, shrewd lips, and wafer-thin square glasses. He stands on the platform, in front of the table, hands clasped behind his back, eyes narrow and fierce.

I feel Victor touch me on the fingertips as I begin to sit. No one else notices, I think... That's the problem when you do what I do. It doesn't matter if you fall for someone and you know it's right – you've got to watch for the gossip.

For the moment, though, I'm watching the hairless guy. He appears to be waiting for the audience to quieten down.

Victor and Herbert take their seats. Somehow – and maybe it's one of these writer things – they manage not to look at the audience. Victor does cast a few glances at me. Is he making the most of the time allowed?

Suddenly the bald man starts speaking and all eyes fall on him. "Ladies and gentlemen, welcome to this most distinguished event," he begins. He has the voice of someone who's been doing this all their life. "Tonight, we have two excellent writers in discussion with one another. On my right, we have Herbert Buxton. A music journalist in times gone by, he has recently turned his attention to writing fiction. His second novel, *The Vindication*, was released earlier this year. On my left, is Victor Gully. Mr Gully is the author of three novels, and his latest, *The Nothing Prince*, has already been tipped for multiple awards. However, it was his debut, *The Church In The Square*, that captivated readers across the world. Tonight promises to be a major literary feast. Two great minds. Two great writers. I'll hand right over to them." The man gently taps his hands together and we applaud, as if sucked into a state of transfixed unison.

I'm soaked in admiration. Filled with it. Buried by it. All I'm thinking about is him... Victor. The way he's sitting. So proud. The way he can't stop glancing at me. The way his fingers can't stop crisscrossing and trembling.

The conversation starts. Everything seems to connect between these two experts on the literary mind. Oh, that bridge is as strong as stone. But his eyes keep wandering over to me.

There's some commotion at the side of the room. Some shouting. But I don't register it. It's none of my business.

It comes closer, but I don't think anything of it.

Victor's eyes flash with alarm. So do Herbert's. They jump to their feet, shouting, screaming.

I stumble from the chair. It's as if I know who it is, as if I've always known.

"Rowan," I just about manage to stutter. "Rowan, what do you want?"

"You're a bitch, Susan."

He's in the same tracksuit as I've always seen him in. Always the same. Except there's something different. Something that's shinier and way more beautiful. It glistens in the light.

"You cunt," he hisses. He hugs me. I don't know why. He's caressing me. Holding me like I've needed to he held for a long time. "You're a lying, fucking cunt, Susan."

Something tickles my belly and I feel myself grow wet. I breathe in the dull smell of blood.

Rowan pulls away. Smiles so desperately. Comes in again. Stabs repeatedly.

I'm groaning, falling to my knees. Lying on the floor. Old ladies are screaming. Men too. I'm aware of Victor's face meeting my own, cradling my neck. I can see spots of tears.

"I'm sorry," I tell him.

"Please...!" His bravado's so fucking gone.

"Victor..."

I see a candle ahead. Lit up. Warming the bitter air. I'm reaching out for it. I'm ready to leave this place. Ready for a new beginning. The flame grows in its intensity. It's suffocating. It makes me sweat.

In the moments before everything turns to darkness, the flame turns into Scarlet's face. I reach out, hope to stroke her cheek. But I'm falling once more. I hope everything envelops me.

James

5 February 1993

Everything turns to dust, eventually. That's what they always say.

Sitting here in my office that's plastered wall-to-ceiling with my successes, right from when I started out. I'm now as old as some of the senior chaps I used to hang around with. In fact, I'm older. I'm much older. I'm sitting, surrounded by them. I want their advice. I want them to tell me what to do.

Right now, I'm hurting.

Scarlet won't talk to me. She won't speak to anyone. She's walled herself up – quite literally. I've gone outside her penthouse a few times, and I can see her shadow shifting around, aimless and lost. She's hurting badly. She's my daughter and there seems to be nothing I can do.

They're all hurting. They're all in pain. And I can't help.

The funeral's in an hour. They're cremating her.

Scarlet, Josephine, and Gina. All together.

I actually saw Gina the other day. Yesterday, I think. Bond Street. Her eyes were moist, vacant, dead. I tried to stop her, but she just walked on by, as if I was nothing. As if she'd never met me.

Oh, I hurt for them. I burn for them. I wish I could hold the three of them. More than that, I wish all three of them were truly mine. Three daughters.

I adjust my tie. Check my watch. I think of what Paul would say – we met at a funeral, after all. He's not able to come, unfortunately. He'd help me through this moment.

I finish the last of my coffee.

Security line the pavement, separating the funeral procession from the general population of mourners. I'm on the inside, my left hand clutching my wife's, my right hand around Alastair's waist. Roger Miser and that bloke, George, are directly in front. Their heads are bowed, so respectfully, so formal; but I can see the trembling in them. There are a few folk behind us, but I don't try to see who they are. I don't need to.

The procession smoulders on, nearing the church like a pin slowly heading for pale skin.

Scarlet, Josephine and Gina stand behind the hearse. They look the most formal they've ever been. Their arms are linked tight, like chains.

Flashes of cameras and the murmurings of reporters are the only things that cut the frozen air.

We're in Ilford. The church is trapped by surrounding concrete, but it looks as though it was situated in the rolling hills of Dumfriesshire. It has that peaceful appearance: so calm, so beautiful.

Susan's parents aren't coming. From what I read in the media... they need a break. Well, I bloody well think it's because the truth has now emerged. Who Susan really was. Christ, I had no idea. How could I have known?

The newspaper headlines were full of it all. They always are. *Susan ----- Stabbed To Death: Suspect Dead At Scene.* Here was another one, all the juicy bits hicluded (a tabloid, you might guess): *Talented Susan ----- DEAD!*

Whoever this Rowan Colt was, why did he commit such a despicable act? Maybe we'll never know. Police investigations are still ongoing. We know he was from Susan's past, from that dreadful children's home. Oh, I'm not a wretched police detective! But at least he's dead: stabbed in the neck with his own knife by a member of the public after he dropped it.

The funeral procession shifts on.

Josephine's shaking. She stumbles, quickly supported by Gina.

The church is typical – like all the others around England, I suppose. Wooden oak doors. Stone crusted with moss. I've been to so many funerals over the years, damn, they blend into one another. Life's one big funeral.

The hearse stops and the six designated pallbearers take their positions as the coffin is wheeled out. They're from the funeral home: I think Roger said something about not wanting to have emotional people lifting the coffin. Getting involved where he shouldn't be – again.

Everything slows down now. We enter the church, heads bowed, as The Beatles envelops us. I receive a programme. I can't bear to glance at the picture of her. As I take my seat – fairly near the front – I'm scanning down the list: prayers, prayers, more prayers; singing; the eulogy delivered by Josephine; then, a bunch of other nonsensical stuff, including a speech from Roger Miser, and then a tribute by a chap, Victor Gully. Now, where do I know that name from...?

Surprisingly, it's all ready to go in less than five minutes. The coffin is positioned. The vicar stands in his robes, all set. The girls – my girls – are at the front.

When the music stops, silence grips us. It's like the beginning of a film from my youth. The vicar briefly bows his head, and then takes to the pulpit.

"Ladies and gentlemen," he says, his voice foggy, "we are gathered here today to celebrate the life of Susan. All of you knew her in some capacity. All of you were blessed to..."

I start zoning out. I feel my wife's gloved fingers stroke my elbow.

A prayer comes, and then a hymn.

Josephine climbs the pulpit, rips open the papers, stares at the audience. I know she won't get through this without breaking down. Yet somehow, she speaks with clarity.

"Susan. How can I describe her? She was one hell of a piano player. She was the quietest member of our group. She was reserved, patient. But she was also the strongest person I've ever known. I only recently found out about her early life. What she went through. The torment. The suffering. The abuse. But she came through it all. I don't know how she stayed so calm, so collected. But she did. She pursued things with strength and honour and –" Josephine falters. "– beauty. I'm sorry, bear with me. Please. She was my friend. She was a sister to me. Fuck, I miss her." She sobs. "Sorry. Sorry, guys. I miss her a lot." She's breaking now. "I will never forget her. Not ever."

She clears her throat. "Susan once said to me: 'When it comes to love, nothing is off the table.' I never understood what she meant by that until recently. She was right. Susan was someone who never faltered. She kept us together she kept us all together. She was the best of us. I will miss her."

She folds up her paperwork, as if it really is paperwork. She nearly trips on her way down, but somehow steadies herself. She looks so fragile, so broken. She's like one of those stick insects that kids have these days. Everything about her is at ease of being ripped like damp paper.

The vicar comes up next and does a few readings. I suppose that's when I nod off again. I look up again when Roger Miser gives his speech. It's nothing too self-centred. How much the team at the record company admired Susan. How much they loved her. All that sort of stuff. He's professional, a hundred percent. When he's done, he dips his head, tiptoes down the steps. On his way back, he briefly touches Josephine's shoulder.

"Now, I would like to invite Victor Gully to speak," says the vicar.

I hear shuffling. Turning my head, I see that a man a few rows behind me is rising to his feet. He's young. There's a bearded gentleman next to him – his father? The young man makes his way to the podium without a single glance at anyone. He's cut off from them all.

Oh, bloody hell. I recognise him. Saw him on the front of one of those literary magazines recently. Yeah. Victor Gully.

"I didn't know Susan that well," he begins, chewing his lip. "In fact, we ran into one another, quite literally. You know how she used to love her morning runs. I knew her only for a few days, but she enriched my life. She did it in ways I could never imagine. I'm grateful that she came into my life, because she changed who I am. Susan was the most honourable, decent human being I have ever known. Those few days I knew her were –" He stops. Gulps. "Susan, I wish I'd known you better." I can hear him breathe. He starts heading back to his seat. All eyes are on him now.

When we file out, I drag my wife over to our daughter, who has ventured off from the flow. She's by one of the graves, out of view, a smouldering cigarette in her grip.

"Scarlet, I'm so sorry," I say, hugging her. She doesn't resist. "I am so, so sorry."

"What's there to be sorry about?" she says back to me. "These things happen. Where's Paul and Siobhan? I thought this was their kind of thing."

"Scarlet, we're here for you," my wife whispers. "We're all here for you."

Alastair tries to comfort his sister. But it's like holding a slab. She just won't respond.

"Susan's dead. There's nothing more to say." Scarlet turns away from us. There's another cigarette being produced.

"Scarlet...!" stammers my wife.

"Let's leave her," I say, taking her elbow. "Alastair, bring the car around. We're not welcome here anymore."

Josephine

11 May 1984

It was a job that was vaguely bearable.

Office work. Plain and simple. Stapling reports. Making tea and coffee. That sort of crap. But it was a job that paid well. Reasonably so. Enough for her to save up. Maybe see a few more countries.

She was finishing late today. The others had gone to The King's Rose to sink a few pints, anything to drown the sorrows of the long working week. It was nearly Six and she wanted to be back home by Seven. Friday night family dinner.

It was her dad who got her this job. She should have been grateful for it, but she had a hunger for what was out there. Beaches with white sand. Starlit nights. Incredibly, unthinkably brief romances.

It took her a few minutes to do a final check on the office, ensure the lights were switched off, papers properly filed away, etc. When she was done, she tugged on the shirt that felt so unnatural on her, and headed out of the building.

The company she was working for was situated on the northern outskirts of Epsom, where suburbia began to melt into London. Her parents lived on the southside of Tadworth, where the open countryside began to beckon.

There was nothing for it, except to walk to the bus stop.

As she'd done for the past several weeks, she began the casual stroll. A few revellers were out, kicking back, embracing the weekend. It was May and it was warm, with the promise of a beautiful evening sun, though Epsom certainly did not have the allure of the Madagascan coastline, nor its bars and cafes.

She smiled at the memory.

She became aware of commotion ahead. Angry voices, though deeply passionate in whatever they were talking about. Viciously passionate. Three women doing a sort of nonsensical, tribal dance on the pavement. Every so often – when a member of the public happened to come near – they would stop their little routine, try to force a leaflet into their hands.

To her left, there was a street that offered a decent shortcut to the bus stop. She should take that. This trio of women weren't completely ridiculous: they looked dangerous, determined. They were hippies, and she should smell the drugs even from here. She'd seen them on her travels, she knew the type. The pathway to the left – she should go down that. But she was a traveller. She'd learnt about strength and compassion. She went straight ahead.

She kept her head down as she passed. She felt one of them press a leaflet into her hands.

"Where the hell are you going?" a voice yelled.

"Not interested," she responded. "Not fucking interested."

"We could be wiped out and you don't care?"

"What's that supposed to mean?" Josephine snapped back at them. A fatal mistake.

The three of them were the same age as her. She had no doubt of that. Years later, she would reflect on their immaturity, their naivety. Many years after that, when she herself was destitute, she would sometimes think of these three.

Two of them had the stereotypical appearance of butch lesbians. Josephine had often seen them outside gay clubs on her travels. Strong, confident bullies. These two wore the hippie gear like it was a joke: the rings, frilly clothes, funny symbols attached on too loosely.

But the third, staying well at the back, she was a serious hippie: dark eyes, unwashed black hair, peace symbols and bracelets. Rags for clothes and differing trainers showed that she was someone who took life on the road as seriously as a mortgage.

"There's a protest on in a few weeks." One of the butch women aimed her eyes at the leaflet she'd passed to Josephine. "Are you going to join us? Will you join the effort to stop American cruise missiles in Britain?"

"Cruise missiles?" Josephine hated questioning. Always too many answers.

"Yeah, the cruise missiles. Have you not heard of them?"

"Not really. I've been travelling."

The other butch woman spoke up. A murmur. "Typical."

The first one took over, all professional. "Look, we won't bother you anymore. You've got our leaflet. If you're interested, we'll see you there."

"Thank you," replied Josephine, waving it in the air, as though trying to summon something. She nodded at them, and then set about for home.

It was only when she was on the bus, crammed alongside the other weary workforce, that she started thinking deeply. She would go along. An afternoon excursion. It would be a break from the usual weekend rigmarole of drinking and silent family dinners.

She'd seen a lot on her travels. She could cope with a small protest.

Gina

19 February 1993

"You conducted yourselves in a highly professional manner," I hear Roger Miser tell us for the hundredth time that morning. Now, though, he adds something to it. "*I* am proud of you. *George* is proud of you. Now, though, you must stand for yourselves. I am arranging for a series of interviews."

"What kind of interviews?" asks Josephine.

"Television and radio."

"How can you say that? At a time like this?!"

We've grown used to Josephine's temper. So much so, it's become normal. These past two weeks, she acts like she owns everything. Nothing's off limits for her. She's become the bully that we were used to.

"I know you don't like this," Roger Miser responds calmly, "but a lot of people are asking a lot of questions. The longer we sit on this, the great the pressure will become.

"Girls, I am truly sorry for your loss. Really, I am. But there are bigger things to worry about right now..."

George – standing at the back, like he always does – watches on with his arms folded.

"If we don't cut this off at the stem, the wound will fester," Roger Miser continues. "It will fester until our limbs start coming off. I know that's grotesque, but that's the bloody truth. We have to put our side of the story out there!"

"Why do we need *our side of the story*?" snaps Josephine. I can see she's fighting back tears. "Why the hell do we need that? She was murdered, Roger. Stabbed in the neck. Murdered by a fucking psychopath. A fucking evil bastard. What more do you want to know? What more do they wany to know? I'll give a fucking interview. I'll tell the world about what happened. I'll tell her how Rowan Colt stalked her, harassed her, threatened her. I'll tell every fucking continent about the abusive childhood Susan had. But I'll tell them how she overcame it. How she pulled through."

"That's exactly what we want!" exclaims Miser.

His office has had a makeover. The fresh scent of peachy paint and the clearing of excess ornaments. That pile of LPs moulding in the corner: gone. That picture with some singer from the 1980s? Removed, cleared out. Everything about this office has changed. Even the air freshener. There's this thing, *minimalism*, which I heard about recently. Something to do with cutting down on the unnecessary things in life. That's what I think Roger is doing. In fact, I'm certain that's what he's up to. The question I'm asking right now: Was Susan's death the catalyst for this?

"We've got interviews lined up for each of you," says George. "Gina, there's this obscure little west country magazine that wants to do a spot with you. I know this really isn't what you're after right now. Something read by old ladies. Roger and I are in agreement, though. This is exactly what is needed. Josephine, you're doing something with the BBC. They'll be in touch within the next twenty-four hours. Sorry, I don't know the full specific details. Scarlet, Fox News wants to interview you. Roger and I have carefully set this one up. Scarlet, I can't imagine how you're feeling right now, but –"

"Honestly, it's fine." Scarlet sits up. Her lips seem to purse for a cigarette. "Christ, guys, I don't know why you're looking at me like that. I'm over it now. She died. She's gone. Murdered, as Josephine has kindly put it. But I'm not going to spend my time grieving and crying. I'll do this interview. I promise. I'll do a thousand interviews just like it."

"Scarlet, what's happened to you?" I find myself whispering. I think I was only trying to speak to myself, but the words have been heard by Scarlet. She pricks her ears up, looks straight through me.

"Nothing's happened to me. Nothing at all."

Even Roger looks shocked. George can't make eye contact with anyone.

"Don't you feel anything?" stutters Josephine.

"I miss her, as you'd expect. That's normal. Isn't it? Should I be expressing another set of emotions?"

I don't think any of us know how to respond. She's so cold.

But it's not that that gets to me. It's the way she continues, unabashed, unaffected, talking nonstop...

"Susan was a dear friend to me. They say that friendship knows no bounds. Certainly, our friendship had a strong foundation." She shrugs her shoulders. "I was reading a book last week on the subject. Very interesting. Some psychologist in New York. I recommend his work to you."

"I think I should draw this meeting to a close," says Roger. He doesn't wait. He tags George along by the elbow, taking him out of the office. I hear him say, "Stiff drink needed."

"I'll see you all later," says Scarlet, rising. She's gone. I swear, I hear her whistling.

"Fucking bitch!" croaks Josephine. "She's a fucking bitch!" She hunches over, trembling.

"Oh, Josephine..." I put an arm on her shoulder, but she doesn't budge. "Josephine, I'm going to have a chat with her."

I find Scarlet outside the front entrance, waiting for a car to turn up. The way she stands, so pointed and tall, it makes me angry – jealous, even. We're all grieving, and she isn't affected at all. She's immune to emotion.

"We need to talk," I tell her.

"We don't," comes her response. "The funeral's over. The lawyers are sorting the will and everything out. What's there to talk about?"

"Why are you being like this?"

"Being like what?"

"Why aren't you grieving?"

"I am." She looks up and down the road. She wants this car to appear. She wants to be away from this.

I grasp her arm, yank her away, drag her along. "I've had enough of this!" I yell at her. "Enough!"

"Get the fuck off me, Gina."

"You'll have to hit me – that's the only way you're getting shut of me."

Opposite the building, there's a hedge, always neatly trimmed. (It might be Roger Miser's doing.) A gap in the hedge leads to a small park, that's nearly always empty. That's where I take her. I pull on her wrist and throw her in front of me. I steer her along like an out-of-control child, move her along the pathways. At the other end of the park, there's another gap in another hedgerow. This one leads to a small woodland path, with overhanging trees. That's where I take her. When I feel I've gone far enough, I spin her around.

"Why the hell are you doing this?!" I scream.

"I'm not crying for her, Gina. I won't."

"How can you say that?"

"She was special to me..." She blinks and the first clusters of tears begin to form.

"I know she was."

"I loved her, Gina."

"I know you did. I know."

"But we'll pull through this." Scarlet is trying to sound confident. She's trying to be strong. It's like the day she first suggested this band to us, back when there were five, when she acted like a leader, pulling us together.

"Scarlet, allow yourself to grieve."

"I am, can't you tell?" Her voice is fragmenting. She's breaking. She's falling apart.

"Scarlet..." It's then that I hug her tight. "Scarlet, it's okay."

The sobs echo through me. I feel her knees weaken. I feel her falling apart. She drops, knees sinking into the floor. I fall with her. I fall so hard that I feel something scrape my knee and the first drips of blood soak my jeans.

"I miss her!" she wails. "Oh, Gina, I miss her."

"Me too."

No further words come from her. No further words are necessary. No further information. Not even any more emotions. Just tears. Tears in the cold air.

We hold each other tight and we don't stop.

Scarlet

3 April 1993

She's not in the driver's seat, though that is something to be expected. Josephine's the one driving. They trundle along in her W124 Mercedes – something she got from a friend last week. Scarlet did complain that she should think about getting a slightly 'richer' car...

The grief is past them now. It's time they moved on.

Trundling behind them is another car filled with the spare musicians and their instruments. It's so mechanical, the way they wrap up their sadness...

The house is a few miles west of Dunwich, situated just outside a tiny hamlet. She went up there a week ago, just to check on it, see if it was still falling down. And it was. Crumbling to pieces. But it'll do the job. It's what the band needs.

They drive and she thinks of Emma. Not Susan, but Emma. In truth, Scarlet's beginning to forget what Emma looks like. It's been years since she's been gone. She's a ghost. A spectre without a face.

Scarlet's thinking about the summer of 1989, when she first realised her feelings for Emma. The two of them were away in Dorset – somewhere down there. It was an art project field trip thing for Scarlet, but Emma tagged along because she wanted a quick holiday.

It was the final night and they – the two of them – were walking along the seafront, the gentle lull of the English Channel washing over them. No words were shared between them. Just looks and connection. That's when Scarlet had that inkling, the beginning of feelings. It lasted less than a moment. The briefest flicker of open souls that passed between them.

She's gone now. Long gone. Nothing more to discuss.

They arrive at the house for lunchtime. Josephine's the first out, directing everyone, telling them where to go. The male replacements and the tech guys (who've arrived in a third car – though Scarlet hasn't bothered to make a note of it) start moving equipment inside.

It's a decent, comfortable-looking place actually. It's about twice the size of one of those cottages you see in country magazines, but with extra space and roof that's had the straw ripped out and replaced with tiles. It's situated by the farmer's field – currently churned up – and the perimeter is covered in rubble and dust. The place is collapsing. In some ways, it already has. The soul of the place has been crushed.

There's no furniture. Actually, that's a good thing. What used to be the living room is now being jammed full of sound equipment. A sofa would have been an inconvenience. Someone starts a backing track, and is quickly scolded by a fattish guy with a red beard – the leading tech guy. Arguments and bickering are the start of a good few days of recording, and Scarlet's confident that this will be the best yet.

She wanders through the house, seeing the three allocated rooms where the technical people will sleep, the one where the male musicians will rest, and the upstairs area where she and the girls will rest their eyes.

There doesn't seem to be anywhere that's untouched, that's not interfered with. Eventually, she finds a small room – must have been a former storage larder – and leans back against the stone wall. It's like being back in her shack again, though with less company than one. She's half a person now.

It's a strange thing, not sleeping in a luxury hotel. They're staying onsite – her idea, actually – to give a strong emotional, connecting theme to the album. A sense that they work, eat and sleep together. No room for pause, no chance of reflection. This is full-on and real.

"Scarlet, come on!" booms Josephine's voice. "Are we having lunch, or what?"

It's the end of the first day and half the songs have been recorded. Scarlet wants to light a cigarette, but her voice is scratchy, hurt, bloodied from the stress. She goes for another cold bottle of water – her tenth. When she finishes it, she feels the stabbing urge to piss. She goes to the only thing that still works in the cottage: the toilet with the broken system.

Slamming the door behind her, she hears Mark – one of the backing musicians – announce that there's a chest of beers he's brought with him. Everyone else cheers. Even Gina. Scarlet feels for a moment that they're not celebrities. She even allows herself the luxury of fantasizing about it. But soon enough, when she re-emerges and joins the troupe, Josephine's talking about their fourth album. One of the other backing musicians – Finn – is listening in detail.

Josephine's got an extra level of concern about her. Since their arrival, she's had a haunted look about her. It's like there's something tugging away in her mind. Her eyes sometimes droop and her hands often flop uselessly at her side.

Finn's quite attractive, Scarlet thinks. Part Icelandic. Well-built. Looks after himself. Not the kind of guy who lounges about all day.

Mark appears, dragging this plastic chest in with him. "Help yourselves, guys," he commands, ripping off the lid. "Beers all round."

Scarlet's first, lifting out a Budweiser can, and bursting the seal. The way she drinks it, Roger Miser might end up getting her to do an advert some day!

The third backing musician – late fifties, the oldest one their – speaks up. He's been quiet throughout the day, but he speaks with an assertiveness, an aggressive confidence, that pressures the room to become silent. "Boys, I've been thinking about going solo. Do you think it's too late for me?"

"Maybe," says Finn. "I don't mean to be nasty or anything like that, but..."

"I think you could. It's never too late." Mark shrugs his shoulders. He's just said those wise words with a crusty sense of resignation.

They eat dinner out the front. A barbeque that Finn has brought: it's one of those small things that will become popular ten years from now, during that wretched hot summer that I'm sure most of you remember. He's set it up with great ease, kicking the flame into life.

They sit on deckchairs, stools and upturned boxes in the overgrown front garden. Burgers and hotdogs, wrapped up in their bread overcoats, are dished out. More beers are provided.

There's something that's too overfamiliar and too damn casual about tonight. She's not used to it. It's an alien world, something she hasn't been to in a long time. She fakes a smile and joins in the jokes, but she doesn't feel connected to it. Josephine and Gina are laughing and falling about themselves. It's clear: they've forgotten who they are. Scarlet can't seem to bond. No matter how hard she tries. No matter if she forces or doesn't force it. She can't fall in this sea and go swimming.

Someone makes a joke about a single that Mauro Lane has just released. She heard it just the other day – melancholy and depressing. She's not offended at the remark: the tech guy obviously doesn't know about her and Mauro. Or maybe he just doesn't care. Either way, she's not offended or hurt.

She doesn't belong in such a casual, friendly atmosphere. She wishes she did. She wishes she could crack open another can, join in the party. But she's frozen solid on the spot. Like an old photograph lost in a loft. She's standing there gathering dust.

Gina

10 April 1993

The way Roger says things these days, whether he's speaking to the press, or chatting over a drink, he's definitely changed. It's like he's lost that edge, that sense of seriousness that sets him apart from most other managers out there.

"I'm really pleased that you've done this," he tells us, leaning back on Josephine's sofa. "Considering what's happened, you've done a highly professional job." He seems to smirk, rubbing his cleanshaven chin with a rough knuckle.

We wait for his next sentence, his next words. The words seem to have a problem coming out.

"Ladies, I know this will be an uncomfortable question, but... we need to consider some rearrangements to the band setup."

"I'm happy to move to the keyboard," offers Josephine. "Are there any objections to this?"

"No objections from me," says Scarlet.

"Nor from me," I add.

"Well, I'll consider that settled," says Roger. "However, we must now consider *additional* members of the band. There are only three of you, after all. We need to bring in additional musicians."

"What you mean?" comes Josephine's question.

"Ladies, we have to move forward. I think maybe it is time that you learned to forget about Susan. Sorry, I know that sounds harsh, but we have to think of the band."

"I can't believe you just said that..." Josephine's face goes a fake shade of purple.

"He's right," I say.

I feel like one of those cool dudes wearing sunshades in these adverts we've had on the telly recently. Funny, at first, but mildly annoying after you've seen it five or six times.

"We can't spend the rest of our lives with an empty chair for Susan. Josephine, we have to push through this. You know we do."

"I'm not letting her go. How can you say that? Don't any of you feel anything?"

"Of course we do," says Roger. "We do. But we have to move forward. Look, I didn't want to say it like this, but now I have to give you an ultimatum: you hire new members for the band, or I drop you after the third album comes out. I don't mean to sound harsh, but you have to see things from my perspective."

"He's right," I repeat. I sound like something from *Logan's Run*.

"Josephine, Susan meant more to me than anyone. I loved her. We have to let her go, Josephine." Scarlet suddenly sounds human when she says this. Disturbingly so.

"Yep," Josephine quietly responds. "Yep. You're right." She wipes the edge of her eye.

"Good." Roger stands up. "Right, ladies, I need to make a move back to the office. Got clients to see. Any idea on who you're going to add to the band? Sorry, stupid question. Look, I know you'll hire the right people. Right, see you in a bit." His mobile phone is out and he's tapping the numbers with his thumb. "Send the car round please. Thanks, mate. Right, girls, see you in a bit."

When he's gone – and I don't know how this happens – we start falling into laughter.

"Fucking dork," says Josephine. "What an arsehole!"

"I just want to punch his lights out sometimes," says Scarlet.

"I know the feeling. The guy is deranged." I hold my breath. I hold it some more. "Anyway, I'd better shoot off myself."

It's then that I realise there only three of us.

Josephine

11 April 1993

I reach the north of London by Six A.M. Good timing, I remind myself. I've planned like a professional. My ex would be proud. Oh no, maybe he wouldn't be. He's probably still crying.

I'm driving to Bradford. I've never really been there before. I passed by it once, years ago. Not the most attractive place. But I need to go there. I need to see it. I have to know where she lived, where she was raised, the life she had, who she loved. I need to know whether she was loved.

Lorries and motorbikes whoosh past me. I hear the deep beats of one of our songs. At least I think it is.

Something else has been on my mind recently: Greenham Common. I was stupid to get involved with that, but, hey, we all do things we regret. I've often thought about that Friday when

I was heading home from that temp office job. What if I took a different route? What if I ignored those protesters dancing on the pavement, or thrusted my middle finger at them? What if I did the right thing, what that voice in my head was telling me to do? What if I walked away... How might my life have turned out? How might things have been different? Would I still be travelling? On some strange continent, maybe running a backpackers hostel? Maybe, maybe...

Life has strange ways of turning out. Now, *that's* one hell of an overused expression, let me tell you.

I pull on the handbrake and look up. The former children's home is caved in; its roof has sunk like a gorge. There's a light pattering of rain that drools down the windows of the car. How did she survive something like this?

I have a contact in child protection services. It's one of the perks of being famous. You make new friends in high places, and you make friends with their friends. I found out the details of the children's home, and here I am, watching the rain slide down the decaying wood and splintered tiles.

It's walled off with tape. Signs warn of the danger of going in. Unstable structure. Sharp objects. Don't bloody go in.

The children's home itself only has one floor and has that murky greyness of one of those council flats. The windows, shattered like broken hearts, show only a dark interior.

"I never knew you," I say.

That's all I came here to do. That's all that's needed. I head for home, the tears washing through my eyelids.

Here I am again, alone. Here I am again, flashing back to a past I'd hoped was buried.

2 June 1984

The bus eventually stopped, its brakes screeching and crying. She hadn't been sleeping, but the movement jerked her awake and she stared at the thronging crowds packing the fields outside the military base. A shiny new sign declared: RAF Greenham Common.

She nodded a thanks to the driver as she stepped off, hoisting her decaying bag over her shoulder.

"Honestly, don't waste your time here," the driver said.

But those words were lost on Josephine, because, like a dragonfly in the open air, she was attracted to the swarm of protesters.

Streams of police officers were on patrol, presumably to ensure nothing got out of hand. A few of them had hands on batons, ready to strike. Music and dancing were vibrating the air. The protesters – all of whom were women – were linking arms, forming lines that snaked through one another. It was the kind of sight that reminded Josephine of her voyage through the west of Africa: the tribal dances and the community spirit. Such beauty.

She watched the procession for a few more moments, and then edged closer... just as there was a break in the routine and the crowd thundered into a roar.

"Josephine!" It was one of the butch women who'd stopped her in the streets, the one who'd passed her the leaflet. Her eyes were glazed over with adrenaline.

"Hi, how are you doing?" she responded, startled.

"Yeah, you missed something extraordinary. Should have seen when we yelled abuse at the Americans. A bunch of them were going in, all in their red, white and blue. We really put them at double speed. Right, Josephine, you'd better join in..."

She edged toward the crowd of women. Two of them were squabbling and getting pushy. She watched them through bleary eyes: they were her age; they should have been at university; here they were, shoving each other on sloppy ground.

Suddenly, one grabbed the other's ponytail and pulled hard, yelling, "You fucking cow!"

Josephine laughed, watched as the fight escalated, eventually pitting two groups of women against one another. She hadn't seen anything like this on her travels...

Posters and banners had been strung up on the fence. *No Nukes. Ban The Bomb. Nuclear Free World.* All in many different colours.

Police officers burst in, prying the fighting women apart. "You carry on like this, ladies, we'll have you nicked!" one of them warned.

It was then that Josephine saw the many hundreds of women gathered, countless more than she'd seen from the bus. They were pressed against the fence, hands linked, facing whatever lay inside. They were transfixed schoolgirls, trapped in the web of hypnotism. Fingers and thumbs fastened themselves through the wire.

Two military trucks rumbled across the base, a scene which seemed to make the girls grow angrier by the second.

Josephine didn't quite know the way forward from here. Did she just ask to join in? Or did she need to speak to an organiser? Were there forms to fill in? She took a deep breath and went up to the women at the fence.

"Mind if I squeeze in?" she said.

A gruff woman – short, stocky – nodded her head and made room. Josephine touched the fence, joined in the growing chant that was gradually turning into a roar. She was a little unengaged at first – a little embarrassed, even – but she felt a passion swell inside her. Her stammering voice became clear and confident, maybe even aggressive. She was part of this lot, whoever they were, like she'd been born for it. She'd never known anything like this before, not even on her travels, not anywhere. Time was lost on her as she joined in the abuse, even taking the lead now and then.

She stayed for several hours, but when the light dwindled and her eyes began to drift, she started back. It maybe hadn't been the best idea to come here. She was glad she did, but she wouldn't be able to come again. Waving a silent goodbye, she began to leave the scene.

She was laughing, trying not to fall over herself. A very strange group of people!

She became aware of a woman walking next to her, on approach. "Great protest, wasn't it?" came a chirpy voice.

"Yeah, it was. Didn't think I'd ever go to one of these. Hold on, do I know you from somewhere?"

"You should." The woman was more of a girl. Timid, quite afraid. Black hair and a frilly, multicoloured coat. "I was with those two nutters when we stopped you on the street."

"Oh, yeah! I'm Josephine, by the way."

"I know who you are. Listen, I really admired the way you conducted yourself today. Not many people can just join a protest, get stuck in. And they seemed to like you." The girl looked back at the thronging mass, still clipped to the fence. When she turned to face Josephine, her eyes grew mildly moist. "Listen, I have something that might interest you. Do you know East Anglia well?"

"Fairly."

The girl passed over a slip of paper. "Can you come to this address at the time listed? I assure you that it'll be well worth your while." She patted Josephine on the elbow, winking. "See ya."

Josephine felt a tremor behind her and realised that the bus was pulling up. She ran for it and just about made it through the door. It was only when she was sitting down that she looked at the paper. It had been crumpled in her grip, its surface littered with folds. The address and the time were there, and so was the icon of this group, whoever they were. She'd seen something similar on her travels, but never did she think she would be running her thumb over the hammer and sickle on a bus in Britain.

She thought about things, about life, about this group. The closer she got to home, the more she became enticed by them. One meeting wouldn't hurt. Surely...?

Josephine

2 May 1993

The invite waits for me inside the fan mail. George – good champ he is – is by my side, helping me to sift through the mound of letters. Everyone wants to know everything about me. It's like the spotlight has tilted on its axis, pointed at me, and now there's no way I can back off. He's rummaging through the letters, complaining how one of those on this "work experience" should be doing this job.

We're in George's new office in Record Company HQ. He's barely moved in: boxes are still taped; photographs are piled up, waiting for sorting.

"This looks interesting," he says, holding up a letter lined with a gold strip. "Definitely not from some teenage kid with the hots for Scarlet..."

I throw him a dark look.

"Take a peek." He tosses it over.

I barely catch it, sending him a vicious scowl as the tiniest papercut opens in the fleshy part between my fingers.

"Christ, it does look official," I hiss, pulling out a typed letter. The ink still feels wet. "Fuck, I've been invited to some music festival up in Shetland."

"It'll be hard to swing that," responds George. "Roger doesn't want the band doing anything at the moment."

"For Christ's sake, George! The invite is for *me*! Just me! Only me!"

"Really?"

"George, do I have to say it a million times? I'm not married to the fucking band!"

His jaw drops. My sudden outburst has taken him by surprise. He's a rabbit trapped by the headlights of a motorbike.

"They want me up there. End of this month. It's not to sing or anything. They want me as this special guest or something. Oh, Christ, George, fuck it. I'm not doing that. Far better things to do."

"Well, why don't you talk it over with the girls? You're having dinner tonight, are you not?"

"Yes, we are. George, you do realise, don't you, that you're starting to sound like Roger? More and more these days."

George stops what he's doing, stares at the floor. He grips his desk, spreading out his fingers. He sighs, tugs on his cardigan with his free hand. He's exactly the same as the day I met him. A formidable, gentle presence. A kindly man, but a heart of cold stone.

"Do you think I should do it?" I ask him. "Honestly, is this something that I should do?"

"It's up to you," he responds. He's as calm as a starry night reflected in the Indian Ocean. "It's up to you, although I would definitely talk to Scarlet and Gina. Trust me, Josephine. You're an individual, a person, someone truly unique. But you're part of something bigger. You're –"

"It's okay, I understand. I know where you're getting at."

"I don't mean it in a bad way..."

"George, I understand. Totally. I think I need to go and have dinner with the girls, see what they have to say."

That evening.

And they're in agreement.

They say what they have to say, including any and all concerns on the subject, in between mouthfuls of the finest Italian pasta (from one of the finest Italian restaurants in Covent Garden). They hope that I'm careful, that I don't do anything stupid or dangerous. But they trust me, and they're quite happy for me to go.

"So, I'll guess I'll go then," I say grudgingly.

More murmured agreement.

It's strange, very strange, how we've grown increasingly silent over these past few months.

"I'm glad she met someone in the end," says Gina. "Victor Gully. A writer, of all people."

"He was indeed," I say. "But she never really got him though, did she? She never had a proper relationship. She never had him. Christ, I even read his latest book. Utter tosh. Utter shite."

"Is that *The Nothing Prince*?" asks Scarlet. She holds a small belch. I can see the contortions kicking off underneath her skin.

"Yeah, that's the one. Utter crap. I mean, who wants to read shit like that?"

Heads turn our way. I've spoken too harsh and way too loud for this place.

"To Susan," I say, lifting up my glass. "You were the most beautiful thing in all our lives. You were everything."

"She was indeed," replies Gina. She goes to reach for her glass, but her fingers seem to refuse to grip the stem. She gulps. "Yeah, she was."

"Actually, did either of your read Gully's first book?" asks Scarlet, wiping away bolognaise sauce with a napkin. She used to do it with her wrist or her sleeve, but she's gone up a gear now. But bloody hell, she still doesn't know how take part in a conversation.

"It's *The Church In The Square*, isn't it?" says Gina. "No, I've not read that one. Didn't it win some kind of debut award or something?"

"I think so."

"When are we going to get these new musicians sorted?" I ask, with a definite demanding nature. "We need another guitarist as soon as possible."

"We'll start it next week," says Scarlet. That's what she said the previous week.

"I don't know about you, but I just want to get out there again, back amongst our fans, blasting our music out."

"Quite right, Josephine." Gina narrows her eyes at me. "Quite right."

James

9 May 1993

I'm the most casual I've been in years. Well, old chap, it is certainly a beautiful day. The sun is out and the air – even at this early hour – feels warm and fuzzy. I've had my breakfast and I'm fully fuelled with coffee. Like Reggie Perrin, I set off at a brisk pace to the train station. Except I'm not as smartly dressed: a t-shirt, fleece, walking trousers and trainers are wrapped around my skinny frame.

I'm heading into London to meet up with Paul. He phoned me on my mobile telephone last night, frantically warning me that his wife was becoming suspicious of us. When I say that, I mean he was properly panicking. Hyperventilating. But I assured him – as I will assure him today – that there is nothing to worry about.

At Sevenoaks Station, I have a brief memory of a time – I can't remember when it was, for the life of me – when Scarlet came home for a weekend. I smile at the memory, but I need to keep a straight face for the train.

It's the usual weekend crowd – I think that's the term, old chum – travelling into London: teenagers, stay-at-home university students, old couples. No one seems focused. Everyone seems distant. Lighthouses at sea. I take a seat towards the front of the train at an empty table. Innocent onlookers gaze at me with a guilty, avant-garde look; I'm definitely a sinner in their eyes. I raise my eyes as the train shifts off. A child complains with a scream and is swiftly reprimanded by their parents.

"Beautiful day, isn't it?" I say to the conductor as he checks my tickets.

"It is indeed, sir. Very much." The thin, weary man, who looks like one of those chaps off *On The Buses*, nods his head and moves on.

The train accelerates through the disappearing countryside. I swear that new buildings are on the rise: here and there, houses spring up like squawking chickens, ruffling their feathers. A shopping centre, reflecting the sun like a giant amethyst, has spread its wings: already the car park is half full with the overeager and families with one-too-many attachments.

By the time I reach London, I'm already planning exactly what I'll say to Paul. Probably I should have said this earlier, but Susan's death has thrown everything off the wheel as of late. Nothing really makes sense anymore.

I wade through the weekend chaos of Waterloo and head for the Tube. I know the Underground like the back of my hand. That's what comes when you spend hours as a student exploring its network. The noise, the hissing, it all brings back memories. Memories of too many nights out, I should add!

I get off at Holborn and head to a Turkish restaurant, which I booked last night. I've never been here before and have no idea if Paul will be able to follow my directions I gave him on the phone last night. I wait outside for a few moments, but soon see the swindling figure of Paul Casselden in the distance. As he gets nearer, I see the worry on his face. He is not exactly – shall we say – the dignified figure one sees at funerals and other such events.

"Paul, there really isn't anything to worry about!" I say to him.

"That's easy for you to say! Christ, James, I think she knows."

"Paul, I want you to take a deep breath. Okay? Breathe in. Breathe out."

"Yes, James, I'm sorry."

"Now, do you feel ready to go into the restaurant, or do you need more time? If you need to, we can take a walk or something."

"No, it's okay. Let's go eat."

I gesture for him to go first. We are seen to promptly, escorted to our table in the half-full restaurant, given menus, get treated with a sense of honour, told that we shall have a waiter who will look after us for all the time we are here. This is a family business, after all...

But we're starting off with a glass of red each.

"Tell me what Siobhan said," I whisper.

"Oh, it was a mixture of things. She was questioning why I kept meeting with you in London. I told her the obvious things: that we were friends and colleagues, that we were catching up. But she said she was suspicious of the number of times we were meeting up, and accused me of not being faithful to her."

"Did she accuse us of having an affair? Did she?"

"Well, no, but..."

"Paul, I really don't think that Siobhan is remotely suspicious of us. Trust me."

"But, we need to be really careful."

"And we are. I mean, we're not seeing each other romantically, are we?"

"Of course not." Paul thumbs the rim of his wine glass. "Sorry, James, I know I sounded really panicky last night and I know I wasn't my best, but I have both our interests at heart."

"I know that, Paul. I know."

"James, could we maybe schedule our lunches a bit less often? I know that seems an awful, horrid thing to say, but I don't want to risk anything."

"It's okay, Paul, I understand." Of course I bloody don't. I feel a knife between my shoulders.

Our dedicated waiter comes over to take our orders. Clearly Paul's been to a Turkish restaurant before, because he knows exactly what he's having: he points at the menu and lists calmly and methodically what he intends to eat. I somehow place my order, blindly, with the mental capacity of a fruit fly.

"What did you order?" Paul asks me, as if a secret part of him wants to humiliate me.

"You know what, I have no sodding idea, mate. Shot in the dark, I should say."

"Whose funeral did we meet at?"

I snigger. "You know, I can't remember. So many funerals over the years, so little time! Can you believe it?!"

I know Paul is trying to bring back the good times, the special memories; but I can see that he has become side-tracked. I think I know what will soon emerge from his lips, but I hold back on striking first.

"I know you went through hell over what happened to Susan," he says. "I can't imagine how painful that was. I really can't. Are you okay?"

"Well, not really, and I don't think I ever will be. Christ, Paul, Susan was almost like a daughter to me."

"James, you must not think like that," Paul warns me, shrinking his lips. "She was not your daughter, James. It's – I can't think of the right word. It's... Damn it, James, it's bloody *toxic* to think like that. She was somebody else's daughter. Somebody else's blood. Don't take responsibility for something that isn't yours."

"I'm not trying to do that!"

"Look, how is Scarlet bearing up over it?"

"She's hanging on." I flash back to the funeral. I think of her stoic, arrogant refusal to join, her defiance against grieving. "She'll pull through. I know she will. In fact, I've got faith that this will pass."

"That's good to hear." Paul starts smiling again.

We see each other off outside the front of the restaurant. A firm handshake. No embracing. We're not going to risk anything. A casual "take care" and an even more casual "see you soon". That will do us, I should think!

I head for the Tube, picking up an afternoon paper on the way. I don't know why, but I've got this real sense of euphoria. I realise I've collected the wrong bloody paper: some tabloid I've picked up. Damn! Blast!

Outside the station, I hear the hissing and the screeching below. Damn! My legs start moving and I dash down the steps, just as the doors of the carriages are opening. I squeeze through and fall back onto a seat.

Pictures of footballers and the latest celebrity gossip adorn my vision. It's oddly beautiful, but the disgust clings to the back of my throat.

There's a lurch and the train starts to move, disappearing into the blackness of the underworld of London, the hands of history.

I don't recognise the people around me. It's not that it's the weekend. No, they're too unfamiliar. Very much so. I'm on the wrong bloody train. How could I have been so wretched stupid? In too much of a hurry, that's my problem! I try to mumble my surprise, but the words don't seem to want to emerge.

I stand up when I feel it brake. The station – battered and bruised – appears in the windows. I get off, temporarily lost as I try to locate the stairs. Or is an escalator? No, it's a set of wretched steps! I head up, and the air seems to be even more suffocating with each inch of ascension.

I'm in an industrial estate of some sort. The whirring of forklifts and the clangs of metal fill my ears. The warehouses and other rectangular blocks, stained to buggery with moss and dirt, are like ants nests, brimming with activity and life.

I start walking. I could use a stretch of the legs. Too much sitting down all day.

There's nothing much to see. Nothing whatsoever. The few people I do witness in their fluorescent jackets milling around, trying to look busy, seem as though they're not quite here. It's all maybe a little bit too much like a fairy-tale.

I see a small café ahead, nearly empty. I go inside, unsure of how to behave in this simplified gloryhole. Two metal tables and a tub of instant coffee. 50P a cup. I think there might be a touch of change in my pocket.

"What'll it be then?" a miserable-looking woman with too narrow a face and very beady eyes asks of me demandingly.

"Cup of coffee, please."

"Take a seat, be with you in a sec."

There's only one blooming seat out, and it seems intent on falling to pieces, judging by the splintering in the metal. I cautiously put myself down and rest my wrists on the table, forming a steeple with my fingers.

"You're not from round 'ere, are ya, darlin'?" the woman says. I turn and watch her spoon some granules into a polystyrene cup.

"No, got a bit lost." Not the cleverest thing to say, I admit. Bloody hell, there is most definitely a scowl in her eyes!

"Fifty pence, darl," the husky form that brings over my drinks tells me.

I hand her the necessary item straightaway. No holding back. I would not dare!

"You do look a bit lost, actually," she says, heading back to the counter. "You do. You've got that face. You're a posh, well-to-do bloke, ent ya?"

"I'm just passing through."

"That's what they always fuckin' say. Just finish your coffee and fuck off."

Don't respond. Now that is something I learnt a long time ago. Keep steady. I want to lash out with profanity, to retaliate. But I keep my cool. I stand firm.

The coffee tastes too good that I even forget it's instant. I'm lost in a world of my own, but somehow I'm still trapped in that awful hotel in Liverpool. I'm still thinking about that woman. And I shouldn't. Bloody hell, of course not!

I don't finish my drink, only getting through two thirds before I taste its true flavours. I dare myself to mutter a casual piece of gratitude behind me and am soon gone. I head back through the industrial pathways. The clanging and shouting are beginning to die down now. I realise that it is indeed late afternoon and most people – well, during a weekday anyway – would be heading home by now. Suddenly there's silence.

Damn. I'm damn-well lost. I look about me. Everything is mostly unfamiliar. I think about retracing my steps, but know that there's little point in that. It would only lead me back to that café and another cup of sour instant. I wander in circles for a few moments, thinking about what to do. I'm a penny caught in hurricane.

I try to resist panicking, but know that every second I spend here makes my arrival time home that much later.

"Christ, where is this Tube station?" I ask, as if somehow I'm expecting an answer.

I see a small group of people up ahead. They look vaguely familiar, but I'm not sure why. They are young, very much so. I realise that they are all in martial arts uniforms – karate robes to be precise. I go up to them, jogging with relief.

"I say, excuse me, do you know where I can find the Tube station?" I ask them breathlessly.

"Sorry?"

"I'm looking for the Underground station. Do you know where it is?"

One of the guys is approaching me. He's tall, athletic. The kind of son most men wish they had. "What is it?" he asks me.

"I'm looking for the train station, the London Underground. I'm a bit lost, you see."

"Why are you checking my girl out?"

"Excuse me?"

A brunette is tugging at the man's arm, pleading with him. "Steve, it's okay," she whispers.

There's a fist hammering its way through the air. I stagger back, wincing in pain and shock as my nerves fill with fire. My right temple is throbbing.

"Christ, Steve!" I hear the brunette yell. "Jesus!"

I know that my tongue is hanging lopsided from my mouth. The collection of karate uniforms laugh like children, except for the brunette, that is.

"I'm sorry, I wasn't trying anything! Bloody hell!" I yell, getting to my feet. Well, there's no point asking them directions to the Tube station now. No point in trying to have some gentle conversation!

I stagger blindly, like a drunk. Hot tears flow like acid. Through the mist, I finally see what I've been hoping for: that familiar ring with the line through it. I straighten up, compose myself, wipe away the moisture with my sleeve, scratch my cheek with my cufflink.

I look back the way I came. Anger flushes through me. I should have said something, stood up for myself.

Now I'm running away. I don't notice myself getting on the train, but I know I'll never forget the eyes of my wife as I walk into our house.

My wife looks so fragile and cold.

"What's wrong?" she questions, as I enter our home.

"Nothing," I say, heading to the cabinet and pouring myself a whisky. "Nothing at all. Nothing." I press the glass against my cheek.

It's been a few hours since the assault, but I'm still shaking. I down the glass in one, refill it.

"Nothing's wrong," I say, but there's no one in the room with me.

Josephine

30 May 1993

I'm glad I did it in the end. It's been a shitting exhausting trip and I'm probably too tired to drive, but – you know what – I'm feeling happier than ever. I've got air in my lungs. Wait, I said that last night...

When the ferry docks in Aberdeen, I don't waste any time heading down to my car. I'm feeling fresh, eager and ready to rock.

Yes, I was a guest. No, I wasn't performing. And no, I wasn't the star of the damn show. But I felt alive. It was some interview – no singing or dancing or complicated nonsense attached. Just questions on my career, my opinion of the music industry, where I think it's going. It was a fantastic night at the Lerwick Festival of Music and Dance. After my event – in a crowded auditorium with wooden rafters – I had a few drinks with the locals and watched a few bands perform. For a moment, I forgot who I even was...

Of course, when you're in my industry, there's no escaping who and what you are.

The further south I go, the more secure in myself I feel. It's not like I was insecure up north, of course not! But I'm a London girl. Always have been. Always will be.

I'm being stupid, driving all this distance. It's too far for someone like me to manage on my own. But I've got more energy right now than I've had in a long time.

Someone like me should really be getting a driver to do all the hard work, but, you know what, I love that addictive sense of freedom. You can do you what you want, how you want it.

Even when I pull into my driveway, after ten hours of hands on the wheel, I feel fresh-faced and eager. As though I've had the luxury of sleep all the way south.

Harrow's looking beautiful tonight.

Later, after I've unpacked and cracked open a new bottle of white, I phone Scarlet and Gina to let them know how it went. They get a load of nonsense about the beautiful scenery, the oomph of the festival, the amount I drank, a little about the locals. But they don't get – and they never will get – details on the man I kissed at midnight.

It was a spontaneous thing, something I never thought I'd do. But it happened. I just saw him in the corner, looking a little bit shy, a vacant look in his eyes. I went over. I talked to him, asked him if he was enjoying himself, then kissed him right on the lips. No one stared. And even if they did, they would have been too drunk – both on alcohol and adrenaline – to notice.

I think about phoning Roger, but decide I can't take his pressuring voice tonight. You know something? I need a bloody night off from him. Genuinely.

My doorbell chimes. I need to get the bloody tone changed at some point. It has this irritating, chirp-like sound that makes me want to tear my ears off.

"Hi!" says my next-door neighbour, Marco.

"Well, hello there," I reply.

"You've got mail," he tells me, handing over a small pile of letters.

"Well, I hope it's not fan mail. That mound of stuff is starting to piss me off."

"How was Shetland?"

"Okay, I suppose. Well, there's hardly anything up there, is there?"

"You're right there. But you had a good music festival, did you? That's what you went up there for, right?"

"It was a fantastic festival, as a matter of fact." I fold my arms, smirking.

Marco's an investment banker. Late thirties. Still with the good looks: sharp black hair and navy-blue eyes. Every time I'm coming up to the house, I see him looking nervously out his window. Sometimes he even has the guts to venture out himself. It's often to give me the paper, or something else that's so ridiculously tedious. For some time, I was mildly irritated, but I'm a changed person. The new me is out for everything. Out for all the good bits and pieces that come with life.

"Marco," I say, tut-tutting. "Marco, Marco. Marco, why do you keep coming over here and trying to talk absolute crap? Why don't you just say that you want to buy me a drink?"

31 May 1993

It's been a while since I've been this way.

When I woke up this morning, all I felt was a desire to come here, to this place. Maybe it was from the glass of wine Marco bought me last night – small, local wine bar; nothing fancy. Or maybe it was from a sense of loyalty. This man – despite being homeless – had shown me the greatest strength I'd ever seen. I feel that the least I owe him is a cup of coffee. I'll take him to a nearby café. Whatever he wants. If we get photographed by a nosy newspaper? So bloody what!

I'm not afraid of what other people think. This is the new me. I don't give a damn what others think. I couldn't bloody care less. Susan taught me those morals. This might be a little bit morbid, but Susan's death has made me realise what's important in life, and what you need to let go of. Sometimes, it's fear. Sometimes, it's an old relationship. And sometimes, it's the truth.

I'm on the street leading up to the cluster of trees. That Little Tikes thing is still there, trapped in the garden. The kid must be too big to ride it now! I take a gentle stroll, as though I'm a lady in some pretentious Jane Austen novel. There's chatter and music coming from within the trees. My heart sinks. The man's been driven out and some yobs have moved in.

Imagine my surprise when I find that there *is* a party going on, but the man – still with that smile – is the centre of attention...

There must be, what, twenty or so people there? No, wait, at least fifty. Several tables have been set out across the forest floor; no, wait, more than thirty tables. And – hold on a minute – there's almost a hundred people gathered. The tables are covered with the food fantasy you read about in novels set in villages in the 1950s: cakes, sandwiches (in triangles), pots of tea and coffee, scotch eggs, sausage rolls. It's a fantasy of the childlike imagination.

The homeless man stands in the middle of it all, every smile directed at him. Except he's different. His hair is cut short and he's cleanshaven. The colour has returned to his cheeks. It's been over a year since I last saw him, but I feel like I know him, like he's a close friend or brother.

"Josephine?!" The man's eyes flicker into beacons. "My word!" He even sounds different.

I go to him. We embrace and I breathe in the gentle scent of aftershave and deodorant. He's in a suit, with two buttons on his shirt undone. He could almost pass for Marco.

"How have you been then?" I ask.

"Oh, fine, fine. I'm supposing you want to know about all this?"

"Yeah."

"I'm leaving the country. Tomorrow. A new life. Canada."

"How...?"

"I helped out a little bit." The woman who's said these words is my height, with a full set of red hair that hangs like a curtain right the way down to her shoulders. She looks at me as though I've stolen him. Christ, is she the girlfriend?

"Josephine, I'd like you to meet Marie." The man's taking control, giving all the orders, all the directions. "Marie made all of this happen."

"Wow, hi," I stutter. My hand reaches forward to take the woman's. She passively takes it.

"About a year ago, Marie came into my life," the man tells me. He says it with an aggressive storytelling stance. He takes the woman's hand, holding her to him. "It was a few days after you came, actually, Josephine. Like you, Marie was lost, ended up wandering around here."

Marie continues the story. "I knocked on his door like some ignorant teenage girl. I asked him the way out of these bloody woods. And then somehow, somehow, I offered to raise funds for him."

"And she was good on her word." He carries on the story like he's full of himself. "Marie got me a flat. Then, lo behold, we started falling for one another. And now we're moving to Canada together. Can you believe that?"

"Tomorrow," says Marie, smiling. I swear that tears are collecting.

"But now, right now, we're having a party," says the man. "And you are most certainly invited!"

The other *guests* have already dug in. Paper plates and plastic drinks do the rounds. Someone's put on a CD and – who could guess – it's our debut album. A few in the crowd recognise me, and, as I mingle amongst them, I suspect that there are a few elements of jealousy and awe. They're do-gooders, wealthy charitable people. Retired investment bankers, headteachers, academics. The right sort. When I chat to them, I think of the person I should have been.

There's alcohol provided – cans of beer and a few bottles of wine. They go quite quickly, but they're drunk respectfully. No one gets drunk. No vomiting or loudmouthed anger. Everyone here is part of a community.

"I can't believe the shack is still here," I say to the man, when I manage to catch him on his own. Both of us stare through the door, as though our respective demons are hidden inside.

"And it'll be here for some years to come I think," he responds sadly. "I can't see it going anywhere. It's starting to melt into the forest. Oh, my name's Joseph, by the way."

"Ha, well you know my name."

"I do."

Joseph puts his hands on my elbows and turns me to face him. "I've never forgotten about you. You're stronger than you think you are."

"Thanks," I reply.

Joseph looks at a shiny, silver watch. He sighs, yawns. "Well," he whispers. "Well," he repeats, a proper man's voice ebbing through, "we should be making a move."

I look at my own watch. It's nearing Five. Yep, they should be heading off.

"Marie!" Joseph calls to his girl. "It's time!"

The party falls silent. The music vanishes like sand in a breeze.

Marie gives a speech, thanking everyone for their support. She sheds a few tears as she talks about life, where we're going, who we are. At the end, she takes Joseph's hand in hers, spills more tears. "For the first time in my life, I'm happy." That's how she finishes.

The two of them go into his cabin and emerge with several bags. It hits me like a stone. They're moving on. They're heading to a new place that's away from here, and I will never see him again. Both of them give me a strong embrace. They walk away, hands linked, going to the edge of the forest. They pass beyond the boundary, swallowed by the light.

Others start moving off. The tables are folded up and the uneaten food and drink is carefully packed into tartan boxes. I watch the whole thing, slightly bewildered, as though I'm stuck to the spot, frozen. Eventually, they start streaming out. There are few goodbyes and chants of "see you" as they depart.

When I'm alone, I find myself with a craving for strong coffee. And maybe a cigarette. I slump to the ground outside the shack; a sense of loss grows inside me like a child. Time to go home.

I hear the sound of raindrops pattering the canopy above.

Scarlet

7 June 1993

She even makes notes this time.

Roger Miser calmly gives them the dates for the tour in October. Two nights in London, one in Ramsgate, and one in Colchester. When he's finished, he smiles, asks them about the new members of the band that they've recruited, and promptly dismisses them.

"Lunch?" Gina offers.

"Thanks, but I'm off to visit family," says Scarlet.

"How are they doing?" asks Josephine.

"They're okay. Well, I suppose I'll confirm that when I see them." Scarlet shrugs her shoulders, steps backwards, nearly bumping into a stack of stools. She allows herself permission to scratch between her legs. Does Roger wince in disgust? Probably.

For once, George isn't in the room. And she's glad of that. He seems to be the only decent gentleman she knows. Few and far between, true gentry seem to be these days.

"I'll see you all in a bit," she tells them. "Roger, is my car outside?"

"Ready and waiting."

She knows they've got used to her just buggering off when she fancies it. She's able to walk blind through this building. She's practically led along by the money and fame. She's not even aware of the point when she's left the company head-quarters and entered the car. She picks up today's fashion magazine from the seat pocket in front of her and sifts through the latest in dresses and respectable dress sense.

"The traffic's busy today," the driver informs her. None of that "all right, love" crap. He says it in a posh tone that's maybe just too upper-class for this job. "I'll try to get you there as soon as you can."

"Take your time," she replies. "There's honestly no rush."

"I love your music."

"Which was your favourite song? Or don't you have one?"

"You know, I have absolutely no idea. Really, I don't." The driver's eyes return to the road. He seems to have made up his mind that he wants to be silent.

By the time the driver has dropped her off at the family home, she's already feeling the gnawing hunger in her belly. Whatever her parents have cooked, she'll bloody eat it. She's ravenous.

She goes up to the door and bangs her frail knuckles on its newly varnished surface.

It's Alastair who answers, looking polite and formal, as is usual for him. He welcomes Scarlet inside, as a guest. Her mother's in the kitchen; she can hear the woman rustling around. Pots and pans, cutlery and glasses: the whole orchestra is at work.

"Hey, it's me!" she calls out.

Her father pokes his head out from the living room, nodding a small hello. "Good trip down?" he asks her. "Lunch is in five minutes." He's yanked back inside.

No demanding questions. Not even from her mother. Just smiles and polite looks. Everything lacks that interrogating tone.

"Homemade pizza," declares her mother.

"You haven't made that in years!" says Scarlet. "When was it last...? Eighty-Eight?"

"I bet it'll be as fresh as ever," Alastair butts in.

Her father comes out into the hallway again. "Well, are you two going to join me for a drink? Hmm?"

Something's definitely off about him, she realises, as her teeth pierce that old familiar pizza base. The sharpness of the tomato cuts into her lips. It's not that he's less critical of her or anything, it's that he's slower, more anxious.

"How are your respective careers?" Scarlet asks her family.

"Fine, fine," says Alastair. "The law's a busy thing to have on your chest, but it pays well."

"I've found that the insurance game is somewhat stressful these days," her father says. "But one pulls through it."

Her mother immediately bursts into a tale of a gardening show she went to recently. A local event. The well-known, familiar characters. Competitions: Who could grow the best roses? Who could manage to keep their small shrubs clipped to perfection?

The conversation flows between her mother and her brother like the baseball bouncing off the wall in *The Great Escape*. But she can see the strain in her father's eyes. It seems about to burst out, showering them all in guilt and shame.

"I was assaulted!" her father exclaims.

"James, we've been through this," his wife says, grabbing his wrist. "The kids don't need to know about it."

"Some karate wannabes in stupid uniforms."

"What the hell happened?" stammers Alastair. "Dad, are you okay?"

"Much better than I was."

"Scarlet," her mother whispers. "Scarlet..." She seems to abandon her voice for a few moments. "Scarlet, not a word of this gets out. Do you understand? I don't want Roger Miser to be talking about it on the nine o'clock news."

"What did you say?"

"You heard me."

"No, I don't think I did. Say it a bit louder." Scarlet's never been one who's able to control her anger, but it's spilling over the edges. "Christ, Mum, do you really think I'd do that?"

"No, of course not, but..."

Scarlet knows everyone's feeling this uncomfortable moment. It's shared like a platter of fresh oysters. She's disgusted at the way no one can speak. She could walk out of here, wash her hands of them. Who could blame her? Who would care?

"I love my family," she hisses. "You know that, don't you? Why would you think I'd do something like that?"

"We're not accusing you," says Alastair. As if his little mutiny in the corner will help things.

"I would never hurt my family, not ever!"

"We're being distracted by the main thing here," says her dad. "Christ, I could have been seriously injured!"

"But you weren't!" protests her mum. "You were a bit shaken, a bit upset! Honestly, James, get a grip!"

Scarlet's dad doesn't respond. He raises a glass of something to his lips, doesn't make contact, puts it down with so much reluctance. Pretend reluctance.

"How's everyone been?" he asks. Is he trying to act like the past few minutes haven't happened? "Scarlet, how's the music going? When is the third album coming out?"

"Next month."

"What's it called?" asks her mum.

"The title isn't important," her father intrudes. "It's the theme that matters. What's the theme of this one? Love and loss?"

"Just loss."

"I'm sorry." Her mother's eyes drop. Everyone's eyes drop. They know what they're digging up. "Scarlet, are you coping okay?"

"As well as I can."

"I know things are hard," her mother drones on, "but believe me you will get through this."

"I'm making efforts. Though it's not something you can exactly sleep off."

"We know that, Scarlet," says her father. "We absolutely do. We're here for you. If ever you need anything. If ever you need to reach out, we're here. You understand?"

"I understand." Scarlet gulps. She's a little girl again. "Listen, I should probably go."

"Please, do stay!" her father pleads.

"It's okay," responds her mother. "Scarlet should take some time for herself. She's a little bit too up there to be hanging around with the likes of us."

"I should go." She doesn't wait a second longer than she has to.

Scarlet

3 July 1993

It's released in the early hours.

She doesn't realise it, but the copies are selling like extra hot hotcakes. Kids and teenagers, stressed and tired parents, irritable nightshift workers – they're all queueing up at stores across London, waiting to get their hands on this new selection of music.

She doesn't realise the popularity she's receiving. Every-one's saying her name. Everyone loves her. It's the kind of love that truly knows no bounds. Feelings and emotions that seep through the fabric of human beings, that break down bound-aries, that push through doubt and self-doubt, that keep a sense of sanity and peace. Maybe she'll never realise it.

She's up, throwing the sticky sheets to the other side of the room. It's been a hot summer so far. She staggers around her home, her lonely home, naked and empty. She doesn't dare turn on the radio or the television, because she's afraid of what she might find: that she is truly popular in the minds of the nation.

The phones rings. It's Josephine. She sounds panicked, afraid almost. Her voice, deep, husky, as it always is, speaks volumes of the soul.

"Yeah, it's out," she whispers. *"Christ, I'm fucking scared, Scarlet! How the hell will we get through this?"*

"We will," says Scarlet. She's back to her old self again, the confident girl who started this whole thing in that café in 1990.

"Scarlet, I know this is going to be something big for us. Something truly big."

"What happens will happen," she tells Josephine. She's got the sternness of a wise old man, someone with a hundred lifetimes of experience.

"Gina's already phoned me this morning. I guess she'll be phoning you soon."

"She probably will. Listen, Josephine, I'm going to hang up. Try to get some sleep. We're gonna need it." She gives the woman a hurried goodbye, then another one, hangs up. Just as she's about to move away, the phone rings again. It's Gina this time.

Four hours later, she's eating her breakfast. It's real posh this one: poached eggs and salmon. Fresh coffee too. But she's set it too weak. It tastes like hot water with a bit of caffeine flavouring in. She looks out on to her street, watching the passers-by and the taxis. She's a new age, feminist Sherlock Holmes, trying to solve the mystery of her success.

And it is *her* success, because she was the one who came up with the idea. She thought of the name for the band. She pulled everything together. If it was Gina who tried to give birth to the idea, well, it might not have worked so effectively...

Already she's done an interview on a local radio station. They'll be talking about that all year. *How did such a small, insignificant station like ours get an interview with Scarlet? How did we do it?* All she knows is that twenty-four hours from now small radio stations won't be able to just interview her on a whim. She'll be far too important. Far too great.

Roger phoned just as she got out of the shower. A full day's worth of appearances has been confirmed. Interview with Terry Wogan at one o'clock, another one with some guy on ITV at Three, and then a special concert tonight to kick off the release.

"Keep it together, girl," she whispers to herself. "Keep it together."

Of course, it's not going to be that easy this time. It's not like the first two albums, where they were – in all honesty – jumping in the water, trying everything out. Now, it's much more serious. Everything has to click into place this time. The fans will cheer and the newspapers will beg for interviews. Private jets will be readied. Hotel rooms will be booked and prepared. The whole world is gearing itself up for the release of this album.

She doesn't realise how the big the queues are getting. That people are pushing each other, that tempers are flaring. She doesn't know that in Liverpool, someone has punched someone else, leaving them with life altering injuries; all because they accidentally stepped on their toes, such was the anger and ferocity of the queue. Stupid, isn't it?

She brushes her teeth... twice. Just to make sure that every-thing is cleaned. That there are no remnants or decay. There's nothing that could possibly make her appear the slightest bit unattractive to the world at large.

Just before the others arrive, she runs a hand through her hair that literally refuses to play by the rules. She wonders why she's blonde. Or why she chose blonde. Or maybe why she was forced to choose blonde. She wants to make sure things are relatively perfect for the hours, days and weeks ahead.

This time the fame feels different. It's lost its peculiar sense of edginess and it's been replaced with something that feels darker and more claustrophobic. She's trapped. Truly trapped this time.

She remembers when she was a small child, stuck in primary school, dreaming dreams of fame and fortune. Imagining herself performing to the world. Wearing cowboy boots and tassels, dancing around under a disco ball, the lights of the universe blasting upon her. Of course, no one told her of the anxiety and the fear, the knuckle-breaking dread of looking over her shoulder. And no one told her of the loss that she would endure.

Josephine and Gina both arrive at exactly the same time. Breathless, hearts pounding. Scarlet can sense it. It's like she knows the two girls better than family.

"We ready?" says Josephine.

"Yep," is all Scarlet needs to respond.

"Car's waiting outside."

"I thought we weren't due on that show until One," says Gina.

"Yeah, but they want us there at least an hour early," counters Josephine. "It's nearly, Eleven, and you know what London traffic is like."

"Let's do it," commands Gina, her voice unbroken and confident. Like it's the real true form.

They descend to the street, straight to a scene comprised of eager, guilty onlookers and a few photographers.

"Here we go," whispers Scarlet.

"Scarlet!" a woman screams from the crowd.

"Scarlet!" someone else – a balding man – yells.

"Scarlet!"

"Scarlet!"

The crowd begins a chant: "Scarlet! Scarlet! Scarlet! Scarlet!"

A security guard – employed by Roger Miser, of course – gestures them to the waiting car.

"They seem to love you, Scarlet," moans Josephine. "It's all about you. If they ever make a film about your life, they should give it the title: *A Life Called Scarlet.*"

Gina laughs at it, but Scarlet feels herself casting scowls. Yet she can't find the strength to stand for herself.

Both shows go swimmingly and they find themselves heading to the launch concert well ahead of schedule. It's in some small venue in north London, far from the thick crowds in the city centre and threatening groups of fans who would swamp the place.

Scarlet sits in the flawless dressing room – *her* dressing room. Everything is set out for her, all the necessary components. And all of it belongs to her. No exceptions. She checks her complexion in the mirror, forces a clueless smile, waits and waits.

It's Josephine who barges in – without knocking, of course – and slaps the table. "Come on, doll, time to get ready. They're howling for us out there."

Yes, dear reader, Scarlet's grown used to the silence. No longer does she hear the crowds or sense the danger. She just glides through it all. Not a care in the world. Not a moment's hesitation at the top of the cliff that overhangs an oasis of the entrapment that only fame provides.

"Let's go then," says Scarlet, lifting up the guitar.

The two of them walk side-by-side down the corridor, the thundering of the audience rippling through the air.

She can't remember the last time she was onstage. It's a familiar and alien feeling to her. She briefly remembers their debut performance, though prefers to shut it out of her mind. She's before the crowd, swallowed by their screams.

Josephine and Gina take their positions, and so do the unnamed male musicians they've acquired.

"Come on crowd, you need to up your game!" Josephine screams into the mike. They howl louder in response.

"I hate it when you do that," says Scarlet, but she hasn't aimed her mouth at her mouthpiece. No one hears her. She's not even sure that they'd care if they did. "Right," she growls, this time pointing everything in the right direction, "let's get on with it."

The first notes kick themselves into life. It's from the first album, one of the all-time favourites. It gets the crowd into an absolute frenzy. Scarlet's voice makes contact and the warmth spreads like a plague.

Her throat feels viciously dry when they're done with it. There's a bottle of water at the front for her, but she can't be bothered to reach for it. It's time for the next blast of sound, one of the tracks from the third album. Time to knock it out.

How will this mob receive it? Aggressively? Will be they a million percent abusive? Bottles hurled at the stage?

Josephine kicks it off. Scarlet counts the beats in her head, bursts into song, fiercely this time. No waiting around. Not a damn moment.

Gina

3 July 1993

I don't like this crowd. Far too aggressive.

Since I lost my faith, I've found myself more and more sensitive to noise. No longer can I see through the screams and the shouts. No longer can I hold it together.

I've been having thoughts of leaving the band. Starting out on my own. Finding my place in this world. Writing my own songs and composing my own music. Or maybe something else. Paint pictures, sketch – like what Scarlet used to do. In that filthy bloody shack.

I smile our way through the six or seven songs we do from the new album, and then we go back to some of the old favourites. The hits from the first album.

I briefly flash back to France, to that small village or whatever it was. Sometimes I'm not convinced it actually happened, that it was all in my imagination. Part of me will always wonder what really happened back then. What the hell did Roger Miser do? What was the exact sequence of events? It's stuff best left to the imagination.

"Come on, you lot, up your game!" Josephine howls. "Up your bloody game!"

Josephine

3 July 1993

After our last song, we're forced to withdraw. Security guards shepherd us to the far-off changing rooms.

I'm thinking that our new additions to the band are bloody amazing. But I'm thinking of this Marco, who I have become quite close to. Christ, we're seeing one another. He really likes me and everything. We're going out for dinner tomorrow. His treat. I can't remember the last time a man's taken me out for dinner.

But there's another man on my mind. The man in the shack. It's not that I'm sad he's left, it's that – I don't even know why I'm thinking like this – it's that he's able to just move on, to leave everything behind, and I'm trapped here in London. Even though I could get on a plane tomorrow, go to Cuba or the Bahamas, I'll never really be free of this. I suppose that's the price of fame.

I wipe the sweat off my forehead and splash my face with water. A careful study of myself in the mirror reveals how exhausted I am slowly becoming. There's no secret: I'm finding it harder and harder to do concerts.

"Roger's reserved us a place at a penthouse bar in Westminster," Scarlet tells me. She's popped her head through the doorway, smiling, or trying to.

"Do you ever knock?" I grumble. But she's already gone. No doubt gone to get herself glamoured and everything.

I do the finishing touches to myself, check my eyeliner. Exhaustion washes over me in waves and it fills me with that familiar beauty of completion. Have I finally made it in life? Achieve all I ever wanted to achieve?

It's Gina who comes in next, announces two things in quick succession: that the car is ready, that Scarlet's brother, Alastair, is coming along as well.

I follow the others down to the Mercedes, which is all ready to go, engine running, driver not looking too happy. The three of us are promptly whisked into the heart of London.

"Is Roger coming tonight?" I ask.

"No, I don't think he is," says Gina. "Unusual, isn't it? Mind you, knowing him, he's probably already there."

"Definitely," says Scarlet.

"No, I think you'll find he won't be there tonight," says the driver. "He's got a couple of meetings or something, so I heard."

"A night off the pressure," Gina whispers in my ear. "Thank God."

The bar itself is within arm's length of the Houses of Parliament. I've definitely heard of it. A place where only the richest of the rich are permitted to know about. It's on the top floor of a building that's packed to the edges with restaurants and other bars. As we ascend stone steps, surrounded by more crumbling stone, I become aware of the gentle scent of cigar smoke. We're shown by men on top hats and tails through solid glass doors with brass railings into a room that's filled with black tables and men and beautiful couples. The young people starting out contrast with the old men with their brandies and smouldering sticks. It's a room that's caught halfway between the old and the new. There's a bar table, all marble, with stools hosting young women in expensive dresses and their male counterparts in semi-tuxedos. There's one guy sitting alone, head in his hands.

Eyes turn our way. We don't need to introduce ourselves.

The black tables are arranged with the carefulness of a French café, but with the gentleness of an old cottage's living space. There are booths at the sides of the room; one is empty, all ready for us to plant ourselves down. Indeed, we're being politely escorted by one of the staff to the vacant booth.

"I hope food is included," says Gina.

"It is, ma'am," our escort tells her. "I will have menus brought out."

"My brother, Alastair, is also due to join us," Scarlet informs him. "Could you bring an extra menu, please?"

"It will be done."

We file in, edging ourselves along the table. I glance back at the bar, look at the guy by himself. I recognise that hairstyle.

"Excuse me, ladies," I say, getting up and marching over. "Marco, what the hell are you doing here?"

He turns, face surprised. "Hey, Josephine! Sorry, I didn't see you there!"

I clasp his hands in mine and hug him. "Now, you're not drinking alone, Marco. Come, join my girlfriends and I!"

He looks panicked and it's like I know what's going to happen even before the voice cuts through my ears.

"Who the hell is she?" a female voice growls.

I turn around to face a fairly attractive girl with long black hair and a sapphire dress. Fury is written across her lips.

"Josephine, this is Lauren," says Marco. "Lauren, this is Josephine. Josephine's an acquaintance. She's in that band, I forget their name..."

"We are *not* acquaintances!" I shout, turning the room into complete silence. "What the fuck do you think I am, Marco?! You fucking bastard!"

"I'm sorry, I should have been more clear with you," he responds, as weak as weak can be. "I don't know how to say it..."

"You've made your point very fucking clear, Marco." My voice is loaded with rage, but I don't care that every single set of eyes in the room is locked upon this love triangle. "*Lauren,* how long have the two of you been together?"

"Two and a half years." Lauren stands with her arms folded. I'm not sure who she's angrier with.

"Josephine, you should go," says Marco. "I'm sorry you had to find out this way. Honestly, I was going to tell you." He's like a blabbering little child.

"It's okay, Josephine, just walk away." Gina's arm slips through my arm.

"I'm heading home!" I hiss. "Someone get me a fucking taxi!" I point at one of the bartenders. "You there, get me a fucking taxi! Now!"

"Josephine, stay and have a drink with us," Gina whispers in her soothing mother's voice.

"I'm not staying anywhere!" I'm sobbing. I'm openly break-ing apart and I don't care if a column or two is written about me in the morning's papers.

"Is everything okay, ma'am?" It's our escort, all gentle-manly, checking on me. He's got a hand on my shoulder – one of the few men permitted to do this.

"I want a fucking taxi! Now!" I'm yelling now. "Get me into a fucking car!"

Alastair appears on the scene – all trussed up – watching things unfold. He looks like he's been caught in a vacant pose. "Whoa! Everything okay?" he asks.

"Take my place, Alastair," I hiss at him. "Sorry, girls, to-night was not the night for celebration. Absolutely not."

My escort assures me that a taxi will be promptly ordered. I stagger backwards, drunk on instability, allow myself to be shepherded to the door. I haven't touched a drop of the stuff tonight, nor do I plan on doing so. Things have simply gone too far for that.

I don't remember the taxi ride home – and I probably never will. When I get to my front door, I slam my cheek hard against the wood. A tear is smudged on the surface. I go inside, stumble through the hallway.

I think – only for a few moments – about that first performance we did in Inverness. So long ago now.

"You're a stupid girl," I tell myself. "Trusting him like that. You're a stupid girl."

4 July 1993

I don't know how I've slept, but I wake up in one piece in my bed. My throat is dry, and I don't know whether it's because I overstretched my vocals last night, or I maybe did have a sneaky drink.

I'm so eager to get out, try to swim through the sunlight, to see whatever is waiting for me. It's how I cope with uncertainty. It's how I survive the heartbreak.

I don't think about all the negative press that will soon come my way. No doubt journalists are writing their columns, getting ready to strike me down. I make myself a quick breakfast, swallow some coffee, forget to brush my teeth, walk down the street, confident. I've shed an old skin. A relationship that was never destined to work – gone.

On a whim, with no particular logical set of thoughts, I set off for Scarlet's shack. The taxi rank at the end of my street – which I've never really used – is filled with the black cars. I take the one at the front, tell him roughly where to go, and I'm on my way.

"You seem quite cheerful today, love," the driver remarks.

I'm smiling wider with every passing second, because I know that with every one of those ticks, I'm getting closer to the grove.

"I'm always cheerful," I reply. "Always."

This is a positive. This relationship wasn't meant to be, and I'm glad I found that out now. Far better than two or three years down the line.

"Well, it's a Sunday mornin' after all," he grumbles.

"It is indeed."

When we arrive at the end of the street, I tell the driver to stop. "Here," I whisper, thrusting a note into his hands. "Keep the change." I dive out, marching swiftly along the pavement, head held high. I don't know why I'm doing this, but I need to see this. I nod at the child's buggy toy, still there in the garden, untouched. The grove welcomes me with open arms.

Yes, it's still there. It's a solid ghost that taunts me. The forest throws around that eerie silence that screams louder than a foghorn. I stop. I feel the emotion washing over me. The shack's door is wide open. Cautiously, I venture inside, not sure of what to expect. And what did I expect to find? Everything's been taken out, cast to the side. Even the flooring's gone: my shoes are slowly being swallowed up by the soft ground.

It's time to move on. It's time to let it all go, put it solidly in the past.

Slowly, I begin to trudge back out of the trees. When I'm back on the street, I pause for a moment, then continue walking. I pass the child's buggy, do a mock salute, wonder if its user is now too big for it.

Life's a hard lesson. But I think I'm learning that now, and it's going to be painful. It'll hurt like hell – as the Americans would put it – but it will be freeing.

I'm at the end of the street and I pause again. It's time to move on, but one last look at the place won't hurt. I turn around and walk back, dipping into the trees like Goldilocks. I'm doing something that's totally out of my mind, but I find myself running up to the shack and slamming my hands on the wall. Tears wash out of me and I grip my fists.

"Are you okay, ma'am?" A soothing male American voice.

I turn around to see a young couple, fingers interlinked, gawping. They're tourists. It's easy to tell: the girl has a map of London twirling between her fingers.

"Oh, I'm fine," I reply. "Just a rough breakup. Came here to clear my head."

"You've chosen the right place," says the woman. "My God, it's so tranquil in here!"

"I'm assuming you're visitors?" I say, voice quivering.

"We are indeed," she tells me. "Just married!" She holds up her left hand, briefly disregarding the map. It flutters to the floor, knocking aside a few fallen leaves.

"How did you end up in here?" I ask. "I mean, this forest isn't anywhere near the tourist areas!"

"My wife and I like to go off the beaten path," says the man. "We take cabs to random places, get to know random people, just go with the God darn flow. You know what I mean?"

"Well, dear husband," the woman complains, misery creeping into her tone, "we should be going. We have lunch booked at that fancy Italian place you wanted to check out, but you wanted to check out a couple of museums as well."

"You're right." The husband waves at me. "Nice to meet you, ma'am!"

"See ya!" shouts the wife.

They head in the direction I came from, two little ants frogmarching through the path of life.

"Unbelievable," I say. "Bloody Yanks." I slump against the wall of the shack, laughing. Maybe I'm laughing too much.

I sit there for what feels like hours, but it's only a few minutes. I know this because I keep glancing at my watch.

An old man with a grey beard and anorak is standing in the distance, arms folded, beaming at me. He's like a homeless Captain Birds-Eye. His trousers are too long, folding over his walking boots. He hasn't got a care in the world, casually moving over towards me, but not in a straight line, but not in a way that makes him appear drunk.

"Beautiful day, isn't it?" he says.

"It is indeed," I answer. "It is indeed."

But I've had enough of new faces today. I don't even acknowledge his look, any displeasure he might have. I just walk out. They say pride goes before a fall, but I've fallen and now I'm rising up like a phoenix. For what seems like an age, I've been moving forward with my life – genuinely. This whole thing with Marco, it's but a small interruption. Time to draw a line under what happened, a scorch mark in the sand. It's time to bring things to a close.

When I'm back, I don't wallow in self-pity. I'm on the phone to Scarlet and then Gina, catching up on the gossip and the news. After that's done, I lean back on my sofa, crave a can of beer, reminisce over old boyfriends and even older travelling companions. I think about so much, all the chances I've missed, all the things I could have been.

9 June 1984

The meeting was held in a disused house near Dunwich. She managed to get there – hitchhiking most of the way – fifteen minutes before the meeting started. The directions proved easy to follow, no issues at all.

The sight of the hammer and sickle draped over the front door, the windows, along the driveway – well, everywhere – unnerved her a bit at first. Several well-dressed men formed a ring of conversation in the front garden, their mouths moving in unison. There were young people, too, milling around, socialising, some even wearing shorts. Others were attempting a far more formal effort: shirts that threatened to thread, trousers (mostly linen), the occasional blazer. But the majority here were of the hippy type: colourful clothes and bandanas, pendants of curious symbols, mouths that couldn't keep shut.

Never had Josephine seen such a strange concoction of people.

"The name's Sally." It was the girl, the one who'd invited her. The frilly coat with its kaleidoscope of colours and patterns still decorated her body. She seemed to smile even more than before, her eyes brighter and alert.

"Good to put a name to the face at last!" exclaimed Josephine.

"Let me show you around." Sally tucked an arm under Josephine's. The two women walked towards the house.

The smell of fresh coffee and Danish pastries greeted her. Sally showed her through a corridor to a kitchen area, where the aromas were coming from. A group of teenagers argued about which cakes and rolls should be planted on which plates. There was a seductiveness about this room. A table, covered with a white cloth, had a range of brittle plates stacked with sandwiches and the like, chocolates, salads. Two coffeepots had also been set up on it, all ready to go.

"We're a very efficient operation here," said Sally. "Oi! Watch what you're doing with that!"

One of the teenagers – a blond-haired boy – gently lowered the head bust of Lenin in the centre of the food table.

"Where's the meeting being held?" asked Josephine.

"It'll be in the garden. They're setting up as we speak. I just thought I'd introduce you to a few people first. Ah, there he is!"

A heavyset man with a blackened beard entered the room. Thick glasses no doubt concealed a lifetime of myopia. He looked bitter, worn down, fed up over so many things. The hammer and sickle was pinned to his breast pocket.

"Meet the leader of the East Anglia Communist Movement, Norris Keel," said Sally.

"Good to meet you." Josephine stretched out a hand; it was swallowed instantly by his. "I'm Josephine."

"Sally's told us all about you," said Norris. "Actually, we think you'd be a great asset to our organisation."

"I'm glad to be here."

"I must first of all apologise for our headquarters. It's not exactly much, but it does the job." Norris chuckled, adjusting his pin badge with a thick thumb and barking out a loud cough. "Well, we'll be starting in a few minutes. I would grab a seat if I were you, before they get filled up."

"We will," said Sally, touching Josephine's elbow. "First, I want to introduce her to my boyfriend."

"Will's upstairs right now," said Norris. "Though I think he's practising for his speech..."

"We'll be a couple of minutes."

"Speech?" stuttered Josephine.

"Sally's boyfriend is our speaker of honour, shall we say. He's just joined our movement as one of the coordinators, but he used to live in the Soviet Union and was part of their Communist Party."

"Come on, Josephine." Sally gripped her harder, steering her up a narrow set of stairs. They went along to the end of a tight corridor, where an open door showed a man pacing back and forth, whispering to himself, as if trying to cast a spell.

"Will, are you going to be doing that all day...?" asked Sally. She rushed through the opening and kissed the smiling figure.

Josephine had had it in her head that this Will would be a man in his mid-twenties, with loose-fitting, hippy clothes, with an unshaven face and ponytail to match, but he was dressed smarter than just about anybody she'd seen here. Slim-fitting black trousers and thin black shoes. A thin jacket – no doubt tailored to his exact size – boasted of wealth and curiosity. A tie, the exact same colour as a gold bar, was tied in a Double Windsor, with a silver tie clip keeping the strands together. His hair was brown, combed neatly and gelled just the right amount. He had a strong complexion, with a muscled physique, but not too much so. As Josephine got closer, she could see a blue watch, with *New York* engraved around the edge. Even from here, she could hear the delicate fingers ticking away.

"Josephine, this is Will. Will, Josephine. I was telling you about her yesterday."

"Ah, yes, the fabled Josephine," said Will. He spoke with a slight Cornish accent, but with an Oxbridge overtone. "Hi, I'm Will Parson."

"It's good to meet you." She held out her hand to him. He took it gently.

"Ladies, I should be getting ready for my speech. Big things to say today."

"I'll head downstairs." Josephine began to retrace her steps.

"Okay, see you down there," said Will, embracing his woman and planting a kiss on her forehead.

When she reached the garden, she found the frivolity she'd seen upon arrival had vanished, replaced with... loyalty? Everyone was in their place on simple wooden seats organised in neat rows, with an aisle through the middle. Much like a wedding. A raised platform with a microphone eagerly awaited its speaker. Norris Keel was on a seat at the back of the platform, checking through some papers. She took the nearest empty chair and folded her arms over her lap.

"He's coming in a second or two," whispered Sally, sitting next to her. "You'll love it when he speaks. He's got such a depth of knowledge about communism. He even puts Norris to shame."

Norris Keel approached the microphone, clearing his throat, the noise spreading across the fields to the horizon. "Good morning, ladies and gentlemen, and welcome to this meeting of the East Anglia Communist Movement. I know that for many of you, this is your first time. I can assure you that you are all welcome here. You belong to this movement, I can see it in your eyes. There's a man I want all of you to meet, a man who has lived in the Soviet Union and given us the opportunity to develop strong links with their Communist Party. Please welcome Will Parson."

Josephine watched as the firm and gentle figure of Will walked up the aisle. He took his position behind the mike and adjusted its height. He ran a finger across his upper lip and scanned the crowd. His voice ran smoothly, not shaking in the slightest, and he delivered each one of his points with enthusiasm. But she couldn't take a single word in, because, in that moment, she was deeply in love with him.

Alastair

4 July 1993

Dear Diary,

It's been one of the strangest days I've had in a long time.

Last night I was at my sister's band's album launch – the afterparty bit. What a sight it was! Especially with Josephine. Oh, that poor girl... I got in just as a fight between her, her boyfriend, and another girl was breaking out. I genuinely had no idea what the hell it was all about! From what I gathered afterwards, she was quite fond of this Marco bloke and this girl that was sitting with him was his new girlfriend. Damn, you should have seen how aggressive Josephine got! I've always been a bit scared of her, a bit nervous, but this was something else. Anyway, I think I am going off track.

I woke up this morning, ever so mildly hungover, but extremely energetic. I went for a brief jog and then spent breakfast going over a few legal papers for next week's court case. I found that I had an itch on the back of my neck, in my mind. Not something that a cream would take care of.

You see, ever since Dad disclosed what happened to him with those karate people, I've been fairly shaken over it. I'm not sure what the specific problem is. Maybe I'll never know. All I know is that I woke up this morning with a determination to have a look at the place where it happened. Maybe it was the family bloodline. The family bloodline calling me to my duty.

So I went there and found absolutely nothing, except for a sign with a crude illustration of a child throwing a kick. (Don't ask me how I got the address.) A metal shutter blocked the entrance to the karate club. I tussled with the edges for a few moments, realising after far too long that the place was bloody closed. I didn't stay for long after that. I started making the long journey back, pissed at myself that I'd missed a morning of hard work.

Things changed damn quickly on the way back though. I was nearly back at my apartment, but stupidly decided to take a shortcut, one that I'd only used a couple of times. Just before you get to my street, there's a sort of leafy suburb-type road, with trees overhanging, casting their shadows over a string of cafes. It's like a scene from one of these campus novels. I slowed down a bit, taking my time with every footstep. At the end of the road lies a newsagent – one that's become increasingly popular with me since I moved here – that has everything you could ever possibly need, and I'm not exaggerating. It was only as I checked my watch that I realised it was closed on Sundays. I'm not sure what I needed to get anyway...

I thought about what I needed to get ready for next week. There was so much to put together, so many little things that needed to be sorted.

I was passing the shuttered newsagents, smirking at my own stupidity – maybe one too many drinks last night. The sound of metal falling, a vicious crash that pounded my eardrums, stopped me in my tracks. It was coming from a small alleyway that ran by the side of the shop. I thought about just continuing on my way, reasoning that it was probably a cat, but then I heard voices. I ventured close to the entrance and was nearly knocked over as two figures ran past me.

"What the hell are you doing?" I snapped, seeing the plastic bags in their hands.

"Amias, what do we do?" A young woman asked. She was barely twenty – I think. She stood trembling. Thick, auburn hair, covered her eyes. Her tongue hung out and her eyes sparkled with panic.

The kid called Amias, his boyish hair in a similar style (and colour) to hers, also looked startled.

"What are in the bags?" I asked.

"Just stuff," said Amias. "Nothing really."

"Doesn't look like nothing. Give the stuff to me, or I'm reporting it."

"You do whatever you want," said the girl. "It's a free country."

"What's your name?" I asked her.

"Tamsyn."

I was struck by how clear and open she was about that. No holding back whatsoever. Actually, I was quite infatuated by her. She was the kind of girl I wish I'd had at university.

"Well, Tamsyn, Amias, give me the bags now," I demanded. "Immediately."

"Or you could let us walk away." Tamsyn grabbed her companion's arm. "Come on, he's my little brother. Think what a criminal record would do for his job prospects!" She started moving away, taking her timid brother with her.

What could I do? I was too scared to do anything. I merely watched them leg it down the road. I watched them become small dots, turning into a side street and vanishing from view.

I continued back to the flat, annoyed at myself for letting them get away, but even more so at the fact that I'd let the family who ran the newsagents down. But what can you do when you're infatuated with a girl with beautiful auburn hair?

James

11 August 1993

I didn't sleep last night, not a wink.

It wasn't the heat of summer keeping me awake, nor the unstoppable barking of next door's dog. It was the humiliation.

The embarrassment of some karate kid knocking me to the ground. I woke up this morning angry, full of bile. I was a bit snappy with my wife on the way out – I admit that.

I'm on the train now, and I'm much calmer. A takeaway instant coffee is clutched in my hand and it's getting colder quicker than I'd like.

I'm not after revenge. I just want to see them. I just want to walk into that karate club, talk to them, ask the guy to apologise. I just want him to admit that he was sorry for what he did. It's not much to ask.

When I get to London, I chuck the dregs of my drink down a drain and toss the polystyrene cup into the nearest bin. I'm aware of how different I look compared to the others: slightly dishevelled, worried, unshaven. Indeed, there are a few dodgy looks I get from the other suits and ties.

I don't take the journey in. It doesn't process. One minute, I'm on the tube, the next, I'm in that industrial estate. I think about going to that dreadful café and indeed I do. There's someone else there this time: a younger woman, probably sixteen. I place my order, rudely, take a seat, and she brings it over to me, slams the cup down, and snatches my money. I take a couple of sips, admire the cheap taste of shop's own coffee granules, and clench my fists.

The industrial estate is empty – completely. How can it be a busy weekday and not a soul or a truck in sight? Beyond ridiculous, I should think!

When I finish my coffee, I storm out, going in zigzags. Spit hangs from my lips. The fury drives me to the darkest levels possible. I'm enraged. I get lost one or twice, but I soon find myself looking at the icon of the kid throwing that stupid kick.

"Come on, you bastards," I hiss, approaching.

I'm taken aback by the white plastic sign. *Permanently Closed.*

"You bastards," I whisper.

There's no point in being angry now. They're gone, moved somewhere else. A new chapter in their lives. I'm sinking to my knees, unable to cry, unable to even think about crying. I lost a chance, that much-needed opportunity at hitting back. Now I'm a wounded man, broken down.

Somehow, I pick myself up. It's going to be a long journey home. I should be as quick as I can. There is work to do, after all.

Gina

12 August 1993

Roger Miser calls us in for an early morning meeting. Album sales. Selling like hotcakes on both sides of the Atlantic. He's very proud of us. We're his girls. His pride and joy. George stands behind him, arms folded, like the proud uncle.

"You're a household name," says Roger, flipping through a magazine. I can't see which one it is, but it's glossy enough to have our names in. "Ten-year-old kids in Wisconsin are dancing to your hits. High School jocks in Nebraska are fighting over you. Genuinely, I'm being serious. Some guy made an insult about your hair, Scarlet, and this other guy knocked him out. Hospital treatment. Cops involved. Bloody hell, you girls are causing a storm over there!"

But I see – we see – that there's something else going on. Roger Miser's lips are pursing themselves. His brown teeth and oiled hair glint in the dim light of the office – actually, they've recently refitted the lightbulbs in here and things are a little bit brighter than their usual ultra-gloomy self.

"We need to think about boosting your security," says George. "I know that's not something you want to hear, but, well, with what happened to Susan..."

"How many months has it taken you to come to this conclusion?" Josephine shouts at the two men.

"These things aren't simple."

"I don't care, George. After Susan was coldly murdered, you should have got us the extra security, there and then. Why didn't you?"

There's an ensuing argument that seems to last for hours. I don't participate, instead staring at the array of books and LPs Miser has lined up around his office. I couldn't care less about the bickering that won't seem to stop. I'm thinking about the letter that came through the post last week: only a few lines, but they needed less. I've received an offer to join another band. They want me to be their drummer, as their previous one has pissed off travelling. It's not an all-girl band this time: two male singers, a female guitarist, a male keyboardist, and then there'll be me replacing the "dopey, long-haired bloke" who didn't have the stamina to stay. Apparently, Africa was more appealing.

I'm weighing up whether to accept it or not. In all honesty, I'm leaning towards accepting it. How will the girls react to it? Will they be supportive? Oh, why am I asking that! Of course they won't! They'll strangle me to death! Maybe not Scarlet, but definitely Josephine.

I've got a meeting with this band later today. We're meeting at The Crown in Seven Dials for lunch. Do they really think that pub grub is going to sweettalk me?

Roger Miser delivers a few more lines, something about potential concerts, then says we're done for the day.

"I'm catching up on my sleep," says Josephine, as we make our way out. There's a new receptionist who flashes her lipstick at us. We all try to hide our disgust.

"See you later," I tell my bandmates.

I've got hours to kill until I meet them, but I decide to head into the city centre early. I don't take one of the luxury limos of Roger's fleet, instead placing myself in a common taxi. I direct him to take me to King's College. I don't think he's in the slightest bit fooled that I'm a student. When we arrive, I head to the bank of the Thames, where a strange group of watercolour painters have been set up. I watch them for a bit, stare at their hands twitching as colour impacts canvas.

I rest my elbows on the rail that lines the edge of the pavement and stare out across the river. It's tranquil right now. No shouts or screams or horns blaring. Why can't more London days be like this?

"Hey, why don't you join us?" one of the painters calls over to me. "We've got a spare set of stuff." He's quite a heavily built man, but he's young. I'm guessing early twenties. He sounds proper East End.

"Oh, no, it's not my thing. I'm not much of an artist." I smile at them and stare back across the river.

"We all started out as amateurs," the man says. "Come on, join us for a bit."

"No, really, I'm not interested. It's a lovely day, though. Enjoy yourselves!" I wave at them and start walking away.

There's laughter and sniggering. I hear someone say, "Posh tart." More laughter.

I take a long stroll to Covent Garden, stopping here and there to look at trinket shops. It starts as looking through eyes of curiosity. It ends with me pacing up and down shopfloors, tired of seeing the same things over and over again. Every shop owner has the same haunted, pissed-off look in their eyes.

I managed to kill enough time to arrive at the pub at exactly Half-Twelve. I glance around, realising that I haven't the faintest idea of what they look like in the flesh. I've only seen their album covers, and there's never much insight you can gain from those.

The barmaid is younger than me, brittle-looking. What's the term they use to describe the likes of her? What is it? Anorexic – that's the one. You can see the bone through the weak folds of skin. Brown hair hangs in threads, splintering. She stares at me with drowned eyes.

"What'll it be?" she says hoarsely.

"Gin-and-tonic, please."

"Coming right up."

My drink is ready in record time. Except there's too much gin in it. Grimacing, I look around at the other occupants of The Crown: deadbeats, loners, antisocial depressives. Everyone here has a sad story to tell: Were they dumped by the girl of their dreams? Neglected as a child? Bullied at school? Survived a plane crash?

A take my drink to one of the barstools at the window and continue the ritualistic slow sipping.

"Excuse me, Gina, right?"

"Yeah, that's me. You're Robin, aren't you?"

Robin – the lead singer of the band – is, as is typical these days, much older in physical form than the photographs on album covers and in magazines. He's slightly overweight, but his scarred Norwegian features push through. There other singer is there as well. I don't know why, but he looks like the younger version of Roger Miser. Maybe it's the face, maybe the posture. I don't know.

The other bandmembers aren't here. The two guys look at me as though I've already been accepted, that this is a casual chat designed to get me in the mood for whatever upcoming tour they have in mind.

"Really pleased to meet you," says the second man. "Brian, by the way."

"Two lagers, please," says Robin to the stick figure behind the bar. He turns to me, gestures us towards a set of stools and high table in the middle of the pub floor. When we're all sitting down, he starts, even before the drinks have arrived:

"So, Gina, we think you'd be a valuable asset to the band. We've seen you performing live – all of us. The way you play the drums, you're an artist. You're someone who has the true calling to do this. I'm not much of a believer in fate, but you're meant for this. Gina, we want you to be the newest addition to our group."

"I thank you very much," I tell them. "I must stress that I have a solid commitment to my group. An absolute commitment. It won't be easy to walk away from them."

"I think you'll find it very easy. Let's be honest, your band-mates, they're deadbeats. Now, before you yell at me, scream at me, call me insults, take a moment to think. Do you really see yourself going anywhere with these bandmates at all?"

"Our third album is selling bloody well. Both sides of the Atlantic. Millions of copies."

"That's classic Roger Miser talk. Do you even have your own opinion of things?"

"There's nothing wrong with the band!" I protest. I'm beginning to wonder if this is even a job interview. Feels more like an interrogation.

"There's also the matter of Josephine." It's Brian who's spoken this time. I know from an article I've read that he's in his late thirties, can barely sing, but he has one of those senses of loyalty that's completely unflinching. He's had a haircut as well: it no longer looks like it's been dragged from the Seventies; it's trimmed instead to the standards of the modern businessman.

"What do you mean?"

"My brother used to know Josephine, quite well. I should probably introduce myself. I'm not Brian Coffey, as I'm advertised in the media. My real name is Brian Parson. My brother, William, used to know Josephine a long time ago."

"In what capacity?"

"You do know Josephine used to be a member of the East Anglia Communist Movement?"

"Yeah, I knew that."

Brian drills his eyes into me. "I'm not having a go at you, but when you find out the truth about what Josephine did, you'll understand."

"I think you've gone far enough, Brian." Robin smiles at me. "Josephine, what we're trying to say is that you'd thrive in our band. It's an excellent opportunity for you. Really build yourself up."

"I'm not sure I would, if I'm honest with you. My commitment is to the girls. Through and through. I wouldn't feel right abandoning them."

"We didn't expect you to agree to anything today, Gina. We just want to make ourselves clear on where we stand. We want you to become a part of our group, a part of our world. You're suited to us."

"I'm tempted by your offer. I really am. Honest to God. But... I need to stick with those two. I'm sorry if that's not what you wanted to hear."

"Completely understandable." Robin dips his head. He produces a slip of cardboard from his jacket pocket. "This is my number. I've got one of these mobile telephone things. Quite handy, actually. There's also the number and address of my manager as well. If you change your mind, let us know."

"Thank you," I tell him, "but I must decline." I decide to take my leave, standing up determined and affrontive. "Thanks for invitation. It's greatly appreciated."

I don't look back.

By evening, I've forgotten about everything, except for what Brian told me. But soon enough, it's at the back of my mind. By Eleven, all I think about is Scarlet and Josephine, and how I need to take care of them.

Scarlet

25 September 1993

They meet in the basement of a coffeeshop in Soho. It's perfect for this discussion, something that's been the subject of mutterings in the press in recent days. Whispers in the background. Myths and rumours. Best to get it out the system loud and clear.

As she takes a seat, she thinks of something else: exactly a year ago today, she was nearly killed by that knife outside LAX. She remembers Mauro's soothing aura of comfort. She's eager to forget about it now, especially him.

Gina and Josephine are waiting for her to start.

It's beginning to turn into Autumn now and the girls are starting to get the colours in their hair. Even Scarlet has allowed her blonde hair to be mutilated with spots of dark red.

"Guys, are we calling it a day?" she asks them.

Their lattes are brought down, placed on the table. No sloppy messes or overflowed cups. No halfwit attempts at creating flavour. Everything here is true to its name and nothing less.

"I've been having thoughts," says Gina.

Oh, if only Scarlet knew the real meaning behind those words...

"I have to admit, I have as well," says Josephine. "I've been thinking of a career outside music."

"We have to come to a definite decision," says Scarlet. She puts a cigarette between her lips and is about to light up, when a stern voice cuts across the room.

"Sorry, ma'am. No smoking allowed."

"There goes that one, then," she mutters. "Right, girls, what are we going to do?"

"I don't want us to split up," says Josephine. "But I can see the two of you are having some doubts about things. I completely understand. But I know Susan wouldn't want us to do this. She'd want us to be out there, performing on the stage. Guys, we're truly big now. You heard what Roger said. We are definitely one of the greatest bands of all time. Better than The Beatles, better than REM, The Beachboys. All of those! We are truly great! Can you not see this?!"

"That's precisely why I want to get out," says Gina. "I'm terrified that we might become too famous. Too great. Too bloody good."

"Why are you so afraid of that?" Scarlet asks her.

"Something tells me... I dunno. I think it's just wrong."

"Then why did you agree to this in the first place. Do you remember? When I sat all of you down in that café and I told you about my idea? Why didn't you tell me you had doubts back then?"

"Because I didn't think we'd get to this level!" Gina's fists turn blue. "How was I to know?! As much as I love the travel and the glamour and the hotels, I didn't really want it that much!"

"You were nothing when I pulled this group together. Neither were you, Josephine. You were nothing but a failed schoolteacher. But I got all of you to function as one. Now I'm going to say this. You're not going to like it, and you'll probably want to punch my teeth out. But let's do this October tour. We've agreed to it. We're contracted to it. We have an obligation. So, I'm going to see you girls on the tour. We're going to make something of ourselves. We'll perform until our hearts stop. That's what we'll do. Any objections?"

The silence hangs colder than the cooling lattes. Scarlet waits as long as she feels is necessary. She takes only the slightest sip of her drink and then leaves.

Scarlet

7 October 1993

The days are good for her. She knows that this is the perfect time of her life, when everything is coming together. She can tell it from the roar of the crowd.

The venue is definitely coming alive tonight. She saw it on the way in: her steady stream of fans eager to get through the door. Revenues from the ticket sales will definitely make Roger Miser happy. She imagines that now: his sneering, milky face.

Ten years ago, when she didn't even really know what music was, she would never have dreamed of something like this. Now she's here, she almost wishes she could disappear again, back to the age of obscurity.

A woman's voice drones behind her: "They're ready for you, Scarlet."

She gives herself one final check in the mirror, ensures that the prettiness in her face won't dissipate, and then heads out of her dressing room. She enters the corridor just as Josephine and Gina are coming out of theirs.

"Let's get this thing going," says Josephine. If she's reluctant, she doesn't show it.

The opening band are doing a few hits. They're this cheapskate boyband from Chiswick. Only one really good hit (which they're playing now). Roger was very generous giving them this opportunity to open up for Scarlet and her girls.

For Scarlet, tonight is just another night on the stage. It's so regular, it's like bloody clockwork to her.

The boyband gets a mildly moderate cheer as they begin to shift off.

Scarlet doesn't think too much about what the stage is going to be like tonight. Even as the roar of the crowd nearly drowns her ears, even as the hissing and the cheering slams against her ribcage, she doesn't stop. It's normal to her now.

The backing musicians take their places and so do the girls, eyes down at first. Josephine kicks of the first notes of their opening song and the release of the hidden talent is complete. It's a big hit with the audience, in the end, and soon enough they're begging for more.

Then comes the big hit from the debut album and it roars out across the Apollo. Yes, dear reader, they literally roar it out. It hits every part of every person there.

"You need to up your game, guys!" yells Josephine, when the song is done.

And they do. Damn – they bloody well do.

There's shifting in the crowd. Like a sort of jumbled Mexican Wave.

The girls start the next song, and the next one after that.

With every note and every passing minute, things get louder. Scarlet begins to revel in it, begins to feel a part of it, begins to wish it would last forever.

Something sails past her, smacks against the ground.

Their music stutters, as Gina yells out, "What the hell...?" Scarlet sees her stumble.

There's a man on the stage, topless, skinny body gleaming in the stage light. He jolts up to Scarlet, starts dancing with her. She's a little put-off, quite annoyed, but she plays along with it.

Their music stutters again, then stops. Josephine's yelling something incoherent, obscure.

The topless man throws his arms up, screams out, "Well, fuck you then!"

The crowd starts booing. More chanting, this time of hatred and bile. More people ascending the stage, rushing toward the girls.

"Scarlet, let's get out of here!" Josephine's got her by the arm, dragging her away from the microphone. "Scarlet!"

The stage lights are out, replaced by emergency floodlights that have turned the place into an action film set.

Men are howling and smashing bottles, fighting with each other.

Scarlet's maybe got a second or two before Josephine and two security guards drag her off the stage. She watches, horrified, as punches are thrown and thrown again.

"Fucking move!" someone hisses in her ear. "Scarlet, now!"

She's not sure who's said it. In the years to come, she'll sometimes reflect, think it might have been Josephine.

She's moved away, deep into the recesses of the building by strong hands. She's aware of the girls being dragged along too. All three of them, and the backing musicians. She's in the cool air now, tiptoes dragged over splintered tarmac that's marked with dried chewing gum. There's a car – not a limo – with its doors open, waiting to swallow her. She's hurled inside and she feels the breath of Josephine sail in next to her.

"Get the others in the second car!" It's a deep voice. One that smacks of decades of experience.

Doors slam. Scarlet feels a lurch.

She still hears the roar of the crowd, only this time it isn't an innocent bunch of sheep, but a furious crowd of raging demons.

Roger has it all worked out. There's a hotel in north London – four-star – that's used as sort of refuge for any stars needing urgent help. He's had it going for the past eight years. Highly useful. He's sent the girls there, a sort of hiding place, somewhere for them to catch their breath.

Three of the hotel suite's armchairs are pulled together in a tight cycle. The girls sit facing one another. (Dear reader, the girls each have their own suites. They're using Gina's, for the time being.) Each of them has a stiff drink in their hands.

"We'll leave you alone," one of the security guards tells them. "Roger Miser is on his way."

The door clicks shut.

"What the hell happened?" stutters Josephine.

"I'll tell you what happened, things fucking kicked off!" Tears clog Gina's voice.

Scarlet feels herself stammer. "We just need to take a few moments, think about things. I know it will be okay. We just – we just…"

"What time is it?" says Josephine. "Christ, let's get some food. I think we need some food."

Gina giggles. "It was a bit like that film, wasn't it…?"

"What film would that be?" says Scarlet.

"*The Bodyguard.* You know, that one with the singer who falls in love with the guy who's protecting her. It was like that bit, you know, when the riot erupts at her concert. We just needed to be carried out and taken to safety, and that would have been a perfect re-enactment."

"Gina!" hisses Scarlet. "Oh, Gina, just shut the fuck up. You don't know what you're talking about."

"Sorry, I didn't mean it like that. I'm just… I'm just shaking."

Josephine's got Gina's hands in hers. Scarlet's somehow find their way in. It's like an ancient ritual and they're summoning the ghosts of the past.

Several moments later, there's a sharp knock on the door and Roger Miser enters, brandishing his unique aura of certainty and caring.

"How are you all bearing up?" he asks.

"As well as can be expected," replies Josephine.

Scarlet sees George skulking in the doorway. He runs a hand through his beard, thick fingers no doubt caught in the grease. Christ, is he in a state of undress? He looks like he's had a night on the town. Shirt untucked. Glasses hanging loose. He looks depressed – clinically so.

Roger seems to get the message. Scarlet imagines herself in his shoes: looking down at three women who have bonded tighter than blood. He knows when to back away, and that's what he does. He's gone quicker than you think.

Scarlet

13 October 1993

She lands on the west coast of Ireland before the sun's properly filled the air.

Shannon Airport is relatively empty and those travelling members of the public who do see her don't get past the sunshades and blonde hair. There is one person – a small child – who Scarlet thinks recognises her, but it doesn't go beyond a smile.

The prearranged taxi is waiting for her. She goes straight for it, her eyes matching with the luxury elements on display.

"You know where to go," she tells the driver.

She watches streets and roads pass in silence, drifting into a trance that never seems to end. Soon they're in deep countryside. There's not much to see here, no company to keep.

Only the occasional passing cars confirm that other human beings exist.

Her hotel is right on the coast, overlooking the roaring, thundering waves. Everything's crashing out there. It's a bed-and-breakfast – clearly not what she's used to. However, there's what looks to be a warm welcome from the girl at reception. A pretty girl as well: the classic Irish redhead from fairy stories. She checks Scarlet in, asks if she has any concerns, any questions, that she's a massive fan of her music.

The hotel is isolated, half a mile from a small village. It's family-run. The parents are away in Canada for a couple of months, leaving the girl, who Scarlet learns is called Felicia, to take care of the place. Not that there's much that needs looking after: Scarlet's the only guest and no one's due to stay for the foreseeable future. That's what the girl tells Scarlet during the checking in process.

The driver helps out with the bags. Well, he carries the lot of them, right up to Room 7 on the top floor.

Where Scarlet's going to be sleeping for the next week looks comfortable enough. Double bed, wooden dressing table, kettle with instant coffees. There's a little window that looks out to the ocean. She stands with her elbows on the windowsill, eyes drooping, thinking of Mauro, getting him out of her head.

The cough of the driver snaps her out of things. "I'll be off now. See you in a week."

"See you."

She falls back on the bed, shuts her eyes, can't fall asleep. She's come here to clear her head, to get everything out. The riot at the concert has spooked her, made her almost think about walking away from it all. That's what she's still thinking now. She needs to be away from it. She needs to draw a line under this fame and fortune, invest her money in a sleepy cottage, lie low for the rest of her life.

She doesn't stay still for long.

"Everything okay?" the girl asks her on her way out.

"Everything's fine. Just going to take a walk."

"Lunch is at One."

"Thanks."

She walks into the breezy air, swayed in all directions. She's not sure where to go, or should she go. Taking a few moments to think about it, she heads towards the village.

There must be ten buildings there at the most. Small houses with no apparent life in. There's what looks to be a post office. And a pub. Everything seems frozen.

"This place comes alive," she mutters.

But it's perfect. She needs to be away from people. Hardly anyone knows where she is.

She can hear the distant growl of traffic, maybe even a shout.

For the first time in years, she's truly alone. Not a feeling. Not a flicker of emotion. The genuine truth.

She's back just in time for lunch. Felicia is standing at her post in reception, clearly bored.

"Hey," she says to Scarlet.

"Hey, I'm ready for lunch now." Scarlet says this with an assertiveness. She's used to getting what she wants – she's entitled to it. The girl complies.

"Follow me through to the dining room," says Felicia.

Scarlet's led through to a room that has that cosy feel to it, something she hasn't felt it years, not since a childhood holiday to the coast where they stayed in a bed-and-breakfast just like this. Ten dark wooden tables, arranged in random positions fill a room with a large window that looks out into the unknown. The walls are filled with various paintings and photographs, topped off by an antique spyglass that hangs above a disused fireplace. A picture of Felicia and her parents hangs above a door marked *Kitchen*.

"Nice little room," remarks Scarlet.

"Spent my childhood here and my teenage years," says the girl. "Now I'm studying in Galway, a free woman, and I get dragged back to this dump."

"I wouldn't call it that."

"Say what you will, but it is."

"Where shall I sit?"

"Did you book a table?" The girl breaks out into a snigger. "Sorry, couldn't resist a bad joke. Sit wherever you want."

Scarlet aims for the table by the window. For a moment, she forgets that she has company. A gentle cough from the girl brings her back to focus. She studies the paper menu in front of her, unsure of how to respond to the allure of Irish cuisine.

"Not sure what to have," she admits.

"I'll tell you want, I'll make you the Irish Stew. It's easy and simple. What do you want to drink? Oh, never mind, I've got a few bottles of Guinness."

"Sounds good. You know, you've not asked about the band yet. By now, I'm usually getting pressured for impromptu interviews from hotel staff, who all want to know about my personal life, my relationships, what kind of wine I drink."

Felicia lifts her eyebrows. "To be honest, I wasn't thinking about that at all. But maybe you can tell me later." She heads to the kitchen, turns back just as she opens the door. "Over dinner."

Scarlet spends the afternoon walking along the coast, letting the stiff Atlantic wind batter her black overcoat.

She's thinking about Susan again. She shouldn't be doing it, because she's done her grieving. But her heart longs for Susan, longs for her soft hands.

She feels the pain in her stomach, the lurches of grief. She's in so much pain that she deviates from her walk and heads onto a beach that seems as wide as a desert. She's aware that the damp sand will ruin her designer shoes, but she's beyond caring about every single thing.

She misses him as well. Whatever Mauro is doing, she hopes he is happy. He deserves it.

As for Emma, well Scarlet thinks nothing of her. She's even beginning to forget what the girl looked like.

She walks for a bit more, gets bored with the endless, repeating scenery, and then turns back on herself, heading towards the village. It looks like it's woken up now. A few people are milling about in their front gardens, faces down. She could be an angel with flapping wings and they wouldn't see her. The pub seems open. She goes up to the entrance, expects to hear harsh accents telling her that a girl doesn't belong here on her own. She finds though that there are only smiling faces and a pretty attractive barmaid who asks her what she's having. Scarlet goes for the obvious choice.

She forgets to use the toilet before she leaves and by the time she's back at the hotel, her bladder's straining and screaming to go.

"Sorry, chat later," she says to the girl, racing up the stairs. She barely makes it to her bathroom before she wets herself and allows a relieved gasp to escape her lungs.

The dining room has changed by the time she comes down for dinner, Seven P.M. sharp. The room is lit with candles and tealights. Somewhere, there's a scented flame. The table by the window has been set up for her: plates and cutlery at the ready. And a glass of red wine.

"Wow," she allows herself to mutter. She's put on a dress for tonight – something dark and red – but she knows that she hasn't gone far enough.

Felicia comes in, all togged up nice. "Sorry," she says, "but the best-dress uniform of the hotel is all I have tonight."

"It's okay."

"I hope you don't mind, but it's a pre-set menu. Garlic bread for starters, then woodfired pizza for mains."

"Sounds tasty."

"Right, I'm getting our garlic bread. Take a seat."

"I'm sorry, *our garlic bread*?" stutters Scarlet.

Felicia smirks. "Take a look at the table. It's set for two."

"Listen, I know what this is. Are you after some sort of lesbian hook-up?"

"Whatever made you think of that?"

"I dunno. Two girls. Alone in a hotel for a few days."

Felicia rubs her chin. "A hook-up wasn't what I was after. Can't two girls just enjoy one another's company over dinner and wine?"

Scarlet's the one who finishes her portion of pizza last. Felicia refills their glasses, milky eyes shooting right at her.

Scarlet knows, full bloody well, that this is an attempt to get her under the covers. Of course it bloody is. She knows she could have this girl, no questions asked, knows that she could go through with it; but she finds herself unable to say yes.

"I heard about what happened at that concert in London," says Felicia. "They really cancelled the rest of the tour over it?"

"Well, it was at my insistence. I came here to have a break from things."

"Shit, I'm sorry."

"Don't be. Actually, I'm thinking about walking away from it all."

"Seriously? Why would you do that?"

"Because, I'm tired! I'm tired of it all." She knows it's the alcohol interfering with her judgement, but honestly, she doesn't care. "I'm tired of the endless touring, Roger Miser, the late-night parties. It's too much. And I can't stand it anymore. I know what you're thinking: that the travelling, glamour, hotels, and all that, it's great, it's fun. But you're trapped. Like a bat in a cage. You're locked in so tightly you can't breathe. The truth is, the one person who made it all worthwhile was Susan."

"I remember watching it on the news. I'm so sorry. I can't imagine what you've been through."

"That's the understatement of the year, Felicia. I loved her. I cared about her more than I cared about myself. It cuts right here, right here." She clutches her chest as though her heart is actually hanging from her ribcage.

Felicia reaches her hands across the table, takes Scarlet's. Scarlet gulps, but then allows her guard to relax once again.

"I've kinda always had a crush on you," says Felicia. "Ever since I first saw you perform. Your first concert in London, I was there. I watched right from the back. God, I wanted to kiss those lips of yours there and then. You're fucking cute, you know that?"

Scarlet gets to her feet, shifts to the other side of the table, and kisses Felicia hard. "Sorry, needed to get that over and done with."

14 October to 20 October 1993

They spend their time eating, making love, watching crappy VHS tapes, and walking along the coast. At first, Scarlet treats it as nothing more than a holiday, a holiday from herself.

There comes a point when she realises that she wants to stay here with this girl. It's the point where she believes that she can let everything go, start a new life here.

One of the nights, she asks Felicia, as they lie snuggled in bed, "Can I stay here with you?"

"Why would you want to?" comes the reply.

"Because I really want to."

"You're serious, aren't you?"

"Of course I am."

"Well, if you'd be prepared to swap the microphone for cleaning pots and pans, then, yeah, you're more than welcome."

On that night, they share their most passionate kiss yet.

On the last night, when they lie together in bed yet again, Scarlet makes promises to Felicia. Felicia touches Scarlet's face with silky hands, devours her with milky eyes.

When the morning arrives, Scarlet wakes up alone. Naked, she stumbles through to the shower and washes last night's activity off her. She goes downstairs to the breakfast room, thinking that Felicia has sorted them out something nice.

But the girl is back in her hotel uniform, face blank.

"Breakfast is just about ready," she tells Scarlet. "Five minutes. There's coffee and cereal on the counter. Help yourself."

She hasn't twigged what's happening. She's still too tired.

"I'll have to cancel my car," she yawns.

"Your car will be here at Nine," replies Felicia.

"What's going on here?"

"You're checking out today. I have other guests arriving later..."

"Hold on a minute..."

"Scarlet, you're a popstar. I'm a poor student doing a bit of parttime work for my folks. We're hardly compatible, don't you think?"

"Hang on a minute..." She rushes up to the girl, cuddles her, as if that's going to do anything.

"Scarlet, please." The girl turns around, holds Scarlet's face in her hands. "Scarlet, you're a beautiful woman and I really like you, but... I thought a lot about things last night and this is a little bit too much for me."

"I want to be here with you."

"I know you do. But I can't. You're a great singer and a wonderful person, and I really hope you find the connection you're looking for, but I know you will."

Scarlet's backing away. "I'm getting my things," she says. "I'm going now. I'm getting my shit and I'm going to the airport. Call the driver, tell him to get here as soon as possible."

"Please stay for breakfast."

"You're chucking me. I'm not fucking staying for breakfast. I'll eat something proper, in the lounge at the airport."

She goes back up to the room, gathers her things, drags them down the steps.

"Where's my fucking car?!" she yells at Felicia.

"You've changed, haven't you?" replies the girl. She's standing behind the reception desk, checking over papers, oblivious to everything else.

"I said I want my fucking car!"

"It's on its way."

She wants to be out of her. Back in London, that's where she's needed. That's where she belongs. A new album needs to be written.

She's not sure of when the driver actually comes, but she's suddenly aware that she's being carried through the Irish countryside once more, moved along by the ferryman. At the airport, she thinks she won't be able to eat, no appetite whatsoever, but she finds herself gorging on pastries and fresh bacon, toasted sausages and crisp coffee. Proper bloody food. An attendant comes at the necessary minute to take her to the plane.

What was she thinking? She smirks as she's escorted to her seat. Stupid bloody idea, coming over here.

As the plane roars into the sky, the ground disappearing beneath her, she finds herself trying to figure out what went wrong. What specific things did she say? Was there something she murmured in her sleep? Of course, the answer is bloody obvious: she *can't* have a normal life. No matter how hard she tries to do normal things and live a normal existence, have normal relationships, go out for normal dinners, something will always go wrong. She'll say the wrong thing, look at someone the wrong way.

She finds herself yearning for him again. It pulls at her heartstrings and waters her eyes.

When she arrives back home, she starts rummaging through her things, getting more and more upset until she locates her little black notebook. She flips through the pages, sticking a thumb on his mobile number. Whether he's still got it, she doesn't know. She punches the digits furiously into the phone. It's ringing. But no one answers.

Alastair

20 November 1993

Dear Diary,

I've dated a few women in my time, but tonight was something else. She turned up, before you ask. She was slim, a brunette. My kind of girl.

It probably wasn't the best idea, but I'd booked us a table at an Indian restaurant in Vauxhall. I'd been there once before, back in my student days. Back when every meal out was a luxury.

Anyway...

So, I'd tried one of those matching agencies; I suppose, just for a laugh. A bit like that episode of *Only Fools And Horses*. When I'd visited their office, I had to clench my jaw shut to stop my face cracking into a smile.

I'm getting off track again.

The rendezvous was on Vauxhall Bridge at Seven P.M. I got there fifteen minutes before and rested my forearms on the railings, looking out across the Thames. I watched the boats come and go, listened to the shouts and roaring cars; I took it all in.

"Hi, you must be Alastair, right?"

I turned around to see a woman with long brown hair combed with exact precision. Ten years from now, I'm not sure what I'll think of her. But in that moment, I was definitely attracted to her.

"Yeah, that's me," I said.

"Hattie," she replied, reaching out a hand.

"It's good to meet you, finally!"

"Same here. I'm famished, let's find this restaurant of yours. It's an Indian place, right?"

"It is indeed." I think that's what I remember saying to her. I think so.

"Good. Link arms?"

I was surprised. I suppose I hesitated too long, because she gazed at me darkly. I gulped and forced my arm into a donut ring.

We walked together into the deep heart of Vauxhall. Several times, I lost my way, but somehow I found the trail of breadcrumbs again.

I remember saying something to her along the lines of: "This is our restaurant. Hope you like it." Not exactly the most romantic thing.

It was a small place, with only six tables and four weary staff. For a moment, I thought I'd gone and booked us into a takeaway. But my fears were short-lived: two waitresses approached us and greeted us in the most cordial, polite manner I have ever witnessed.

Hattie seemed impressed, anyway.

Finally, finally, we were sitting down, a glass of wine before each of us.

"So, what do you do for a living?" was her first question.

"A lawyer."

"Oh, that's cool. I wish I had the brains to be a lawyer."

"So, what is it that you do for a living?" I asked her.

"I'm in hospitality. Hotels, as a matter of fact. I'm working at reception in one of those hotels right in Westminster."

"Oh, which one?"

"I'm not telling you. Let's get through dinner first."

You get the picture. It was a fantastic date. I was relaxed, totally relaxed. Everything seemed to be going to plan.

It was as we were having dessert and coffee that things took a turn for the bizarre. I was halfway down my cup, listening to her tell tales about the hotel she worked at in Prague, when I saw two familiar faces whoosh past on the street outside. Tamsyn and Amias. They didn't see me, at least I don't think so. They were chatting away to each other, in the brief glimpse I caught of them. Then they were gone.

"Earth calling Alastair!" Hattie stroked my chin as she said these words. "What's so fascinating out there?"

"Nothing," I responded.

"Then focus on me."

I think that should conclude my diary entry for today. Hattie has told me that she wants a second date.

Yet all I'm thinking about now are Tamsyn and Amias. Why should I be obsessed with them? I hardly know them, except for a fleeting conversation. Yet as I write these words, all I want is five minutes with them. Correction. I want five minutes with Tamsyn.

Scarlet

20 November 1993

She takes yet another look at her date for tonight, realises yet again that he's attractive, and allows herself to relax.

His name is Raymond and he owns an international fashion brand. He's in his mid-thirties, but he looks eighteen. He works out every day, with a membership of five private gyms in London. But what he loves most of all is running in the early hours along the bank of the Thames. Like Susan used to do.

She'll admit to herself. Well, she'll admit to anyone that it's been a hard year. A bloody hard one.

Yet now the conversation – about fashion, of course – flows as smooth as water from a pixie's imagination.

He's a good guy. A friend of Roger's set them up on a blind date. These things – as Scarlet has found out in the past – often turn to disarray. But tonight, things seem to be working. Everything is connecting.

It's the perfect ending to this year. There's a song somewhere in this moment, but it doesn't need to be sung. Not yet, anyway.

1994

Herbert

17 January 1994

I'm not too happy with the funeral arrangements. Poor Wallace Rodriguez deserved far better than the Nine A.M. slot on this freezing morning. But the world is what it is. My time in America taught me that.

I'm in King's Lynn to may last respects to the former deputy editor of my first magazine. He was old when I met him. God knows how he managed to keep on all these years.

Trudging out of the small hotel that seems to be splintering at the scenes, I suppress the urge to swear at myself. What I really want to say is this: Why the hell did I come back? In America, I was the man I've always been destined to be. Young, strong, slim. The perfect mix. Now, what do I do? My journalism career has pretty much dissipated. I write novels for a living now. And not very good ones.

Anyway, I'm complaining again...

I arrive at the church just as the other mourners are beginning to gather. A few handshakes and deepest sympathies to the close family. I think I met the wife once, a long time ago, just before I left Wallace's magazine. Slowly but surely, I begin to get to mingle and introduce myself. A couple of people have read my work, but I don't have any major fans. And of course! This is not the wretched place to be discussing literature!

The hearse pulls up — fresh off the factory line, by all appearances — and the funeral director steps out, dipping his head. He looks worn to the bone, threading, decomposing.

The coffin is propped up on the shoulders of thin pallbearers and carried into the church. We begin the process of filing in, our eyes downturned.

I've never been much of a fan of funerals – who is? But several of my newfound novelist friends say they've always found inspiration in the bleakest moments of life.

I stay at the back, keeping my eyes unfocussed. There are nice tributes from the immediate family and the vicar delivers a moving testimony. After the service, we head to a seniors' social club twenty minutes down the road where Mr Rodriguez frequented in his final years.

The social club is a large cabin with a plastic floor. A single room, with adjoining toilets and a kitchen, has that old musty scent to it. Fights in the school canteen. I smirk at the memories. Christ, I hope I don't have to stay here too long. It's depressing. Honest to God. A buffet table of sandwiches and drinks breaks the dreary silence. I pick a small selection, grab a glass of fruit juice, and start the mingling process.

After a while, someone approaches me. She must be the youngest person here. Obviously, a distant relative or a friend of a friend of the family, because there's not a single tear present on her cheek. In fact, she looks quite jolly.

"I'm Milly," she says. "You're Herbert Buxton, right?" She holds out a hand. Christ, she must be sixteen, seventeen at the most.

"Yes, I am." I take it, but release my grip quickly.

"I've read both of your books. I loved them both. I'm a big fan."

"Thank you! I'm glad to see someone's been buying copies. How did you know Wallace?"

"My mum used to work at this club. She's in ill health right now, so she wasn't able to make it, but I wanted to come along. Show support."

"That's a great thing you've done. What did you think of the service?"

Milly takes a moment to think. "I thought it was okay. Though I'd hoped for a bigger turnout."

"Yeah, me too."

"It is what it is."

We both fall into that awkward silence. The last time I was like this was when I met the head of my first publisher. That was one awkward afternoon...

I rest my hands on my thick chest, smile at Milly. "I think we should begin to mingle with others..."

"Sounds good to me."

It's only when she's walking away that I curse myself. Maybe I was a little too aggressive.

Already, I'm getting ideas for the new book...

I take dinner at a local pub – the name of which has been long rubbed out. Partially cooked steak pie and a pint of ale. I'm like a character in that 1920s detective story I've not got around to writing yet.

I keep thinking that I'm going to bump into people from the funeral, but no familiar faces dare themselves to appear.

I'm thinking about my time in America, back in the 1960s, when the roads were as open as people's feelings. For years I crisscrossed that country, interviewing all manner of musicians. Country And Western, Rock And Roll, Classical. I would write up my interviews, send them to whichever magazine I happened to be working for at that particular time, move on. Just a shame that the work dried up. One day, I was travelling through Kentucky; the next, I was on a plane back to Britain.

I've often dreamed of going back. I'd like more than anything in the world. But I'm in my fifties now, married, with a family. I can't just get up and go. I can't be my younger self again, free, no connections. Some things just aren't possible.

With that sad note in mind, I slowly finish my dinner.

18 January 1994

When I arrive back at my house in London's Hillingdon, I find that my wife and two teenage stepsons are not present. I search the cluttered hallway, hoping that I'll find a note or something. But I find I'm too lazy to search. It was too long a drive back from King's Lynn and my legs muscles are beginning to cramp once again.

I inch my way through to the only tidy room in the house: my study. Here, I find that my wife has left a pile of folded laundry and an assortment of crockery which we've been pledging to take to the charity shop for months. Typical Audrey: using my study as a storage depot.

I stifle a yawn as I fire up my Packard Bell Statesman. I've been putting a few notes together for the new novel, should I ever get around to writing it. Somehow, I think it will be a long time. As I sit here, my legs and arms throbbing, I try to let the ideas flow, but nothing is coming. I step up and shift around a little, rolling my heels against the ground. Something catches in the edge of my vision. My answering machine's red light blinks away. I start playing the tape.

The first two messages are requests for interviews, but the third is from an old colleague of mine. We worked together at the last magazine I wrote for, just before I switched to fiction.

"Hi, Herbert, it's Randall, how ya doing? How's the world of fiction treating you? Listen, I've got something that might interest you. I've booked a table for lunch tomorrow. I'll have you picked up at Half-Twelve. Trust me, Herbert, this will be worth your while."

I play the message again. It's odd, Randall Portman reaching out to me like this. If there's an opportunity, he's the sort of bloke who'd seize it for himself. Odd. Anyway, he says he's going to pick me up tomorrow. I'll see what he has to say – it's probably an invitation to some party or other. I'll see what he has to say.

"I'm home!" Audrey's voice calls out. "Herbert, you back yet?"

"In the study!" I answer her.

She comes in, shopping bags making her knuckles white. "Hiya," she says. "How was the funeral?"

"As well as funerals can go," I tell her. "Where are the boys?"

"School."

"Oh yeah. Don't know why I asked that question."

"I thought we'd go out for dinner tonight. How does that sound?"

"Sounds great. Actually, I've just had a message from an old colleague. He wants to meet me for lunch tomorrow, says got something that might interest me. He's even picking me up from the house."

"That's very generous of him. I take it it's Randall?"

"You guessed it in one."

I stand up, shift across the room, and hug Audrey tightly. "It's good to be back," I whisper. "You know I hate going away, don't you?"

"Of course, I know that. When we married, you promised me you'd cut down on the travelling."

"And I have."

"Good." Audrey pulls back and looks me in the eye. "So, whatever Randall wants to offer you, make sure it fits with your promise."

"I will."

19 January 1994

The black cab pulls up five minutes earlier than expected. Randall Portman steps out from the backseat, beckons me in, goofy smile on his face.

"How was the funeral then?" he asks me, as we set off.

"It was okay. Bit of a lonely, sordid affair, if you ask me." I'm back to speaking in my journalist tone. I don't dare do it near my wife. I've got that flamboyant, confident streak back. "Not many people turned up."

"Yeah, I tried to make it myself, but I was held up with personal business. The wife's been having a few issues at work recently. Anyway, I was there in spirit."

"So, what's this opportunity you've got for me?"

"All in good time, all in good time." Randall fiddles with his extra-large glasses and strokes his thin pale face.

I've always found that Randall's body language doesn't match his intentions. He's the kind of man who looks weak on the outside, but behind the brittle armour is the most deceptive, manipulative person you'll ever meet.

We're only in the taxi for about ten minutes before we reach our stop. It's a Thai restaurant I visited ten years earlier. Was it a classical violinist I was interviewing? Or was it the lead singer of that dreadful West German punk band, the one who overdosed in 1991?

"I thought this place closed down years ago," I remark to Randall as he pays the driver.

"Not quite," he replies, leading the way in. "Though the owner has fucked off back to Thailand."

On the outside, I see indeed that the lettering has changed. It's bold, colourful Eighties hues have gone, replaced by sharp lettering all in black. On the inside, though, everything appears just as I remembered. The tables, draped with that crisp cloth, are all set with the appropriate cutlery. The red carpet still has that feeling of dust crunching beneath my feet. The pictures of the owner – well, former owner – with various important people are still hanging on the walls, like memories you can't quite shake off.

"I have a booking for two, name of Portman." Randall spits through his teeth as he says this to the waiter who greets us.

"Follow me."

As soon as we're sat down, Randall does what I've always known him to do: orders a bottle of French wine and two glasses. Whatever restaurant you see him in, whether it's Nepalese, Nigerian, Indian, he'll order French wine. That's the way he does it. I know that there's no point asking him anything until we each have a glass poured. When one of the many waiters scurrying about finally puts down two glasses and adds the dark red liquid, I know I only have to wait until he takes the first sip.

"So, what have you brought me here for?" I ask, when it's done.

Randall produces a magazine from his jacket. He flips through it, raises his eyebrows as he stops at a particular page, and thrusts it across the table.

"What do you think?" he says. "It's this month's edition, by the way. My magazine."

Three women stare up at me from an image that's been spread over two pages. I recognise them immediately. The one with the blonde hair, the lead singer, looks so cold, the way she sits perched on the stool, elbow digging into her knee.

"We did a feature on them to kickstart the year," explains Randall.

"I know them. I met their keyboardist, Susan, the night she was killed."

"I'm sorry, I heard about that."

"I only met her briefly, but she was one hell of a character, Randall. You would have liked her."

Randall takes another sip of his wine. One of the waiters comes to take our orders. Randall, being the excess of personality that he is, does it for both of us. "Trust me," he says to me, "I know you'll like what I've ordered."

After a few minutes, Randall's tone seems to drop. "Well, I have an offer for you, something that may, or may not, interest you. My magazine was recently contacted by a certain Roger Miser. You know the name?"

"I've heard of him."

"Well, he's been working on this idea with the band to have a journalist follow them for a lengthy period. Basically, following them around, taking notes of their practice sessions, their banter, creative thought processes, that sort of stuff. We got sent the paperwork a few days ago. I thought of a few people in my magazine who might be suited to it, but..." He sighs. "Unfortunately, no one has really got the time to commit to such a thing, but you do."

"Well, Randall, I'm a fulltime novelist now."

"And how's the latest book going? Have you written any-thing yet?"

"Well, I've been making notes..."

He laughs, right at me. "I've read both of your books. They're great, don't get me wrong, but we both know your heart belongs in music journalism. And we both know you're determined to get back to America. This job will allow you to do just that. All you'll need to do is follow the band around for three years –"

"*Three* years!" I exclaim.

"Yes. Follow them for three years, take notes on their various deeds, that sort of stuff, and at the end write a ten-page piece for my magazine. You'll be paid half a million for the work."

"I have to admit, that does interest me."

"Good."

"Though I want to see the paperwork first."

"Of course."

I'm not lying here. This sort of thing genuinely interests me. But then the harshness of reality hits me: my wife. I promised her.

"How much travelling is involved?" I ask.

"Well, you'll obviously be covering their tours across the country. I think they've got a few things lined up this year. You'll also be doing the international stuff as well. They're a major band. I've heard it said that they will define the Nineties."

"The thing is, I promised my wife I'd cut down on the travelling."

I think he's going to spill his wine, the face that he pulls right now. "Oh, never mind what she says! You're your own man, Herbert! And the money at the end will surely make her happy, won't it?"

"You've got me there. Alright then, I accept – well, as soon as I see the contract."

"Good. I'll have it delivered to you tomorrow." Randall smiles, that childish grin he always does when he's scored a major victory. "You'll be meeting them next week."

I'm eager to respond in some way, some form, but I don't need to. He's said all my words for me and I don't need to utter another word.

Josephine

20 January 1994

I'm woken in the early hours by the shouts and screams of Year 8. Bullying me, mocking me, ripping me to pieces.

"Hey, miss, we made you cry yet?!"

"Aww, poor miss! Poor, poor miss!"

Then, I hear Mr Merton's voice in my ear. Yet another one of his fits at me. *"Josephine, what's happening with this Year Eight class is your responsibility. Your fault. You've got to be consistent in your approach. What I saw when I walked in was a class out of control. You've got to be consistent. Consistent..."*

"Consistent!" I hiss, covering my ears. "Be fucking consistent!" I sit up in bed, scrunch my knuckles.

It takes me a while to properly wake myself up. Part of me refuses to do so.

I check my alarm clock. It's Three A.M. Half the world is asleep. The girls are coming later to discuss this writer guy who'll be covering us for the next three years. It was Roger Miser's idea. A way to give our band a unique twist, a major selling point. Why the hell not?

Christ, it feels like summer. My pyjamas are crunchy with sweat; so are my bedclothes.

I stagger through my home, legs unsteady. Tears are coming, there's nothing I can do about that. Sometimes, you see, I have these dreams about my teaching days. They always find a way into my thoughts, like ants.

"I'm fucking consistent now," I say to the air. "Consistent as a fucking ruler."

They'll always want me to play by their laws.

I'm so on-edge now, I can barely stop myself falling over. Before I know it, I'm grabbing my running shoes and outdoor gear, pulling them on with a lack of care.

It's icy and they haven't gritted the pavements. Several times, I nearly stumble, but once I reach the end of the street, the ground becomes a little more stable. My feet smash against the tarmac harder. I turn corners blindly, imagining what it was like for Susan. This is the closest I'll ever feel to her.

Hours later, I face the girls in my living room, having given them the full briefing. Of course, they were informed of the detailed arrangements late last year. It's still a shock to them though, judging by their mute faces.

"I want you all free to speak your mind," I tell them. Part of the failed schoolteacher in me rises to the surface. I just need a cane. "Is anyone nervous about partaking in this because of Herbert Buxton's association with Susan's death?"

The girls look at each other, like lost birds.

"I have to admit, I am a bit uncomfortable with this," says Gina. "I understand it's not his fault and everything, but..."

"We need to talk to him," says Scarlet. "Before he starts his little project, we need to have a bit of a chat with him, get to know him a little bit."

"We'll be doing that next week," I reply. "Roger's booked us a table in some fancy restaurant. If we like him, he officially starts his project at the beginning of February.

"Well, I can do that." Gina leans forward, hunches on the sofa.

"Good," I say. "Excellent. Scarlet?"

"Fine with me."

Hours after they're gone, I find myself transfixed in a state of boredom. And it's easy to explain. I don't exactly have a life. I have no boyfriend, no real friends. I live for the band. I live for meetings with Roger and George, deciding in which direction to take things, deciding on so many pointless endeavours, deciding of whether to decide.

Yet another cup of coffee appears in front of me.

I think about a time when I did have a life. When I was in touch with my emotions. During my travels. When I was on that beach in Madagascar, open to the world.

I allow myself to laugh out loud, revelling in those memories. Of course, I find myself going beyond those sweet moments. The summer of 1984 calls out to me, refusing to be put aside.

10 June 1984 to 22 June 1984

She thought about him the day after she met him. Within hours of getting up, she was obsessively daydreaming about him. She knew it was foolish and idiotic, but she didn't care. She was energised, happy, fulfilled. She had air in her lungs, moisture in her eyes.

Throughout the working week that came and passed like a firefly, thoughts of his beautiful physique filled her with pleasure and motivation. All assigned tasks in the office were done. All managers impressed beyond belief.

As the days passed, the realisation that he would never be hers began to bite. Not painful. Not uncomfortable. She'd known it all along. She began to come to terms with it, and did so very quickly.

On the evening of Friday, 22nd of June, she was alone in the office sorting out the last of the files. She hummed some T. Rex to herself as she put worthless files away in neat little spaces. When she was done, she locked up, trudged outside, tried not to think about the worthless job.

Will Parson was on the other side of the road, gazing at her thoughtfully. His bum was resting on the bonnet of a car. A Mercedes. Her boss had one similar to it.

The man had something in his hand. A silvery card of some sort. As she approached, he handed it to her.

"Congratulations, you're a member," he said. "What do you think?"

It felt as heavy as steel. She ran her thumb over the full form of her name, etched in the metal. Below it, also carved, the hammer and sickle. Also included, in smaller scars: *East Anglia Communist Movement.*

"Your membership card," he explained. "Don't worry about fees. I've paid the bill for you – you're a member for life."

"Oh my," she stammered. "Oh, I don't know how to thank you."

"Well," said Will, standing up, "you can start by allowing me to take you out for dinner."

20 January 1994

The phone is ringing.

I'm standing, looking through the window, though I don't see what's on the other side. I don't think I'll ever see.

The phone is ringing, louder and louder.

I pick up the receiver. It's Roger.

"Hi Josephine, just phoning you about some tour dates. I'll call the others later. You've got a U.K. tour in March and later this year, you're doing South Africa, Australia and New Zealand. Three nights in Johannesburg, two in Sydney, and two in Auckland. From what I've heard, it's going to be a fantastic run."

"Good, that's what I want to hear," I say. "Honestly, that's great."

"How are the girls feeling about Herbert Buxton?"

"They seem okay with it. It'll take a while, but they'll get used to him."

"Mr Buxton, I think, is a little nervous about it as well. But I spoke to him on the phone just now and he seems to be confident and happy about things. Let's just see how things play out. If it doesn't work out, it doesn't work out."

"That sounds like a plan," I say.

"How are you holding up anyway, Josephine?"

"I'm fine. Never been better. Just cracking on with things as best I can."

"That's the spirit. I know you've had a rough time of things recently, but it's encouraging to see you pull through. You're a strong woman, Josephine. Never forget that."

"How can I?"

Scarlet

24 January 1994

She knows he's disappointed, though not heartbroken. She can see it in his eyes. He's annoyed at the fact that he won't get to date the lead singer of this amazing band anymore, but he's not going to cry himself to sleep tonight with a broken soul.

"You're a nice guy and everything, but it's just not working out for me," she tells him. "I hope you understand…"

Raymond purses his lips, shrugs his shoulders, makes some attempt at a reply.

Thankfully, the coffeeshop they're in is largely empty, though a couple of businessmen, trapped in suits since the early Seventies, are discussing some deal or other. It's nearly Three in the afternoon and the exhaustion can be felt in the air.

Scarlet clasps his hands, tells him she's thankful for everything, and proceeds to get up and leave.

Roger's booked a restaurant that is vaguely familiar to her. As the others turn up, she begins to recognise the features: lines of lanterns crossing the ceiling, bamboo cubicles, diamond wine racks. A sad smile crosses her lips as the memories flood back. Mauro took her here two years ago. That was the time Eugene popped by as well for a visit.

They're gathered on the pavement outside. Josephine and Gina are on the lookout for him, eyes glancing across the flow of traffic.

Roger and his young lady have also come along. They look angry, though there's a sense of merriment in the way they have their emotions connected.

"Is George coming?" asks Gina.

"No, not on this occasion." Roger checks a pager on his belt.

A taxi pulls up and a large figure emerges. Slightly over-weight, meaty hands, and a thick beard, Scarlet almost doesn't recognise him.

"Hi, you must be Scarlet, Gina and... Josephine?" he seems to stammer.

"Yeah, that's us."

"I'm Herbert Buxton."

Scarlet's unsure of whether to reach out and shake his hand, but she forces herself to do so.

"Shall we go in?" says Roger, shifting his wife towards the entrance.

She's lost that look of a professional model. Looks as though she's put on weight.

Josephine's the one to take over, as she always is. She lunges forward, takes Mr Buxton's hand, tells him she's really glad beyond belief to meet him.

The party enters the restaurant, edging themselves through the entrance. But Scarlet's thinking of nothing except Mauro. Reminders of what she could have had leave scars in her sacred memories. But she's a girl who's determined to pull through. She won't fail. She won't back down. She goes in with a smile on her face and shows a full heart of questions.

As she sits down with her girls, Mr Buxton, Roger and his woman, she begins to accept that she'll never truly find happiness. She had it with Mauro, but she threw it away. With this sort of stuff, there are no second chances.

She keeps her smile high as Mr Buxton discusses his years in America. She guesses that it's part of his pitch, part of his selling plan to get the band to really take him onboard, to get their full seal of approval.

"Certainly an impressive career path to date," Josephine remarks, when he's finished.

Scarlet's thinking about the time, years ago, when she was reading about him in a magazine or a newspaper, she can't remember which. It was his debut novel, wasn't it? Yeah, they were on their way to Inverness. When it was all five of them.

Gina and Josephine prod him with questions as their dinner and wine goes on. Roger occasionally interjects with official comments and even more official requests.

Herbert Buxton seems like a man full of life. A man who wants nothing more than to succeed at what he's doing. Yet, she finds herself hating him.

Surprisingly, he doesn't talk about his fiction. Maybe he knows about the pain this will cause.

Scarlet doesn't know why, but she's blaming this bastard for Susan's death. Of course, there was no way he could have known, but the hatred bubbles inside her. He's so distant from the band. He's an outsider, a distant star. He wasn't here at the beginning, back in that coffee shop when she started all of this. He's an intruder. Someone who knows how to violate. He doesn't belong here and he never will.

Marianne

1 February 1994

These past few months, every morning, without exception, I worry about my husband. His behaviour's becoming more and more erratic. Since he disclosed to us last summer what happened to him, getting punched in London, slowly but surely there's been a change in him. For one thing, he's been joining and leaving karate clubs. He stays a month, then he leaves, joins another one. The cycle continues, a never-ending charade of kicks and cries.

Today, the day before we go to visit Paul and Siobhan, I'm sitting in our back garden, trapped by the freezing darkness, sipping the last of my instant coffee, and I'm worrying deeply about my James.

I can hear him rummaging around in the house, sorting something out. I hear him muttering something about where the washing powder is located.

Alastair's worried sick as well. He's been coming home a lot, nearly every weekend, to help out. Even at the expense of his social life. He never asks to be thanked, never complains, even when his father is talking nonstop about how much he adores karate. Alastair's very dedicated, unlike Scarlet.

Scarlet's another story altogether. I know, I know, I shouldn't say this about my own daughter, but she's always been distant from others. Nothing's ever been right about her. Even her name... It should have had two ts at the end, but, oh no, James wanted to put a unique spin on things.

I'm going to be stuck all day with him tomorrow, though at least Alastair will be there to help out if things turn really bad. I need to get out for the day, some peace and quiet. Even if it's just for the morning, I need to be away from the house.

I head back inside and play the wife again to my husband.

"You're up early," he says, drinking his smoothie. I don't think he's going to bother tidying up the splashes of bananas and blueberries strewn about the place.

"You know we've got a big day tomorrow, what with our car journey..." I don't bother to continue. Drying sweat clings to his eyebrows. He's been doing his Four A.M. runs again. I thought he'd give them up, but, ah no.

"I'm absolutely fine. I'm going to be working from home today. Hope that's okay..."

"It's perfectly fine with me. Actually, James, I was thinking of going out today for a few hours. Meet up with a couple of friends for coffee or something."

"Go for it. Honestly, I'll have plenty to occupy my mind. How about we get a takeaway for dinner or something?"

"Sounds good to me."

I'm glad to be out of the house. It feels like a release, like I've escaped from prison. Wandering along the street, I take note of the gradual stirrings of the working population. There's a sense of everything in this world clicking into place.

I set off for the train station, every part of me unsure of where to go. Waves of commuters are already pouring into the building, newspapers rustling like rattlesnakes.

I check the departures board. Anything that's not too far. It's easy enough to choose. Royal Tunbridge Wells. Not too far. Shouldn't be too long on the train. Mind you, I'm not someone who often travels by rail. I book a return and make my way through the maze of commuters to the platform.

I know British Rail isn't the most efficient organisation on the planet, but this morning at least, the train is on time. I manage to fit myself into a crowded row of seats and take a few deep breaths. The train moves and shifts.

Scarlet was never the daughter I was supposed to have. I know it's a sickening to say, but I should have had a beautiful blonde, with a smooth complexion and deep blue eyes. I was deprived of that. Starved of my right to have the child of my dreams.

Hmm. I didn't know that many people worked in Royal Tunbridge Wells. A fair few come here, as it would appear. I'm the only one who doesn't have a workplace to go to, as it would seem!

The coffeeshops and bakeries are only just cranking up into life. I wouldn't call it clockwork, more like a shuffling of a teenager's limbs as they slowly wake up.

I know something will have to be done about Scarlet. After all, can this really go on? Can we tolerate her eccentricities? I need to ask and answer these awful questions. Questions which burrow right to the centre of my brain. Questions I'd rather didn't exist.

The world seems to pass me by here. I'm surrounded, trapped, a woman with plenty of regrets.

Alastair

2 February 1994

Dear Diary,

Well, we arrived at the Casselden's house safely.

We're doing things slightly different this year. I suppose Mum and Dad are getting a bit old to drive there and back in the one day. We're staying at their place for a couple of nights. Maybe we should have been doing this in previous years.

So, we had a good trip up today. Mum was a bit reluctant to let Dad take the wheel, though he did succeed in doing the last leg. It's all political with him. He can't be seen to lose.

Something has changed in him, that's for sure. The sense of pride that I've always seen in him has begun to dissipate. I don't think he's become the shadow of the man he once was, but he's certainly been shown the door.

When we arrived, Paul seemed to be getting out of the house slower than usual. He'd lost that energetic twinkle in his eye. Indeed, when we sat down in their living room for the customary talk on insurance and the like, Paul struggled to complete a sentence.

At dinner, with only one bottle of cheapish French wine to share between us, there was a discussion of politics.

It did get to that stage, in the end, when all the conversation died. We spent the night in front of the television, all eyes glued to various happenings on the screen. We ended up sitting through half an episode of Eastenders. Ever since the Mitchell brothers appeared, the show has grown more and more depressing with each passing day.

Eventually, we decided to have a nightcap of brandy in near silence. Siobhan made a quick joke about the local council not collecting bins on time, but everyone found it hard to laugh.

One interesting thing did happen though. As we readied ourselves for bed, the next-door neighbour's radio blasted out one of Scarlet's songs. We felt it through the walls and the ground.

"There she goes again," Paul remarked.

I'm not sure how to conclude the diary entry for today, except for the obvious thing: I'm worried about Dad.

James

3 February 1994

After we finally get away from our respective wives, we start the arduous journey to the pub. Not as a couple – that flame has long since been extinguished. We're happy with the way things have gone for the both of us.

"Do you remember this time four years ago?" Paul asks. "You know, when Scarlet came into the house, the band still a figment in her imagination? I have to admit, I was restraining my laughter. But look how far she's come."

"And look at the pain she's endured."

"I know. Susan."

"Sometimes, I don't even know who she is anymore. It's almost like… I can't say it, Paul. It's almost like I don't have a daughter. It's almost like she never existed."

"You should never say things like that, James. She's your daughter. Don't ever forget that fact. She's your daughter."

The pub's right ahead. Our pace quickens.

Not many drinkers are in tonight. Only a few regulars, hunched at the bar, give any indication of some sort of human presence.

"Take a seat," Paul commands me. "I'll place our orders for drinks."

I find a secluded spot: one that I've been meaning to try out for ages. It's a booth buried in a stone corner, cobwebs hanging over it like forgotten Halloween decorations. There's hardly any light and it feels colder than outside. I sit on the cracked leather bench and move around to the far side.

Paul returns shortly thereafter, two pints of stout in his grip. "Here we are," he announces proudly. "Here's your poison."

"Cheers." I wait for him to sit down before I raise my glass.

"Cheers," he replies. "Christ, James, why did you have to pick this shitty part of the pub?"

"I'm a man of mystery, what can I say?"

"That you are indeed."

"I'll be honest. I've been acting out quite a bit lately."

"I noticed." Paul smirks. "Your level of conversation has gone somewhat downhill. Anyway, mustn't fret. Mustn't indeed. It's to do with this martial arts nonsense, isn't it? If you want my advice, put the fists down. Put martial arts out of your head. If you cut that crap out, you'll find yourself feeling better. Believe me, I know what I'm talking about. You might not think I do, but believe me... I do."

"But will I truly be able to let this stuff go?"

"You can and you will. Step back, think, reflect. That's my advice. Take it or leave it."

Something about this makes sense. I lost focus a long time ago. Now, I've been put on the right path. The past months and weeks stretch out behind me. I see how I've gone wrong. Maybe not completely so, but in time I know I'll see the mistakes I've made. I know I've slipped up. If I'd reported my assault to the police, instead of engaging in this martial arts extravaganza, then maybe, just maybe, I'd be more normal.

4 February 1994

It's Siobhan's idea – maybe to inject some fun and excitement into things – but Paul and I both latch onto it: going out to this upper-class café in the city centre for breakfast. I suppose it makes a change from the usual.

Paul drives us in, his monologues about insurance enthralling us all. He's the bloke I know from the 1980s once again. He's the man who could command the world with the click of his fingers. The man I fell in love with.

The café is right next to Strawberry Fields. Paul has a moan about the local parking arrangements as he tries to find a place to leave the car.

Immediately, I'm struck by the presence of the café, totally in love with it. It's called St Catherine's, and it certainly lives up to the name, judging by the silky covers across the tables and the brittle glasses.

We're shown in by a smiling Asian woman, ponytail hanging straight down her neck.

Siobhan takes charge. "Hi, I phoned yesterday with a booking," she says. "Name of Casselden."

"Yes, we have you here. If you will follow me…"

We're taken to a table right by the window. Fresh orange juice is immediately provided for us and I can already smell the coffee brewing. The waitress provides us with crisp menus as we take our seats.

"You've certainly gone really posh," my wife remarks. "Siobhan, we're definitely splitting the bill."

"It's all on me," Siobhan insists.

"You sure?" I ask. "This is such a treat! I feel that we must contribute in some way!"

I suppose – looking back – that I shouldn't have been so argumentative. I should have lived in that moment. Had I known what happened next, I would have been more chilled out. Oh, how I've wished that I could have lived those few moments differently. How I wish!

Paul gets up from his seat. I don't notice the alarm in his face. I'm too ensconced in the battle for the bill. He moves past me in a flurry. I'm thinking he's going to the toilet or trying to hurry the staff up.

"Where's Paul off to?" Siobhan wonders out loud.

He's storming outside – part of me thinks he's tired of the arguing. He heads straight for a newsstand and lifts up a broadsheet, flinging over the pennies like he's got no time left.

"I think they've got papers in here," I say to him, when he re-enters the café.

"You need to read this," he tells me. "You need to read it. Now."

I scan the headline, but refuse to take anything further onboard. It's too painful to contemplate.

"What the hell...?" My wife snatches the paper from me, horror creeping into her eyes. She does it – something I wish she wouldn't do. She reads those awful words. *"The Secret Communist: How Josephine..."* She can't utter the surname. *"...Joined The EACM and Ripped It To Pieces.* James, look at this!"

"The EACM... that's..." Siobhan clutches her chin.

"It's the East Anglia Communist Movement," I tell her. "Collapsed in Eighty-Four." I sit back, shocked to the core. I'm taking a long glance at my wife. We're going to be on our way soon.

"Paul," I say, resigned, "have a lovely breakfast. We need to be getting home."

Herbert

4 February 1994

Well, this is certainly one for the books. I'm being genuine here – in case there's any misunderstanding. I'm sitting in an office, eyes flickering between Roger and George. They lean over the girls, who are sat like dolls before them.

Josephine – for once – is utterly silent. She hasn't issued a single word since she arrived.

It's Four in the afternoon, yet it feels like everyone's just emerged from sleep. No one will sleep tonight.

I can see the distress in them. See the heads in hands. See the look of shock and betrayal on Roger's face.

And what am I doing? Taking notes. Taking notes and daydreaming about getting back to America.

"You understand how serious this is," says Roger. He's cut out the various pages that the article appeared on, stapled them together with all the care of the world's worst teenager. "There's no way back from this."

"We really should have been told the full details of Josephine's involvement with this communist group," says George.

"How did someone find out about this?" asks Scarlet. "I mean, Josephine's always been very guarded about her personal life. She's not one to broadcast that kind of information."

"You're in the public eye now," replies Roger. "You don't have secrets anymore. My theory is, someone from this East Anglia Communist... whatever it is... has spoken out. Why they waited all this time, I don't know."

"I don't understand why this is damaging," says Gina. "The organisation wasn't illegal, it's been broken up. To be honest, all this article says is that Josephine was a member for a short while. I've read it twice over. There's nothing that suggests she committed a criminal act or broke the law or anything."

"That *is* true," says George, "but everyone associates communism with the Soviet Union. It's that association, that link, which makes things difficult. Roger and I can't tolerate things like that. We have to give serious consideration to our future partnership."

"You can't drop us over this!" snaps Gina. "Christ Almighty, there are far worse scandals out there to be caught up in!"

"Put yourselves in our shoes," responds Roger. "Try it. See what conclusion you come up with."

An argument ensues. I watch both sides fight and back down, rise up and lose. It's a pantomime for the lame. There are raging references to Josephine's teaching career, her numerous boyfriends, and everything in between. Eventually, the deadlock is broken – by the good woman herself.

"There's another way out of this." Josephine gets up, wipes away tears. "Drop me."

"Don't be stupid, we're not fucking dropping you," says Gina. "We're not, are we, Scarlet?"

Roger continues his speech, hands digging into the edge of the table. He says things so calmly that I'm taken by surprise. When I've seen him on television, he's always so stressed, so full of anger and focus. Yet now, he seems almost at peace. "The international tour is off," he tells them. "South Africa is cancelling your tour dates, and I'm pretty sure Australia and New Zealand will be following."

"If I left the band, would they reconsider?" Josephine is visibly trembling.

"It is possible," says George. "Though highly unlikely."

"Then get rid of me. Cast me to the side and forget about me. Put me out of your minds." She rises to her feet. Christ, she can barely move in a straight line. "See ya."

Gina calls after her, but it's too late. Scarlet shrugs her shoulders.

"As I said, there's no way back from this," says Roger. "What do you expect us to do?"

I watch the great man go to a dingy cabinet in the corner, yanking out a bottle of whisky and a dusty glass. He swears to himself, his thin form stiffening.

"I remember when I first met the lot of you," he says. "Didn't know what the hell to think. I believed that you were something different. I believed that you'd define a generation. I remember when it was the five of you. Now... Girls, I don't know what to do."

I stop taking notes. There's no way I can go any further. There's nothing more to put down. Nothing more to be said.

"We're done," says Miser, swallowing everything in one.

I stand outside, taking in what's just happened. It doesn't occur to me that this contract of mine might just fall to pieces.

A few cars pass by, their drivers oblivious to the drama that's happening in the building less than a hundred feet away.

Gina and Scarlet – I presume – are doing the formal paperwork. George sent me outside to wait. I suppose, as a writer, that's all you do. Hang around, waiting for the good stuff to happen. Waiting for the nonsensical bitchfight to break out.

They're taking way too bloody long. It's been half an hour. Can't take that long to sort the ruddy forms out, can it?

I'm craving a cup of coffee, begging for one in my head. Something to keep me going.

I take a few deep breaths, see that there's a guy selling rolls and cups of coffee across the road from me. There's no sign of the girls. I think they'll be a while. I fish a few coins out and head over. The bloke – way too overweight – nods as I approach.

"What'll it be then?" he asks.

"Black coffee. Do you have any bacon rolls at all?"

"I do."

"I'll have one of those."

I wait for my order to come, eyes on the doors to Roger Miser's headquarters. Is he still with that blonde piece? I keep wondering. When both pieces are in my hands, I find myself wandering in circles, anxious for the unknown to emerge.

It becomes an hour before I realise it, and still they have not come out.

"Should I just go fucking home?" I growl to myself. "Christ, I'm fucking going home."

I never had nonsense like this when I lived in America. Oh, here I go. Down memory lane once more. That bloody reggae singer and the time I spent in his home, listening to all manner of stories. I was young, handsome, fit. I was at my peak.

The doors burst open. Scarlet comes first, followed by Gina.

"A word," says Scarlet, pointing behind me.

Gina's walking off the other way. She's moving quickly, the kind of speed you would have if you were enraged. Not angry. Not annoyed. Enraged beyond belief.

Scarlet pushes a palm against the small of my back and propels me along. Coffee spills over my wrist as I nearly drop the cup.

"Christ, calm down!" I hiss.

She brings me to a stop, turns me to face her, and I look into those steely eyes that make no damn sense.

"You're still going to fulfil the terms of your contract," she tells me. "The band is still together. Well, it's been reduced somewhat. Gina's staying. I'm staying too. And so are you. We don't have Roger Miser anymore. He's dropped us. You will complete this contract. Did you take notes during that meeting?"

"Yes," I say sheepishly.

"Good. They'll be part of your final report, I imagine. You will be paid in full, that I promise you. That's what Gina and I were sorting out. Gina's not too happy about it, but you can't have everything."

"I'm gobsmacked, genuinely."

"Good." Scarlet grips my arm. "Right then, are you coming for something to eat, or not?"

She doesn't need to lead me this time. I blindly follow. One of her many drivers pulls up, right by where we're walking, and she tells me to get in, though not firmly this time. As we drive away, I take a final look at the record company building, but I barely see it.

Josephine

23 June 1984

He asked her the question, calmly, politely, with a degree of respectful sarcasm: "What made you want to become a communist?"

They were eating Chinese food. Not the takeaway standard, but rich and beautiful. A restaurant with too many stars in Sutton, all kitted out. Chopsticks so brittle that they threatened to snap in two. Wines whose vintages were beyond luxurious. She'd never experienced such things before. Here she was, locked in a trance of love and envy. Damn, she wanted him.

"I'm not sure," she replied. "I suppose that I've always had an interest in the communist system, how it ensures everyone gets the same opportunity."

"On your travels, did you ever get to the Soviet Union?"

"No, unfortunately."

"It's an amazing country. I don't think that I have other words for it. Stunning. Incredible. Their system works beautifully."

"I definitely want to visit."

"You may well get the chance." Will placed his chopsticks on his plate and dabbed his lips with a napkin. "I think you're a great communist, Josephine. Quite frankly, you are one of the best I have ever seen. You are passionate about people, dedicated. If it wasn't for my girlfriend, I would be dating you in an instant. Believe me. Let me ask you another question, if I may. How would you feel about a communist system in Britain?"

"I don't think it would be allowed. Thatcher might have something so say about it."

"But – assuming the EACM got into power – do you think such a system would work?"

"Yes, I think it would." Josephine took another sip of wine and smiled, trying to win his affections, though she knew it wouldn't push through.

"Good. There is definitely a place for you in our new world."

She was so focused on his flawless beauty, she didn't think about the meaning of those words.

"What made you go travelling?"

A question she could answer far better. "I've always had such a strong desire to see what was out there. I've always been an explorer. A wanderer. Ever since I was a kid. Mucking around in the trees and bushes. I've just had that Captain Cook sense of curiosity."

"Fantastic. What was your favourite country?"

"Madagascar."

Will leaned back in his seat. He signalled to one of the waiters. "Another bottle of this fine stuff, please." He shifted his weight forward and looked right into her eyes. "So, tell me about Madagascar then?"

"I'll admit that it was mainly spent on the beachfront. Loved it. Met a variety of interesting people. It's hard to describe it..." She was struggling with the words.

"It's okay," said Will. "It's okay, you don't have to finish. I can tell it meant a lot to you. The emotions are spinning around in your head. The memories. It's hard to process it all. I understand."

When the bottle was brought over, Will ordered it uncorked. "Best to let it breathe a bit," he told Josephine.

"What made you want to be a communist?" she asked.

"A lot of things."

"When did you realise it was the system for you?"

"Let's enjoy this dinner. Then I'd like to show you something." He raised his hand, summoning the same waiter over again. "I'll need to leave my car here tonight," he said. "I trust that's okay? Good."

They continued the meal without any further intensive questions. She found herself trying to suppress the smiles, trying to hold back the tides. He was suave, attentive, a dream of perfection. Her stomach was doing knots, dancing the tango.

After dinner was over, Will told another one of the waiters to organise a taxi. He helped Josephine with her coat and escorted her outside.

"What would you like to do now?" she asked. "I was thinking, we could go and see a film or something, if there are any late-night showings?"

"Come on, dear, you know I have a girlfriend. You know I can't just do that. There is, however, something I'd like to show you. Come with me. I've got a hotel booked for the night. Twenty minutes away. This will be worth your while."

Josephine felt herself swept up. Swooning. She knew that nothing about this made sense, that something was deeply wrong, but she'd fallen for him, way too hard. She was hurting for him, desperate to be with him. Desperate for just five minutes alone with him.

When the taxi arrived, he opened the door for her and tipped the driver straightaway.

His hotel was right in the centre of Epsom, a blustery spectacle of lights that seemed to outshine everything around it. In the years ahead, she wouldn't remember the trip from the taxi to his suite on the top floor, but she would recall the popping of the champagne cork and the way he escorted her to the sofa, his calmness as crisp as the bitterness of the drink he gave her. When she was bent and broken after a long day of teaching and being abused, she would think of this night, the bits that would come to her.

"What would you say if a communist system was installed in our country?" he asked her, when they were settled inside his suite. "Hypothetically, of course."

"Well, it would be interesting. Though I don't think anyone would vote them in."

"Do you think it would work though? Efficient?"

"I suppose – hypothetically – it would."

"What if – hypothetically, as you put it – a communist government were to be installed overnight in London?"

"How would that ever happen?"

Will smiled, poured them more champagne.

She found herself looking around the suite, although she would barely remember what she'd seen in the years to come. The marble floor, the shelves with their bottles of spirits and glasses, the chunky fridge where Will had retrieved the champagne from, and the silver cooler standing between their outstretched legs.

"Do you ever want to do something, really do something for the future? For your children? For society? For this country?" His tone had changed now. He sounded demanding, almost aggressive.

"Yes, I suppose I do."

"There's a small contingent of the EACM who want to do something radical for this country." Will put his glass down and stood up, began pacing across the floor. "The EACM is a great organisation, don't get me wrong, but the majority of its members lack ambition, motivation. In fact, communists across Britain lack ambition. I want to give communists their day. I want Britain to be a communist society, fair for all. Josephine, my dear, this small group of us want to take over, by force."

The fear hit her in the stomach, then in the neck. "What?" she stuttered.

"You're showing the same reaction my girlfriend had when I first mentioned it to her. There's nothing to be afraid of."

"Why would you do something like that?"

"Because I'm a man who loves radical change. Sometimes, one has to force that through. I learned that during my time in the Soviet Union."

"You're talking about... well, treason. How do you plan on doing this?"

"I want to know if you're in with me on this. Are you?"

"I honestly don't know what to say." She was perplexed, confused.

Many years later, she would look back on this moment, think about what could have been, the other path she could have taken. But in that moment, all she felt for him was deep love, widening with every moment, every second.

"I'm with you," she told him. "I'm with you all the way."

Will grinned. He came to her, wrapped her in a hug. She could smell his peachy aftershave, something which comforted her more than anything this world could offer.

"I'm in," she repeated.

"Good. Tomorrow, I'll pick you up and take you to our... operations centre, I think that's the appropriate word for it. There are two people there who you won't have met yet, as they're not in the EACM. But I know you'll get on well with them."

She was a trapped princess in a fairy-tale. Her knight in shining armour was prodding her with champagne.

"I'm in love with you, Will," she said. "I can't help the way I feel. I can't fight it." She fought against herself, but she couldn't hold it in. She jammed her lips against his, tasting his moist tongue, her nose brushing against his cleanshaven cheek.

He didn't pull away immediately, but when he did, the look of shock and regret was hanging from his eyes.

"Oh, Josephine, you can't just do that!" he hissed. "Josephine!"

"I'm sorry. It's just, I've loved you since the moment I set eyes on you. I can't imagine anything else! I want you! I need you!"

"Josephine, Josephine. What do you expect me to do?" He gripped her hard by the shoulders. "Oh, my dear, what should I do?"

"I'm sorry. I didn't mean to push things. You know the way I feel now."

"Look, Sally's part of this little group, I should make that very clear."

"It won't affect anything. I'm absolutely committed to this. I promise you. I will commit to this."

"Good. That's what I want to hear." He leaned into her again, planting a kiss on her forehead. "Now, I suggest you get home. Grab some semblance of an early night. I'll pick you up around Eight tomorrow."

24 June 1984

In fact, he was on time. She saw him pull up across the road from her bedroom window, his brakes squeaking. He gave her a quick wave and she bounded down the stairs, out of the house.

"Beautiful day, isn't it?" he said, as she got in.

"It is indeed."

He was wearing a grey breasted suit, with a scarlet tie. He had two badges attached to his fabric: the hammer and sickle, and a small image of Lenin.

He drove off, immediately diving into a monologue on the 1917 Revolution, as though last night had never happened.

They left Epsom, heading west, passing through Oxshott and Cobham, bypassing the north edge of Guildford. Saturday drivers, some with families, seemed to bask in the English sunshine, as though it was the only moment of happiness they'd ever known. When they arrived in Ash Vale, Will gave her a flash grin.

"Nearly here now," he said.

They turned off into a housing estate of some sort. Large tower blocks, rising like compound fractures, made her feel like she was an ant. The estate looked dead, beaten up. She saw a few lowlifes stumbling across broken pavements. A gang of skinheads, faces potted with self-loathing, stood around a pile of skateboards, drinking cans of lager. One of them nudged the grass with the tip of his Doc Marten.

"Right here," said Will. He'd stopped before one of the blocks.

"Canterbury Tower," remarked Josephine, eyeing the name of the building, hammered just above the first floor flat.

"Indeed. Let's head up to the top floor."

"You mean, it's up there...?"

"I bought the flat for our movement," said Will. "It's the perfect place to operate from. Believe me."

"You're going to leave the car here?"

"Yes." His confidence was concerning.

"But, it's not exactly safe, is it?"

"It's perfectly safe. I've done it a hundred times before."

He led her to the entrance porch. Cigarette packets and rusted cans nearly tripped her up as she followed Will into a lobby where graffiti coated every surface. The scent of urine and sight of several used condoms nearly made her gag. He hit the button marked up on one of the lifts and cogs somewhere began to whirr like the Soviet working apparatus.

"How can you have a headquarters in a place like this?" she croaked. "It reeks of piss!" She wrinkled her lips at the sight of a used need by her left foot.

"Trust me, it's the best place for it."

The lift doors opened. A black woman, plastic bags in each hand, trudged out. Her eyes lit up when she saw Will.

"Good morning, Mrs Gleeson!" he boomed. "How are you?"

"I am well, Mr Parson. How is your family?"

"They are well. Brian has just started this new job. Office worker, of all things."

"I am pleased to hear that. I should be going, Mr Parson. Have a wonderful day."

"I will indeed, Mrs Gleeson." He touched the woman gently on the arm, and then began to shepherd Josephine into the lift.

"How long have you based yourselves here for?" she asked, the doors closing on her feelings.

"You seem more interested in where we've situated our headquarters, rather than what we're all about."

They began to ascend, every movement a heartache. Every lurch a stab in the back of Josephine's feelings. She loved him and she couldn't have him. She adored him and she couldn't be with him. She needed him and he would never be there.

Used tissues, dirt and vomit clustered the floor of their little capsule. Josephine shut her eyes, trying to close out the horrors by her feet.

When the doors opened, Will strode out, she tagging behind him. They went along a stained carpeted corridor.

"Here we are," said Will, stopping before a door marked 1510. He knocked the wood firmly.

Sally was on the other side, her face beaming. Josephine had to watch the couple embrace, the joy in their eyes.

"Come on in!" she said to Josephine. "Come on now!"

Josephine did the right thing. She faked her own happiness at life, silently lied about her own joy. Anything to keep the pretence up.

The flat was another world. Not some poky shithole she'd imagined, but like one of those penthouses in New York. (She'd read a story about life in New York penthouses in a magazine, just before she'd set off on her travels.) Shiny wooden floorboards, smartly painted walls, several framed pictures of Lenin hanging on the walls, the scent of fresh coffee, the low hum of patriotic music. It had the scent and the feeling of a log cabin retreat.

"Everyone's in the lounge," Sally informed them.

Will led the way once more, barging through a glass door (made completely of glass) and into a room with red leather sofas, two Soviet flags standing either side of a large emblem of Lenin, and a table with some sort of a silvery tea set on. There were twelve others gathered, some of whom she recognised. The sofas were pushed up against the walls, with the table pitch perfect in the centre of the room. Everyone was dressed smartly, the males and females alike, smart suits, with the hammer and sickle proudly displayed on their jacket pockets.

"Take a seat," said Will.

Josephine saw a space appear between two women, their smiles begging her to join them. She smiled back, adhering to their request. She muttered a silent "thanks", and then turned to face Will and Sally, who were standing between the two flags.

"Thank you all for coming," he said. "I appreciate that this meeting has been hastily arranged, with only a few days of notice, and I know that on a Saturday, you would all rather be with your families, but the reason I have organised it is to go through our plans for the big day. And also, we need to welcome our newest member, Josephine."

Sally quickly took over. "We will change the world on the Thirty-First of August, at Nine A.M. That is the date and time where everything will change. You each know your position. You each know what you're supposed to do."

"I want to go through the plan one more time," said Will. "The night before, the Thirtieth of August, we will check into the Orion Hotel outside Euston Station. What is our official story? Craig?"

A man younger than Josephine, with eager, rosy cheeks, seemed to jump out of his seat. "We are attending a funeral of one of our dearest comrades."

"Excellent. Well done, Craig. At Six A.M. on the Thirty-First of August, we will meet for breakfast in the dining room of the hotel. What do we do after we have finished our break-fast? Diedre?"

The woman to Josephine's right spoke up. "We head to our rooms, retrieve our weapons."

"Excellent!"

"Sorry, weapons?" stuttered Josephine. "Weapons?"

"All in good time, Josephine, all in good time. At Seven-Thirty A.M., we will head over to Trafalgar Square, where I have reserved us a table for coffee. What is the name of the café? Michael, enlighten us."

"The Fishban Coffee Shop," said the oldest man here. He was rough around the edges, unshaven, light blue eyes, like glaciers.

"We will stay in the Fishban until Nine A.M. At precisely Nine A.M., we will leave the coffee shop, head straight to Downing Street. We go up to the gates, stand in front of them as a single line. Then I will give the signal to attack. Alesha, what is that?"

The woman to Josephine's left barked out a loud cough and stood up. "You will give a clear nod of your head." She spoke with a deep Welsh accent. Of all the beautiful communists in this room, she was slightly overweight, with bulging eyes and a rough ponytail.

"Excellent. That is what the signal will be. A clear nod of the head. When you see that, you take out your guns, and pour bullets through the gates. Craig, you will then plant your explosives and we'll blow it open. We go in, continuing to shoot. Shoot, shoot, shoot. We'll have them taken completely by surprise. We push forward going straight for Number Ten it-self. There's not much of a plan after that. We'll fill the whole building with bullets, kill that bloody Thatcher... You all have the full briefs on what happens next. You've all trained for it. When we're in control, we'll make a broadcast to the nation, explain what's happened. Tell them that this country belongs to communists. The way it should be!"

"Yeah!" a few of the audience cried out.

"Are you ready to become true communists?!"

"Yeah!"

"Are you ready to kill capitalist pigs?"

"Yeah!"

"Excellent! You're all great soldiers, true warriors, freedom fighters. You all hold a special place in my heart, a truly special place. We have chifir ready for serving. Make sure you help yourselves to a cup. And –"

"Sorry, but have you all lost your fucking minds?" snapped Josephine. "Do you have any idea what you're fucking playing at? Do you? You think you'll just be able to walk in there, shoot the place up, tell the country and the world that Britain's now a communist state? What about the British Army or the Ministry of Defence? What about the Americans or the French? You think they'll sit by and do nothing?"

"We've thought about that," said Sally. "When they hear our message which we will broadcast, they will come flying to our cause."

"I genuinely believe that many more people will flock to our cause," said Will. "In fact, I don't believe it – I know it."

"You're insane, all of you. You're fucked up." Josephine stood up, began backing away. "Will, don't do this! Please! Will, I love you! Please, don't do something stupid!"

"A new world beckons," he replied calmly. "We want you to be a part of this world. A leader in it. Come, now. Sit. Have some of this tea."

"Fucking no way!" she cried.

Two of them stood up, began to move towards her.

"Get away!" she screamed. She went for the door.

"After her!" someone shouted.

She yanked the door open, ran blindly, stumbling and tripping down the corridor. She reached the doors of the lift and her fist punched a slimy, greasy, sickly button.

"Please open! Please open!" she howled.

The stairwell was opposite. She should go for it. Thuds against the floor. A ping behind her and she stepped back.

Alesha's red face popped into view; she was gunning for the lift. The doors snapped shut in her face. Cogs, the machinery whirred once again. Josephine gulped as the lift began its descent. She was gripping the filthy floor, heaving. She watched the numbers on a faded electronic display slowly count down. She sprinted out as soon as the doors opened, running into the light of the day. She didn't look back. She kept pounding the ground. Did the gang of youths swear at her, call her a name? She would never be able to recollect. She kept going, eyes on the ground. Only when she had left the estate far behind, did she dare to slow, risking a glance behind her. Nothing was coming after her.

She started walking instead. Trickles of sweat clung to her skin.

"Everything okay?" a man asked. A kindly gentleman, flat cap and everything.

"I'm okay," she said. "Had to run for my bus."

"Take care. You don't look very well, lady."

She continued walking. She could feel that her shoes were broken. Cracked. There was a pain in her stomach, the discomfort of being hungry.

The terror was gone, but she was shaking out of love. Will, she would give anything for him. She was fighting back tears, gulping.

"I don't want to do this to you, I don't want to do this to you, I don't..." She gripped her hair as that phrase repeated itself in her head. She couldn't betray him. She couldn't stab him in the back.

She paced around in circles. She paced some more. Then she cleared her head.

Two Weeks Later

She found out the full, sordid details from the lead detective himself.

On a Saturday afternoon, he came over, sat down with her and her parents, evidently trying to be kind. He looked rough: someone who'd dedicated every minute of his working life to this job, someone who'd given everything, sacrificed his family. Burnt-out. Ruined.

Her mum holding her left hand, her dad holding her right, she listened.

"William Parson had been on our radar for some time, ever since he came back from the Soviet Union," the detective explained. "We had some idea of what he was planning to do. Several members of the East Anglia Communist Movement had expressed a few concerns about his extreme views. We knew about the rented flat in Canterbury Tower, but we couldn't prove anything. Couldn't even get a search warrant.

"When you came into the station, we had the cause to… pay a visit to the flat. Five of them were there and they knew that their game was up – they confessed everything. Over the next twenty-four hours, we managed to arrest them all at their home addresses, with the exception of William and Sally. We eventually tracked them to a…"

Josephine couldn't stomach any more of the acid truth. Sometimes the pain and the rage got too much, too bloody much. She half-heard about how William and Sally had holed themselves up at a farm near Plaistow. She didn't want to hear about how they'd blown themselves up, turning the farm buildings into dust.

She felt she was living their story, burning in the loss of the only man she'd ever loved.

For weeks, she cried. She lost the job at the office – in all honesty, she didn't care. The police would regularly fill her in regarding the investigation. Despite her name being cleared, the weight of guilt consumed her.

One day, she made a decision to go travelling once again, back to the tropics. Back to the ocean. But her parents told her that running away wouldn't solve anything. She needed to do something constructive, contribute, build a life.

At the end of the summer, she made a decision. She would right wrongs. She would save others. She would use the pain of her grief, the agony of her loss to help others. She would heal. She would look into the eyes of young people, try to get them to change their ways. She would teach.

Gina

6 February 1994

"I hope you understand my reasons," he says to me. "Right?"

"I'll pretend to. It'll take me some time to work things out though."

Brian Coffey, real name Brian Parson, smirks at me over the rim of his pint glass. He seems to have put on a little weight since I last saw him, and he looks much older as well. He's gone a bit greyer, put more red in his cheeks.

"I think what you did was fundamentally wrong," I tell him, trying to keep my voice strong, but I know it's splintering and he can see it too.

"Was it? You're very lucky that I haven't revealed something even more shocking."

"What could be more shocking about being a hidden communist?"

"Christ, Josephine was a member of the EACM for a very brief period, although she'd been having a few dealings with them beforehand. No, it's what happened after. The full story of what happened between her and my brother."

"Did you go to the papers for revenge?" I ask.

A few drinkers in this dingy East End pub glance at us. I'm not sure exactly where we are. When I contacted Brian, he gave me an address and even offered to pay the taxi fare.

"When you hear about what she did, you'll understand why I did what I had to do," he hisses in response.

"Your band kicked you out, didn't they? I mean, you've gone down in the world since I last saw you. Why would someone who'd risen to the heights be drinking in a shithole like this? So, I ask you again, Brian, did you go to the papers for revenge?"

"Yes!" he shouts. "I fucking did! You have no idea what she did. What she did to my brother and his girlfriend."

"Why didn't you go to the papers about that as well?"

"I can't. There are legal reasons why I would never be able to have that published. But I can tell you."

"Then fucking tell me."

"Why are you so desperate to know?"

"Tell me!" I yell at him.

"Both of them died because of her!"

"Your brother and his girlfriend?"

"Yes!" Brian's rubbing his chest. "Christ, they both killed themselves. They both killed themselves. They're both gone."

"It must have been hard for you..." Oh, here I go. Acting like a bloody counsellor.

"I need some fucking air," he says, shuffling to his feet. "Excuse me…"

I go after him. There's an unknown anger in me now. For some reason, it makes me think of Scarlet. He's wheezing, slumped against the door pane, arms folded.

"Hey, you okay?" I ask.

"I'm fine. Been under a lot of stress lately."

"Tell me what Josephine did."

Brian smiles. Tuts silently. Blinks. "She stabbed my brother in the back."

"Tell me everything."

Slowly, his story comes out. Bits and pieces at first, words and sentences coming together. I stare and listen in horror. I'm tempted to join the nobody drinkers inside, let my life turn to waste. I'm sickened. Betrayed.

"I won't believe it," I tell him, when he's done.

"You'd better," he responds. "You'd better. You coming in for a drink?" He lunges forward, hand on the inside of my thigh. "How about we go somewhere after? My place for instance?"

I bat his hand away. "Oh, fuck off. Seriously, you fucking creep, piss off."

He sniggers as he backs off, stumbling back into the haze of stale beer and cigarette smoke.

I reach Josephine's place in a fit of denial. I smash a fist against the door, calling out her name. When she doesn't answer, I yell it out.

It's only after ten minutes that I rest my forehead against the windows, using my hands to block out the glare. Her living room's been stripped bare. Everything. Bare shelves and scars on the carpet from the feet of those sofas.

"Josephine."

Mist from my lungs clings to the glass.

Marianne

12 February 1994

I'm not sure exactly what I felt when I heard that Roger Miser had pulled out. Yes, of course, a part of me was relieved – I'm not going to lie about that. I was sad as well. My daughter's dream was beginning to crumble, fall apart, dissipate. No one wants to see their child fail at something. Of course not!

Anyway, I'm having this somewhat lucid conversation with a colleague of mine, Polly Haven. We've both met for lunch at a local café near to my house. We do this occasionally. I suppose you could say that Polly and I have become friends.

"Sometimes, I don't know what to say or do when it comes to Scarlet," I say.

"I don't envy you. My son, Nick, is just like that. A dreamer. Wants to be a photojournalist. Travel the world. See the sights. He'll never achieve it though. I do worry about him. I really do. He is who he is."

"We should encourage them in their youth, whilst they don't have to bear any sense of responsibility. Whilst they're young and silly. Whilst they don't have the weight of the world on their shoulders."

"Poetic imagery, Marianne." Polly guzzles down the last of her soup, stares at me. "How is James doing?"

"He's a lot better, actually. I think he's finally snapped out of this karate nonsense. Thank Christ."

"That's good to hear. I was worried about him. It's good to hear he's back on the straight and narrow. Speaking of which, how's Alastair by the way?"

"He's doing well. He's moving to Vancouver next week."

"Oh, yes! For some reason, I thought it was at the end of this year. I suppose you have your Christmas plans made?"

"Absolutely. We're going to be looking at flights tomorrow."

"Excellent. Oh, how are Paul and Siobhan?"

"They're okay. We stayed with them for a couple of days this time, instead of going there and back in the one day. Well, we had to leave early because those allegations came out about Josephine."

"Now, that *was* something!" Polly fills out water glasses from the china pourer (a dirty, clay object so out of place with this establishment) and shivers. "Fancy becoming involved with bloody commies! Unbelievable! I always thought that Josephine was a bit shifty..."

"Did you ever see them perform live?" I ask.

"No, never got the chance. My daughter did though. Last year, I think. They're a very strange bunch, I'll give that to you. They only emerged, what, four years ago...? Three albums in four years."

"My daughter's a creative individual. Never could focus on anything. Always away with the fairies. And that godawful shack of hers... Abysmal. Dirty, vile, a bloody eyesore. I was glad when they moved it to that place in London."

"Yes, I heard about that." Polly sighs. Her makeup seems to twitch. "It must have been hard for you, finding out about Josephine."

"You can say that again. I kept the newspaper." I lean back in my seat, turn my head quickly, reach for my handbag. I fish around inside, fingers eventually clutching gold, turn, look up, and a familiar shadow passes my vision like an old curse. Christ. Bloody hell.

He's older now and the family that walks by his side shows how the years have cut into him.

"Are you okay, Marianne? You look in shock."

"Oh, I'm okay." I face Polly again. "Polly, dear, shall we get the bill?"

It turns into late afternoon by the time I get rid of her. We spend a good hour shopping and I get irritated with our third excursion around Woolworths. After seeing the latest high heels, I manage to see her off.

"See you in a bit!" I shout, giving a last wave.

Unfortunately, despite wandering nearly every inch of Sevenoaks, I don't find him. He's an old ghost, a disappearing act. When was I last saw him? 1976? 1975? An old boyfriend from university. Someone who told me he loved me more than anything. Someone who promised me the world. I told him to find himself someone better.

"You deserve better than me." Those were my words to him. Poorly chosen.

Regret tastes viler than lemons. It burns at your throat, cuts into your skin. The knowledge that I could have lived a different life, one of love and adventure, that hurts.

I find myself in the middle of Sevenoaks with my hands in my hair, trying in vain to hold back the tears. But he's gone. He's disappeared into the cold air with his family.

When I return home, I find my husband dashing around the rooms excitedly. For a moment – oh, Christ – I think he's gone back to karate.

"What is it, James?" I ask. I'm feeling grouchy.

"Nothing. Except..." His face breaks into yet another grin. "Except, I've managed to secure a contract in Canada. Pack your bags, Marianne, we're upping sticks!"

Herbert

7 March 1994

I suppose, really, this chapter should be called: *Twelve Meetings With Scarlet*. Though it is somewhat unclear. It implies that I'm the one having the meetings with her, rather than Scarlet having twelve separate meetings with twelve separate record producers.

The first meeting is in Camden Town. Two smiling old men receive her in an office that looks like the set of a Roger Moore Bond Film. They hear her case, how she'd be a valuable asset and all that. But they smile even more and politely decline offering her a contract.

As we walk out of their office, Scarlet gives a meek smile, huffs. She waits until I've finished taking notes and then head for the nearest taxi rank.

"I miss the limo," she remarks. "Oh, well."

Gina's silhouette appears ahead. She takes her time moving towards us. Tiredness lingers in her eyes. "What they say?" she says.

"They turned us down." Scarlet folds her arms. Her leather jacket crinkles. "Oh, well, to the next one."

Just then, my mobile phone rings. I mutter my apologies, fish it out. "I'm expecting a call from my wife," I say. "I have to take it." It takes me a few moments to find the button. "Come on, come on!" I hiss. "Ah, there we are!" I'll miss payphones! Whatever was wrong with them?!

"Hi, how are you?" my wife's voice croaks through the wires.

"Yes, everything's fine. You said you were going to call me about something?"

"Yes, I need to head over to Chelmsford. I'll be staying the night. It's for work."

"Oh, that's a bit lastminute, isn't it? Is it to do with that conference?"

"Yep. You know what the education sector's like."

"Okay, I'd better not argue, considering you're a head-teacher."

"Yep."

"What time are you back tomorrow then?"

"About Eight in the evening."

"Okay. I take it you'll be gone by the time I'm back."

"Yep."

"See you tomorrow. I love you."

"Love you too."

"Have you quite finished?" Scarlet asks me.

"Sorry," I reply, putting the device away.

"Good." Scarlet tugs at her frayed sleeves. "Right, let's head to the next one."

We head to Covent Garden, exchanging the orderly streets for art venues with their twists and turns. Scarlet leads the way and I follow several steps behind, at the ready to take notes.

The next record company has an office right next to Seven Dials. The two men running it are younger than Scarlet, much younger. I've heard a few things about them. The Leighton Brothers. Ambitious. They're focused on even younger, naïve artists, so I have heard.

As we enter their office, one of them tells a short tale about a lunch he once had with Tony Wilson. They sit us down, not in their office, but in their lunchroom, give us instant coffees each. One of them – the youngest – calmly tells Scarlet that the company has considered their proposal, but ultimately must reject it.

"We hope you understand," says the youngest. "It's nothing to do with your talent, which I know is totally superb. It's to do with your... affiliations. I'm sorry."

"Though we wish you nothing but the best." The eldest pipes up his friendly tune. "You are a highly talented group and we know you will do well."

The younger brother scowls at this last comment, almost baring his teeth.

"We should go," says Scarlet.

That's the way it continues.

The girls go in. I follow. Polite conversation follows. Sometimes over coffee, once over lunch. But it always ends the same way. A flat, firm rejection.

Scarlet's face gradually changes, from one that is hopeful and full of joys, to one that can barely focus, one that is blind to everything around her. After the twelfth one is done, she sinks to the pavement and grabs her own hair.

"You okay?" asks Gina.

"Not quite," replies Scarlet. "Looks like we're on our own."

I suddenly feel a sense of vulnerability. If they close down, I close down.

"Right, I need a drink." Scarlet stands back up, takes a deep breath, runs top teeth along her lower lip. "Then I think call it a day. You can go home, Herbert."

"But I think that this is a good time to interview you. The perfect time." I'm whinging like a kid, I know that. I shouldn't be so pathetic. But there are things you can never help.

"Go home," she tells me, sterner this time.

"I'll see you soon." I'm defeated. It's best not to argue.

"Have a night off from us." Scarlet seems to be composing a new song right in front of her. "You'll need your rest."

There's a stack of mail waiting for me when I get through the front door. Bills, mainly. The usual crap. The price of living in London. Though I'm earning more than enough to cover it all.

I get the coffee going and type up my notes for the day. It goes methodically and I find that I'm putting a little creative inspiration into it. It's almost as though there's a fictional band involved. Unreal concerts. Imaginary afterparties.

Scarlet and Gina are other people, very much different; better people. Damn, am I even saying that? Notes done, I shut down my computer and push back, screwing my eyelids shut. Everything stops.

The way my house is, I feel more alone than during my youth. My wife and children, they should be here. I find myself pacing the floors, as though I'm hunting for little people hidden behind coat stands and inside draws. (Honesty to God, I once had an idea for a novel on that. Something I'm glad I didn't follow through on.) I head to the kitchen, with the intention of taking out an extra bag of coffee, but find myself dashing back to the study.

I don't know why I'm doing this, but I go through an old storage box that's placed high on one of the shelves. It's from my last year as a fulltime music journalist.

"It won't be there, you silly old duffer," I groan to myself.

Old notebooks, hotel napkins, an LP, a ridiculous number of pens, and a whole other assortment of paraphernalia. Yep, it's gone. Of course it is. No... wait. Is that it?

The scrap of paper is stained, beaten up, degraded, mutilated. Oh, how poetic I can sound. How bloody so! I run a thumb over it, trying to think about what to do. It's my escape from London. My ticket out of here. My window to another life.

The guy who gave it to me said there's always an opportunity for someone like me at his magazine in the States. One hell of an opportunity.

I think about phoning the number, seeing what happens. Move the family out there, that's what I need to do. But loyalty is the second strongest force this world has to offer. I'm not going to abandon Scarlet, even as her band, as her world, falls apart. Even as everything collapses, I will not leave her.

"Put it away," I whisper to myself. "Put the thing away."

Alastair

15 June 1994

Dear Diary,

It's been something of a long day, you can say that.

This morning, I flew into Los Angeles, just as the sun was casting its first rays. Tomorrow, upon my departure, I'll also be flying through those early beams of light.

I took a taxi to the city centre, dropped my things off at the hotel, and then set off for Venice Beach. It took more than two hours to make my way there. The driver and I were sharing the anger and frustration, an invisible link between us, as the traffic stopped and started around us.

Josephine was waiting for me in the prearranged spot on the beach, right beside the skatepark, checking her watch. When she saw me, she folded her arms and narrowed her eyes. "Late," she said.

"Traffic," I replied.

"For a lawyer, that's a shit excuse." She uncrossed her legs and stood up, wiping sand from the backs of her legs. She came forward and embraced me, threw a hug around me. "It's good to see you again, Alastair. How've you been?"

"I've been okay."

"How's the job?"

"It's going okay. Lots of paperwork and all that. Getting used to the new legal system. God, you have to do everything all over again."

"Sounds a bucketful." Josephine looked around her, as though she had every moment at her disposal.

She'd changed. The annoying, quite aggressive woman I'd known had mellowed. Her skin, her eyes, her smile, all so relaxed and peaceful. Here she was, in a light blue dress, sun-shades resting in her hair, as though she was just another member of the public going about their daily business.

"Shall we go for coffee?" she asked. "There's a place just up the road."

"Absolutely."

We walked off the beach, moved along streets filled with surfing boards, joggers, streamers and loud music. Josephine led the way and I followed behind. She took me to a café sandwiched between two water sports shops; snorkels and surfboards threatened to tip from the edges. The café looked like one of the sets from *Back To The Future*, tables cut neatly to the edges, that classic American diner look. On the outside, at the front of the café, a couple of tables were positioned roughly on the pavement. Salt-bitten wooden things, they were a contrast to the orderly Cold War setup inside.

"I don't want to sit in there," remarked Josephine. "Too claustrophobic. Let's sit in the fresh air. Please, take a seat, what do you fancy? I'll go inside and place an order."

"Black coffee," I said.

"Excellent. We'll grab lunch somewhere else. Can't stand the food here." She smirked and went inside.

Two joggers shifted past, shadows passing over me. No smiles. I watched young couples and beat cops walk on by, eyes drowned out by the sun. This place had a feeling of paradise on Earth. Scarlet loved it, I know that much for sure. It was in this interview she did on the radio once: *"It was heaven, I don't think I've felt anything like it."*

"Won't be long," said Josephine. She sat down next to me, shifted her chair closer to the table.

"They don't look busy at all," I remarked. "I mean, considering it's..." I gestured outwards.

"You don't know this part of the world at all, do you?"

"I guess I have some catching up to do."

"That you do." Josephine touched my forearm. "So, thank you for agreeing to see me."

"Is this business or pleasure?"

"Business. Strictly business."

We stayed silent for a few minutes, as the world carried on in front of us. Two men in lawyer's shirts strode past in a hurry, jackets slung over their shoulders. There was a disturbance as our drinks were delivered: mine, a coffee not as hot as the day; Josephine's, a strawberry milkshake already decomposing from the heat.

"I'm free of it all," she said. "For a long time, I was trapped. Imprisoned by endless world tours and relationships that faltered before their first step. Now, here I am, with all the money I could want, in a place where the sunshine is always on. I just did it, Alastair, I just walked out. No one cares over here. No matter your background, no matter your tragedies. Everyone's like, 'We don't give a damn.' I can start again. That's what I want to do, what I need to do. I've decided to set up a music magazine."

"And you want to help me set it all up for you."

"Not exactly. Alastair, I want you to become my personal lawyer."

"Josephine, Josephine," I gasped. "I have a job, in Canada. A job I love very much. A job I'm good at. A job I know I'm meant for."

"I can pay well."

"I'm sure you can, Josephine. But... look... I don't know how to say this. Don't you remember that party? The one where you had that breakup? Christ, Josephine, I was worried – genuinely worried – about that escalating into a fistfight."

"Really?" The woman took a loud sip of her milkshake and her eyes seemed to wander straight through me. "Honest to God, mate, you need to get some perspective. Plight of the Third World and all that. Jesus. Look, I can pay you three times what you're earning now. All the perks. Fancy car. Five-star restaurants. You name it."

"But maybe I don't want that. All I've ever really desired is a normal life. Friends, family, a good career." I stopped in my path, knowing what I was about to say would hurt her a great deal. "I've looked into your world enough times to know I want no part of it. It's scary, it's disturbing. Drugs, violence, abuse. Why would anyone in their right mind want to step inside?"

She hesitated. I knew she realised that I was right.

"Then why did you fly all the way down here if you aren't comfortable with this world?" she asked.

"I honestly don't know. But I'll say this to you: take a step back. Enjoy life. Don't try to make your mark anymore. Have a milkshake on a day like this and just... relax. Like you said, you have enough money, you have enough of everything. You've earned a decent bit of rest and relaxation. Enjoy life."

With my speech made, I stood up, handed down a dollar bill. "This is on me," I said. "Josephine, I'm going back to my hotel, back to my life, back to my world. Take care of yourself, dear." I started walking away, just like that. I returned to my new life, a normal life of an expat, just like that.

As I mentioned at the beginning, it's been something of a long day.

Josephine

15 June 1994

Utterly useless. I smirk, watch the lawyer disappear into the distance, swallowed by the crowd. I allow myself to laugh, to rejoice for a few moments. The day's getting on. I should be going. I'll overheat if I'm not careful.

I cradle the remnants of my milkshake, twist up the dollar note that Alastair left and place it under the glass. I sit for a few moments, watch the day wear on, and then decide to head for home. I wander away from the sea, my eyes cast forwards. I'm not the person who looks down anymore. I'm not the girl who'll back down. Well, I've never been. I throw out a hand as a taxi passes by and its red lights shoot into life.

"Beautiful day, isn't it?" the driver asks me at some point during our journey. He's not the typical Angelino cab driver. Silver-haired and shrewd, he looks like he's been snatched from the world of academia.

"It is," I answer.

"The way they treated you was awful."

"What?"

"The British media. I read the story and I thought, What the heck? So you were a member of the communists in the Eighties? Who gives a damn?"

"Unfortunately, Roger Miser."

"Ignore him. He's an ass."

"I'll take that onboard."

He doesn't say anymore. That's the rule in this part of the world. No unnecessary conversation. He knows what he needs to know. Nothing more is needed.

Just then, my apartment block comes into view. It's five floors high and has that strange apparition, whereby it fits into the surroundings, but also alienates you when you stare at it too long. It's apparent marble-white surface reflects the viciousness of the sun's glare.

"Right here, that'll do," I say, handing over a few dollar bills. "See you in a bit."

I head inside, running a hand over the back of my neck, as if it will heal me from any sunburn I've got. I've downsized quite a bit. My top-floor apartment (not a penthouse) has all the amenities, comforts and extremities that I need.

The area I'm now living in, Pacific Palisades, is full of the well-off, but it lacks the attention-seeking celebrity cult. Here, I can walk along the street, have some coffee, smoke a cigarette, and no one will call me out. In Pacific Palisades, I've had the chance to truly disappear.

I'm on the top-floor landing, gently pushing the key inside. I hear the door opposite to mine rustle. A voice cries out to me: "Hi!"

"Sorry, you startled me!" I respond, but my tongue catches in my mouth.

I've seen her a couple of times in the local area, but I had no idea she lived here. She's tall, higher than me, with blonde hair hanging loose and a tanned complexion. She's got a smile that's kinder than charity and jeans that seem a little too tight on her.

"I'm Sanne," she says.

"Josephine."

We shake hands. She's got beautiful blue eyes. In many ways, she reminds me of Scarlet.

"I've just moved in," says Sanne. "Only two weeks ago. I used to work in the bank in Stockholm, then I got offered a job here. Working in America has always been my dream."

"So, you're Swedish then?"

"Is it obvious?" She grins with perfect teeth.

I don't know what to say. I feel like a childish idiot. I feel like I'm caught between two walls, slowly being crushed to death.

"I need to go and meet a friend for coffee," she says. "Catch you later."

"Catch you later!"

When the front door is shut behind me, I allow myself the right to curse at what an idiot I've been. I can't open my mouth when I really need to. I'll need to apologise to her at some point.

"Josephine, Josephine," I say to myself. "You're a big fool."

It's then that I hear my fax machine whirring into life. I dash through to my office. Well, it's a room with a desk in and a few other things. I'm hopefully picking up a new computer next week and then there'll be some rapid rearranging of the furniture. This is my new life and I'm going to make a success of it. The piece of paper is hanging out, flopping around. I yank it up, stumble.

It's a message from Gina. Her name is the first thing I see, scrawled at the bottom. It's almost like I'm subconsciously blocking the rest. It's a poorly worded message, written in a hurry. Roger Miser's dead. A stroke or something. She hasn't asked how I am.

I throw the fax down and head back outside. It's not that I feel anything; it's that I want to see if it's in the papers already. There's a store nearby that sells British papers. They usually have a copy of *The Telegraph* in. Guilty pleasures for an expat, I suppose. I take a fast walk to the shop. The heat presses down on me.

The guy behind the counter greets me with a heavily accented hello. I smile, slightly exasperated, worried even more so. I start perusing the newspapers and I don't even need to find the British ones. It's on the front page of every outlet. Roger Miser's face, eyes sharp. I could pick any one of them, but I select a copy of *The Times*, which promises reviews of Miser's life and times inside. I snatch a copy up and hand a few coins over on my way out.

Back at my apartment, I start reading furiously. I take in paragraph after paragraph, trying to make sense of the tragedy. He was found by his wife, dead and naked in the bathtub.

Emotions never play ball and today is no exception to the rule. I sit on the edge of my bed and I fall silent. With each passing moment, I turn another page and another and another. Every moment is a curse and a blessing. I find out things I didn't know about Miser: his early childhood in Yardley Wood; his first marriage; his very deep love for Elvis.

I hear my fax going again. I walk through and examine the message. It's from Scarlet. Only a few lines.

They're interested in us again. We're getting offers from record companies. You can come back if you want. Scarlet x.

"And why the hell would I want to?" I say out loud. I scrunch the paper into a ball and chuck it away.

I'm laughing now. I go back to my bedroom and resume reading. The opinions become boring before long. It takes a full five pages before I get to the other news. This new film *The Lion King* has opened up in cinemas – there's a small piece on it by an overenthusiastic moviegoer. A lot of other uninteresting stuff. I'm about to fold it shut when something catches my eye.

It's in the obituaries. There's an official one of the great Roger Miser, written by Herbert Buxton. All flowery and full of praise. But there's something else there, right at the bottom. If I'd read the paper in a hurry, I would have missed it. I peer in closer.

I don't know why, but I start reading it out: "*Hiram Merton, headmaster of Rainham John Graham Comprehensive School, has passed away at the age of Sixty-Three. With a career spanning more than four decades in schools across Britain and elsewhere in the world, he was known as being an affectionate and caring teacher, always going the extra distance for his students. He had the ability to push students beyond their limits, encouraging them to pursue their dreams. He never gave up on anyone, something many of his former students will remember. As well as a teacher, he was known for his support of trainee teachers, turning many of them into professional educators. He will be sorely missed by everyone at Rainham John Graham and no doubt by all those who have worked with him.*" I gulp. "*Hiram Merton. Born Fourth of February, Nineteen-Thirty-One. Died*

Thirteenth of June, Nineteen-Ninety-Four." I fall back on the bed, thumbs brushing my eyelids. "You bastard. You're gone now. You ain't coming back, you shit."

Emotion sweeps across me, digs into me. Hot tears flow. The last links with my past are beginning to die. Who remembers me now? Mr Vernon perhaps? The awful little shits I tried to teach? Even if they do remember, they probably couldn't care. Most of them have probably got kids of their own, stuffed away in some council flat. I couldn't care less about them. They mean nothing to me. They never did.

16 June 1994

The next morning, I'm woken by a loud thumping. Shouting through the walls. I sit up, alarmed, thinking that there's an intruder or a mugging. I jump out of bed, running to the front door. It's coming from just outside, right on the landing. Carefully, inch by inch, I open the front door.

It's Sanne, furiously grasping her doorhandle, shaking it and yanking it. She is – presumably – swearing in her native tongue.

"Are you okay?" I ask.

"I'm fine. Just, this door. Can't open it whatsoever. A nightmare."

She's in running gear that's soaked through. Beads of sweat trickle down her bare shoulders. She's muscled all over, well put together. Her blonde ponytail brushes against her turquoise running top.

"Hold on, let me help out." I can see that she's got the key jammed in the lock. Gently, I clutch the handle, rotate the key, and it begins to open. "I think you were turning the key the wrong way."

"Oh, that explains it!" she exclaims. "Thank you so much, Josephine!"

"No worries."

"Thank you, thank you! Listen, I'll catch you later, I need to get a shower and go to work."

"Sure, catch you in a bit."

As soon as I'm inside, I realise that my focus has gone. Literally, I can't concentrate on a single thing. Christ, she's cute. Not that I'm inclined that way! Though I'm slightly tempted. Just a little bit.

The day wears on and I find that I don't end up doing much. I take a walk and get another paper, but there's nothing new about Roger Miser. Just a few more trips down memory lane with other patrons of the music industry. Lead singers of bands, solo artists, even sound technicians. Everyone's got their own personal story, their own encounter. And these little stories fill the papers. There's even one from him... Mauro Lane. Patronising git. Self-centred piece of writing on how his *casual relationship with the great man altered* his *pathway*. Arrogance, utter arrogance.

17 June 1994

The next day, I switch on the television after lunch and find myself face-to-face with the police announcing that O.J. Simpson is a fugitive. A warrant has been issued for his arrest. There's a part of me that thinks this might be a film, but the seriousness on the police officers' faces as they're briefing the media tells me that this is deadly serious.

Despite this, I'm thinking of Sanne. Today has been hard. When I woke up, it was a matter of curiosity. Now, it's starting to hammer at my heart. What the hell is happening? I'm not... inclined that way. I'm not one of... those...

Later, much later, I watch a live feed of Simpson fleeing from the police. I don't look at it for long, because I'm running from something else.

Look, I'm not one of those closet homosexuals, one of those tragic celebrities who've spent their life hiding away, and now they're having their moment of awakening. I'm not one of those. All I know is that I can't stop thinking of her. Yes, yes, I'm sexually attracted to her. And it's not right, I know. Of course it isn't.

I go out by myself to a local steak restaurant for dinner, order the tastiest meat on the menu and a glass of the most expensive wine – red. Thoughts of her become more extreme in my imagination and it gets to the stage where my food tastes of ash. Everyone around me is whispering about O.J. Simpson, but I'm shouting about Sanne in my head.

I want her. I need her. Already the images of us living happily together are popping into my head, refusing to leave. She's so beautiful and sensual, it's unreal. By the time I get around to paying the bill, I'm already fantasizing about getting physical with her.

But when I get back home, all pretence is gone. I hear activity behind her door, footsteps, but I don't have the courage within me to go and knock and invite her over for coffee. Instead, I become a weak sock and sidle back into my apartment, shutting the door.

Later that night, another fax comes through. Gina's begging me to come back. I reply almost immediately. *No thank you.*

18 June 1994

I wake up with regret in my chest. But I have a determination to make things right. I'm like Roger Miser on a Friday evening.

I do something out of the ordinary. I put on my running gear and set off. I can feel the warmth of the sidewalk through my trainers. Around me, there are other female joggers, stuck in their own worlds. I know Sunset Boulevard is like this: full of isolated runners. When I get back, I'm hunched over, wheezing. I look at her door, think about knocking, decide against it, head into my own home. Deep breaths. That's what I'm telling myself.

I take one of these organic breakfast things that have become popular and fresh green tea, and then watch the day turn from orange to yellow from my balcony.

Maybe it's time to be impulsive. I dash back inside, get a pen and paper, scribble out a note. *Dinner sometime? Josephine.* I nip across the hall and pass it under her door, then scurry away like the bit where the prisoners escape the camp in *The Great Escape*. I'm more of a Richard Attenborough than a Steve McQueen.

An hour later and she still hasn't responded. I'm braced for it, ready for the inevitable punch to the gut. I mean, all my relationships have been a disaster so far, why should this be any different? Wait, no, I shouldn't be thinking like that. It's not even a relationship. I don't even think I'm asking her out. I'm just a bit curious.

Eventually, I get bored and venture out. I think about knocking, but think better and decide on my favourite coffeeshop instead. I drink two espressos, one right after the other, watching lovers arm-in-arm and hand-in-hand walk past, gazes fixed at the floor and one another. Everything is in its place.

The café I'm in is only ten minutes' walk from my apartment, but it feels like it's in a different world. That's what this place is. It's not one community, it's many, all lumped together into a collective. There's a feeling of the constant unknown. Never knowing who you'll meet or where you'll end up. It's the nearest place to paradise there is.

I'm alone, but that's not necessarily a bad thing. I came here to start again and that's what I'm going to do.

I pay the bill – or, the check – and slowly return home. Yes, that's it: home. Not that useless, grey island, but here, bathed in the sunlight. This is home.

When I open my door, my left shoe catches something and slides backwards. I nearly topple forwards. I nearly swear a little too loudly, but I manage to right myself. There's a slip of paper on the floor, a perfect square of white that's been stained by the dust from outside.

Oh no.

Gingerly, I reach down, expecting the full punch in the face of that two-letter word. But...

Yeah, I'd love to! Tonight? Sanne.

I'm over the landing in the blink of an eye. Knuckles pound on the door. She answers in a silk dressing gown. Her hair's ruffled up, shaken like a moth. She looks sleepy. There's no makeup, but she doesn't need any.

"I'm sorry, did I wake you?" I say.

"It's okay. I went for an afternoon run and took a beauty sleep afterwards. Why I look so tired! So, yes, dinner tonight?"

"Yeah, absolutely. About Seven?"

"Sounds great!" Sanne yawns, showing perfect teeth.

"There's a cool place nearby." I'm thinking of the steakhouse. "Are you fussy about food?"

"Not particularly. We Swedes like any kind of food there is!"

"Good. I'd better get on the phone, get us a table sorted. I'll pick you up, say, at Half-Six?"

"That would be great!"

I give her a quick wave, turn away, glance back just as her door closes.

Christ, have I done it? Have I got her? Or maybe it's wishful thinking.

I want to jump with joy, but is this too good to be true? I slow myself down, start thinking methodically, pick up the phone, dial the restaurant, secure a booking for two.

The rest of the day passes in a daze. With every moment, with every millisecond that passes, I'm finding it harder to breathe. I try some yoga postures I learned, but nothing helps.

The moment comes like a freight train and punches me so hard I have to wash my face before I go to the door. I'm in a t-shirt and light jeans – am I underdressed?

"Damn it, Josephine, put something nicer on," I complain to myself.

No time. I hear the door opposite opening.

Deep breaths. I start walking to the exit. Even deeper breaths.

She's waiting for me in a dress code that seems copied from that catalogue I was considering launching when I first moved out here. A brief flight of lustful imagination. She wears a white shirt with open cuffs and green leggings that stop short of black ankle boots.

"Hi!" she says.

Her hair's uncombed. It hangs like the definition of neatness, straight down on three sides.

"Love your hair!" I exclaim. "What products d'you use?"

"None," she replies. "I have natural Scandinavian hair." She flashes her teeth. "Shall we?"

"I hope you like what I've booked," I say, as we leave our apartment block.

"I'm sure I will, but the company is what I'm forward to the most."

"Me too."

"It's not far. Just around this street. Actually, I think you will like it. You're a red wine drinker, I take it?"

"Absolutely!" She stops me where I am, a hand on my elbow.

"Good! There's a vintage you need to try. I'll order us a bottle."

I'm completely stupefied. Struck with numbness. I gently run my left hand on hers, smiling as hard as I can.

"I'm famished," she whispers. "That's what you English say, isn't it? Famished."

The restaurant is nearby. I can smell the fumes of sizzling meat.

She walks ahead, as if she knows the place better than me. I follow behind, entranced, totally absorbed, too focused.

The steakhouse is brimming with people. I can see their heads from the sidewalk opposite, bobbing up and down, teeth in their food. I know now that it's my turn to take charge.

Suddenly I begin to stagger. Memories of a meal with Eugene come back. Didn't he take me to a steakhouse once? A way to thank me for all the love and support I gave him?

The restaurant is rectangular, long and slim, with its tables arranged in exact places, lined along the walls, edge to edge, corner facing corner.

The waitress – who I've learned is called Eugenia – greets us with a smile.

"You know who I am!" I say to her, trying to be witty. This is one of the few occasions when my sense of humour is recognised.

Eugenia rolls her eyes and directs us to a table. She hands out leather menus. They're so smooth, it's as if they've been custom made just for us.

"I'd like a bottle of that wine I was having last time. Can't remember the vintage... If you could get that and two glasses." I gesture for Sanne to sit first.

"I know the one you're talking about," says Eugenia. "I'll sort it out for you. Don't worry. Just relax. Act like you're on vacation."

"I like it," says Sanne, wrapping her hands around one of the tealights on the table. "It's a beautiful restaurant."

"I'm happy I've met you."

"I'm happy too." She pulls away, but her framework seems to relax. "So, I listened to your music. My God, you guys were really good! I know about what happened, with that communist nonsense."

"Ah, I should have mentioned that earlier."

"Oh, don't worry. To be honest, Josephine, I don't care. What happened, that's in the past. All I know is that I'm happy I have you."

Eugenia reappears, holding the blessed bottle in her hands, like it's Christ reborn. "Your wine," she remarks. "I've uncorked it and it's ready for you. Shall I pour?"

"Go for it," I say. "Sanne, what do you fancy having?"

"Medium-rare steak," she tells Eugenia. "With everything that comes with it."

"I'll have the same."

We both hand our menus back at the same time. I think we're both pretending to look past one another, but I'll never be sure.

I don't pay attention to how good the wine is. Or even if it's the right one. I can't – literally can't – take my eyes off the angel in front of me. The way she's bathed in candlelight, the way the rim of her glass touches her lips and her eyes still make contact with me, I don't care about what's around me.

"So, you're from London," she says. "Is it a cesspit like they say it is?"

"Not exactly. There're some nice places. The Mall. Embankment. Actually, there's a small grove right in the middle of a housing scheme. It gave me a lot of comfort during the dark times."

"Do you want to talk about it?"

"Not really..." But I find that I want to. I spill the beans and spill everything else. Robert. Eugene. Marco. And all the other boyfriends. The hurt. The bitterness of the backstabbing. The sleepless nights where I clawed at the pillows, digging like an animal.

"Shit, I'm sorry," she says, when I've finished. "Men, eh?"

I hear a whisper from behind me. Something along the lines of: "That's her! It's definitely her!"

"What are you doing next week?" asks Sanne. She lifts up the bottle, leans in closer, appears to examine it, pulls away.

"Not much."

She puts the bottle back down and leans forward, her sparkly eyes centimetres from my own. I feel her fingers slide over my own.

"I'm going away next week. Elko. It's a town in Nevada. I'm going to meet up with a contact there. I've been thinking of starting up a consultancy business. I'm going away Tuesday night, coming back on Saturday. I was thinking, would you like to come along?"

"Yeah, absolutely! I'd love to!"

"It's about ten hours' drive, so we'll need to head off very late on Tuesday night," she whispers.

"We'll share the driving."

"I didn't think you rich people drove!"

"I'm not like other rich people."

Our conversation seems to hang from a tightrope, not pointing in any direction. We talk about anything that happens to be worth discussing: the L.A. Riots, the latest paperback releases, the weather, the best wines, Bill Clinton.

I find that the steak is tougher than the previous night and the wine tastes sour. I gradually relax, but my throat refuses to loosen.

She's so beautiful, too beautiful for me.

"Do you fancy taking a walk?" She puts her knife and fork at 180 degrees on the plate.

I haven't realised that everything is gone from my circle of porcelain. I raise my hand, snapping my thumb and forefinger, that all-American signal, one of impatience.

"You bet," I respond.

I hand over a generous tip as we walk out. It's chilly. For a moment, I believe that I'm back in London during late October. Actually, it's like that January at Rainham John Graham, when it was so cold that I started losing the feeling in my fingers. Actually, maybe it was because of the little thugs abusing me at every bloody opportunity. Well, perhaps a lot of things caused my fingers to go numb. At least now I'm with far better company.

"We need to have a little chat as well," says Sanne.

Gulp. That's the response, isn't it? The appropriate one? The one you use when you're about to be horribly, atrociously rejected.

We walk and we walk some more. I'm getting the feeling she's in a hurry. Her shoes are sounding heavy on the floor, as though they're digging to the core.

"Sometimes you can barely look at me." Her tone's changed. She sounds stressed, angry, as though she's annoyed, as though she has the greatest hatred towards someone. "And I'm wondering why. You like me, don't you? But you're scared, terrified of coming out. You can't admit that you're a lesbian."

"I don't know what to say."

"Listen. Listen carefully." She puts her hands on my waist. Her eyes... so soft. "Do you want me? Truly?"

"Yes," I reply. "You're what I want."

"Then prove it."

"How?"

"Kiss me."

"Let's go back to mine."

"No, here."

"Kiss you here?"

"Yes."

"But..."

"Yes, we're in public. And it's here I want you to kiss me."

"Shit." I jump forward, pull her close, shove my lips against hers. "I want you, Sanne. I fucking want you."

"That's more like it!" She throws her arms around me. "We're not having sex tonight, I'm going to make that clear. If you want me, you've got to commit to me. There is no easy path." She holds out her hand. "Take it," she whispers. "Take it. Prove it to me."

I don't feel nervous, not one bit. I'm surprised. I'm afraid of this change that's taking place within me. Afraid of what might happen.

Our fingers link and I'm so scared of looking into her eyes. I don't want to face up to the fact that she might feel the same way I do. I don't want to feel I have to trust. I don't want to feel. But I'm starting to cross the boundaries between us.

People stare at us as we walk, but they don't gaze our way for long. This is Pacific Palisades and everything goes here. I'm not afraid anymore. I don't think I'll ever be afraid again.

21 June 1994 and Onwards

The past few days have been a total bliss. We've been out for coffee, taken strolls along the streets. Normal couple stuff. It feels strange to be so normal, so everyday. To be able to fit in.

Sanne's been adamant on us not pushing things too far too fast.

"We need to take it slow. It's imperative that we take it slow."

It's a phrase that repeats like a broken record, over and over again without a single interruption. But I find it cute. Actually, it's oddly arousing.

Sunday night she came over, and I cooked her dinner: a stir-fry with any number of things randomly thrown in. We ate it on my balcony, watching traffic and people pulsate through the night. Our hands linked like copper chains, we allowed the world to go on below us.

Just being next to her fills me with something that's indescribable. I'm truly happy with her. More than I've ever really been.

It's the night of our departure to Elko and she knocks on the door exactly when she said she would. Two large, hefty leather bags, one in each hand.

"Ready?" she whispers.

I hoist up my rucksack with my little finger. "Everything I need."

"Good. Right, let's head to the car."

When we've left the lights of L.A. behind us, Sanne starts whistling. I'm presuming it's an old Swedish tune, a tale of romance and adventure.

"You have a beautiful voice," I tell her.

"Thanks."

"I'm ready to go to the next step."

"And what would that be?"

"We're going to be sharing a bed. I want to do more than fall asleep with you."

"I know. Let's see how things play out."

I want to say that I'm able to stay awake, but my eyelids are heavier than iron ingots. I think I doze off against her shoulder.

I wake up to one of the brightest days I've ever known.

We pull into Elko just as shops throw open their doors and car engines giggle into life. I'm still as sleepy as shit and barely notice Sanne swing the car off the road, pulling us to a firm stop in front of a motel.

"Come-on, sleepyhead," she taunts. "Your room awaits."

I follow her across the carpark to a small hut marked *Reception*. Letting her go inside, I try stretching, but quickly realise that I'll cancel my ineffective yoga membership.

She seems to be arguing with the guy behind the desk. I don't think anything of it... until she starts jabbing a finger at me. I've never seen her angry before and it's not something I want to get used to! Her hair flops in every direction, flicking around like wet spaghetti. I'm about to see if she needs help, but she suddenly hands over a wad of notes. She comes out, throwing her arms in the air, sighing, saying a few expletives towards the sky.

"You okay?" I ask.

"Yeah, yep," she mutters. She's got the bags gripped tight. Her pale Scandinavian skin turns extremely white around the knuckles. "We're in Room Fourteen."

The motel has two storeys and our room is on the first floor, right at the end. She leads the away and I follow blindly behind her.

"I've seen the movies," she says. "You know, when the bad guys are on the run and they hide out in places like this."

I'm not used to this basic nature. All my hotel rooms have been filled with the latest glitz and glamour, with bowls of fresh fruit and chilled champagne. I've always had room service five minutes away, and all the company and solitude I could possibly need. This has a bed and a shower room.

"Listen, I need to meet with my contact," she tells me. "I'll be a couple of hours. Grab some sleep. I think there's a diner down the road if you want some breakfast."

"Okay, sure."

"I'll be as quick as I can." She leans in, kisses me.

I wave her off at the door and sit down on the bed. I fall backwards like a brick, curl my feet up to my chest.

The next thing I know, Sanne is sitting next me, leaning over.

"Hey, sleepyhead," she whispers, planting a kiss on my nose. "You know what time it is? It's nearly Eleven!"

"How long was I asleep for?"

"A few hours. But I bought us breakfast."

"What –?"

"Bagels and muffins, and coffee." She points to a few paper bags on the floor. "Come on, tuck in, my treat."

"You fancy going out tonight?"

"Love to!" She ruffles my t-shirt, shoving a kiss on my neck. "Actually, there's this great place I know. It's a quick walk from here. Great seafood. I take it you like seafood?"

"Yeah, I love it."

"Cool." She leans close, rests her head on my chest. "I'm happy with you."

"Me too."

"Right, you. Breakfast."

I don't think there's any way to describe the next two days. We spend every moment together, never a second apart. We take walks, drink coffee, eat food, fall asleep. I have to admit, I was a bit unnerved when we first shared the bed together, even though there was no physical contact beyond a close cuddle.

I think I'm beginning to fall in love with her. I don't know why this is, considering I barely know her. I guess some things just refuse to make sense.

In the hours we spend in Elko, I find that I'm forgetting about my past life. The band, the concerts, the afterparties – it's almost like they belong to another person's memories. It wasn't that long ago I was talking to Scarlet's brother about launching a magazine. Another time. Another life.

On the Friday night, something changes. We're both buzzing from the red wine we've been guzzling all night. We enter the motel room, me thinking about sleep before our long drive back. Her hands are on me like vices and she gently swivels me around to face her. I'm trembling, but I've never been so sure of anything. Every last barrier between us drops.

We're on the road back to L.A. before the sun's had time to rise.

"Beautiful little city," she remarks, as Elko disappears in our rear-view mirror.

"Not as beautiful as you," I say.

"You're too kind."

The empty road opens up before us. We're swallowed by the darkness.

"Fancy doing dinner tonight?" I ask.

"Maybe." I can hear her swallow. "The thing is, I'm not sure if I should."

"What...?"

"I can't be with a woman who refuses to let things go."

"What do you mean?"

"I can see it in you. You're refusing to let things go. It's in your eyes."

I'm protesting immediately, even though she's shaking her head. "That's bollocks, Sanne!"

"It's not and you know that. Whatever happened in your past, you have to let it go. You have to release it all, put it all behind you."

"I've done it. I promise you, Sanne, I promise you."

"Then prove it."

"Just tell me how to!"

"I want to see how you respond to this." Sanne slows the car. She drums her fingers on the steering wheel, looking like a disappointed angel. "Josephine, I love you."

"I –"

"Before you say those words back to me, think about what they mean. And be fucking sure that you mean them."

"I don't need to think. Sanne, I love you too."

The car gradually comes to a stop. No rush on the breaks. A gentle, smooth grinding on the wheels. Her hands are still on the wheel. All I can hear is her breathing.

"Do you really mean those words?" she whispers.

"Yes. With all my heart."

She leans over, digging elbows into her belly, pursing her lips, fastening them around mine. "I trust you. This is the start of something new."

"I feel the same way."

The next three weeks seem to pass in countless moments. I can't believe how quickly I'm allowing myself to grow close to her, but I can't stop.

In the evening, when she comes home from work, we go for meals and drinks in bars. And she refuses to allow me to pay. I try arguing, but I give up. At the weekends, we dine in some of L.A.'s finest restaurants, and then we go dancing until the early hours, coming home just as dawn breaks.

The days begin to blur into one another, like jam and marmalade. She takes her holiday allowance and we use it to fly out to Hawaii, visiting every island in the chain. No one notices us, no one stares. We kiss in a street in Honolulu and not a single person utters a remark. We go swimming and make love in the ocean. We hike and have photographs taken in each other's arms. No one cares.

When we're back in Pacific Palisades, we resume our routine of dining and clubbing. Sanne has to go away for a quick meeting in San Francisco, something she insists on doing by herself, but she's back a day earlier than she planned, and her smile is brighter than ever. She tells me that she's done a massive new deal for the company she hopes to launch someday. In celebration, she takes me out to this new Latin restaurant that's opened up in Malibu. It's a Wednesday night and we make the stupid mistake of going clubbing afterwards. By the time we get back to our apartment block, it's time for her to get ready to go to work.

The summer begins to draw to a close, but we soon focus on planning our winter holiday. Sanne wants to take me to Sweden to meet her family and go up to the north of the country. She's thinking of renting a cabin up there, where we can have a private few days after Christmas.

"Trust me," she says over dinner, "my parents are a handful! We'll need a few days to recover from them!"

On the first day of September, I receive a letter through the post inviting me to New York for an interview with a magazine. I'm a bit reluctant to accept it, but Sanne persuades me. Actually, she's really insistent.

We part ways in front of LAX, sharing a simple kiss.

"See you in a few days," she says.

"I want this to be over and done with."

"And it will be sooner than you think. Come back to me as quick as soon can."

"I won't be a second longer than I need to."

We kiss again, fingers linked and parting with an electrical suddenness.

In New York, I'm met by the deputy editor of the magazine, who drives me to the hotel himself. On the journey through the thronging traffic, he tells me the story of how the magazine came together. Two college friends on a drunken night out in the late Seventies trying to chat up girls: somehow the idea sprung from that. The idea grew into fifty copies of what was supposed to be a one-off edition of a music review magazine. Ten years later, it was a major player in the industry, attracting music journalists from all over the world. Herbert Buxton had even done a couple of pieces for them. It's an interesting story, but I get bored when he keeps going on and on about three writers he believes should have worked for the magazine.

It takes me a while to recognise the hotel, but then it all floods back. The Olympia Restaurant. The lobby. The busy, almost chaotic atmosphere. I keep expecting to turn around and see the girls, eager smiles and trembling fingers, ready to strike chords and blast out music. But all I see around me are businessmen and lawyers.

When I check in, I ask the girl behind the desk if Mr Bellini still works here.

"He left last year," she informs me. "Works in Canada now, if I'm not mistaken. Anyway, your room..."

Later, I do the interview and get ferried back to the hotel. It's on the journey back that I realise I've been truly forgotten. Everyone's going about their business. Everyone's trying to make their name. I already made my name – and a scandal as well. Now I can disappear into the crowd.

I don't know how I pass the rest of the day, but somehow, I get through it. Somehow, I wind my way through the hours, somehow occupy every single second.

The next day comes and I'm taken back to the airport. All I'm thinking about is her, getting back to her. Falling asleep with her.

She's there to meet me at the other end. We embrace, cuddling like we haven't seen one another in years. She's bought herself a new car. A four-by-four. She laughs and jokes about it: "Something the new deal's given me!" She tells me about this deal as we drive back: "It's already bringing in so much money!"

When we get back, I make a proposition to her. We're in the hallway, at the point of no man's land between our apartments, and I'm desperate to tell her. I was thinking about it in New York, but no it's threatening to spill over the edges.

The words catch in my throat, but I eventually blurt them out: "Sanne, do you want to move in together?"

She's got her key in her lock and I can tell she's biting her tongue. "Is that really what you want, Josephine? You really want to make that kind of a commitment to me?"

"Yes. I don't need to think about it. I know it's what I want. I know this is how I feel. It's what I truly, deeply want."

"Then let's do it."

"I love you, Sanne."

"I love you too, Josephine."

It's October and there's a definite change in the weather.

I take runs in the morning – maybe it's a tribute to Susan, maybe it's not. In the evening time, I take walks, sometimes with Sanne, sometimes alone. But I'm happy, truly happy. I've got Sanne. I've got the best companion I could ever hope for.

We continue our routine of dinners and clubbing. I know that I'm becoming the woman I've always known I could be.

She showers me with gifts and she tells me that she loves me more than anything. I do the same, but I try to go the extra mile. It becomes a sort of competition: who can give the most. But there's no need for a winner.

We've completed the paperwork and she's moved into my apartment. We're thinking of buying a house, but we're not in a rush. For the first time in my life, things are actually working.

One day she sends me to get a few groceries, but when I get to the store I find that I've left my purse behind. I quickly dash back, and find a startled Sanne standing semi-naked in the lounge.

"Sorry, forgot this," I say, lifting up my purse from its regular resting place on the coffee table.

"Ah, shit," she says.

A semi-naked man emerges. He's perplexed, astounded, face opened wide. Then his lips turn into a crooked smile. "So, this is her then?" he says. He's got black, dirty, ragged hair. He looks fit, but his body is covered in gruesome, green tattoos. He wears jeans with every known stain and a smouldering joint threatens to burn his knuckles.

There's a moment where we all pause and we don't know how to proceed any further. We stand in a triangle of insecurity and unknown emotions.

"I asked you a question, Sanne!" the man shouts. "Is this her?"

"Yes, this is her," says Sanne. Her head bows itself.

"Fucking hell, couldn't you have done better?"

"There's nothing wrong with her."

"She's a total fuck-up, Sanne! Don't you know anything about her? All the shit she's done? Haven't you read what was in the fucking paper earlier this year?" He puffs his joint and the stench fills my throat. "Anyway, I don't give a shit. You dykes are a fucking mystery to me."

"Josephine," whispers Sanne, "Josephine, I'm so sorry."

"Is this a joke? Did Scarlet come up with this?" It's a pathetic line from me, but it's all I've got.

"No. This is real. Josephine, I'm so sorry I deceived you. I'm so sorry. I can't imagine what you're feeling right now."

"Why?"

"She was a drug dealer," the man tells me. "How the hell do you think she paid for everything? The new car? The expensive meals? Did you really believe it all?"

"That's enough, Dan." Sanne jabs a finger at him. "Enough!"

"Fair, fair." He raises his hands in the air, a mock surrender.

Sanne comes towards me, holds me by the shoulders. "Josephine, I'm truly sorry."

"All of this was a lie?" I stutter. "All of it?"

"Josephine, I'm a businesswoman, and my boyfriend is my business partner."

"This can't be happening." I'm falling back to 1991, when I woke up to find Robert packing his things and just fucking off. "This can't be fucking happening! Sanne, I love you!"

"I'm sorry. That shit I said in the car, I know I shouldn't have said it. I was curious about what it was like to be with a woman. Oh. Hmm." Sanne takes a step back, looks at Dan, turns back to face me, plummets into laughter. "Fuck, I don't know why I'm being so caring! Josephine, you really are a slut in the bedroom? Jesus!" She takes a bottle of beer off Dan and raises it up, downing it quickly.

"Honest to fucking God, Sanne!" shouts Dan. "Don't swallow it so quickly!"

"We're heading to Mexico," says Sanne. "Retiring there. Putting our feet up, as you Brits say. You've really given me a lot of moral support over the past few months, babe. I hope you know I appreciate that."

"What if she talks?" says Dan.

"She won't. She loves me too much." Sanne comes close, brushes a finger down the bridge of my nose. "You won't tell anyone, will you? Of course you won't." She sticks her tongue out, lashes it back in. "Bye."

"Hold on..." says Dan. "We've not got everything packed."

There's some shuffling about as they gather their things and leave. Both of them give a silent wave. When they're gone, I head into the bedroom, expecting to find everything ruffled and ruined; but it's all so neat and, respectful. It's almost as if they genuinely care.

I go out for coffee and come back. I knock on Sanne's door and am unsurprised to find it swing open, revealing a flat stripped of everything, even the carpet.

I go back into mine, dig out the phonebook and send faxes to Gina and Scarlet. I'm coming home. That's the gist of my message to both of them. I'm returning. If they want me, they can have me. If not, then that's fine. Within the hour, I hear from them both. They both desperately want me back.

The heartbreak hasn't hit me yet, but it will soon enough. Even as the tears fill my eyes and tickle my jawline, I don't break down. Even when I'm sitting at one of the bars that we used to frequent, downing my fifth shot, I don't feel the betrayal. When it reaches me, it will pull me to the ground, drown me. Right now, though, right now, I'm focused. I'm focused on going back to where I belong.

I'm coming home.

A week later, by which time the apartment has been sold and I've got a hotel booked for a few weeks in London, I'm waiting in the early hours for the taxi to take me to the airport. It seems like I'll be standing here for hours, but the cab spots me in the distance, seems to race towards me.

"Airport, please," I command.

"Good to see you again!" says the driver. "You won't recognise me, but I gave you a ride a few months back."

"Oh, yeah, I think I remember you," I reply, as we set off. "Actually, could you take me back? I'd like to see the place one last time before I leave. Take me once more around the place."

"Know exactly what you mean." The driver takes us down a street, then another one, then another, and we're soon coasting past the apartment block. "Didn't work out then?"

"You could say that."

At the airport, he drops me in the exact spot where Sanne once saw me off. I briefly look around for her, but I realise if I do that, I'll be spending years doing it.

I need to get out of here. I should never have come in the first place. I should never have allowed myself to fall into the trap of believing that someone genuinely cared about me.

Why didn't I see it? The trip to Elko: Why was she carrying those two large leather bags and why didn't she bring them back with her to Los Angeles? The lifestyle should have raised alarm bells as well. She always insisted on paying for things, never allowing me to treat her. Sometimes when we went clubbing, I saw her talking to well-dressed men. Only for a few moments, mind you. I assumed that they were hitting on her, but the formal handshakes and nodding of heads, and the secrecy, all makes sense now.

I did nothing except make a stupid mistake. I saw what I wanted to see, not what was there. I saw only the beautiful hair and the soft eyes, not the shady behaviour in the background. I don't think I'll ever really forgive myself for what happened. I don't even think I'll ever fully understand.

Gina

19 October 1994

She's changed. Wow, she really has.

She's lost some of the fat around her waist and her eyes seemed to have gained a new sparkle. She emerges into Arrivals with thicker, stronger, heavier steps. A few people stare our way, but it's Scarlet they seemed focused on. Not Josephine. And Herbert Buxton's ten feet away, at the ready to make notes.

"Girls, how have we been?" she asks. She kisses me hard on the cheek and slaps Scarlet on the elbow. "Hey, Herbert," she says to our writer friend.

"It's good to see you," says Scarlet. "I'm sorry you couldn't make the funeral."

"Oh, well, I'm not much good with that sort of stuff any-way. Thanks for picking me up from the airport, by the way."

"Driver's outside," Scarlet tells her.

We plough our way through the crowds of Heathrow through to the mad rush of taxis. Our car is not one of the luxurious, smooth limos, but a taxi with *Pre-booked* written above the windscreen.

There's not even an offer to help us with the bags. Huffing and groaning, Josephine does it all by herself.

"How was America?" I ask, as we clamber inside. "We've selected our new record company. Nice group of people." I mentally pause, collect my thoughts, continue. "We definitely want you back."

"And here I am," she replies. "I'm eager as anything to get started."

"You're okay and everything?"

"What about? You mean, all that communist shit?" She smirks. "Honest to God, I'm okay. Though, I'm amazed that you want me back."

"That's the way the industry works," says Scarlet.

"You sound like Roger Miser."

We're getting close to the hub of London. There's some sort of children's street party happening. It's a bit too early for Halloween, so why are they all dressed up in those costumes? Oversized pumpkin suits and extra-large skeleton outfits stand out like pinpricks against the grey, smoky atmosphere.

"So, how's the world of writing then, Herbert?" asks Josephine.

"Oh, just bits and pieces at the moment." He looks up from his notepad. "Hopefully, I'll have a good article to put out there."

"Let's talk about it over lunch."

"You haven't got time to relax," says Scarlet, leaning over her shoulder. Somehow, she suits the front passenger seat. "We've got a gig coming up. Up in Edinburgh. Saturday, Twenty-Ninth of October."

"This is news to me!" I exclaim. Actually, I'm really pissed off. Since we signed with this new record company, Scarlet's taken on decisions for herself, doing whatever she wants with the band, putting us up for five new albums and deciding on their themes. She's even written some of the tracks.

"Better get practising," she tells us both. "It's our come-back special. Right, Josephine, we need to drop you off at your hotel." She turns to face the front again.

I mouth *fuck* at Josephine, who smiles back and shoots up her eyebrows.

The car pulls to a stop in front of The Savoy. I go out with Josephine. I tell Scarlet that I'd like to have a catchup with her at some point, see how she's holding up. Scarlet decides not to join us. She's got work to do, apparently.

"How have you been?" I ask Josephine, as we head into the lobby. "Now we don't have the other two to worry about."

"I've been holding it together. It's been a rough ride in the States, but I'm better now. Just need to relax, stick my feet up, try to switch off for a bit. I'll get there in the end. I'll bloody get there. Hold on, be a minute." She goes up the reception desk and starts checking herself in. When she comes back, she invites me up for coffee.

"Can you believe it, I have to get approval from manage-ment to take you up to my room?!" she exclaims. "Dear God...!"

Herbert

29 October 1994

After breakfast, I get a few moments to myself to go over the notes I made yesterday. We flew up yesterday, and, be-tween armfuls of champagne in the lounge at Heathrow, I managed to get a few sentences down on paper. With a cup of instant coffee in my cramped hotel room, I make notes on notes, trying to get down anything else I might have forgotten from the boozy trip up.

I'm aware that this has to be turned – somehow – into an article for a magazine. And not just the scrawls I've made these past months, but the pages and pages I'll generate over the next two-and-a-bit years. It's all got to come together and I have no idea how it's going to happen. Is this the same feeling I had when I wrote my first novel?

The girls are planning to go on a daytrip around Edinburgh before the concert tonight. I'll be accompanying them, ten paces at the rear.

I feel as though I've been living several lives this year: my own emotions, Scarlet's, Gina's. Even when Josephine was across the sea, I had this connection to her. Since Roger Miser's funeral, these bridges have only grown stronger. Is it that I'm a father figure to them? Or is it that I'm desperate to have daughter figures?

There's a knock on the door and Scarlet doesn't even wait for me to answer. She barges in, face pale, cigarette fumes filling the space in front of her.

"Ready?" she questions.

"Always."

"Then let's go."

I snatch up my notepad and pen, shadowing her, following right behind.

Gina and Josephine are waiting in the lobby. The renewed sense of fame and recognition is slowly but surely hitting them. I can see it in their faces. That feeling of not knowing what is what, who is who. The band has only been apart for a few months, but they look like they're reuniting after ten long years.

Josephine's carrying a map in her hands; it's dangling from her fingers like a flab of skin. "Anyone fancy trying out one of the local cafes or something?" she asks. "They do good coffee round here, so I've heard."

The others aren't impressed. They shrug their shoulders. They'll go along with it, but they seem dismissive. I watch them begin to file out, whilst innocent onlookers don't participate. I make a few notes, but stow the notepad quickly in my coat. I don't know how, but I just know it's not the right time for words.

The girls are reminiscing about their early days. They're walking side-by-side, with Scarlet in the middle. This would be the perfect photograph, the most beautiful image you could ever get. But it lasts for an instant and then it's gone.

We stop at a café on Canongate. I think I recognise it, the dome-shaped cups and the very fragile glass windows. I think I took a faded rockstar in here once for an interview, years ago. I sit on a separate table, with cooling mint tea served to me, watching them talk about the night ahead and their fears and dreams. My pen flickers against the notepad, though I don't there's anything from today that I'll use for the grand finale.

"Why don't you take the afternoon off?" Scarlet says when we leave. "I mean, we're not going to be doing much. Just going to lunch and seeing a few sights."

"That's gold material," I reply. "Trust me, I'm never bored with this sort of stuff. This sort of stuff, grabbing coffee, having lunch, the everyday stuff, is exactly what the readers will want."

"Suit yourself."

Of course, dear reader, I am bored. I'd rather be at home, readying myself for a trip to the pub. But I'm here, with a group of girls I barely know, following them around the city. Of course, I know this will be a gem for the final article, but I can't help the fact that I don't feel I belong here. I'm thinking once again of America. The only place that ever felt like home.

Scarlet

The truth is, she's realised that this city reminds her of lost love.

She leads the group from trinket shop to trinket shop, but she's always looking elsewhere. She's thinking of him. She expects him to appear from nowhere, to forgive her. But what she did to him was unforgivable. She should never have kicked him away. He'll never come back. He's away in America, a new life at his disposal. He'll never come back, not in a million years.

Mauro told her once that he'd come here, to Edinburgh, for a childhood holiday, said every minute of it had filled him with joy. Yeah, he'd told her the story during one of their Saturday night evenings at home, a luxury Chinese takeaway and a bottle of the finest red in front of them.

"How did Miser's funeral go?" asks Josephine.

"It was okay. Big Church service, then we went to the crematorium. Then to his home. Big send-off. Champagne and everything. Quite a gathering. Very convivial."

Actually, it was a nightmarish episode. George got pissed beyond belief: three glasses of champagne and a whole bottle of Miser's whisky. A drinking competition erupted at some point in the afternoon and by evening the entire place was ripped to shreds. Scarlet stayed behind to help Roger's widow tidy up. There were some tears and a few cuddles, followed by the two of them opening up one of Miser's prized bottles, followed by them waking up naked in the same bed the next morning. Of course, it didn't go any further than that. There was too much pain, raw wounds cut too deep.

But she doesn't tell Josephine that. How can she? It's a step too far.

Gina

I think it's too soon for us to be back together, but I don't have a say in things anymore. I've given up even trying to take charge.

We spend a few hours exploring the cobbled streets of the Old Town. There's a cute little garden we visit, built right into the side of the street, which we're unable to get into. Scarlet takes particular interest in it, particularly as to why it's only open on Sundays. She mutters obsessively about it for a few moments, before we decide it's time to move on.

We visit more trinket shops, get our photographs taken in different places, and soon find ourselves in need of lunch.

"I know this really cool Italian place," suggests Herbert. "It's a bit of a walk, but you know, it might be right up our street."

"Have you been there before?" I ask.

"Once. About ten years ago."

"Fuck it, why not?" says Josephine. "Is the food any good?"

"It's okay. Not first-class, but it's okay."

"Let's go for it," says Scarlet.

We pass young families, tiny stalls selling useless crap, a few bagpipers, an Asian performer throwing something ridiculously high in the air and catching it on a piece of string. We cross the big bridge that overshadows the train station. On the opposite side, we find ourselves trapped by a protest; it takes us a few minutes to succeed in our liberation.

The restaurant's an obscure-looking building. If I've got my history right, it was once a townhouse for the wealthy. Three levels: two above ground, one below.

"The Mother Rome Restaurant," states Josephine. I don't know if she's displeased or severely impressed. Everything's the same with her.

"Come on, girls, let's see if they have a table!" chides Herbert. "Come on!"

Okay, it's not as luxurious as I remember, but the smiling waitresses in white shirts and the gruff-looking man standing at the back with his arms folded behind his back give the restaurant a sense of order.

"Do you have any availability? For four?" asks Herbert.

"Yes. Please." One of the waitresses has now approached us and is guiding us to a table in the corner. I don't think her English is very good.

There's a couple at the table next to us, hands linked, eyes locked on one another.

"Let's get a bottle of wine for the table," says Josephine. "Your best Italian red!" she commands the waitress. "Four glasses."

The girl nods, eyes down. She tells us in broken English that she'll be back for our orders in a few minutes.

"Nice place, Herbert," remarks Scarlet. "Okay, I'm impressed. Seriously."

The couple next to us are talking about the man's job. I learn that he's a lecturer down south and he's thinking of taking up a position in Glasgow, though he's not so sure about it. The woman replies that, as she lives in Glasgow, she expects a definite commitment from the man. She doesn't sound too happy about it.

If we didn't have money, we would consider the prices in this place very dear. Even though the menus have been stacked on the table and not handed out to us, even though the cutlery has a tiny bit of dust on it, even though it takes ten minutes for the wine to come back, and even though the wine is not allowed to breathe before it's dumped in our glasses, this is a place of moderate luxury.

I order lasagne and the others order spaghetti. Herbert has spent five minutes convincing them that spaghetti is a must for eating out in an Italian restaurant.

There's little bit of hostility next door. The woman is questioning, interrogating the man. I can't help but listen in.

"Look, all this stuff about you being a lecturer in journalism, it sounds too good to be true," she's telling him. "Do you actually have a job?"

"Of course I do!"

"But it's not adding up for me," she replies. "What about this thing in Glasgow? Have you actually been offered a position up here?"

"That I exaggerated a bit on. I've messed this up, haven't I?"

"You did. You know, I was really hesitant about breaking up with you, but I'm now glad that I am! You're a dick!" She stands up, kicking the seat behind her, storms out.

The man quickly jettisons some money on the table, runs after her.

They confront each other on the pavement outside. He's throwing his arms up in the air, presumably trying to explain himself. In one, viciously swift movement, she strikes him across the face.

"Now that was a proper bitch slap!" says Scarlet. She slams her hands violently on the table and laughs out loud. "Fucking hell!"

"How are you girls feeling about tonight?" Josephine asks us. "You nervous? You should be! This is our comeback special!"

"How do you think they'll receive us?" I ask. "Scarlet, do you think the audience'll applaud? Or tell us to piss off?"

"I don't think that'll happen," replies Scarlet.

When the food arrives, I don't think any of us have any appetite. It's a labour to get through it, especially as Herbert continues with his notetaking. But I begin to think that the reason for our tight stomachs and anxious, dry mouths is because of what tonight will bring.

Only one person heckles as we emerge onstage, but they're quickly drowned out by the most loveable crowd we've ever had. We stand in the limelight, and so do the backing musicians, and there's a little bit of muttering between us as we get set up.

We break into our opening song – from our first album – and the crowd roars even louder. I think we've met their approval.

"You need to up your game!" Josephine tells them, when the song is done. "You need to up your bloody game!"

Scarlet

30 October 1994

She waves them off at Edinburgh Airport and heads towards the taxi rank, unaware of the many pairs of eyes checking her out.

It's going to feel strange, travelling alone once again, but this event has been on the books for a couple of weeks: she's being interviewed on a local radio station. The new record managers thought it might be a good idea: she should spread her roots to the smaller figures.

She can't even believe that the Leighton Brothers have snapped up the band, considering the way they initially cruelly rejected them. But the band is safe and allowed to prosper once more.

She thinks of a lot of things as she rides a taxi to the city centre, but there are many other things she'd rather didn't exist in her life. Many other things she'd rather cast to the depths of her dark imagination.

She checks into a new hotel just next to the railway station, on the edge of the Old Town. It's the most basic place she's stayed in for years: a single bed, a kettle and assorted teas, and a handwritten notice which states breakfast starts at Seven A.M. and finishes at Nine. She quickly brushes her teeth, debates whether to have a cigarette, but slurps some water instead.

She takes a brisk walk to the radio station, where she's met by the producer, who doesn't offer her any refreshments whatsoever. She's surprised at how brief the interview is – less than twenty minutes. A few questions on the upcoming album and how they're coping with the revelations around Josephine. When she's done, they all give her a polite smile, tell her that she's been a wonderful guest, and then show her to the door.

As she slowly wanders back to the hotel, she feels a knot inside. It's the realisation that they're not big players anymore. Of course, their albums are still being bought and they've got another record deal, oh yes, but they're no longer adored and wanted by every soul out there.

She's not too sure what to do for dinner tonight. She's got no friends, no companions, no one up here to sit down and have a coffee with. She's got the loneliness of a walker hiking along the edges of a cliff, but the appeal of a dancer on a stage in New York. She opts for a takeaway: poorly cooked pizza and a coke. Not once, as she stands inside the kebab shop, does anyone ask if she's that singer. She detects a flicker of recognition from someone next to her, but she's invisible in here.

She knows before she even gets back to the hotel that she won't be able to sleep tonight. She takes a walk, stops somewhere for a drink, has a photograph with a couple of eager fans, but finds herself unable to do much else to alleviate her frustration.

She needs to kick some life into all of this. She phones up Josephine and Gina, but can't get through to them, leaves messages instead. She asks them both, politely, that she would appreciate any contributions and ideas that they might have for the next album.

Herbert

3 December 1994

I'm caught in the worst downpour ever. Just as I step out of Hillingdon Station, I narrowly avoid a fresh soaking from the heavens. I quickly take shelter underneath a canopy that once protected the coffee place here – before it was closed down by the local council.

I'm holding two heavy bags of Christmas shopping: wine, boxed pastries, chocolate biscuits, cans of beer: a typical Christmas at the Buxton's. I start whistling to myself, relieved that I've got a short break from the band.

They're good girls, all three of them. Bright little things. I've tried repeatedly not act like a father figure, but I have to admit, I'm doing it more and more often. I care about them. I'd go to the end of the world for them.

The rain begins to die off and I decide to chance it, walking the half kilometre to my house. My wife is heading out as I pass through the door.

"Just off to visit May," she informs me. "I'll be back in a while. Dropping some Christmas presents off. The kids are away for the day."

"Got some of the Christmas goodies," I respond. "Fancy going out for a meal later or something?"

"I can't," she replies. "I'm really sorry, but I don't know how long I'll be at May's."

"It's okay. We'll do something another time."

"Okay. Sure. Listen, got to go. See you later."

I quickly disassemble the bags and stumble through to my study. In less than an hour, my notes from the past two months are fully typed up. I do a quick check on all the writings I've made over the course of the year, file them away in my precious manila folder, and realise that I'm ready for the holidays.

I settle into the living room and crack open a bottle of red wine. A 1989 Bordeaux vintage. I let it breathe, smell the fumes. After a few moments, I partially fill up a glass, and fall back into my armchair.

I should probably give George a call at some point. I know that he was like a brother to Roger. Since the funeral, he's become withdrawn. He runs the record company, though not very well, as they keep losing people. I don't think he's cut out for the job.

I hear the front door click open. My wife calls out my name.

"In here!" I say. "Living room!"

She comes in, still in her overcoat, throws a newspaper down at my feet.

"How's May?"

"I didn't go and see her."

I lift the bundle up. Oh, drat, it's not a newspaper. I'm holding a brown folder that's held together by greyish string.

I'm cursing at myself, wondering what I did. Who the hell is suing me?

"I need you to sign them," she says to me. "I need you to do it right now."

"What the hell...?" The stem breaks in my hand and the wine spills. The stain will never come out of this chair that belonged to my grandfather. "Divorce papers?! Sorry, Audrey, is this some sort of joke?"

"This has been coming a long while," she tells me. "Herbert, I can't be with someone like you... And I think you know it hasn't been working..."

She moves into a lengthy monologue, detailing how she's been having an affair with another headteacher for months, how she believes that her children need a stable father figure in life, not someone who writes "silly nonsense" for a living, how she needs a fresh start, that she doesn't love me anymore, that she's glad that we gave it a go, but it's time for us to both move on. She'll always treasure what we had, but she can't keep things together anymore. She wishes me luck and she's quite happy to let me keep the house. She just wants her freedom and a few books and ornaments, but she'll leave me everything else. I'm to have no access to the kids.

What else can I do? I'm like Tristram Shandy – in my view, a weakling. I put my signature where it's needed, and then get another glass from the cabinet. A refill later, I allow the shock to hit me.

Well, I was never a family man. I go through to my study, yank up the phone, call Gina.

"*Oh, shit,*" she says. "*Are you okay?*"

"I'm fine. I just need you here. I don't know why, but I need you here."

"*I'm on my way.*"

"Come as quickly as you can."

She ends up arriving late in the afternoon, around Five. I've had a couple more glasses since then and I feel mildly tipsy. I fake a smile as I welcome her in.

"You okay?" she asks me.

"I'm fine," I answer back. "Actually, my wife left me, but apart from that, I'm okay."

"Oh, shit. Are you drunk?"

"No!" But as I say this, I stumble backwards.

"Herbert, I need to go," she replies.

I reach after her, but she ignores me, disappearing through the door. I try to rise up, fall back, find myself identifying patterns on my ceiling.

1995

Josephine

5 May 1995

I've been putting it off for weeks, but it's come to a point where it's now or never. As I enter the restaurant, I think about chickening out and dashing back to my flashy new apartment in Chelsea, but something inside me tells me to take this chance. I can always back out later.

Gina's set this up. I don't know whether she feels sorry for me or if she genuinely wants to help.

The restaurant looks vaguely recognisable. I think Roger might have taken us out here once. In the early days.

One of the waiters approaches me. Does he recognise me? I think so. I think there's some familiarity in his smile and the way he blinks.

"Hi there, I have a booking," I inform him. "Someone called Gina made it."

"Ah, yes," he replies. "Come with me. Please…"

My date tonight is someone called Jason. He runs a small import and export company; it's headquarters are situated somewhere in the forest of Canary Wharf. We've already met briefly, when Gina introduced me to him in March. He's attractive: tall, shortcut hair, shaven. I don't know whether I could be in a relationship with him, or whether I even want to give it a go, but I suppose it doesn't hurt to have dinner.

The waiter shows me to a table at the back, where Jason is already sat, a glass of water in front of him. He stands up and places a kiss on my cheek.

"It's good to see you," I say. "I hope I wasn't too late."

"No, it's okay. I was early. Please..."

"You're such a gentleman!" I swallow a deep breath as I sit down. "What are you drinking? I'll order us something."

"No, please, let me..." Jason pulls the waiter to the side and whispers something in his ear. There's a quiet nod from both sides and then my date sits back down, fiddles with his cufflinks, and asks me how my day's gone.

"Oh, nothing much," I say. "Went over cover design for the next album cover with Gina and Scarlet, and then went for coffee with a friend. Apart from that, it's been a fairly quiet day."

"When's your next album coming out?"

"They're aiming for a November release."

"Wow." Jason leans forward. "I ordered a bottle of this restaurant's best red. I want to make this a very special evening."

"What vintage?" I ask him.

"Surprise."

"So, what made you choose this restaurant?"

"Actually, it was Gina that suggested it." Jason looks up as the waiter brings over the bottle. It's uncorked with a soft plump in front of us. "Chateau Nenin. Nineteen-Eighty," he tells me. "Very good vintage."

Our respective glasses are filled up to a quarter. I'm about to reach for mine, but Jason raises his hand, tells me to let it breathe properly.

"You can't rush art," he says.

"It's going to be a long evening," I reply.

"So, what got you interested in music?" asks Jason.

"I've always been doing in on and off. Then about five and a half years ago, Scarlet got the five of us together in this small café, where she proposed the idea of a band. To be honest, I thought it would crumble at the first hurdle, but..."

"Interesting."

"I'm digressing a little bit. I should be asking a lot more about you."

"No, please. I want to know about this band. You said there were five of you. Sorry if I sound ignorant. I'm not exactly engrained in the music world. I know very little about it!"

"I started with Scarlet, Gina and myself, and two other women, Susan and Emma. Emma walked out and moved to America before the band had even properly started. Susan was murdered. Stabbed to death."

"Oh, I'm so sorry. When did it happen?"

"Two years ago."

"It must still be very painful."

"You could say that. But what's in the past is in the past. Susan was never the one to quit on things. Never the one to back down. She was stronger than most people in this world."

"You don't have to talk about this if you don't want to." His hands touch mine.

"She wouldn't want me to be talking like this during a date. Let's enjoy this evening. Who knows where it might lead? But let's enjoy what tonight has on offer. And let's have some of that wine."

"I think I can manage that."

I find I enjoy the company. He seems like a nice guy. Gracious. Caring. Full of laughter. Attentive. Beautiful.

When we part for the evening, I feel elated. So much so that I tell my taxi driver to stop half a mile away from my new home, giving me the excuse to walk. I take in London's moist air, breathing it deep, feeling it fill my blood.

As soon as I'm in, I pick up the phone. Jason doesn't answer, so I leave him a message: I definitely want a second date with him.

But it's later that night, as I lie facing the ceiling, my heart pounds so fast it turns to jelly.

It's too good to be true. He's too loyal, too handsome, too gentle. I don't deserve someone like him. What the hell does he see in me?

He hasn't phoned back. I know he's probably doing the same as me right now. He's looking upwards, thinking through exactly how he's going to chuck me. He's not the kind of guy who would just write a quick note; no, he would want to do a methodical job of this.

6 May 1995

I wake up at Six A.M., hit the ground outside. I don't know whether I've done this to honour Susan's memory, but it feels good to have this kind of a start to the day. When I get back, it's Quarter-Past Seven and the light on my answering machine is blinking.

I take a gulp, rewind the tape, and start playing. It's from him. His calm, relaxed voice.

"Thanks for your message last night. You know what, I really enjoyed myself as well. I'd love to have a second date with you. I was thinking how about next Saturday? There's a great Turkish restaurant I know about, which I think you'll like. I'll book us a table if you want. Anyway, we'll talk on the phone later and discuss it."

The receiver's in my hands and I'm dialling his number before the sweat has finished trickling down my spine.

Scarlet

10 June 1995

When the interview is done, she goes to her dressing room and makes a call to Josephine. It's only five minutes, and that's all that's needed. A few details about the next album, making sure everything's ready, checking for any overlooked details. Strictly business.

She's effectively free for the day. Nothing else requires her attention.

The Leighton Brothers set this interview up: a slot on a breakfast show, ten minutes long. And very, very early. Nothing fancy, but both Leightons were enthused by it.

After she's finished in the dressing room, she's escorted out to Newcastle-Upon-Tyne's streets, where a taxi is waiting for her. The driver stubs out his cigarette when he sees her.

She's staying in a Holiday Inn at the outskirts of the city. She'll always remember how Roger Miser would get the girls booked in to only the most luxurious hotels. Now, well, she's stuck with the riffraff.

Her stomach's rumbling. It's a result of the stress and the fact that she was being interviewed at Six A.M. without any breakfast.

She thanks the driver when he drops her off at the hotel entrance and yawns her way inside and up to her room. A quick splash of her face to rub the last of the makeup off, and then she heads back down to the lobby where the first scents of breakfast are beginning to emerge.

The breakfast room is small, too cramped for her likings. She ate hotel pizza in there last night – something she'll never do again. The train from London arrived in Newcastle after a three-hour delay, and she arrived at the hotel just after Eleven P.M., no doubt looking like a starved zombie. She would have eaten anything at that point.

The buffet is out: cereals, toast, fruit and hot drinks. There are a few steel bowls labelled: *Bacon, Scrambled Eggs,* and

Sausages. Perfect. But when she goes over, she lifts the lids to find that they're empty.

"What the hell?" she mutters. She's a bit annoyed. She checks her watch. Just after Seven. It says on the placard in her room that breakfast commences at Half-Six. "Excuse me!" she calls out. She jogs out to the lobby, where an elderly man is stacking things behind the reception desk.

"Yes, ma'am, what can I do for you?" he asks.

"There's no hot food out," she tells him.

"Oh, I'm sorry about that. It will be out momentarily. We've had some new staff join recently and they're still getting used to things. I'll go into the kitchen, check on things."

"Okay, thanks." She returns to the breakfast room. Blindly, she fills up a glass with orange juice and piles a bowl with clumps of cereal. There's no one else here. She's alone.

For a single moment, she's the person she used to be. She's the freedom-loving girl in the leather jacket. She's the girl that used to interrupt her art college lecturers, telling them that writing essays on the Glasgow Boys was a waste of time. She's the wild, blonde-haired girl rumoured to have slept with Sofie, that Dutch fine art doctoral student who did the occasional lecture with them. Scarlet smiles over that memory.

Where's Sofie now? What's she doing with herself? She must have finished her doctorate by now.

There's the sound of shuffling feet. A woman enters the breakfast room, pushing a short trolley with several large, steaming bowls on. Even from here, Scarlet can smell the cigarettes. She watches the her fill up the steal domes on the buffet counter with eager eyes. Eventually, she can't hide from the calls of her rumbling stomach anymore. She goes over, snatching up a plate from the neat pile next to the coffee machine. The woman, who has this short-cut hair and a fine golden necklace, who has dead eyes and the beginnings of age and wrinkles on her cheeks, looks at her as she starts filling up her plate.

The woman looks vaguely familiar. She probably worked at one of the other hotels Scarlet's stayed at the past, but she's too recognisable for that. Scarlet knows her mouth has dropped open when the penny finally drops.

"Sharmaine?!" she gasps. "Sharmaine Bateson?!"

"Hi, Scarlet."

"How have you been?"

"Fine. Sorry the hot food's been late coming out. If there's anything else you need, just let me know."

Scarlet wants to ask: "What happened?" But she knows that she shouldn't, even though she's now full of caring and love for this stranger. Instead, she meekly smiles.

"I've got to get back to work. Enjoy your breakfast." Sharmaine waddles off. She's put on a bit of weight: her black trousers barely fit her.

Scarlet grabs some cutlery and returns to her table, finding that the delicious bacon and eggs taste of cold ash.

Dear reader, you can see something has changed in Scarlet. It's like she's become aware of the world around her, for the first time in her life.

She doesn't know how she's able to get through her breakfast. She tries and fails to put out of her head the image of the broken woman she knew years earlier. She looks over her shoulder at the kitchen. The scent of cigarettes is still there, but it's in her head now, locked in, imprisoned.

On her way back to the room, she stops by the reception, asks what time the taxi's coming to pick her up.

"One in the afternoon. You've got your room up until then, so there's no need to worry about checking out."

"I might go for a walk actually. Explore the city a bit."

When she's back in her room, she lies back on her bed, realises that she should have had an extra cup of coffee. She sits up, goes to the window, stays there for a couple of hours. She's about to pull away and sling on her coat, when she sees Sharmaine. Smoke drifts over her shortcut hair, covering her head like a spinster's veil. She waddles across the hotel car-park, then sidles across a road to a bus stop. The cigarette's been put out, but Scarlet sees her pull another stick out. She can see the woman cursing as a bus pulls up. Number 33. The vehicle moves off, drags on the ground. Only the empty bench remains.

Scarlet eventually takes her walk just before noon. She doesn't go very far. Just enough to fill her lungs. When she returns, the taxi's waiting and she's got five minutes to grab her things.

Gina

22 July 1995

It's smiles all around. We've probably got five minutes or so before the drinks arrive, considering we're in one of the swank-iest clubs in Soho, confined to leather sofas. Glittering glass jar fountains surround us and we're showered with orange light. A youngish bloke is busy mixing cocktails behind a polished wooden bar. Bottles of vodka, whisky, flavourings, all shaded in blue light, hang from the wall.

I'm sitting with my new guy, Jeff, facing Josephine and Jason. There was an awkward silence at the beginning of the evening, but now that the introduction barriers are out of the way, we find ourselves freeing up.

The bottle of champagne is delivered in a delicate silver cooler and four fragile glasses are placed on the black tree trunk table that separates our sofas. Jason fills our glasses, Josephine's first.

"To your new album," he says. "A toast!"

"To the new one," says Jeff. "It'll be your best yet!"

"Did Scarlet say she was going to join us?" asks Josephine.

"Does she need to?" replies Jeff.

"It would be nice for her to be here," I say to him.

"But it's nice to have a break from her once in a while." Josephine sips her champagne. "Good stuff. I think I might get a bottle of this for myself."

"What do you think of Scarlet?" Jeff asks. "All of you, what do you think of her?"

"I think she's okay, actually," says Josephine. "We've never really been on the same level and there have been times we've disagreed, really argued. But she's actually okay. Sometimes, I get the feeling that she's hiding stuff."

"I've always found her a bit vague, if I'm honest," says Jason.

"You only met her once, when I introduced you to her." Josephine seems a bit mad at him.

"But it's like she's never quite there, if you know what I mean."

"I absolutely agree." Jeff cracks a smile and reaches for his glass. "I watched that interview she did recently, you know, the one on that breakfast show? What's that expression? A rabbit caught in headlights. I'm surprised she was able to utter a single word."

"Look, maybe we should move on from this subject," I say. "I'm a little bit uncomfortable discussing this."

"You're right." Jason slouches and rubs his forehead. "You're right, I'm sorry."

Jeff touches my elbow. "I went to Blockbuster yesterday and rented a tape. *When Harry Met Sally*. Can't stand Meg

Ryan, really can't, and this was no exception. She's a dreadful actress. Godawful film as well."

"Then why the hell did you watch it?" asks Josephine.

"Curiosity mainly. Wanted to see how the other half of the world live."

"On that note, I need the bathroom," I say.

The club seems to be filling up a little bit. Two girls in way too short dresses are doing slow movements on the dancefloor. I can see that one of them is wearing a tiny golden crucifix.

I freshen up before leaving the bathroom. As I walk past the barman doing the tricks with the cocktails, I spot a familiar face on a sofa. He looks happy with himself, content. Next to him is a woman with thick blonde hair and skinny bare shoulders. She's facing away from me, but I can tell she's beautiful. The man recognises me, but quickly focuses his attention on the woman with him. I do something stupid and go over to them.

"Hi, how have you been?" I ask.

Victor Gully does not look at all pleased. A scowl creeps across his lips. "What do you want?" he snaps.

"I just wanted to say hello, see how you're doing. There's a group of us over there. You're more than welcome to join us if you want."

"No, thank you. Can I get back to my evening now?"

"I didn't mean to interrupt, sorry. Enjoy your evening." I head back to my table.

Jeff's stood up, concern in his eyes. "You okay? What was that about?"

"Oh, it's just someone we used to know." To Josephine: "Victor Gully."

"Oh, Christ, he's here? Guys, let's finish our champagne as quickly as possible and get to the restaurant. I don't want to be here a second longer than we need to."

Josephine

19 August 1995

I check my bag one last time and then go around the apartment, checking and rechecking the windows and doors. When I'm done, I sit on the sofa, hands shaking.

Jason and I have gone from strength to strength over the past few weeks. I don't think I've ever felt so close to anyone. Gina keeps saying that we're a good match, even Scarlet does as well.

He's moving to Cornwall next month to launch his own business. He's been wanting to do it for years, so he tells me. It obviously means that we'll be physically apart, so I'm arranging to buy a place near to his.

He tells me that he wants to commit to me and I know I want the same. And that's what today is all about. We're going to visit his parents in Taunton. We're even staying the night in their house. How long is it since I've done that? Can't remember. It wasn't even with the loser I used to live with.

Jason drove there last night. I'll be heading there today. It's good that I'll be driving there alone: that way I can panic and cry in complete discretion.

It's Seven in the morning; there are a couple of hours before I need to set off. I take the Tube into the heart of the city and find myself wandering the gift shops of Covent Garden. All the niceties and cute little ornaments seem to beg me to buy them. I get a couple of glass orbs with fuzzy illustrations on them and head back towards the Underground station.

My head's really in the clouds this time. Blonde hair catches my eye, but I don't register it. It's when I hear her voice that I stop, look across to the other side of Seven Dials and see Sanne's hair fluttering in the air of London. She's with that guy. Dan, wasn't it? He's had a bit of a haircut and he wears a pristine white shirt, unbuttoned at the cuffs. Both of them are staring through the window of a clothes shop. I can't help but look at them both. They're oblivious to everything around them. Their hands are locked together. She's stroking his cheek and he's rubbing the small of her back. I can't believe that's them! It can't be! She turns and our eyes connect, but I'm moving away.

As I drive over there, I think about them, envisage their beautiful, peaceful nature. I soon forget about them, soon put them out of my head, out of my mind's sight, gone, buried.

My heart's hammering like an earthquake as I pull up in front of their house. Hopefully it's the right one. Yep. 10 Williamson Road. This is it. Deep breaths. I allow myself a moment to contemplate what's about to happen. This is a very serious relationship. Maybe it's too serious.

I step out of the car, check myself in the mirror, straighten myself up.

It's an old house. Two storeys. Grey stone. There's an archway, emboldened by white paint over the edge. There's a heavy-looking doorknocker on a dark wooden door, so damn medieval. I grasp the ring and slam it down twice. A few moments later, Jason appears.

"Come on in!" he beckons. He leads me inside.

His parents emerge from adjacent rooms. They have bookish looks, like they've spent all their lives swallowed by the written word. I used to know someone like that once, during my travelling days.

"I'm Ralph," says the father.

"Lilith," says the mother.

I shake hands with both of them. "It's so good to meet you!"

"How was the trip over here?" Ralph asks. "Traffic okay?"

"It was okay. A few holdups as I left London, but nothing terrible."

"Well, we have lunch just about ready," says Lilith. "Are you hungry?"

"Very much!"

"Good." Ralph clears his throat. "Well, I've got a bottle of red to open and breathe, so why don't you head through to the living room? Would you like a drink of some sort? Tea? Coffee? Sherry? Brandy?"

"Coffee will be perfect."

Jason takes my arm, starts moving me through. His mother tells us that she'll get some coffee ready. His father follows us in, one step behind. He's a little bit shorter than Jason and has his grey hair and beard neatly trimmed. He wears a brownish short-sleeved checked shirt and formal black trousers and shoes. There's not a hint of nervousness or anxiety around him.

The living room is quaint. A couple of bookshelves fill one corner, but the titles are fraying. Maybe it's because I'm so used to seeing them in top class hotels. The wallpaper seems to be peeling, brown on the other side. A lampshade hangs from the ceiling, badly in need of a small dusting.

"What do you do?" I ask Ralph. "Sorry, very vague question. I mean, your career, job."

"Oh, I'm a retired general practitioner. My wife is a law lecturer at Bath University."

"What area?"

"Criminal law."

Lilith returns. A tray is rattling in her bony grip. There's a cafetière filled to the top and four cups. "We only have decaffeinated coffee," she informs me.

"Oh, that's perfect!" I say. "Please, let me help you." I reach up, but Lilith has already placed the tray down on a small table next to the bookshelves. She jams the plunger down and fills up the cups. I offer to help, but I'm gently rebuffed.

We all drink slowly. Jason tells his parents the latest in his plans for his business. He's excited. I watch him with admiration and I know he can sense my gaze on him. Damn, I really like him.

"Lunch should be ready in a few minutes," says Lilith. "I've prepared roast lamb."

I start rubbing my belly, cheeks clenching. I apologise to my hosts, tell them that I've had a spot of indigestion recently. Is there a nearby pharmacy where I can get something to settle my stomach?

"Yes, there's a chemist down the road!" says Jason's father, looking worried. "Please, let me take you there."

"No, it's okay!" I insist. "I'll be back as soon as I can."

"When you leave the front door, turn left, walk to the end of the street, and it will be on your right. You can't miss it."

"Thank you!" I stand up, wiping invisible dust off my sleeves.

After I've left the house, I allow myself to sigh loudly. They seem like nice people, trustworthy. You might even say *honourable*. I shove those thoughts to the side for the moment, continuing to touch my stomach. I twist my face into a collection of agonising moments. Only when I'm far enough away do I straighten up. I'm not ill, far from it.

"Damn," I curse, when I realise that I've left my mobile phone in London.

I keep walking, looking about for a payphone. I pass the chemist at the end of the street and see that there's a traditional red booth just outside its entrance. When I'm sealed inside, my shaking fingers pick up the receiver. I take a few breaths, insert a few coins, and start typing in the number for Scotland Yard. It's odd that I know it off by heart, right?

I considered doing this last year, when I came back to England, but couldn't find it within myself. I'm going to report Sanne and her boyfriend. They're drug traffickers, after all.

My finger intends to press down the last digit, but my brain hesitates. I put the receiver back down and step back. Nope, I'm not going to let those two drag me into their world. They'll get caught sooner or later, but I won't be involved with them anymore.

When I return, lunch is ready. Both parents ask me how I'm feeling. I tell them that the antiacid is working. I'm ten times better.

It's late afternoon and I'm in the garden, my eyes darting around the broken and unbroken flowerpots. They're lined up on either side of a stone path that ventures from the door to a small overgrown pond. The grass needs a cut and the fencing needs a lick of paint. There's a coiled hose that's been left to gather dirt and rust. I wonder how long it's been there, trapped, forgotten about.

I feel Jason next to me and instinctively lean into him.

"How are you finding it?" he says. "Parents aren't too fussy over you, are they?"

"No, they're all right," I reply, touching his elbow. "They're really nice. I really like them."

"I think they really like you as well. They're taking us out for dinner tonight, their treat. It's nothing fancy. Just this new Indian place that's opened up."

"Fantastic."

He kisses me lightly on the forehead and goes back inside. I'm left by myself with the birds for company.

At dinner, I find myself beginning to loosen up. The tension disappears as quickly as the first glass of wine. The restaurant has a humble feeling to it: the right number of other dinners, the correct lighting.

Ralph and Lilith ask me about the band. I give them the short version of its history.

I enquire about their histories, how they got into their respective fields.

"I always wanted to be a doctor," says Ralph. "When I was a child, I would pretend to diagnose my classmate's medical problems. We had toy doctor stuff in the classroom. I suppose I stopped laughing when I got to university and found there were so many assignments, reports and procedures!" He chuckles.

He gets serious as the main course is served: four portions of chicken tikka masala with boiled rice. His tone fits the monotony of our meal. After he qualified, he did some overseas work in the Congo before returning to England, where he met and married Lilith. He worked at two surgeries in Bath before settling in Taunton, where he practiced at a centre less than a mile from his house until his retirement.

I realise that I'm truly happy. Do I have, do I really have a stable partner, maybe for the first time in my life? I glance to my left – repeatedly – at Jason. I know his mother sees it.

20 August 1995

His parents see me off from the pavement. Ralph gives me a peck on the cheek and Lilith hugs me really tightly, as though I'm a long-lost sister. They go inside, their firm but frail bodies holding it together. Jason holds me to him, hands around my waist. He's staying for another two days. I think he said something about visiting some childhood friends.

"I love you," he tells me.

"I love you too," I reply. "Have you got your mobile with you? I'll call you when I'm back in London."

"Yeah, sounds good."

We kiss and draw apart. I stroke the base of his chin and sit in my car. Before I know it, I'm on the network of roads back to London. I'm fighting back tears, but they're droplets of joy. I'm so happy. I never thought I'd experience this amount of life. Finally, finally, I've made it in life. Finally!

I stop at a service station to call Gina and Scarlet. No particular reason. Just to say hello. I ask them if they want to meet up tonight. There's a new swanky bar that's opened up just outside Leicester Square. Would they be up for it? Gina's very keen. So is Scarlet, though she doesn't show the greatest enthusiasm for it. I say I'll be there for Eight P.M.

The day increases in beauty the closer I get to home. The journey becomes a sense of blissful ignorance. I daydream about the early days of the band. I laugh at the memory of our first performance, when we thought no one would turn up. I think of the time Scarlet got us together, over five years ago, in that wretched café to propose the idea.

I pull up in front of mine just as my stomach starts rumbling for lunch. When I'm inside my home, I think about what to prepare, but decide to head out for something to eat. I've deserved it. I'm celebrating.

I quickly change my clothes and walk to the Underground Station. Right at the last minute, I change my plan. There's something I've got to see first.

When I'm on that familiar street, I do a nod towards the child's buggy, still unmoved after all these years. Still grounded. Still immobile. The grove – still with its familiar collection of natural shows – welcomes me back. I step through the mystical, fairy-tale nature of the place to find that the cabin is still there. I venture towards it. Cautiously, I step through the entrance. It's a place stopped in time.

I think of the homeless man who lived here once, the comfort he gave me, how he saved me.

"It's time to let you go." That's all I need to say. I turn on my feet and return the way I came.

But when I'm at the end of the street, something makes me stop. I turn around and quickly make my way back into the grove, back to the shack. I place my hands on the wood, let out a few sobs.

"Thank you," I whisper. "Thank you."

Time to go.

I turn away from the building, for what I know will be the last time.

Sanne's staring right through my eyes. "Hi, Josephine," she says. "Long time, no see. How are you?"

I can't react. I can't do anything, because violent hands grab me from behind and spin me around. Dan stands there, moisture clinging to his eyelids.

"Hey, fuck off!" I yell.

He throws a punch at my stomach. I keel over, gasping. My vision goes black.

"Why didn't you fucking say hello to us?" snarls Dan. "You think we didn't see you? God, you're an ignorant little cunt, aren't you? Sanne, keep an eye out. Make sure no one disturbs us."

"Sure, babe."

I'm lifted up. Dan puts his fingers around my throat, drags me along the dirt. Suddenly things feel enclosed. That's because I'm in the shack.

"Stay the fuck there," he hisses, throwing me down.

I land like Christ on the bed, my spine slamming against the hard edge of the wood. He grabs me again, turns me over.

"Hold still. Don't move a fucking muscle."

I feel his fingers around my belt, fumbling with the clasp. Another punch goes into my left side. I can't think. I can't take onboard what's happening. It doesn't process with me.

There's a moment when I blurt out, "Please."

He responds at some point, but I'll never really know when: "Fuck no."

Eventually he lets go and I hear him zipping himself up.

"Enjoy that?" he sneers. "I did."

Sanne appears in the doorway. Is there a flicker of remorse in her eyes?

"I thought I told you to keep an eye out?" says Dan.

"Are you done?"

"Oh, yeah. She's definitely a piece of meat."

"What if she reports us?"

"She won't, trust me. She's not that sort of girl." Dan looks at me. His face is sweaty. "You won't talk, will you? And even if you do, by the time the cops come looking, we'll be on a plane home. Take care, hun."

Sanne kneels down next to me and puts a finger on my cheek, which she slowly strokes along its surface. She kisses me on the forehead and both cheeks, clutches my hands and lets go very quickly. Then she follows Dan out, as though I never existed.

I get up, try to walk. My legs catch in my crumpled trousers and I tumble to the floor. I rise again and stagger out of the shack. I attempt to scream for help, but nothing comes out. It's like my mouth has declared its going on strike.

The world won't stand up straight. The sky is an ocean, an endless ocean. The trees are mountain ranges, unthinkable peaks. My world seems to rotate around me. One last time, I try to scream, one final effort, but I'm falling. My head smacks against cold dirt. I gasp, just as everything shuts down.

Herbert

14 September 1995

I get to the recording studios before the girls – something which is unusual. I've been increasingly getting the feeling that they're pushing me away. I thought they knew what this whole thing was about! I'm supposed to be accompanying them as much as I can! Every juicy titbit increases the chance of this article being the... What was it Roger used to say? *The ultimate business.*

The Leighton Brothers are all set up. They've decided to host the meeting in one of the actual recording rooms, the largest there is. A large, circular table has been moved in. By the looks of things, we're going to be in here for a few hours. Philip, the eldest, is going through some paperwork. Keith, the youngest, is pacing up and down the room. You wouldn't think in the slightest that they're related. Philip is calm and methodical, ambitious yet cautious. Keith is impulsive, too much of a risk-taker, a chaotic individual who's been told too many times to slow down and think things one moment at a time.

"How long are they gonna be?" asks Keith. He puts a cigarette between his lips, holds up a flame.

"They won't be too long," replies Philip. "You need to take a few moments. And smoke outside, please."

"Fuck." Keith grudging lowers the lighter, rips the stick from his mouth.

"Why are you making notes?" Philip says to me.

"I'm just going over my notes actually." I hold up the pad to him. "See?"

"Every time I see you, you're writing on that fucking thing. Christ, you're beginning to piss me off."

"Jesus Christ, mate."

"I don't know why we're continuing this on from Roger." Philip yawns and thumps the stack of papers in front of him.

"My contract is with the band," I tell him.

"But I own the band. Roger might have treated them like royalty, flown them first-class, let them stay in the best hotels, but that's stopped with me. They do as I fucking tell them. Why are you shocked, Herbert?"

"Well, the way you're talking about them."

"What, really? If I told you that I think Scarlet is nothing but a lesbo slut, what would you do about it? Nothing. You see, Herbert, you're in my little pond now. You're all in my pond. You do what I do, when I tell you to do it. Now, I'm happy to let you continue with your notetaking. Go for it, mate. But remember, you work for me now. You all work for me."

The long-haired guy who sits cross-legged at reception knocks on the door and enters. He's breathless, tired, with the appearance of someone who simply doesn't want to be there. He looks around at us all, but focuses his gaze on Philip. "Sir, they're here," he informs him.

"Send them in," says Philip.

The lout nods and shuffles back the way he came.

"Keith, can you call up accounts tomorrow and get rid of him?" Philip says it like he doesn't mean it. "He's making us look bad. The next time you decide to employ someone, run it past me first, okay?"

"Sure."

When the girls arrive, Keith's all smiles. Philip doesn't even look up. He tells them to be seated and the meeting commences. Well, the meeting is him. He tells the girls everything that's going to happen, how the album will be released, a few performances he's got lined up at the end of November.

Philip dominates this place. I've seen it in him before, but this is a new level. He's scary, truly aggressive and sadistic in his mannerisms.

Josephine seems less than her usual self. She's been a lot like that recently. More reserved, eyes focused down a lot more. I don't know whether she's having problems with this new boyfriend of hers.

When the meeting ends, Philip leaves the room, followed by his brother.

"Well, that concludes things nicely," grunts Scarlet.

"See you later, guys," says Josephine. Her hair's a mess, straggled in all directions. She walks out, face pointed at the floor, as if she's afraid that the ceiling will collapse onto her.

"Is everything okay with her?" I ask Gina.

"Beats me. It's hard getting through to her at all."

"Should I go after her?"

"Nope, just leave her. She'll be fine."

"Gina, can I go over a couple of things with you?" asks Scarlet. "Herbert, you might want to stay for this as well. I'd hoped Josephine would stick around, but, oh well..." She opens up a crinkly new diary. Black leather, with virginal white pages. "Right, the album launches on the Twenty-Fifth of November. And we're doing a performance that night at Wembley Stadium. On the Twenty-Sixth, we're at Alexandra Palace. Herbert, we need to decide where you're going to be for this. My feeling is that you're best placed in the front of the audience; you'll get a good angle of the stage."

"It won't work that way. I need to be behind the scenes with you, to get close to your feelings, to listen to the small talk. That's what this whole project's about!"

"He's right, Scarlet."

"Nope. I want him in the audience." Scarlet's lips are sealed. "I want him to see us as the fans do. He's spent far too long up close with us. Way too long.

"Now, for the main stuff. On the Saturday, we're due to kick off at Nine P.M. I suggest we meet at my home at Six for an early dinner. That way, we can get to Wembley in plenty of time. On Sunday, meet at mine at Five, then that gets us to Alexandra Palace a few hours before we start strumming chords."

"Sounds like a plan," agrees Gina.

"I'm still stumped why you want me in the crowd." I know I sound petulant when this plea shoots from my mouth.

"Remember what you're contracted for." Scarlet tuts and lets out a laugh. "Mr Writer, go and do something useful."

"Is that my cue to leave?" I grumble. I don't wait for an answer. I grab my coat and start walking.

When I'm outside, I'm not sure which way to go. Camden Town's traffic is starting to build up. Horns blare and tempers drift along the roads and pavements. Children – who really should be in school – are dragging at their parents' arms. A man with an armful of leaflets is doing his best to dish them out, but he hasn't taken the hint that no one is interested.

There's a payphone further down the road. I fumble in my pocket for some loose change. I open up the booth, something that requires considerable strength as the door sticks. I push a few coins in and dial Victor's number.

He answers after two rings. *"Yeah?"*

"Hi, mate, it's Herbert. How have you been?"

"What the hell do you want, Herbert?"

"I just want to check up on you."

"Herbert, I'm fine. Actually working on a new novel at the moment."

"That's fantastic! Listen, I was thinking, why don't we grab a drink or something?"

"I don't think that's a good idea."

"Why not?"

"Well, look who you're associated with."

"Look, if you're worried about the girls, they won't be coming. It'll be just the two of us. They won't even know I'm meeting you."

"I'm trying to turn over a new leaf here. Start again."

"That's good. I'm really pleased for you, mate. I just want to have a catchup with you. Writer stuff, that's it."

"Okay. Let's meet at that pub in Seven Dials. I forget its name."

"Sounds good. Around One?"

"Perfect. See you then."

I mutter a silent vow of gratitude to the entity up and step out of the phone box. Josephine's standing with her arms folded, leaning against the wall.

"Up to much?" she asks me.

"Nothing, I swear. Just catching up with an old mate."

"Was it him?"

"Who?"

"You know the guy I'm talking about."

"I don't, actually."

"Victor Gully."

"Well, I'm going to meet him for a pint. A quick one, mind you."

"Is he still shaken over Susan?" she asks.

"Well, of course he is. Look, are you thinking of joining us?"

"I wouldn't mind seeing him."

"You sure?"

"Positive." She winks.

"Josephine, can I ask are you okay?"

"Fine as I can be."

"Are you sure?"

"Herbert, you're not my father. Stop acting like you are."

"Sorry, I didn't mean to sound like that."

She looks hurt. Just for an instant, just for a withheld breath. There's pain, sadness, twisted knots in her eyes. I don't do anything about it. What can I do? Not a single component of me reaches out.

"Let's grab that drink, then," she tells me.

We make our way through London like two ghosts. That's an idea for a story... if I ever decide to descend in my values of self-respect.

"London's a beautiful place, isn't it?" she says at some point during our journey.

"I've never really noticed. I much preferred America. Back in the good old Sixties, when everything and everyone was innocent. Oh, Josephine, it was like another world. You could be whoever, whatever you wanted."

"Why did you leave the States, if it was that great over there?"

"Work dried up."

"Ah, the best excuse." She smiles meekly, puts her hand on my arm. "Do you know why I left America? A fucking relationship. I made a stupid mistake. Let my guard down, let the wrong woman into my life."

"I didn't know... I didn't know you were... a..."

"A lesbian? Well, I'm not really one of those. I just made the mistake of dabbling in that area. And look what happened... She did a lot of damage to me. She broke me, tore my heart in two. She did a shitload of damage to me and I don't know if I'll ever recover."

"But you've got this new guy in your life." I've met Jason once. Mature – a lot more so than when I was at his age. He's perfect for her. Really, he is. "You should be happy. You deserve to be happy."

"To be honest, I don't know what the hell he sees in me. His parents adore me. I've no idea why. Christ, I wish they hated my guts."

I don't know how to answer her. I don't think anyone would.

We continue in silence, before Josephine pulls me into a bus stop. She flags the first one that comes along.

"Come on, Herbert, you've never been on a bus before?"

Thankfully it's one heading in roughly the right direction.

When we get to Covent Garden, the shops are in the full swing of business and the tourists are taking their photographs.

Josephine seems to shudder when walk across the Seven Dials junction. I swear that she clinches my arm just that little bit tighter.

"We've got a bit of time," I tell her. "Do you fancy a cup of coffee or something?"

"I'd like that."

We find a place off the junction: the kind of place where someone like me would typically make notes for their next novel. Years from now, they'll have lots of cafes like this across town centres and university campuses. It's one of the funkiest places I've been in, with bags of coffee stacked across walls and baristas who are still effectively children.

We sit at the back, our heads bowed.

When it's time, we head to the pub. I spend about ten minutes hunting for Victor Gully. Only when Josephine's ordered our drinks and is sitting impatiently do I realise that he won't be turning up. I should have known. But I'm an old man, trapped in the traditions of old ways. Maybe I don't understand the level of hurt he's endured; maybe I never will.

Scarlet

25 November 1995

She's been worried about Josephine, but it's not something she's willing to admit. The new album came out this morning.

Philip phoned her earlier: there were queues spotted outside HMV just prior to opening time. He seemed quite confident about things. Of course, she knows that it's not going to be nearly as good as the last one.

She sits in her penthouse, cuddled up in several layers. The weather outside is too cold, something she curses. It's not good weather to release a new album. It needs to be summer, not so much for the atmosphere of the concert, but for the mingling and one-night stands that happen after. She's learned that these things don't happen as much when the pavements are caked in ice.

Her stomach rumbles, the consequence of having two bananas for lunch. Just like art school, when she was skint every second of every day.

She's not doing anything today, except for waiting. She knows what Ted Bundy went through in his final hours. Waiting for the moment when the executioner would throw the switch. She'll die tonight, that's for sure. She'll fall on her cross.

Josephine

25 November 1995

I feel Jason's fingers stroke the back of my ear and I pull in closer to him.

"How are you feeling about tonight?" he whispers.

"Nervous," I respond. "How about you?"

"Same. I've never watched you perform before."

"Well, you'll finally get the chance to."

We're sitting in my living room. Fresh coffee and biscuits are on the table. It's a picturesque scene from one of those home magazine covers.

"I'm very proud of you," he says. He pulls, back holds my face in his hands. "You're so beautiful, Josephine."

"You don't have to say that."

"You've made me really happy. You're a part of me."

"That's so sweet."

"I'm a man who knows what he wants. And what I want is you." He shifts back, pulls something from his pocket, an object that fits within his fist.

I stare at the ring of diamonds and feel myself stop. I don't know how long I drag the world to a halt around me. He's waiting for an answer. He's patient, yet annoyed.

"Jason," I stutter. "Jason... Do you really mean this?"

"Yes."

"Are you really sure?"

"Yes. I know this is meant to be. I know we're meant to be."

"In that case, I accept."

Neither of us can quite take onboard what's just been said. To me, this is dreamlike. I think we did a song on this theme. Was it the first album? Might have been. I pull him close, hug him so tightly.

"I've never been so happy as I am right now." He lifts out the ring and gently pushes it over my finger. "I love you, Josephine, and I always well."

"Do you really mean that?"

"Without a shred of doubt."

We hold one another, tears on our faces. It's the moment every girl dreams of. It's what every girl desires more than anything in the world. I can tell he's overjoyed. The way I feel right now, I can't explain it.

The moments are all too long and yet all too brief. Before I know what's happening, I'm seeing him off at the door and I'm trying to fight back the tears.

"See you in a few hours, on the stage," he whispers. "I love you."

"I love you too."

Hours later, I walk onto the stage with the other girls – and our backing musicians. The others see it, but I know that it's probably just puzzlement in their eyes.

We do two songs, favourites from our first album. We get applause, not as rapturous as what we got before my communist secrets found their way out, but it's cheering all the same. Well, it's far better than booing.

Herbert

25 November 1995

Actually, I'm having a better time than I thought I would. I did a few of these things before, back in America. I'm with the fans, laughing and cheering as the music washes over us.

Jason's a few feet away. I swear I saw tears in his eyes as Josephine came on. Happy tears, though.

I'll have a few things to write about tonight, that's for sure!

They do a song from the new album. It takes time for it to be absorbed at first, but when it is, the crowd's happier than they were earlier. Any new song needs time to sink in.

I've seen plenty of concerts over the years, but this has to be the most intense. Almost too intense.

"Well, it's been a great night!" Scarlet says eventually. Moisture covers her shoulders and arms, her face and neck. She's breathless. "One more song for you. One more song, guys."

It's one from the second album, the one that all the schoolgirls like to sing. When it's finished, the crowd whistles. Clapping shakes the foundations of Wembley.

"Thank you, thank you!" Josephine pulls a mike off a stand and clears her throat. Wembley doesn't fall silent, but it lowers its voice. "Thanks for coming along tonight! You see, it's an extra special evening for me. Not only am I firmly back in the music fold, but... my boyfriend, Jason, proposed to be this afternoon and I accepted!"

The crowd sends out a round of cheer.

Josephine lifts her right hand. "But the truth is, I'm not good enough for him. He thinks the world of me, but I wish he didn't. I'm nothing but a slut and a whore." She leans down, picks up this golden envelope. "One guy in here is going to be very lucky. One lucky guy. I'm going to toss this into the crowd. Whoever catches it, well, they'll get a night they'll never forget." She leans back, hurls it as far as she can.

I don't know why I'm so optimistic, but I really think that the crowd, out of pity, won't go for it. But they do. They scramble over one another, pull each other apart, rip into one another. I stand there, horrified. I shut my eyes, hoping, just hoping, that this isn't true.

Scarlet

11 December 1995

Philip and Keith seem to be leaning over her. They're on the other side of the table in their plush meeting room, but it's like they're breathing into her face. Keith's panicky, flexing his fingers, taking rapid sips of water. Philip, on the other hand, runs his fingers through paperwork. She can sense the anger and fury coming off him.

It was all over the papers, every single detail of it. Not a single shred left out.

Philip's now writing a few details down. His reading glasses hang on the edge of his nose, like a suicidal cliff jumper about to leap to their death. Occasionally, he peers up at her.

Suddenly, he shouts out, "Keith, if you can't handle this, please leave!"

"Sorry, Philip." The older Leighton takes a few deep breaths, but he still looks purple in the face.

"That's better." Philip goes back to writing, his ballpoint pen scratching like a dog.

He stops. His pen levitates and he gently slips on the lid. He places it alongside the document and removes his spectacles, folds them, slides them into his front jacket pocket.

"So, who was the lucky guy?" he asks. "Painter or something from Croydon, wasn't it?"

"Yes," replies Scarlet, "something like that."

"I'm assuming Josephine won't be joining us?"

"No."

"Where is she?"

"She's at home, I think."

"Probably comatose on the floor in a pool of vomit. I take it you saw the headlines?"

"Who couldn't have? Believe me, sir, I'm so embarrassed. What she did, throwing that envelope to the crowd, it was unacceptable —"

"I'm not talking about that. I don't know whether you read the Sunday papers, but I happen to. Great story about Josephine on the piss on Saturday night. Got kicked out of a wine bar in Soho. She hurled a bottle at the barman, just missing him. Then she proceeded to vomit... well, just about everywhere. Police let her off with a warning. She should count herself lucky."

"She needs help."

"Oh, on that we agree. She needs serious professional help." Philip presses his fingers together, blinks a few times. "Scarlet, you know what I'm going to say to you."

"Yes, sir. I understand."

"Good. I want her gone within two weeks."

"I understand, sir."

"I will say, though, you and Gina handled yourselves well on the subsequent performance on Sunday night. But then again, with Josephine out the picture, it was probably far fucking easier."

Scarlet holds back the sobs. "Sir, I will tell her by the end of the week."

"You have the opportunity to do it right now." Philip nods his head at the door.

Josephine shuffles inside. Her hair is plastered with dried vomit and dirt. She's in a t-shirt that reeks of fresh body odour and cigarette smoke. Her eyes are bloodshot and makeup is strewn down her cheeks.

"Nice of you to join us," says Philip. His fake smile drops into a frown. "You're still drunk, aren't you?"

"Sorry." Josephine sits down, leans forward on the table.

"Scarlet..." He raises his eyebrows at her.

She swallows a deep breath, puts a hand on Josephine. "I'm sorry, but I have to let you go."

There's no fighting back this time. All the warlike posturing is gone from the woman.

"I understand," she whispers. "Scarlet, I'm so sorry. I'm so, so sorry. I've messed up, haven't I?"

"It's okay. Don't apologise."

"You did mess up," says Philip. "You're very lucky you didn't screw things up for the band on Sunday night. Believe me, Alexandra Palace nearly cancelled. You are so fucking lucky." He purses his lips, bares his teeth. He kicks his chair behind him, jumping to his feet. "Do you have any idea how much you embarrassed me?! You vicious little slut! You fucking bitch!" He grabs Josephine by the throat and hurls her at the door.

"Hey!" Scarlet stutters. "That's…" She can't utter another word. It's like everything's been completely caught in her teeth.

"Fuck off!" screams Philip. "Keith, can you get security, get this waste of space out of here?"

Keith moves over to Josephine, flabby arm deployed, locks it around her waist. "Come on, darling, let's get moving."

Philip seems to count a few beats. Calmly, he sits down, runs a forefinger under his nose, and grimaces. "I sincerely apologise for that," he says. "I hope you understand."

"There was no need to get –"

"Physical? Yes, there was. Scarlet, Roger Miser sheltered you from the harsh truths of this business. Welcome to the real world. It's going to be a painful experience for you, a short, sharp shock."

"How are sales of the new album?"

"Adequate," he replies. "Adequate."

The door opens and two men tread inside. Happy snarls on their faces. Pride and arrogance on their lips, if such things can ever be worn together. T-shirts with *Choose Life* stuck on the front and black jeans, cheap aftershave and greased hair. Philip waves a hand, not even sending a glance in their direction, and they leave sheepishly.

"What are you doing tonight?" he asks.

"Nothing much. Glass of wine or something. See what's on the box."

"Come over for dinner. My wife makes the best Spaghetti Bolognese you could possibly imagine. Trust me. And home-made garlic bread to go with it. She's Italian, you see. Very traditional, comes from a very... ornate family. Anyway, I'll send my driver to pick you up. Say, around Seven? Yes, that's a good time. Be ready."

"Thank you. I appreciate the offer." She wants to add her firm declination, but Philip waves his hand.

"I look forward to it. Oh, and don't mention what's just happened with Josephine. I don't want my wife finding out."

The afternoon twinkles on, the sun blasting its light across London. She watches it like the curious little girl she once was. Watches how it makes the streets seem to glow. Observes how the freezing air makes Londoners huddle together. She was one of them at some distant point in her life.

Sometimes she thinks of her days at art school. It's where her looks came from, where her pale eyes and shortcut hair became welded to her personality. She reminisces, then and there, about the relationships during those months, the ones that worked, the ones that didn't, the ones that should have worked.

She should count herself lucky – she knows that. How many young girls get the kind of dreams she's had? How many long for the stage, for the openness of New York, for the travel?

Yet she wishes – sometimes – that she never had this. It feels in a sense too big for her. Like she was never meant to experience it.

The problem is... when she reminisces, bad things come along as well. Awful memories. Things she wishes would stay buried. And there's one more than any other she wishes was truly gone, something that she actually paid the police to forget about.

He comes at Seven, right on the dot. His Mercedes pulls to a stop and he emerges from the rear, giving a friendly wave. He's changed from his Bond Street shirt, jacket and trousers into jeans and a zip-up jersey with a faded red t-shirt underneath.

"Come on," he says, now waving her inside.

They don't drive far, only about twenty minutes. It didn't occur to her that someone as repulsive as Philip Leighton could have his homelife so close to hers.

He lives on a suburban street that's surrounded by tower blocks. Like an island in the ocean of poverty and distress. It's like the set of *Coronation Street*: all the cobbled houses clumped together, nailed against one another. His house is at the end. Over the red brick wall, she can see the basis of an overgrown garden, one that's been left to rot and fall apart.

"See you later," he says to the driver. "This way, Scarlet."

A door that's way too snug between crumbling burgundy bricks flings open and two small boys run out. Philip nearly topples over as they wrap themselves around his legs.

"You boys grow with every day! Another six feet!" He hoists both of them into his arms and carries them to the door.

He's joshing. He's laughing. He doesn't look like a man in his forties, instead a guy who's grown younger, a big kid.

A woman in an apron, a sunburnt yet tanned face, a tight bun with a free-flowing complexion, reaches out a hand to Scarlet. "Hi, I'm Marlene. You're Scarlet, aren't you? It's so lovely to meet you."

Philip and Marlene link hands across the table, their eyes on Scarlet. Marlene's cracked open a new bottle and filled their glasses. She looks flushed, watery eyes blinking away the stress and dirt of the day. Philip leans back in his chair, dragging a fork across the remains of his bucatini. A plate of focaccia still steams on the table. They've put the kids to bed, clearing the atmosphere for tonight.

Philip's just finished the story of how he and Keith launched his record company in 1977. She knows he's skipped a lot of the sordid details, but she'll fill in the blanks later with rumours and gossip that float around the music world: loans with bad interest, threats, abuse, intimidation. A few weeks ago, she heard a story that he raped a female singer in 1979.

"Scarlet is definitely a singer of the future," he says. "Roger Miser – bless his soul – launched her career. My job is to raise it to the next level. And it can be done."

"I met this man when he came to visit Rome." Marlene strokes her husband's shoulder. "I was a student working at this gallery. Eighteen, I was. He comes in..." She's clearly struggling to find the words: maybe her English isn't that good. "He comes in, and he goes straight for me. He asked me out for a drink. He was very clear about it, that he wanted to have a drink with me, and wouldn't leave me alone until I said yes."

"I bought her a few drinks, and then three weeks later, I asked her to marry me."

"I said yes immediately."

She realises, after a short while, that they're a typical couple. A normal, average husband and wife. A relationship that could stand the test of years and decades, whatever trials came along. She knows that they love one another, truly and deeply. She knows that there's nothing that could rip them apart. She knows that they're dedicated to one another, knows that they would die for one another if it ever came to it. It's the sort of love she wishes she had. Wait, she did have it at one point.

He pops into her head with that calm, sweet smile of his. A life lost.

Marlene's prepared some traditional ice-cream. "The exact same recipe they use in the village where my mother comes from."

Scarlet finds that she likes it more than she should. It's smooth, crispy, floats down to her belly. She thinks about asking for second-helpings, but is too frightened of being seen as rude. Philip's wife serves fresh Italian espressos in pristine little cups, but Scarlet takes one sip of hers and fights back the urge to gag.

Both of them see her off when the evening comes to a close. Marlene's phoned a taxi. It appears sheepishly at the end of the road, lights blinking.

"Thank you for coming tonight," she says to Scarlet, planting a kiss on each of her cheeks.

"No, I should be the one thanking you!" Scarlet replies. "I've really enjoyed myself. Thank you so much for the meal!"

"The pleasure was mine. I'd better go upstairs and check on the children. It was lovely to meet you, Scarlet!"

When she's behind the door, Philip puts on a grimace. "You're not the biggest fan of Italian food, are you?"

"Not really, but your wife's cooking was excellent."

"I've no doubt it was. Listen, I'll give you a call tomorrow, okay? Your taxi's waiting."

He's gone the second she turns away. The driver glares at her, visibly jams his finger against his watch. She starts moving, relieved that the evening has come to a close.

Gina

12 December 1995

When I was really young, around five or six, I became really famous for five or six seconds. Long story short: I was in a choir at school that was invited to appear on Blue Peter. We did a rendition of some hymn – can't remember for the life of me which one it was. Then they interviewed the headmistress and a couple of the girls on the plush sofa. I remember wanting to be sat there so badly, but since these girls were the chosen lead singers of the choir, with their soft voices and even softer faces, they *had* to be the ones who had their fifteen minutes. As I mentioned, I got five or six seconds. As the camera pans over our little group in the studio, you can see me, on the end, the tall kid, just briefly. But I'm there. No one in the world has caught on to this. I receive hundreds of fan letters every week, but no one has deduced the fact that I've been famous before.

This I tell George as we sip our way through our instant coffees in polystyrene cups. He listens, bemused, but he listens.

He's been managing the record company okay since Roger Miser's passing, but he looks so sad, so beaten down, so withdrawn. There's still that grandfather-like sparkle in his eyes and I hope it stays there.

"You do surprise me," he says at last. "Very much so. Is there any way that I could find that footage?"

"Check with the BBC Archives."

"I might do."

George has asked to meet me. He said on the phone last night that he waned to talk to me about something that was "too important to leave any longer." We've met in this workman's café on this industrial estate somewhere.

Eventually, the small talk stops and we gaze into each other's eyes.

"What did you want to talk to me about?" I ask.

"I wasn't sure who to talk to about this, but... take a look." He passes me an envelope. It's golden, much like the one that Josephine threw into the audience. I hold it between my fingers gingerly. Somehow – and I'll never figure this out – I know what's inside. "Go ahead," he whispers, "open it."

Everything written down confirms my suspicions. To be honest, I'm not surprised with half the things I'm reading. It's like they've always been there, waiting to reveal themselves. When I'm done, George dips his head.

"I'm sorry you had to read this," he says. "You could say that this is a confession."

"Don't apologise. Don't ever apologise. Thank you for this."

"I'm heading out there next month. I need to say my own goodbyes. I need to seek forgiveness."

"Why? It was all Roger Miser's doing!"

He gets up, downs whatever's left in his cup. "But I was there," he says. He leaves without a word of goodbye.

I'm about to run after him, but stop myself very quickly. I need to let him do what he needs to do.

Josephine

16 December 1995

Jason bows his head, trying to wipe away the tear marks.

"I'm so sorry about everything," I say. "I know it doesn't mean much to you, but I'm so sorry."

"It's okay." He grasps my hands. "I know it sounds stupid, but I really want to give this another shot. I know, I know..."

I hold his fragile face between my hands. I'm fighting back tears, really going to war with them. "You deserve so much better than somebody like me."

It's the first time we've properly talked since I threw the golden pass. Sorry, it should be capitalised now: Golden Pass. That's what the media are calling it. I've cleaned myself up a bit, but my eyes are still puffy and my skin is still etched with tiredness.

"I know I'm asking the world of you, but please give me this chance," he pleads. "Josephine, I love you, more than anyone else. Give me this chance. We can pause the engagement, if that's what you want, take a step back."

"Jason, why would you do that? Why?"

"Because I love you. I don't want anyone else in the world."

We're hugging. I'm crying into his neck. I want to tell him everything, but I can't. It's blocked tight. I can't utter a single word. I can't. No matter how bad I want to spit it out, it won't come.

"I love you so much, Jason, more than you will ever know."

"I love you too, honey."

"What time are you setting off tomorrow?" I ask.

"Early. Around Eight."

"Listen, I need to have a think about things. I'll come to your hotel tomorrow at that time and let you know. I just need time to think things through." I check my watch. "That's ironic. It's Eight A.M. now. Twenty-four hours. Jason, I need these twenty-four hours to myself. I need time to think."

He holds me tighter. "I'll be waiting."

We kiss at my front door and then I slump back into my living room. I'm so lazy it's unreal. I pick up the remote, but don't have the energy to switch on the telly.

I know he deserves better than me. Damn, I wish I'd never met him. I know that he needs someone who's strong, who's decent, who's honourable. Not someone like me.

I suddenly feel the urge to go after him. "I'm sorry, Jason, I don't know what I was saying. Let's start over." But I control myself.

I go for a walk, then another walk, then take lunch at this local pub. I don't think anyone recognises me. I don't care if they do. I manage to abstain from alcohol. When I'm back home, I drink my way through three bottles of water.

I fiddle with the Christmas tree and clean out my coffeemaker. All the while, the sense that I have to make this awful choice presses on my brain. I can't fight it off. I can't pull it down. It's there, a knife in my brain.

I remember our first date. Remember now normal, how mature he was. Think about how safe I felt with him.

Dinner is chicken and rice, marinated with oils and spices. I've got this new recipe book that gives you thirty different ways to cook chicken and other meats. I've found it therapeutic, very much so, since the attack.

I think about the future. What would happen if we really made a go of it? What would our children – if we had any – be like? It's not that I can't see myself living a happy life with him, it's not that. It's just, I don't see why I deserve him.

I can't eat, so I force myself to. By the time I've swallowed the last few strips of meat, there's an urge to vomit.

I take another walk, try to get the food to wash through me. I end up going past his hotel and spot him in the restaurant. He's staring at an empty plate. When a waitress moves it away, he smiles up at her, and then droops his head again. I could go up to him, right now, tell him I love him.

No, I need to think some more.

Later that night, just before I go to bed, I take out a piece of lined paper. I hold my trusted fountainpen, gripping it like a vice, and write possibly the most random thing of all.

A memory floods me. It was years ago now. I witnessed Scarlet's father kissing another man. A horrible memory. It's so vivid and I want to cut it out. But I'm writing it down on paper, telling every sordid detail.

When I'm done, I read it through. I'm shocked how candid and gratuitous I was. I fold it up into crisp rectangles and seal it in a golden envelope. I place it in the far-right corner of my desk, in between two porcelain penguins.

I fall asleep and then wake up straight away. I've found that I've reached out to him, hoping amongst hope that he's there, but of course, he's not. It's hurting that I've already – in a sense – chucked him.

17 December 1995

But when I awaken, I'm full of anger and determination. I won't let anything come between us. I'll tell him everything, about the abuse I received as a trainee teacher, about the rape. I'll tell him every last detail. He'll get it. He'll understand.

I'm out the door, pulling on my coat and gloves, and I'm running to the hotel.

Screw Sanne and the others. Damn them! I'm strong and I won't let them beat me!

My feet stumble and shake, and I know it's a sign that I need to take up running a little bit more! I see the hotel up ahead. Is that him? Yes, it is! He's loading his bags into his car. He's got that awful grey overcoat I've been begging him to get rid of.

"Jason!" I cry out. "Jason!" I throw my arms around him.

I think I've caught him by surprise. He stumbles and strokes my neck.

"I'm sorry about yesterday," I say. "I'm so, so sorry. I'm better than that. I'll be a better person. I want to give this a go. I really, really want to. I love you."

His face seems to crack with emotion. "Let's have breakfast." He takes me by the hand and leads me into the hotel. It's the kind of place familiar with business travellers and indeed there are a few of them hunched over plates of scrambles eggs and bacon. It's a buffet setup. A waitress – it might have been the one I saw tending to him last night – asks his room number. When we're finally sat down – he's taken me to a table in the corner – I grasp his hands in mine.

"Jason, you were right about everything!" My voice is a panic, a total panic, but I don't care, because I want him. I need him.

"I'll be back in a minute," he tells me. He goes up to the counter and returns with two bowls of porridge and two mugs of black coffee.

"I love you and I promise you I'll never let you down again."

"Josephine, my Josephine," he whispers, stroking my chin. "You're so beautiful and I should count myself lucky. But... I don't know how to say this. I didn't sleep last night. I thought about you, a lot. I kept picturing you on the stage. The way you threw the golden envelope out. Do you know what it was like for me, to read all about that kid screwing you backstage? The thing is, I'm not angry with you over it. I should be, but I'm not. Do you know why? Because that was completely out of character for you. Something triggered you to do that. I want to know what it was."

"I don't know why I did what I did. I can't explain."

"The thing is, Josephine, there has to be some sort of an explanation. I need to know."

I picture Dan's face and Sanne's smug grimace. I want to open up, to let him know everything. But it's a block in my mind. Nothing comes through. There's nothing to pay the ferryman. I clam up, suffocate, and tears drip into the porridge.

"I just had a moment of insecurity." The words hang in my mouth.

"That's not it," he replies. "Come on. Are you going to tell me what's going on?"

"I can't."

"Then I hope you understand I can't be a part of this relationship." There's no emotion in him. "Goodbye, Josephine." He gets up. "Breakfast is paid for. Help yourself to as much as you want." He walks and I turn my head to watch his figure dissipate.

1996

Josephine

9 January 1996 and Several Subsequent Days

I write it down. I write it all down. My experiences of teacher training fill up three sides of A4 paper. But I make stuff up. Like how a group of the boys accosted me in the corridor and sexually assaulted me. Like how my mentors took turns at physically attacking me. A whole bunch of other stuff. It's not a problem, because this letter will never see the light of day. Here, I've sealed it, in a golden envelope, which I place in the corner of my desk. It's sealed and it's locked away and there's no way anything from it will get out.

I lean back, smirk, imagine the shock on my mentors' faces if they ever saw what I'd written, and get myself ready. I'm meeting Scarlet for coffee. I'm not sure what she wants to talk about, but she's insistent.

I did something stupid that morning, when he left me in that hotel. I sat there for five minutes like some blithering idiot. It took me five minutes more to finish my porridge, and ten minutes more to finish his. Then I went to the buffet and piled my plate high with bacon, sausage and eggs. I ate it as quick as I could, and then went up again and got even more fatty nonsense. A third time and a fourth time, until I was pushing things down my throat, forcing them down. A fifth time, a sixth time and a seventh time. People were staring as food dripped from my lips. The staff dragged me out in the end. I heaved everything up in the car park, in the exact spot where his car had been parked.

I'm still processing the breakup, still waking up every morning and expecting him to be there. A solid, secure boyfriend. A proper, real partner. Someone who would have my back. Someone who would have loved me. I'll always be thinking about what might have been, even as I sit in the coffeeshop and order caffeine and cake.

The café is situated a mile from where I live. It's somewhere I often liked to have my morning fix, but ever since the Golden Pass Incident, I've found it necessary to avoid the place. But today I'm lucky; no one points out to me.

She turns up late. I think it's around twenty minutes. I wave at her and she comes over.

"Can I get you coffee?" I begin to ask, but she's completely silent.

She puts herself in front of me, buries her face in her hands, runs fingers through her blonde hair.

"What's going on?" I ask.

"How've you been?" comes her voice.

"I've been okay, I guess."

"I'm sorry to hear about Jason."

"It's fine. These things happen. How are things with you?"

"Listen, I didn't come here to talk. You're not going to like this, Josephine, but I – the band, I mean. We need a fresh start. We need to be in a position where we can safely move forward and pursue our ambitions. Josephine, I need you out of our lives."

"What?"

"I know that you've stored a few things at the record company. You've got twenty-four hours to clear everything out. You're not to contact me again. You're not to contact Gina. You're not to contact anyone in the band or associated with it." She produces a document that looks so ridiculously legal. Lawyers' names are on the front (I recognise a couple of them) and there's fancy letters after their names. "Philip says that you need to go through this." She starts moving, stands up with every intention of being firm.

"Aren't you going to say goodbye?" I shout after her.

But she ignores me.

"Scarlet?!" I yell. "Scarlet!"

Someone shouts back at me, some coffee-drinking pensioner: "Jesus, sweetheart, keep your voice down! I'm half-deaf and I can still hear you!"

There's a clattering as one of my feet catches a chair and sends it tumbling to the ground.

I don't remember getting home. I'm in a daze, permanently disconnected from the world, cut off completely.

Even though I sort of understand why Scarlet's done this, it doesn't make it any easier.

I go through the document. I spend the afternoon and evening trying to come to terms with its contents. I'm not only banned from contact with the band and record company, I'm outlawed from attending any of their performances or going anywhere near any of their properties.

I understand, I really do.

But, fuck, I'm angry. Retribution weighs on my mind. I'm on my feet, back on the sofa, walking around again. I'm hyper, full of life, full of energy.

I'm not letting this go. Berserk with rage, I dash into my study, and lift up another one of these Golden Passes.

"Payback time," I whisper, just as there's a thumping at the door.

It's Herbert, out of breath, red-faced. "I came as soon as I could," he splutters. "Are you okay?"

"Fine," I respond. "Yourself?"

"I'm okay. I'm worried about you, Josephine."

"Don't be. Honestly, I'm really okay."

"Are you sure?"

"A hundred percent. Listen, why don't you go and be with the others. I'm just bad news. I really am."

He comes close. I don't register this, but he's holding me close. He's a father figure, far better than the one that raised me up. I know I shouldn't be doing this, but I'm crying, breaking down in front of him. I know how utterly pathetic I must look, but I can't help it. I'm so broken inside. There's no sense of feeling, nothing. I'm so broken.

"What will I do?" I blubber. "What the fuck will I do?"

"You'll find something," I'm told. "Keep your head down, keep focused. You will find an opportunity. You will."

He goes at some point. I'm not sure exactly when, but it leaves a painful vacuum behind, one that latches onto me. I'm holding the thin air in my hallway.

When I'm in my living room, I burst into a fit of rage.

And it's a rage that continues over the next few days.

I take my allotted time in the record company to collect my belongings: a pair of shoes, two paperbacks, and a single framed photograph taken of us in 1994. The Leightons aren't in the building, neither are Scarlet or Gina. Even the receptionist seems to have pissed off somewhere.

On the way out, I yell, "I'm off now! See you later!" Whether they're skulking away somewhere or just taking the absolute piss, I don't know. Either way, I don't hear a response from anyone. I'm Miss Bloody Invisible.

Over the next few days, there's a moment in time when I'm glued to the television. I think it was just after dinner, after I'd gone through my second glass of wine. I wanted to smirk, but I wanted to cry every tear that I could, when I saw the way-too-young presenter doing a mini-report on the band.

They're going on a tour across America: New York, Los Angeles, Phoenix, Dallas, and New York again. Scarlet's the one being interviewed. My, I think sometimes it's possible to forget how beautiful she is. She's stunning. She's delicate.

I know what I've got in my possession. I still have contacts who could get it out there. The media would enjoy themselves. They'd love to rip things to pieces.

I should just face it: I want revenge. I want retribution. I was cut out of the circle. Excised. That bitch will pay. She's going to suffer for it. She'll understand my humiliation.

I'm in my study. I think it's in the early hours, but it could be four days later. I'm holding up the Golden Pass. What's in here will destroy Scarlet's reputation. It will wipe it off the face of the Earth. Rub it into nothing.

I smile at the thought of the band in tatters.

But I can't imagine myself pulling the trigger.

George

26 January 1996

My French is lousy – always has been – but that doesn't stop me from trying it with the taxi driver who picks me up from the station. He gives me that look that tells me he's seen way too many Englishmen on their travels.

It's late afternoon. I arrived in Paris yesterday and took the train down this morning. There's no rain, no floods, no other threatening weather, no disruption, no drama. My stomach's rumbling for lunch.

Yet I'm getting a different kind of butterflies as I approach the town. Everything's the same as I left it. I remember, because I was the last one to leave.

Christ, we were young! We were stupid! We did crazy stuff! Okay, we weren't that young, but we felt like we were in the throes of youth. We felt like the world belonged to us. In a sense, it did – the world revolved around the town that summer. And we owned this town!

I shouldn't be so proud. In recent years, I've grown more disillusioned with who I was in those days. Roger Miser and I were close friends back then.

I was here, over twenty-five years ago.

Now, if you knew Roger Miser in those days, bloody hell, he was your best friend. Vibrant, full of energy, aggressive when he needed to be. Full of himself.

I was here, in the summer of 1980.

I know that old phrase: *The Summer That Changed Every-thing*. And I've had a few of them believe me. 1969, 1974, 1977. But it was the summer of 1980 that really did change everything for me.

I shouldn't reminisce like this. A lot of pain came out of those weeks, but it really made me the person I am today.

The driver pulls up in front of the hotel, gruffly tells me the fare, which I pay in full (as well as a small tip). There's no point haggling in France.

The hotel – the only one in this town – has had some renovations. I see they've repainted the walls and inserted new glass in the upstairs windows. It's like there's been an attempt at a transplant operation.

I won't ever forget staying here, the riotous nights that we had, the parties, the laughs, the tearing of the paint from the walls. We were insane in those days.

But it's inside that things start stirring up painful memo-ries. How can I forget the day when Roger and I turned up and flashed our ludicrous smiles? How can I bury the memories of us walking through town, our gazes flickering towards every half-naked woman?

The interior of the hotel has changed since I was last here, although the wooden reception desk is still in its present place. I think it'll be a long time before every solid memory is taken from here.

Oh, blast! They've still got the same keys. Great, chunky wooden things with oversized metal components.

"Are you okay sir?" says the receptionist lady.

She's young – too young for a place like this. Part of me thinks that I'm responsible for the way she is. She shouldn't be working here. Is she familiar? She might be. Maybe I saw her when she was a child.

I shouldn't get distracted. After all, I'm here for a reason. I'm here to... Actually, I don't know what I'm here for.

The staircase, with its hand-carved banister. The book-shelves in the first-floor corridor, still rammed with their 1950s editions of magazines no one wants to read anymore. The place is beautifully preserved. Too much so.

I haven't been placed on the second-floor room I was in the last time, but the one I'm in on this occasion has all of the same comforts.

Why did I come here? This place has nothing except grief and pain. Oh, why am I being so self-pitying? I was part of the group that caused the pain.

I drop down on the single-size bed, drop my bags, drop my eyelids, drop my head into my hands.

I saw it. Behind the reception desk. That picture of Roger Miser, fresh-faced and bright-eyed, all smiles.

There's no way I'm going to reveal it to you. That's something you'll have to wait for. What happened during that summer was complicated and complex, a messy affair. But I'm not here to tell my story. I came here to make peace.

I need food. It's strange, I thought I wouldn't have an appetite.

I know where to go. There's a café next to the hotel, the one Roger Miser and I used to frequent for breakfast and sometimes lunch. Gingerly, I leave the hotel. I must look like a man with many guilty secrets! It's definitely the way I'm trudging out.

The café still has its unreadable name scrawled above the windows. I go inside. I suppose I'm expecting voices from the past to yell out, but all I see are two men in business suits sitting together, fish in front of each, going through a set of papers with graphs and statistics on.

There are tables with red crisscross covers and polished wooden chairs. There's something new: a glass counter with pastries and cakes on proud display. Thankfully, I don't recognise the lady who's on shift. But it worries me that she's the same age as me. Was she here, back in 1980? I bloody hope not.

I try my French and succeed in ordering a ham and cheese croissant and fresh coffee. Simple pleasures like these are enough for me these days. I eat at the same table – the one right by the window – where Roger and I used to sit. We'd plan our day here, which women we'd sleep with, which parties we'd consider attending.

Back in that summer, the streets outside were jammed with all manner of people. Everyone knew who they were, where they belonged. Even us visitors knew where we belonged, our place in the food chain of life. Well, everyone except us two.

The lunch is grander than the miniscule portions we used to get here: fresh salad and crisps go with the overdone pastry. I just about manage it. The coffee is a little bit on the sour side, but it's bearable.

After lunch, my intention is to go for that gentle touristy walk, but there's a destination already locked in. I try to fight it off, but it's like wrestling a bull. Twice, I nearly trip. Three times, I have to steady myself.

It's January and it's so bloody cold. I should have worn gloves. Even before I'm at the school, tears are creeping out of the corners of my eyes. I wipe them away with trembling fingers.

And here I am. Before the ruined buildings. My fingers curl around the railings as I gaze at the place. The playground overgrown with weeds and litter. The broken doors and windows. The sagging roofs and faded copies of the school's logo.

Have you ever wondered why Roger Miser gave Scarlet and the girls their chance? Why do you think he invested so much into them? Why do you think I displayed such enthusiasm and awe when I first heard their music? Do you seriously think I liked listening to their Godawful songs? Roger Miser and I were trying to make amends, though neither of us will ever admit it. That's why Miser gave them their big break: atonement. That's why he gave them a three-album deal: a way of saying sorry for what happened in 1980.

I'm looking out, tears spewing uncontrollably, like a rainstorm.

"I'm sorry," I say. Then louder: "I'm sorry!"

It's no use. Those voices are long-gone, disappeared, consumed by the past. All that's left is anger. And tears. Tears that should never have been cried.

James

11 March 1996

Of all places, it happens to be on Bond Street. London's Bond Street. Words associated with the megarich and royalty.

I'm in London for a few days, firstly to catch up with my daughter, and secondly to meet up with Paul and Siobhan. I'm heading up to Liverpool in a few hours and intend to spend my stroll on Bond Street trying to find out something nice for them.

I pop into a few of the shops, but I don't buy anything. I'm getting more and more impatient; there's an iron fist of determination within me to get something nice for my friends. And I'll succeed.

In Vancouver, my wife and I are finding ourselves utterly confused and frazzled by the number of shops there are. It's like there's too much choice. I've been hearing that this internet thing might allow you to shop from the comfort of your home, but wouldn't it make things even more confusing? Marianne seems keen on it.

A voice rings out hollow.

I think it's just some drunk.

But the tone is too firm. Too secure.

"Bow to your sensei!" the voice repeats, a command that could silence the sea.

I turn around to see a shortish man ten or so feet away. He's gone grey, completely so, but he's still got that fighting figure, that look of aggression in his cheeks.

"I'm sorry?" I splutter, but I know who it is. It's not the kind of guy you forget.

"You may not have trained with me in decades, but I am still your sensei! Bow!"

People are staring. Curious, goggle-eyed children and their equally disturbed parents watch.

"It's so good to see you again," I stammer. "How have you been?"

"I told you to bow." He's come up close to me now, eyes cutting into me. He grimaces. "Do it."

I dip my head, bend my waist. "I'm sorry, Sensei. For-give me."

"You may be a high-flying executive professional," he says, "but you are still my student. You may have left karate behind, but you are still bound by its code. I am still your teacher, James, don't ever forget that."

"I'm sorry, Sensei."

"There is no need to apologise. Just be aware of who you are, and who I am. Have an enjoyable day."

"Good day, Sensei." I bow and when my head returns, he's in the distance, fading into the crowd.

I move away quickly, anything to avoid the prying eyes. I get off Bond Street and find this small coffeeshop where a swift espresso helps to take the shock off my mind.

What the hell just happened?

By the time I reach Euston to get the train up to Liverpool, there's something else that should be incredibly concerning to me, far more so than bumping into some silly teacher from decades past, except I don't hear the murmuring in the crowds and I don't see the eyes fixed on the display window of the television store.

Even as my carriage is slowly but surely dragged north, I'm oblivious to the story that's slowly breaking.

Josephine

13 March 1996

It's the way he says it: devoid of emotion, lacking commit- ment. He says it in one tone, one voice. He doesn't give a damn. He knows I'm ruined – I can see it in his eyes – but he's not going to risk lifting a finger.

"I'm sorry, Josephine, there's nothing we can do."

"It's okay."

Craig Hinchliffe, my solicitor, grimaces. He opens his briefcase, takes out a small stack of papers, and quickly returns it.

"I'll be in touch as soon as I hear anything," I'm informed. "However, I strongly advise you to settle."

"Thank you. I'll consider the options."

My solicitor gets up to go. He straightens the strands of his wispy hair and lifts up his overcoat from the sofa. "Is there anything else I can do for you?" he asks.

"Nope."

"In that case, I'll see you later. Have a good evening."

"Thank you, Craig. Goodnight."

When he's gone, I dissolve into tears. I'm not crying over the fact I'm being sued. I'm angry that I made a stupid mistake, a silly error of judgement. On Thursday, in my rage, my blinding rage, I picked up the wrong envelope to send to the media. Not the one of Scarlet's father having a secretive gay fling, but my exaggerated account of what happened at the school. It's like a comedy: one careless mistake and I've kicked a wasp's nest.

Everything's coming back. So much crap I hoped was buried. Over the past few days, the media's had a field day with the abuse I received as a trainee teacher. Several former pupils – including the one who sexually assaulted me – have been giving interviews. Apparently, I was "totally ineffective", "insecure", "a nightmare".

Why – oh why – didn't I open the letter up to check? Of course, it's simple. I forgot about the other one. I casted it out of my mind.

Now, here I am, on the verge of ruin.

It's amazing how it takes less than a week for your life to turn upside down. Thoroughly amazing.

I haven't heard anything from the girls. Even Herbert hasn't been in touch. Understandably so. After all, I've done an enormous amount of damage to the reputation of the band.

Philip Leighton was on the radio yesterday, saying that I was an "unhinged, dangerous woman". I know what he's doing: distancing him and the band from me. Protective measures.

14 March 1996

The next morning, I'm on the phone to Craig, telling him that I want to settle. Rainham John Graham is prepared to accept £100,000, as well as a public apology that I will release to the broadsheets and the majority of tabloids.

I'm feeling more relieved with every second. I've conceded defeat, but I'll be able to go home in one piece.

I even consider treating myself to a fancy meal out somewhere; maybe Herbert would like to join me.

When Craig calls in the afternoon, I assume it's to work out the final details of the settlement, but I can tell by the tone in his voice that he's worried, deeply worried. The school have withdrawn their offer.

"I'm sorry," he says. *"Josephine, I'm so sorry."*

"It's okay."

"We'll be in touch regarding court dates. I wish there was something I could do."

"It's fine. Just keep me updated, okay?" I hang up.

Sanne's there in front of me. Her boyfriend as well. They stare at me, laughing and sniggering. She's got that same tender, beautiful grin that she had when she left. I blink and they're gone, but their taunting auras are still there. *Auras.* That's definitely the right word. Evil, twisted *auras.*

Herbert

18 March 1996

This isn't a good idea — and there's probably a dozen or so distinguished colleagues who would advise against it — but I record every detail I can of this meeting. Philip is politely telling the girls what's happened to Josephine. I think I hide the shock, but the way Philip occasionally glances over at me, I know that the mask is slipping.

When he finishes, he curls his thumbs in the direction of Scarlet and Gina, as though he's a headmaster about to cane two truanting schoolchildren. "Do you have anything you want to say?"

"Is she going to be okay?" asks Gina.

"That's not your concern," he replies.

"How's it going to affect us?" asks Scarlet.

"It shouldn't. I've got my lawyers on hair-trigger alert. If anything does happen, they'll be able to react very quickly and stop or, at the very least, minimise any damage. Certainly I wouldn't worry about Josephine. She's pretty much destitute and you'll probably find her mopping the floors at Somerfield before long."

"I think we've got our priorities wrong," says Gina. "Our first thought should be her, making sure she's okay."

"And why?" snaps Scarlet. "After what she did? She jeopardised our safety. She put us all at risk. All because she had a grudge against that stupid fucking school. She deserves what she's getting. I don't give a fuck about her, Gina. And you shouldn't either."

Silence fills the meeting room. Even Keith in the corner quietens himself. Only the scratching of my pen reminds me that there's still life in the world.

"Do you think this is what Susan would have wanted?" says Gina.

"Don't you dare bring her into this, Gina," hisses Scarlet. Her knuckles are as pale as her hair. "Don't you fucking dare. Just don't."

"I think we all need to calm down." Keith comes over, raises his hands, tries to cool the simmering tensions.

I can sense the red-hot loathing that forms a bridge between Scarlet and Gina.

"Gina, that was a mistake," says Philip, tut-tutting under his breath. "I suggest you apologise."

"Why should I?"

The fight turns into petty bickering. I get two thirds of the juicy details. All the while, I know that I'm going to have to somehow bring this into the finished article.

Officially, I stop following the band on the last day of January next year. The magazine wants the article by Valentine's Day. Then, who knows what?

"That's enough!" snaps Philip. When he raises his voice, he sounds shrill, like he's got an iron gauntlet latched around his windpipe.

The girls fall silent and focus on him.

"Good," he whispers. "Good. Now, the important news is that Josephine's *little accident* hasn't affected album sales, or anything else. In fact, I've been called up quite frequently over the past few days. You're getting a bunch of incredible interview offers. I think that now Josephine is out the way, people want to know *your* stories. Ladies, I think we need to seize this opportunity."

"He's right," says Keith.

There's more bickering between Scarlet and Gina, but eventually things turn to business. Interview requests need to be accepted, a small tour organised, a new album planned.

In the last moments of the meeting, I fight the urge to piss. When Philip methodically ends the discussion, I dash out to relieve myself. When I return, the girls have left. Philip's gone as well. Only Keith remains, chewing on the skeleton of a green apple.

"Do you fancy a pint later?" he asks me.

"No thanks," I reply. "I've got plans, mate."

"How about another time then?"

"No thanks, mate. Listen, I've got to go now. Work to do."

Call me paranoid, but I make sure I'm not followed on my way to Josephine's home. It's strange, but who would follow me anyway? Maybe Philip Leighton. I mean, just look at the way he treats his brother...

I check my notes on the bus, trying to put together a story, trying to figure out if I'll use this in the magazine article at the end. In all honesty, I'm starting to look forward to the completion of this project. Three years was way too long for this. Three months would have been more appropriate. I've got piles and heaps of notes at home. Damn, it's going to be impossible to sort out.

Josephine looks slightly the worse for wear when she opens the door. Dark rings hang under her eyes and it's clear that she's been crying.

"Hey," she just about manages to croak.

"Are you okay?"

"Take a wild guess. Anyway, why are you here? I'm not supposed to have any contact with you."

"No one has to know."

"Come on in, for Christ sakes."

Her home smells fresh, clearly sprayed with one of these new fancy cleaning products you see on the news. It soon becomes evident why: cardboard boxes line the corridors.

"You're leaving?" I stammer.

"I've got to give up the apartment. No choice in the matter. Legal bills and all that. Plus ,I'm going to owe the school five-and-a-half million in damages."

"Oh, shit."

"Yes, shit."

"Where will you go?"

"I'm not sure yet. Probably a bed-and-breakfast for a few nights, then I'll see what happens."

"Why don't you come and stay with me for a bit?"

"Herbert, I don't think that's a good idea."

"Why not?"

"Let's have some tea."

Her kitchen, like the rest of her apartment, is stripped bare. A few cups, a kettle and a bag of dried milk lie in the corner of the worksurface.

"Sorry, had to give the fridge away," she tells me. "Powdered milk. I hope that's okay with you."

"I'm sure I could live with that."

She casts me an aggressive look. I don't think my joke has worked with her.

"I won't have you winding up in a b-and-b," I tell her, trying to be firm, though my voice is splitting apart. It's not as firm as it was back in America. Ever since I left, it's grown progressively weaker. "I want you to stay with me. You can stay as long as you need."

"Why would you want to have me in your home? Why would you do this for me?"

"Because I care about you, Josephine. I care about you."

"You're not in love with me, are you? Please don't tell me that. Please. You're old enough to be my –"

"I get it. Josephine, I get it. I'm not in love with you. I just care about you deeply. Look, maybe I pushed it a bit too far. I didn't mean to overstep the mark. I just want to look after you."

"But I'm not your responsibility." She moves towards the kettle, but doesn't switch it on. "Herbert, you have a job to do. You have a contract to fulfil. Tell the story. Tell it in its completion. You're capable of it and so much more."

"Am I? I thought about it a lot on the bus here. I don't think I'm cut out for this."

"Why not?"

"I feel daunted by it all. How the hell will I put three years' worth of notes into a magazine article? I'll have two bloody weeks to do it!"

"You'll find a way. I know you will."

She puts her hands around the back of my neck, looks into my eyes. I can see the distress and pain behind her pupils. She looks so sad, so dejected, so worn down, so fed up of everything, so ill, so torn up.

"You can do anything you want to, Herbert. You're not a spent force."

"Oh, but I think I am."

"You're not." She runs her fingers through my hair. "You're a good, decent man, and you deserve nothing but the best."

"Thank you."

"You should go now, Herbert. Go and live your life."

She takes my hand in hers and leads me to the door. Another smile comes my way and she gently shuts the wood in my face.

1 April 1996

Two weeks later, I find out on the news that Josephine has been made bankrupt. I don't even read the full article in *The Times*; I barely skim my way through. I fold the paper up and toss it in the corner.

I find that I'm working more efficiently now. The ideas are coming together. The strands of the story are beginning to weave into a beautiful pattern. I've plotted a rough outline of the article, leaving room for the stories that I'll gather over the next few months.

Next year, I'm returning to America. That slip of paper I have hidden in the box on my shelf: it's a number of an old contact. I phoned them up last week, told them what I wanted, told them that I wanted to work in the States again as a music journalist. I have a wealth of experience to offer. Last night, I got a phone call: there's a job waiting for me in San Diego, starting at the beginning of March next year. It's nothing as glamourous as what I used to do, but I'll get to interview musicians and do a bit of travelling around the country. It's just what I'm after.

As for Josephine, why the hell should I care? I'm being an arrogant so and so, but I need to think about myself. My marriage is gone, my family is gone, and soon this contract will be gone. I need to think about what I want in life; I think it might be the first time I've focused on myself.

Keith

14 July 1977

"Congratulations, both of you are going to New York."

Keith noticed Philip smirk at the announcement. He almost sneered himself, but quickly tightened the muscles in his cheeks and lips.

"You're joking, surely?" was Keith's response. He knew both he and his brother looked daft in that moment, daft as two rubber doorknobs.

"I don't joke about anything," replied Barry Farringdon. He gently tapped his cigar on the stained ashtray that was an eyesore on his otherwise clean and tidy desk. Barry's thick glasses and three-piece suit, cotton tie and Italian shoes, trimmed moustache and bulging stomach, gave him the look and complexion of sheer superiority.

Keith and Philip looked up to him unquestionably. Given the fact that he was a strong believer in them, given the fact that he'd given both of them high-level roles in his record company, well, there was no reason for them not to get down on their knees and worship him. Barry Farringdon was a god in the music world. Revered and respected by bands and musicians from London to Manchester to Newcastle, his name was one to be feared and admired.

"When are we heading off?" asked Keith.

"The day after tomorrow," said Barry. "Very early flight from Heathrow. Make sure your bags and stuff are packed."

"Is anyone coming with us?" said Philip. "From what you've said, Mr Farringdon, we're going to need a little backup. I've never been to New York. I don't know my way around the city."

"It's okay. It's okay. You'll be met by my American lawyer, who will be there to provide the necessary legal support."

"We'll get it done, sir," said Keith, "by any means necessary."

"Just be extremely careful. You're both very clever men, but you're also young and inexperienced. Don't take any chances. Don't do anything stupid."

"You can trust us."

"I'm counting on it."

It had been late last night when Barry Farringdon called, asking him to come into the office first thing and to bring his brother too. Farringdon had sounded panicked, alarmed. The moment the two brothers were seated on the ancient leather seats, he'd told them everything:

One of his bands – only established last year – had done a concert a few weeks ago in New York. Massive turnout. Yet, despite the ticket sales, not a single penny had come through to London. The company that ran the venue had not returned any calls. He wanted Keith and Philip to go over there and try to see what was going on.

Barry Farringdon looked at the end of his tether. Wrung like a chicken. He put out his cigar, sighed, coughed. "Listen, I trust the two of you with this," he said. "Go there, find out what's going on, come back. You've got a week there to get everything sorted. This is not a holiday. This is serious. Right, head downstairs. Barbara's got the flight tickets."

Keith led the way out. He was glad to be away from Barry's claustrophobic office. It was too much: the leather seats and primrose-themed carpet, the red fabric sofas and array of strong spirits on the white shelves. Shelves that seemed to be constantly suffering from their repainting. He headed down the brown carpet staircase, followed by his brother, to where Barbara, who looked like she'd been nicked from high school, was painting her nails.

"You reckon this is big, like dangerous?" said Philip. "I'm a bit worried."

"Don't be. Everything will be fine. Listen, you go home, I'll collect the tickets. I want to see if Barbara will allow me to buy her a drink."

"I wish you wouldn't do that. Barry wouldn't like it."

"Barry doesn't need to know. Anyway, head home, I'll take care of everything here."

Alastair

19 April 1996

Dear Diary,

The fax said to come as soon as possible. Scarlet and I have never had the best of brother-sister relationships, but the message from her was brief; it seemed clustered with panic. She – or rather this Philip Leighton – organised my flight over the Atlantic.

I landed at Heathrow in the early hours and was met by these two Leighton Brothers. They were polar opposites in every way, shape... and form. Keith Leighton was a short, squat guy, with a slight bulge in the stomach and a reddish face. He looked worried and anxious, frequently glancing around his person. Philip Leighton was the complete opposite: calm and composed, dressed in a three-piece Armani suit. Clean-shaven with his ungreased hair cut short, he had the appearance of a model, respectable businessman. But I've heard rumours about Philip Leighton for years, even before Scarlet signed up to him. He's a despicable, aggressive, manipulative bully. A contact of mine back in Canada told me once that Philip had driven another record company owner to suicide after threatening to seize his business.

No, I've never liked either of the brothers.

I'm sitting in my hotel room half an hour away from midnight as I write these words. I'm trying to keep them fresh in my mind. It's been – shall we say – an interesting day. I can't begin to describe it, but I'll do my best.

So, the Leighton Brothers drove me from Heathrow to their company headquarters in London. Keith was driving and Philip sat next to me in the back, where he proceeded to grill me on the ins and outs of my legal career so far. He wasn't too intrusive, but he seemed to want to know everything.

I have to admit, their offices were far smarter and better-looking that Roger Miser's. Cleaner, more pristine, fresher. A pretty receptionist greeted us as we walked inside. A lobby with plants and abstract paintings made me feel like I was back in my legal work experience.

"Hi there, dear," said Philip, "how are you doing?"

The receptionist smiled. "I'm very well, sir, how about you?"

"I'm okay. Listen, dear, I've got to sign this gentleman in."

She handed over a small clipboard and asked me for my name and signature. I put the necessary information on and Philip subsequently escorted me deeper into the building. Keith walked several footsteps behind, sheepishly. I was taken to this meeting room, which Philip informed me was used to discuss important contracts and tour planning.

"Keith, go and get some coffee going. I think we all need a cup." When his brother had left, Philip turned to me, letting out a lengthy sigh.

"Is Scarlet here yet?" I asked.

"Oh, she'll be coming, don't worry, but I'd like to have a proper meeting with you first, go over a few things. Forgive me, I never asked, how was the flight?"

"It was okay. Thanks for the tickets."

"Not a problem. Anyway, let's get to business. So, doubtless you've heard of what happened regarding Josephine?"

"I have."

"Josephine's issues with her teacher training days nearly caused serious damage to this record company and to the band." Philip chuckled and shook his head. "I shouldn't laugh at this sort of stuff. It's hard not to though when you think of Josephine trying to cut it as a teacher. But anyway, what she did could have made major trouble for our reputation."

I can't remember much else of what he said. He seemed obsessed with the prestige of the band and that it was his highest priority to protect it. He mentioned a few other things about the importance of safety for girl bands and not allowing any sort of misogyny to take place, particularly when it came to concerts.

I remember clearly what his last line was: "Alastair, Scarlet and I have had a little chat, and we'd like you to become the legal representative for the band."

"Excuse me?"

"Six-figure salary, certainly a lot more than you're earning now. I guarantee this will be worth your while."

"Mr Leighton, I don't have any expertise in this area. I don't know the first thing about being a legal representative for a band."

We argued back and forth for a bit. I have to admit it, the guy was intimidating. We had a little pause when Keith brought in the coffee, but then he resumed with extra ferocity. He was so determined to get me to accept it.

Finally, Scarlet came in, two bloody hours after I'd arrived.

"Nice of you to finally come!" I snapped.

"Sorry, I was held up," she responded. "Honestly, I'm really sorry to have kept you waiting. Have you accepted the offer, Alastair?"

"I haven't accepted anything and I've no intention of doing so!"

I'm aware how visibly furious I must have appeared. I probably embarrassed myself somewhat, particularly when I stormed out. To be flown halfway across the world and bullied into accepting a contract! Unacceptable!

I'd been booked into a hotel at Heathrow and I turned up expecting my reservation to have been cancelled, but found that everything was still in place. I took a long shower, sat naked on the bed with a glass of whisky, and tensed up. My left fist clenched itself up like a vice and my throat felt cracked.

I thought that Scarlet wanted to see me! To spend time with me, to catch up. A wretched lie. She wanted me on a professional basis.

I'm tired of being used for professional purposes. I'm tired of being an object: someone who fills in forms and ensures the smooth conduct of business dealings. I've had enough of it all.

As I write these words, I'm considering a change in direction in life. Something different. Something unique. I need a fresh beginning.

Gina

12 July 1996

George reached out to me recently to let me know about his trip to France. Only took him half a year to do it, but I'm glad he did in the end. He still hasn't opened up about what happened back in 1980, but I can see it's hurting him. When I saw him last week, I could see the pain in him. Even underneath the burning sun in the beer garden in Ruislip where we met up, he looked so cold and forlorn.

I'm thinking about that face right now as I step onstage. Someone shouts: "Communist! Fucking communist!" They're quickly drowned out by the cheering.

This will sound strange, but I've no idea where we're actually performing. We've been crisscrossing the country since the end of June on a whirlwind tour that the Leighton Brothers put together. It's our comeback from Josephine's backstabbing act. This is the new *us*.

Scarlet's looking tired. I can see the weariness in her as she takes her position. The guitar hangs too loosely from her and her shoelaces seem on the verge of coming undone.

"Thanks for coming tonight!" she bellows out. "You all good?! I don't hear you! I don't fucking hear you! Come on, fucking roar!"

And we kick off. An old favourite to start with.

Oh, and I'm back on the front row. Now that Josephine's gone, her guitarist role has been given to me. One of the backing musicians now sits with the drums: he's a thickset bald bloke with gritty hygiene; I don't even want to describe it.

As the night progresses, I'm finding that I'm becoming increasingly tired. I'm sleepy, losing concentration with every second that passes. I get a wrong note, but thankfully it's not noticed by anyone; I fucking hope not. My eyelids start to slip. My feet become jelly. My t-shirt is soaked through with sweat and focus.

The lights and the sound blur together, a splintered kaleidoscope. Everything falls apart and falls together.

The edges of Scarlet's figure begin dissolve. I glance at the backing musicians, finding that they too have lost their sharpness.

And suddenly the concert's over. The lights go up and we file off to the sound of whooping and applause.

I need to sleep so badly. I swear, if a bunk appeared before me, right here in the corridor, I'd go and collapse on it.

"You okay?" Scarlet's got a hand on my shoulder. I can feel her sweat through my thin t-shirt. She smells musty.

"Yeah, just a little tired. It's been a long tour."

"You can say that again."

Despite my tiredness, I'm the one that pulls Scarlet into a tight hug. Somehow, I find the energy to jump in the air and let out a loud cheer.

Both of us see Herbert at the same time. He's dressed in perhaps the most casual manner I've ever seen: t-shirt, loose-fitting jeans, and... trainers. It's a little snug on him, but he does look relaxed and comfortable, which is a massive change. He's aged as well. It's sad to see it on him, but it's there, and there's no mistaking it.

"I need my bed!" I blurt out. "I'm exhausted!"

"You look it," says Herbert.

"There's some champagne in my suite," says Scarlet. "I don't know about you guys, but I fancy a glass or two before bed."

Technicians are moving around us in their rehearsed chaos. Everything has to be packed away with absolute precision, ready to be loaded onto the coach. The Leighton Brothers like to do everything via coach, though of course Scarlet and I get our own private transport.

"When are we speaking at that school?" I ask Scarlet.

"I think it's late September."

Philip – as part of his rejuvenation project for the band – has arranged for us to do a talk at Josephine's old training school, Rainham John Graham Comprehensive. He believes that this will clear up our image: we are a band that needs to move forward, a band that seeks forgiveness. When he first mentioned this to us a few weeks ago, he was full of irrepressible joy. You should have heard him!

"We shouldn't view what happened as any sort of setback!" he said. "We should take this opportunity to build a strong relationship with this school, to work with young minds!"

This was the first time I saw him break his calm demeanour. I've never seen so much joy and eagerness! What else did he say? Oh, how can I forget!

"I had a fantastic conversation with the deputy head-teacher, and she's very interested in our band. *Very* interested."

It's the way he said *very*. So obnoxious and arrogant. It's easy to laugh about it, but this guy is in charge of us. He tells us where we play, what we do, where we eat, who we can mingle with, how many glasses of wine we're allowed to have.

When Josephine's legal case was eventually sorted out, Philip got talking with the school. At first, it was an apology, then it became a love letter.

"I'm very tired, guys, so I'm going to head to the hotel," says Herbert. "I hope you don't mind."

"Go for it," says Scarlet. "Goodnight, Herbert."

After the journalist leaves, I stifle a yawn, and begin to shuffle towards the exit.

"Do you fancy playing a game?" Scarlet asks me.

"What?" I stutter.

"A game."

"Well, not tonight, Scarlet."

"Of course! Tomorrow, after breakfast. We don't leave until lunchtime, so we have a few hours. There's a basketball court in the hotel. I'd like to play a game with you."

"I haven't played basketball since... school," I say. "Um, yeah, okay, let's play a game."

13 July 1996

To my surprise, the next morning, she doesn't bother to turn up. I eat breakfast alone, waiting and hoping she turns up.

"You're going to miss breakfast," I mutter.

I'm about to go up and snag some pastries and one of the cartons of juice that they have – anything for Scarlet – when she appears and makes straight for my table.

"Sleep in, did you?" I chide.

"Not quite. I was planning, in my head. Do you remember a while ago when I said that I wanted to do five albums with the Leightons?"

"How can I forget? You were bloody insistent about it."

"Well, I've had a change of heart. I want to do five albums, in total."

"In total?"

"I'm going to inform Philip of my decision. We will do one more album. Our best one. Give it your best, Gina, give it your absolute best. Our fifth album will be our crowning jewel."

"Scarlet, are you out of your mind?"

"I'm not out of my mind. This is what I want."

"After everything we've been through?"

"Precisely." She sits down in front of me, smirks. "We've lost so many people. There's been hurt. Too much hurt. I can't take that stuff anymore. Emma, Christ knows what happened to her. Josephine, bankrupt and ruined. Susan, dead! Roger Miser, dead! My old mentor, Sharmaine Bateson, living like a pig. It's too much, Gina!"

"And that's why we should keep on singing, keep on fighting, for them!"

"Gina, Gina, I know how deeply you care, but my decision's made. I'm going to do one more album, and that's it. If you want to continue the band, go for it. But I'm doing one more album, and there will not be another. Besides, I only ever wanted to do five albums."

"What?"

"Five was enough for me. One for each of us. Hold on, excuse me." She goes up to the counter and fills a plate high with food. When she comes back, I can tell she's acting like nothing's happening.

"One for each of us then?" I feel like I'm interrogating her as I say this.

"Five albums. One for Emma. One for Josephine. One for Susan. One for you. One for me."

"You're so stupidly self-centred, Scarlet, you know that?" I'm about to launch into a tirade of abuse, but I start seeing things from her point of view; it all makes an annoying sort of sense.

"So, we'd better start planning the fifth album then," I say. "Where would you like to do it?"

"How long do you think it would take to write a few songs and put music to them?"

"A month, if I get the peace and quiet to do it."

"Good. Excellent. I'm going to talk to Philip when we get back off tour. There's a small town on the west coast of Scotland, forgot its name, not too far from Glasgow, that would be ideal for us to record in. I've had my eye on the place for some time."

"You know what's best, Scarlet, I trust you."

"I know you do." She shrugs her shoulders, smirks again. "I need coffee."

Keith

16 July 1977

They were met – bleary-eyed – by Barry's American lawyer at JFK Airport, who promptly introduced himself as Randolph Nichols. He was a short, squat man, with a shiny bald head and a puffy face. He shook hands with them, asked them how their flight was, and escorted them to a waiting car outside. After handing a few dollars to a moustached attendant, the lawyer gestured for them to get inside.

"Thank you so much for the support you're giving us," said Keith.

Philip wasn't paying the remotest bit of attention. He'd always been a distracted little child and now even as a young man, he was no different: gazing around at the terminal, drip-fed on it.

"It's my pleasure," said Randolph Nichols, as he turned on the ignition. The car rumbled, croaked into life. "Right, let's go." The lawyer lit up a cigarette and started moving off.

Keith briefly looked over his shoulder, watching the airport disappear behind them and they were swallowed by the towering city.

"Wow," muttered Philip. "Wow. Wow. Wow."

There was much to be impressed by. Maybe too much. Keith simply couldn't believe it, simply couldn't fathom how this had happened: he was in New York. Around them, buildings rose up like teeth. Floors and floors of brittle windows, seas of yellow taxis thronging the roads, smoke and steam coming from hotdog stands, newspaper stands with angry capped men shouting abuse, a newly married couple emerging from a church and cheered by a packed crowd, and... so much more. Too much for him to note down. Far better than bloody Gillingham anyway.

"They do they this is the city that never sleeps," remarked Keith.

And it bloody was. The forbidden fruit of the music world.

No one responded to his comment.

"I'll drop you guys at the hotel. I expect you'll want some rest. I'll pick you guys up at, Seven? Would that be okay? For dinner?" Randolph quickly glanced at both of them. A thick steel ring glinted on his ring finger.

"That would be wonderful," said Philip. "Where's the best place to eat?"

"Philip, this is not a holiday," snapped Keith. "Forgive my brother, Randolph, he didn't mean any disrespect."

"Oh, that's no problem! No, I appreciate you guys want to experience the best of the city whilst you're here. I know a few good places. I'll reserve something."

The world around the car seemed to open and close around them. The buildings threatened to collapse on them. The eyes of those on the streets peered their way.

Keith wasn't the world's expert on cars, but from what he could tell, they were in a Ford Cortina. Maybe not the right kind of car for a lawyer, but it had a strong sense of sophistication. Both front seats had plenty of room, enough for him to lock his knees, but poor Philip looked distinctly uncomfortable in the back, scrunched up and crushed.

They slowed down almost to a crawl. Horns blared and howled. Shouts and flaming tempers floated around like the exhaust that clogged the air.

Keith had a vague idea of where they were: on the approach to Brooklyn Bridge.

"Oh, I didn't mention," said the lawyer, "but there's a good restaurant in the hotel where you're staying. I think it's called The Olympia? I've eaten there a couple of times before. Pretty darn good stuff."

"Well, why don't we eat there tonight?" proposed Philip.

"Good idea." Keith broke into a grin. "We are here on business, after all."

It was another half-hour before they pulled up at the front of the hotel. Guests – definitely the well-dressed of society – flooded through the foyer. Philip grabbed their bags from the boot and Keith watched him – quite irritated – as he did a quick count of their belongings.

"Okay, I'll see you guys in a few hours," said Randolph. He looked out at the clogged street, cursed. "Damn traffic... I'll see you guys later."

Two large cops walked past them, batons tapping against their kneecaps. The lawyer nodded at them and one lifted his sunshades. He looked uncomfortable, stretched-out lips forcing his face into a mild grin.

"Have a good one." Keith sighed and patted Randolph on the shoulder. "We'll catch you later, mate." He walked into the hotel, closely followed by Philip

Pretty girls with hair tied into tight buns stood to attention behind the desks. Their eyes were unfixed, darting around from person to person, businessman to businessman.

The lobby, despite its openness, seemed to close in on them. It was mighty, extraordinary, a metal rod right up his spine. He watched slim ladies pass him in colourful dresses, shifted on by their older husbands, all of whom had their hair neatly trimmed and seemingly treated with every sort of chemical available, all of whom were puffing away.

"Nice view here," he quipped to his brother.

In truth, the hotel freaked him out. He saw the rich and powerful, the famous and silver spoon lucky.

"Excuse me, Mr Leighton?" A young man – maybe a little older than Philip – stood there in a badly fitting bellboy suit. He seemed visibly nervous, unable to make the slightest bit of eye contact.

"Yes, that's me," said Keith.

"Mr Farringdon has sent a message to the hotel regarding –"

Another man, this one in a three-piece suit, approached, putting himself between the bellboy and Keith, waving his gloved hands in a sign of stern formality. "I'll take over from this," he said. "Mr Bellini, could you take our guests' luggage and transport it to the Presidential Suite? Gentlemen, if you will come with me, there is complementary coffee in the Executive Lounge. The manager would like to personally welcome you to the hotel."

"That sounds great," said Philip.

"Indeed." Keith smiled as the three-piece suit with the wispy, grey hair led them in the direction of an elevator.

For a moment, he thought that he might have been out of his depth, but then reminded himself that this was New York. In this city, apparently, everyone felt six feet under.

Alastair

1 August 1996

Dear Diary,

It's here, it's official.

Disbelief is the wrong word. There's just no way to describe how I'm feeling.

Anyway, I am getting overexcited. I am a lawyer: I need to slow down, analyse the facts, and put everything into order.

It was one of those typical days where I was working from home: cases to prepare, reports to type up, as well as a few phone calls. The day went very quickly: everything was completed by lunchtime, which meant I had a free afternoon.

I went to one of my favourite coffee places in Vancouver, which I know always has a free seat or two, regardless of the time of day. If you haven't been to Bill's Best Coffee, then you absolutely must: hand-carved tables, shelves embedded in the walls stocked with magazines and books, homemade chocolatey pastries, paintings and drawings from local artists hanging from the walls, and the best damn espressos in the world. Anyway, I am getting distracted.

So, it was just after lunch, and I took a walk to Bill's for a short, sharp shock of caffeine. In I went, waving hello to the students/part-time staff behind the counter, picking up one of the English papers from the spindly metallic stand by the entrance. I quickly placed my order for a double espresso and a chocolate croissant, and sat at one of the tables by the window. I pushed back into the deluxe leather chair and held up *The Times*.

"What?" I stuttered. "Scarlet…"

They were breaking up. Scarlet's face – drawn out – sadly, silently proclaimed the news. One more album, and that would be it.

Suddenly my espresso was cold and the croissant was beginning to go soft.

I suppose I knew this day was coming. Like all bands, there comes a time when things fall apart. With any endeavour, any dream, any idea, there will come a moment when it begins to disintegrate, collapse into nothingness.

"How did all this happen?" I found myself asking out loud.

I swallowed my cold espresso, chewed on my pastry, and then somehow focused my mind away from the chaos that was unfolding half a world away.

I'm considering giving up this diary. It's too much, way too much for me. Too much responsibility. Too much to take care of. I'm done with it all. When I finish for the day, when I'm ready to relax and put my feet up, all I want is just a quiet evening, a quiet life. Is it too much to ask?

Herbert

18 August 1996

I look up from my notepad as we approach the Erskine Bridge.

"Fucking tollbooths," snarls Keith. "Bloody hell." He curses again as he squeezes the brakes and we gradually pull to a halt.

We've been driving since the early hours, setting off from London at Four A.M. It's been a tiring trip, with too few stops.

The girls travelled up yesterday: a flight up to Glasgow and a luxury taxi over to the town where the recording will happen. Christ, what's the name of the town again?

Keith, myself and the backing singers are heading up in a minibus. It's jammed with recording equipment, luggage and cans of beer. There's hardly any room for us to move around – thank God I'm in the front next to Keith.

Philip's brother leans out of the window and hands change to a young lady in the tollbooth. We're waved through and soon find ourselves travelling across the great expanse of the Clyde.

"One hell of a view," I remark.

"Why the hell did you travel up with us?" asks Keith. "Why didn't you go with Gina and Scarlet?"

"I thought about it, but I wanted something else to add. I've spent so much time with Gina and Scarlet, and... well, you know who I'm talking about. But I want to add a few things about the backing singers and the record managers. Something to spice up the article."

"That's good you're thinking like that," he says. "You know, you seem so happy these days. I can't figure out why."

"Well, when I hand in this article, I'm moving on. I'm going back to America."

"Oh, right. Got your plane tickets sorted?"

"Not yet."

"It's quite warm today," Keith remarks. He fiddles with one of the dials below the radio. "The A.C. even doesn't fucking work properly."

"Is Philip coming along?" I ask him.

"He says he might come towards the end, once it's all done."

"I would have thought he'd come a lot earlier, but..."

"Yes, my brother is like that. He just likes the afterparties and the glory of it, but never the hard work."

"That sounds like him."

"Beautiful view, isn't it?" remarks Keith. To our left, the Clyde opens up into a tranquil abyss; to our right, the skyline of Glasgow glistens.

When we reach the other side, Philip's brother just about misses the turnoff and curses loudly.

"You've done a great job getting us up here," I say. "Are you sure you don't want me to take over?"

"Quite sure," he replies. "Thanks anyway."

"How long to go?" I ask.

"Another hour and a bit I'd say. I came up this way last year for a weekend, so I know the rough layout of the place."

It's going to be a hot, humid afternoon. Already, I can feel beads of sweat gathering behind my earlobes. Well, that's probably due to the wretched air-conditioning. Keith's not taking it too well. I mean, being overweight like he is isn't good for staying cool. He's starts finger sweat out of his eyelids. I turn away, disgusted.

"What was he like?" I'm asked. "Miser. Roger Miser. What was he like?"

"I thought you'd know," is my answer.

"Philip was the one who had all the meetings and dinners with him. I only met him a couple of times. What was he like? What was he like as a person?"

"I'd say he was committed, strong. I wouldn't say he was wholeheartedly a good man, but he was a dedicated chap. It isn't my word you should take though. Ask Scarlet and Gina. They knew him far better than I ever did."

"I might just do that," he whispers under his breath. "I just bloody do that."

The town is called Muirgyle and it rests playfully on the banks of the Clyde. It's a town that seems to have seen better days: we drive past two ice-cream stores with the words *For Sale* gathering mould and dirt on their fronts. A beach –

vacant, except for a few dogwalkers – looks like it's been left to rot, with twigs, rubbish and crap cluttering the sand. Indeed, the whole place looks like it's been beaten up.

"A friend of mine used to come here as a kid," says one of the backing musicians.

"Where's the place?" I ask Keith.

"At the edge of the town. Oh, here we go..." Keith turns the wheel to the right and we shoot up a narrow street.

I stop worrying and fretting. I become as chilled and calm as I was in America. Embrace the now.

This will be one of my last major engagements with the band. After this, it's meetings to discuss the release of the last album and a few concerts. They're doing a short farewell tour next March – too late for me, but I'll have everything I need. Their final album comes out in January.

I think this use to be a Victorian beachside pleasure zone at one point. The historian eye that I have spots the authentic carvings in the walls of homes: dates from over a century ago. They probably had a better time than we're having.

"Hold on," mutters Keith, "I think..." He brakes harshly, prompting complaints from the back, and turns into a tight-fitting driveway.

It's a small mansion, with an oval-shaped garden in front of it and ivy clustered beneath the windows. The brickwork is the colour of damp sand; it's like a mud hovel but with form. The building is three storeys tall, with large entry porch and a small side entrance. The roof seems to be sagging: I can see that part of its apex is dipped.

There's plenty of space in front of the house, enough for several minibuses to park and offload stuff. Two cars are already there – small hatchbacks. Philip said something about a couple of sound technicians heading up by themselves.

"We're here," moans Keith, switching off the engine. "Right, let's get the stuff offloaded."

"Why don't you go and relax?" I say. "Have a coffee or something?"

"I'll have a drink when everything's been sorted out. Right, guys, let's get this done."

I step out and stretch. It's then that I become aware of Scarlet and Gina sitting on the lawn. Both are in t-shirts and jeans, flat-out.

"We're finally here!" I call out to them.

"Then head inside!" responds Scarlet. "We'll be in in a few minutes!"

"Very welcoming," I whisper to myself.

"Lunch first!" shouts Scarlet. "We've ordered some stuff."

"Pizza?" one of the technicians says.

"Much better!" replies Scarlet. "You'll see!"

It's then that I notice the string of five tables and accompanying seats on the grass. Oh dear, what have they got planned?

Scarlet sees me looking. "It was Mr Leighton's idea."

"What?"

"Go inside. Honestly, Herbert. Just go. You'll see it."

I start following the trickling train of human beings inside. Everything seems to grind to a halt, and then move on, and then break down again. Oh, I'm being melodramatic.

The entrance porch is nothing special – I think it's a recent addon, judging by the finely cleaned glass and fine-cut, shiny porcelain tiles beneath my feet.

But inside, I have to stop myself from letting out a gasp. I'm greeted by a large room, at the centre of which is an enormous, dark bronze model of a roaring lion. It's a circular room, with three other doors leading off from it: one straight ahead, one to the left, and one to the right; all at equidistant intervals. Chessboard tiles, roughcut and crumbling at the edges, form the floor. The ceiling is painted white – a recent job, any wally could tell that. Not a very good job, in that dried drips that have made their way onto the dark green wallpaper.

You can tell I've watched one too many documentaries on old houses.

A man, poorly dressed, and with evidently very little sleep, emerges from the door on the left with a stack of papers in his arms. "Hi, guys," he says. "Um, Philip told me to give you this..." He flicks his way through the papers and takes out one of the white sheets. "Okay, here it is..." He holds it out to us, seems to pause, then gives it to me. "Your room allocations."

One of the guys laughs. "Where are Scarlet and Gina sleeping?"

"They're staying in a local hotel, Guy," says the fatigued bloke.

"They should be sleeping here, with us lads!" responds Guy.

I want to snap at him, but restrain my anger.

Guy (full name, conveniently, Guy Hawkes) is the chief sound technician. He's only twenty-five, but acts like he's a teenager. I met him yesterday and from the first instant, I couldn't stand him. Obnoxious, aggressive, always talking down to everyone. The first few hours of the trip up, he yawned and told everyone how much he fancied Scarlet. I confess, it was a bit of a laugh at first, but then it grew tiresome and annoying. Thankfully, he fell asleep after Preston. Hmm, I don't know whether Guy Hawkes is his real name, or if it's made-up: something to give him a shot at fame.

"Anyone fancy crackin' open a few beers?" he shouts. "Come on, boys, I think we've earned it!"

"We've got stuff to get on with," says Keith. "Okay, thanks, Rupert," he tells the tired man. "Right, guys, come on, let's get started. Herbert, can you give me that piece of paper? Cheers. Listen carefully, here are your room allocations...!"

I feel a tugging at my elbow. Gina twiddles her finger and tells me to come with her. I follow her blindly back into the sunlight. Scarlet's still lying on the lawn, face staring up to heaven.

"Sorry, they're a handful!" I say.

She's not laughing. "Look, Herbert," she whispers, "I've been worried about you recently. You look exhausted. Are you okay?"

"I'm fine, Gina. I'm heavily focused at the moment. I just want to get through the next few days, then I can relax a bit, focus on America."

"That's good. I'm really pleased for you. Honestly, Herbert, I hope America works out for you."

"Why is I'm getting the feeling you don't want me here?"

"Herbert, that's not true."

"Gina, come on!" I'm starting to lose my temper. I know, I know, I've had a long trip and maybe I should rest, but the Dambusters have broken the seal and anger is flooding the towns and cities of my mind. Very poetic. Maybe that should go in my new novel. "Look, Gina, I really need this for the article."

"Just don't strain yourself, okay?

"I won't. I promise."

I calm myself as quickly as I can, deep breaths, trying to slow my heartrate, trying to calm my mind, trying to focus on the words that I somehow need to put down, trying to dream the American Dream once again, as futile as it may be.

Another vehicle is pulling into the grounds of the house: a large van with a cartoon image of a moustached chef on each side.

"It's okay, Scarlet ordered it," I'm told by Gina.

"I did indeed!" Scarlet's right next to us. "A special treat for us all, to kick this thing off in style!"

"What the hell is it?" I ask.

"Tapas and champagne. Only the finest."

"Where the hell did you get it from?"

"It's in Glasgow. A tapas restaurant in the Merchant City. Thought I'd have some delivered out here. Come on, Herbert! Cheer up! Gina and I have been hard at work setting up these tables!"

I don't know what's got into this woman. Her eyes are ridiculously wide open, full of energy. She seems to have gained a healthy amount of bulk: possibly from working out, I don't know. But – as ever with this woman – she's become a different person.

Two blokes get out. They don't need to confirm Scarlet's identity: I can see in their eyes that they know who she is, what she is. One of them opens the side door of the van and out comes silver tray after silver tray.

Everyone's coming out of the mansion, emerging like disturbed termites. Guy's eyes seem to be widening with every moment.

"Come on then!" Scarlet yells at them. "Food's ready!"

The silver trays are piled on the table, along with crystal champagne glasses and ten bottles of the bubbly stuff. I approach the table, along with the other men. I think – I know – that there's a sense of disbelief among us. One glance at the vintage of the champagne confirms this.

"Shit," mutters Guy. "Fuckin' hell, girls, you've done us proud!"

"Of course we have," says Scarlet. She nods at the men from the restaurant. One of them tells her that he'll be back around Six to pick up the detritus.

I've got the worst stroke of luck assigned: I find myself sitting between Guy and Keith. The former keeps whispering to me about how sexy he thinks Scarlet is. The latter is too scared to do anything about it.

Champagne corks are popped and the glasses are filled.

Scarlet's positioned herself at one end of the table. She raises her glass. "To the final album!" she calls out. "The final album!"

"Yeah, yeah!" shouts Mick.

I take an uncomfortable sip and flex my ankles.

"I just want to say a couple of things." Keith rises to his feet. "I'm very proud of each and every one of you. We have a difficult week ahead, but we will make a glorious success of it. I know we will. I believe in us! I believe you!"

Gina breaks into a smile, lifts her glass. She gazes at me, winks.

19 August to 25 August 1996

On the Monday, I'm woken by the sound of clanging and things shifting around. I sit up in the single bed in my room, conveniently located on the top floor, right at the end of the building. It's cosy, but stuffy, and there's only one small window. But thankfully there's a tiny writing desk.

I curse when I realise it's nearly eight o'clock and curse louder when I realise I forgot to set the alarm last night.

I gather some clothes and sneak along to the shower a few doors down. I spot Olly; he's carrying a couple of guitars, whistling to himself.

"Sleep in, did you?" he taunts.

"Very funny," I grumble.

"You missed breakfast. There's a few things left in the kitchen, but you'd better hurry up. We're starting in five minutes. Guy Hawkes, where the hell are you with the kit?"

"Coming, coming." Guy's raspy voice filters through the wood and stone like a bad cough.

I quickly shower and change, wondering if maybe I should check into a hotel. But I have a loyalty to these people. Maybe that's a fault – it most probably is – but this is the last major event I'll do with them. I owe it to the girls to be around them, to record as much as I can. I waddle back to my room, retrieve my notepad and pen, and head to the kitchen.

There's a narrow set of steps that connects the top floor to the second floor. A bad design, very bad. It's like descending a ladder, so much so, that I take it extremely slow. How Olly, one of our junior, inexperienced technicians, got those guitars down is anyone's guess.

I make it to the kitchen just as one of the backing musicians is beginning to move a plate of pastries in the direction of the bin.

"Hold on!" I command. I snatch a few of them up. "Any coffee?"

"Sorry, mate, it's all gone. I think there's some instant somewhere. Anyway, mate, I've got to shoot off."

"Yeah, sure. I'll be through in a few minutes."

I eat breakfast as quickly as I dare, careful not to get indigestion. I'm not as young as I once was. Maybe I'll get some of that youth back once I'm in America. I rub the crumbs off my lips.

The recording studio has been set up in the living room, which is the obvious place for it given its size and ease of access: back in the large circular room, you take the door directly in front, and you'll find yourself in a room with a grand fireplace, bookshelves (empty), French-designed windows, and ancient rugs which have been rolled up and put to the side.

I stand at its entrance, leaning casually on the doorframe. Scarlet is busy directing people. An electric guitar is strapped around her neck and she wears a serious face. Gina also wears her guitar, but loosely. Backing musicians are all in place. Everything is ready to go. Guy is checking a bundle of cables. He gives a thumbs-up signal to Keith, who is standing at the back, arms folded.

I jot a few things down, look up, see Guy with his hand around Gina's waist.

"Oy! Knock it off!" I yell. I storm over, jab my finger against his throat. "You're overstepping the mark, mate! Cut it out!"

Guy gives me a hard shove. I stumble backwards, fall to the ground. My notepad and pen shoot off in opposite directions. He towers over me, like a giant.

"I'll teach you a fucking lesson, you old bastard!" he hisses. "You fucking has-been!"

"Guy, that's enough!" screams Gina. She stands in front of him, blocking him from reaching me. "Guy, come on! I don't think he understands."

Scarlet's standing to my left. "What the hell's going on?" she demands.

Gina pulls off her guitar. "Scarlet, Guy, let me talk to Herbert outside. Five minutes." She holds down a hand to me. I shrug it off and pull myself up.

Keith comes over. "Right, guys, I suggest we take a quick breather before we start."

Gina puts an arm on my shoulder and starts leading me out.

"I'm sorry, I couldn't stand idly by," I say. I think I sound like I'm whimpering. I probably am. "The way he was touching you, completely inappropriate...!"

"For Christ's sake, Herbert! Guy and I have been going out for a few weeks!"

"Oh, I'm sorry, I didn't know."

"It's okay. Look, I know you're trying to be a good guy and everything, looking out for us, but you need to take a step back. Go home, Herbert. You don't need to be here. Honestly. You really don't. You've got more than enough material for your article."

Disappointment and rejection are a massive punch in the gut. I can't help the feeling that she's right. Of course she is.

"Give me a few minutes to gather my things, then I'll be off," I tell her.

"Herbert, take as long as you need."

"I hope it goes well this week."

There's a sense of pity in the way she purses her lips. "Safe travels home, Herbert. Try to get some rest, okay?"

A few hours later, I'm on a train heading back to London. I don't feel it at first, but gradually relief spills over me.

Maybe I've been getting a little too close to the band. It's been two-and-a-half years since I started shadowing them. Two-and-a-half years where my focus has become blurred. I need to refocus, to get myself together.

When I get home, the first thing I do is drink a pint of water and power up my computer. I start writing. The ideas are flowing and it's all coming together, beautifully.

As the week passes, I find I'm becoming more and more distracted. Words start slipping and the ideas lose their sharpness.

I need to be with the band. Regardless of whether Gina thinks I'm overworked or not, I need them.

I take the earliest train possible on the Sunday. When I reach Glasgow in the early afternoon, I take a taxi straight to the house. I'm expecting the driveway to be jammed, so instruct the driver to park outside the entrance.

I'll say hello and then sort out a hotel for the night. No big rush.

I hoist up my rucksack and walk into the grounds of the mansion. No cars or vans are present. Did they finish early? I go up to the front entrance, expecting it to be locked, but find that it swings open.

"Hello?" I call out.

I roll my eyes. Maybe they went out for lunch. I decide to head upstairs and take a short nap in my room. I feel like a student coming back to his parents' home for the summer. When I'm on the top floor, I yawn and rub my eyes.

The room is still the same as I left it. I forgot to take my wretched alarm clock home with me. Grumbling, I pick it up and stuff it in my bag.

"Just cut it out will you!" Gina's voice is sharp and tearful. "You've been going on about it all fucking week! Can't you just knock it off, Guy?"

"Why should I? He was fucking looking at you like a piece of meat. I don't like people disrespecting my girl like that."

They start shuffling down the corridor. Footsteps creak through the wood.

"Look, Guy, I want to make this work between us. I really do. But this can't keep happening between us. What are you gonna do if I'm performing and some guy checks me out? Are you going to beat the living shit out of him, there and then?"

"I'm sorry. I'll try to be better. I just don't want that dirty old fucker ogling you again."

"What did you say?" The next words come from me. I'm standing in the corridor like The Man With No Name. (I'm the biggest fan of *The Good, The Bad and The Ugly*.)

"Christ, here he is." Guy spits on the ground in front of him.

"Guy, come on, leave it." Gina's got one foot on the staircase; she's tugging his elbow, trying to get him to follow. He shrugs her off.

"I sincerely apologise for the misunderstanding the other day," I tell him. "I messed up, mate."

"What are you doing back here?" he says. "Thought you'd fucked off back to London. Snivelling little cunt that you are."

"Mate, I don't want any trouble. I left a few things up here. I came to collect them."

"Guy, come on, the others are all at the restaurant," says Gina. "Let's go and join them."

"Fuck the restaurant. I don't fucking care. I think he wants a piece of me."

"Guy, I'm not interested in any trouble," I say, as firm as I can. I've always been a pushover. I've never been one to stand my ground. I'm shaking, tongue caught between my teeth, and I know he sees it.

I do the only thing I know I can do: I back away. I retrace my steps, but I don't go back to my room. I'm craving – desperately – air. At the end of the corridor, there's a door that leads to a small balcony. I've been there out there a few times during my brief tenure here; today is the perfect day to use it to collect my thoughts. The balcony's small, maybe a little too much, with an area the size of three telephone booths. I pull the door open, step out and breathe in the fairly unpolluted air. I rest my elbows on the stone railing, try to stop the panicked tears from making a scene.

I shouldn't have come back.

He's followed me.

"I don't want any trouble," I say to him.

"You're nothing but a has-been," he sniggers, slapping both my shoulders. "Piss off back to London." He makes an opening, mocking gesturing me back inside with a meaty hand.

I head to my room, barging my way inside angrily. I'm sick and infuriated. I've been bullied enough. Do I go purple? Is it possible, or is it only in cartoons that it happens? I leave my chamber, go back down the corridor.

Guy and Gina are hugging on the balcony. He's got her sweet little face in his hands. He leans forward kisses her on the forehead.

"Give us some privacy," he tells me.

"After you apologise to me."

"Are you taking the fucking piss?" He breaks away from his girlfriend, starts advancing. "You want to fight with me? Right here, right now?"

"No, I want an apology."

"Fuck you," snaps Guy, silencing Gina with his right hand.

I close the gap between us.

"You're nothing, Herbert," he tells me. "You're a has-been, you're a yesterday's man. You're absolutely nothing, but a dirty old bastard." He takes a step forward.

I put up my hands. I feel his thumb and forefinger make contact with my throat. I shove him as hard as I can. I think I can just about see the panic in his eyes as he trips backwards. Gina screams as he collides with her. I screw my eyes shut.

I open them, finding only an absence in front of me. They're gone, and so is part of the stone railing lining the balcony.

I tiptoe to the edge, look down. Guy and Gina are sprawled out on the ground, like makeshift crucifixion re-enactments.

"Guy? Gina?" My voice comes out like dried grass. "Guy! Gina!" I fumble my way outside as quickly as I can, kneel down next to them. Both sets of eyes are open in shock. "No!" I cry out. "No!"

I have very little time to decide what to do next. An impossible choice. I don't think I'll ever know what gives me the strength to pick. I go back into the house, retrieve my rucksack, leave. Thankfully, I'm not spotted. I don't think so.

I pass through street after street, each one blurring into the next, and to my relief find a taxi. Deep breaths. I compose myself, smile.

"To Glasgow City Centre," I command the driver.

The shock doesn't hit me until hours later, when I'm on a train heading south. The horror of what I've done, the serious trouble I'm in. I make sure that I show no emotion. I'm aware that sweat is soaking my shirt, but I can't allow it to affect my business-like aura.

Keith

18 July 1977

The company offices were located in the heart of Brooklyn and they set off just after dinner to avoid the worst of the rush-hour traffic. Although the lights burned and blazed away, although the thronging metropolis tempted them with alcohol and whores, although the hotdog stands and the bars and the shows stroked their shoulders, Keith managed to stay focused. Throughout the late-evening journey they were taking in Randolph's car, he never once looked up: his focus was on the bundle of documents in his hands pertaining to the overdue payment. Barry Farringdon's British lawyer had also put together a legal letter, which Keith was reading through for the tenth time.

"Have you met these people?" asked Keith, glancing to his right. The lawyer blinked at his words.

"No, not yet," said Randolph. "Don't worry."

"How can you say that? They're ripping us off, mate!"

"Well, to be honest, they're probably a bunch of college kids doing a summer job."

"Let's hope. How far away are we?"

"Not too far. Not too far. Gee, you know my father used to work around here during the Great Depression?"

"You can tell us the story over drinks later." Keith turned around to face his brother. "What did the fax say from Barry?"

"Oh, it was just to wish us luck." Of course, Philip's mind was lost in the streets around them.

"We're here," announced the lawyer. He turned off and they headed down a dingy side street. Overflowing rubbish and several half-dressed tramps filled the place with dread and despair.

"Christ, let's just get this done," said Keith. "Then shoot back to the hotel for cocktails."

"Their office is right at the end of this block," said Randolph. He slowed the car to a crawl as they approached a thickset brick wall that marked the termination of the street.

Two children were playing a game of tag next to a skip. Oblivious to their filthy surroundings, they played on.

"This is some place to have your head offices," remarked Philip.

"They said they'd meet us outside." The lawyer unclipped his seatbelt and opened the car door. "Shit, I hate waiting around like this. Shit!"

"It's a bit shady." Philip opened one of the rear doors and shunted himself out.

Keith was nonplussed, without a care for anything. To him, it was just another hiccup to sort out. He merely leaned against the car, went through the documents in the folder again, ensuring that everything was accounted for.

"Did they give us a door number?" he asked Randolph.

"Nope! They said they'd meet us out here on the street. God damn!"

"Very fucking disorganised. Fucking useless." Keith was tempted to scrunch the paperwork in his steel grip.

"Hold on..." Randolph raised a hand to quieten him. He was staring intently at one of the doors that had been built into the stone a lifetime and a half ago.

Three men emerged, all in overcoats, all with their eyes tilted towards the ground. Keith noted their leather gloves and crisp leather shoes, their perfect knotted ties and rigid thin necks. They spread out and formed a line, Orion's Belt; all with black hats.

"Follow us," one of them said.

"Yes, of course." The lawyer was stammering. He hiccupped and coughed loudly.

"Are you okay?" asked Philip.

"I'm fine. Let's follow these guys."

They were shown down a narrow corridor filled with dim red light. Wallpaper peeled off the walls like rotting orange peel. The carpet felt lumpy, like that feeling of stones wedged in your shoe.

"Here," one of them said, rapping his leather knuckles on a door.

A voice inside told them to enter.

As soon as they were inside, Randolph gasped and seemed to want to force words through his mouth.

"What the hell is going on?" Keith asked him.

They were in a room a little bit larger than Barry Farringdon's office. A man dressed in a similar manner to their escorts sat at a desk smoking a long cigar. He appeared not to register their arrival. On the walls were shelves and shelves and shelves of trophies and awards. *Community Leader 1956. Lead Charity Fundraiser 1971.*

"These three gentlemen are here to see you," said one of their escorts. "About this rock concert."

"Thank you." The man rose, straightened his jacket, and approached like a cat. "So, you two are the guys from England then...?"

"That's us," said Keith. "Well, let's get to business then –"

"No, no, no. You're in *my* office, in *my* town. You two guys are young, so I'll forgive your ignorance. Now, I know in England, you do business with each other with a pat on the shoulder and a cup of Earl Grey. But to me, you ain't even dayroom."

The man walked back to his desk and stubbed out his cigar on a silver ashtray. He was thick around the waist, with red cheeks and wrinkles on his forehead. He had thinning brown hair and a number of jewelled rings lost in the chubbiness of his fingers.

"Look, it's been a long day and I'm tired. Here is your money…" The man picked up an envelope next to the ashtray and handed it over to them.

Keith opened it, ran a thumb through the notes inside, unsure of how exactly to laugh. "Sorry, is this a fucking joke?" he hissed. "There's about seven-hundred dollars in here! We're owed seventy-thousand dollars!"

One of the escorts snapped: "You treat him with some God damn respect!"

"It's okay." The man raised a hand. In an instant, the tension among the three escorts cut out. "It's okay, they're two ignorant young men who don't know their right from their left. Gentlemen, there's your money. Go back to your hotel, relax, get laid, I don't give a damn."

The lawyer spoke. "Excuse me, sir, may I have a word with Keith outside in private?"

"Go ahead. Maybe you can talk some sense to him."

"Keith, with me please."

Keith told his brother to stay where he was. Gripping the folder and envelope in each hand, he followed Randolph Nichols back into the corridor.

"Keith, I need you to listen to me…" The lawyer pulled the door closed and nudged him a few steps along the carpet. "Keith, take the money. Take the money and let's get out of here."

"Randolph, I'm not afraid of these guys. I've got a legal letter right here!" He angrily flashed the folder at eyelevel. "And you shouldn't be afraid as well! You're a damn lawyer! At least I thought so."

"Keith, we need to take the money and we need to get out of here. The men in there don't play by the rules. That legal letter you've got… wipe your ass with it. That's how much use it is. These men play a whole different ballgame compare to you and I, son."

"Mr Nichols, you really aren't making the slightest bit of sense."

"Christ, Keith! They're the God damn... *mafia!*"

"Oh, come on!"

"I mean it, Keith. If we don't take the money and leave, all three of us will end up at the bottom of the Hudson."

"Mr Nichols, you're a jabbering idiot. If they were the mafia, I'm sure that the police would be on to them."

"Trust me, Keith." Randolph looked quickly back at the door. "Keith, we need to get out of here. There's no way you're getting any of that money. Trust me on that. It's probably secured in a warehouse under armed guard. Be grateful you're getting the seven-hundred. Believe me, Keith, don't fuck with these guys. They'll rip your God damn teeth out and feed your testicles to dogs."

He knew that there was no use arguing. The lawyer clearly had his mind made up. Useless, pathetic nobody. His eyes were locked and serious. No ifs, no buts. "Alright then," he said. "Alright, Mr Nichols. Have it your way. But Barry Farringdon will rip you to shreds, mate."

The lawyer led the way back inside. "Apologies, sir, but there was a misunderstanding!" he told them.

"Yes, I was unclear on a few things," said Keith. "I'm sorry."

"Excellent." The thickset man coughed into a clenched fist. "Keith, I don't ever want to see you again. Fuck off right outa here. You come back here, I'm gonna bust ya."

"Let's go," said one of the escorts. He pulled open his coat, revealing a pistol sealed in its holster.

"Please, there's absolutely no need for this!" the lawyer pleaded.

"Just fucking move," said the escort.

As mobsters nudged them towards the door, Keith glanced back. The man was lighting up another cigar, disappearing into a cloud of smoke. Their eyes met for a moment, just a moment, but Keith detected a sense of loss and longing, a tough fragility. He wanted to reach out, lend a comforting hand, but the humiliation and anger was blinding him. This Don with the cigar, this bloke who'd reduced him to nothing! Hatred was such a strong word, but he felt it now.

When he flew home, he knew that Barry Farringdon would most likely kick him out. He would be jobless, destitute, ruined. All because of this cigar-smoking prat.

"I'll get you for this," he wanted to say.

But by the time he'd found the strength to move his tongue, he was outside on the street. The mobsters slammed the door shut behind them. A woman – scarcely dressed – walked past them, high heels digging at the ground. She looked broken, the way she examined them with those cold, dead eyes.

"We need the money!" Keith yelled at the lawyer.

"Be grateful we're all in one piece!" shouted Randolph. "Christ, I need a damn drink! Guys, get in the fucking car. I'm taking you back to your hotel. Seriously, get on your plane, go back to England, and just fucking forget about this. What's the worst that's gonna happen? You get fired by Barry, you move back in with your Sainted Mother. If you rub these guys the wrong way, they'll tear your God damn tongue out." He yanked open the driver's door. "You coming, or what?"

They left the side street and headed back towards Manhattan. Things hadn't stopped: New York was still full of energy and light. Keith, however, felt disconnected from the extravaganza around him. He was nothing in this place. He'd been degraded to a clump of wet sand. He was a slice of rotting fruit, a crushed ant.

The lawyer dropped them off at the hotel without a single goodbye.

"I'm heading to bed," said Philip.

"Goodnight. I need to go for a bit of a walk, stretch my legs. I'll see you in the morning." He went back outside, stood for a few moments observing the traffic.

Why did everyone seem like they had their own successful life story? Even the cab drivers crawling past appeared content.

"Excuse me, sir, are you okay?" It was the manager who'd helped to check them in. He must have just got off-duty: top button undone and tie twisted at a funny angle.

"I'm fine. A little worn-out. Actually..." No, he shouldn't be going that path... "Actually, I'd like to report an incident of organised crime to the police."

1997

James

15 January 1997

We're holding the party at a plush hotel on the banks of the Thames, with a full view of the Houses of Parliament. It's best-dress, no exceptions. Bouncers stand at the ready, their gloved hands prepared to do justice to those who get a bit too nosy. Celine Dion is playing in the background: *Because You Loved Me.* I like it. One of the biggest singles of last year.

My little girl turns 27 today. I can't fathom it. I've braved the courtroom, challenged dangerous judges, but I feel like I'm in the dock now. Scarlet has turned 27. It doesn't seem at all real!

I watch her have her photograph taken with the Leighton Brothers. She's sandwiched in the middle and Philip has an arm around her bare shoulders. Flashes fill the room, then she's shepherded over to a corner, where a journalist lies in wait. Even from here, I detect a few of the questions:

"How has your band coped since the death of Gina – ?" "What are your future plans after the band breaks up?"

I sip my champagne and head to where Alastair is facing the glass. I catch sight of George doing his rounds. We nod at each other briefly, exchange our smiles.

A few other people whose faces are ever so slightly familiar are milling around, and I do my best to send off quickfire greetings, but I know that I'll never meet every drop of social satisfaction.

How do I describe the function room? It's the perfect size for this event: everyone has space for themselves and three invisible friends. Pinkish red sofas and polished, bright wooden tables with wine and nibbles give with the feeling of a diplomatic extravaganza.

"Enjoying yourself?" Alastair asks me, as I take my place beside him.

"You don't sound like you are," I respond.

He gestures with his glass out to the lights on the Thames. "It's times like this that I realise how big the world is."

"The world's a big place, but it's not that big. Come on, now, come back to the party. This is your sister's big day."

"I just wanted to have a quiet family dinner."

"Oh, Alastair, you know that can't quite happen. Scarlet's a little too... big for that now."

"She's always been a little too big for anything."

A male voice is shouting, "Let me past!"

Instinctively, I shield Alastair from any danger. Not that I need to, of course. It's some rambling, shaking bald bloke in a three-piece suit, clearly having had one too many tipples. He's trying to force his way past the red rope, fighting with the bouncers; they're well-trained, pushing him back like a tsunami destroying a shantytown.

"You're trying to silence me!" the man shouts. "You won't fucking succeed!"

"Get him out of here!" snaps Philip Leighton. He's jutting forward from Scarlet, arms out, as if he's ready to fight this guy to the death. "Security, please remove this man!"

"I'm not fucking going anywhere! My daughter! My beautiful daughter! Killed herself because of the monster you worshipped, Scarlet!"

"Alright, that's enough!" yells Philip. "Get this man out of here, right now!"

The intruder is American. He's got the appearance of someone who was once calm and collected, but is now chaotic and lucid. I realise that, because I've known people like him: men who've lost everything. I watch on as he's dragged out; he fights back like an animal, but the bouncers are wildebeest who lynch him along kicking and screaming.

Philip calms everyone down, smiling and joking, waving his hands, calling for a sense of decorum to return. The party returns to normalcy so quickly, it's as though not a peep was heard from the intruder.

"What the hell was that all about?" Herbert Buxton's standing next to my ear, eyebrows fluttering. "Very bizarre..."

"How have you been, Herbert?"

"Oh, very well, just so busy. Only a couple of weeks left with your daughter's band before I round up."

"You're off to America soon, aren't you?"

"Yep. Can't wait. Everything's fully confirmed. Just got to write this article. My final day with the band will be on the last day of January, which is when the album will come out. I don't know about you, James, but I think that's poetically beautiful."

"Indeed."

"I need to shoot off now. Got to get a few groceries and then grab an early night. Being interviewed on radio in the wee hours tomorrow."

I hold out my hand to him. "Have a good night, Herbert. Thank you so much for coming along. It means a lot to me and to my daughter. She's having a difficult time with the grieving process."

"I'm glad I've been able to help. See you soon, mate."

"Bye."

After he's gone, I tell Alastair that I'm going to mingle and suggest he does the same. I nod hello to a few people I vaguely recognise from functions that Scarlet has invited me to over the years.

It gets to the point where I know I've outstayed my welcome. She's not five anymore. She doesn't rub her hands in paint and pull silly faces. She's a woman grown. I go to her before I leave, give her a small peck on the cheek. Does she actually register my presence? I'm not so sure.

When I'm back out on the streets, I feel the horrid chill make its way down my spine. Thankfully, my hotel is fairly close, less than half a kilometre; but it feels ten or so miles away.

A group of men and women – twelve, I think – are laughing a little too loud on the opposite side of the road. Early thirties? I think so. They're inebriated, but not overtly pissed. I was like them once, back in the day!

Whispers cross through the late-night traffic, barely audible over the din of tyres scratching on tarmac. My ears prick up and I turn to face the group. They seem to recognise me. They're pointing at me, jabbing fingers in my direction, laughing even louder. Did I know any of them in a court case?

"It *is* him!" one of them yells, a brutish man with a balding head, yet very slim fingers. I can see all the detail all the way from here.

"Remember me?!" another man shouts. "Remember?" This one is well-built: one too many sessions in the gym, anyone can see that. "Fucking hell, I don't think he does! I gave you a slap once, remember? When you popped by our karate club a few years ago? Remember?"

"Guys, I'm really not interested, I don't want any trouble." I turn away and continue walking.

"Here that? He doesn't want any trouble! Go on then, you sad old fucker! Fuck off home!"

"Provoke me all you want!" I shout back. "It's not going to work!"

Profanity and insults are hurled in my direction, but working in the insurance game has given me a thick skin. I actually find myself laughing about it when I get back to the hotel.

As I lie in bed, I think of nothing except my daughter. I know that these past years we've grown apart. My wife feels it too; perhaps that's the reason why she didn't come along. I know, I know that fathers and daughters routinely fall out and move apart – I get that! But with Scarlet, it's different. If there was a gulf between us when she was born, there's a whole world dividing us now.

Is it time that I let her go?

Scarlet

31 January 1997

She's glad to see that the news of the final album has made the front cover of *The Daily Telegraph*, but she's angry that the paper hasn't featured a tribute to Gina.

She's performing tonight. Not sure where, but she's doing a single performance to mark the last album making its mark on the world. It's the last one she'll do before the farewell tour.

She's asked Philip not to phone her. She doesn't want to know how well or badly the album is doing. Actually, she doesn't care. Since Gina's death, she's lost any commitment to it. All she wants to do is say goodbye, let it all go.

What will she do next? She's thought about setting up a charity for Rwanda. She's also been considering presenting a documentary series or hosting a talk show. It's strange, isn't it, dear reader? That after seven years, Scarlet has so many choices at her disposal. She can appear on T.V. shows, launch her own business with great ease, start a solo career if that's what she wants. There's nothing off-limits to her.

She could even go and give talks in schools, if that's something she really wants. She's already done it, after all.

She wanted to cancel her talk at Rainham John Graham Comprehensive after Gina's death, but Philip got very persuasive and subsequently aggressive. She did the talk in front of a hundred or so schoolkids, all of whom ogling her. Afterwards, it was tea and biscuits with the head and deputy head, as well as Philip.

What was it the deputy headmistress said? *"Music can help empower trainee teachers to develop their teaching practice."*

Alena Nunthorpe was a chubby Welsh woman in her early fifties, with bulging eyes and the breath of a former smoker. Scarlet didn't like her from the first moment of seeing her. Too much fat around the middle and a highly aggressive posture.

Just before the meeting ended, they discussed Josephine.

"She was a troubled individual," said Alena. "I was Head of English at the time and the Senior Mentor for all the trainee teachers, so I saw her quite a bit. Poor girl, I really pitied her."

Philip gave out a small cough. "I'm very sorry about what happened. I can't imagine how difficult it must have been for the school, then and recently."

"Then there was what happened a few years ago," said the headteacher, Lambert Howard. "I only joined the school after my predecessor's passing, so I do not know the full details, but –"

"Are you referring to the motorbike incident?" said Alena.

"Yes. She came by the school on the back of a motorbike – I think it was her boyfriend or someone who was with her. She started harassing members of staff and pupils. Mr Merton was on the verge of calling the police, but she suddenly rode off. Anyway, that's water under the bridge now. What matters is that we've been given a wonderful opportunity to develop teaching practice..."

Scarlet shuts the voices out. She understands now – even though she doesn't agree – why Josephine did it.

The new album came out this morning – that's all she knows. She wants to be kept in the dark, she wants to be in blissful ignorance.

She's being picked up at six and driven straight to the venue. No frills. No messing about. Straight there. Do the performance. Get back. She's not even going to have time to see Herbert, though he'll be there in the audience, making his incredulous notes.

It's mid-morning. She never bothers to check the exact time. She's at home, on her own, waiting for things to happen.

The buzzer to her penthouse rings and she lets them in without even bothering to check if it's Philip Leighton or Magwitch. She waits for whoever it is to come up. When they knock on the door lightly, she assumes it's Keith.

"Hi Scarlet."

"Is this a joke?"

"I know it's been a long time. How have you been?"

"How can you just come back here, like this?"

"If you'd rather I went away, I will."

"No, it's okay. Just come on in."

It's been years, but Emma still looks the same twenty-something woman: naïve yet mature, caring yet self-centred. She's become more beautiful, graceful. Scarlet can do nothing but stare intently at Emma gliding through her penthouse like a floating tissue.

"It's so good to see you again," says Emma, sitting down on the nearest available armchair. "How have you been?"

"I've been fine. Where have you been travelling to?"

"All over the place."

"I'm imagining this," Scarlet tells herself. She screws her eyelids shut, opens them. There's only an empty chair left in place. "Bitch," she utters. "You bitch."

Hours later, feels like days later, she's backstage. She's adjusting her makeup, sorting her hair out, checking her complexion. She's anxious to get tonight over with, just so she can head back and crack open a bottle of wine.

She vaguely recognises the dressing room. She's been here before: the first performance the band did in London. Who was it who doubted whether anyone would turn up?

The backing musicians are all at the ready. She can hear them fumbling around in the adjacent dressing room, muttering to each other, cursing.

She's trying to think of what she needs to say to the crowd, how she'll calm them down. She doesn't have time to go over her thoughts, because Philip pops his head in.

"It's time," he tells her, before disappearing.

She takes the long walk to the stage, heart hammering. In a few hours, though, it'll all be over. She pulls apart the curtains, wades through the fabric, and emerges into the spotlights. Cheers and clapping surrounds her, but she can see and hear that the crowd is not as big as it normally is. Definitely half as large as it normally is?

"How's everybody doing tonight?" she says into the mike. "Are you ready?"

The crowd half-roars a response.

She glances behind her as the backing musicians take place.

"Before I begin, I want to share a few words about Gina." She bows her head. "She was an inspiration to me. An inspiration to each and every one of us. Someone highly principled, someone who always did what she believed was right. Someone –"

"Just play the fucking music!" someone yells.

"Yeah!" someone else calls out.

"We didn't come here for a fucking eulogy!" a third voice shouts.

One of the backing musicians strums a few chords. It's okay: Scarlet's not taken by surprise: she knows the music inside out. She'll always know it. Her voice comes out at just the right time and it seems to calm the hissing of the crowd. It's an old favourite, from the first album.

But when they move on to one of the songs from the last album, the behaviour of the throng changes. They don't boo or swear, but it's like they become insecure in themselves.

As the minutes pass, she feels the words slipping. The songs seem to hate her. She forgets a couple of the words, gets a few of the lyrics mixed up. She knows why: the girls wrote most of them. Maybe it's their way of punishing her.

When the concert is over, the crowd applauds and cheers, but not with the love and devotion that they used to have. It occurs to her that the vast majority have been fans from the very beginning, committed veterans to her cause. Now their strength and compassion are beginning to wear out.

There's no escort back to her changing room. She slumps down in the seat, sweaty and tired, fed up and bored. She wants this whole thing to be over. She wants the band to be finished, to be nothing, to be fed to the sharks.

She wipes her face with a flannel and cries out no tears. She buries her face in the table, wishing that she could have a normal life.

Paul Casselden – arsehole that he is – was right about so many things. That February day seven years ago: he was bloody right. A normal life, being one of the crowd, there's nothing wrong with that.

She looks up to see Emma reflected in the glass. "Can't seem to shake you off, can I?"

Emma shakes her head. "Nope. You aren't getting rid of me that easily."

Herbert

1 February 1997

Officially at one-second-past-midnight, I stopped following the band. And what a way to go out as well! Some concert! A pity about the heckling and abuse. But she did okay, considering.

I'm up at six o'clock in the morning, ready for what's in store for me today. I think about cancelling, and maybe that's something I should take seriously. I'm a grain of sand dancing in a storm, though, and I can't resist being pulled.

After a quick breakfast of porridge (trying to get healthy) and orange juice, I pull on a pair of old jogging trousers and a t-shirt that hasn't been worn since 1984.

Winding my way through the early morning moments of London's Underground maze, I take company among the leftovers of last night's partygoers and the drug addicts passed out on the floor.

I'm dressed like a dirty old man, because that's precisely how I want to appear. I don't want people to recognise the great Herbert Buxton. Even though he'll soon be gone and on his way to America, even though he'll quickly be forgotten around these parts, he does not want to take the risk of standing out and drawing the wrong kind of attention.

I wind up in Peckham and follow the well-worn route that only I know so well. It takes me through side streets and subway crossings that seem to linger in the darkest recesses of my imagination. You never know, they might find their way into one of my books someday...

I turn on to the street, whose name I can scarcely remember, and see that she's already outside.

"So, you're leaving me then?" she taunts, tossing her cigarette.

"Duty calls," I respond. I go quickly up to her and pull her close.

"Honey, this is very unprofessional." She giggles, but I can tell she's being completely serious. "Baby, people might see us."

"Darling, this is going to be my last appointment with you," I say. "I'm leaving the country in a few weeks."

"Oh, where to?"

"America."

"But our sessions..." Her thick Eastern European accent is so soothing and arousing, yet it can be nagging and irritating. She comes closer and closer to me, breathing the nicotine remnants into my mouth. "When are you leaving, baby boy?"

"First day of March."

"Well, there's plenty of time for us to meet again."

"I won't have the time, my dear. Catching up with old friends, finishing my article, that sort of stuff."

"Oh. I hope you come see me, baby." She runs a finger down the back of my neck.

"I really won't have the time. So, are we going to head upstairs?"

"Yes." She takes my hand. "Come up with me, baby."

I know where I stand now. I'm swallowed whole, consumed, crushed. Everything melts together: I'm in the building, up the graffitied stairwell, inside her flat. Money's exchanged at some point, but I learned long ago how to block that exact decrepit moment out. In the next conscious instance, I'm on the street, making my way back home, unwashed and filthy.

I started visiting her after my divorce. It's a treat every two months, something that has kept me sane through the heartbreak and disappointment of a lost marriage.

When I'm home again, I allow myself to get emotional. The loss hits me harder than I'll ever allow myself to admit: my wife and stepchildren, my Peckham whore, and Gina. Over these past few months, my mental strength has improved, so much so that I'm able to push the incident out of my mind.

I'll know fully understand how that happened and I'll never be able to confess. I'm too much of a coward for that. I wouldn't be able to face prison, or the prospect of my life and career ripped to pieces.

These days ahead, I need to focus. Get this article written, get it sent off. They want it by noon on Valentine's Day. They've said that they want it sent via this *email* thing. I know Scarlet's managed to work her way around it, but I still find it jolly confusing. Anyway, it shall be done.

Scarlet

22 February 1997

She stands – she thinks – almost on the spot where her trusty little shack once was. She has her arms folded behind her and, despite the cold, she's wearing a scrawny tank top and a pair of fraying, thin trousers. A cigarette lies dead on the ground; wisps of smoke crawl their way between frozen bits of grass.

She had many happy hours in this spot, with her coffee machine and paints, fruitful imagination and explosive sexuality.

This is supposed to be a happy weekend, a time of celebration and family. She's done something that might be stupid or clever: she's bought her parents' old house. At the start of the year, she realised that it was time for a change. Having a penthouse in London is great, dear reader, but it's too much for her. At night, she looks across the road and can see some famous musician practicing their chords. She needs a step back from everything. She needs a space to collect her thoughts.

The house suits her down to the ground. She grew up in it, after all. It's the perfect distance from London, enough space for her to relax. With all the money she has, it's a sort of... retirement. She's moving in at the beginning of March.

This is a weekend with all the family gathered in one place. Her parents and Alastair will be heading back to Vancouver on Monday.

Her parents kept ownership of the house when they moved to Canada, but they've been growing increasingly frustrated with the costs. Scarlet made an offer to buy it and they've graciously accepted.

She looks up and sees Emma there, smiling as always. Right there on the field, standing with the same posture as Scarlet.

"I was wondering if you were ever going to turn up," says Scarlet – not to Emma, but to Herbert Buxton. She knows he's right behind her.

"I couldn't fail to."

"Did you get everything done you needed to?"

"Yep. Article sent in, money received, travel plans fully sorted."

"That's good. I really hope things work out for you. You deserve it, Herbert."

"Thank you."

Scarlet remains where she is, doesn't turn around, dear reader. She expects Herbert to go, go to the station, get the train to London, forget about her, about the band, about everything. But he stays exactly where he is. She can feel his breathing.

"Years ago now, just after we properly got started, I made a payment," she tells him. "Do you want to know who I made the payment to?"

"Lots of bands and singers make payments all the time," he responds.

"It wasn't to do with the band, it was to do with me. I paid two police officers to keep quiet. I went to Eastbourne, handed over money so that they'd keep shtum. Do you want to know what I wanted them to keep shtum about?"

"I don't particularly want to know, Scarlet."

"When I was a kid – really young – I made with friends with an elderly neighbour. I'd go over there, into his house, without my parents knowing. He'd show me pictures of when he was young, of his grandchildren, all that stuff. Weeks and weeks this went on. Then one day, this man took me for a walk. We ended up down there..." She points, blindly, in some direction. "There's a small ditch up that way, at the side of the road. I don't know whether it's still there, or if they've filled it in. But he took me up there, told me he wanted me to see the beauty of the English countryside. Something along those lines. And I suddenly got so scared. I thought he was going to hurt me, I really did. Maybe he was going to hurt me, I don't know. I panicked. I panicked so hard, and I... pushed him. Not hard. I was a kid, such a young kid. You know that phrase? *You don't know your own strength.* I didn't think I could hurt someone. He stumbled, fell backwards, fell into the ditch. I watched the sheer terror in his eyes as he collapsed. His head smacked against a rock. It sounded like when you dig your thumb into an apple. Christ, Herbert, the way he lay still, it still sickens me. The next thing I knew, there was a police officer standing there. He must have seen everything. He placed a hand on my shoulder and then pulled me into this tight cuddle. I'll never know why, but he took pity on me; he covered everything up. Of course, it came with a price. The man was known to be a bit of a pervert. The policeman thought that I was some sort of child prostitute and that's why I'd gone walking with the man that day. Every so often, him and one of his mates would call me a hooker, tease me when I walked down the street. It went on for years. Can you imagine that? Every morning, waking up filled with dread, waiting to hear 'hooker', 'prostitute', 'slut'. When I launched the band, I decided to pay him off, in the hope he'd be quiet. You see, Herbert, we all have our secrets. This one's been burning me inside out all these years, and I wanted to tell someone – anyone – about it. You seem to be the only person I can fully trust."

She turns around, knowing exactly what she'll see. "I'll miss you, a great deal," she tells the empty space. "Take care."

She goes back to the house, feeling dazed yet relieved that Herbert Buxton has gone. She'll never see him again – and she hopes, prays that it will be the case.

Philip Leighton's car is outside – he must have arrived whilst she was out for her walk. When she enters the house, there he is, chattering away with her brother and parents in the living room The Casseldens are there as well, already sipping away at the coffee. When Philip sees her, he gives her a quick wave.

"I just need to have a quick word with Scarlet," he says. "I'll be back in a few moments." He takes her back through the front door.

"Thanks for coming along," she says. "It means a lot."

"It's my pleasure. I just wanted to mention a couple of things regarding the incident in January at your birthday party. I trust you're okay with what happened?"

"Yes, I'm fine. Who was he by the way?"

"That's what I wanted to chat with you about." Philip looks around him, as though he's extra careful about any potential extra ears. "There are a few legal limits on what I can say to you, but his daughter had dealings with Roger Miser in Nineteen-Eighty, in France. The gentleman's daughter died as a result of these... dealings."

"What?"

"Scarlet, that's all I can say. I wish I could tell you more, but there are legal clamps on what can come out of my mouth. Please ensure that you don't tell anyone what I've said."

"Of course, yes."

"I thought it would be the legal, responsible thing to keep you informed, though I cannot divulge too much; I hope you understand."

"I understand."

"I'm going to head back in now. Don't stay too long out here. It's freezing."

Scarlet

14 March 1997

She forces herself to emerge from the dressing room and grudgingly pulls on a smile. Even from the backstage corridors of the Roundhouse, she can hear the restlessness of the crowd. She gulps, curses herself for eating too much dinner, and strides towards the stage.

The crowd are waving and cheering, eager for her to get on with it. She decided earlier to kick the evening off with one from the latest album.

"How are we doing?" she asks the audience. "You know, I can't believe it's come to this! Our farewell tour, ladies and gentlemen!" Really clumsy, ignorant, arrogant words.

She's always tried to live in the moment and tonight is no exception. Yes, it's the start of the farewell tour, but it's also just another concert. Just another night on the stage, with the spotlights over her head and an iron hand supporting her back. She has everything she needs: a voice, music to go with it, and a crowd to blast her on.

Someone screams out from the audience, "Just get on with it, darlin'!"

"I'm about to," she replies. She turns behind her, gives a nod to the musicians.

She's always loved that feeling, when those first chords are struck and the energy that gets released. Every time she's gone on stage and those first notes sound out, the euphoria that accompanies them is like nothing else in existence.

Not today though.

There's booing from the crowd. At first, just a few hoots, then the venom comes. She's taken aback by the profanity and the hatred.

"Go on, bitch, fuck off!"

"Slut!"

"You're fucking rubbish! Fucking hell!"

And she's so shocked and horrified that she can't help but let out a whimper. One of the backing musicians grabs her by the elbow, pulls her away. "Come on, Scarlet, let's get out of here. Come on!"

Next moment, she's in her dressing room. A security guard from the venue puts down a cup of sour instant coffee right in front of her.

"What the hell happened?" she asks. Her backing musicians are around her, as well as Keith. None of them seem to know what's going on.

"I think there was a footie game on earlier," says someone. "I think there were a lot of hooligans in the audience."

"That's very expert of you," she answers back. "Everyone, get out. Just get out!" she howls.

Her reflection is shattered, splintered. Everything about her is cracked.

"What have I become?" she moans. "What the hell have I become?"

"Things never last forever," says Emma, leaning over so that her chin is on Scarlet's shoulder. "It's the way the world works."

"We gave it a shot, didn't we?"

"That you did. That you did."

"I miss you."

"I miss you too."

Keith

23 July 1978

The paperwork was completed, signed and dated. Keith stepped back, raised his glass of only the finest champagne, and proposed a toast: "To a great future!"

They were in Barry's old office – since refurbished – celebrating the signing of Keith's first band.

His brother – smart and a little more confident – stood at the side.

The band – two women and two men – sat before him. Keith had signed them, his first band, his first success, his first proper foray into the music business.

And only the finest champagne to wash everything down. Only the very best.

"Not too many glasses, I'll warn you about that!" he told them. "Don't forget, you're off to Mexico tomorrow on tour!"

The lead singer, Fred Bangor, a vibrant young man too young for twenty, stood up, holding his glass to the sky. "Mr Leighton, I wanted to say a massive thank you. You've made all of this happen."

"No, no." Keith shook his head. "No, guys, come on. Your talent has won through."

"We owe you a lot," said Fred Bangor. "Keith, Philip, from the bottom of our hearts, thank you."

"Well, if you want to thank me, smile in front of the cameras downstairs. Now, for God's sake, finish your champagne!"

They went downstairs, Keith lightheaded, Philip no doubt the same. They did the photoshoot in the newly built reception area: pink sofas, grey carpet, bright crystal lights hanging from the ceiling: the perfect crescent moon for pictures that would appear in the paper. Journalists were there too, wanting to know everything about this new band that had smashed its way on to the scene.

Of course, Keith himself was modest about his involvement.

Yes, he'd suffered the humiliation of being sacked by the revered Barry Farringdon. Yes, he'd launched his own record company soon after with only seven-hundred U.S. dollars. Yes, he was now enjoying the lucrative pleasures of having signed his first band. And yes, they were heading off on a worldwide tour! But he was very much modest about his success.

To him, the best part right now was standing at the back and watching his first success make themselves triumph.

His new secretary stood at the other side of the room, a package in her hands. This one was slimmer, with dark pretty eyes and breasts that stuck out just the right amount. He'd slept with her a few times, but he wasn't too fussed about making any solid commitments. She was a good secretary, kept things running. She was standing still, likely waiting for the main commotion to die down before she approached him.

He wished a journalist would quiz him on his reflections. After all, it was exactly one year since he'd returned from New York emptyhanded. He'd grown a lot over the past twelve months, really matured. He didn't drink as much, he exercised more, and had generally made himself a better man.

And this new band, ready to take on the world! They stood proud, holding their glasses, absorbed by the flashes of camera bulbs. He was a father watching his children fly the nest.

Eventually, he grew tired of his secretary standing there and waved her over.

"This came for you," she informed him, passing the package over.

"Thanks. Actually, could you leave it on my desk?"

"Certainly, sir."

"Thanks." He went over to his brother, patted him on the shoulder. "This party could be better, Philip," he remarked. "Could you head to the basement? There are a few bottles of champagne down there. I think everyone needs an extra glass."

Later, when everyone was gone, Keith sat alone at his desk. Had Barry done the same, kicking back like king of the castle, whenever he'd sent a band on their way to achieve glorious success? Basking in that sense of melancholy and joy, the hope that your children will do you proud? It was Keith's turn now. He was the man of the hour, the man of the moment, the man of this century.

He lifted up the package and started opening it.

"More fucking fan mail, I expect," he groaned.

It was the size of one of these VHS tapes he'd seen mentioned in the news a lot. At least, he thought so. But it was so damn hard to open: the tape was thick and would hardly budge. Eventually, though, he managed to tear a wide enough hole to access whatever was inside.

Something hard fell into his palms.

"What the hell?" he muttered. It was a ring: heavy, chunky silver, with a red jewel. "What on earth?" He let it fall, let it dent the wood, a strong metallic kiss.

A small, envelope, just like the size he'd used to send secret messages to girls he'd liked at school, came out between his finger and thumb. He opened it, knowing that this was some sort of hate mail from a disgruntled nobody.

Dear Keith,

Unfortunately, your lawyer is in five or six pieces and scattered across the Bronx.

It's been a year since you came to visit us in Brooklyn. Do come back when you're able. We have missed you.

Sincerely,
The Don

Keith didn't utter a sound. He tipped forward, rested his forehead on the desk. He couldn't cry, but tried to scream out something that may have resembled remorse.

Scarlet

31 August 1997

She leaves her hotel room at ten o'clock, fresh-faced, with her makeup installed. A couple of hotel staff brush past her as they stride furiously down the corridor. In 1992, they would have stepped to the side for her. They would have shown themselves as honourable, respectable souls, dear reader, who so avidly give way for the Queen of Music. That's not the case this morning. As she walks down the stairs, she is the one who has to stand aside: people are moving this way and that, pushing into one another and her. Nearly everyone's on their phone, jabbering away frantically. She was aware of the commotion at breakfast, but now, as she enters the lobby, she senses panic and shock.

She makes her way outside, where the car will be picking her up. She's in Swansea to attend an inaugural event. Philip Leighton has launched a special collaboration with a teacher training centre in the city.

What can she say? After that disastrous performance at the Roundhouse, the remainder of the farewell tour was scrapped. Soon after, Philip Leighton officially severed their business relationship and the band was formally disbanded. But he went further: scrapping his record company and setting up a new venture with Alena Nunthorpe; essentially, it's using the power of music to help trainee teachers develop 'reflective practice', whatever that is. Scarlet's been invited along to the opening of the new centre in the heart of Swansea.

She turns her head and notices that everyone seems to be glued to a television above the reception desk in the lobby. Curious, she goes back inside.

On the screen, a grim-faced reporter is informing his captive audience that Princess Diana is dead. A car crash in Paris.

Scarlet's stumped. She's feeling a deep sense of sadness and pity for the Royal Family. Such tragic, tragic news. Christ knows how this Tony Blair bloke's going to handle it... But she can't be worrying about this sort of nonsense.

A horn sounds outside. Her car's waiting for her. She flashes a wave and heads outside.

"Heard the news?" she says to the driver.

"Oh yeah, absolutely awful," the driver replies. She looks at Scarlet through the rear-view mirror. "Make sure your seat-belt's on, love.

The centre is situated at the waterfront. It's pristine and beautiful. What would Gina say about it? A Bond villain's paradise.

Scarlet is dropped off at the main entrance and is left to make her own way inside. It's a circular building, a self-contained academic construct. According to what she's heard, it's a place *where the teachers of tomorrow can develop their practice in a diverse environment.*

For all the *critical reflection*, there's very little direction in this place. She's standing in front of an information desk, too afraid and embarrassed to ask the staff behind it where she needs to go. Around her, there's a hub of activity. Everyone's going in their own direction.

"Scarlet, yes?" A suited official hands her a lanyard.

"That's me."

"If you'll put this on and come with me, I'll take you through..."

She's shown to a lecture theatre that's far more formal, far more mature, far more orderly than anything she encountered at art school. Actual rows of seats with fabric surfaces; a platform with a podium and mike; a steel-coloured projector on the ceiling. This is so posh, it's unreal. Did Alastair go to a place like this?

Audience members are taking their seats, one by one, but she won't have to worry about getting booed off this time. They look too respectable.

Alena is standing behind the podium, shuffling through some papers. Philip Leighton is behind her on one of the three seats that have been set up on the wooden platform. He gives her a smile as she sits next to him.

Five minutes later, when all four clocks in the room mark eleven o'clock, Alena begins. She gives out only a few sentences, ordering a minute's silence in response to today's news, before handing over to Philip Leighton. He tells his story: how he was awakened to the enormous potential of collaboration, how this has been an enormous and powerful journey for him. It's actually quite a beautiful speech.

Scarlet's asked to say a few words, and she's very careful with what she tells the audience. She merely agrees with everything that's been said and informs the crowd that she looks forward to seeing how things develop.

When the event is over, a coffee reception takes place in the main lobby. She stays for a few sips, speaks with a couple of journalists, and then returns to the hotel. Her accommodation is situated at Llandarcy Junction; it's a noisy, but bearably comfortable ride back.

She enters the lobby, yawning noisily. She's so tired, she doesn't hear her name being called. The words turn transparent when she pushes the button for the lift.

"Don't you ever recognise me?"

"What the hell are you doing here? You know what the –"

"Well, since you're no longer signed with Philip, the rules no longer properly apply," says Josephine. "I got in contact with Keith. He told me you were staying here."

"Josephine, if you've come to cause trouble, I'm not interested."

"I'm not here to cause trouble whatsoever. Scarlet, I came to say goodbye."

"Goodbye then."

"Scarlet, please. Can't we just part as friends?"

Josephine seems different. She's lost weight, but in a good way. She's built-up. There's colour in her eyes. She's got her hair done: it's combed with absolute precision; flecks of gel keep everything in line.

"Where are you going?" asks Scarlet.

"The south of Argentina," she replies. "I had some inheritance money come in and used it to buy a place down there. It's time for a fresh start. You might call it an early retirement. You never know, I might write a book or something."

"That's great. When are you heading off?"

"Just now. I'm flying tonight."

"Well…" Scarlet looks past her, then to the ground. "Well, safe travels then…"

"Look after yourself."

"You too." She turns back to the lift and then spins around to call out to Josephine, but she's walking away.

Scarlet watches as she enters the summer air and seems to dissolve in the sunlight.

1998

James

2 February 1998

Well, it's that time of the year again. Our trusty visit to Paul and Siobhan. I admit, we haven't been too sharp about it these past few years. This year, however, I've made a renewed commitment; except this time, we're not the ones doing the travelling: Paul and Siobhan have flown over to visit us.

They're still jetlagged – that much is obvious. They sit in my living room, performing at their upmost best to stay wide awake, but it's a losing battle. I've made them fresh coffee from my new stainless steel cafetiere, but it's not enough.

Marianne asks about their flight and they give murmured responses. A half-hour delay from Heathrow, but that's Heathrow for you. Alastair quips that if you haven't suffered a delay at Heathrow, you're not a real traveller.

There's part of me that wants to burst in, rant on about insurance. It's childish, right? But I stand back, because Alastair's doing the talking.

These past two years, he's become far more mature than I could possibly imagine. He'll be a far better man than I'll ever be. There's a rumour – unconfirmed, of course – that he's got a new girlfriend. I'm sure he'll introduce us eventually.

Paul and Siobhan have definitely aged since I last saw them. I can see the strain in their eyes, the weakness in their skin. As we sit here, Paul gives me the occasional glance. We know what we both had, but it's something that needs to be consigned to the past. We know that we cannot share so much as a hug. Nothing can happen. Maybe nothing should ever have happened.

The conversation has now moved to Scarlet and the band. I don't like them talking about it, because it's still too raw and painful. Seeing news reports of my daughter getting booed off-stage makes me curl into a ball. Can any father tolerate seeing his daughter treated in such a way?

I'm about to suggest plans for lunch, but I hesitate. I pause, observe. I realise – as I have done all along – how lucky I am. I have a family, close friends, and a life in a glorious city. Everything I could ever possibly want, it's right here before me.

"I'll put some more coffee on," I say, "then I'll make us a booking for lunch. What are you in the mood for?"

Josephine

3 June 1998

I'll never tell anyone where I am, or else there would be no point in living here.

It's the early hours, just after four o'clock. I'm walking along the promenade of this new town I live in, staring up at the twinkling sky. In the months I've been here, I do this at least once every week. Doubtless a few curious eyes have drifted in my direction, but there's nothing here to drag me back in time. No one knows who I am or what I was, or what I've done.

I came to this place once, on my travels all those years ago. I hooked up with a fellow traveller and our brief fling turned into a serious relationship, all within two days. Sometimes the two weeks I spent in this town – of which you will never know the name – feels like two years.

The cold wind bites against my cheeks and throat. I've got umpteen layers on, yet the frozen ether cuts into me as though I'm completely naked.

A dogwalker passes me and we give each other a short nod. We know each other only as passing ships in the night, as romantic as that might sound.

I reach the end of the promenade and rest my elbows on the railings, peering at the distant mountains, capped with shadows of snow. That handsome traveller and I used to cuddle in this spot, before sneaking back to the lodge.

I allow myself a small laugh. Our relationship ran like clockwork. We arrived on the same day, stayed in the same room at the lodge, fell for each other at the same time, left this place in the same moment. I can laugh about that, because what's the point in living otherwise? I'll never forget him, for as long as I live.

After I said goodbye to Scarlet, I took a detour on the way to the airport. I stopped at Jason's house, perhaps with the hope that he'd come outside and take me back in his arms. I knew what I was expecting; even so, my heart broke in two. I looked through the window, saw him laughing and joking with his parents. There was a woman sitting next to him, fingers stroking his palm. They looked so picturesque, so perfect, so content. I walked away, throat dried out from the crying I was suppressing.

Since I moved to this place last year, I really feel like I've been given a new lease of life. For the first time, possibly since I had the ability to reason, I haven't felt stressed or in danger. There's no chance of anything coming back to hurt me. Nothing can. Nothing will. And if Robert or Sanne or Sanne's boyfriend decide to show up, I'll fight. I'll fight and I'll win.

The past has no place here and I refuse to allow its presence in my life anymore.

I take one last look at the stars, remember my years with the band, remember those nights performing to those screaming audiences, and then turn back the way I came.

1999

Scarlet

3 June 1999

She doesn't converse with Emma that much anymore, though sometimes she wishes she could still hallucinate. She doesn't know what really happened to Emma, though someday she hopes she will.

Since she's stopped singing, she's done a variety of things: launching a charity, a few stints as a guest host on a couple of gameshows, developing her own perfume which has gone down well with the New York crowd. She was even considered for a slot on *Have I Got News For You*, but someone presumably talked to someone else and they were very quick to give her a firm *no*.

Life has breezed on for her these past two years. Everything and everyone have moved forward. She sometimes still feels like the innocent sweetheart who gathered her girls in that café in 1990 to announce her grand idea. She's still stuck in that moment, but the world has moved forward and people have changed. It's the way the world operates, the way it's destined to pin itself together.

She spends her days shut away, planning this thing and that. Today is just like any other. She's sitting in the family home – well, *her* home. She's writing a speech that she's due to give in Swansea next week. It's not like writing lyrics though. It comes slowly, like frozen clumps of fat. She's supposed to be talking about her reflections of working in the music industry and how it can be applied to assist with the development of trainee teachers. Philip Leighton is one-hundred percent ecstatic about it.

She goes through to the kitchen, where many a family gathering had a focal point. She switches on the kettle and tosses a dusty teabag into a pristine cup. She's cut down on the coffee, considerably. When the tea is made, she returns to the living room and surprisingly writes the remainder of her speech in less than half an hour. There's a temptation to put in something about Josephine, just to ruffle a few feathers; but no, that would be going too far.

She's heard unsettling rumours about Josephine, stories that she's had a relapse into alcohol and taken a further step to cocaine use. But they're just whispers. There's nothing in the papers, nor this *internet* thing, where many people seem to get information from these days. She knows that Josephine is still living in the depths of the south of Argentina, safe from all influences both good and bad.

It's Scarlet who's the one most at risk – and she knows it! That's why she only has red wine in the house. No vodka. No gin. Nothing that could shipwreck her.

She reads her speech through, and then reads it out loud. She practices like she's rehearsing one of the hits from the debut album. She sees her audience, imagines herself amongst them, but then the curtains close.

2005

Scarlet

6 January 2005

It's only a small audience this time: twenty people gathered on a crisp morning in a poky café, sipping coffee. The lights are on low, but the spotlight is, once again, on her. She sits on a thin stool, going over her mental notes. She knows what she needs to say and exactly how she needs to say it.

And guess who's got the privilege of interviewing her? None other than Victor Gully. He's put on a bit of weight, but he's also gained several more novels, the most recent of which has been nominated for prize after prize. Since the new millennium, he and Scarlet have been talking. At first, it was letters. Then it was a phone call. Then they met for a cup of coffee. Finally, they've struck up a close friendship.

The audience are a clustered gathering of former fans. A couple of them are wearing the merchandise t-shirts launched in 1992. They're no doubt all enthusiasts, definitely eager for their five minutes with her.

There's no need for security of course. Who after all would want to harm her? She's vanished from the public eye. Everyone's more interested in Atomic Kitten or Busted, or this Girls Aloud. Who listens to her voice anymore? Who puts on one of her CDs in the car on the way to work? Who plays her music on one of these iPods, earphones wedged in as they amble down the street?

Victor Gully starts. He gives an introduction to the event and asks for donations to the supporting body. (It's been planned for over six months, all Gully's idea.) Then he fires the first question, right at Scarlet: "Fifteen years ago, in this very café, in this very spot, you first proposed the idea of forming a band with four other remarkable women. Josephine. Gina. Emma." He pauses. "Susan. Did you ever envisage a journey like the one you've had?"

"Not quite," she replies.

The question-and-answer session officially lasts for forty-five minutes, followed by ten minutes of questions from the audience, and then a half-hour of signing autographs. It's great to be amongst fans, even if it's to chat with them and ask them what their favourite hits were. She has a cup of coffee from the same make of cup as she had all those years before: smooth and unremarkable.

When the event is over, Victor Gully gives her a lift home. He tells her a little bit about the book he's writing: a biography of Susan, that he's simply going to call *Susan*. It's part of his healing process. He's going to keep it simple, no fluffy non-sense. It's going to be about her strength, wisdom and courage. It's going to be about how she overcame great adversity to achieve the extraordinary.

But when they arrive at her house, Scarlet tells him her thoughts sternly: "No. Don't do it. You didn't know her as much as we did. Stick with your novels."

She goes into the house and retrieves her guitar and trusty leather jacket that's become even more torn these past five years, even though it's been residing in her cupboard. She's going to play a few notes in the spot where her art shack once stood. As she goes back outside, Victor Gully emerges from the car; he looks desperate.

"At least promise me you'll think about it," he says. "I won't mess it up."

"Victor!" She slings the guitar over her back, the strap catching her neck in a mild pinch. She grasps his shoulders, looks him right in the face. "Victor, you're a nice bloke. You're a good man. You loved Susan – no one's doubting that. But you need to move on. Write a cracking new piece of fiction. Really go for it. Don't waste any more time with us. Move on with your life. Get married. Have children. Live a great life. You've earned it, Victor."

"But, Scarlet..."

"Goodbye, Victor." She turns away from him and starts walking.

"Scarlet, where are you going?" he calls out behind her.

She keeps walking. The shouts become fainter and so too does the light. She lights up a cigarette, puts her hands in her jacket pockets. She hears him yell out once more. She hears every word, but pretends not to.

Acknowledgements

A Life Called Scarlet has been a major undertaking and there are countless people to whom I am indebted.

First and foremost, my family.

I thank Richard Selwyn-Barnett for his advice, support, inspiration, and introducing me to so many people in the art, writing and music scene. There is no way this book would have come into fruition without him.

I also thank Noel Boyd, Jamie Harris and Raedan O'Dubhghaill for their friendship and practical feedback on earlier draft versions of the book.

I want to send my appreciation and gratitude to the following organisations for their support, both in feedback and opportunities to discuss *A Life Called Scarlet* with a wide audience: Oxford Writing Circle, SubdriftNYC, Helensburgh Writers Workshop, Round Lemon, Isolation Be Gone, Poetry Lit, 105 Publishing, North London Film Studios, and Dove Tales. Special thanks also goes to Vessy Mink for giving me an appearance on Music Train.

I want to thank the following for numerous areas of support: Lynette Jackson-Edwards, Laura Bremner, Jean Rafferty, Glen McCoy, Eddy Foreman and Ray Evans.

Notes

Front cover created using Canva.

Front cover background designed by Loganyouth Studio.

www.ingramcontent.com/pod-product-compliance
Lightning Source LLC
Chambersburg PA
CBHW072033190726
48294CB00005B/1242